The Count
Of Chartres:
The Reluctant Crusader
A Novel

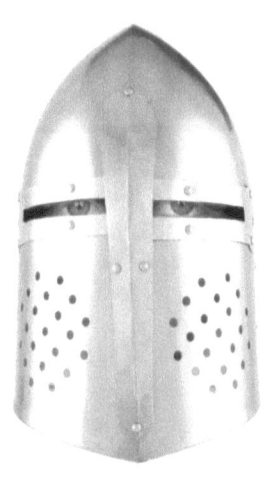

Cover art by Ying Tiun, Shanghai, China;
Maps by Eureka Cartography, Berkeley, California
(mapmaker@maps-eureka.com; www.maps-eureka.com).
Chanterai por Mon Corage, Chanson de Femme, Chanson de Croisade, found in *Songs of the Troubadours and Trouveres: An Anthology of Poems and Melodies,*
edited by Samuel N. Rosenberg, Margaret Switten, Gerard Le Vot.
Illuminated initials: The illuminated capitals are from the *L'Ornementation des Manuscrits au Moyen-Age* (*The Ornamentation of Manuscripts of the Middle Age*),
a French book published in 1894.
Illustrations are in the public domain,
and every attempt has been made to contact current stakeholders.

Digital Editions (epub and mobi formats) produced by Booknook.biz.

Also by TIMOTHY MERRILL

Winkies, Toilets and Holy Places: One Family's Story of Life on a Sabbatical — Europe, Istanbul and Bethlehem/ © 2008 by Timothy Merrill / All Rights Reserved

Published in both print and electronic format by iUniverse, www.iUniverse.com,

and available on Amazon, www.Amazon.com

The Temporary Typist: A Novel

© 2013 by Timothy Merrill/ All Rights Reserved

Paperback available from Lulu Press (www.Lulu.com); e-book for Kindle on Amazon.com.

For Jeanie

The Count of Chartres:
The Reluctant Crusader
A Novel

CONTENTS

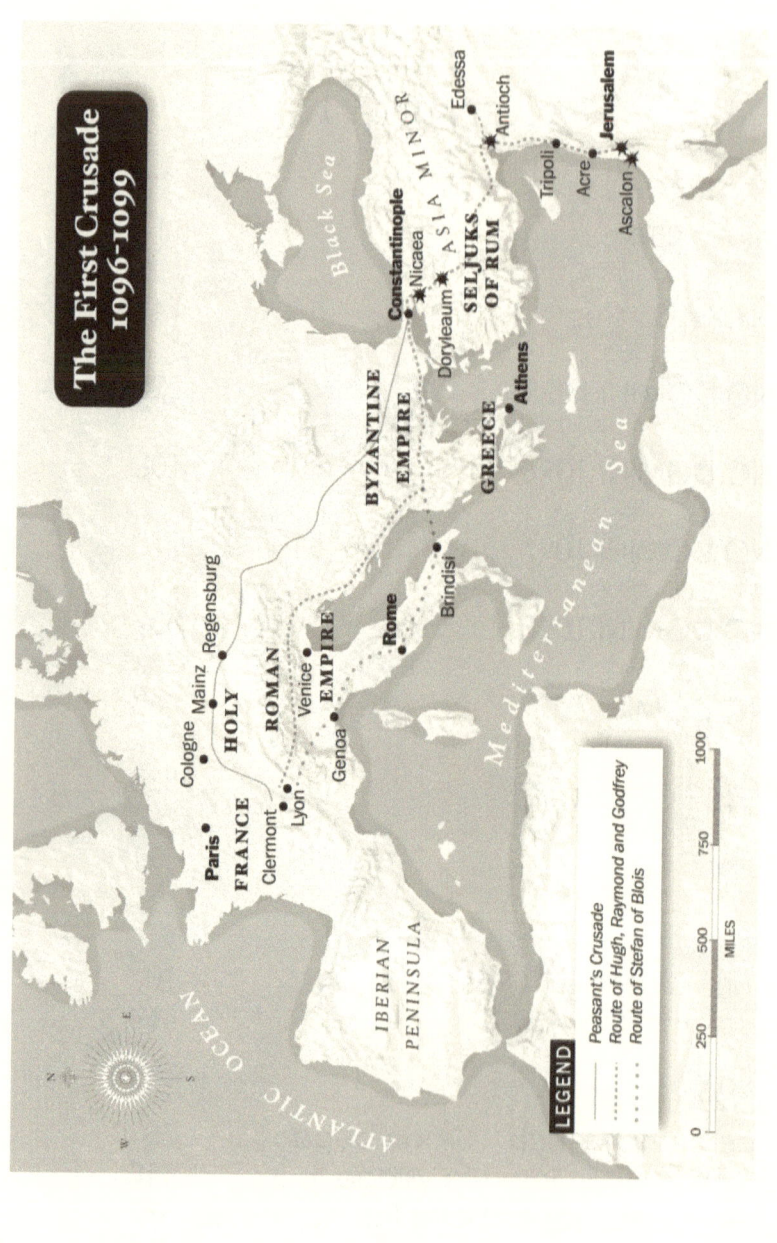

The First Crusade
1096-1099

ATLANTIC OCEAN

IBERIAN PENINSULA

Paris •
FRANCE
Clermont •
Lyon •

Cologne •
Mainz •
HOLY
ROMAN
Venice •
Genoa •
EMPIRE

Regensburg •

Rome •

Brindisi •

Mediterranean Sea

Black Sea

BYZANTINE
EMPIRE

GREECE
Athens •

Constantinople ★
Nicaea •
Dorylaeum ★
ASIA MINOR
SELJUKS
OF RUM

Edessa •
Antioch ★
Tripoli •
Acre •
Ascalon •
Jerusalem ★

LEGEND

—————— Peasant's Crusade
·············· Route of Hugh, Raymond and Godfrey
·············· Route of Stefan of Blois

0   250   500   750   1000
MILES

CHARACTERS

Aban Arslan, sultan of the Seljuk Turks, and the leader of the
principal foe faced by the Crusaders from the Bosporus to Antioch.

Addie, or Adelaide Bartholomew, is a principal character in this story.
She was a young widow with a daughter (Clare) to care for. She
also had a sister, Arletta (Lettie) and a brother, Peter. They heard
Peter the Hermit preach, and decided to follow him on his
"peasants'" or "people's," pilgrimage to Jerusalem.

Adela, Countess of Blois and Chartres, daughter of William the
Conqueror, and Stefan's wife.

Adhemar, the bishop of Le Puy, was the papal legate on the First
Crusade, and an influential figure during the crusade.

Alexius I Comnenos, Byzantine emperor, 1081-1118 A.D.

Anna Comnena, daughter of Emperor Alexius Comnenos, living in
Constantinople.

Arletta Bartholomew (Lettie), younger sister of Adelaide. Aunt to
Clare. Sister to Peter. Joins the Peasants' Crusade.

Baldwin I of Edessa, brother of Godfrey de Bouillon, was a leader of
the Nobles' Crusade, and later a regent in Jerusalem.

Bernard of Clairvaux, 1090-1153 A.D, founded the Cistercian Order
and was less than 10 years old when the First Crusade captured
Jerusalem. He was commissioned by the pope to preach a second
crusade, a crusade which came into being in 1146, and which failed
miserably.

Bohemund, was a Norman from Italy and a principal leader of the
Nobles' Crusade. Known as the Prince of Tarranto, and later as the
Prince of Antioch, he did not go on with the crusade to Jerusalem,
staying instead in Antioch as its regent. He considered himself
Stefan's rival for the affections of Princess Anna Comnena.

Clare, a young girl who, with her mother, Addie, is a member of the Peasants' Crusade.

Fulcher of Chartres was a chronicler of the crusade, a young priest with a gift for writing. He is the narrator of the story—a story which he tells to Bernard of Clairvaux who is contemplating a second crusade. (See **Bernard of Clairvaux.**)

Godfrey de Bouillon, one of the leaders of the Nobles' Crusade.

Guy de Monteil, a relic seller, grave-robber, joins the Peasants' Crusade with his good friend, Pons de Rodez. Both he and Pons are principal characters in the book.

Hugh of Vermandois, one of the lesser leaders of the Nobles' Crusade and a brother of King Philip I. He did not fulfill his vows at Jerusalem.

Ivo, bishop of Chartres, a brilliant jurist and prolific writer. He opposed King Philip's repudiation of his wife, Bertha.

Peter Bartholomew, was a brother of both Addie and Lettie, and, like his sisters, joined the Peasants' Crusade. Peter often had visions of Saint Andrew.

Peter the Monk, also known as Peter of the Cowl or Peter the Hermit. He was a leader of the Peasants' Crusade, attracting thousands of followers because of his preaching and apocalyptic vision.

Philip I, was the long-reigning king of France (1060-1108 A.D.). He also known as "the Amorous," and had many run-ins with the pope and Ivo, bishop of Chartres, because of his affairs.

Pons de Rodez was a relic seller, grave-robber, who, with nothing better to do, decided to join the Peasants' Crusade with his good friend, Guy de Monteil.

Pope Urban II set the First Crusade in motion with his sermon at Clermont, France, in November of 1095 A.D. He died before Jerusalem was captured by the Crusaders.

Raymond IV, Count of Toulouse, sometimes referred to as the Count of St. Giles. He was very wealthy, as well as pious and one of the older leaders of the Nobles' Crusade. He was married to Elvira.

Robert Curthose, or Short Breeches (also Duke of Normandy), was a
brother of Countess Adela, and the oldest son of William the
Conqueror. The king of England at the time of our story, however,
was his younger brother, William. Curthose was one of the leaders
of the Nobles' Crusade, but in name only.

Robert II, Count of Flanders, a minor leader of the Nobles' Crusade.

Stefan, Count of Blois and Chartres and one of the wealthiest men in
France. He was one of the leaders of the Nobles' Crusade, husband
of Countess Adela.

Tacitus, imperial envoy, loyal to Alexius I Comnenos.

Tancred, the intemperate nephew of Bohemund, was a minor leader
of the Nobles' Crusade; later, he claimed the title, Tancred, Prince
of Galilee.

Walter Sans Avoir, sometimes known as Walter the Penniless, was a
leader with Peter the Hermit of the Peasants' Crusade. The two
leaders separated with their respective followers. The behavior of
Walter's followers caused considerable trouble for the Peasants'
Crusade. Peter and Walter reconnected near Constantinople.

INCIPIT PROLOGUS

October, 1139 Anno domini
The Cluny Abbey, Duchy of Burgundy

N NOMINE PATRIS, ET FILII, et spiritus sancti. Amen. It is a joy to the living and even profitable to the dead when the deeds of brave men, especially those fighting for God, are read from the written records or, retained in the recesses of the mind, are solemnly recited to the faithful. Those still living in this world are themselves inspired to follow God and embrace Him with enthusiasm when they hear of the pious purposes of their predecessors and how in following the precepts of the Gospels they spurned the finest things of this world and abandoned parents, wives and their possessions, however great. As for those who have died in the Lord, they received the prayers of the faithful who are still alive and who, when they hear of the good and pious deeds of their forebears, bless the souls of the departed and in love bestow alms with prayer on their behalf— whether they, the living, knew the departed or not.

This is how my little book, *History of the Pilgrimage to Jerusalem*, written about forty years ago, begins. Quite wordy, in retrospect. But it's relevant now, as you will see, because of an unexpected visit one day last spring. I was in the chapel of the abbey after terce where we'd just sung the divine office. It was comfortable, quiet and cool there within the stone walls of the nave. Truth be told, I was sound asleep on a wooden chair—my brothers had left me alone—when the sacristan poked me in the ribs and whispered that

I had visitors awaiting me in the cloister gardens. I couldn't imagine who they might be, for I've outlived my family and hadn't had any guests for several years.

"Alright, then, Brother John," I said, clearing my throat. "Tell them I'm coming." The mousy little fellow hurried away while I grabbed my walking stick, a root from a fallen oak, and made for the gardens. When I stepped into the white sunlight of that spring day, I saw four clerics conversing privately a short distance away. As I approached, they looked up, and, since I was moving slower than a three-legged turtle, they immediately rushed to my side.

"Ah, this must be Fulcher," said the tallest one, smiling broadly. His dress identified him as a monk: a simple, faintly embroidered green cloak with a cowl, clasped at the front, and beneath this an alb of coarse, undyed wool. His face was angular and clean-shaven; his body lean and wiry. A Latin cross of pewter hung from his neck on a silver chain. I judged him to be nearing fifty.

"I am," I announced, bowing as low as my physical condition allowed—which was not much. He was not a common monk— clearly my superior in rank, although not in age.

He bade me be seated with him on a nearby bench. The religious with him, somber in black cassocks, the simple garb of common priests, hovered nearby like a coven of crows. The monk folded his hands in his lap and looked at me with curious eyes and said, "I am Bernard, abbot of the Cistercian monastery of Clairvaux."

I was so surprised, I started coughing and gasping for breath. Doesn't take much to startle an old man like myself, I guess, but this was astonishing news nonetheless. I'd heard of this man ... that he'd written many books—none of which I've read, but I've heard that many others have—that he was something of a mystic, that he was very pious and serious and that he had no interest in climbing the hierarchical, ecclesiastical ladder. Some said he could be pope if he wanted to, but he didn't want to. Like I said, he was a mystic. He was a personal friend of the pope, and a defender of the faith against heretics far and near. What could such a man want of me?

I didn't know what to say, and in any case it didn't matter because it took me a few moments to stop coughing. Once a cough gets going, it sputters for a while under its own inertia and, by the time I had calmed down, I'd almost forgotten how or why the coughing fit had started. But when I did, I ventured to say something I hoped would not sound too silly.

"I've heard of your good books—good *works*," I said, "and of your disputations with Abelard—"

Mon Dieu! That was the *wrong* thing to say. Abelard! At the sound of that one name, Bernard's adjutant and the other clerics began clucking and cawing as though a bone was lodged in their throats. They looked away, embarrassed—for me, no doubt. The abbot himself frowned and interrupted me quickly.

"—Abelard's mind is brilliant, but his spirit is dull," he said sternly. "I can think of no one who can think logically to the wrong conclusion better than he!" The abbot's eyes, once alive with curiosity, now were narrow and concentrated. His eyebrows veered into a V at the top of his nose, making him look like a hawk. I then recalled others speaking of Bernard's moral force; it was evident now as he spoke. "What he writes and teaches is theological trash—heresy—yet the students of Paris flock to hear him, notwithstanding, like he's the apostle Paul himself. They read his ..." Here Bernard stumbled, forgetting the work.

"*Sic et Non*," I suggested. The truth was that Abelard was well known and well-liked here at Cluny and our abbot, Peter, was a friend of his. They'd argue about who was first Peter and who was second Peter. Our abbot thought that he himself, being older than Abelard was "first Peter." It was an ongoing joke with them. No one else thought it was funny.

"*Sic et Non*, quite right," Bernard exclaimed. "*Yes and No* ... they read this insipid heresy and go mad over it—completely enamored and completely misled. But he has a quick mind, grant you, and perhaps the best intellect in the Church today, which is precisely why he's so dangerous. Actually, I am on my way to Sens now to convene a synod where I believe his writings will be condemned, as they should be."

He had been speaking rapidly. He paused now, out of politeness I think, to see if I wanted to respond. But I was still blubberstruck by his presence and had nothing to say. "Anyway, the Church has more to fear from its scholars than it does from its servants," he went on. "No one ever accused heretics of being ignorant, uneducated simpletons." He raised his right hand with a pointing finger. "But we must always choose Scripture over sophistry!"

"*Sed quae stulta stint mundi elegit Deus, ut confundat sapientes*," I said, quoting the apostle. God has chosen the foolish things of the world to confound the wise! The abbot beamed.

"Yes, yes," he said. "Exactly!" Then he leaned closer. "Fortunately, I have not come to Cluny to discuss theology or philosophy."

"What then?" I inquired.

He whispered: "History!"

"What?" My hearing was not so good. "History?"

"History?"

The abbot smiled at my confusion. "The pope has just given his approval for the Knights Templar. You may have heard of my little book *In Praise of the New Knighthood*?"

I had not. He seemed disappointed but continued undaunted. "But even the military strength of the Knights Templar will not be enough. Not enough. I'm afraid the Latin kingdoms of the east are slipping away from us. It's difficult, you know, for us to maintain our influence there, and the churches, cathedrals, monasteries, cities and governments, not to speak of the priests, bishops, archbishops, monks and canons—well! Just everything is in grave danger from the Saracens. It might be necessary to organize another crusade to the Holy Land."

This was the second surprise of the afternoon. My hand went to my throat, but, thankfully, no coughing spell ensued. "Another pilgrimage to the Holy Land?" I was thinking, "Isn't one pilgrimage enough?"

"Yes," he replied. I observed now that Bernard's eyes were a barometer of his emotional temperament. At first, they seemed *curious*. Then concentrated. Now they were clarified, like the purest crystal. "Like the first pilgrimage of 1096-1099." He hesitated for a moment, and then I understood the purpose of his visit. "You were a pilgrim on that first crusade, were you not, Fulcher?"

I nodded. Indeed, I was. I had been a part of that crusade from its very inception. But it was many, many years ago ... too many to think about. My venerable head ached from such thinking.

"Tell me a little about it," he said, as though I should be able to summarize in a few brief sentences the tumultuous events of four rugged years that happened more than forty years ago.

"Where do I begin?" I asked. "I don't know ... Good Lord! That was a long time ago." I rubbed my hands anxiously. Perhaps I was trying to wash them from having anything to do with whatever Bernard had in mind.

The abbot came to my rescue. "What were conditions like then?" he asked, hoping, I suppose, to prod my memory. Could I recall the events of long ago? Really, when you live the life of a contemplative, you lose track of time. Summers and winters had come and gone, and it had been years since I had thought about that nightmare of a pilgrimage in the late '90s.

I had to give him *something*. "At the time," I began, hoping my memory would improve as I spoke, "the country was suffering from severe local famines and acute shortages of vital necessities. Swineherds and sheepherders had nothing to do—disease had killed their herds and flocks, you know. Poor harvests had raised the price of corn out of the reach of the needy; greedy merchants lost no time in taking advantage of the general misery. There was little rye; bread was scarce and expensive; the poor and orphaned, abandoned by nature, if not by God, were left to eat roots and wild herbs. Cattle were sold at a low price for they were too costly to feed. Terrible portents abounded in the heavens. The skies were barren and neither the prophets of Ba'al nor the zeal of an Elijah could effect even the smallest cloud or a drop of rain. The sun turned to blood and the moon hid its face. The stars, unanchored from their celestial moorings, fell upon the earth in a maelstrom of fire. Seeing these wonders as signs from God, the peasants searched their hearts and confessed their sins."

"And the knights and the nobles?" Bernard asked.

"Were at war with each other," I replied, beginning to warm to the subject. "Not being satisfied with the wealth they had, they tried to increase it by whatever means necessary and possible."

"The Truce of God?" Bernard was referring to an ecclesiastical proscription of all petty wars and fights between Wednesday evenings and Monday mornings in memory of Christ's passion.

"Increasingly ineffective," I said. "The nobles satisfied their bloodlust by annexing the fiefs and castles of their neighbors by force: lord against lord, vassal against vassal, knight against knight. They were all Christians; they all took the sacrament; they all recited the *Pater Noster;* and they all left church to go kill their brothers who were likewise Christians, had taken the sacrament, recited their prayers, and so on."

The abbot nodded gravely and waited in silence. "We in the Church—both east and west—watched with alarm as Christian lands fell like ripened fruit into the Islamic basket," I continued. "The very gates of Constantinople were threatened. It was risky to undertake a pilgrimage in those days because the holy sites were in Moslem hands. The Holy Sepulchre was destroyed and then rebuilt. Pilgrims were molested as a matter of policy. Some were circumcised and their blood splashed over the altars of baptismal fonts. The bellies of others were torn open and their entrails removed. Some were tied to posts and shot with arrows; others were compelled to bare their necks while their scoffing attackers made a game of seeing if their extruded heads could be severed by a single stroke of a drawn scimitar."

Bernard and his party digested this news uncomfortably but were determined to hear more. "And the pope?"

"The pope had his own difficulties," I explained. "Guibert, as you know, was insisting on his claim to the chair of St. Peter, much like the recent dispute between Innocent and Anacletus which you helped to resolve. For months at a time Urban was unable to stay in Rome—"

"Fulcher, Fulcher! This is what I want you to do," said Bernard, waving his hands in front of me to stop my narrative. "Gather your notes of the pilgrimage and submit them to me for study. You were an eyewitness, were you not?"

I nodded. "A chaplain in the army of Count Stefan of Blois and Chartres," I said.

The abbot and his party stood. I followed their lead. "Send your most vivid recollections as soon as possible, by next fall at the latest. Is it possible?"

My most vivid recollections! I was terrified at the thought. Advanced in age and as feeble in body as I was in mind, how could I remember such things? As though he could hear my thoughts, Bernard inquired: "You have written a history, have you not?"

"*Historia Hierosolymitana,*" I replied. Perhaps my hesitation was obvious. Frankly, I didn't want to do as he had requested. My *History of the Expedition to Jerusalem* was more a collection of notes than a book. But you don't say no to Bernard of Clairvaux!

"Splendid," he said and they left me alone in the garden.

"Splendid," I said, calling out after they were gone. "Splendid! Just splendid!"

That was at least five months ago. Bernard will soon have my manuscript. But I must add this further word: If I have been able to achieve some small literary accomplishment, however meager, it has no doubt been obscured by the vulgar additions and emendations of my collaborator in this project. The person to whom I refer is the author of the *Gesta Francorum,* a brother who wishes to remain anonymous and with good reason! While the classicists here and at Chartres prefer an elegant, elevated Latin, the contemporary idiom of my colleague corrupts the language, not to speak of the reader, in the most base sort of way.

I must further state that I cannot be held responsible for a manuscript which I have yet to read in its completed, final form. I am in the awkward position of writing a prologue to a text the contents of which remain, at least in part, a mystery to me. My final draft went to the author of the *Gesta* and from him directly to the copyists. I fear that this edition contains matters about which I would blush to speak. I have no doubt that those wretched villains in the scriptorium have wickedly embellished certain passages appealing to their licentious natures and have thus rendered otherwise decent readings indecent.

Know, therefore, that my purpose is to glorify God as He has made known His deeds through the courage of the Franks, and to record this event as one of the greatest achievements in providential history. *Beata enim gens cujus est Dominus Deus ejus!* Whatever is uncovered in the following narrative that is edifying and uplifting may be safely attributed to my own hand; on the contrary, whatever is odious, base and vile may be ascribed to my collaborator and those monks whose minds dwell on perversion and not on the things of God. *Exsurge Domine, adjuva nos!*

EXPLICIT PROLOGUS

ANNO DOMINI

1095

CHAPTER ONE

The Emperor, the Princess, & the Count

Constantinople
June, 1095 A.D.

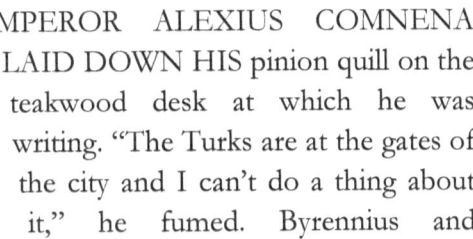

MPEROR ALEXIUS COMNENA LAID DOWN HIS pinion quill on the teakwood desk at which he was writing. "The Turks are at the gates of the city and I can't do a thing about it," he fumed. Byrennius and Melissenus, senior advisors to the court, hovered nervously nearby, their hands clasped and heads tilted toward his imperialship. They were dressed alike in flowing hooded robes of blue and green wool, with gold chain stitching, and tassels—to distract demons—on the hems and arms. The hoods were pulled back and lay flat on their backs below the nape. Both men were pointy-faced with pointy, scratchy and feathery white beards. They were in the palace library where Alexius did his thinking, talking and writing. The emperor was a reflective type and the advisors were accustomed to listening to the man sort through his ideas aloud. Alexius thought. Alexius talked. Alexius wrote. Seldom in any other order.

"The danger isn't as great as you suppose," said Byrennius, the taller of the two. He walked around the front of the desk to face the emperor. The desk was situated in the center of the tapestried room. Behind the emperor were enormous curtained windows through which the glow of the early morning sun bathed the room in a warm aura. "The Turks have yet to cross the Bosporus, and that's no small feat."

"A feat they'll accomplish soon enough unless I get some mercenaries," Alexius responded, looking up from his papers to address the older man. He was not usually so ill-tempered. On the contrary, when he wasn't irascible, irritable and irrational, he was a calm, dignified man of middle age with a gracious and effortless manner to which he added discipline and self-control. He was medium height. His hair was short. On his head was a small crested crown with a few inlaid gems. His eyes were intense and his expression severe. The face was lean, cheekbones accented, and his beard trimmed. A mustache flowed downward from his nose, drap-ing the corners of his mouth and meeting the beard below. He was dressed informally with trousers and a blouse over which was a tunic of deep blue but patterned with orange and green colors and fastened across the chest with a gold chain. He pushed away from the desk and stood, explaining: "The Petchenegs are useless, half-breed Turks. The Bulgarians despise us. And I can't recruit from Anatolia because the entire province is overrun of Turks."

"But the Varangian Guard—"

"Full of Anglo-Saxon refugees from Britain who don't like the Normans any better than we, and unruly, undisciplined Norsemen," he said. He turned toward the windows. "I have a small army, and if I wish to enlarge it, I've got to coddle half-breed Turks, fleeing Saxons and some maniacal Normans who believe it's their destiny to rule the world!"

"Father, you are becoming … overwrought," cooed a soft voice from across the room. The men turned to face the speaker: It was Anna, the princess and daughter of Alexius and Empress Irene. Melissenus and Byrennius were quite accustomed to her presence since she often functioned as an informal advisor to the court, a position she enjoyed not only because of familial connection but also because of the acuity of her mind.

"Come now," she said, approaching her father gently, "sit down again, and finish the letter." The emperor grudgingly returned to his desk. "Finish the letter." His daughter had a way with her father. It was both a power she exercised with caution and an influence to which Alexius knew he was susceptible. Like many fathers with daughters, he was aware of his natural tendency to be tender—and gullible. "I have every reason to be irritated," he complained. "Aban Arslan has marched through Anatolia like a hot knife through butter. Dorylaeum, Nicea, Nicomedia, Pelecanum, Chalcedon, and Chrysopolis—"

"Aban Arslan is a monster of your own creation," Anna said. "I warned you against writing that letter to Malik Shah. It's better to scheme against known enemies than by assassinating them taking your chances with unknown ones." Byrennius and Melissenus exchanged glances. They could never address the emperor in this manner under any circumstances. But Anna was not one to hold her tongue.

"You were against that letter, it's true," Alexius sighed, "but you favor *this* letter?"

Anna nodded. "The bishop of Rome can help us. He's the one to whom you must turn."

"The bishop of Rome!" Alexius laughed and looked at his advisors. "Which bishop of Rome?"

"Urban, of course, your excellency," replied Melissenus, although he was sure that Alexius himself knew this. "Guibert is a fool. He'll never be the pope, don't you agree, Byrennius?"

"Exactly," the counselor advised. "Besides, Guibert held a council in Rome which condemned clerical marriages." The Eastern church, ever since the Schism of 1054, had permitted the clergy to marry.

"Well, Urban it is," said Alexius, taking the parchment in his hands. "Here Melissenus, read this for faults and give me your opinion." He handed the draft to the learned man who began to read silently.

"No, no," Alexius said impatiently. "Aloud!"

Melissenus did not mind the emperor's harsh manner. He had known Alexius since the early days when Alexius was a field general serving Emperor Michael, fighting against the Norman Roussel in the Anatolian mountains. The emperor could be compassionate. He was not always grumpy as he was now. When he captured Roussel, he had been ordered to put out the old warrior's eyes. But it was an injury Alexius could not allow the man to suffer. Melissenus had been attached to Alexius' army then and had been with him ever since. He was accustomed to variations in the emperor's mood; it was a small thing with him. So he adjusted the document in his thin hands to catch the morning light and began to read.

"To His Holiness, Urban, Bishop of Rome, grace and peace through—"

"Here, give me that," said Alexius, standing quickly and taking the manuscript from Melissenus. "I'll read it myself." He began to skim its contents as he strolled around the room.

"Let's see," he murmured, "thanked him for lifting the ban of excommunication and advised him that we've now included the bishop of Rome in the patriarchal diptychs, an omission not by any canonical decision but through sheer carelessness ... Latin churches in Constantinople are free to follow their own rite, he should find that agreeable ... Regret the addition of the *filoque* to the Creed, but Latin is such a theologically impoverished language compared to Greek that philosophical subtleties are best expressed in the language of the New Testament ... No, no, better omit that ... Christians in the East are threatened by Islam. The Turks are at the gates of Nova Roma, pilgrims to the Holy City are continually harassed, and the city of the Lord is in the hands of infidels ... shortages of available men to fight the forces amassing on the Asiatic side of the Bosporus ... could you use your good offices to recruit mercenaries to help us defend against the infidel and recover lands that belong to the empire?" Alexius looked up. "There, did I overlook anything?"

Bryennius, Melissenus and Anna shook their heads and shrugged. "This letter," said Alexius, satisfied, as he prepared the wax for the imperial seal, "may be the salvation of the empire. All we need are a few mercenaries, a group here and there to augment our own forces so we aren't stretched too thin, and we rout the Turks, and with the help of God, perhaps retake at least the western frontier of Anatolia. Ha!" The scroll was sealed.

"Have this letter rewritten with the changes and returned to me," he said to Bryennius. "Now, where is the count from Chartres?" he asked, looking up.

"The count from Chartres?" Anna said, unaware of her father's plans.

"Yes, my fair princess, a fine young man of Chartres, one of the wealthiest men of France who has now been in the city for a week to promote trade between our city and France."

"A Norman!"

Alexius put his arm around his daughter and began to walk her toward the door of the chamber. "Yes, yes, but we mustn't hold that against him. He is quite different from all the Normans I've met—you'll see—and I've arranged for him to take this letter back to France and convey it to the Bishop of Rome!"

"A Norman is a Norman," she said.

"My daughter, you judge men too quickly! A slight fault, but a weakness that devalues your counsel to me. Ah, here he is now," he said as the study doors swung open.

"Count Stefan of Blois and Chartres," announced the page. Anna was curious. She had learned to trust her father's judgment, but her own prejudices, unlike his, were generalizations born of actual experience rather than casual hearsay. Therefore, she disagreed with her father's assessment, believing herself to be open-minded and painfully impartial.

The count stepped into the room briskly, and kneeled before Alexius with a flourish, kissed the emperor's proffered ring, and then arose. *He is decisive and has manners*, Anna thought, coming to a quick, perhaps reluctant, conclusion. "Your excellency, it is a pleasure to see you again," the count said warmly, smiling at Alexius and nodding in the direction of Bryennius and Melissenus. He had not yet noticed Anna who had positioned herself near the doors to observe this man from Gaul undetected.

"It's most gracious of you to carry a message from us to your pope," said the emperor. The count, Anna observed, was rather tall with a frame that was lean and muscular. His head was covered with lank, blond hair, and his Norman face, she admitted, was pleasant and well-fashioned. He moved with ease and she thought he might be good with a sword. She wondered what sort of a lover he'd be.

"This is yours," said the emperor to the count as a page stepped forward, bearing a small but exquisite, hand-carved box. "A small gift of appreciation to soften the hardships of your journey and to express my gratitude."

Stefan, a wealthy man himself, was nevertheless surprised with the gesture. "Most generous of you," he said.

"Not at all," Alexius replied. "Tonight you will be a guest in my palace and we shall have a dinner in your honor." He approached Anna who now shrank from the introduction she knew was about to happen, fearing that her most cherished and dependable prejudice may indeed be precisely that—a prejudice. She didn't feel comfortable in any situation in which she was denied the strength of her opinions and the solace of her preconceptions. Her father arrested her ere she left the room.

"Anna, you must meet our guest," he said, as he motioned for her to approach. She walked toward the count who had turned about to meet her. She was startled: He had the deepest, Bosporus blue eyes she'd ever seen.

"This is my daughter, the princess Anna," Alexius said. "She'll escort you to your quarters for the remainder of the day. I'm sure you'll find them suitable. I, myself, am unavailable for the rest of your stay," he said, returning to his desk. "A polo match this morning in the Hippodrome and boar hunting this afternoon in the Bulgarian forest." Anna bowed slightly, smiled at the count, and turned to leave.

"Good day, your excellency," Stefan said.

"Until this evening, then," replied the emperor as the two of them disappeared into the corridors of the palace.

They walked silently through an elaborate, covered portal and down a barrel-vaulted vestibule that looked out upon the imperial gardens. The walls of the impressive colonnade were marked at intervals by ornately decorated rectangular pilasters that extended to flowery capitals beneath the cornice. Inlaid between pilasters, vigorous mosaic murals depicted the founding of Constantinople and the building of the palace. Artisans were laboring on the figure of Constantine.

Anna wondered if the count was ever going to say something. Then he spoke: "Your father is a very generous man," he said, awkwardly. To Anna, he seemed ill-at-ease.

"You have to understand," Anna replied in Norman French, "that in the east, parsimony is the unpardonable sin. Here, one's reputation depends entirely upon splendor, opulence and magnificence and the more excessive, the better."

"And the emperor does it so well."

"He does it *too* well," said Anna, keeping the walking pace brisk. "Sometimes he treats foreigners like yourself better than he does his own people."

They walked silently. It gave Stefan an opportunity to observe the princess. She was beautiful—but princesses are supposed to be beautiful. That was not so remarkable, then. Still … her hair was dark and fine and wrapped around a pleasantly-formed face of eyes that were green, and a nice girl's nose that was appealing, and the effect was a countenance that was confidant and opinionated. Her skin was fair and unblemished. She walked quickly with her chin high, a woman of bearing and purpose, Stefan thought. And education. She speaks French.

"You speak French," he said, restating his thought.

"You observed," she replied.

"You don't like me."

"Yet another observation," she said, not breaking stride. Stefan skipped a step to catch up with her.

"Where did you learn to speak French?" he asked, amused by her impertinence. Anna stopped suddenly and turned to him. "I am an educated woman. I speak and read French, Greek and Latin, and I can read Arabic. Does that surprise you?" She didn't wait for his response even though he was about to speak. "In my country, as in most countries," she continued, "women do not receive an education, and if they do, it is very little and only to make them agreeable companions for their husbands. I am well-educated so that I will not need a husband." She started walking again.

"Certainly a princess is in no need of a husband," Stefan rejoined, not to be put off.

"You are correct, but my father doesn't realize that an educated princess is the worst kind. Men, especially princes or nobles, do not like educated women."

"Why not?"

"Because educated women are powerful women, and they do not like powerful women." They sat down on a wooden bench in the garden surrounded by ornate floral patterns, brilliant blossoms, and singing birds. They had lapsed quite unconsciously and unintentionally into a conversation.

"My wife reads Greek," said Stefan.

"And do you like her?" Anna asked. Stefan was silent.

"You men," said Anna, pressing her point. "Educated or not, you are so strong, manly, you … you like your muscles and your weapons. You build towers one day and tear down monuments the next. You're always doing something powerful and impressive. It's all very physical and coercive. But women, we don't understand or employ power that way. We can't—for obvious reasons, really. But an educated women, thinks about it. She understands her essential weakness in comparison to men, and so she uses her power in other, more effective ways—more effective, I say, than a man's power. For a woman, at least a smart one, *persuasion*—the ability to persuade—is true power, and believe me, if a women has honed the art of persuasion, nothing will stand in her way. Such a woman is dangerous, and men instinctively understand this. Don't you see?"

Stefan had to confess that he didn't. Anna continued: "A man can change what one *does*, but a woman what one *thinks*! And if you can change what a person thinks, *then* you can change what a person does. Men have a hard time doing that, so they go off to war. Always. It's just the way things are."

"Really?" Stefan inquired.

"Really."

"You don't know as much about men and women as you think," said the count. "I know for a fact that not all men behave—or believe—as you say," said the count.

"When is that?" she asked.

"When a man woos a woman," he replied, grinning. "A woman taken by force is no conquest, only that woman who gives herself freely."

"A woman never gives herself to be a wife freely," Anna said. "To be a mistress perhaps, but never a wife."

"Nor a man to be a husband,' Stefan added. "To be a lover perhaps, but not a husband."

✠✠✠

Stefan was amused by their encounter and looked forward to seeing the princess that evening. During the day when he thought of her, he couldn't remember too much about her except her eyes—and hair. He realized then that he had been more interested in her ideas than in her looks. That evening, however, when he was seated on the dais between the emperor and Anna, he recalled quite clearly her appearance. She was not hard to look at. Her eyes—again the eyes!—and her nose, delicate, and lips undulant as an archer's bow. Small hands and graceful feet. Breasts … well …

They did not speak much throughout the evening. The dinner was festive, boisterous and entertaining, and the occasion had attracted many of the Byzantine aristocracy. "This is Constantine Doukas," said Anna, introducing him to one of the young nobles present. He made the acquaintance of many such dignitaries on this night, and even addressed the crowd to give them greetings from France. His reception was cool, but uniformly polite, and Stefan surmised that, like Anna, they were not accustomed to considering a Norman their friend. But it was not their friendship that the count desired, and moreover, Stefan possessed an affable nature that enabled him to discard frosty manners and be comfortable in even the most awkward of circumstances.

He was also intrigued by their dress, manners and customs, and this curiosity allowed him to pass the time pleasantly. The food, on heavy trenchers, was exotic, more so than the food to which he was accustomed. They preferred lamb, but goose was served on this evening with condiments of wined cheese sauce for fowl, and currant sauce for meats. Other platters held leeks with walnuts, fried artichokes, figs, and dates stuffed with eggs and cheese. For desserts, there were plum tarts, pears with carob cream, and fried Valencia oranges. Mulled wine was plentiful and it flowed freely.

Presently, tiring of this, he excused himself intending to return quickly, and stepped onto a torch-lit portico to inhale the fresh air floating off the sea. A half moon was slung low over the Asian hills across the Bosporus, and its rays painted a jagged and sparkling course across the night water. Then he noticed a presence at his side. It was Anna.

Stefan pointed in the direction of the moon and said: "You cannot credit your father with the generosity of this view, now can you?"

"No, but this city … it is a beautiful city," she said, not looking at him.

"The dinner tonight was both generous and thoughtful," Stefan added. "Another example of the eastern tradition of—how did you put it?—splendor and magnificence."

Anna sighed. "The emperor knows nothing about finances. It's a small wonder there's any money in the treasury at all. A few years ago he devalued the coinage and it was a disaster. But, although we suffer many things, we do not suffer from a want of finances. My father taxes our people to their limits, he forces the aristocracy to make loans, he confiscates property from the nobles and the Church, and he imposes fines rather than putting people in prison. Somehow, he holds it all together ..." Her voice trailed off.

"You don't want to be a wife?" Stefan said, inspired by a sudden flash of intuition. Anna shook her head.

"Constantine Doukas?" he asked, guessing.

She turned to face him. His soft eyes staring directly at her stopped her cold. She nodded and looked away.

"Let me tell you a story," she began. "Several years ago, the Italian Norman, Robert Guiscard, enraged because my father broke off the engagement of my brother to his daughter, sailed across the Adriatic with his son Bohemund, landed at Avlona, and laid siege to Dyrrhachium. It was then the summer, and it was October before my father arrived to defend the fortress. In those days, the only troops available for my father were the Varangian Guard, mostly Anglo-Saxons and no match for the Normans. The next spring, Robert marched his army along the Via Egnatia toward Constantinople. He himself had to return to Italy, but he left the campaign in the hands of Bohemund who was to secure Macedonia and Greece—which he did. Although my father had no army but some well-paid Turks and Venetian ships, he was still able to free Thessaly. But when Robert returned, he and Bohemund destroyed the Venetian fleet and would have threatened Constantinople had not Guiscard died and his sons not quarreled over the inheritance. Bohemund forced his attentions on me at a time when I had foolishly accompanied my father to the battlefield."

She stopped her narrative and turned toward Stefan. "So you see," she went on, "I don't like Normans. In my experience they are horse's arses, really." She turned to leave. "When I met you this afternoon, I'm afraid I was rude, *uncharacteristically* rude, I might add, but I was irritated because you, a Norman, from the moment I saw you, did not seem to match this preconception. It would have been easier for me if you did."

Having said this, she returned to the hall. Stefan clutched the marble railing and watched the moonlight dance upon the waters of the Bosporus. Interesting girl, this Anna, he thought.

CHAPTER TWO

The Monk

The Auvergne, France
November 22, 1095 A.D.

INETEEN WAR HORSES FROM THE Ardennes thundered down a dampened trail in the forest of the Auvergne, beating up the earth, churning up the dark, volcanic soil of the *Chaines de Puy* and spraying it to the side. These black, snorting steeds glistened with sweat. Powerful forelegs carried their riders through the forest like the steeds of Apollo across the sky, their muscles rippling with every stride. Their nostrils were flared and moist. These beasts were not merely animals used in battle; they were themselves *instruments* of destruction. Trained in the art of war at the court of Blois, these magnificent creatures were fearsome in combat. A properly trained war horse could mean the difference between life and death; indeed, a slow horse often meant a fast death.

They rode in pairs: five forward, four in the rear, and a single horse in the center. Each charger except one bore a knight equipped for battle—ribbon-tipped lances holstered vertically. The speed at which they now traveled would not be maintained for long; these ponderous animals were not built for pursuit. But this particular morning, the knights were on exercises—pushing their steeds to the physical limits. They would stop to rest at Lac de Chambon before continuing.

In the center of the band, a man and a woman were borne by a powerful Pegasus whose full, snowy mane, sweeping tail, and regal carriage—even at full gallop—bespoke its pedigree and training. The youthful paladin was attired exclusively in black including a full, high-collared blouse. His left hand held the reins, and on his right hand he wore a gauntlet on which was perched a sharp falcon. Its beak pierced the wind as they trammeled forward through the deep forest. Except for a sword belt and an emerald-studded sword, the male rider was wearing no military regalia as were the other knights. Yet he rode with the bearing of a knight.

His companion sat astride the same horse, pressing hard against his back, her arms about his waist and mittens of Celtic wool on her hands. Her long, flaxen hair trailed in the wind as did a purple cape which fluttered over the flanks and buttocks of the horse.

As the party raced through the Auvergne, leafless, spiny trees and evergreens with tapered branches were only spectral images in the early morning fog. It was cool; breath from straining horses vaporized in the air. The night rain lay in crystalline droplets upon fallen leaves and forest grasses. The soggy trail sometimes was potted with puddles.

Under a thick canopy of pines and oaks, the small coterie of knights approached a bend in the path and took to the inside, leaning in the direction of the curve. It was not a path actually, but a roadway—an old imperial road that had been built in the age of republican Rome when an aggressive senate was building empires on the fringes of the world. In Gaul, they had carved roads across plain and through forest. Even throughout the Auvergne, one could still see the granite stones that had been laid as curbs, and occasionally even the roadwork itself was visible. In the Chaines de Puy these links to civilization were still used, but the Roman markers were usually buried under centuries of history-enriched soil or overgrown by untamed brush.

The knights had no sooner negotiated the turn in the roadway when a loud commotion arose. Curses filled the air. Horses panicked. The startled warriors belatedly reined their horses to a halt, but not before several had crashed into each other, tumbling their riders to the ground. One knight lay motionless in the underbrush several feet from the path. His helmet had been knocked off when his head hit the earth. Another sat nearby nursing a gash in his leg. Within seconds, a well-disciplined military unit rushing at top speed had been reduced to disarray. Snorting stallions stomped about and pranced in place.

Flying around the curve in the path, and the path itself obscured by the forest, the platoon was surprised to come upon a donkey and its rider plodding along in the same direction as they. Even more curious, the commotion, clashing and clanging of metal and armor had startled neither the rider nor the beast whatsoever. They would have continued clopping forward were their way not blocked by a knight who, having succeeded in passing them, turned about to confront them. While several of the band dismounted and began the awkward task of putting a disheveled knight back together again, this knight nudged his high-stepping steed directly in front of—and above—the little ass and its rider.

A knight on any horse is a fearsome figure to a person astride a donkey. But on a war horse, the effect is even more dramatic. Moreover, the eyes of a knight are virtually obscured by the flattened nasal of his conical helmet. One fears what one cannot see. In this case, what could be seen was the kite-shaped shield which hung from his left arm and a gloved left fist which grasped the still-holstered lance. His right hand held the brass-polished handle of his battle-tested sword.

"You fool!" said the knight. "You should've let us pass! You must have heard us coming even if we didn't see you. Why didn't you get out of the way?"

The fellow on the donkey wore the dark brown wool habit of a monk. The robe was gathered at the waist by coarse twine, while the cowl was drawn completely over his head so that his face was hidden. The faceless monk appeared anonymously drab. His habit was soiled and dirty. Boney and fleshless hands, elongated fingers fitted in chalky skin, lay folded across his lap. Soil was encrusted under jaundiced fingernails that had grown to an inch. His calves and feet were bare; the toenails had begun to curl. He carried no bag or provisions.

The forest was quiet except for the stamping and pawing of horses. The monk said nothing, sitting quietly upon a donkey even more nondescript than he. It was a chestnut animal with white points upon the face and below the knees and hocks. Its face was Benedictine: long, dour and sleepy.

"This one isn't talking, my lord," the knight said, irritated. He drew his sword and moved his horse beside the donkey. Sitting sidesaddle as he was, the monk's back was to the knight. The soldier leaned forward and placed the flat of the sword against his head. But the man in the cowl didn't flinch.

"You are being rude but I shall be courteous," said the knight, keeping the sword to his head. "We are from the court of Blois and Chartres. This is our lord, Count Stefan." With his sword he pointed to the man riding under their protection. "In all of France, save the king himself, there's none more skilled and courageous than he. His possessions are vast and his power is great. Some of his closest friends are the bishops in the Church." The knight waited again. "Perhaps you have friends in common," he said ominously. He brought the sword again to the monk, pressing the blade against the cowl and spoke, this time with more force, "Now, monk, who are you and why did you refuse to yield so that this little inconvenience could have been avoided?"

The donkey, no ass of Balaam, said nothing and made no move and its rider was equally speechless and motionless.

"Perhaps you need some encouragement to speak!" The knight moved his sword to the monk's back and began to push its point into the woolen material.

"Wait!" cried the lord. Stefan brought his white stallion forward and, as the interrogator moved back, he and his lady slowly circled the monk. The count had been observing the proceedings closely.

"I think I know this man, Gerald," the count said. "He is one of the *prophetae*, a mystic and a hermit. You've heard of them, surely. He's performed many miracles. He preaches to the peasants—not with authorization of course—but they believe him to be a holy man, a wise man who can settle their quarrels and show them the way to God." Stefan paused, surveying his vassal for signs of recognition. "From Amiens, isn't that correct?" If the count expected an answer he received none. "Well, no matter," he said with a wave of his hand. "This man has done us no harm. He's probably en route to Clermont like us. We shall pass single file and wish him Godspeed on his journey wherever he is going. Come along." Stefan turned his horse and moved away from the monk to allow his knights to form rank before and behind him. By now, the knight who had been thrown to the ground had been reintroduced to his horse. The party regrouped.

The ass and its rider plodded far down the path, becoming graying figures in the misty distance. They were not lost, however, to the vigilant eye of Gerald, the lead knight. With a shout he spurred his horse, gave it a solid slap in the flank, and sped toward the vanishing pair with the rest of the knights in close behind. Quickly they recaptured the distance lost between them, but this time there was no trouble. One by one they thundered past the monk although the wide-bodied war horses came perilously close to bumping the little donkey and dislodging its rider. Soon distance between the knights and the donkey-riding monk increased and the loud thudding of the horses hooves became a muted rumble, and then an echo until quickly it was quiet again in the forest of the Auvergne.

"Steady, Kioko," said the man in the cowl. "Easy, now," and he stroked her ears affectionately. At Lac de Chambon, the prophet dismounted and walked into the shore water until the water wet the hem of his robe. In the early morning the lake was placid and pale. Lowering his head, the prophet drank from cupped hands that brought the lake to his mouth. The water spilled through his fingers wetting his graying beard.

Kioko and the prophet resumed their journey. The trail led to an exposed ridge giving them a sweeping view of the mountains and valleys of the region. Although patches of cloud lay inert in distant meadows and vales, the monk could clearly see the Chaines de Puy, a string of porous domes, rocky cones, wooded craters and high mountains—volcanoes of millenniums past. Surrounding these domite formations were verdant folds of forest and glade. The strange but natural marvels indigenous to this area made the Chaines de Puy a wonder to behold and often inspired not a little apprehension in the souls of its superstitious inhabitants. Far away at the edge of the lowering sky and slightly to the northeast were the cliffs of Clermont, the impressive ridge beneath which lay the city.

"Let's go, Kioko," murmured the monk. He made some quick clucking noises. Kioko's ears twitched and the ass plodded forward. They descended the ridge and soon were in the woods of the Auvergne again.

✠✠✠

The pile of shirts, linens, pants and under-tunics at the base of the evergreen with the spreading limbs and ample boughs belonged to the bathers in a nearby pool. The clothes had been discarded quickly and carelessly. The foursome happened upon the pool by mere chance. They saw steam rising in the cold of this autumn morning and had investigated. They found a large natural and shallow basin of heated water. Pons and Guy, although aware that in this region such ponds were not uncommon, had never seen such a phenomenon themselves, much less taken advantage of its healing properties.

The bathers were two men and two women and they played like children, joining hands, dancing in circles and singing songs they remembered from their childhood in Provence. The music and the laughter rose on the late morning breeze to the tops of the weather-beaten pines above them.

Tiring of this, they paired off. They were quite naked and having a grand time until one of the girls screamed. Perhaps it was more of a shriek. Guy, startled by this, looked up and turned around. Pons and his lady were likewise gawking. On the water's edge not far away, stood a monk with the cowl drawn about his face. The girl who was with Guy dislodged herself from his grasp and crossing her arms about her chest backed away to the deeper part of the pond and sank slowly into the thermal waters. Pons and his friend, already submerged to the shoulders, stayed that way. Guy was startled and stepped back to put more distance between himself and the monk, but tripped, lost his balance, and fell. After much splashing and paddling about, he came to a stable, upright position, sitting in the shallow water, his mouth agape at the sight of the hooded intruder.

The stranger stood motionless.

"We aren't doing anything," Pons said. "These women are our wives."

"And which one of these delectable creatures is your wife?" the monk inquired.

Pons and Guy immediately indicated Guy's startled companion. Seeing their mistake, they simultaneously shifted their pointed fingers to the other woman, realizing instantly they had repeated their blunder. "This one," Guy said, attempting to save the situation, "is the devoted wife of Pons, while this one here is *my* woman."

"Now you add false witness to the sins which have already been put to your account. Even if you were telling the truth, have you not uncovered the nakedness of your neighbor's wife and they of their neighbor's husband?"

"What do you want?" asked Guy.

"I want nothing. The question is: What do *you* want?"

Pons spoke: "We're just simple pilgrims from Provence. We're on our way to Clermont because we heard that the pope is going to speak. There's talk of a pilgrimage to Jerusalem. Guy and me—we've lost everything. The crops failed during the drought, and food is expensive. We survived on fish, frogs, eels, a few roots and herbs. We have little pleasure except what we can create for ourselves. If there's going to be a pilgrimage, we want to be a part of it because there's nothing left for us here. It would involve no sacrifice." He hesitated. "We have nothing."

The monk spoke quickly. "But that's where you are wrong. It's not a question of whether you will offer a sacrifice, but what that sacrifice will be. You've chosen to sacrifice your virtue rather than your flesh. You want to be pilgrims to the holy places, yet you are not holy yourselves. You must seek good and not evil; hate evil and love good that you may live." With these words, the monk disappeared into forest.

"He may have been the Devil himself for all I know," Guy muttered. "He sure smelled like the Devil!" He reached impishly for his lady, but she pulled away. "I've never been more than twenty miles from the place of my birth," he said petulantly. "Now I take a trip of a lifetime only to have some filthy monk scare me to death!"

"I think it's time to go," said Pons.

"Let's get out of here," Guy said, concurring. He leapt adroitly out of the pool, raising his angular, naked body above them. But when he left the pond, he was surprised again.

"*Mon Dieu*! Our clothes are gone!"

CHAPTER THREE

The Pope, the Bishop and the Priest

CLERMONT, FRANCE
November 23, 1095 A.D.

OR CENTURIES, THE TOWN OF CLERMONT slept quietly in a luxuriant valley of the Auvergne between the great tableland mesa of the Chaines de Puy to the west and the Montagne Bourbonnaise to the east. Evidence of pre-historic volcanic activity spilled over the mesa, dotting the area around Clermont with domes of cracked rock and rugged buttes of scree and talus. Although not the least of the cities of Gaul, the town was overshadowed in both economic and ecclesiastical importance from the very beginning by Lyon to the east. It had been called Augustometum in the early days of Roman Gaul when enterprising legions had extended the empire to its limits, giving towns and villages the nomenclature of Roman deities and emperors. For a time, the town was referred to as the Cite d'Auvergne. But since the third century when Saint Austremoine, the apostle of the province, had come up the Allier, it had been the seat of the bishop. The town came to be known as the "bishop's mountain," or *cleric montagne*. People were soon calling it in the Latin *Clermontensus*, or simply Clermont.

Actually, there was no mountain except Puy de Dome to the west. Britons, Normans or other strangers passing through would always ask, "Where's the mountain?" And the townspeople would patiently explain. When Austremoine first arrived, there was no church. He chose the highest ground in the village as the site of the first house of God. Since then, the town had grown and the church had been built and rebuilt several times over, always on the same site.

When travelers descended the western hills, they saw the town of Clermont in the center of an agricultural patchwork of cultivated fields. But most striking of all was the dark edifice rising above the center of the town. It was constructed of dark volcanic rock—black lava—hewn out of nearby quarries, the first time lava had been so used. Tradesmen and engineers from Amiens, Beauvais and Paris had provided the expertise and design; the townspeople, their sweat and very lives. The result was a stunning black cathedral with cross-topped spires, a cathedral that brooded over the city casting spells and shadows of the supernatural. Set as it was upon the high ground of Clermont, the flat, red-tiled domiciles of the city formed a colorful pedestal for the lava jewel of the Auvergne. As all streets and roads led to or emerged from the cathedral, the apparent omnipresence of the *cathedrale noire* evoked a sort of perverse, fearful pride: their cathedral was black; their God was stern; and now, not only was it the seat of a bishop, it was the temporary home of an ecumenical council of the universal Church.

At the sound of a knock, Pope Urban II turned away from the shuttered window of the cathedral study, releasing the embroidered, velvet curtains that had been held aside by his chubby, bejeweled hand. Realigning alb and chasuble, he glided across the room toward the door—head and garments motionless as though scores of tiny feet underneath those clerical vestments were rolling him along.

A thin-voiced page announced Adhemar, bishop of Le Puy. He entered with a flourish and made a hasty demonstration of obedience to the pope.

"Mon ami, mon ami!" The pope beamed lavishly as he held Adhemar at arm's length as though his friend had changed in the four months since he had seen him last at Piazenza. "You're looking well. The famine obviously has not caught up with you. Gratia Dei." Urban laughed.

In fact, there was no evidence of corpulence in the physical appearance of Adhemar whatsoever. To the contrary, he was lean-faced and the small muscles of his Roman countenance, coupled with a principled jaw, suggested firmness of character without hardness of spirit. The eyes were decisive and keen with life.

"It is always good to see you, your Eminence," said the bishop of le Puy.

"Adhemar! Let's not be so formal. It is I, Odo of Chatillon! Odo, who nursed you through the quadrivium! Odo, who fed you Plato, Plotinus and Augustine. How many times did I chase you out of the gardens when no one at the abbey knew where to find you? And I would find you, reading Boethius or the like!"

The pope released the bishop and moved toward the desk. He turned partially to face Adhemar again. "*De consolatio philosophiae!*" he said, laughing. "Ha! Philosophy never consoled anyone! Drives you mad, I say. That's what it does. All questions and no answers. You end up being either a lunatic or a saint—perhaps the one being the condition of the other, eh?" He laughed again bois-terously.

Adhemar smiled with reserve; not at the pope's attempt at levity but at the revelation that some people grow to resemble their names. Odo. The roundness of the letters, the pope's rounding, balding head, bulbous nose, spherical cheeks. Even his eyes, large and globe-like ... and the rotund, portly waist. The pope looked like an Odo; he couldn't be anything but an Odo. Never, for example, a rakish Philip, with its slashes and straight lines. Even his pontifical appellation suited him: Urban, or VRBAN, with the open V and the open A and N, the beginning and the end, the round B in the middle.

"Here we are again, your Eminence," he said, waving in the expanse of the room which was now the pope's headquarters while he was at Clermont.

The pope sat down behind the hand-carved oak desk in the center of a room sacredly aromatic with the sweet scent of polished woods and embroidered tapestries. The pope, leaning over some papers, motioned Adhemar to be seated, and they sat together in the companionable and comfortable silence of friends.

Presently the bishop of Rome spoke. "This matter with Philip is going to be a nasty business, Adhemar," he said with a sigh. "The man—what a rogue! He abandons Bertha, the wife of his youth, for Bertrada du Monford, who has in turn left her husband, the Count of Anjou—and the two of them expect the Church to stand up and applaud." The pope leaned away from his desk, and opened his palms toward Adhemar in frustration.

"And the word is out—although we can't confirm this—that he's involved in another adulterous affair with God knows who. We talk to him, we threaten him, we beg him. For two years this has been going on, yet he steadfastly resists our efforts to resolve this. Now the council will condemn his actions with Bertrada, and I shall be forced to draw up papers of excommunication."

"I doubt that the king will allow his disobedience to go that far, your Eminence," said Adhemar, insisting on formalities. "Philip may be a proud man, even a man given to occasional excesses of the flesh. But he is also a *practical* man. He knows that he cannot function as the regent of France if the country is under the interdiction of Rome, not to speak of his own personal excommunication. He'll come around."

"He's a proud man," said the pope, nodding. "As for excesses of the flesh, the man's brains are in his pants ... I don't think he's a *practical* man. That's where he differs from Henry. If I went to Canossa in the dead of winter like Gregory, could I expect Philip to show up standing in the snow for three days? Never! Henry was proud, but he was practical; he knew what he had to do, even if, and especially if, his own interests were at stake."

Adhemar, who could number listening among his virtues, sat mute, admitting that Urban's assessment was essentially correct even though Emperor Henry, eighteen years after Canossa, was presently excommunicated.

"What is that commotion?" Urban asked. In the distance, beyond paneled doors and in the unknown recesses of cold, stone corridors, came a faint cloud of dissonance, a disturbance. Urban shrugged and went on. "Therefore, I have prepared myself for the likelihood that I will not have his support for the pilgrimage. He will *not* raise an army, he will *not* provide funding, he will *not* encourage his lords and vassals to join us. In short, he isn't going to do a blessed thing! While his servants fulfill their vows at the Holy Sepulcher, Philip will be in Paris sleeping with Bertrada or someone else. He has no substance, he is bad for France. Alexius wants me to send him an army and I can't even get the King of France to button his trousers!" He stopped, glowering at his papers. "He is a fool," he muttered.

Adhemar looked aside in amusement at this display of episcopal exasperation. The bishop of Rome did have a temper.

After a few contemplative minutes had elapsed, Adhemar rose, stretched himself to his full height and approached his old mentor. "You may be certain that we will do our utmost to secure his cooperation and, failing that, engage ourselves all the more assiduously to ensure a successful conclusion to this pilgrimage." The pope smiled. Adhemar always expressed himself well. He was a bishop with the manners of a prince.

The commotion they had heard before had by now swollen like a gathering storm, boiling to the very doors of the study. An interruption was imminent. The pope arose and stepped out from behind his desk. Adhemar was about to go to the doors when they quickly swung open. Adhemar eased to the side of the study to observe. Into the office stepped a page and two brutish knights sans helmet and hauberk but bearing an argumentative young man between them. He was a priest, average height, slight of build and not a line on his face. His full length, black cassock was slightly askew. Urban motioned for the guards to release the cleric and excused them without a word. Released, the priest rotated his vestments so that the column of fasteners faced front as they were supposed to.

The distraught page put it this way: The priest had attempted to penetrate the security of the cathedral, asserting it was necessary to see His Holiness in person in order to deliver an urgent message. He had escaped the guards momentarily and was re-apprehended en route to the bishop's study. Believing His Holiness to have already been disturbed by the ruckus, the page felt it his duty to offer this explanation and await further instructions.

Urban dismissed the page, a scurrilous chap who appeared personally affronted by the whole affair. He turned on his heels dramatically and padded out of the room, drawing the doors shut behind him.

The harried priest dropped deferentially to his knees and remained still with head bowed. Pope Urban II shuffled toward him until the papal sandals were directly beneath the supplicant's gaze. The pontifical toes, round and ruddy, peaked discreetly beyond the hem of his alb. The terrified priest, inexperienced in the ways of both the Church and the world, momentarily forgot what protocol required at moments such as these: the bauble on the toe or the ring on the hand. In ecclesiastical *terra incognita*, his eyes fixated on the bejeweled toe, but his heart hoped for the papal hand.

Sensing movement, the priest raised his head and saw Urban's extended hand. Joyously, he clasped it firmly and thankfully, and kissed the proffered ring.

"What is your name, my son?" asked the pope.

"Fulcher of Chartres, your Holiness," he replied, head bowed again.

"Come, come," said Urban, "get up and be seated." Urban floated back to the desk and busied himself with his robes while the young man took his place in Adhemar's chair.

"Now, tell me what happened," Urban prodded.

The young priest turned to look at Adhemar, then back at the pope, and back again to Adhemar, sweeping the room for details, anything familiar.

"It's all right," said Adhemar. The bishop remembered when he was a young priest, visionary and inexperienced.

The cleric began his story. "This morning, I went to the cathedral to pray—which is my custom, even back home in Chartres, I visit the cathedral rather than saying prayers in the village church. I went to the cathedral for prayers and following my prayers I stayed to write." He looked at Adhemar as though he must explain. "I like to write, you know. I have been writing about my journeys south from Chartres to Clermont, and I carry a writing box with my parchment, ink and quills—which I don't have now. It must be in the cathedral, I must be sure—"

"—After you finished your writing," Adhemar broke in, sensing that the narrative was digressing.

"After I finished my writing, I left the cathedral, crossed the commons toward the Rue de Gras. As I was walking down the street, I saw a monk coming my way on a donkey, very slowly for the Rue de Gras is very steep, you know. I didn't think much of it until he drew closer. I saw that he was very dirty—I mean, extremely filthy by any standards. His face was striking, sort of ... strange ... long, swarthy, dour. As we were about to pass one another in the street, he spoke to me directly. 'Father,' he whispered. He had a very low voice, not really so low, but commanding, like the thunder you hear no matter how far away it is, you hear it and listen. He didn't speak loud, but it was a voice that compelled me to listen. 'Father,' he said to me, 'I have an errand for you, an errand at which you must not fail.'" Fulcher stopped his narration, thinking that perhaps the whole thing sounded too preposterous.

"Go on," Adhemar urged.

"I had no idea what he was talking about. It all seemed very mysterious to me, and why me? But he pulled a leather pouch out of his cloak and handed it to me. He said, 'You will find the vicar of St. Peter in the cathedral chambers. You must deliver this to him immediately. Do not open it. Show it to no one; give it to no one.' And then he gave me a bag of clothing which he said to give to the needy. After that, he left and I am standing in the Rue de Gras with a bag in my hands. I went back to the cathedral to pray in the Chapel of St. Venerand. I decided I should do as I had been told. But I was stopped in my attempt by the guards and only by persevering was I able to make it to this door. If I have erred, Holy Father, I have erred in faith."

Fulcher unbuttoned his cassock and withdrew from within its folds a pouch which he slapped on the desk. "Here it is," he announced, sitting back in quaking relief. The satchel was not touched. The three churchmen stared at it as if it were an object of veneration.

When the pope stood, Fulcher arose and together they walked to the door. "Go in peace, my son," said the pope. "You have done the right thing," and placing his right palm upon the taller priest, he gave the young man his blessing. Fulcher bowed to accommodate the blessing from the diminutive pontiff and then left without a further word.

Adhemar joined the pope who remained motionless by the door thinking. "Peter is here, Adhemar," said Urban somberly. "Peter the Hermit, Peter of the Cowl. I want you to find him and bring him to me."

CHAPTER FOUR

The Peasants

DELAIDE BARTHOLOMEW TUGGED FIRMLY AT the rope binding the cloth and deftly made a knot and tested it. It held.

"Let's see if that's better, Lettie," she said to the girl. Arletta grimaced as her older sister hefted the bale of wool fabric and helped her into the shoulder harness they had improvised.

"How many more trips must we make, Addie?" she asked. "I don't know if I can walk another mile." The two women were wearing plain blouses with long-sleeves rolled up to the elbow, and kirtles of homespun linen over which were full-body aprons with pockets. On their heads were white caps; on their feet, sandals.

"One more" Adelaide said, trying to be cheerful. She took a handkerchief to her brow and sopped up the perspiration that had gathered there. "One more, and then all the cloth is at the market." They were going to the abbey market at Cordes where all the goods brought to market on the backs of the peasants were exempt from tariffs. Goods brought to market in carts were subject to three deniers, and goods brought in on shod horses were taxed two deniers per beast. So Addie, her sister Arletta, her brother Peter and her daughter Clare had made several trips to the market to sell their homespun cloth, staggering up the dusty red road to the walled city which sat on a high hilltop aerie above the valley where they pastured their small flock.

In a year in which famine had stalked not only her flock but also her family, every denier saved was a denier earned. They grew enough food in their garden to support the four of them throughout the year and Addie was confident they would survive the winter. They had managed to keep a few chickens, but they could not afford a cow, so they had to buy their milk although they could scarcely afford to do so. In famine, the price of everything went up. They often went without milk, for it was more important to purchase other supplies, such as salt, than it was to have milk.

Addie believed that the sheep would be their ultimate salvation. At first, following the death of her husband, they had simply taken the wool to market. Then, with money saved from the sale of the wool, they purchased a single loom at which Addie could weave narrow strips of cloth.

Clare helped tend and feed the flock. Peter sheared the sheep with Ollo's prized shears. Addie and Lettie washed the raw wool in large tubs and then carded it prior to spinning. The wool was then spun into thread by the two of them while they watched the flock in the fields. Soon the thread was spooled and woven into cloth.

But the work still wasn't done. The fulling was done by Addie and Peter treading the cloth in troughs. The heavy, dripping cloth was then hung on hooks in frames, so that when the cloth was dry, the material would be stretched to the exact size desired. Lettie and Clara brushed the cloth with teasels in wooden hand frames to raise the nap. The long process was arduous, requiring a singular effort of both limb and body. More than once, the family was tempted to desert the enterprise altogether. Now the four of them stood in the shadow of the snow-capped Pyrenees, ready to trudge up the hill to the fortified city of Cordes. Each bore a burden according to age, strength and ability.

"I wish Ollo was here," said Lettie in a twangy Provencal accent as they started out again.

Addie wiped the perspiration from her brow. Even in November, the sun shone warmly in Languedoc. The scarf tied over her head was damp at the forehead. Except for a few wisps behind her ears, it covered most of her auburn hair. She had asked her brother to cut it to keep the curly mop off her neck. It felt better that way when she was working. So Peter took his shears and clipped her hair like a yearling lamb. The sleeves of her blouse were rolled high to free her hands and arms for labor.

"He's not here and nothin's gonna bring him back," she said. She stooped when she walked, the cloth stacked high on her back. There wasn't a pebble in the road within a six-foot swath that she didn't observe. She recognized every stone, boulder and mud-hole along the way. Her shoulders ached and she could feel the muscles of her upper back tense as she shifted the load she carried. It would be three days before she stopped walking askew after this was all over.

Ollo was dead. He'd been dead for two years now. Ate some infected rye and died of ergot. The priest had given him last rites, but Addie couldn't afford a proper Christian burial in the church stone yard, so she loaded his body into a borrowed wagon and left by herself for the mountains with nothing but food and a shovel. She buried him with no help from anyone in a place known only to her and God. She wanted it that way. When she returned, she never mentioned it again. There was work to do.

He was only 26 when he left his wife and 7-year-old daughter, four years older than Addie. But he left a piece of land and a small flock free and clear. He was a freeman, given his freedom as the dying wish of his lord, Guiliaume de Castres, who was in dire need of good works ere he faced his Maker. Together, and with the help of Peter and Lettie, even little Clare, they had tilled the land and built up the flock.

Addie set her ochre-freckled, sunburned face upon Cordes. Her eyes were fired with determination. Her family kept pace, for Addie was conscious of their ability. Her brother, Peter, was a strapping lad of 17 with a rosy complexion. He had been doing the work of a man since he was 13. The dark-haired Lettie, his sister, was becoming a woman. Slender at the waist, and chest budding, she sometimes tired under the strain of the daily demands of work. But she completed her share of the chores; she had no choice—there was too much for Addie or Peter to attempt by themselves. Clare was a child, impish and playful, yet a fragile, delicate creature. Still, she insisted on full participation in sharing the burdens and responsibilities of the Bartholomew household, and Addie made sure that her time was well-spent.

When they returned that night to the mud-hovel they called home, they were 100 deniers richer. Now they would have to make it through the winter. It would be difficult, especially if the season was harsh. Peter, however, told his sister the next morning not to be afraid. St. Andrew had appeared to him in a dream. The saint had told him that neither plague nor pestilence, arrow nor famine would come nigh them, for he had a work for them to do.

Addie scoffed, as she always did, at Peter's visions. He expected it and it no longer hurt him as it once had. No one believed in his visions. But that he saw visions was a fact that seemed to comfort his family. It was typical of Peter to dream dreams, and if Peter could still see visions in the dead of winter, staring into the jaws of starvation, then all was well. Peter's ecstasies were the one constant in the Bartholomew's fast-changing world, so Addie didn't mind even if she did seem irritated by them from time to time. "Just don't say anything to the priest," she warned her brother.

✠✠✠

The massive oak doors of the cathedral with enormous iron hinges closed with a clunk behind Fulcher as he stepped into the late-morning light. The sun was bright, the sky deep and endless and the air biting and rare. The winter equinox approached and the sting of an autumn breeze caused Fulcher to wrap a cloak about him for warmth.

No matter. Fulcher himself did not feel the chill. When one has received the blessing of the pope, one pays scant heed to other things. Fulcher felt that his entire life had been a prelude to this one morning in which, in the providence of God, he had been chosen to be an instrument of God. He had experienced this feeling once before when he had been ordained and consecrated by his bishop, Ivo, two years earlier. The episcopal blessing had indeed been an inspiration, but the papal touch was pure joy.

In this exalted state, the young priest passed through the rectory gardens and into the city square where autumn leaves danced in the swirling wind. Here the streets of the town spread out like spokes in a cartwheel. Fulcher reviewed his options: the Rue de Gras where merchants displayed a variety of wares including handcrafted boxes, carvings, rugs and embroidered cloth, and vendors sold food, and farmers brought their vegetables to market. Today fresh vegetables would be scarce, for the season was quickly passing, but street chefs were preparing a fine assortment of savory meats and delicious sweets. He might try the Rue des Chaussetiers, however: cloth, stockings, garments there. Perhaps the Rue de la Coifferie: more clothing shops plus hats. Or the Rue de la Boucherie: butchers here offered such viands as stag, hare, beaver, badger, otter, partridge, beef, pork, mutton and lamb. The carcasses were displayed appealingly on spiked racks, but alas, it was too noisy and odiferous, and besides, Fulcher was not hungry.

Fulcher started across the square toward the Rue de Gras. With the council in session, the relic sellers and merchants were turning a tidy profit, and they might, in so doing, salvage a disastrous year. Visitors from Normandy, Provence, Burgundy, northern Europe, Britain, Spain and Italy filled the square and the stalls of the city markets. Many were religious—in Clermont for the ecumenical session, 300 for the council itself and many hundreds more in town as observers.

A few hermits, anchorites and anchoresses came out of the hills to hear the pope, and the major monastic orders were represented, all attired in the appropriate ascetic and monastic garb:

Benedictines and Cluniacs arrayed in black, Cistercians in white. The female counterparts wore a feminine version of their respective monastic orders: Benedictine and Cluniac nuns were attired in white under-tunics, black gowns and veils with white wimples around the face and neck, while Cistercian nuns were dressed exclusively in white *cucculae* over their habits. People called them the White Ladies. Some baldheaded and discalced Carthusians could be seen wearing coarse hair-shirts and scanty tunics.

Thus, the markets of the Rue de Gras were full of holy orders, a perambulating patchwork of black and white. Fulcher had no purpose and little money. But he browsed along the cobbled street nonetheless, inspecting the merchandise, making mental notes as to quality and cost. The markets and goods of Chartres were generally superior, he thought.

To his right on a lower step of the steep street, Fulcher saw nothing but baskets, large and small, woven no doubt by a local craftsman with the special reeds of Provence. He was about to take a closer look, for they were very attractively crafted, but the two Cistercian nuns, with whom in his shopping he had temporarily cast his lot, had already spotted them.

He was not prepared for what happened next. The nuns leaned forward to inspect a particularly large and handsome basket—a basket used for the transportation and storage of melons and fruits. The lid was so large that the nuns took positions on either side of the vessel to lift the cover together.

This they did, but its removal revealed a hairy, male Provencal, clad in nothing but a broad smile. "Bonjour, nonettes!" he said, giving the nuns a slight wave from his cramped position in the basket.

The Cistercian White Ladies recoiled in fright, startled not only by the surprise itself, but, of course, by the nature of it. It's not every day a nun, Cistercian, Carthusian or otherwise, gets a gander at a naked man. A great cry went up, and townspeople quickly gathered to see what the fuss was about.

Seeing—or hearing, it should be said—their fright, the hapless Provencal panicked and stood upright in the basket, fronting the nuns in *nudum nudendum*. Stumbling out of the basket, he pushed between the nuns who were as immobile as Lot's wife, and dashed through the market to the cheers and shouts of onlookers and passersby.

"Stop that man! Put some clothes on him!" Fulcher shouted as the bare-arsed man disappeared into the milling throng. "Put some clothes on him!"

Fulcher elbowed through the townsfolk to come to the aid of the nuns. One had collapsed to the ground and was reciting the Lord's Prayer: *Pater noster, qui es in caelis, sanctificetur nomen tuum; adveniat reqnum tuum, fiat voluntas tuas, sicut in caelo et in terra.* Fulcher saw immediately that she was temporarily beyond help.

The other was still standing, but sinking fast. Fulcher lunged at her, catching her mid-swoon and eased her to the earth and into his grasp.

"Are you sensible now?" he asked when she revived. He took her head in his hands and forced her to look into his eyes. "Feeling better now, are you?" he asked.

She couldn't look at him. She placed her head against his chest and clung to him. "*Peccavi, peccavi, peccavi!*" she said. "*Mea culpa! Mea culpa! Mea maxima culpa!*"

"Sister!" Fulcher said, shaking the nun quickly and vigorously. *Lord have mercy*, he thought. Once again, *terra incognita!*

"Father, I have sinned, hear my confession." The nun was whimpering, on the edge of incoherence. "You must hear my confession." Fulcher looked up at the amphitheater of faces that had ringed the three of them. But there was among them not a single priest who could be of assistance. "Move away, please. All of you, please, move back," he shouted. "Give us some air now!"

The crowd quieted and stepped back a few paces, but did not disperse. Fulcher turned his attentions to the woman in his arms. "Father, I have sinned. Hear my confession!"

"Sister," Fulcher began, "Confession must be confidential and anonymous. Let's get you back to your—"

She shook her head earnestly. "Father, I saw it!"

"What, sister? What did you see?" asked Fulcher gently, unknowing.

"It," she hissed. "It!"

"What? You had a vision?" Fulcher turned to the crowd again. "She's had a vision! Move back now! Give us some room here. She has had a vision!"

Certain of the people started to smile and not a few giggles sprinkled the air. The priest faced the Cistercian nun again. "You've had a great shock," he began. "Now you must rest. We can talk about what you have seen later."

"*Peccavi! Peccavi!*" She lifted her face to Fulcher's ear. "I saw it," she whispered.

"What did you see, sister?" He whispered back.

"The *instrumentum concupiscientiae*, Father!" She paused and then put it another way. "The *membrum carnalis!*"

Oh! ... OH! A vision indeed! Fulcher coughed, and could feel his blood rising to his face. The *membrum virilis!* Of course! The townsfolk must have overheard this exchange, for they laughed and jeered. "I saw the same thing the sister saw," said one wag to another, "but it didn't look like much of a vision to me!" Fulcher released the nun immediately, stood and surveyed the crowd indecisively. "Take care of your sister,' he said to the White Ladies in the throng. And he fled down the Rue de Gras, his black robes flapping furiously.

The Provencal had been apprehended by Guerin d' Marchaud, an importer of cloth. He was seated on the tiled street in an upright fetal position and leaning against the wall of the merchant's shop. Someone had given him a blanket.

Pushing through the press, Fulcher approached the man. "What's the meaning of this?" he demanded with a touch of asperity. He felt an obligation to pursue this matter as far as he could.

"I didn't mean to scare those nuns, Father," replied the Provencal. "If I had clothes I would be wearing them. But I don't."

"What's your name?" said Fulcher.

"Pons de Rodez," he answered. "My friend and I are from Provence."

"And where are your clothes?" inquired Fulcher, asking the obvious question.

"It's a long story, Father."

"I have the time," said Fulcher. "I have the time."

"We were bathing."

"You were bathing? Whatever for? No one takes a bath without a reason."

"As I said, we're from Provence. On our way, not far from here, we found a pool in the forest. We were tired from our journey and were less than a day from Clermont. We thought we should take advantage of the warm water. So we bathed. But when we went up to the bank to retrieve our clothes, they were gone. Poooooffff!"

"You bathed in the pools of the Auvergne? The *lacrima diaboli*—the tears of the Devil? My God, it's a miracle you only lost your clothes and not your souls!"

"Yes, Father, it is a miracle," Pons said.

"Yes, it's a miracle," Fulcher repeated. "Where are your friends?"

"My friend, Guy de Monteil, is still in the hills. I came into town early this morning before dawn looking for clothes. But when the light came I was in danger of discovery and jumped into the basket, yes? And was discovered, you know, anyway. Can you by any chance find us some clothes?"

Providential! Fulcher remembered the mulish-looking monk. "I think I can help you,' he said. "I'll be back.'

Fulcher stood and spoke to the merchants. "I'll be back shortly with some clothes."

At the rectory, Fulcher recovered the clothes the monk had given him. There were underclothes, shirts and pants for two men. That would do. There were also women's garments; someone would need them in due time, Fulcher thought.

For yet a third time that day, Fulcher departed for the Rue de Gras.

CHAPTER FIVE

The Pope and the Monk

CLERMONT, FRANCE
November 25, 1095 A.D.

HEN JOHN LANGLOIS, BUILDER OF the choir of St. Urbain at Troyes was hired as the master builder of the cathedral project at Clermont, he immediately made two far-reaching decisions. The first was to abandon the traditional rotunda design patterned on the Pantheon of Rome and made famous in France by the exquisite spirituality of the Palatine Chapel at Aix-la-Chapelle. Rather, the church was modeled on the *basilica* and consisted of a central nave with two aisles. The interior of such a building could more easily accommodate large crowds, such as the council which was now in session. A transverse nave crossing the main axis so as to form the shape of a cross completed the final shape of the cathedral during the period when many architects were experimenting with a style they called Romanesque.

His design was not without problems, however. Langlois' nave at Clermont was daringly high and a decision had to be made about the roof. Typically the nave was covered by laying wooden beams from one wall to the other, which could then be left exposed or covered by a coffered ceiling. The disadvantage of such a roof was that it limited the size of the nave, and the wood was liable to catch fire.

Langlois made a second decision. He opted for a stone-vaulted groined roof the success of which depended upon a precise knowledge of three-dimensional geometry and an ability to calculate the curve of the vaulting. On the day of the cathedral's dedication, Langlois' diagrams could still be found etched in some of the stones. The bishop elected to leave them there as a reminder of the artist's skills.

Two days after Fulcher gave Pons a new wardrobe, the bishops of the council convened for a final evening session in the rib-vaulted nave of Langlois' cathedral. The bishops were attired in full ecclesiastical regalia. This session was a mere formality; the business of the council had been completed the day before.

In this final assembly, the council seated over 500 people—bishops and secular observers. Pope Urban II said the mass in the torch-lit nave. Benedictines from Monte Cassino chanted psalms. The antiphonal performance was both solemn and sublime. Fulcher's heart was full of joy. It was consistent with his ebullient nature that Fulcher could be in rapture upon hearing only a few notes canted by some Italian monks in a minor French cathedral.

To the impassioned mind of the Count of Blois, however, the mass was merely sacred drama, impressive to be sure, but firmly rooted in *this* world, not the next. Whereas Fulcher's interest in the mass was *theo*logical, Stefan's was *christo*logical: Fulcher saw the face of God and was uplifted; Stefan, the hands of Christ and was condemned. The bloodied Christ above the high altar reminded him of sin—his own—and guilt. Fulcher was sanctified and blissfully unaware of it, Stefan was condemned and shamefully aware of it. He knew he was in need of salvation: to be saved to sin again. *Ut gratia abundet.*

They both stayed to hear the canons of the council read in their entirety following the mass. While the reading was customary, it wasn't particularly interesting. Several of the aging bishops fell asleep and remained seated upright only because they were supported by younger clerics. Sixty-one canons covering a wide range of ecclesiastical and cultural experiences had been adopted by the council. The *Pax Dei* was reaffirmed; new regulations against simony were enacted; clerics were forbidden to drink publicly in taverns; all Christians were to receive ashes during Lent; men were to abstain from intimate relations with their wives on certain holy days; and excommunicates were not to be buried in Christian cemeteries. *Et alia.*

Dominating the interest of the council, however, was the second Canon pertaining to a plenary indulgence: *Quicumque pro sola devotione, non pro honoris vel pecunie adeptione. Ad liberandam ecclesiam Dei Hierusalem profectus fuerit, iter illud pro omni penitentia ei reputetur.* This Canon was the cornerstone of Pope Urban's great vision of a pilgrimage to Jerusalem because it provided that the successful completion of the journey would offset all sins, past and present.

While this indulgence was unprecedented and was by itself sufficient to fire the desiccated imagination of restless knights, Urban went on to completely modify the concept of *pilgrimage*: the pilgrim in this enterprise *would not only carry the staff, but the sword!* The implication was obvious: this was not merely a pilgrimage but a crusade! The pilgrim would be armed!

The council was astir. Bishops marveled and openly discussed the ramifications of what amounted to a sweeping theological revision of the pilgrimage ideal. The excitement generated among the knights and nobility was intense. The pope's announcement meant that the knight was no longer required to give up his *soldierly* vocation in order to enjoy the *spiritual* benefits of a pilgrimage. Indeed, his mandate as a soldier of Christ was a call to fulfill that vocation. Whereas he had once shed the blood of his brother and was condemned, he could now kill an infidel and be praised! The guilt-ridden knight, so in need of salvation, could now become the agent of his own redemption: with a single sweep of his sword he could save both the soul of a Saracen and the soul of a Christian— his own!

Salvation, Fulcher understood, was what this pilgrimage was all about: the salvation of the *pilgrim*, the salvation of the *Church*, the salvation of the *holy places*, and even the salvation of the *infidel.*

Especially, the salvation of the pilgrim. This was not simply a just war—perhaps not a just war at all, in the classic Augustinian sense—but a *justifying* war: Should the pilgrim fulfill his vow at the Church of the Holy Sepulcher, he would receive a full pardon for his sins; Should he have the good fortune to die gloriously in battle, he would reap as his reward the eternal salvation of his soul.

Urban argued persuasively for the pilgrimage along several lines. First, the economic and social conditions in France created a favorable climate for a pilgrimage. Famine and poor crops had impoverished the nation. This, in turn, led to the very bloodshed the *Pax Dei* was designed to stop.

Then, too, the church in the East was in serious danger due to the Islamic threat. The Turks were at the gates of Constantinople. Emperor Alexius was begging the West for military assistance. An army of God, a *militia Christi*, Urban reasoned, would be an appropriate response to this request.

Finally, it was well known that travel to the holy places in Palestine had become very dangerous. Christians were no longer granted access to traditional sites. The holy places languished in neglect and suffered from the irreligious abuse of the infidel. Against Islam, whether in defense of the holy places, the eastern borders, or Latin and Greek rite churches, Christendom appeared ineffectual and powerless.

Power, Stefan understood, was what this pilgrimage was all about: the power of the Roman bishop versus the Constantinopolitan patriarch; the power of the military forces of western princes against the armies of Turkish sultans and emirs; the power of the cross against that of the crescent; the power of Christ against the power of Mohammed. The pilgrimage was a contest of power, and for Stefan it would never be anything else. An unalterable law of the world, Anna had said.

✠✠✠

As the last "Amens" still hovered about Langlois tribunes, the pope and his aides, Bishop Ugolino of Ostia and Cardinal Diego of the Italian curia, left the nave and followed a labyrinthine course of corridors and stone, cold and rutted stairwells to the pope's subterranean quarters not far from the cathedral crypt. The pope's aides helped him get out of his papal robes and prepared a fire in his chambers. He prepared a mug of strong mead. This night was the capstone of a career in which there had been many such high points. Born Otho de Lagery of a noble family in Chatillon-sur-Maine in 1042; student, canon, and archdeacon at Rheims; monk under Abbot Hugh, and later prior of Cluny; transferred to Rome and became pope by acclamation only seven years ago.

Urban was drinking his mead and leaning into the fire when he heard footsteps. He reached for a small piece of wood and was placing it on the flames when he tensed and held the log still.

"Bonsoir, Pierre," he whispered, placing the wood upon the fire.

"Good evening. Holy Father," replied the visitor. "How did you know it was I?"

The pope straightened and turned about in his chair to face the gloomy cavity of a cowl and a man in the habit of a monk. Urban smiled and shook his head.

"Three things, Peter," he said brightly, thrusting three fingers in the face of the monk. "If you wish to put a fright into bishops and prelates with nocturnal peregrinations in their private quarters, you must first take a bath. Second, eat something besides fish, and third, trim your toenails. When you moved off the carpet, I could hear the scratching." He paused. "Besides, I more or less expected you to show up. I have the sermon you sent."

"Good," said Peter. "I want to talk about it." Peter removed his hood and, drawing a stool, scooted close to the pope. They conversed for a few moments about persons and events they had in common in their personal histories. Odo and Peter had both been educated at the cathedral school at Rheims, but Peter left before Odo and went to Cluny. Unhappy with the strict regimen of Abbot Hugh, he left before Odo arrived and retired to the hills to begin a solitary life as a hermit, venturing into towns and villages only occasionally and then only to thunder dire imprecations against those who had committed various breaches of morality. Yet, in spite of the isolation of his vocation, he had remained in contact with prominent figures in the church. Peter the Hermit was a name remembered by all—and not always pleasantly.

"Terracina," said Peter.

"Terracina," the pope agreed. "The last time we met.'

"And the last time we talked about a pilgrimage," Peter quickly added. "Let me shoot this arrow while the target's in sight. Can I have some of that mead?" Urban waved his hand in a way that granted permission, and Peter got himself some drink. Then he sat down again on his stool. "These are momentous days. I don't want to cause no trouble or anything. The pilgrimage is really, well, it's really important. But there're people in Cluny who will recall—if they are reminded—that the pilgrimage was *my* vision and that I allowed you to—how should I put it?—'Appropriate' it for the Church only out of respect for the apostolic office and, anyways, because I couldn't see no conflict with going ahead with my own plans anyway."

"And I have a few arrows in my quiver that will not miss their mark either," said the pope irritated. "You don't *allow* the Church, anything. Your ideas aren't your ideas to market or sell, withhold or give away as though you own them. You're a servant of the Church. And you probably have forgotten that your own plans, Kioko, are doomed to inevitable failure. You have neither the skill nor the means to get *yourself* to Jerusalem, let alone hordes of pilgrims! In fact, I'd be surprised if you could get out of France!" He laughed, and took more drink.

Peter winced at both the reference to his name and his past. Those who knew him well insisted on calling him Little Peter, a reference to his height. In the Picard dialect, the name was Kioko. He had given the name to his donkey, hoping that he would not be called by the same name as that of his ass. He was wrong. But most stinging was Urban's mention of Peter's previous attempt to travel to Jerusalem. He had come up against the Turks and forced to return. It had been a bitter disappointment.

"Your Eminence," the monk said earnestly, "now listen to me. The pilgrimage you're talking about to this fancy council of bishops is not a pilgrimage of the *people* but of knights, nobles and princes. No room for common people who, with faith in their God and courage in their hearts, have no other desire than to see Jerusalem and walk the streets which Jesus walked. And the piety and holiness of the church, you must agree, is not in the nobility, but the peasantry. Right? I'd stack up one peasant against a hundred nobles any day of the week. Yet, you told your bishops to keep the people at home, when it is *their* participation on which depends the very success of this effort. Isn't that right?"

"What do you want?" asked the weary pontiff.

"The people must be a part of this pilgrimage and God has called me to lead them. Give me your permission to preach the pilgrimage, give me the money to do it, and I'll personally ensure that the pilgrimage achieves its goals."

The pope stood quickly and confronted the monk. "That's out of the question!" he said hotly. "I repeat, out of the question! You see yourself like a Moses leading the Israelites out of Egypt? The treasury of St. Peter is not at the disposal of itinerant monks." Urban flapped his arms in frustration. "You walk in here in the dead of night and think you can steal away with the resources of the Church and for no better reason than you think you can scare up a pilgrimage and you think you can lead it!" Urban sat down on his bed, aggravated and shaking his head in disbelief.

Peter answered coldly: "St. Peter said to the lame man, 'Silver and gold have I none, but such as I have I give unto thee. In the name of Jesus of Nazareth, rise up and walk.' The apostle had power, but no money; you have money, but no power. You've staked your reputation and that of the Church on this enterprise, and you don't even know if the lame man is going to walk. And if there's even the slightest suggestion that this whole idea, which you've represented as your own, was in fact the vision of an itinerant monk—as you say—your dreams will disappear like so much smoke in the wind. All I want is for you to broaden the appeal to include the people, authorization to preach and the financial means—"

"Absolutely not," said the pope. "Moreover, I myself—as you well know—am preaching to the people tomorrow. If this pilgrimage is anything, it is a pilgrimage of the people."

"Only certain people," the monk corrected. "The poor and the infirm must stay at home. The women likewise have been instructed to remain behind. You have already disqualified seventy-five percent of the population. Penance, when it is offered, Holy Father, should be offered to all people."

"Don't try to instruct me in the Christian faith, Peter!" Urban said. "And do you really want women on this pilgrimage? Really? You want women thrown in with 100,000 lusty knights, who, after two days, not to speak of two years, of celibacy, can think of nothing but—well, you understand what I'm saying. You're mad … or foolish. Maybe both. Probably time for you to leave now!"

The monk stood. He pulled the cowl around his head and cinched the rope about his habit. "I am a prophet. Your prophet, Urban. I have a letter from God. The people will follow. I have taken the pilgrimage before. The poor—men, women and children—who have no lords and protectors deserve this opportunity."

The pope went to the fireplace to stoke the embers. "You have a letter from God?" he said. "And where did you get a letter from God?'

"It doesn't matter," said the monk. "Where did the Church get all the wood it says is from the True Cross? Where did it get all the milk from the breast of the Blessed Virgin? Where did it get all the teeth from St. Peter? It is not a question of wood, of milk, or of teeth, but of faith. If the people believe it is wood from the cross, milk from the Virgin, a tooth from the mouth of St. Peter and if that belief motivates them to good works, then the value of the relic is authenticated. The point is, if the people believe I have a letter from God, and if that belief causes them to put their faith in me, I can lead them to faith in God."

"The people will have faith in you," Urban replied, "until you get to the Bosporus—if you get that far. Then they'll be ready to stone you for taking them into the Islamic wilderness to die. And they will die, there's no doubt about it."

Peter was not finished. "Odo, I know this: without faith— death-defying, mountain-moving faith—nobody is going anywhere. The question here is: how do you plan to give faith to the Franks tomorrow when you speak? The truth? The truth does not always inspire faith; sometimes one lie in the service of the truth achieves more than a thousand truths ever could. Didn't God Himself use deception to defeat the Devil by disguising deity in the form of a Man?"

Peter paused and folded his hands thoughtfully before continuing. "Best thing," he said, "stick to the text I gave you. Be careful! Don't talk about alliances with the East. Best not mention anything about bringing the church together again. Talk politics and theology to the bishops and princes but when you talk to the people tomorrow in Suger's field—well, they don't care. Alexius can go to hell as far as they're concerned."

Odo, seeing Peter was not leaving, wearily brought out more ale and poured himself another. "Want some?" he asked. "Northumbria's best."

Peter was gazing at the crucifix above the bed. "No," he replied. "Are you listening?"

"Yes, of course." Odo raised the mug to his lips. "Continue."

"Keep it personal. Tell them they are living in the last days. That the Turks are the devils of the Antichrist. That Jerusalem is besieged by the infidel. That they themselves hold the solution to the final victory. That the millennial kingdom is about to be ushered in and that they can have a part in it. Show them their death and the unassailable reasons why they must die. If you give them a reason to die, you give them a reason to live … and to fight, and then—" Peter the Hermit punctuated his final words by shaking a pointed finger at the pope, "you will have your pilgrimage!"

The monk turned from Urban and disappeared into the night. The pope never saw him again.

CHAPTER SIX

The Sermon

CLERMONT, FRANCE
November 26, 1095 A.D.

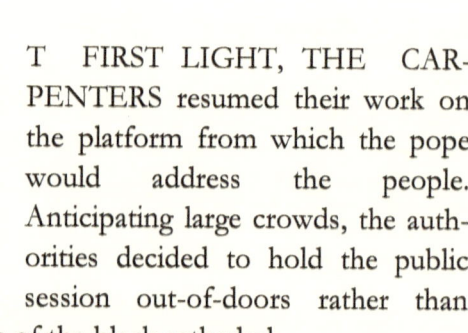

T FIRST LIGHT, THE CAR-
PENTERS resumed their work on
the platform from which the pope
would address the people.
Anticipating large crowds, the authorities decided to hold the public
session out-of-doors rather than
within the confines of the black cathedral.

The Council secured a field beyond the city by paying
thirty solidi to Suger, its owner. At the base of a series of
rocky domes and ridges, the workmen built an elevated
stage large enough to seat several score of ecclesiastical
and secular luminaries including local bishops, members
of the curia, papal nuncios and not a few of the princes
of France.

Early that afternoon on a grey and chilly day, the
crowds showed up as expected and invited guests
arrived: Hugh, the count of Vermandois and brother of
the Capetian king, Philip; Robert of Normandy, Stefan's brother-
in-law and brother of William Rufus of England; Count Raymond
of St. Gilles and his wife, Lady Elvira; Count Stefan of Blois and
Chartres and his wife, Lady Adela; and many other scions of

French nobility. The laity, of course, were outnumbered by religious dignitaries such as the bishops of Lyon, Le Puy, Paris,
Amiens, Rheims, Rouen, Chartres, et alia. The English were
represented by Anselm, the Archbishop of Canterbury, who found
it convenient to attend the council and escape—if momentarily—
his difficulties with William II. It was a source of no little
amusement to Stefan that the archbishop, in the infinite wisdom of
those who arrange such things, was seated next to his wife who was
the sister of William II, the king of England. The afternoon might
not be so dull after all, he thought.

The pope's speech was an event the community had been
anticipating for months. Now everything was ready. A podium
stood at the end of a small runway that went into and above the
crowd. The special guests were seated on tiers adorned with
Venetian tapestries and striped silks on one side while the
Benedictines from Monte Cassino occupied a series of terraced
benches on the other. Beyond the altar, which was centered directly
behind and several steps above the podium, were three large
crosses, the center cross the tallest. Mounted upon this cross was a
larger-than-life Suffering Christ, a work of art commissioned for
this occasion and wrought by Martin, a woodcarver from Anjou.

Stefan looked out on the gathered throng as the Benedictines
lifted up the strains of the TE DEUM. He estimated its number to
be in the thousands. The crowd huddled in clusters according to
family, village, ethnicity and geographic regions: Provencals here,
Normans there, Picts, Brits, Italians—all with their own. And, of
course, religious everywhere.

The chants faded and the pope arose slowly in heavy clerical
vestments and padded down the runway to the lectern where his
speech awaited. It's going to be a long afternoon, Stefan thought
wearily as the masses cheered the pope wildly. He had sat through
papal speeches before. Brevity was not one of Urban's virtues.

"Race of the French," Urban began, as a vision of the monk
arose before him, "race living beyond the Alps, race chosen and
beloved by God, as is radiantly shown by your many deeds, dis-

tinguished from all other nations as much by the situation of your lands and by your Catholic faith, as by the honor you show to the Holy Church; dearest Sons of God: I, Urban, Supreme Pontiff and by the permission of God prelate of the whole world, have come in this time of urgent necessity to you, the servants and children of God, as a messenger of divine admonition. We want you to know what grievous cause leads us to your territory, and what need of yours and all the faithful brings us here."

Count Stefan glanced sideways at the archbishop. He was smiling benignly and hanging on every word. Across the dais, he spotted a clerical scribe, Fulcher, the young priest from Chartres, scribbling furiously.

"A grave report has come from the lands around Jerusalem. You must hasten to carry aid to your brethren dwelling in Jerusalem who need your help for which they have often entreated. The Turks, a foreign race, a race absolutely alien to God, have attacked them, as many of you already know, and have advanced as far into Roman territory as the Arm of St. George. They have seized more and more of the lands of Christendom, have already defeated them in seven times as many battles, have reduced the people with sword and raping and have carried off some as captives to their own land. They have cut down others by pitiable murders and have either completely razed the churches of God to the ground or enslaved the people to the practice of their own rites. These men have destroyed the altars polluted by their foul practices. They cut open the navels of those whom they choose to torment, they tear out their most vital organs and tie them to a stake, drag them around and flog them before killing them as they lie prone on the ground with all their entrails out."

As the pope recounted the evils inflicted by the Turks upon Christians, the mood of the crowd became ugly. In diverse pockets of the milling crowd, Stefan could hear muffled chants: "Death to the infidel! Death to the infidel!" Urban raised his arms for silence and continued.

"Race of the French," Urban began, … "A grave report has come from the
lands around Jerusalem. You must hasten to carry aid to your brethren
dwelling in Jerusalem who need your help for which they have often
entreated." (pp. 71-72)

"On whom, therefore, does the task of avenging these atrocities lie, if not on you, upon whom above all nations God has bestowed outstanding glory in arms, magnitude of heart, litheness of body and strength to humble those who resist you?"

Stefan realized that Urban had captured the crowd. This was not typical papal ranting. The shouts for the slaughter of the Turks continued. Urban silenced them again.

"Therefore, with earnest prayer, I—no, not I, but God—exhorts you as heralds of Christ to repeatedly urge all men of all ranks whatever, knights as well as foot-soldiers, rich and poor, to hasten to the land of the Savior's birth and exterminate this vile race and aid the Christian inhabitants." The rhythmic shouting had begun again. Urban raised his voice speaking as loud as his ample lungs would allow. "Listen carefully: For all those going to Jerusalem, there will be remission of all sins."

The crowd, ready to dispense judgment, had been strident and vocal; the crowd ready to receive forgiveness became quiet. "I repeat: All who go to Jerusalem will be granted the remission of their sins if they come to the end of this fettered life while marching by land or crossing by sea, or in fighting the pagans. This I grant, through the power vested in me by God."

In the heavens, cliff hawks and peregrines circled on currents, screeching in the numbing silence that now covered Suger's field. Serfs and nobles alike cataloged both their sins and their virtues and were humbled. The husband remembered the serving girls with whom he had slept and the wife recalled her adulteries. The peasant woman thought of the eggs she had stolen and the curses she had uttered. In a world in which survival and salvation were the primary occupations of life, the prospect of eternal salvation in exchange for participation in a pilgrimage to the city sanctified by the Savior Himself, struck the thousands dumb with wonder. The pope spoke again!

"Jerusalem is the navel of the world, a land fruitful above all others, like a second paradise of delights. The Redeemer of the human race made it famous by his birth, embellished it by his death, left his seal upon it by his burial, glorified it by his resurrection. This royal city, placed at the center of the world, is now held captive by her enemies and is enslaved to pagan rites by a people who do not know God. Not only do these people not acknowledge God, but from them shall spring the Antichrist. And it is clear that Antichrist will wage war not against Jews or against Gentiles but, according to the etymology of his name, against Christians. And if the Antichrist finds no Christians in Jerusalem, just as today when it is thought that there is scarcely a single one in that place, there will be no one to resist him, nor any whom he may rightly attack. According to Daniel and to Jerome his interpreter, he will pitch his tent on the Mount of Olives, and it is certain that, according to St. Paul, he will sit in Jerusalem in the temple of God as if he were God. The Evangelist cries that Jerusalem must be trodden down by the Gentiles until the times of the nations be fulfilled. Dearest brethren, these times will only be fulfilled when through you, with God working with you, the power of the Antichrist will be broken. For the end of the world is at hand. But first, before the coming of the Antichrist, a renewal of the Christian empire is necessary so that, when the Evil One prepares to advance, he will find opposition from those who are readied to defend the faith. Therefore, listen carefully: Let those who wantonly wage *private* wars against the faithful, now devoutly wage a *public* war against the infidel!"

The pope paused until his message had been carried to all his listeners. And then he added, "For this is the will of God concerning you." As the people heard his words, the multitude erupted in thunderous applause and echoed his words: "It is the will of God. *Deus vult!*"

The Roman pontiff signaled for silence.

"Let those who have been robbers, now be soldiers of Christ, for this is the will of God concerning you." Again came the response: "Deus vult! Deus vult!"

The litany continued. "Let those who once fought against brothers, now rightfully fight against barbarians, for this is the will of God concerning you." The response was immediate: "Deus vult! Deus vult!"

"Let those who have been exhausting themselves to the detriment of body and soul now labor for a double glory, for this is the will of God concerning you."

From the Provencals, Normans, Italians, Picts, Celts, Brits; from those on rocky ledges, those perched in trees, those sitting on meadow grasses or sloping hillocks—the cry was the same: "Deus vult! Deus vult! Deus vult!"

"Let nothing delay those who are going. Let them settle their affairs, collect their money, and when winter has ended and spring has come, zealously undertake the journey under the guidance of the Lord, for this is the will of God concerning you."

It was masterful oratory. Every stanza lifted the frenetic crowd to higher levels of ecstasy. Once again he filled his expansive lungs, this time for a final oratorical thrust.

"Jerusalem pleads for liberation and calls upon you to come to her aid. It is, in fact, principally from you that she demands help because, as we have already said, upon you before all other nations, God has bestowed outstanding glory in arms. So take this road for the remission of sins, assured of the unfading glory of the kingdom of heaven."

Pope Urban moved slowly away from the lectern as the chanting began anew. "Deus vult! Deus vult!" As he began his return to the papal chair beneath the gonfanon-decorated baldachin, he turned to face every segment of the surging masses, waving his blessing and nodding a pontifical benediction. The enthusiasm was as unexpected as it was unprecedented. Urban had never witnessed a scene such as this. The multitude, beset by poverty and famine, fighting and bloodshed, were transported on flights of rhetorical fancy to the *eschaton*. Urban had presented a vision of their apocalyptic destiny. They saw themselves, not as servile peasants whose vaporous life was without meaning, but as persons of history, as the children of the millennium standing on the threshold of a new age, an age which they themselves had the power to usher in. A Pons, or a Guy, and the thousands of their compatriots, could play a decisive role in providential history! It was their destiny! It was the will of God! Deus vult!

Urban's heart was strangely moved. He recalled his encounter of the recent night: Yes. Babylon will fall! It has become the dwelling place of demons, a haunt of every foul spirit, a haunt of every foul and hateful bird, for all nations have drunk the wine of her impure passion. She shall be burned with fire, for mighty is the Lord God who judges her.

✠✠✠

Bernard pushed the Gesta Francorum *aside and turned to my* Historia. *"You seem to feel that the pope undervalued the importance of his own speech, or at least his rhetorical ability," he said. We were in the Scriptorium and had stayed up late to study the opening chapters of my work and the* Gesta. *The oil was running low in the lamps, the wax was gathering thickly on the candles, and my energy was fading like a flower in the afternoon sun.*

I nodded. "I don't think Pope Urban ever realized the importance of connecting Jerusalem to the true goals of the crusade. In my mind, Jerusalem was of secondary importance to Urban—"

"Secondary importance? Are you sure of this?" Bernard had made his reputation by being skeptical.

"No, no, no. Pope Urban never understood the fuss. All he really hoped to achieve was to ingratiate himself to Alexius and begin to forge ties once again with the East and the Eastern Church. He didn't understand, as Peter the Hermit most certainly did, how crucial to the success of his military aims was the millennial enthusiasm of the people. No one was more surprised than he by the response of the masses to his appeal at Clermont and the subsequent furor it created. He had hoped to light a fire, true enough, but a fire that could be contained ... and controlled ... by adding a little fuel now and fanning it a bit then. In his wildest dreams, he could never have foreseen how the fire would flame out of control. He had—"

"—committed eschatological arson!" Bernard interjected.

"Yes! It was out of his hands. The world, for good or for ill, would never be the same."

✠✠✠

As the outcry continued, Pons and Guy could see from their distant vantage an ecclesiastical figure step out on the dais and approach the pope who had taken his seat on the papal throne. The figure first knelt and then stood before the pontiff. The Provencal peasants saw the pope lift up, for all to see, a linen tunic on which was a crimson cross, on both front and back. The pope then gave the cloth to two white-gloved deacons who fitted it to the cleric's robe. Pons and Guy could see that the pope was speaking to the figure, but they could not hear what was being said. A murmur swelled among the thousands as word filtered through the crowd that the person taking the cross was the bishop of Le Puy and that he was taking the vow of a pilgrim.

And indeed it was Adhemar, for he arose and was escorted by the pontiff himself to the podium to be presented to the Franks. They saw that he was wearing the sign of the cross. Urban II raised his arms, heavy with clerical raiment, and announced loudly to them: "Adhemar, Bishop of Le Puy—CRUCESIGNATUS! CRUCESIGNATUS!"

The roar of the masses was again spontaneous and enthusiastic. A thunderous descant began anew: *"Crucesignatus! Crucesignatus! Deus vult! Deus vult! Deus vult!'* The two churchmen turned to each other and embraced warmly. "Mon ami, mon cher ami," the pope whispered affectionately. "You are the first crusader!"

Moments later, Adhemar the Crusader led the people in the *Confiteor.* The Benedictines concluded with the *Exaudiat Te Dominus:*

The Lord hear you in the day of trouble!
The name of the God of Jacob defend you!
May He help you from the sanctuary,
And give you support from Zion!

May He be mindful of your sacrifice,
And favor your burnt offering!

And far away, with those words echoing mellifluously in his ears, a monk on his donkey turned for Provence, his face solemn and eyes blazing with apocalyptic fire.

CHAPTER SEVEN

The Count

OUNT STEFAN OF BLOIS WAS NOT among those who stepped forward to receive the blessing of the pope or to take the cross, or to otherwise commit to an enterprise that as yet posed more questions than answers. That he had remained anchored to his seat on the dais was itself a tribute to the man's resolve, for he was not only eclipsed in enthusiasm by his knightly peers, but, also, he was badgered unmercifully by the hectoring of the woman beside him.

"You must arise at once and take the cross," she whispered, as Count Raymond of St. Gilles promenaded before the admiring eyes of the thousands in Suger's field. His wife, Lady Elvira, looked on, beaming. "This is embarrassing," said Adela, noting darkly Elvira's wifely pride.

"Don't be ridiculous," said Stefan resolutely.

Adela took a softer tack. "Stefan, *carrissimus*, what is the problem?" She put her right arm around his shoulder and stroked the nape of his neck with her experienced fingers. "This is an opportunity for heroism, honor and glory. One must take these chances as they're given!" She felt the muscles tense. "This is no time for indecision!" she added, digging her nails suddenly into the flesh.

The count jumped slightly in both pain and surprise. He raised a hand to his injured neck and turned stiffly to face his wife, locking his stubborn, blue eyes on the I-am-so-angry-I-could-spit eyes of his wife. "I am not being indecisive! I've made a decision; it just happens to be one of which you don't approve." He paused, lowered his hand and looked away from her. "My mind is quite clear: there will be no judgment on this matter until we've looked at this carefully and given it some thought!"

Shouts of "crucesignatus" rang out again as Count Raymond arose bearing the sign of the cross. Urban had recruited yet another prince. "Details," Adela hissed. "We can take care of details later! Decisions! What we need are decisions!"

Adela continued to exhort her husband but with no success. Stefan would not make a decision that would necessarily involve the administration and disposition of vast sums of money on the basis of papal rhetoric alone. For Adela, wealth and position were mere trifles. The crusade raised before her the specter of battles and banners, victories and spoils. The pope's oratory took her back to her father's many campaigns when she would wait in childish excitement for the Conqueror to return to Rouen when they lived in Normandy. She would go hunting for deer or boar and would ride with him through dark forests or gladed meadows. He would tell her of his many adventures and glorious battles. "Courage," he told her when she fell off her horse, "is an act of the will. It's something you do, not something you feel. It's being willing to pay the price." Being courageous, she always got back on her horse after a fall.

"I want to be a knight like you!" she said.

He laughed. Once, when they were walking, he picked some wild, white daises and gave them to her. "Adela, can a flower be a tree?"

"No," she said solemnly. "But I would rather be a tree."

"It takes as much courage to be beautiful and fragile as it does to be strong and daring," her father said. She remembered his eyes passionate and paternally warm and how they embraced her. "Someday, you will be a princess, and you will marry a knight."

But her knight refused to be budged, although she herself was reeling with joy and excitement. The battle was on! Her Norman blood stirred with anticipation.

✠✠✠

"Gentlemen! Gentlemen!" said the count of Blois, attempting to gain the attention of his friends. On the same day that Urban had delivered his proclamation of a pilgrimage to Jerusalem, the nobles and princes were the guests of the pope at the castle of Fulk, a wealthy local count, for a bacchanalian evening of dinner and entertainment.

They assembled with their wives in the castle's great hall beneath exquisite paintings and ancestral banners. While the pope himself had declined to attend his own dinner, his legate, Adhemar, presided over the festivities and sat at the head table beneath a makeshift baldachin with Anselm of Canterbury, Ivo of Chartres and five representatives of the Italian curia.

A salt stood before the seat of Adhemar and the other guests were arranged according to protocol below the salt and at tables covered with a white linen overlaid with an elegant, turquoise runner from the Orient. Table fountains spouted wines and fragrant waters from elaborate, sculptured turrets.

It was a banquet indeed! The tables were laden with platters of fresh fruit, chargers overflowing with meats in pepper sauce, venison in frumenty, and partridge and quail. Flagons of wine, ale, mulled apple and pear cider were prepared to slake their considerable thirst.

Waiting upon the guests to ensure that no gastronomic need went unsatisfied were a number of servants supervised by the steward. Serving girls brought food from the kitchen. The carver had prepared and served the meats, the panter had sliced and readied an exotic array of breads and pastries, and the butler had ameliorated weakened and discolored wine by adding the appropriate spices, or *coloure de rose* as needed. It was his inspired service with the butts of ale and wine that ensured an evening of creative and animated discourse.

At Stefan's table, the conversation had drifted to questions of supplies, armies and leadership. On the latter issue, Raymond of St. Gilles, the oldest among them, had pressed the view that the pilgrimage at its present conceptual stage appeared to be nothing more than an *a cephalous* collection of undisciplined armies. Hugh, the king's brother, shared that position, but Robert of Normandy believed that Raymond was merely maneuvering to assume the secular leadership of the armies himself, should the need for such a leader become apparent.

"Gentlemen, gentlemen," said Stefan. He fingered a slice of partridge, dipped it into a lentil gravy and dropped it into his mouth.

"Gentlemen," he said, wiping the corners of his mouth with a linen, "it won't work."

"What won't work?" asked Raymond, a veteran of the wars of the Spanish Reconquista and unacquainted with the notion of things not working.

"Having a leader, at least a lay leader, of this pilgrimage."

"Why not?" Raymond persisted. When Raymond had a question, it was generally not without cause. He was no fool. At the advanced age of 53, he was respected for both his wisdom and experience. More than once he had successfully led his Gascon and Catalan forces over the Pyrenees against the Moslems in Spain. He had battle scars to show for it and had lost an eye. He wore a black patch over that eye and women somehow found it attractive, a device Raymond was not loath to exploit. Last year, he had taken a little dark-haired, olive-skinned slip of a girl to be his wife: Elvira, the out-of-wedlock daughter of Alfonso VI of Leon and Castile. He was, then, experienced in both the ways of love and of war.

Adela beamed. The men were listening to her husband. "To begin," answered Stefan, in measured and familiar tones of rationality, "we could never agree on who that leader should be. Any one of us here at this table is capable of commanding the combined forces of our individual armies." He reached for a goblet of red wine.

"But who should it be?" he asked, looking at Raymond. "There are no obvious choices here and no obvious basis on which such a choice could be made."

"Consider Robert, for example," he continued, pausing to take a sip of the wine. "The Count of Flanders is as strong in spirit as he is in body. He is very well-acquainted with the affairs of the East through the work of his father who made the pilgrimage nine years ago. He knows Alexius and his army is simply the best." The youthful count with the soft eyes appeared pleased with these words. He was an eager fellow, ruler in his castle for only three years, but he had steadily acquired a reputation for keen administration and scrupulous fairness.

"Or you, Raymond. As the veteran of many battles in Spain and elsewhere, you're certainly the most experienced among us. When I was a lad, my friends and I used to make up our own *chansons de geste* based on stories our fathers told us of your bravery and courage. Your compassion and sense of fairness are legend; your soldiers both love and respect you; and your army is easily the largest."

Raymond of St. Gilles, the count of the prosperous city of Toulouse, raised his cup in Stefan's direction and nodded with the hint of a smile, perhaps a smirk. With the patch over his eye, it was sometimes hard to know for certain whether Raymond was behaving somberly or in jest.

Stefan continued to list the possibilities. "Hugh would also bear the title of *Dux Militia* with honor and dignity. The count of Vermandois is the son of King Henry and therefore comes from a long line of nobility which could be of essential importance in our relations with Alexius. And, as brother of King Philip, no one could fault our selection of Hugh as commander of the armies." Hugh lowered his eyes, not believing a word of it; he didn't want to look at the others for fear of seeing the disbelief registered on their faces as well.

"And you, Godfrey, why not elect you our commander?" Stefan liked Godfrey best of all the princes at their table. Godfrey was young, but already admired by his peers for his fearless spirit and bravery in battle. He had been a captain in his early youth, leading men twice his age into war. But his interest in war was tempered by his love of learning. He could speak and read Latin as well as German. He was a knight's knight: high born and well-mannered. Godfrey shrugged at Stefan's questions, smiled and said nothing. Stefan laughed and continued: "Godfrey is fearless: who else would pursue his enemy into the Lateran of Rome and slay him on the spot?" The group laughed heartily at Godfrey's embarrassment. "Lord of that impregnable city of Boullion, he has shown everyone that he could lead a force large or small to victory."

Stefan remembered his brother-in-law: "Robert would also be an excellent choice. As the eldest son of the Conqueror, the count of Normandy certainly has the financial and human resources to lead the pilgrimage. Perhaps he can even resolve his disputes with his brother and persuade the English to participate!"

"The English are whiners," interjected Adela.

"They may be whiners, my dear sister," said Robert with feeling, "but they come by it naturally. Their king—our brother—"

"—is the biggest whiner of them all!"

There was no love lost between Adela and her brother. Robert's love of women was exceeded only by his love of wine. His wine-addled brain had provoked more than one difficulty with his peers. It had not helped that his father, while lavishing love and affection upon Adela, had scornfully referred to Robert as Short Breeches (or *Curthose*). He was indeed short and stocky, but strong of limb. He had a penchant for dining upon venison and fowl and strong drink, thus making a bountiful body but a barren spirit.

Short Breeches continued to speak: "You have omitted one name from your list, Stefan—your own." Robert turned to the others. "No one can wield a sword like Stefan, and no one has the financial resources as does he, and his piety and devotion to the church are well-known."

"I wholeheartedly agree with my brother: my husband would be an excellent choice," proclaimed Adela. While Lady Elvira glowered, the men laughed good-naturedly.

Stefan rushed in to save the situation. "You can see for yourselves the problem. Even if we could ourselves—here at this table—come to an agreement, and it's not at all clear that we could, do you think for a moment that the Flemish would submit to the leadership of a Provencal? And would the Provencals obey a Norman?"

"In fact," he went on, summarizing, "the only way we can work together *is to work together.* If we can cooperate, a leader is not needed; if we cannot, a leader will not help."

"We have a leader anyway," said Hugh, speaking up. "Adhemar."

"Adhemar is not our leader," said Raymond. "He is the papal legate. In matters of faith and religion we are bound to obey him. But His Holiness did not intend Adhemar to make military decisions."

"True," said Hugh, "But if His Holiness thought we could not cooperate, he would've appointed a leader."

"Yes, but that is not within his power to do," Raymond countered. "This is our decision. We may appoint whom we choose."

"I don't think so," said Godfrey de Boullion, popping a fig stuffed with cinnamon egg into his mouth. "It is within his power, for if I understand the pope correctly, what we have here is not a *secular* army, but a *sacred* army; not a *secular* cause but an *ecclesiastical* cause. When Raymond took the cross this afternoon, he committed himself—as did I—to pray at the Holy Sepulcher and to be a soldier of St. Peter! Therefore, I assume that the pope believes it is completely within his purview to appoint a commander of the armies if he believes it to be necessary."

"Yes, yes," said Stefan. "Godfrey is absolutely correct." He leaned forward intensely, a goblet of red wine still in one hand. With his free hand, he translated his spoken words into animated gestures. "My lords, remember this carefully: what you heard this afternoon at Suger's field was not the whole truth."

"What are you talking about?" asked Raymond, curious, but careful. He was reluctant to be drawn into the continuing conversation.

"Raymond, the pope has received several letters from Emperor Alexius, one as recently as five months ago—I know, because I hand-delivered it from Alexius myself—requesting military aid from the West. The emperor is desperate. The Turkish bastards are on his doorstep and he can't do a thing about it. This pilgrimage hasn't been called to rescue Jerusalem, but to rescue Constantinople and to restore to Alexius the territory his own armies couldn't defend!"

"The pope is using us as mercenaries?" asked Hugh of Vermandois.

"No, no! How can we be mercenaries when neither Constantinople nor Rome is going to pay us a single damned denarii? The reality, my lords, is that not only are we *not* going to get paid for fighting the emperor's war, but the pope is asking us to foot the bill!" Stefan finished, but he felt a pang of remorse for speaking thus against the father of one of the most exquisite creatures he had ever laid eyes upon.

"He's right! Holy Mary, Mother of God!" swore Robert of Flanders. The rest sat in stunned silence at Stefan's interpretation of the day's events. Even Adela, never reluctant to plunge into a conversational void no matter how sacred, was given pause—not so much by her husband's statements, as by the obvious respect with which he was treated by his peers.

"That's the beauty of this whole scheme," Stefan continued to argue. "The pope can simply issue a declaration of war and perhaps insist that Alexius pay the bill. But he doesn't do that. Instead, he recruits a pilgrim, not a soldier, but gives him an indulgence and a sword. Voila! He has a soldier after all! And a soldier of St. Peter at that!"

"And why shouldn't Alexius pay the bill?" asked the brother of King Phillip.

"He should, and we're not going to let him get away with it," whispered Stefan. "From the pope's point of view, however, there's only one reason: *reunification*. The pope hopes to reunify the empire and the Church, and heal the Schism of 1054. By giving Alexius the military aid he needs in the form of a pilgrimage and underwriting the cost in coins, not to speak of human life, the pope hopes to establish enough goodwill to begin negotiations toward reunification."

With the exception of Stefan, they had all taken the cross that afternoon. Stefan's view of the pilgrimage was disheartening.

Raymond spoke up: "Then what was all the talk about the Antichrist and the holy places—"

"Rhetorical bombast," Stefan answered. "Either the pope knows his Cicero or someone wrote the speech for him. Do you think the peasants would've listened to a sermon filled with talk of reunification, the Eastern church, and giving the Greek emperor a helping hand? Not even you, Raymond, would've danced to the altar had the pope proceeded in such a fashion. The speech was an *objet d'art*, a rhetorical masterpiece. I've never heard him do better."

"I, for one, am not convinced,' said Raymond, piqued at the personal reference. "I believe the defense and restoration of the holy places is vital and long overdue."

"And I agree," said Stefan. "And I have no doubt that Urban sincerely desires the liberation of Jerusalem." He paused to survey his comrades. "But you should know from the beginning that this pilgrimage would never be called for that reason alone. This endeavor, as worthy as it is, hinges primarily on Urban's relationship with the patriarch and emperor of Constantinople. Everything else is secondary."

Their conversation now turned to military matters: the size of the armies including foot-soldiers, horses and knights; lines of supply; suitable routes to Constantinople. Tiring of this, and continuing all the while to empty flagons of wine, the nobles' thoughts turned to matters of a lighter nature until—long after

Adhemar and the curia had departed—the revelers could scarcely think at all and Count Fulk's guests gaily staggered away.

✠✠✠

Count Stefan and Lady Adela departed only a few minutes after the Bishop of Le Puy. Complaining of a fever, Adela had to persuade her husband to break off the conversation and to flee up five flights of narrow, twisting stairs to the luxurious bedchamber Fulk had provided for them in the keep of his castle. Beautiful oak floors were overlaid with bearskin rugs, a fire blazed in the fireplace, and the canopied bed covered with heavy blankets and soft pillows seemed inviting.

"I was proud of you tonight," Adela said as she snuggled against his body. Adela hoped his heart was not as cold as were his feet. She rested her worried head on his chest in the hollow below his shoulder, and inside his nightshirt a nimble finger traced a lazy design on his warming flesh.

"But you were not proud of me this afternoon—is that what you're telling me?"

"Let's not talk about this afternoon. That was a long time ago."

Stefan turned to face her, rolling her head off his chest. "This afternoon, you disapproved of me in no uncertain terms; but this evening I'm in favor again. It's like my life is defined by whether or not you are proud of me."

Adela turned away from him. "I'm sorry I said anything," she said. "I was just happy being with you tonight, that's all."

"Well, I was not happy being with you this afternoon. You have to take me as I am, Adela. You didn't marry your father!"

In an instant, Adela sat up angrily and whirled to face her husband. She was wearing a delicate night robe, a gift of her mother, Matilda, who had purchased the pale, maroon silk from the Genovese. Now, a lace strap slid off her left shoulder revealing a breast that heaved in agitation as she spoke. But somehow, inexplicably, that bare breast facing Stefan as a half moon globe in the mellow glow of the fire, mitigated the effect of her anger.

"I know I didn't marry my father," she said, her voice rising. "Your problem, Stefan, is that you can't accept me for who I am! It's just so hard for you, isn't it, to accept the idea that thinking isn't your exclusive domain."

Do you like her? Anna had asked. Stefan pulled Adela down to him and put his hand on her exposed breast, caressing it. They lay face to face, peering into each other's deep, dark wells of volition and passion.

"But you're wrong, darling," he whispered. "It is my exclusive, sole domain. It's the exclusive, sole domain of all men; it's heresy to believe otherwise. Women were not born to think, they were born to love!"

Adela ignored this and wrapped the bedcovers tightly about her and snuggled closer to him. She slid her hand between his legs and began to massage his aroused body. "Thinking and loving are two parts of the same sword. One's the grip, the other the blade," she whispered. "Good thinkers make good lovers. *Cogito, ergo amo, carrissimus.*" She paused to let this intelligence seep into his brain. "On the other hand," she continued, "it's no fun to fuck an idiot, is it? Which is the way you've been behaving lately!" She withdrew her hand and turned away from him.

Stefan said nothing. He wanted to weigh his words carefully. He had learned, he believed, that in his dealings with his wife it was better to speak a few well-chosen words than many ill-chosen ones; she could flush out illogicalities like a dog hunting quail. His knowledge of this had obviously failed him now, however.

He reached for her in conciliation. "You have to admit that you're not going to find a husband who has been more patient than I have been with you. Count Raymond would've had you flogged and put in stocks this afternoon."

"You want me to be like that little whore, Elvira?" Adela asked, knowing he wanted no such thing.

"Of course not!"

They lay facing each other again. Stefan could not seem to drop the subject. "Just be sure that when you use your considerably gifted mind, you don't try to make all the decisions before I've had a chance to think about it—that's all." He kissed her nose quickly punctuating the sentence.

Adela said nothing so he went on. "If I am going to raise an army, if I am going to ride to Constantinople, if I am going to fight the Islamic infidel, if I am going to scale the walls of Jerusalem, then it seems to me that I should be the one to make the decision about it. This afternoon, you arrived at a conclusion before I uttered one word on the subject, and before we had a chance to discuss it."

These words cut to the quick and Adela felt chastened. And further, she was angry that she had allowed her impetuosity to lead her into an error which she could not reasonably defend. She was quiet. Then, "You're right, Stefan," she murmured, "I'm sorry and it won't happen again, I promise. I just got so excited … all the people … the pope … and I wanted to be a part of it. I would've taken the cross on the spot and you didn't seem interested and everyone else was excited … I lost control … I'm sorry. It really won't happen again."

"Until the next time," Stefan said.

"No, I mean it. Never again. I trust your judgment."

"So if I decided not to go to Jerusalem, you wouldn't object?"

"Of course I would object, carissimus! But I don't believe for a moment that you won't go. You're the best soldier in France." She put her head on his shoulder again. "I didn't marry my father, but you're very much like him … much more so than Robert … Robert is so spineless. You were telling everyone tonight that Robert could command the armies. Ha! You were lying and you knew it, I knew it and he knew it! Robert can't even manage his own affairs let alone someone else's. That's why he owes William so much money. You'll go; you have to."

"I don't like leaving my affairs in the hands of other people."

"YOU take care of the pope's business and he'll take care of yours." Adela tried to be reassuring.

"The Church is one of the largest landholders in France and I don't think they'd mind expanding their holdings at my expense."

The countess raised herself above the count and looked square into his eyes. "Stefan of Chartres, don't be so cynical. I can manage your affairs. You know that."

"Of that I have no doubt, Adela!"

"In fact, I'd like to manage one right now..." and she kissed him lightly, and then again. "How am I doing?" she asked softly. She didn't let him answer, but kissed him again. Their mouths met openly, impatiently and receptively.

"I thought you had a fever," Stefan whispered.

"I do," she answered. "Feel how hot I am." She took his hand and moved his finger across the crown of her head, down her flawless face, and around her waif-like neck. Continuing, she led his princely hands to her breasts where they lingered touching, caressing, arousing. Then she guided his searching hand across her body until it finally rested in a warm, moist and moving darkness.

Stefan moved adroitly to sit astride his wife. He looked at her, touching her face lightly as though it might not be there, it was so perfect and therefore so unreal. Her eyes, slightly large and set above high cheekbones, watched him, followed him, unthinking. Her hair, golden and fine, lay brushed across their pillow. He touched her again. There is a mathematical purity to the female body, he thought, or at least something geometrically curious and interesting. Not like the male body, essentially rectangular, straight lines and a shaft. Her breasts, identical golden orbs, were parted like twin suns setting on opposite horizons. Breasts, areolas, nipples: circles within circles within circles ... globes ... ovals ... cones ... no straight lines but hazy curves leading nowhere and everywhere, and the triangularity where the inner thighs met the torso, the Pythagorean perfection of the pubis. With any luck, the sum of her hypotenuse would be equal to the sum of his right angles.

Later when they lay in post-coital drowsiness, she said to him:

"So maybe we can do this again?"

"But not now," he said, and he parted her flaxen hair and kissed the nape of her neck. "Goodnight, carissima."

"Goodnight, crucesignatus!"

✠✠✠

On Christmas Day, 1095, anno Domini, Count Stefan of Blois and Chartres, in the company of Fulcher who had been appointed his chaplain, took the cross at Chartres Cathedral, Bishop Ivo presiding.

Two deacons approached and placed over Stefan's head a white linen cape which bore the red cross in both front and back. When fitted on the count, it extended slightly over his shoulders and down his arm and fully down his back and over his feet as he kneeled. He was covered with the sign of the cross. Then Fulcher, the chaplain, solemnly approached the bishop who — with great pomp — bestowed upon him the pilgrimage charter which Stefan had himself written after seeking the counsel of advisors and his wife.

Fulcher turned to face an expectant congregation, most of whom were standing in a nave swept with incense and bathed in candle's glow. They were Stefan's political benefice, the people who had reaped the good fortune of his protection and even-handed administration. As Fulcher prepared to read, Stefan remained on his knees, arrayed in knightly attire that was now covered by the cross. His helmet rested on the stone floor of the cathedral. His head was covered with a hauberk, a leather cap which extended across the forehead and to the base of the skull. Beneath the stole of white linen, an apron of mail was attached to the hauberk and encircled his neck providing protection where the helmet could not. The single-piece suit of mail was gathered at the waist by a finely detailed sword belt studded with fine jewels. Bishop Ivo, deacons, archdeacons, and acolytes observed as Fulcher read:

I, Stefan Henry, Count of Blois and Chartres, being solicitous for the salvation of the souls of myself and my parents and mindful that on the

Last Day, when, at the advent of our Lord Jesus Christ, all men must rise again with their bodies and be ready to account for their deeds, those who did good deeds will go to eternal life but those who did evil deeds will go to eternal fire,

In order that my lord, the blessed Peter, to whom God gave the power of binding and loosing and the keys to the celestial kingdom, may deign to open the doors of the celestial kingdom to myself and my father and my mother and other ancestors of my family, do solemnly affirm my irrevocable vow to undertake the journey to Jerusalem as a penance for my sins, and roused by the love of the Holy Spirit, to go to the Holy Land there to fight and kill the enemies of Christ and to cleanse the place in which the Lord Jesus Christ deigned to suffer for the salvation of the human race.

Stefan's attention began to waver under the weight of Fulcher's ponderous rendition. Did he not know well enough these words which he himself had written? Could he forget that November afternoon at Suger's field? "Take the cross!" Adela urged. "Take the cross! Take the cross!"

He could see it clearly now. Adhemar and then Raymond and Hugh and Robert accepting the blessing and acclamation of the pope while he was shrinking smaller and smaller on the dais. Then in the crowd, the thousands, he saw—he was seeing now again— hatred! Malevolence! It was a throng possessed, screaming and ranting: "Deus vult! Deus vult! Crucesignatus!"

Stefan's head swayed as he tried to focus on the textured granite slabs that lay like coffin lids beneath his bended knees—it could be *his* coffin. Perhaps it *will* be his coffin, not long from now.

"My lord, my lord," said Fulcher. "Are you well?"

Stefan looked up. His chaplain was kneeling in front of him and had grasped him roughly by the shoulders. "Are you well, my lord?" he asked again.

Stefan glanced down at his hands which were bleeding. "You fell forward and cushioned your fall with your hands. You have cut them somehow," Fulcher explained. Stefan nodded, dazed.

"I'm sorry, Father," he apologized. "Just a bit of dizziness, I'm afraid." He took the cloth Fulcher offered and wiped the blood from his hands. "I'm fine, Father, really. Let's continue.'

A grim-faced Bishop Ivo had not moved an inch, but was observing carefully. Fulcher put his hand on Stefan's shoulder in a gesture of reassurance and then stood to resume the recitation. Stefan thought of how embarrassed Adela must be.

Suddenly he desired to be with Anna.

Since divine mercy has inspired me that owing to the enormity of my sins I should go to the Sepulcher of Our Savior, in order that this offering of my devotion might be more acceptable in the sight of God, I decided not unreasonably to leave as alms a designated sum under an agreement herewith attached for all the houses of Cluny in the Duchy of Aquitaine and the Counties of Poitou, Blois, Bourbon, Nevers and Auvergne.

In taking this vow, I forswear the love of wife and kindred, the affection of friends and loyal servants, and undertake gladly the sufferings of this journey as but a small measure of the suffering of our Lord who, though he was rich, for our sakes became poor;

The affairs of state and family I leave to the administration of my devoted wife, Adela, daughter of William of Rouen, to direct in concert with the provisions of the agreement aforementioned and herewith attached.

I have left a designated sum, to ensure that each day of my absence a candle shall burn before the Statue of the Virgin Mary on my behalf. I have also directed that, in the event of my death, the Office of the Dead shall be said on my behalf and in my memory on each anniversary of my birth for fifty years.

Should, for some unthinkable reason, this holy and solemn vow be renounced, I have irrevocably declared that a substantial portion of my resources revert to the care of the Church.

These arrangements must remain unchanged and are established by the validity of this charter with the authority of my silver seal; they are confirmed by the affirmation of suitable witnesses.

[By my hand) Stefan Henry, Count of Blois and Chartres
Christmas Day, 1095 anno Domini

Bishop Ivo rendered the final blessing after which the count arose, cradled his helmet under one arm, and with his other hand on the hilt of his sword, turned and descended the steps of the altar, the cape with the sign of the cross trailing behind. He walked briskly down the long central aisle of the nave toward the rose window and the great western doors as admiring throngs on both sides strained for a glimpse of this the most famous of the *crucesignati*. Stefan continued, paying no heed, eyes forward and unwavering, until at last he had quit the cathedral and stepped into the bracing winter air of the December night. A stable boy had readied his white stallion for him. Stefan paused and looked back toward the cathedral briefly. He could hear a choir of boys singing, an angel chorus announcing the Nativity. *Gloria in excelsis Deo.* The scent of incense lingered and co-mingled with the cold night air.

He put on his helmet and stepped to the steed. In one swift-flowing motion, he mounted the beast, wrapped his cape about him and rode hard into the numbing darkness toward the Three Rivers.

✠✠✠

Adela watched as her husband descended the steps of the altar, but quickly lost him as he strode down the center aisle of the nave. The throng was too dense, and in her attempt to jostle for a better position, she was instead merely shunted aside.

She maneuvered toward the north transept and found refuge momentarily at the base of one of the four massive pillars supporting the crossing and lantern. Then, stepping away from the fluted column, she moved toward the ambulatory as the choir sang the *Gloria.* The crowd was so large that it had even spilled into the ambulatory, and, insofar as she could determine, it had completely surrounded the altar.

She migrated steadily down the ambulatory until she reached a small wooden door at the rear of the altar. Quickly she opened it, stooped slightly and entered a narrow stairwell leading to the crypt beneath the cathedral. Closing the door behind her, she wrapped her cloak about her tightly, for it was bound to be even colder in the cave than it was in the church. On the landing at the top of the stairs a single torch was lit, but as she peered into the lower darkness, it seemed to be the only one. She took a candle from the basket provided, lit it by the torch, and began a descent into the crypt.

It was but a short distance down the stone steps. There was not much to see. A small chapel was situated at the east end of the cave, but otherwise the furnishings as well as the architecture were exceedingly spare. The crypt of Chartres was, in the words of the clergy, "the Virgin's most preferred residence on earth." Adela could not verify that now, and indeed, the last thing she wished to happen was to have a visitation from the Blessed Virgin. Coming to the crypt was a poor idea, she thought.

The crypt is a place of worship. Except for a few paintings on the walls, there's little to distract the pilgrim. The monk or the pilgrim enters the crypt willing to accept the fact that nothing is happening. In such an atmosphere, the monks are passive, allowing the unmarked space and complete silence to enfold them in a sort of ecstatic sublimity.

Adela very seldom achieved ecstatic sublimity on her own, however; ecstasy was something better *shared*, she believed. She held her candle aloft for a better look. The flickering light cast eerie shadows on the curved planes of the undercroft vaulting. Gloomy catacombs are also better shared, she allowed. Wandering to the north side of the crypt, she waited at the sacred well into which the early martyrs of Chartres were said to have been thrown. She peered into the murky darkness but could not see the bottom. She knew it had a depth of about 130 feet. Where are those denarii? she mused. Rummaging through her clothing, she managed to produce a small coin. She looked again into the well, holding the light to best advantage, and then with her free hand holding the coin above the void, she released it. She counted: one … two … three … four … five … six—ah! She heard a faint, faraway splash.

Suddenly she sensed movement behind her, but before she could scream, a gloved palm had grabbed her across the mouth, stifling any cry she could utter. The candle fell from her hand and slipped to the floor extinguishing the light. She was startled, but not afraid, even though the assailant had her quite firmly within his grasp.

"Quiet!" he whispered. She relaxed. The man released his grip. Adela pivoted within his grasp and reached for his face to feel its grainy texture. She touched his hair and thrust her fingers deep into its rangy mass. She was, she knew, in the arms of Philip, the excommunicated King of France. She obeyed him. She was quiet. Then she kissed him, long, and with passion.

CHAPTER EIGHT

The King

CHARTRES, FRANCE
December 25, 1095 A.D.

OME," SAID THE KING, TAKING Adela's hand. "This way." He tugged at her ... Then, tripping, she lurched forward after him as he strode away. They moved quickly through the dank darkness of underground anterooms and crypts noiselessly, except for the soft pad of their leather slippers upon the granite flour of the coarse stone. Then they found a door. Philip lifted the latch and they swooped into a chapel not much larger than a tomb. The king caught the scent of candles; he saw a golden aura caused by candles lit at the altar. They stood now at the edge of the light. The chamber was bare except for an altar and crucifix behind it on the frescoed wall. A crack in the fresco that started above the crucifix seemed to meander intentionally to the cross disappearing behind it and emerging jaggedly again at its foot. Then it weathered out like a dry branch of a tree toward the floor. In the cold, thick walls to the left of the altar, a niche held a small statue of Madonna and Child.

Philip closed the door slowly. Adela heard the iron latch fall. She pulled her cloak about her and shivered. In the silence, they clung to each other, and then kissed again, grabbing each other as though they knew their passion would be short-lived and inevitably frustrated or interrupted.

"Someone's coming," Adela whispered, breaking away. She leaped lightly to the side wall and was pretending to admire the Madonna when she heard the latch again, and the door creaked opened and Ivo, the bishop, entered without so much as a sidelong glance at the pair, genuflected before the cross, and then whirled about.

"So here we are," he said, straightening up and adjusting his stole. In the half light of the candles, his gaunt features made his thin face hollow and his countenance stern. He clasped his thin hands together and placed them ceremoniously in front of his thin body. Jutting his narrow, pointy chin slightly upward he added: "The only question is *why* are we here?"

Ivo's speech was as lean as was his body. He was of the opinion that it is the lean and thin of the world who are the logical, analytical and rational ones, and the corpulent ones of the world who lack those same qualities but who compensate in passion, intuition and emotion. The thin, who have made themselves that way through deprivation, are the sour, unpleasant ones—godly in practice, ungodly in temperament; the fat, who have satisfied their desires with the pleasures of the world, are the happy and contented ones.

"I loathe you," Philip snarled, approaching Ivo in a manner calculated to be menacing. It irritated Philip—this overbearing manner of Ivo—the coldness, the superiority and the piety. This is what Philip couldn't abide, the sort of piety that denied and devalued human nature, that implied that to be a good person one had to be more than human—by which was meant refusing to act upon one's human urges and desires. So if one feels like eating, one doesn't eat; if one feels like drinking, one doesn't drink; if one feels like playing, one doesn't play; if one feels like fecking, one doesn't feck. One can eat when one doesn't need to or want to, or drink when one doesn't need to or want to. But to confess that God made a woman for a man, as a glove is made for a hand, and then to say that it is better not to put the hand in the glove, and that a hand is more of a hand if one doesn't, made about as much sense to Philip as the suggestion that a fire is more of a fire if it does not burn down the thatch hut. It never occurred to Philip to resist his passions. Oh yes, he had discussed these matters often with the Church. There was perhaps no regent so intimately familiar with the Holy Mother Church as Philip. But, as he explained to more than one churchman, he never felt divine when he attended the bishop's mass; he only felt human and guilty. But he always felt divine, incredibly divine, with a Parisian wench, wrestling about in the wet juices of their love. That's divinity precisely because it's so utterly human. It was a dangerous philosophy for novices and monks of the flesh, and it also provided more than one woman an excuse to surrender, since she was, in surrendering, surrendering not to profane humanness, but to perfect humanness, and therefore to something inexpressibly divine.

"Should I be surprised?" Ivo replied, turning his head to follow the king as he approached, locking his steel-cold eyes on his. "And should I care?" Philip began to circle him now, deliberately and slowly. Adela watched only a few short feet away, inching closer to the circle of these two men who were now taking the measure of each other

Ivo continued, moving away: "You married Bertha, the wife of your youth, but only because it was advantageous. Then you seduced Bertrada, the wife of Fulk of Anjou, and asked me to assist at the nuptials, which of course I refused to do. Although you claim a divorce from Bertha, it is not a divorce recognized by a General Council; and now, in fact, you are excommunicated by the decree of Clermont. You have broken the laws of the church, the laws of God, and the laws of consanguinity." Philips eyebrows arched slightly at these words, but he said nothing. Then said the bishop:

"There is a certain fidelity that I owe to you, but by virtue of the highest fidelity of all, I have been faithful to that course of action designed to bring about both the salvation of your soul and that of your crown." He reached the door and turned stiffly to leave. "If there is no other purpose for this meeting other than to express our dislike for each other, then I bid you good night!"

Adela rushed forward, putting her tiny white hands on the bishop's arm, her voice soothing. "Oh no, you mustn't go yet, your reverence," she said. "There is no reason now for these disagreeable things ..." She directed him back toward the yellow light where the three of them stood tightly, their faces partially obscured by the mask of darkness. "All of this is in the past ... there is no ill will now, is there?" She gave the king a nudge. His head shook in agreement.

"What, then, shall we talk about on this fine evening?" asked the bishop of Chartres.

The king began: "I've heard rumors that you want to build a new church."

"It has been discussed."

"Oh, it has been discussed! It has been discussed! It's been discussed in Rome, in Paris, in Saint Denis, in Beauvais, in Laon, and yes, it has been discussed in Chartres. Every bishop with a church, every archbishop with a cathedral, every abbot of a house has been discussing a new church. The old Romanesque churches are old, cold and dark. Everywhere I go now I hear the clergy talking about building a new church, a new cathedral, a new house of God. And why have they been raving so? Because of the new science, the new mathematics, the new geometry." Philip's gestures became grand and expansive. "Don't you know, bishop—you surely do—that we are standing at the threshold of a great—no, a massive—revolution in science and knowledge permitting things only dreamed of before?" He paused to take a breath.

"What do you dream of, bishop? Do you dream of writing books? becoming a great canonist? becoming archbishop, cardinal, or even pope? Are these your dreams? No, these are not your dreams, Ivo. You dream of mortar and stone and stained glass and exquisite statuary. You dream of a cathedral twice as big as the present church and three times as high. You dream of a clerestory in the clouds and spires piercing the heavens. You see wide ambulatories and huge, fluted pillars taking the eye upward to the throne of God himself. You see thin walls reaching unimaginable heights pressed out by new methods of vaulting and supported by external buttresses ... a nave larger than the largest filled with the villagers and townspeople, serfs and barons, and the princes of both the world and the church. You see yourself saying mass at the high altar in this the most beautiful and largest cathedral in the world. Don't you, Ivo?"

Ivo had not moved, and Philip was directly in front of the bishop again. "Have I left anything out?" said the king, finishing.

"The choir, the lantern and the transepts," said Ivo.

"And how will you pay for the construction of this new church?"

"I don't see that it is any of your business."

"I want to help," said Philip. "I want to help." The king felt better. The bishop was on the defensive. The bishop was vulnerable. The church was his soft underbelly, the point where he could be attacked, the point at which the prelate was not so lean. Philip chortled to himself. The bishop had condemned his predilection for women; but the king had exposed the bishop's predilection for beautiful churches. Like throwing off a wife, the bishop would cast off his church in a moment if he knew he could have a more beautiful one. His mind was already filled with lustful thoughts of another building, more expensive, more beautiful, newer, young and fresh, rather than old, thick and cracked.

"The building of a new church is still many, many years away, and in any case, it's a project that won't be undertaken in my lifetime, and even if it were, it could never be completed in my lifetime."

"But even to commence the construction of a new cathedral, greater than anything before, the greatest in all of Christendom! That would be wonderful for you, am I not telling the truth?"

Ivo said nothing.

"But, you can't pay for it ... you can't pay for it."

"Nonsense!"

Philip crouched into the face of the bishop and whispered slowly and distinctly: "You can't pay for this new church of yours, can you, Bishop?" He straightened up. "The rents on the fields, the taxes, the denarii and solidi, and the contributions of the peasants and villagers, won't even allow you to buy the limestone mortar and you know it."

The king went on: "Now, Adela here,"—he pointed to her— "came to me with a problem. Seems that you put considerable pressure on her husband to go to the Holy Land. And she's wondering why. A wife who says goodbye to her husband when he goes on a pilgrimage says farewell with weeping and wailing as though she will never see her husband again. There are many evils that lurk on the road to Jerusalem, not to speak of the Saracens these men will face this time. Stefan is an excellent soldier, but it is a long journey, and there will be many battles with the infidel, many walls to scale, cities to destroy. So she wonders why you put so much pressure on her husband to leave her and she comes to me for protection and advice. And then I remember something curious. If Stefan is killed in the Holy Land, most of his wealth goes to the church. Who helped him draft that agreement, Ivo? Why, it was the great scholar and canonist of Chartres, Ivo himself! Oh, his wife and his family are taken care of, but Stefan is a wealthy man, great lands and many castles. I doubt there is scarcely a man in France with the wealth of Stefan. So Adela is worried, and I am worried because there isn't any chance that you seduced Stefan into going to the Holy Land because you think, maybe even hope, he may be killed and die a martyr, and then, regrettably, all his wealth will fall into the lap of the church, into your lap, Bishop, the sort of wealth that would enable you to hire the architects, and master builders, tradesmen and artisans to build your church. Now that's not something you even think about, is it, bishop? And your little logical mind wouldn't argue that, since building the church is the will of God, and since you don't have enough money but Stefan does, that it might be the will of God *if the Church assisted Stefan to his martyrdom?*" Philip was shouting now. "You wouldn't even think of such a thing, would you, bishop?"

The bishop broke away angry. "That's preposterous."

"Lady Adela doesn't think so," Philip replied. "It makes abundant sense to her."

"You're mad!"

"You say that the Church has never murdered anyone? That all priests are celibate? That the Church has never subverted the truth for financial gain? Are you saying this is preposterous, or is it only preposterous that you haven't thought of this little scheme yourself?"

"I am not staying to hear more of this!" Ivo attempted to cross the chapel to the door, but Philip prevented him.

"Let's just suppose that what I have said is completely farfetched. If it is, then there's nothing to worry about. But if there is a grain of truth to what I've said, then it's my duty to defend Lady Adela and protect her interests. Now let's suppose there was a way to finance your new church that would not require the martyrdom of Stefan of Blois. Wouldn't that enhance his chances of living? Yes, it would. And that is what I propose to give to you: a way to fund the building of a new church without taking control of Stefan's land."

The bishop stepped over to the Madonna and stroked the marble figure. "How?" he asked.

"The Holy Lance."

"The Holy Lance?"

"The spear that pierced the side of Jesus—"

"I know what it is; what about it?"

"What if I could get it for you?"

Ivo laughed.

"If you had the Lance, the poor and rich alike from all over Christendom would flock to Chartres and pay to see it. Not just this year, but in perpetuity!"

"But how are you going to get it?" Ivo asked, still smiling.

"That's my affair."

"And the *quid pro quo?*"

"If I deliver the Lance to you, you will assure Adela that no action will be taken against her husband while on the pilgrimage."

The bishop turned to Adela: "I cannot assure you that your husband will not die on the pilgrimage." To the king: "And I resent the implication that the Church would have anything to do with such a scheme."

"Come, come, Bishop. You are too sensitive. Let's put it this way. You and I sign a covenant in which I deliver the Holy Lance and you deliver Stefan's lands to Adela should he die. There is nothing complicated about it."

"I will do no such thing."

"Yes, you will, because if you don't, and Stefan dies, I shall seize his property by force and you'll have neither the land nor the Lance."

"You can't do that!"

"And what will the Church do against me? Raise an army? The knights of the Church will be in the Holy Land. Will the Church excommunicate me? Ha! I am already excommunicated."

The bishop paced the width of the chapel for a few minutes. In the musty hush of those quiet moments, they could hear midnight bells ringing up and away from them. Philip stepped back into the darkness waiting impatiently, while Adela stood near the altar in the light like a *sanctimoniale* over whom both God and the Devil might be fighting.

"You get me the Lance and in return Adela gets my commitment not to murder her husband. And if he dies anyway?"

"If he dies, he dies. In that case, the land reverts to his widow, and you get the Holy Lance. But be reasonable, Bishop. This covenant removes any possible motive the Church might have to, er … hasten … Stefan's death."

"And what if you can't deliver the Lance?"

"I'll deliver the Lance," the king said resolutely.

"So in reality, you are not offering me a deal, you are instructing the Church on a change in plans. No matter that Stefan has just sworn a solemn oath, no matter that his signed instructions are in the keeping of the Church. This is not an agreement you seek; this is an edict you are making. You dare to command the Holy Church of God! I shall gratefully receive the Holy Lance if it is offered to me by anyone. But as for the life or death of Stefan of Blois, I have no jurisdiction over such matters."

He walked to Adela, shaking a bony finger in her face. "And as for you, Adela, I would be very careful. Damnation already awaits him," nodding at Philip. "Be careful lest a similar fate befall you." And with that he left them.

ANNO DOMINI
1096

CHAPTER NINE

The Bartholomews Meet a Goose

Late Spring, A. D. 1096

OTHER, IS THIS JERUSALEM?"

Adelaide Bartholomew did not answer her child's query if for no other reason than it had been asked so many times before. But she, too, had seen the town—visible across the flat landscape of Picardy. She did not know its name; she did not want to know or need to know. The journey had taken them through many such towns during the past six weeks. It was not Jerusalem, however; she knew that for certain.

Whatever the name of the village, Peter the Monk was certain to attract more pilgrims. Addie knew the routine. They would find an uncultivated field beyond the town, throw up makeshift tents, cook a supper of gruel or barley cakes, and then gather with friends around a fire and sing, or dance, or share the experiences of the day. They would clasp their aching feet, caress and massage them until they felt better again. Then they would spread some straw and lay down upon the earth under a cart or in a tent and drift off to sleep.

But Peter would go into the village to preach. At dusk, he would take a spot on the church steps, or a bridge, or in the market, and when the light of the lavender-scented evening had paled, he would fill his lungs with evangelistic zeal and begin his harangue.

"The end of this age is at hand," he would roar. "The Second Coming of Christ draws nigh. You have seen the signs in the heavens and witnessed the weeping of the earth. Floods and pestilences have tormented you. Your fields are barren, your stomachs are empty, and while you await the return of prosperity and do nothing, the city of the Lord languishes under the weight of pagan iniquity and occupation. Repent and change your ways. Come with us now to Jerusalem to free it from the infidel and establish with the help of God a New Jerusalem on earth!"

Of course, he said much more. But in this age of visions, it was rhetoric on the same theme. Addie knew. She heard his sermon in Castres of Provence when he spoke, barefoot and cowled, at the river's edge. His presence was entrancing. His deep-set eyes were like eyes that saw only her; his words thundered only at her. The name Jerusalem stirred powerful emotions in her. She felt transformed by hope, by images of a heavenly city descending from the sky to the earth, of bright angels wearing the purest white playing

"Peter would go into the village to preach. At dusk, he would take a spot in the church steps, or a bridge, or in the market, and when the light of the lavender-scented evening had paled, he would fill his lungs with evangelistic zeal and begin his harangue" (p. 110).

trumpets of gold. Her heart quickened at the thought of stepping in the steps of Jesus! Of living in a land that flowed with milk and honey!

Normally, Addie would have dismissed the idea of leaving her village as utter nonsense. Her work was in the fields, with her sheep and her wool. She could care for her family better by staying in the sunbaked lands of Provence and Languedoc than by traveling with a band of visionary ne'er-do-wells. Others could go to worship at Jerusalem. Not she. They themselves could not afford to go, nor could they survive such an expedition.

But her thinking changed. They now appeared to have no future in Provence. There was no reason to stay. Every night they threw roots and herbs into the stew pot, but they still went to bed hungry. But it was not because of a shortage of food. The problem was that the greedy bastard merchants were hoarding the grain until the prices were higher. While shopkeepers got fat, her family was suffering. Therefore, if suffering must happen, it may as well happen while traveling to the city of Jesus! They could not worsen their misfortune by following Peter the Monk and they might improve it.

So they sold what they could, managing to buy a cart and a nag to pull it, and joined Peter's band two weeks later. But when Addie prepared to leave, together with hundreds of other peasants in the valley, a curious thing happened in the local economy. The merchants, seeing their market disappearing, lowered prices— slowly at first, and then they came tumbling down. Sheep sold for pennies. For Addie and her family it was a mixed blessing. She could buy the grain she needed, but it was difficult to get a good price for her animals. So they left with five sheep and a few coins in their purse and their unsold possessions loaded high on a two— wheeled cart. The rest she left behind. And when tears creased her face, she didn't look back. Not when they rolled their cart through the land of cypress and cicada did she look back. Nor when they left the vine-clad plains and dry, stony hills of Provence did she look back. Nor when they traveled up the Rhone River valley; not at Grignan, Lyon, or Dieulefit; not in the forests or billowing wooded hills; not in town or undulating countryside. She would never look back, she thought.

"Mother, is this Jerusalem?" Clare's voice was insistent and imploring.

"No, Clare, it is not Jerusalem!" her mother answered. "Was the last town Jerusalem?"

"No," Clare whimpered.

"Was the last town Jerusalem?" she asked again.

"No."

"And will the next town be Jerusalem?"

"No."

"That's right! We will not be to Jerusalem for many weeks, so no more questions from you!" Addie swatted her child's head playfully and lifted her up on the cart. "Here, you ride for a while and rest until we get to camp." She glanced at the distant town. "And when we get close to the village, be sure to hold out your hands." People loved to give alms to the dimple-faced little girl.

That night, Peter the Monk preached and Addie knew that when the light of the next morning broke, a small number of souls willing to forsake everything and tramp to Jerusalem would appear in the fields and that a significant amount of money would fall into Peter's treasure chest—money from the wealthy who could not go, or preferred to pay the way of someone else.

✠✠✠

The same afternoon, in the wood hills above Laon, Pons and Guy lay hidden in a thicket along a narrow road which twisted and coiled to the small Cluniac monastery of St. Jean not far away. They were dressed in brown wool breeches, linen bandages for leggings, and a tunic with close-fitting sleeves and belted at the waist. Not the dress of thieves and robbers, but they were not, as yet, thieves and robbers.

"Shush!" Pons said, as Guy attempted to fold up his sleeves above his wrist. The thicket stirred. "You know the plan, so be quiet."

Guy removed his cap to be less conspicuous and waited. Two monks in habits and cowls approached, carrying large leather satchels slung about their shoulders. Pons and Guy hunkered closer to the earth.

When the monks were abreast of their position, the two Provencals flew out of their nest like hawks and swooped upon their startled prey. The monks cried loudly against the outrage, but Pons and Guy, producing some twine, bound the monks after first divesting them of their robes and purses. They then donned the robes themselves and left their own tattered clothing for the monks. They examined the satchels.

"What have we here, Pons?" asked Guy, as he pulled a reliquary from the purse.

"That is a sacred relic of the abbey and you had best leave it alone," shouted one of the monks.

"Sacred relic indeed!" scoffed Pons. "About as sacred as a chicken bone in a kettle of soup!"

"And here is the money you have collected from the poor today, oh?" said Guy, rummaging through the coins at the bottom of the satchel. The monks struggled violently to free themselves,

"You are robbers and cheats, and your souls will roast in the fires of hell if you take so much as a single coin."

"Hey Guy, 'ave you noticed how fond our monkish friends are of the expression 'the fires of hell'?" asked Pons as he held up a reliquary to the afternoon light streaming through the oak trees.

"Pons, this is what I think," said Guy approaching the monks who were still thrashing about on the ground like fish out of water. "Now, look at these monks here. They are the cheats and robbers, oh? Right?"

Pons nodded as Guy continued: "The bones of the saints, the wood of the Cross, the milk of the Virgin! Look's like pig knuckles to me, birch or oak wood, and calf's milk. I think, Pons, that we be doing the Church a service, I really do."

"How's that, Guy?"

"Well, now, if indeed these articles be genuine, then we are only serving the Church when we sell them for a fair price to the pious who rightfully place their faith in them, mind you. But if they be false, why then, the profits we make from our treachery will justly advance the cause of the pilgrimage which His Holiness has proclaimed and in which endeavor we are now vouchsafed to pursue."

Pons stared at Guy in astonishment. "Where did you learn to talk like that?"

Guy sniffed and said, "It was something the bishop said when Frederick of Arles took the cross in a ceremony at the church. I remembered, that's all."

So Pons and Guy left the monks trussed up in the forest and emerged on the road to Laon as Cluniacs themselves, anticipating eagerly the crowds that would flood the marketplace tomorrow, crowds that might buy their relics. They whistled and sang as they walked, not feeling the least twinge of guilt. On the contrary, in times of economic distress, they often relied on their wits to supplement what divine providence had been unable or unwilling to provide.

That night, however, found them in a cemetery.

"I don't like this, Guy," said Pons nervously. The cemetery was in a woods beyond the eastern and ancient walls of Laon, walls built during Caesar's Gaul. The cemetery was recent, however, and was the sacred burial ground of the Jewish community which had grown to a collective of considerable size and influence in Laon.

"Put a lamp on yonder branch," said Guy, pointing to an oak. "It will keep the spirits away." Pons hung the lamp and returned to the corona of light in which Guy was digging.

"We don't have enough relics," Guy explained. "We need bones, Pons. I've explained this before. We can't kill a pig because we would have to steal it and that's more risky than digging up this grave. Besides, pig bones would be white and clean. Relic bones need to look old. And we can't dig up the bones of some poor soul in a Christian cemetery. So the bones of these Jews are perfect.

We'll sell them as relics! Sort of ironic isn't it? Making money for the pilgrimage to Jerusalem off the bones of Christ-killers!"

"But bodies, Guy. I don't like digging up bodies!" Pons wiped his dirty, mud-caked face with the sleeve of his tunic.

"Jews, Pons, Jews! Killers of Christ, worse than the goddern Turks, Pons. The Turks don't believe in the son of God, but the Jews—the Jews are killers of the son of God! Don't you understand that?" Guy hissed at Pons, and struck his spade deeper into the soft earth, dampened by spring rains. The earth coated his hands and filled the crevices under his fingernails. "You know what I've heard about them Jews?" Guy asked, grunting as he dug. "They got tails, you know ... you can't see 'em, but they're there alright. And hemorrhoids, all Jews got hemorrhoids 'cause they said when Christ died 'His blood be upon us.' They is always bleeding, Pons. And they smell funny ... but the smell goes away when they're baptized."

"Do their tails disappear when they're baptized?" Pons asked.

"I don't know," Guy said. Just then his spade hit something solid. They excavated further and then lowered their lamps to the dismal scene they had uncovered. It was a body, no doubt about that. The two bent low to clear away the mottled soil to reveal the skeletal remains. When the corpse lay exposed before them, they stood upright out of a slight, if not real, sense of respect as well as to rest from their labors. Then Pons reached for the skeleton. It lay in the form of a human being, but the sinews and ligaments binding piece to piece had long since decayed. Hundreds of bones now lay neatly arranged in the shape of a human as though someone had attempted to reassemble the form.

Pons hefted a leg bone, examined it briefly and then placed it in his sack and took an arm and another leg. Guy watched with curiosity.

"Jesus! What the feck are you doing?" he asked.

"Let's get this over with and get out of here. We need some bones, so let's get some bones."

"What are we going to do with big bones like that, you idiot?" He grabbed the bones and threw them into the grave. "We can't sell big bones as relics. How could we explain the possession of the leg bones of St. Anthony or an arm of St. Simeon?" Guy bent to the earth and fussed with the skeleton. Then, standing up, he said, "Hands, feet, fingers, toes, teeth——that's all we can use." He held up some small bones to the terror-widened eyes of his friend. "Get rid of those. You get the hands, and I'll do the feet." They laid their sacks on the ground above the grave and, jumping into the cavity, began to finish their task. With a stone, Guy chipped some teeth from the skull and dropped them into his sack.

✠✠✠

The next morning, the air was blue with wood smoke, and the field dotted with tents resembled the encampment of an army. Addie surmised their total must now be near ten thousand! And growing daily ... and all of them preparing for another day's journey. Carts were tied down, horses tugging at their tethers, oxen lowing and cattle bellowing. Ox teams were yoked to carts and wagons. A cadre of agitated and shouting monks rushed down the road and through the fields, searching for something they had apparently lost. Addie could hear the shouting above the bellowing of the animals. The cart lurched forward when Addie gave it a halfhearted tug, cutting ruts in the soft earth. Peter grazed the rump of the horse with a hazel switch and soon the cart was on the road, its wheels turning again toward Jerusalem.

They overtook a band of new pilgrims, about forty or fifty of them. All women and children. Each carried a sack of provisions on their back, and a walking stick in their hand. At the foot of their procession was the most beautiful white goose Addie had ever seen. Clare jumped off the cart and ran off to see it.

"Your goose is beautiful," said Addie to one of the women leading the group. "You must be happy to have him with you."

The woman was barefoot, as were all of their company. She was dressed plainly in only a *sorquenie* thrown over a plain dress. She wore a small *chapelet* on her head. There was an air of the religious about her. The woman looked quickly at Addie and then flashed a big, vacant smile. "Oh, no," she said excitedly, "This is not my goose, or our goose. It does not belong to anyone." She looked at Clare who was scrutinizing the strutting fowl. "Don't touch the goose, dear!"

Addie hesitated, puzzled. "If the goose doesn't belong to you or anyone else, then why is it with you?"

The woman replied: "Ach! We don't know where this goose is come from. Lord, one morning, there it was in the village—out of nowhere. It just came from the sky." The woman's eyes grew large as she described the miracle. "God sent the goose, friend. God sent the goose to us." She glanced to the sky and then back to Addie. They had fallen in step together. "It's the same story for us and the others. No rain, no crops, dead cattle dying standing up. Then this holy fowl flew in, and if it didn't rain till the fields were soaked, the cisterns full! Well, 'twas our salvation for sure, that I kin tell ya. When this happens, I know that this goose is a divine goose, sent from heaven to guide us."

"Mmm, God gave you a guiding goose … a goose guide?"

"That's right, dear," the woman said, beaming.

"And are you going to Jerusalem, too?"

"Oh yes," she replied. "We heard Peter preach, but when he left, the village was very undecided. Many believed the men should stay to take care of the crops that had now revived. But we believed the goose was filled with the Holy Ghost and would lead us and show us the way to the Holy Land."

"A godly goose guide with the Ghost! Glory be! That *is* miraculous," Addie exclaimed. "What happened then?"

"We waited for days and days … you never can tell when God is going to move, you know. For days that goose doesn't leave the village. We waited impatiently. Why, miss, we had packed our carts and prepared you know, because we were anxious to leave for the Holy Land, but the goose with the Ghost was in no mood for travel. 'Twasn't the will of God, we guessed. One day—saints alive!—it took to fluttering, and then waddled down the lane out of the village, and we followed it at once not wishing to grieve the Holy Ghost."

"The goose guide is going to lead you to the Holy Land?"

"But how does it know the way?" Clare asked.

"It's a goose with the Ghost, child," the lady said. "And if the Holy Ghost don't want us to go to the Holy Land, then we'll be somewhere else, wherever the goose and the Ghost lead us."

"What if it should fly away," Clare continued, "fly off until you can't see it?"

"Then, child, that would stop us in our tracks, and we'd stay put until the Ghost comes upon us again. There!"

She had an answer for every question. She was quite devout.

Then she said, "Say, have you seen any Jews yet?"

Adelaide thought for a moment. "I don't believe I've ever seen a Jew. Heard about 'em, I guess, but never seen one."

"Why, you've never seen a Jew?" the woman exclaimed. "You will, child. You will. I hear there's been trouble."

"What kind of trouble?" Addie asked. She hadn't heard about any problems and she wasn't sure she liked this woman.

"Well, the Jews control all the money, and the nobles are trying to raise money for the pilgrimage, and the Jews won't give it to them—except at a high rate of interest of course. There's going to be blood, I know it, I know it!' The woman sniffed, touched her nose and continued: "You know what happened in our village a couple of years ago? Well, I'll tell you. There was a little boy, darling little fellow, his name was Guilluame, yellow hair, pleasing face, son of a ploughman and learnin' to be a skinner. One day, shortly before Easter and the Jewish Passover it was, he disappeared. He was last seen going into a Jew's house. They found him eight days later on Wednesday of Holy Week. They had shaved his head and stabbed his little body. The boy's mother and our priest said the Jews did it as a re-enactment of the death of Christ 'cause they know Christ was the Messiah and the Son of God. A maidservant working in a Jewish house saw the whole thing through a chink in the door. They seized the boy after a synagogue service, gagged him, tied him up, pushed a ring of thorns around his head, bound him on a cross, drove nails through his left hand and left foot, stabbed him in the side and poured scalding water all over his body! Your children aren't safe around Easter anymore, that's for sure."

"But is that what really happened?" Addie asked. She hadn't formed an opinion yet.

"Of course! In my village!" cried the woman. "Oh, oh! here's a problem!" The Holy Ghost had squared off with a mongrel dog and a great flap with honking and barking and shouting and screaming ensued. Addie dropped back to let the woman and her group handle the crisis and then waved as they continued down the road in pursuit of the white-feathered deity.

"What does one feed the Holy Ghost?" Lettie wondered aloud after they were gone.

Addie, who had been staring at the departing company, broke out of her trance, and laughed. "Hush, child. God will take care of the Holy Ghost.

"I don't know if it was a divine goose or no," Peter grumbled, looking at the soles of his shoes, "but if it was, I just stepped in the divine dung of Holy Ghost." Addie lunged at him to hit him, but he ducked and she missed. But then brother and sister fell in step together.

"I had another vision last night," Peter said.

Addie glanced at him. "Saint Andrew?" Her brother nodded. The apostle had appeared to him, he said, bearing a sword. "He said that he had a great task for me to accomplish but that, before I did great things, I must be faithful in small things. I should be prepared, because soon something is going to happen, something for me to do."

"What does it mean?" Addie inquired. Peter shrugged and ran down the road after Lettie. "You're as mad as that awful woman," Addie called out after him.

Addie could still see the women as they continued their journey behind the Spirit-filled goose. But that afternoon, the band departed from the primary trunk of the pilgrimage choosing instead a meandering road that disappeared into a wooded vale. "The Holy Ghost has found a better route than the one we're taking," she speculated.

CHAPTER TEN

A Murder

Year 4856
Year 1028 of the exile

"WE ARE A PEACEFUL PEOPLE," said the rabbi to Peter the Monk. Yekuthiel, son of Rabbi Joseph the Elder, twisted the tassels of his prayer shawl anxiously. "But what we hear from Rouen disheartens and discourages us." They were meeting in the study of the rabbi in the synagogue at Rameru, a Burgundian town not far from the German frontier. The rabbi was old, thin and smallish, wrapped in heavy, oversized velvet robes. A Star of David pendant hung from his neck, resting on his chest just beneath the frayed ends of a wispy, ashen beard. Atop his head, he wore a small, round-trimmed hat with a peaked crown.

The room was ablaze in the candlelight of menorahs, candelabra and thick, beeswax candles on pedestals. Scrolls were stacked on the floor beneath bookshelves crammed with tattered histories and commentaries of the *yeshivah* scholars, and copies of the Talmud and other sacred books. There were more scrolls in bins in a corner of the room, and next to the scrolls, the *kuppah*, or collection box. The desk was cluttered with parchment, quills and ink bottles, and the walls were covered with rich, silver-threaded tapestries. The chamber was a slovenly hovel of keen intellectualism where prayer and theology, science and faith mingled in amiable creativity.

"What have you heard from Rouen?" inquired the monk matter-of-factly, although he knew what the rabbi was about to report. The two sat in straight-backed chairs opposite each other as they were indeed opposites of each other. The Jew, a man of wealth and means; the monk, a man of poverty and no means. The Jew, a man of refinery and manners; the monk, a man uncouth and ill-mannered. The Jew, a man of learning; the monk, a man of intuition.

"Our brothers reported that pilgrims have attacked our community in Rouen, and that some of our young men were forced to undergo baptism, and others were killed. We have heard of similar disturbances where your pilgrimage has traveled ... outrageous behavior. The violence must stop ... I don't know how, but it must stop. We fear for our brothers and sisters in Germany and the Rhineland."

Peter listened to the rabbi impassively, staring at him with an intensity that would have unnerved most, but not Rabbi Yekuthiel. His many years had sifted out fear and vulnerability. He neither intimidated nor was intimidated.

"I have thousands upon thousands of pilgrims with me, rabbi," Peter said. "They are like sheep without a shepherd. They are penniless and without masters, footsore farmers, women, children, harlots, liars, murderers, fake monks and weepers, fit-throwers, hymn-chanters, and purse-thieves, old men of tired, gentle blood, and young men with hot, ribald blood—thirsting for adventure. I can hardly control the actions of them all."

The old man sighed. "But is it so impossible to restrain the impetuous? Your Church forbids such actions against us."

"What the Church forbids and what the people practice are two very different things," said Peter.

The old rabbi lifted his hand feebly and smiled. "Let's not quibble ... we shall never agree on this." He shifted his body in the chair and leaned slightly toward the monk. "Your undertaking requires finances ... it's a heavy financial venture. It's a burden to you constantly. You think about it night and day. You preach in the cities of northern France and you will preach in the Rhineland and, while you may not turn converts away, you don't want more pilgrims to join you, now do you?" He laughed nervously. "You have too many souls to take care of already ... too many mouths to feed, too many criminals to manage, too many women to control ... ah, the women ..." His voice trailed off.

Peter was about to speak when the rabbi resumed. "You preach because you need money. I know, I know ... I understand how this must be. So we will help you with your money problems, if you will help us with ours. Relieve my burden, and I'll relieve yours." Peter was silent, gazing into the sad eyes of the rabbi, not seeing there the centuries of affliction, the hurt, the pain. Candles flickered.

The rabbi pushed himself out of his chair and shuffled to the desk, gathering his robes about him. He rummaged through some papers until he found the sheet of parchment he had been looking for. He showed it to Peter.

"This is a letter to our confreres in Germany," he said, "advising them to give you similar monetary assistance as you proceed through the Rhineland. In return, we must have from you your solemn vow as a Christian to allow my people to live unmolested and in peace."

The monk took the parchment, read its contents, and placed the letter in his lap. He said that he appreciated the suggestion provided it was offered with the understanding that he could make no such vow. It was a promise he could not guarantee.

The rabbi returned to his chair. "You are a person of influence. The people listen to you. You are their spiritual leader. You hold them in your hands. Surely, at your word, the bloodshed and the offense against our customs and faith will stop!"

"You give me too much credit, rabbi!" said the monk, agitated. He stood and paced about the room, lifting a commentary from the rabbi's bookshelves. "These are hotheaded pilgrims whose entire lives have been spent in fighting and wars of one kind or the other. Not even the Holy Father could get them to stop the slaughter *of their own people*. Put a few Christians together, give them some property and before long there's bound to be a war. Now, if they cannot be restrained from killing their *Christian* brothers, how can I stop them from killing *your Jewish brothers*? And don't forget, I am but one part of this effort. Walter Sans-Avoir has a large following and he's headed for Hungary. Vollshalk and Folkmar have followings of their own. I have heard that Count Emicho of Leningen is gathering still more in northern Germany. I may be able to exert some influence over those who are with me now, and those who may join me in the future, but of the other groups, I cannot say.

"Another problem. These pilgrims have left everything, given up everything, to travel beyond Christendom to drive out the Moslem heathen from the Holy Land. Yet, inside Christendom is an enemy who is equally repulsive—"

"Ach! We are not your enemy. We are different, but not enemies …"

"Oh, yes, yes! *I* can make that distinction," Peter replied, replacing the commentary on the shelf, "but the peasants can't. Moslems, heretics and Jews are all the same in their eyes. They can't understand why they should travel thousands of miles to fight the Moslem, but be forbidden to fight the killers of Christ who live right under their noses. There's a certain logic to it. And I fear that some indeed—as you suggest—will use this pilgrimage as an opportunity to avenge the blood of Christ … It is not easy for me. I cannot always control them. They possess a rationale, however *ir*rational, that drives them mad."

Rabbi Yekuthiel stood and wrapped his robes and shawl about himself tightly. "So you do not want our money?"

Peter shrugged. "What can I do? But you misunderstand me. I do want your help because your money will give my people a reason to stop the harassment. They have a reason for war, we must give them a reason for peace. Your money does that. My point is: without this money, I can do nothing. With your gift, I can *attempt* to protect you, but cannot *guarantee* it … So we will take your money if you offer it. The Lord doesn't care where the money comes from. The money of a heretic or a Jew is as good as the coin of a saint if it is used to achieve His will. Doesn't the Torah say: 'They intended it for evil, but God intended it for good' ?"

Rabbi Yekuthiel ignored the reference to Scripture and went to the door and opened it. Two young men entered carrying three cloth sacks. They went to the desk and untied one of the sacks and dumped its contents on the surface. Hundreds of silver coins spilled across the desk while the monk watched.

"What you see," said the rabbi, "is 250 *zekukim* of silver. The other bag contains another 250, for a total of five hundred *zekukim* of silver. The third bag holds five pounds of gold. See for yourself."

✠✠✠

Count Stefan loved the challenge of the impossible, and the difficulty of transporting thousands of knights and soldiers thousands of miles over sea and land to Palestine intrigued him. He might prefer not to go at all, he might prefer that Alexius manage his own affairs; but having taken the cross—however reluctantly— Stefan now felt an enthusiasm he had not experienced for many years.

Stefan strolled to the window of his spacious bedroom high in the keep of his sprawling castle. He was dressed casually in flat shoes, maroon *chasusses*, breeches, and an airy silk blouse. His golden hair was parted in the middle and fell naturally in slight waves at the face to the nape of his neck. He peered out the narrow window. The fortress was situated on a towering bluff facing the south, overlooking the Loire River at Blois. Here the river channel was wide and shallow, and it flowed languidly to the sea. On both sides of the river lay miles of undulating hills, cultivated fields and pasture for sheep and cattle.

The impossible! Never in the history of mankind had there been an attempt to transport so many men so far to achieve a specific military objective. Not in the days of Rome when the farthest outpost of the Eternal City had been Britain or Ireland. Not in the days of Alexander, whose reach extended as far as his knowledge of the world. Never before! Stefan shook his head in wonderment. How reckless! It would require intrepid recklessness!

And yet, while the impossible can never be achieved without recklessness, it must never be attempted without preparation. Preparation! A prepared man can afford to be a reckless one, but the preparation must come first! The count left the window and returned to his writing table. Picking up his quill, he continued to write:

> *Our nobles have already begun to make preparations for the autumn departure. Hugh of Vermandois, the brother of King Philip, is putting his meager affairs in the hands of his countess. Godfrey de Bouillon, Duke of Lorraine, is raising money by bribing Jews, selling estates on the Meuse, and promising his castle to the Bishop of Liege. Count Raymond has recently acquired the rich marquisate of Provence. He has connections with the royal house of Spain by his marriage to Elvira of Aragon. The count is old; I do not believe he intends to return from Palestine. He is leaving his wealth in the hands of his son, Bertrand, and selling other lands, or pledging them, to raise money. He'll have the largest army of us all, I think. Robert Curthose, my brother-in-law, is trying to raise money by pledging his duchy to his brother, William Rufus, the King of England, for ten thousand silver marks. The two of them have been feuding for years.*
>
> *Coinage is a major problem. It is simply not possible to transport all of the supplies that will be needed on a venture of this magnitude. Supplies, therefore, must be purchased, not bartered, along the way. For this we need a considerable amount of coins at the ready. Fortunately, we have discovered that as we put our land and buildings up for sale, coinage has begun to reappear from abbeys, monasteries and churches where it has been hoarded for years, even centuries.*
>
> *I am assigning specific responsibilities to my chief vassals, dividing their duties into four areas: transport, food, the army and shelter. Everard of Le Puits has transport. He'll provide carts, baggage wagons, oxen, mules, extra wheels and axles and the tools to repair them. Guerin Gueronat will feed the army. He will purchase grain, oil, meat, salt, game and wine for the journey, at least as far as Constantinople, and estimate what will need to be purchased along the way. Caro is commander of the army under my overall*

direction. He will secure palfreys and war horses, armor, bows, spears, swords and lances, etc. Turning peasants into foot soldiers and bowmen requires armor and weaponry, and a knight who loses a horse must be given a replacement. Caro will gather the beams, pulleys, wrenches, spades and hammers for the miners and engineers. Geoffrey Guerin will recruit tentmakers, and put in a store of canvas, poles and tools.

I write to reassure you that plans to come to the assistance of Constantinople are well underway. In this you should take comfort. I look forward to renewing our acquaintance. I had no idea when I left your glorious city, that I would ever see you again. The thought of seeing you gives me pleasure.

The count signed his name at the bottom of the page, folded the parchment, placed it in an envelope, and sealed it with wax, applying his personal imprimatur. He then summoned his secretary and gave him the envelope. It bore the inscription: *Anna Comnena.*

✠✠✠

"Here's what I got, mamma," said Clare one day, pulling her hands out of her apron, opening them to show a few coins.

They'd taking to begging on occasion. As they crossed into Germany, they were footsore, weary of body and already beginning to experience shortfalls in grain, food and money. Adelaide Bartholomew's store of food was perilously low. If a meal had to be missed, Peter and Addie gave up their portions to Clare and Lettie. The miles had chewed the leather soles of their shoes to shreds. So they fashioned straps of leather to the soles and wrapped them around their feet and ankles. Addie was hoping for new shoes soon. They should have brought an extra pair with them, she thought ruefully.

Foot soldiers, tired and hungry, protested shortages and brought their complaints to Peter. He compared the entire throng to the children of Israel who, delivered from Egypt, preferred to be in Egypt hungry than to be in the wilderness free. When the hunger became severe, the peasants often took to plundering the homes and villages of the countryside, stealing, tearing down, setting fires and committing mayhem. Peter was unable to stop it.

Thus, Peter the Monk was unable to deliver on the halfhearted promise he had made to Rabbi Yekuthiel. Peter's way was to assume that what was the will of God didn't need the will of man to achieve it. "God's will be done," he would say, arching an eyebrow sternly, not thinking about how—exactly—God's will was to be accomplished among men on earth.

At Metz, Peter met the Count of Leningen. Emicho had been preaching the crusade among the Bavarians and Rhinelanders, saying that he was the long-awaited Last Emperor—the last in a line of emperors beginning with Constantine and extending through Charlemagne. The legend was not new. Someday, the legend went, an emperor would arise and lead an army into battle against the Jewish Antichrist at Jerusalem. At the conclusion of the battle, Jesus would descend to the Mount of Olives and designate the Last Emperor as the ruler of the temporal millennial kingdom. Emicho claimed to be that person; that Jesus had appeared to him in a vision telling him that he would reveal himself to Emicho at Constantinople.

In Speyer, Emicho and his followers forced Jews to undergo baptism or die. Eleven refused and the count had them killed. One pious woman drove a dagger into her stomach rather than be killed by a Gentile. Local Christians marched on the synagogue and burned it to the ground, but not without first seizing the Torah and trampling on it in the blood of those who had died. The violence here ended quickly, however, when the bishop, a righteous man, used force against Emicho, and quickly hanged the leaders of the mob.

But the infection took hold, spreading throughout the entire body of the pilgrimage and even inflaming the emotions of Christians who had lived in peace with their Jewish neighbors in the cities of the Rhineland *for years.* The next day at Worms, a similar riot occurred. The Jewish community itself was divided between those who thought they were safe in their homes and those who sought the protection of the bishop. An unruly mob of pilgrims bolted from house-to-house slaying men, women and children. Seven days later, they forced the bishop to give up those who were hiding. The Jews, preferring death as a Jew to life as a Christian, died with the *Shema* on their lips: About eight hundred souls died at Worms and were buried naked in common graves. Those who were not killed in the melee were stripped and dragged to water for baptism.

It was in Worms that Guy killed his first Jew. Not that Guy was accustomed to killing. It was not just the first Jew he killed—it was the first human being. Guy's experience with violence was very limited, although he was a man of fiery temperament. He had always worked in the fields. Even when his lord had battles to fight, like the last time in Spain, Guy was left in Provence to take care of the crops. He had bloodied his fist on the face of many a friend or foe in a drinking establishment, to be sure. But these quarrels were more likely to involve a serving girl or a question of honor, rather than a dispute over a fine point of theology. Religious matters were never worth fighting about, he judged; and as for the Jews, why, he had never seen a Jew himself. He had only heard tales about them—how they slaughter babies, and how no child was safe with them, how they controlled the houses of money in Provence and the north of France. And although he had seen drawings of Jews with Devil's horns, he had never seen one—until now, until Speyer.

Guy considered Emicho to be slightly mad. The count could talk of nothing but the Jews. No one mentioned Jerusalem in his camp, no one talked about liberating the Holy Places. And certainly no one among these pilgrims gave a peck about helping the emperor in Constantinople.

Guy would no doubt have been peaceful in his encounters with Jews had not a riot occurred. Feelings were running high against the Jews in Worms, and the greater the slaughter, the greater the sense of moral certitude. When one kills another human being, there must be a powerful justification that accompanies the slaughter—unless one is simply mad. It never occurred to anyone, certainly not to Guy, that murder is the ugly handmaiden of madness. Guy assumed that since so many Jews were being killed, they somehow deserved their fate. God would not permit it to be otherwise. *Deus vult!* Even the Jews, themselves, appeared to accept their suffering as part of the peculiar burden of their own history.

Guy witnessed the slaying of many Jews. They saw old men and young women actually pull back the collars of their garments to bare their throats—inviting their tormentors to drain the blood from their bodies. And so their attackers did. The shedding of blood created the thirst for more blood. The killing, and the cries of women and children continued, until it numbed his conscience and diminished his ability to think. He succumbed to the blood fever that had infected his companions. He, too, became—mad.

Their party was sweeping through the streets bent on mischief, when they came across a young man hurrying along the walls. They accosted him roughly and when the youth whirled to face his captors, death was in his eyes. He was a gaunt boy of whose skin was almost blue with death. His yarmulke rested on short, dark hair, and phylacteries were strapped to both his forehead and left forearm. His shirt was open at the collar exposing a slender neck around which was a prayer shawl. His lips were thin and tight. To Guy, he appeared an odd creature, decidedly alien to anything they had experienced. The boy spoke as a man, as one who knew his fate. He stumbled away from the mob, backwards, to the wall of the house where he had been caught and faced his attackers, calling them bitter and arrogant; their purpose in going to Jerusalem— barbaric.

"You are all a pack of idolaters, and you believe in three gods!" he screamed, as the gang threw him to the ground. But the rabble held back when the boy began to pray: "Look and behold your servant, O Lord," he wailed, "and see what we are doing to sanctify Thy great name, in order not to exchange you for a crucified scion who was despised, abominated, and held in contempt by his own generation, a bastard son conceived by a menstruating and promiscuous mother."

At this, there was a tremendous outcry and furor. Guy felt a dagger pressed into his palm. The Christians fell upon the lad like a pack of dogs; there was a glint and whir of silver sheen, a dagger finding its mark. The point pierced the tender skin and sank fully into the soft upper belly of the youth beneath his heart. The boy's eyes widened in the surprise of death and his mouth opened … then his body relaxed and lay lifeless on the ground. Blood oozed through the wound, soaking his linen tunic in a widening circle of blackness and crimson, until it dripped onto the bricks and into the dust of the street.

Guy's hand released the dagger as though it had suddenly become as hot as a firebrand. The perpetrators of this crime were quiet. They stared at the boy and slowly backed away from the scene, murmuring among themselves. The stillness was broken when Pons pushed through the swarm and rushed to the fallen youth. He pulled the dagger out of the body, cast it aside, and rolled the boy over on his face. Then, inexplicably, and to the wonderment of his cohorts, he straddled the body and reached down to grab the Jew boy's breeches. With a yank and furious twisting, he pulled them down to the ankles, exposing his buttocks. Pons stared in surprise for an instant, and then whirled upon his companions. His face was hot and moist. He looked in anguish at Guy and then burst through the mob and back into the street. This Jew had no tail, nor was there a sign that there would ever be a tail, or that there had once been a tail. No tail.

✠✠✠

The worst was still to come. At Mainz, the peasant pilgrims were forced to camp outside the gates and stay there because the burghers would not allow them inside the city walls. Under pressure from the Jewish community—now terrified by reports they had received from Worms—the bishop forbade entrance into the city and promised to protect the Jews from the savagery of Emicho's forces in accordance with the Church's teaching. But someone within the city opened the gates at night and Emicho's forces stormed through the town creating confusion and general mayhem. There was no doubt about their intentions and Jews immediately went into hiding.

A meeting was arranged for the following morning in the chambers of the bishop. When Peter of Amiens (known as Peter the Hermit or Peter the Monk) and Emicho arrived, Bishop Ruthard and Rabbi Kalonymous ben Meshullan were already there. The rabbi spoke first:

"Hundreds of innocent lives were taken in Speyer and Worms … shown no mercy!"

Emicho shrugged. "It was unavoidable," he said. The count was a short, nervous man of sharp, sunken features, and empty, pale eyes that continually darted and flitted about, like bats in an empty cave. Emicho disliked meetings, and endured them by fussing and fidgeting with his hands. He rarely smiled, and when he did, one saw that he was lacking a front tooth.

"It was avoidable! It was all avoidable," shouted the rabbi. "Speyer was avoidable. Worms was avoidable. And Maintz is avoidable. What business have you here with us so far from your route to Regensburg and Constantinople? You have gone out of your way for no other purpose than to shed Jewish blood and steal our money!"

"The entire pilgrimage is out-of-our-way, rabbi!" The rabbi's anger fired the count's hostility. "These people could be in their villages right now, husbands with their wives, women in their homes, men in the fields, children with their playmates. But they hear the voice of the Lord calling them to Jerusalem to liberate its shrines and to drive out the heathen. And if the Jew inside of Christendom itself can help us finance the pilgrimage, we see no reason to refuse."

"But no bloodshed, Emicho," said Bishop Ruthard, a timid man, but honest one who attempted to do what was right. "Your pilgrims must vacate the city and return to the fields. You and your leaders can remain within the city to make arrangements."

"We do not want vengeance," said Peter. Turning to the rabbi he said, "There can be no mistake. Jews and Christians, well, we can hardly be friends—"

"Not true! Jews and Christians have lived in harmony for many years in most of these towns. We'd have peace today if it were not for outsiders like both of you!"

Peter continued. "But it's not our purpose to avenge the blood of Christ or to visit upon the children the sins of their fathers."

"You evidently do not speak for your friend, Emicho, or for your followers, because everywhere you go, you leave a trail of carnage. Jews dying in the streets, Jews murdered in their homes, Jews slaughtered in the synagogues," replied Rabbi Kalonymous bitterly.

"Unfortunately, that has happened," said Peter, concurring.

"You are aware, as is the bishop, that the canons of the Church expressly forbid the persecution of the Jew?" the rabbi asked.

"Yes," said Emicho, "and that means nothing to these people who—"

"These people—" the rabbi was shouting again, "—these people are here because they listened to the pope and to the preaching of this prophet. Why do they now—*suddenly*—have no ears to hear what both their church and their prophet say unto them? That I ask you: why is that?"

Peter intervened, stepping between the two of them. "Rabbi, we're not here to argue—"

"I am!" the rabbi countered. "If your people were being rounded up and killed for no reason other than a religious one, would not you be arguing? Are we not otherwise like you? Are we not like each other? Don't we take tea in the afternoon? Don't we bake bread? Don't we love our children? Don't we pray to God? Oh, you accuse me of being argumentative, and this I say to you— you Christians are the most argumentative, quarrelling people I know."

"—The realities are clear to all of us."

Kalonymous continued quietly now: "You carry letters to us from the Jewish communities in France—Sully, Troyes, Rouen— seeking our cooperation in return for safe conduct. But your promises are of no more use than parchment for covering jars. Unless you leave the city and leave us unharmed, you, too, will have to pay the price."

"Ah," said Emicho with amusement, "A Jew threatens a Christian?"

"No, a Christian threatens a Christian," the rabbi replied. "I have sent a messenger to King Henry giving him notice of these troublesome events. His reaction, to put it mildly, was controlled rage. He has sent this epistle for you, bishop. Perhaps you would like to read it now and share it with the count." Rabbi Kalonymous produced a missive and gave it to the bishop. "The realities are clear to us all, isn't that what you said, Peter?" The rabbi smiled as the monk nodded.

The bishop read the letter in silence. Then he gave it to Emicho whose studied expression remained unaltered as he perused its content.

"This letter poses no problem for us," said the count when he had finished the reading. "We do not intend to do you harm. In fact, we want to help you—on a *quid pro quo* basis, of course. If you provide for our needs while we who bear the cross remain here, I can see no reason why hostilities need continue."

"I have anticipated your conditions," said the rabbi. "I have six hundred *zekukim* and seven pounds of gold to assist you in your venture. Half will be delivered now and the other half when you are beyond the city walls."

Emicho was silent and walked slowly around the rooms as the others watched. Then he stopped in front of the rabbi and smiled.

"No," he said.

"No?"

"No, but your offer is generous. You have shown yourself to be peace-loving. We do not want to place a burden upon you. Instead, these are our conditions. I wish to address the entire Jewish community in Mainz, to thank them for their generosity. They should assemble in the bishop's courtyard tomorrow at noon and bring with them any offerings which they may wish to contribute toward our holy venture. I will appoint a few trusted men to collect the monies which will go into our treasury, and that being completed, I will speak to them, and then we will leave the city. What say you to this?"

"I can't bring my people out of hiding! They are afraid."

"And very vulnerable," Emicho added. "Urge them to go to the bishop whom they know is their friend and someone they can trust. Tell them to gather in his courtyard. In this way, I can guarantee their safety because my own men can protect them against those who might wish to storm the walls of the court."

The rabbi said that he would take the count's message to his leaders. If their response was favorable, they would gather in the bishop's courtyard at noon on the following day. If their response was unfavorable, the rabbi would meet the count in the same courtyard at the same time, alone, with six hundred *zekukim* and seven pounds of gold.

"I hope you will not disappoint me," said Emicho.

That night, the pilgrims, all wearing the emblem of the cross on their garments, began looting and pillaging in the city. The burghers, eager to defend their shops and homes from such destruction, put up a fight and in the ensuing riot a Christian was killed. A cry immediately arose that this death was the fault of the Jews.

News of the rioting and the death of the pilgrim reached Rabbi Kalonymous and the elders gathered to debate the question of aid for the pilgrims. Fearing more turmoil if they did not accede to the demands of the count, they agreed to bring their money to the court and gather the Jewish community in the bishop's courtyard to hear what Count Emicho of Leningen had to say. The count was a German, and the bishop was a friend. They had no alternative.

The next day, when the morning was still cool, entire families gathered in the open space of the ancient courtyard. Hundreds upon hundreds crowded within the yard, perhaps over a thousand. Not long after the noon hour, Emicho's soldiers entered the courtyard and moved among the families with sacks and treasure chests inviting them to give generously. The Jews gave liberally and fearfully, praying as they dropped their coins, pearls and jewelry into the chests.

The soldiers then quit the yard, and locking the gates, rejoined Emicho who was mounted on his war horse in the square before the Church. He wore an iron breastplate, and a helmet with a nasal almost obscuring his face. He gripped a holstered lance in his left hand. Peter was there also, mounted—Kioko with him still. Rabbi Kalonymous and the Twelve Elders of the community were led outside of the courtyard and stood facing Emicho. At this, as though a signal had been given, the surrounding streets were immediately filled with armed mounted soldiers, previously hidden from view. They now emerged, their meaning apparent.

Rabbi Kalonymous was furious and began stomping his feet in the dust, tearing his clothes, and shouting profane and obscene things at the count, the monk and the bishop.

"You can't do this, Emicho! It is against the Church!" Bishop Ruthard protested, stepping forward. Peter the Monk, likewise was angry. He leaped from Kioko and stood before Emicho, grabbing the reins of his massive horse: "If you do not repent of this, I will renounce you and your pilgrimage to the emperor and to the pope. You will have no chance to survive. You must stop this at once."

Emicho raised his hand in the air for silence. To the bishop he said: "This is for the Church." To Peter he said: "I am the emperor!" To Rabbi Kalonymous he said: "Convert or perish. It's as simple as that. Receive the true baptism for the remission of your sins, or perish lest you persist further in your iniquity."

The rabbi was stunned. He stopped his raving when he realized the truth. He asked for an opportunity to speak to his people. "Thirty minutes," he said, "and then I will return with my answer."

The count agreed and said they would wait. Rabbi Kalonymous strode swiftly to the courtyard gates accompanied by a dozen soldiers. He turned and snarled, "Alone!"

Emicho nodded, and the rabbi entered the courtyard to converse with his people.

CHAPTER ELEVEN

The Rabbi

Three Days after the New Moon of Silvan

HEN THE COURTYARD GATES CLOSED behind him, Rabbi Kalonymous walked steadily in the soft rain toward the center, pushing through the throng like Moses parting the Red Sea. Over one thousand souls had crowded into the bishop's sanctuary to hear his words.

The rabbi lifted his robe-heavy arms and began to wail: "Oh God of Israel, there is one God and the Lord is our God; to whom shall we liken Him? O Lord, God of Israel, will you completely destroy this remnant of the house of Israel? Where are the signs and wonders which our forefathers related to us saying, 'Did you not bring us up from Egypt and from Babylonia and rescue us from our oppressors?' Why then, have you forsaken and abandoned us now in our hour of need? Why have you given us over to the evildoers of Edom so that they may destroy us? We are a nation despised and pillaged. You have uplifted the shield of our enemies and given them strength against us. We cry out now in anguish, our ears are seared with the cries of our brothers, the staff of our might has been broken, the glory of this sainted community is humbled."

The rabbi lowered his arms and bowed his head in silence, and at this, a general wailing began as each Hebrew lifted his own prayers to the skies. Presently, the rabbi signaled for silence and said, "We who have dwelt together agreeably in life shall not be divided in death. The wrath of God has been kindled against His people. All our wealth did not help us, nor did our fasting, self-affliction and charity. No one has been found to save us. Not even the holy Torah has protected us."

The people wept quietly now as the rabbi continued: "There can be no questioning of the ways of the Holy One of Israel," he cried. "Blessed be His name who has given us the Torah and the grace to be slain for the sake of His Holy Name. Happy are we if we fulfill His will, for we who die are destined for the world to come where we shall sit in the kingdom of the saints. Indeed, dying now, we exchange a world of darkness for a world of light; a world of sorrow for a world of joy; a world of time for a world of eternity."

Someone jumped to his feet and shouted the *Shema*. Another stood and pressed his fist against the leaden sky and cried, "I will die a Jew." A tumult was developing. The rabbi asked for silence. "Examine your knives to be certain of their ritual purity. See that they are not defective, that they have no notches. My life soon is over. I must go beyond the gates where I will attempt to address the crowd. There will not be much time."

A voice called out. "Wait, Rabbi! We will be first." A husband and wife stood and pushed through the crowd to the center where the rabbi stood. Kalonymous moved aside. The man was surely in his third decade of life as was his wife. Her blond hair and his hair and beard were now soaked by the rain. They embraced frantically and wept. Then the man pulled a knife from beneath his shirt, and kissed its blade. Placing the point of the dagger under her left breast, he held it there as he supported her with his left arm. They were looking at each other when suddenly, he thrust it into her heart. Her body immediately went rigid and then relaxed. Her head fell back as he gently lowered her to the ground, weeping hysterically. Standing beside her fallen body, he shouted again, "I will die a Jew." He thrust the blade into his own heart and collapsed upon the body of his spouse.

Rabbi Kalonymous bent over and touched both of them gently as their life was leaving them. Then he straightened and said, "Do what you must do, quickly."

With that, the crowd dispersed within the courtyard. Houses of grandfather and grandmother, husband and wife, and children separated into small conclaves where they could be together. In the slaughter that followed, fathers bound their sons as Abraham had Isaac, and offered them to God, while mothers refused to listen to the wailing of their daughters. Some preferred to bare their necks and have a loved one draw the blade across the throat. One sacrificed another, and in turn that person killed another, until brothers and sisters, teachers and pupils, mothers and suckling child had poured their life upon the ground. The blood of the husband mixed with that of the wife, the blood of the father flowed with that of the son, the blood of the bridegroom was married to that of the bride, the blood of parents with that of the children, until the life-blood of families co-mingled with family upon family, bringing the entire community together, even in death.

Rabbi Kalonymous returned to Count Emicho outside the walls, closing the gates quickly behind him as his people barred them from the inside. Emicho's stallion was pawing and snorting, as nervous as its rider. Emicho asked Kalonymous for his answer.

"We are the children of God,' the rabbi said calmly. "We cannot convert to become what we already are."

"Children of the Devil is what you are!" Emicho cried, raising his sword in the air as his horse reared, forelegs pawing the gloomy air. But as the crowd and the soldiers surged forward, another voice was heard over the rabble. It was Bishop Ruthard, who had taken to the steps that ascended diagonally along the exterior wall of the courtyard. It was raining harder now.

"You must stop this crime!" he shouted, leaping a few granite blocks higher on the steps. "Stop! In the name of God and the Church, stop!"

The soldiers hesitated, and Emicho reined his horse under control. Then he signaled for silence. The bishop continued:

"There is no need for this action. It is a violation of the laws of God and the Church. It is not for us to visit upon the children the sins of their fathers."

"Christ-killers!" someone in the crowd shouted. A peal of thunder split the air.

"The heavens do not want to witness this sacrilege. Rabbi Kalonymous did not kill Jesus. He and the Jews of this city have in every way befriended the Church of Christ. They have lent their aid to support you in this noble cause that takes you to Jerusalem. They have lived peaceably among us, and you who are the townspeople of Mainz know this is true!"

"They kill our children, steal our money, charge us interest," shouted an anonymous voice.

"Devils," shouted another.

"The Church forbids this," Ruthard cried, "and you are in disobedience to the Church and the Holy Father who has sent you on this journey. And those of you in this city should realize that you are destroying the very source that has helped to make you all prosperous."

"Jew lover!"

The crowd became ugly and pressed to the walls. Bishop Ruthard, fearing for his life, fled up the stairs and along the wall, not once glancing upon the grisly scene in the courtyard below. A few peasants seized stones and flung them at the fleeing cleric, but the bishop escaped.

The mob was now beginning to force the gates. Emicho shouted for them to pull back. As the crowd rolled away, Rabbi Kalonymous stood alone.

"The hand of the Lord is heavy upon His people," intoned the rabbi, "but it is heavy against us in mercy. It shall be heavy against you in judgment."

He staggered the few yards that were between him and the monk and looked square into the eyes of Peter the Hermit. "They say you are a prophet and that you have a letter from God ... Does that letter tell you to kill children? Old men and young women?" He turned to Emicho and said in a stronger voice: "And you, Emicho, you say you have had a vision. God is going to make you his Emperor, his Last Emperor. God has chosen you, passing over Charlemagne and his sons, to rid the earth of the Antichrist."

Emicho's men had ringed the feeble, old rabbi as he spoke what he knew were his final words. His body shuddered in the cold, as the rain continued to pelt it. "And in this vision, Count Emicho, did God tell you that you must pave the way to your coronation with the bodies of babies and nursing mothers?"

He turned again to Peter. "I am a prophet, too, Peter." He raised a decrepit finger in the face of the monk: "And I say unto you, you have brought these people into the wilderness to die. They will die, but you, Peter, will not die. No, you shall live to watch the strong brought low, women die of fear and children perish without mercy. You will live to see this judgment come to pass so that your heart might be humbled and your arrogance and pride punished. All will die, save yourself and a dozen souls, one for each of the houses of Israel. And you will know in that hour of darkness that there is but one God ... And when you die at last, you will die in disgrace."

The rabbi whirled upon Emicho. "And you, godless prince of darkness, you who would be the Last Emperor—you shall be no emperor at all. You shall die before you even reach the city of the Emperor, and all who are with you shall utterly perish."

Emicho dropped lightly from his horse, and gave the reins to a foot soldier. He walked slowly toward the rabbi, sword in his gloved hand. The rabbi, clutching his sopping garments at his chest, shuffled backward feeling for the gate behind him. The guards cleared a path for him because they knew that the rabbi's fate was in the hands of the black count.

The mob became quiet as the rabbi began to recite a psalm:

He that dwelleth in the secret place of the Most High shall
abide under the shadow of the Almighty. I will say of the

Lord. He is my refuge, my God, in Him will I trust.

His back was to the gate now, crushed against its wooden beams. Emicho stopped before him, sword pointed to the ground. The rabbi continued:

Thou shalt not be afraid for the peril at night,
nor the pestilence at noonday—

Emicho's sword flashed as he pushed its blade through the body of the rabbi, pinning him to the gates. The count stepped back as the rabbi struggled to stand and lift his arms in the pose of crucifixion.

In thy presence is fullness of joy; in thy right hand, bliss forevermore.

The rabbi slumped upon the sword, jarring it from the gate, and the body fell upon the earth without a sound.

Emicho motioned for the soldiers to remove the body as he walked briskly to his horse. When he had mounted it, he turned to the crowd and said, "Did not the Lord say on the cross that there was a people not yet born who would come to avenge his death with their steel lances? Did not the Lord say before he was killed that from over the seas would come a new race which would be God's instrument of vengeance? We are that people," Emicho cried. "We are that chosen race that God has called to avenge the death of the Lord. It is our duty and our calling to slay the pagan here in our homeland before fighting the infidel beyond the sea."

The throng cheered as lightning suddenly illuminated the murky afternoon and thunder peeled away layers of pent-up terror in the hearts of men. "Open the gates," cried Emicho, as he galloped his steed a distance of fifty yards from the gates. He turned the banner-decorated beast about as soldiers struck the gate with a battering ram. It did not withstand the blows for long. When it was certain that the gates would fall with a final, crushing slam, Emicho spurred his charger and raced toward the gates as his men opened them wide.

CHAPTER TWELVE

A Raft in the River

MICHO DID NOT GET TO Constantinople just as the rabbi had foretold. He took his army into Hungary and advanced to Weiselberg where the gates were closed at King Colomon's command. Weiselberg lies at the point where the Leitha and Danube rivers conjoin and is surrounded by marshes and swamps. Determined to penetrate the city, Emicho spent six weeks constructing a bridge and then initiated a successful assault upon the city, breaching the walls with little difficulty.

Too little difficulty, as it turned out. Once inside, the Hungarian garrison guarding the city, sprung a carefully conceived ambush and Emicho's army was routed and put to flight. Emicho himself was killed, while William of Nelun, Drogo, Thomas and Clarebold fled to southern Italy where they later joined the army of Hugh of Vermandois. The count's head was severed, thrust upon a pike, and posted outside the city gates as a warning to other warlords thinking of subjugating the town.

Of these developments, the Monk knew little until many weeks after the fact. He was unwilling to leave the Rhineland without preaching the crusade. Since most of the Germans were loyal to the anti-pope, Guibert, Pope Urban II did not count upon a great number of pilgrims from among the Germans. Although his coffers were overflowing, the monk was eager to supplement their funds to protect themselves in the event of an emergency. On a pilgrimage such as this, there were always emergencies.

The French, Normans and Provencals, anxious to proceed to Constantinople, were unhappy with the slow pace. The pilgrims needed to keep moving in order to take advantage of the generosity of the town folk along the way. They had exhausted the limits of German hospitality where they were. Walter the Penniless decided to proceed without Peter. Most of the French went with him, whereas the newly recruited Germans, Swabians, Lothangarians and Rhinelanders remained with the monk until he was ready to move forward.

The Bartholomew family did not go with Walter the Penniless because Peter had been asked by the monk to stay with his entourage as an aide and guard. Peter disclosed to the monk his vision of St. Andrew. The monk was greatly impressed by this and thought the youth to be conscientious and spiritually receptive. The monk put his thick-veined hand on Peter's shoulder and said, "I am the old man dreaming dreams; you are the young man seeing visions. This is what the prophet Joel foretold. God is pouring out His Spirit on all flesh." Later he told the youth in a fatherly way that he himself was Eli; the young Peter was Samuel. He should always say to St. Andrew, "Speak, for thy servant hears."

The monk was not the only one to whom Peter divulged his revelations. They were also whispered into the tender and receptive ears of a young Rhinelander maid whom Peter had overtaken one rainy day on a section of muddy road not far from Metz. She was a sullen child of rounded features, whose eyes were red from crying, Peter thought, and so he took pity on her. She was walking alone, and when Peter asked why, her full lips closed resolutely and she looked away.

Peter left her then, and pretended to run out of sight. But instead, he circled around, hiding behind carts and horses, darting between the advancing pilgrims, bobbing up and down with his hand firmly on his cap, straining to keep her in sight. She wore new leather shoes, he noted, and her clothes were fresh and sturdy. He noticed a section of well-tanned, bare leg between the tops of her shoes and the bottom of the mannish trousers she was wearing— bare leg that was mottled with dried mud.

Peter stayed near her into the evening hours, determined to know where she camped. But that night she did not join a camp. Instead, she bedded down near the Rhinelanders, yet away from them. He saw her lift a bulky satchel from her shoulders and lay it on the damp ground beneath a tall oak. She gathered wood for a fire, and soft evergreen branches and sweet grasses for a bed. She had bread to eat, and she carved out a chunk of cheese with a thick knife. There she huddled with a wrap about her shoulders, her back against the oak, staring across her own fire, to the fires of the pilgrims.

He greeted her again the next day, and she smiled faintly. "Hildegard von Metz," she replied when Peter asked her name. Her head tilted slightly and a breeze blew wisps of raven-dark hair away from her face. When she said her name, she looked at Peter for an instant and the youth stammered and looked away.

He saw her every day for a week. Their conversations were awkward because he could not speak her tongue, and her knowledge of Norman French was slight. Through her, however, he brought back to camp the knowledge of new words and a new language which he shared excitedly with Addie and the girls. Lettie and Clare asked him many questions about the girl, but Addie said little. "She should not be traveling by herself," Addie commented crisply. "It is not safe." Peter interpreted this utterance as permission to invite Hildegard to become a part of their camp.

After a week on the road, the redness of her eyes had disappeared, and Peter thought she seemed to look forward to their visits. Her mouth opened to laugh, or speak out. Her teeth were white and perfect, not yellow and ragged like Peter's. At first, he felt foolish and awkward around her, but not so foolish as to stay away. But the feeling soon dissipated; Hildegaard seemed not to notice or care about his teeth or awkwardness. And when one day, she doubled over in laughter, and laid her thin hand on his waist to steady herself, he felt she had accepted him as her friend.

"Hildy," he said in a pleading voice, "you must live with us." He took her hand, but hesitated. Peter heard cartwheels creaking as pilgrims passed by, dogs yapping in the distance. The afternoon sun felt warm on his skin. Green and black flies buzzed loudly over a pile of horse dung at their feet. When he tugged at her hand slightly, she took a step toward him. He grabbed her bag, flung it around his neck, and they ran furiously down the road kicking up stones and dust. Clare and Lettie begged her to stay that night when the fire had died down. She stayed again the next night. The following day, Addie took her in her arms and whispered, "Stay." After that, she remained with them every night.

Peter, meanwhile, was employed by the monk, and could look forward to a steady flow of denarii each week, an income for which Addie was grateful. Nevertheless, after the procession had journeyed east along the Danube and through Regensberg, Addie announced that she intended to sell the horse and cart. "At Odenberg we'll be at the Hungarian frontier, and from there on, we'll need the money."

In this, Addie proved to be perceptive. Crossing into Hungary was a pivotal point for the pilgrimage. It marked the beginning of the isolation of the pilgrims. Previously, the pilgrims could count on some measure of sympathy and understanding from the communities through which they passed. Now, such a reception was not assured. The language was foreign, and religious rites were different as they moved into the eastern empire—customs were strange and sometimes frightening. Addie had had a taste of this even in Germany where the pilgrims often had been ridiculed for giving up everything to embark on a journey of such folly— Urban's Folly, they said. After crossing into Hungary, the isolation was pronounced. They could only hope that whatever privations and losses they suffered would be made up by the generosity of the emperor at Constantinople.

Addie foresaw this development. "We'll sell the cart and horse," she decided. The cart had traveled many miles and was constantly falling apart. Fortunately, they had been able to employ a wheelwright for serious repairs, but this would no longer be possible. The leather straps around the wheels were continually snapping, the axles would give out any day. So they would leave as much as they could behind, find someone with a wagon to carry what was possible, and they themselves would walk. Some of the money from the sale of the horse and cart would be spent on shoes.

The pilgrimage had assumed a different flavor for Addie now. She was in the company of strangers. Gone were the familiar tones of the Provencal dialect, for few of the Franks were with Peter now. This loss of the familiar made Addie as uncomfortable in spirit as the traveling made her weary in body. She and the girls were tired of walking on bruised feet, tired of depending upon people for food and clothing, tired of begging, tired of the newness and strangeness of foreign sights, smells and sounds. Sometimes, Addie didn't want to be where she was. Memories of Provence and of the fields and the sheep and the wool overwhelmed her, and the distance of both miles and time ameliorated the memories of the harshness of the winter past. It had not been so bad, she thought now. She despaired of seeing France again, of feeling the southern sun beating upon her freckled skin. She yearned for her neighbors in the valley she had called her home. Jerusalem lay before her, but visions are ephemeral things: sometimes they are an uplifting power pulling one onward, sometimes a crushing weight driving one into despair. The fulfilment of a dream is an accomplishment, not a gift that is given you, Addie was learning. The monk's preaching kept her hopes alive, but the monk hadn't told her that dreams fulfilled depend upon work achieved. "Faith without works is dead," he told her once, a quotation from St. James. She hadn't understood that dreams were achieved in little pieces, the product of a few big triumphs now and then, but mostly tiny labors performed every day. Labors like walking twenty miles on a good day and good roads; finding firewood; begging; sewing; making barley cakes interesting; raiding orchards for fruit; peeling and slicing vegetables; and repairing the cart. Clare expected Jerusalem to be around the next bend in the road; Addie only expected another bend in the road.

The journey to Jerusalem, therefore, had ceased to be an act of devotion that existed as something separate and distinct in her life—as something she was doing that someday would be set apart, examined and remembered. No, *it was now her life*. There was nothing else and there would be nothing else. She had no notion of when they might reach Jerusalem; she only worried about where they would spend the night. It was *going* to Jerusalem, not *getting* to Jerusalem that was the act of devotion to which she had committed her family.

Addie, Lettie and Clare now traveled in the rear of the procession with the baggage train and the closely-guarded money chest. Arriving at Semlin, they were almost to the Bulgarian frontier. Semlin was a small, walled city, not strongly defended, and ideally situated in rolling farmland. Here the pilgrimage would spend a few days, Peter announced, to rest and renew. The monk had hoped the markets of Semlin would be open, allowing pilgrims to purchase supplies and food.

No sooner had they arrived than ugly rumors began to circulate concerning the treatment of the pilgrims who had passed before them through Semlin with Walter the Penniless. When the Germans saw the weapons and clothing of sixteen men hanging from the ramparts, they knew that trouble had preceded them. They were incensed. A certain Geoffrey Burel, a leader of the Germans, wanted to attack the city at once, but Peter would not hear of it. "This is not our matter," he said firmly. "We need to conserve our supplies, enlarge our resources and get safely to Constantinople. There will be plenty of fighting after that."

All might have gone smoothly if a quarrel hadn't broken out in the market over the price of a pair of shoes. Words were spoken, which led to pushing and shoving and quickly a full scale riot erupted which became, in turn, a pitched battle. Burel would have none of the monk's counsel now. Under his leadership, the able-bodied pilgrims constructed a makeshift ladder and scaled the walls, opened the gates and flooded the city in a massive attack.

Four thousand Hungarians were killed, and many wagons full of provisions were captured.

Addie benefited from the raid, because Peter, in the thick of things himself, purloined a cart and a burro to pull it. It was not as large as the one they had previously owned, but it was in better shape, and at least one of them could ride while the others walked. It was a gift which Addie received with mixed feelings, for she was unaccustomed to accepting blessings which had not been gainfully received. Still, the sight of the little wagon and its animal was welcome and Peter loaded it with grain, food and water.

The monk was now anxious to leave; the rest he had hoped for would not be realized. Certain that King Colomon would send troops to quell the uprising, he ordered the unwilling band to prepare for an immediate departure, even as the sun lowered in the west. When Burel resisted, the monk flew into a flying rage of such terrifying intensity that Burel, mollified by the success of his foray into Semlin, had neither the will nor the courage to resist the diminutive Picard. The camp got on its feet, lit their torches, egressed quickly from the pleasant fields of the Semlin valley and marched toward the Sava River and Bulgaria, an exodus not unlike the night flight of the children of Israel to the Red Sea.

✠✠✠

When they reached the Sava river at first light, Peter's band of several thousand frantic peasants found that the churning river, swollen with spring rain, was unfordable. Wherever they looked, the opaque water, saturated with dark soil, root particles and tree branches, pounded the banks with a roar, and stampeded downriver and out of sight. There would be no parting of these waters and perhaps no crossing at all.

The monk conferred with Burel and then disappeared. Burel quickly sent out teams into the woods that lined the river bank to fetch wood for rafts. Camps were hastily set up and the women cooked gruel and porridge and fed their fare to any able-bodied peasant who needed strength; tools were brought out, tree limbs hacked down and stripped. Some crews worked solely on the rafts, taking the prepared poles and lashing them together with twine and securing main beams with pegs and spikes. Others prepared a place upstream at the river's edge where the rafts could be launched. Burel tried to calculate how far downstream the raft would travel before a landing could be made on the other side. It might be a half mile or so before the crossing could be made, and Burel sent scouts to ensure that the launching point would give them at least a mile to navigate downstream. As a precaution, a rear guard was set at the wood's edge to watch for a possible attack by the forces of King Colomon.

Burel also built a very large raft to accommodate animals, carts and wagons. Peter worked on this raft because it would also transport the money chest across the raging river. Burel had a special plan to get this raft across the river safely. A strong party would be sent across the river trailing a rope behind them and anchor it on the other side. This would be the guide rope. They would then return, trailing another rope, the pulling rope, which would be attached to the raft itself. The guide rope would pass through special rings fastened to the raft itself, thereby allowing the craft to move freely along its length until it reached the far side. The second rope would be winched from the other side and pull the raft across—guided as it would be by the first rope.

The camp took on the character of something alive and fatally desperate. Never had the immediate objective been so clear and urgent. The Hungarian pharaoh, Colomon, was behind them, the river was before them. The work progressed at a feverish pace throughout the day and into the night. By morning of the second day, the pilgrimage was ready to begin the adventure across the river. But Burel was uneasy, and he confided this to the monk who had reappeared. "Bulgars, Pechenegs and Kumans," he said nervously. "They're somewhere over there."

But the monk said nothing.

"We saw some on the rim yesterday, probably mercenaries in the imperial army," Burel added, scanning the bluff across the river for signs of life. "But maybe not."

The monk ordered the banner of the cross to be hoisted atop rafts where it was possible, and signaled that the crossing should begin. The camp was collapsed, wagons moved into columns and pulled as near to the water as possible, makeshift pens were dismantled and the animals herded to the river. At the sight of the swiftly-moving water, the animals balked, brayed, lowed, bleated after their kind, and everywhere was heard the sound of men shouting at the beasts, prodding them forward. Raftsmen shouted directions for stabilizing their vessels, sought help in pushing off from the river bank, and cheered when each raft cleared the beachhead and broke out into the river.

The rafts rode the river like a farmhand on a wild bull, bobbing and dipping perilously as the river slapped and tossed them about at will. Strong men armed with poles and oars had to fight with all their strength to keep their raft under control and out of danger. Addie felt a tightness about her throat as she watched others step onto the frail timber. Water of this force and power was unfamiliar to her. Nothing in her experience prepared her for the fear that swept over her now as she felt the spray in her face. The river was dark and deep, and the expanse was wide. She could never cross this Jordan, and even if she could, the other side was no promised land, that was for sure. She looked away, and saw Lettie stroking the pink ears of their little burro. Her sister was still a child, but unafraid. Only a few years separated them in age, but Addie was an adult, Lettie a child. What made the difference? Addie wondered. She was the one afraid; Lettie seemed undaunted as did Clare. The pilgrimage itself had been monotonous to the girls. "Is this Jerusalem, mother?" For Lettie and Clare, this river, and the raft building and the danger, had injected into the experience a sense of purpose and achievement. The adventure and excitement were new commodities of life to which the young girls thrilled and on which they seemed to thrive.

"Come on, Hildy, it's time to go," Addie said murmured to the dark-haired girl standing beside her. She removed her sandals, tucked them into her sack, and stepped slowly down to the river bank. She watched her feet sink into the earth and felt the mud push up between her toes. She brushed her hair behind her ears and looked back for Hildy, giving her a hand. Hildy came down confidently and helped Lettie who guided Clare. Moments later, they were on the raft with three other women, heavy women Addie noted grimly, and three strong oarsmen. The raft seemed buoyant, but dipped and lurched with every movement, and muddy water flowed over the floor of the craft as the corner dropped below the river and then surfaced again. Addie looked hopefully at Hildy and Lettie, raising her eyebrows as though to say, "What can we do?" She grasped Clare's fleshy hand firmly and they sat down together in the center of the raft, knowing full well that they would not make this short trip across the river without getting wet.

"Haven't you ever been afraid, Hildy?" Addie shouted. Hildy turned to Addie. She nodded. "Plenty of times, Addie," she shouted back, smiling. "Enough to know that fear is friendly. It keeps me alive." Addie looked across the river to the distant shore. Someday, she would ask Hildy what she meant.

The men pushed off, and Addie thought it marvelous how the perspective changed only a few feet from the river bank. They were moving away ... only five feet, but away from this place, and toward another place ... they were leaving something behind. Their life—whatever it had been—was getting smaller, only twenty feet now, but it made a world of difference, and their future was somehow getting larger. Addie enjoyed the emotion of progress; the river was a crossing point; a boundary traversed, a step beyond territory conquered. They had traveled this far, and she had not looked back, except now. Except now. To see how far they had come. Fifty feet.

The current pulled them out into the river, and the strong poles pushed them slowly in the direction of the far shore. She could see hundreds of others there who had already made the crossing. They had passed through the waters; they had not overflowed their frail craft. They would be safe. She tried not to look at the river, at its endless depth, at the death in the water. When she did, her throat tightened and her mouth became dry. She glanced down at her daughter instead and stroked her fair head and patted her back. Her daughter would comfort her.

Suddenly, the raft lurched. They were hung up on a dead tree that was mired in the river. "Push here," shouted one of the men. The river water slapped against the stranded raft, spraying pellets of water into the air and against their faces. They huddled close, shivering in wet clothing, and turned their backs to the pounding until the creaking and groaning craft was dislodged and pitched back into the current again. The oarsmen pushed and poled, compelling the vessel to reel and roll across the Sava River. When they landed, they disembarked like bleating, terrified sheep, and charged nervously up the river bank, sliding in the mud. Atop in safety, they clustered in triumphant hilarity, arms wrapped around one another, and laughed and whooped at their bold accomplishment caring little about the grainy mud and grime that streaked their windswept faces and limbs.

Peter Bartholomew lashed the money chest tightly to the floor of the cargo raft under the watchful sight of the monk. This vessel carried four cows, two wagons, the chest and a dozen polesmen to get it across. Ropes were checked and rechecked, and joints and splints tested for strength. Men on the far side were preparing to winch the craft toward them. The guy rope appeared to safely pass through the iron rings on the raft ensuring that it wouldn't get swept downstream. Peter glanced at the banner fluttering above them. The wind was from the east, but was not strong. A cry went out from Lothar, an oarsman. The men signaled the winching to begin. The men on the raft plunged their poles into the river bed, and leaned on them ferociously, pushing the craft away from the bank as the men on the far side pulled the vessel toward them.

It was sort of a miracle that the raft was river-worthy, Peter thought. The timbers were so huge, and the entire contraption cumbersome and heavy beyond imagination. But they were afloat! The guy rope strained against the iron rings, but Peter could mark the distance they traveled as the rope passed through those rings. Men on the Bulgarian shore were winching with all their might, their curved and aching backs to the river, and the muscles in their arms and legs writhing like snakes. A team of others had grabbed the bare rope itself at river's edge and were pulling and tugging in a war against the river. Some of them lost their grip and footing and fell into the mud, but they jumped up quickly and resumed their effort.

At first Peter didn't understand the significance of the raft he saw upstream of them. Then, as he watched curiously, the danger became apparent.

"Look there!" he cried. He dashed to the edge of the oak deck and pointed to the raft lurching down the river above them.

On the shore, the monk threw back his cowl to see better. Inexplicably, he had not halted the launchings upstream in order to avoid a possible collision; now one appeared imminent. The men on the cargo raft, ploughmen from Normandy and foresters from Bavaria, saw the peril immediately and began pushing hard on their oaken poles to propel their enormous raft out of the way. The pilgrims on the oncoming raft had now been alerted to the danger as well. The word spread quickly up and down the river bank on both sides as the curious and afraid lined the shore to view the outcome.

Addie and her family, and Hildy, heard the shrill voices of alarm, too. From the bluff above the river, they could see the cargo raft rolling in the current. And they saw the smaller vessel of planks and beams, bearing a small huddled mass of souls, careening toward it, bobbing wildly like a piece of balsa wood. She put her hand to her lips; but her mouth was as dry as the desert, and her cheeks as hot. In the easterly breeze, her hair was swept away; the river mud had dried a dirty white paste on her face, and it had cracked and peeled.

"Oh, God!" she whispered, as Hildy clutched her arm and the girls stood close. "Oh, God, no!"

Peter knew there would be a collision even while they struggled to avoid it. As the advancing craft came closer, Peter could see the fear in the eyes of the riders; they were preparing for the worst, hoping to grab a plank or beam should they be tossed from the craft. When they collided, the cargo raft tilted violently causing the animals to spook and crash the pilings that had contained them. They went quickly, bellowing as they disappeared into the river. The smaller raft bounced away momentarily after impact, but then the river hammered the two vessels together again, this time with crunching force. Peter saw the joints running lengthwise across the craft open up slightly. The platform, now in a weakened condition was pulled apart by the tension from the rope through the rings, and the pounding of the raft upon it, chewing and tearing at the weakened seams of the raft.

Peter saw now that the money chest should have been secured on a smaller raft of its own in the event of an accident such as this. Then, the chest could have been released and it would have been able to float to safety at some point down the river. But lashed to the main flooring of the cargo raft itself, its destiny was bound to that of the larger vessel: it could only survive—or sink.

Peter knew what the chest meant to the pilgrimage: its survival was critical. The raft was coming apart. He grabbed a section of rope and attempted to somehow lash the chest to the guy rope, hoping that even if the raft was lost the chest would sink into the river like an anchor and be retrievable. But the vessel was coming apart too rapidly to accomplish this maneuver successfully. Peter, realizing this, could now only attempt to keep his balance, as the raft, splintering and cracking, was catching the power of the river's current. Some of the men had already jumped, preferring to leave the fractured raft on their own terms rather than wait until it might be too late. Some had grabbed the guy rope and were waiting for rescue. This was not possible for Peter, who now felt the cold and realized he was going into the water. He grasped for the chest and for a moment had climbed atop of it, but the river bullied him off, and sent him plunging headlong into the current. The water felt cleansing; somehow it was better to be totally wet and completely immersed than to be simply annoyed and irritated by it. The river had won this battle, he thought grimly as he struggled to keep air in his lungs. He pumped with his legs and thrust his chin forward, his hair streaming back. Although his lungs seemed hot, he consciously refused to release the air within them. He could not, he must not.

Suddenly, his head shot above the river plane, and his mouth opened wide for air. He could not call for help, because his body demanded air as the first step of salvation. He gulped the clean, cool air, and it rushed like a sweet wind into his lungs and gave him fresh strength. He pushed it out again quickly, gathered another lungful of it, and would have then called out, but the river snapped him away. He was thrown against a piece of the raft.. But before he could seize it, the darkness became numbing; he felt like a prisoner in irons being beaten unmercifully. His body was twisted and tormented; his legs would not move; cold, sinewy hands were grasping at his throat; a great millstone sat upon his chest. He cried to St. Andrew, but in the deepness he heard no voices, and saw no light. His soul fainted, and his courage melted away.

CHAPTER THIRTEEN

Terror in the Church

NNA COMNENA RECEIVED THE LETTER from the Count of Blois on the day of Constantine Dumas' funeral mass. The service was held at St. Sophia's on the easterly bank of the Golden Horn, o'erlooking the narrow strait. It was marked by the solemnity accorded such affairs when heads of state gather and the Patriarch of Constantinople presides. Robes brushed the polished floors, and miters bobbed above the crowd like whitecaps on the Bosporus. The vast space of the cavernous church, which, at the beginning, had been filled with light, cool air, was quickly permeated with pungent incense when the ceremony began. Anna was with Constantine at St. Sophia's as everyone had expected she would be, but they had not anticipated that it would be at his funeral, rather than their marriage.

Such are the strange twists of life. The youth had died when thrown from his horse in an unusual accident, the kind of mishap upon which the fortunes of the world turn. Comforters quickly pointed out to her that Theodosius II had died similarly, and that, for good or ill, the Chalcedonian Creed came into being. One does not know the purpose of these matters, Melissenus told her, one only does the best with what one has. It was a decidedly heterodox opinion from a Hellenist for whom teleology was everything.

The common folk who lined the road from the church and the Hippodrome to Constantine's column were of every class, and they stood quietly, bareheaded in the morning sun, gently pushing and shoving, for a glimpse of the princess whose heart, they imagined, must be wrecked upon shoals of sorrow. Her figure could be seen, but her handsome face was hidden behind a black net veil. She had shown little emotion throughout this ordeal and had made no public pronouncements. Her sorrow was the sorrow of one human being for another, as one would grieve for a friend who has had the gift of life snatched prematurely away. She inwardly regretted her inability to show more visible expressions of loss, but in truth, she could not mourn as someone who had lost a lover or a husband. Their spirits had never touched in this way, for a melding of neither reason nor passion had occurred; therefore, his death had not represented a rupture in a union that others supposed to exist. No tearing away of a kindred soul, no fissure in a great love. In their thoughts, attitudes and manners, the two had always remained two, and individually, one of two. Now she was simply one of one, and, therefore she felt no pang of grief, no injury of loss. She felt only sadness for him, only horror that he, or anyone, should have the threads of his life clipped by the Fates at so young an age.

Anna received the note with gloved hand as she was leaving the church through the Emperor's Gate for the procession to the tomb and she read it as the imperial carriage bowled toward the tomb, a half mile away. She did not recognize the count's seal, but when she read his name, her hands trembled slightly, and—even more curious—her eyes clouded with moisture and dropped their tears upon the parchment, smearing the ink. His letter was unexpected and brought to her mind the knowledge that he had been thinking of her, for whatever reason, thus echoing her own thoughts of him. The tears were no especial mark of affection for the Norman count, but she was touched that he had written. And if there was a male in the world in whom she now had the slightest interest, it was the Norman. Such a truth says less about her feelings for him as it says about her state of mind, generally, when it came to men. There were none that fascinated her, and not even Constantine Dumas had held either an intellectual or romantic hold upon her.

She had adopted the air of a woman who, not having a man of sufficient appeal, decides that a man is not needed at all, and that she can manage well enough without one. Constantine Dumas was dead. She had not *needed* him, but now, in any case, *could not have* him. Stefan of Blois was alive. She could not *have* him either, she knew, but she suspected, with a reluctance that bordered on pique, that perhaps she *needed* him.

✠✠✠

Alexius, hearing that the hordes of peasants had crossed the Sava River and into the empire, sent instructions to Nicetas, the governor at Nish, to provide an armed escort for the pilgrims. Although these were scarcely the soldiers he had been hoping for when he appealed to Urban for help, he was bound to provide assistance to these who had vouchsafed their intention to make the pilgrimage to Jerusalem. Such was the polished side of the coin. The other side revealed an emperor who was worried about the effect of thousands of hungry peasants upon the peace and well-being of the villages en route. It was as much for the safety of his own subjects as the safety of the pilgrims that he ordered the governor to keep them under his protection. Walter the Penniless had already arrived with the French, Normans, Brits, Gascons and Provencals. But Alexius was not convinced the Germans, Slavs and Lothangarians would be so well-behaved.

The monk ordinarily would have chafed under these restrictions. But, in fact, the imperial troops could not have arrived at a more opportune time. The disaster at the Sava had left the pilgrimage vulnerable, impoverished, demoralized and lacking in discipline. The peasants were scarcely a fighting force. Less than one hundred knights were counted among them, and the men on foot were completely untrained in the art of war, excelling only in shouting loudly and cursing bravely.

But many in the pilgrim's camp treated the emperor's troops with suspicion: Their language was foreign, and their forces clearly superior. The monk realized that the imperial forces could not be considered their enemy for the simple reason that one does not have the luxury of considering a force overwhelmingly superior to your own as your enemy. They may not be your friends, but they should not, however humiliating, be counted as the enemy. In any case, the presence of Nicetas' guards gave Peter's weary band a sense of order and security which the monk, by himself, had been unable either to guarantee or assert.

No sooner had the troops been attached to the pilgrimage than they were withdrawn for a civil emergency at Nish. No one mourned their departure, but their absence reintroduced questions of survival. Food was the pressing problem, and with the money chest at the bottom of the Sava, the peasants were left to their own cunning.

Addie had little interest in food. The loss of Peter in the Sava had hollowed her cheeks and darkened her eyes, her face taking on the appearance of vacancy even when spoken to. Her tears had dried up long ago, as though her sorrow had been fed and was now being weaned. But Hildy and Lettie knew that the deepest anguish is the kind that is so profoundly unutterable that it pains the body in its yearning for expression, and tortures the mind in its endless *repetition* of expression. They walked silently on the long road to Nish, the three of them alone, arm interlocked in arm, a weary Naomi supported by Ruth and Orpah journeying through bitter Moab to the Promised Land. Little Clare played ahead of them, occasionally pointing people to Addie who sought her out and murmured words of comfort. But Addie paid scant heed to these comforters of Job who presumed to know her sorrow.

Addie came to life only on behalf of Clare. The child needed food and water, and her grief was not so deep as to render her completely unable to function. When, therefore, a group of Lorrainers decided to forage the countryside for berries and nuts, she decided to accompany them and to take Clare with her. Hildy and Lettie stayed at the camp.

They hoped to find meadows of juniper or dog rose shrubs, or even a farmer's field where a sympathetic serf might be willing to donate grain. Soon enough, they passed through scattered woods with sycamores and oaks that had freshly leafed out, and sun-bathed meadows teeming with elderberry bushes and heavy with the berries they hoped for. They worked quickly. Addie's nimble fingers danced through each bush skillfully, sensing at the slightest touch a cluster of berries, clasping it firmly, clipping it, and slinging it into her capacious, fruit-stained apron. When her smock was full, the berries would go into the baskets she and Clare had brought along.

Clare's plump hands were clumsier than her mother's, but no less eager. The fruit she picked went either into the basket or her mouth. She would get sick, her mother warned.

"Would I die like Peter?" she asked, looking at her mother solemnly.

Her mother's hands stopped their frenzied gathering instantly. She froze, as though by some divine caprice she had been turned into a pillar of salt. It was the first time she had heard someone say Peter had died. Died! She glanced at her daughter's face now streaked with berry juices. Clare was staring at her earnestly, her eyes widened by the question, her head cocked to receive an answer. Addie reached for her and pulled her close, encircling her within her strong, dark arms. "No, my precious, precious little girl," she cried, feeling hot tears for the first time in days. "No, not like Peter." She held Clare tight, and Clare, rather than resisting, sensed that her mother needed to hug her more than she needed the hug, and so stayed in the embrace. In the giving of comfort, one often receives more than one gives. So it was with Addie who, in wrapping Clare around her heart as though to calm the child's fears, in so doing, brought new peace to her own.

The peace was short-lived, however. There was motion on the crest of the hill above them. Some horsemen were approaching perhaps a half mile away, descending the gently sloping hillock. Addie watched as they guided their horses on the path, twisting among the berry plants and the brush. Addie turned back to her work, heaping her basket higher with fruit, and searching the bushes for berry-bearing branches. But Clare soon nudged her. "Look there, mother!" About eight horsemen had flushed a peasant out of the brush and had encircled him, taunting and striking him with their poles.

"Come on, Clare," Addie said, gathering up her basket and apron. "Let's go." She wanted to retreat to the woods where they could more easily hide. "Stay low, and follow me. Leave the berries here, and we'll come back." Addie untied her apron and then stashed it and their baskets under the brush. Then they darted away.

The men were not soldiers, but Petcheneg landholders and farmers armed with bows and arrows, whips and poles. They were a tribe of Turkish origin who had settled long ago along the Danube River valley, and had been aided by the Seljuk Turks. Alexius had often employed them as mercenaries. Now, however, they spread out across the meadow to harass the foragers, using whips and poles whenever the Lorrainers were discovered. Their voices grew louder and their tone more violent as Addie and Clare continued to crawl toward the meadow's border and the safety of the forest. A horseman passed so close that from their position flat upon the ground they could've touched the hoof. The crack of their whips sliced through the air, cutting through the fear to the marrow of their courage. One horseman after another passed, until Addie and Clare could not move for fear of discovery. The Petchenegs were apparently rounding up everyone they could find, rousting peasants from the brush like dogs flushing quail. Indeed, the Bartholomews would soon either be discovered or they would be saved; they knew not which.

Moments passed like hours. Hope gave way to fear, and fear to confusion. Then it was over. Suddenly, the brush parted, and a Petcheneg's pole goaded the two of them to stand. Addie stared up into the steel eyes of her captor. He was heavy, and his horse huge, perhaps fifteen hands high. She was not sure what he was saying, but his lips curled back cruelly revealing a thick red tongue, and gaps in his yellowed teeth. He looked away to bark something to his friends. In that moment, Clare opened her mouth as wide as her jaws would permit, and leaped to her feet shrieking, deciding it could do no more harm to vocalize her dread than to remain silent. The Petcheneg backed his horse away from them, raised his right arm and cracked his whip. Addie turned as she saw it coming and moved for Clare. But it caught her across the shoulder and Clare across the face, drawing a welt and a line of blood. In a fury that rendered her devoid of reason, Addie grabbed the man's pole and would've wrestled him off his horse, but the man laughed and knocked her to the ground. Addie hit the earth hard, face down, and tasted dirt mixed with blood. Turning over, she dug her heels into the ground and propping herself up with her arms behind her, crawled upside down, as it were, away from him.

Their attacker dismounted, and rushed upon Addie, straddling her and pinning her to the ground. He grabbed her by the hair, and, holding her head immobile with one hand, let her feel the force of his open hand with the other. Addie's head snapped violently at this assault, but she did not cry out. She had tears aplenty for Clare and for joy and comfort, but no tears left for sorrow. The man thought not to hit her again, but instead laid a dirty, heavy hand roughly upon her breast and held it there, staring at her uncertainly. Addie returned his gaze into his bloodshot eyes without flinching. Whatever the man was thinking, he thought better of it, because he released her and returned to his horse.

Addie and Clare were herded into a clearing where the others had been detained, and then the entire group, numbering about sixty, were marched en masse down the pathway, and over a small knoll to a chapel fashioned with the timber from the nearby woods. It had once been a sturdy structure of beams and pillars on a stone base, but now, although still standing, it had fallen into disrepair. They were ordered inside, an action which confused Addie, but most seemed to think it was a good omen. The interior of the church was stripped of all furniture. Incense burners were gone as were the altar and chairs. The windows were high in the Byzantine style, but the glass had been broken out by rocks. On the stone floor Addie could see the ashes and cinders of fires that had formerly warmed travelers who had happened by. Now, the church was being used as a barn: it was full of straw and grain, and, judging from the odor, it was also a sheep pen by night. The fires were those of the sheepherders, she thought.

The pilgrims moved about uneasily, filling the church which had been built for a congregation of about this size. There were some men in the group, but they were elderly: that is why they were picking berries. The women were both young and old and some had their children with them. The abandoned sanctuary they were now in, echoed with their high-pitched chatter. One woman of about thirty years, who identified herself as Gilda from the Rhineland, attached herself to Addie and protested: "They won't do us harm in a church, now, you know." Her eyes were large and red, and her thick lips trembled as she spoke. She said more, but Addie couldn't understand it all. She was learning different tongues and dialects with Hildy's help, but there was much that still escaped her. But fear is an emotion that requires no language, and Addie saw clearly that this woman feared for her life, as did the others.

Fear takes on a proportion larger than it might ordinarily when in the presence of the unknown. And it was the unknown that was responsible for much of the dread of these moments. None could fathom the intention of their persecutors, not to speak of their motives. Had they known the reason for this behavior, they might be able to set their minds in opposition to it. They would be able to devise a plan to resist, or seek an opportunity to adjust their circumstances. In this unfamiliar situation, however, they could not be certain: To resist might be foolhardy if they were about to be released; To surrender without a fight might be equally foolish if they were to be harmed.

With the first acrid whiff of smoke, the intention of their captors became clear. The Petchenegs put torches to the straw around the church, and archers had shot flaming arrows upon the dry roof. Addie heard them drop like hail. The same bows that sent arrows to the roof would send one into the heart of anyone who ventured to escape, if escape was even possible. The inevitability of their fate hit them like a thunderbolt. They stormed the doors, but were unable to break through. The windows were too high, and no means could be discovered by which to reach them, or implements found with which to ram a breach in the side of the building. Even if they could do this, they realized, their chances of survival were slim.

While they were assessing their chances, arrows flew in at the windows and fell upon the straw, lighting it immediately. Although these early flames were extinguished, the Petchenegs continued to rain arrows through the open apertures until it was impossible to control the blaze within the building. The flames consumed the straw greedily and lapped at the interior walls, sliding higher and higher up its sides. Pigeons which had been roosting on the upper rafters, flew away, fluttering through the windows to freedom. "Oh, if I had wings to fly," Addie thought bitterly. "The bastards can't do this! Why has God forsaken us?"

Addie enclosed Clare's hand in hers and they leaned together against an outer wall near the front of the church. Now, the heat forced them to move away from the wall. The air was filled not only with smoke, but with the fearsome wailing of souls who knew they were about to die, who saw mortality staring at them, who realized that every decision made in life, every turn of fortune, had somehow led them inexplicably to this place, the place where they would leave this earth and fly to their Creator. Had they been sufficiently pious, they might have paused to consider the content of their faith. But piety in the midst of extremity is a rare commodity, and none possessed it on this afternoon. Indeed, Addie, normally acquiescent in matters of faith and morals, now pulled Clare roughly toward the front of the church, where the altar had stood, to confront her Creator in these final moments of her earthly life and to charge Him while she was still in this outraged frame of mind, with outrageous abdication of His duty toward His creatures. She could, she allowed, be held responsible for her sins, although she did not feel herself to be such a bad person, but what of this child? What *possible* justice was being served in the sacrifice of a child of seven in a circumstance of unmitigated cruelty and horror? Why should a child suffer in this world? You are quite willing to take credit for good crops, good health and prosperity, and now You shall have to take the blame for this suffering. And if You do not want the blame, I shall no longer give You praise. O God, save us! What am I saying? "Clare, try not to breathe much, and hold your shirt over your mouth, like this, here, see?"

"I can't breathe, Mother!"

"I know, child," Addie answered. "Do as I said." The church was darkened by the smoke which thickened and billowed upwards. A beam had fallen from the rafters and more were sure to follow. She could make out only the barest outline of the huddled mass of pilgrims in the center of the church. She pulled Clare around the side of the choir, and leaning against its wall, slowly sank to the floor in exhaustion. Her chest felt tight, and she had a feeling of wanting to breathe deeply, that above all she needed air. Instead, she tried to breathe slowly and shallowly. She hugged Clare and enfolded her tightly to her bosom, and kissed her head. "Are we going to die, mother?" Clare asked drowsily. "No, child," her mother answered. "The angels are coming to take us to Jerusalem ... We're going to Jerusalem." The child was growing listless and weak. Addie laid her head upon her daughter's and relaxed, as though to go to sleep. She closed eyes to avoid the irritation of the smoke. She tried to get comfortable, moving about to adjust her body against the protrusions in the wall.

That's when a thought intruded on her consciousness. Her eyes opened wide, even in the blinding smoke, and she sat upright as though she had been awakened with a splash of ice cold water. She quickly moved Clare aside and whirled about in the darkness, fumbling with her hands and fingers to touch what her back had been so uncomfortably feeling. Hinges! Her fingers deftly explored the outline of a hinge. A door! She moved a foot and spread her palms open flat and ran them up and down on the wall. The latch! The latch! There must be a latch! Slivers of wood pierced her hands, but she felt nothing but the urgency of finding that which always accompanies a hinge: a latch.

And then her hand was upon it! A door! A door? A crypt? *The church has a crypt!* She stood up and grabbed the latch, but it wouldn't release. She tugged and pulled at it with all her strength, but, in fact, her strength was rapidly ebbing. The door would not open. Oh, God! Why show us a door, if it is a door which won't open? At the moment of abject failure, she leaned her head against the door stopping her struggle and nearly fell headlong into an opening. The door turned inward, not outward!

"There's a crypt!" she cried to the others. "A crypt!" She heard no response, and, in any case, had neither the time nor the energy to attempt a rescue of others. She grabbed Clare and urged her to follow. "Clare child, come with mother now. We're going to be safe." But the child's body was limp. Addie knew she was alive. She picked her up and dragged her into the opening and held her with the child's head over her shoulders. Addie felt for the first step with her feet and then the next, confidently moving down, closing the door behind her. She did not want the Petchenegs to know anyone had found the door should they bother to investigate. She remembered, and now understood, the fear in the eyes of Jewish mothers in Mainz before the slaughter. She wondered if mothers weren't the same everywhere: Jewish mothers, Norman mothers, Flemish mothers, Moorish mothers. Aren't we all the same, and doesn't God love each and every one of us?

The air in the crypt was clean and cool. Addie laid Clare beside her and listened for a heartbeat. The girl was alive and breathing. She would revive! Addie breathed as deeply as she could and rested on the stone pavement. When perhaps ten minutes had passed, Addie heard a crash so huge that the ground seemed to shake. The roof and walls had collapsed. She heard no cries, just the sound of the fire consuming the timber. It was over.

Addie left Clare to explore the crypt. Her eyes had adjusted to the darkness and she now noticed a fissure of light. Closer examination revealed a small door in the stone that led to the outside. But Addie was not yet willing to test this newfound opportunity to gain her freedom. They must wait until darkness, or at least several hours. She groped about in the darkness to become acquainted with their surroundings. The knowledge might be useful. She ran her hands over an unknown shape; she could feel its line, its curvature, a roundness ... boards ... slats ... a cask! She moved on. There was another such shape, another cask! They were in a wine cellar, or a crypt that was also a cellar. There had been wild grapes in the meadows. A vineyard used to be here. Perhaps the church was built over the cellar when the drought came. That had been many years ago, she thought. No scent of wine lingered now. She returned to the reclining form of her daughter and gathered her in her arms. The child stirred.

"Have the angels come for us, Mother?"

"Ssssh ... we must be quiet for a while," Addie whispered. Then speaking into her ear in the softest tones: "The angels are not coming for us, but they're here watching us now at this very moment!"

Clare said nothing for a few moments. Then, without moving her head, she spoke again: "Is an angel watching me?"

"Yes, darling, an angel is watching you, and he's the most beautiful angel a girl could ever have. His eyes are like jewels that can see everything, and his hands are the strongest of the strong, and wings that can take him anywhere. And the best part is that he's your personal angel watching over you." Addie desperately hoped that it was true, Oh, Peter, Peter, where was *your* angel watching over you?

"I'd like to see my angels sometime," said Clare, moving in her mother's arms.

"I would too," said Addie, sighing. "And fly away, far away, right now!" She stroked her child's hair, and brushed it away from her face. She could barely see the form in her arms, but the touch of her fingers upon the girl's silky skin was a pleasure for which she was thankful. "But right now we must wait until it is safe to leave."

"I'm hungry and my stomach hurts," Clare whimpered.

"We'll have food soon, don't you worry. All that's important now is that we're safe, and that we have each other." They stayed in the crypt for several hours, pilgrims from Provence in a little Bulgarian cellar, afraid, tired and alone. They passed the time rocking gently to quiet songs that Addie hummed, or by resting. After one such nap, Addie sensed a change in the atmosphere, and soon she could hear the patter of rain, and the sizzle of the water upon the embers — still hot — above them. She ventured to the small passageway she had discovered earlier, and tried the latch. It gave. Fearfully, she pushed it out ... just a crack. She pressed her eyes to the crevice and peered out. She could see nothing but rain gathering on the stone, and water running off the beams, or hanging in droplets upon stems of grass. It was still raining. No sound of movement or human activity. She pushed the panel ajar and crawled out of the cellar. The door was, as she surmised, built into the stone base of the church and had been partially obscured from view by shrubbery. But the grass and brush had suffered in the fire, and even now as she ventured forth, she could sense the warmth of the earth on her palms.

Glancing in all directions, she made sure that they were alone. Each step was preceded by the utmost caution, until—risking all, she was fully outside the confines of the crypt and sitting upon the ground with her face to a glowering sky casting showers upon the earth. Addie closed her eyes and opened her mouth, allowing the rain to fall upon her parched tongue and elevated her open palms to the heavens in the posture of prayer. Rain gathered in her hands, which she lowered carefully to her lips. Then she drank.

The church was in ruins. Clouds of ghastly vapors rose to the sky from a charred pile of twisted beams and posts. She did not want to explore the grisly scene. She knew what she would see. She wondered how God would exact vengeance on the perpetrators of such a deed. She marveled at the agnosticism that must be necessary for people like the Petchenegs to do something so dreadful. They must not believe in God at all, she thought. They're godless pagans, infidels, as the monk warned us. They have no god to fear, or else the god they serve is a terrible god ... or in any case stronger than the one who failed to protect these whose flesh lies upon this ash heap. Then she remembered Mainz. Oh, dear! Addie turned away from the sight. Suddenly, her eye caught movement on the crest of the hill.

She whirled around and dove for the stone wall, positioning herself to observe. People were approaching on the roadway, coming straight toward her and the church! ... Two of them, she could see now. They were not on horses ... they were ... monks! Addie saw them stop on the road: They had seen the incinerated church. They started to run toward her, but Addie knew they had not seen her. They approached the church and dashed up the stone stairs to the sanctuary floor where they encountered perhaps the most gruesome sight they had ever seen. Addie judged the scene to be terrible judging from the exclamations coming from the men. Addie inched closer, staying low beneath the stone base of the building. Now she could hear their excited chatter. Her heart froze when she heard them. She gave a shriek and jumped up from her stance beneath the wall into plain view and moved toward the monks, causing them a fright.

"*Aidez nous, s'il vous plait!*" she cried. "*Nous habitons a Provence. Nous somes des pelerins a Jerusalem.*" Then she collapsed on the ground.

The monks stared in disbelief at the sight of life among the dead. Then they ran toward her, jumping to the ground from the top of the wall, only a few feet high. They lifted her to a sitting position and one of the monks cradled her safely in his arms. Addie grasped him and looked into his face. The monk pulled back his cowl, smiled, and said to her:

"*Bonjour, madame! S'appelle Pons, et mon ami, Guy!*"

At those words, unmistakably Provencal, Addie closed her eyes and surrendered to an ineffable peace. Her body went limp in the arms of Pons, the relic-seller.

CHAPTER FOURTEEN

Constantinople

July 2, 1096 A.D.

ORD OF THE DEATH OF the sixty peasant pilgrims spread like the fire that had killed them: extraordinarily fast and out of control, inflaming passions and inciting the pilgrims to violent deeds. All the men of the Lorraine, Germany and Bavaria, blazed into the Bulgarian countryside setting fire to mills, and pillaging whatever village and settlements that happened to be in the path of their incendiary fury. Nicetas, the governor, residing at Nish, attempted to negotiate a parley with the monk, and at the same time, Peter tried to calm the raging emotions of his own people. The governor, a man facing the uncontrollable rage of a people unjustly treated and who were by nature inclined to violence, was remarkably reluctant to grant the market privileges the monk requested. Without the markets, the peasants, choosing between hunger and thievery, would surely choose thievery every time, and undoubtedly add to it, wantonness, debauchery and general mayhem of destructive proportions.

Nicetas agreed to give markets to the pilgrims on the condition that hostages remain with him until the multitude had left Nish.

The monk agreed to this demand, and turned over a dozen men, including Geoffrey Burel. When the monk's band of thousands straggled out of Nish days later, the hostages were released.

Regrettably, the respite gained at Nish failed to satiate the Germans' hunger for revenge. They continued to set fire to the mills, provoking an attack by imperial troops on a deserted stretch of road beyond Nish. The troops, pouncing on the rear of the pilgrimage, captured the baggage train and a large number of women and children, including Addie, Arletta, Clare and Hildegard. By now, this shepherd-less flock of bleating sheep which Peter the monk had at one time referred to as God's Little Lambs, were uncontrollably in pursuit of pasture wherever they thought they might find it.

The monk was able to secure the release of the baggage train. The wayfaring multitude then trudged to Palanka, and it was at Palanka they were able to rest.

On the third night of their sojourn, Addie saw Pons again. She and the girls had spent the day parching grain and shopping in the town markets. The summer sun had set late, slipping away unobtrusively, but firing the cloud-layered sky in shades of flaming orange, lavender and crimson. Hildy gathered some sticks in the near-darkness and kindled a small fire, a congenial blaze around which they sat quietly, leaning against the baggage wagon, bodies aching and spirits sagging, chewing *soksel*, a Bulgarian bread, and drinking tea. Their existence consisted of extremes: hot days and cool evenings; joy in the morning, sorrow at night.

"Good evening, Madame!" Addie looked up at the stranger who had appeared in the fringe of the fire's light at the corner of their wagon. Pons stepped closer, holding a cap in his hands, and Addie recognized at once the special features of the person who had rescued them days before. He was not in his monastic habit. Addie invited him to sit down.

"I didn't recognize you," she said, realizing that she did not know this man's name. Did she know it once, but had forgotten it?

"I was a monk when you saw me last," Pons said, laughing, and sitting down across from Hildy. He took some of the *soksel* Addie offered, and broke off a piece and gave it back to her.

"But you are no longer a monk?" she asked, stating the obvious. She was glad to see this man again, if for no other reason than to satisfy her curiosity about him.

"I am not always a monk," he confessed smiling, tilting his head toward her. He offered her some wine.

"I haven't adequately thanked you for your heroism," she said, pushing it away.

"Nay, now, see here! It was nothing. Have some of this, the healer of body and soul!"

Addie hesitated, but then drank a small draught at first. Its taste was familiar upon her tongue and she allowed the sensation of it to flow past her mouth slowly, and down her throat. She was sitting face to the flame with her knees drawn up and her exposed elbows resting upon them. Her dress was tattered at the hem and her feet bare as was a portion of her arms and neck. Her face was a story of character and resolve: the strength of a Deborah or the cunning of Diana. She gave the wine back to him and stared directly into his eyes.

"Truly, it was something," Addie said, swallowing the last drop. "I never expected to see you again. I thought you were an angel, the guardian angel, you know.'

"Truth, perhaps it was God, maybe it was merely good fortune. I cannot tell about these things."

"I can tell: It was God!"

"And it was the devil who got you into that fix?" Pons asked.

Addie was quiet. Then Hildy spoke: "Sixty people died, but you were spared. Lettie and I stayed with the baggage train that day, or we might have been with you. God was good to us, wicked to others. The truth is, the devil didn't get you into that trouble; the devil doesn't operate on that grand a scale. We get ourselves into enough trouble, he needn't bother. And if there isn't trouble enough, God provides the rest."

"How can you say that, Hildy?" said Addie, surprised.

"God digs the pit which we fall into, and then rescues us from the fate He Himself created."

Addie would have none of that. "How do you know so much, Hildy? There are things I don't know. But there are things I do know, and I know that God sent Pons to us that day. Anything else ... I don't know ... God didn't save Peter, God didn't save the sixty in the fire, and God didn't keep us from the soldiers at Nish ... When I saw those Negs riding beside our wagons, I knew something bad was going to happen. I could feel it, I could see it in their eyes. They were yelling unintelligible things, but I knew it wasn't good. Then they stopped us and separated the baggage wagons from the rest and moved all of us. When one of the soldiers ordered us from the cart, I told the girls to get off, but when I got off, one of the Negs grabbed my arm and I went mad ... pounding on his chest and kicking and hollering. I just didn't care anymore—which scares me when I look back on it. I could've put my girls in danger. But I couldn't stand it. At that moment, nothing, absolutely nothing, mattered except hitting that soldier. I was like the cloth I use to wring out water on the face of a sick child. You twist it and wring it until there isn't another drop ... That was me, all the moisture wrung out of me. It was over. I was done."

Addie stared impassively into the flickering light, her face glazed with fatigue. She pulled her shawl around her.

"Some are going back," Pons said, putting another stick on the fire.

"Back?" Addie looked sharply at Pons.

"Back to Provence."

"Not me," said Addie firmly. "There's nothing to go back to, and besides, going back would mean I've wasted all this time and effort. I think it would be more dangerous to go back alone, than to go forward with the others."

Pons saw tears in her eyes, which, in the firelight, sparkled like fine jewels. 'We'll be in Constantinople in a fortnight," he said encouragingly.

"It can't be too soon," said Addie.

✠✠✠

Pons' powers of prognostication proved in this case to be correct. The remaining distance to Constantinople was passed in relative comfort. The women pressed to Sofia where markets were available. They camped in verdant fields where food was plentiful. At Philipolis, the monk preached to expectant crowds which swelled daily. He told the Greeks of their misfortunes. He compared the throng of pilgrims to the children of Israel who had endured the valley of Baca in search of the waters of redemption. The Greeks responded with warmth and generosity. Their largesse enabled the travel-weary pilgrims to load their wagons with grain and corn and to purchase clothing and blankets.

The wheels of the wagons crunched steadily in the dry dust of the road to Constantinople. They sat on their possessions patiently, accustomed to watching the miles inch by slowly and never asking anymore if the next town was Jerusalem. Their bodies shook and swayed with every sturdy step of the oxen, lurching here and bumping there. At the end of the day they were tired without having taken a single step. Their bodies had moved laterally as many miles as they had moved forward.

They arrived at Adrianople and soon were in the Belgrade Forest, traveling parallel with the Aqueduct of Valens. The pilgrims were in a buoyant mood. Families sang, and children played eagerly in the road and ran alongside of the carts and wagons playing with sticks and balls. And when a loud cheer, sustained and swelling, arose among the pilgrims miles before them, rolling upon their ears like the thundering of an ocean wave, Addie knew that Constantinople was in sight. Soon, their wagons also creaked to the crest of a ridge below which lay the princely city of Constantine, and beyond the city, the beautiful, deep blue sea of Marmara.

It was the kalends of August.

CHAPTER FIFTEEN

Crossing the Bosporus

JOURNEY THAT HAD BE-
GUN IN the spring now came to
a momentary halt in the late
summer. The city, excellent and
fair, that lay below these
wandering children would nourish
them like a mother the infant at her
breast, until they were strong and
healthy again, and impatient to move on.
Constantinople was the last major outpost of
Christianity, and to leave it would be to embark
upon lands held by the infidels themselves. The
sojourn at New Rome would be the time, if ever
there was a time, to choose between the leeks and
garlics of Egypt and the wilderness of Zin that lay
ahead. But, for many of the nomadic exiles,
Constantinople was a heaven of sufficient worth and
glory as to persuade them that any further effort would
be a needless risk of property and life. The grandeur of
the city was enough to satisfy even the most avaricious of men.
Battles had been fought, privations experienced. One need not go
further in order to suffer for Christ. Surely a celestial reward had
already been achieved in the name of people like Adelaide
Bartholomew, and any additional suffering would be
supererogatory and count little to a person for whom mere
entrance to heaven would suffice. To cross the Bosporus was to

commit to the journey. Until now, every peasant and ploughman could turn back. Once in the land of the sultan, however, they must either conquer or perish; they would either die en route, or pray at the Church of the Holy Sepulcher.

Walter the Penniless, who had arrived in Constantinople two weeks before Peter, came out to meet the monk before he reached the city's massive walls. There they embraced on the stone roadway and together they advanced toward the city. Camps would be set up outside of the walls because Alexius had forbidden the pilgrims to camp within the city. Their numbers, in any event, prohibited this. With Peter were thousands of the Alemanni, and Walter had led an even greater host of Franks, Provencals and Normans ahead of the monk. Further, they had been joined by some smaller groups of Lombards and Longobards from Italy. Many other nations and regions crossing the Adriatic from Apulia were marching the Via Egnatia to Constantinople.

"I don't like the incursions of these innumerable armies," the emperor grumbled. "They are savage in their fury, fickle in their minds and too willing to settle their disputes with violence."

"They are an impetuous and passionate race," Anna replied. The two were leaning over his desk surveying maps which showed the position of the camps outside of the walls.

"True, true, but their chief vice is avarice. They covet everything they see and desire everything they cannot have.'

"I have seen their camps, you know. It looks like all of the barbarians from beyond the Adriatic to the Pillar of Hercules have burst in a solid mass into Asia bringing everything with them," Anna observed pointedly.

"Impetuous," Alexius muttered, "and unless they are stopped right now, they are going to be very difficult to control." The emperor, tired of examining the charts, strolled about the study.

"The challenge, father," Anna broke in, "is to bridle their impatience until the nobles arrive from France."

"And they haven't left France even yet—"

"The pope said they would leave on the Feast of the Assumption."

"Even if they *have* left, they will not arrive until late fall and if the mountain passes are treacherous, it may be spring before they see Constantinople. And crossing by sea may be impossible before spring."

"And how shall we live with thousands upon thousands of peasants outside of our walls until then?" Anna wondered aloud.

"They shall not step a foot within the city walls, there's no question of that."

"Perhaps they should cross the Bosporus and set up a pilgrim city there until reinforcements come from the west," Anna suggested.

"The Turks will kill 'em. That's like putting meat in the jaws of a lion and asking it not to chew."

"But we will send them over with some divisions of our army," Anna argued.

"It's an act of aggression. At least Aban would view it as such."

Anna strode purposefully to the table and began to search among the charts and guides. "Look at this," she said. Alexius joined her. "We could convey the entire lot of them across the Bosporus and march them to Nicomedia, around the gulf and down the southern coast to the Civetot."

"Too close to the Turkish frontier," Alexius said, unconvinced.

"We put our mercenaries there only a few years ago. It's protected by the sea to the west, it's at the mouth of the Dracon, to the east are hills and forests, and the area is fertile. It's ideal!"

Alexius paced again in silence. "It will be more expensive to keep them supplied if they are at the Civetot."

"It may be more expensive to keep them here," Anna countered.

"Perhaps you are right," Alexius conceded. He sat at the desk and placed his hands upon it palms down and leaned back to give the plan some final thoughts. Anna left him alone without leaving the room. The emperor had many advisors, including Byrennius and Melissenus, but Anna was, of them all, the most trusted. In spite of her youth, she understood obtuse and shadowy matters with a clarity that suggested that experience piled upon experience only clouded, rather than polished, the eyesight of wisdom.

"We shall abide by our original plan," Alexius said finally, arising. "The pilgrims will stay outside the walls, and if they cannot be constrained there, we'll ship them across the Bosporus."

"We shall need a meeting with the leaders," Anna remarked, not surprised by her father's decision.

"That we will," replied Alexius, "and their leader is a monk, a monk who preaches, who is regarded as a worker of miracles, a prophet."

"They say people pull out the hairs of his mule expecting a miracle."

"Ha! Better be a hairy mule! They'll need every miracle they can get!"

"It'll be a naked mule before they get half way 'cross Anatolia."

✠✠✠

The following morning, while the air was still cool on the palace terraces, Alexius, Potentate of the Eastern Empire, received his visitors from the west in a small imperial chamber. The emperor was seated on a small throne flanked by bodyguards in armor and posting hauberks. Anna stood nearby as Geoffrey Burel, Walter the Penniless, Reginald of Lombardy and Peter the monk entered. The Lombard and Burel stood erect looking forward. Burel's face was sharp and angular, thin lips drawn in a flat line and closed, impounding strident opinions better left unsaid, as though using his mouth as a cage for a prowling tongue. The Lombard, a youth like Burel, had unsheathed his sword and posted it now like a third leg, tip on the marble floor, holding the hilt away from his body. Thus he stood, feet apart and chin up.

But Alexius was not interested in these pretenders. He turned instead to Peter and Walter, the aged ones. Walter, taller than the monk, was clad in Roman sandals and a wool tunic that still bore that stains of Macedonian mud and Bulgarian dust. Light red veins spidered across his upper cheekbones above a sprawling beard that was white like a winter snow. In his hand, he held a walking stick made of olive wood from Palestine, the gift of a wealthy Norman patron. The monk, older than the Penniless, was barefoot in a monk's habit, cinched at the waist by a cord. His cowl was thrown back and across his shoulders he carried a long sack. His face dragged sternly from the crown of his head to the wispy ends of a straight beard, interrupted only by a pinched nose and deep-set eyes. They stood before the emperor as Moses and Aaron before the Pharaoh. Alexius half expected the Penniless to throw his olive-wood staff upon the ground and turn it into a writhing serpent.

Alexius, his hands resting comfortably upon the arms of his throne, spoke evenly and formally. "Gentlemen, I welcome you to Constantinople in the fullness of Christian love and charity. Your presence here is witness to the cooperation that is needed between East and West in order to defend ourselves and all of Christendom against the Islamic heresy.

"This city, and therefore your city, is in danger. The Turks are only days away and the fiendish bastards spend their days and nights devising evil ways by which to bring this ancient city to the ground. This is the city of Constantine to whom the Lord was revealed like Paul on the road to Damascus. This is the city that has hosted the great councils of the church—Chalcedon, Nicea—as well as certain synods within our very walls. Nicea is now in the hands of the infidel, and, of course, we need not remind you that the very roads upon which our Lord once walked are now trodden under foot by the same evil men. So I speak from my heart when I say that we in Constantinople welcome you and rejoice to receive you among us."

Alexius stood and descended two small steps and greeted each man, speaking to them. "You are Peter, a man of God," noting that the monk still had an aversion to cleanliness. "Your many works and the news of your preaching has preceded you," Alexius said cordially. Just then, two pages entered the room bearing satin pillows and small chests. Alexius opened one box to reveal scores of gold coins. Reginald and Geoffrey peered eagerly.

"As a sign of good faith, please accept these gold bezants and be assured that we will continue to supply what you and your armies need as those needs arise."

Anna smiled at the enthusiasm with which Burel and the Lombard accepted the bezants.

The monk spoke: "We humbly accept your gifts, but we ourselves do not come bearing gifts except our devotion to the holy places and our resolve to drive out those who now blaspheme those sites."

"On the contrary," replied the emperor, "you have left all your possessions, your country and homes and families. I have heard of your many hardships and tribulations. You have given much and will give much more in the future. Come, sit here with me at this table."

They moved to a large table on which lay maps of the city and of Anatolia. "First, what are your present needs?" Alexius asked. Anna hovered nearby.

"Markets," Burel answered immediately.

"And you shall have them," the emperor answered.

"Grain, cheese, wine, oil," Reginald added.

"All available in the markets," said the emperor firmly. "But, as you know, there have been problems ... mills set on fire, markets plundered, villages pillaged. You shall have markets, but your people must camp beyond the walls and they will not be permitted through the gates or into the city itself. If they do, they will be arrested on the spot. I will permit fifteen wagons to enter the city and two men per wagon for the purpose of purchasing supplies. The carts must enter the city by the south gate where each wagon will be assigned an imperial guard. They must enter in early morning and must leave the city by noon. This is not negotiable."

"We also need livestock, sheep, goats, cattle," Walter said quietly. "These would be a source of milk, cheese, butter, and meat. And chickens, eggs!"

Burel disagreed: "What are we going to do with livestock? The Turks are less than 100 miles away. We need horses."

Walter spoke: "If we can't feed the people, you'll have no men to ride the horses."

"The Turks are fifty miles away," said Alexius. "Look at this map. The Turks are in possession of Nicea here, and of all the territory beyond the gulf of Nicomedia, here." He traced his finger across the parchment. "The empire is in control of the southern, coastal strip, and that's all. So far we've been successful in keeping the Turks at bay, thanks in part to the low range of mountains between the coast and Nicea and the Anatolian plains. My point is: What exactly are your intentions? Why do you need horses now? Are you prepared to cross the Bosporus and engage the enemy?"

"Yes," said Burel and Reginald.

"No," said the monk and the Penniless.

Alexius touched his hair, smoothing it back, passed his hand over a finely clipped beard, and then rested both of his hands on the oak table. He looked upon each of his guests without rancor or emotion, but with an air of parental clemency. "So, you are going to fight the Turks! You are ready to fight the Turks?"

Burel and Reginald stood with furrowed brows and mouths clapped shut. The emperor looked at his daughter. She swooped to the table.

"What do you know about the Turks?" she asked. The question had an edge of scorn. "The Turks who are camped beyond the hills are not peasants who have left their villages to join a pilgrimage. They are not villagers you have been fighting as you trampled through the vineyards of Bulgaria. They are *soldiers* trained in the art of war, and the Seljuk Turks have been at it for sixty years. Their archers are second to none; as soldiers, they are well-fed and hardy; they're cunning and their savagery knows no bounds. They will kill anything if it still breathes. Your women will be raped and then slaughtered. Babies will have their bellies slashed. Boys and girls will be taken into captivity and raised as Mohammatans—"

"—We come in the name of the Lord," said Burel heatedly. "God will help us!"

"God is always on the side of those who win," Anna replied with asperity. "God favors those who are prepared, those who have the larger army. The presumption that God is on our side is one I'm willing to make only when we engage the enemy with superior forces and preparation."

"How many men do you have right now, ready to fight?" Alexius asked, resuming the interrogation.

"Three thousand," said Reginald.

"Fifteen thousand," said Burel.

"And how many of the Alemanni?" Alexius inquired.

"About ten thousand," the monk answered,

"Twenty-eight thousand," said Alexius, "and of these how many be knights?"

"Two hundred."

"A thousand."

"Another thousand," said Peter.

"Let me tell you," Alexius said. "You have nothing. That's why you do not need horses now. You need sheep, goats and chickens as Walter has suggested. And sheep, goats and chickens you shall have. You are going to wait until additional and stronger armies from France, Britain, Italy and Germany arrive. Until they arrive, we will give you what you need."

Like a dark cloud that cannot hold its rain, Burel could be silent no longer. "My men did not walk over a thousand miles to sit and do nothing," he argued.

"That is your problem," said Alexius pointedly. "You certainly can control your own people, can't you?"

"They are not his people," the Penniless warned, looking first at Burel and then to the emperor.

"I was chosen as the leader of the Franks because the people are tired of being told not to fight."

"They are being told not to fight, because we have not met the enemy, Burel. King Colomon was not our enemy until we robbed his people at Semlin; Nicetas was not our enemy until we set the mills on fire; Alexius is not our enemy and his advice is sound.

We'll stay here until our brothers arrive, and together we'll cross the Bosporus and together we'll confront the enemy."

Walter spoke with finality.

✠✠✠

Peter stood at the window where he gazed past the golden dome of St. Sophia, past the Hippodrome and the Serpentine Column to the hazy azure waters of the Bosporus. A fog as dense as a thundercloud had fallen over him, filling every pore of his being with confusion and fear. Walter, he could see now, was much more capable of leading this multitude than was he. This business was not the task of a prophet. A prophet should sound the call to arms, but not take them up himself. As he looked beyond the sea, Peter experienced a fleeting kinship with Moses. He was not a Moses, but he was like Moses, he thought, in many ways. Like Moses, he stood before an imposing body of water with hordes of impatient people demanding transport. Like Moses, he was unsure that he'd ever see the Promised Land. Like Moses, he regarded the pilgrims as a hardhearted and stiff-necked people prone to the worship of false gods and forever complaining against the one true God. Like Moses, he felt that he and he alone was responsible for this unruly mob of a congregation. Like Moses, he knew he was about to enter a land were provisions were uncertain and the enemy lurked on every hand, and like Moses, he wondered if this generation would ever see Jerusalem, or whether indeed, it would be only their children who would claim the city.

The monk was more than willing to accept the advice of the emperor. He was no longer the firebrand he had been at Clermont. He sighed deeply, remembering the early days of ten months past when he had felt the flame of millennial fire burning in his heart. He had proclaimed the pilgrimage, moved the hearts and minds of men and women, effected great change and initiated a great movement by the sheer power of his words and the personal force with which he invested them. He was then—in those days, wasn't it long ago?—a seer of shadowed reputation, a prophet whose name evoked wonder and fear in villages and valleys from the Pyrenees to the plains of Lille.

Now, the tumultuous journey had labored a weariness into both his flesh and spirit, and he unwillingly recalled the troubling words of Pope Urban II that November night in his chambers. He had been a youthful Jacob wrestling an angel of God. Now he was in the span of ten short months a feeble Israel wondering if his spiritual children would survive to carry his bones to rest in Amiens.

✠✠✠

The arrangements which Alexius offered proved to be unworkable, but through no fault of his own. The peasants were, as Burel predicted, restless and impatient. While the Greeks were generally sympathetic to these homeless waifs who had sacrificed everything for the sake of a spiritual enterprise, the pilgrims traded too freely on their generosity by engaging in frequent acts of violence. Within hours of settling into their camps outside the walls, they began to raid neighboring towns, rampaging through farm and villa, and even stealing the lead from the roofs of churches. Their actions were indiscriminate and widespread making control and enforcement by the imperial militia practically impossible.

Alexius allowed this to continue for a week until, frustrated beyond measure, he saw clearly that the passionate multitude could not stay at Constantinople. Therefore, on a single day, the entire enterprise was transported across the Bosporus. They began a frightful journey along the north shore of the Gulf of Nicomedia toward Nicomedia itself. Even then, the pilgrims could not restrain their lust for possessions, sacking and plundering houses and churches along the way.

The rabble by now had become divided in their loyalties. The Alemanni elected Reginald of Lombardy as their leader. Burel commanded the others. Still, they traveled together as the imperial army would not permit them to divide. They continued to march past Nicomedia, along the southern shore of the gulf westward toward the Civetot.

At the mouth of the Dracon, in a fertile and pleasant district, they settled into the fortress, a defense established by Alexius several years earlier for his British mercenaries.

There they were to remain, Alexius said, until reinforcements arrived from France.

✠✠✠

"And did they stay there?" Bernard asked.

I shook my head sadly. The removal of the pilgrims across the sea was the turning point for this enterprise. Had they stayed in Constantinople, they would have enjoyed both the protection and the resources of the emperor. Now, in the absence of strong leadership, they did not understand the advantage of their position, and they were removed like an ugly wart from the skin. Alexius' plan was wise but unrealistic. It failed to take into account the temperament and millennial enthusiasm of the pilgrims. Anna's plan, on the other hand, was practical but fatal. It failed to recognize that these children of Gaul were in no position to make decisions for themselves. What they needed was an emperor strong enough to resist discontent. Instead they got a princess interested in expediency. Still, if the armies of the French nobles arrive if time, even Anna's plan could work."

CHAPTER SIXTEEN

Stefan is Given a Sword

Chartres, France
September 1, 1096 A.D.

OUNT STEFAN OF BLOIS AND Chartres stood stiffly and awkwardly facing his wife in the Great Hall of his grand castle at Chartres. The dread day of departure had rolled in as quietly and predictably as the fog on the Three Rivers marsh. Stefan now faced the rigors of farewell, a ritual for which he felt himself extremely ill-suited.

"I'll go, then," he said, shrugging. Adela stepped closer. Stefan glanced about quickly. His vassals were waiting, standing about like hobbled horses. Everard of Le Puits, Guerin Gueronat, Caro Asini and Geoffrey Guerin. Across the dim hall, Alexander, his chaplain, and Fulcher, the priest, huddled.

Adela placed her small, white hands on his shoulders, and looked up into her husband's eyes, smiling. "We've already said all the goodbyes we need to say."

Spring and May, violets and nightingale,
summon me to sing,
And my fair beloved makes me a present of love so sweet
that I cannot refuse.

May God grant me grace to rise so high that I might hold her
naked in my arms before I go overseas.

Stefan embraced her quickly and signaled to his men that he was about to leave. An image of his wife rose up in his mind, flushing his face. He was sitting beside her naked form touching her lightly and tormented by the ridiculous thought that it was a form he might forget. They had taken possession of each other for the last time in the frantic way of last-time love; every caress given and every kiss received was a blow against their mortality, a frenzied dance of life before the dance of death.

They walked together to the heavy, oiled doors of the hall and stepped outside into the damp morning. Stefan examined the surroundings carefully, the large courtyard of jostling servants and wives to see their husbands off, children crying, guards on the upper battlements and singers wailing. Footmen stood ready with banners, and the saddler had prepared his charger for the departure. The blacksmith had reshod the horse, and the groomsman had carefully brushed out his coat until it was smooth and soft as goose down. The scene was familiar enough, but Stefan stared as though he were seeing it for the first time. Some people have the good fortune of knowing when an experience will be the last of its kind and can therefore linger to enjoy it as though it were the first. He felt the rolling gravel under his feet, and twisted his toe into the earth to plant himself firmly there. The creeping ivy on the stone wall, covering cracks and crumbling mortar, walls beyond which his army of ten thousand had assembled; Robert of Flanders had marched south to join him, and Short Breeches had arrived also, raising an army with the 10,000 silver marks his brother King William had given him in exchange for the Duchy of Normandy. The other nobles had already departed: Count Raymond of Toulouse with Bishop Adhemar of Le Puy; Goffrey de Bouillon, Duke of Lower Lorraine; and Hugh of Vermandois. The blood strength of the west had been drained, leaving only skeletal forces in place and only King Phillip of the barons and nobles.

Stefan started for his horse. "Wait," cried Adela. Stefan stopped and turned around. A servant had appeared with a large flat and narrow box about six feet in length. "A gift for you," said Adela. The box was placed upon the courtyard ground and as soldiers and family gathered round, Stefan unlocked the silver clasp and lifted the lid. Within the chest was the most beautiful sword and scabbard Stefan had ever seen. The hilt was made of precious metal and studded with jewels. The grip was covered with velvet and held in place by thin leather cords. The scabbard was equally beautiful. "I made the belt myself," said Adela. "See here, my hair." It was elaborately embroidered into the pattern of the belt, and interlaced with gold and colored threads.

Stefan could not say anything. He gently lifted the cruciform sword from the case to examine it carefully. This was not a ceremonial sword. The hilt was perishable; the count knew he would use this sword in battle. The blade was of brilliant steel, and when he laid the sword across his hand, it balanced perfectly, the walnut-shaped pummel provided just the correct balance.

"The steel of Poitiers, and made in Saragossa," Adela said. On the pommel was an intricate design of a pelican, symbolizing Christ, shedding drops of blood to feed its young.

"And there are relics," said Adela, pointing to the pommel, "A tooth and toenail." Stefan looked at her. "I don't know which saint," she said lamely.

"It's magnificent," Stefan said, looking at the sword closely. On one side of the blade the words "Deus vult" had been etched into the steel and thin strands of gold had been hammered into the engraver's marks.

Stefan drew his hand away from the blade and noticed a sliver of blood across his palm. He touched the blade with his finger; its edge was razor sharp. Adela retrieved a thread from the fabric inside the sword-case. She glanced at Stefan who grasped the sword firmly by the hilt. Raising her hand, she held the thread by her thumb and index finger, and then—tossed it gently into the air.

Swifter than Normandy lightning, the sheen of the steel blade flashed, slicing the fragile thread in two. Stefan watched them fall upon the ground and then, grasping the hilt of the sword in both hands he raised it above his head and shouted:

"*Fortissimus!* You shall be called *Fortissimus*, for you shall make me strong, courageous and powerful!"

He placed the sword in its scabbard and strapped it around his waist, adjusting it on his hip until it felt right. Then his horse was brought to him and he mounted it quickly, as did the others. Looking down upon Adela he said, "Farewell, milady. Tend to our affairs wisely." He spurred his steed and the men rode across the courtyard to the castle gate and across the drawbridge amid great shouts and a thunderous clamor. On the other side of the bridge, and before joining the encampment of the army not far away, he reined in his horse, and turned it about for a final wave to his wife.

The daughter of William the Conqueror had already disappeared within the keep of the castle.

If my body goes to serve our Lord,
My heart remains faithful to her.

✠✠✠

Three days before the pilgrims were transported across the Bosporus, a curious event began to unfold in the mid-morning hours in the camp of the Provencals. Pons and Guy had settled into an indolent routine to which they had become accustomed since arriving at Constantinople. Not allowed into the city, they had abandoned their practice of selling relics, and instead had depended upon the largesse of the emperor, preferring the sin of sloth to that of robbery and pillage like many of their fellows. Today was not unlike most days: the morning sun had already twisted the chill out of the hazy air, and men sat in idle groups sharpening their wits as well as their weapons. The smaller numbers of women were never allowed to dawdle, nor would they have considered it: meals to prepare, clothes to be mended, grain to be parched, and—men to be pleased. Ah! Men to be pleased. Addie knew who these women were, as did Guy and Pons. They attached themselves to the pilgrimage like leeches. You could try to get rid of them, but they always reappeared, dark-eyed and sorrowful, slinking about the edge of the camps at night. Addie did not talk to them, and reckoned that each person must answer for their actions, while Hildy went to great extremes to help them when she could. "If God is a God to any of us, He is a God to them," she said firmly.

Pons and Guy had resorted to the shade of an oak tree that was situated on a small rise from which they could see the seawater to east, and the walls of the city to the north. They sat swatting at flies and bugs, with their backs to the tree between high-ribbed roots that spread out from the tree like fingers grasping the soil. Pons had his longbow and arrows to repair, restring and tighten in preparation for an archery lesson he was to give to Addie later this very day. It had been her idea to learn to use a bow when she saw the obvious application of such skill for supplying meat for her family. The pilgrimage had halted; possibly, it would not resume its Jerusalem-bound journey for many months. Addie had no intention of passing time idly. She would learn to use the bow.

A rider approached beneath them at some distance, clopping methodically through the camp, until he was close enough for the two men to inspect. His erect manner, and the red coat and cap identified him as an imperial herald; he was announcing some kind of news. Pons and Guy relaxed: a new edict from the emperor or more information about the great move in three days across the Bosporus. Pons stood and pushed on the end of his longbow to snap the twine in place. They heard the herald shout the name of Adelaide Bartholomew. Flies buzzed dizzily, leaves in the branches above them stirred restlessly. They listened. The herald shouted her name again.

Pons dropped his bow and let it fall under the trees, and leapt across the grassy slope, jumping and dodging logs and rocks in his path. Guy followed less aptly, but just as successfully, until they both accosted the herald in the road, who was startled at this sudden epiphany to two panting, ragged men in his way.

"What need have you of Adelaide Bartholomew?" Guy asked, swallowing another gulp of air.

The herald scarcely lowered his chin to acknowledge the presence of the ruffians before him, but he said: "That be none of your concern."

"We can take you to her if she is in no danger," Pons offered in a cooperative tone, eager to learn of the business of the court of Alexius with Addie Bartholomew.

"Her presence is required at the court," the herald answered.

"At the request of whom?" asked Pons.

"The emperor himself!"

The herald followed Pons and Guy through the Provencal camp, twisting among tents and wagons, dodging dirty-faced children and barking dogs. When they were near Addie's tent, Pons ran ahead and called out to her, and then disappeared inside. A few moments later, he came outside followed by Addie and Hildy.

"You are Adelaide Bartholomew?" the herald inquired officiously. He had the stern, pinched countenance of one who relished his occupation if for no other reason than he realized it was as high as he would advance in his social standing. Being a herald is what he was called to be, and the knowledge of having found his perfect place in the will of God lent to him an air of righteousness bordering on conceit.

Addie was fearful. "Yes, my lord," she said.

The messenger informed her that she was required to come with him to the court and that she would ride with him on his horse. Addie said she would get some things, but the man said they must leave immediately.

"I will go with her," Pons announced.

"No, you will not," countermanded the man.

"I would like that very much, if he would come with me," Addie said.

Guy remained behind with Hildy, Lettie and Clare, while Addie mounted the herald's stallion, and Pons, borrowing a horse, followed. They waved goodbye, and left in a stiff gallop, disappearing in the direction of the city.

They rode hard through the Golden Gate, the hoofs of the animals pounding hard on the swept pavement, and clattering loudly as they passed through the gate itself and into the city. Within fifteen minutes, they were at the Hippodrome and St. Sophia, and—not slackening their pace—they pushed their beasts forward through the walls of the palace court as imperial guards stepped aside to give them passage.

Pons was forbidden to enter the palace, but Addie was taken inside where she encountered opulence of a magnitude she had never before experienced. Had she been unconscious and returned to her senses within these walls, she would have sworn she was within the Pearly Gates themselves, so beautiful was this splendor to her eyes. Finely colored frescoes, jewel-studded doorways, glistening marble, flowering plants and rushing fountains. These sights made her head light, for this experience of the extraordinary and unusual was taxing her energy as severely as the long days pushing toward the imperial city.

They passed through a door where a page announced her name and she saw dimly a seat with a person seated on it. Instinctively she understood this to be the emperor himself, and she clutched her throat in wheezing apprehension. When escorted to the throne itself, she dropped to her knees both in respectful homage and out of sheer exhaustion.

She felt a tug at her arm, raising her to her feet. She turned and saw the monk.

"Peter!" she gasped, putting her hand to her mouth. "What are you doing here?"

Addie had never seen the monk smile, and now, when he did, it changed his appearance in the same way the sun changes the landscape when the clouds part. He appeared soft and gentle, and his eyes were kinder when joined by an upturned mouth.

"Don't be afraid, Addie," the monk whispered. "The emperor desires you to meet someone." They turned to the gilded doors. They swung open to reveal a slight, halting figure standing there.

"Peter Bartholomew," announced the page.

Addie's heart tripped a beat at those words. She leaned forward with a gasp, and then screamed with joy when she recognized the form in the doorway as indeed that of her brother.

Uncomprehending, she moved toward him but was arrested by a lightness of ecstasy that drained every drop of strength from her body leaving her an empty vessel. Her legs became as water, her eyes closed, and her head fell back. She slipped to the floor with a groan.

That evening Peter told his story again by the light of the campfire. Pons and Guy, Lettie, Clare, Hildy and many others had joined them to celebrate the return of he who was dead and was now alive.

He told them that he was wrong to stay with the raft as long as he did, but he thought he could secure the money chest. He remembered nothing after going under the water except that he felt he was flying, arms outstretched, over a field of exquisite wild flowers where children were playing and girls were picking blossoms. He could see in the distance a church, surrounded by walls, and behind it a large mountain. As he drew nearer, he saw a figure leaving the church. It was St. Andrew. The saint spoke to him. "There are many things that I have for you to do," he said. "I will show you more." The saint then disappeared and when Peter awakened, he was in a thatched hovel where a peasant woman took care of him. He lay there a week with a fever, and a gash on his head. He was later escorted to Constantinople under imperial guard. He asked to see Peter the Monk, who then arranged the meeting. The emperor also gave him ten gold bezants.

Three days later, Peter helped his sisters and Hildy load their possessions and ferry across the choppy Bosporus. They marched with the multitude to the Civetot where they established camp again.

They had not been there for even a fortnight when the Turks attacked.

CHAPTER SEVENTEEN

The Bartholomews Meet the Turks

September, 1096 A.D.
The Civetot

HE DRACON RIVER VAL-
LEY IN which Addie Bartholomew settled was bounded by
wooded hills molting into gold,
umber and crimson, which converged
several miles from the sea at its upper
end in a pass leading to the lake district
near Nicea. Not closer than two miles
from the indigo Marmara, the valley
flattened expansively to the sea. The
river, tumbling from the mountains and
through the pass, snaked through the valley and into the
marshlands where it then multiplied into flat, clear streams with
yellow, rusty pebbles at the bottom. Addie was happy here, if, for
no other reason, than it was a place where they could find shelter
against the winds of autumn and the cold of winter. The passion to
see Jerusalem had cooled, like embers cool in an unattended fire;
Peter was with her now, and remarkably, his reappearance had
changed her thinking. Having him back made her life complete; the
pilgrimage had become unnecessary.

Peter was no longer in the service of the monk. The chest of
bezants, zekukim, jewels and precious stones was somewhere at the
bottom of the Sava. The monk did not have any work for the

young man. Still, Peter was privy to conversations unheard by most. He told his sister, for example, that the monk had fallen into disfavor among the peasants and that the French were following Geoffrey Burel whose leadership was far more energetic and whose millennial vision seemed like that of the monk's in the very beginning. The monk had grown cautious. This, at least, was the view of the young men who, in such close proximity to the Saracens, were fairly aching to dip their swords in blood. In the ten months in which they had been traveling, *they never had been applauded for the warlike posture they had often assumed.* Now, they were within striking distance of the Turks, and they yearned to begin a legitimate offensive against a legitimate enemy.

Addie was accustomed to such talk, and she, too, felt a sense of optimism, rather than fear. But she did not approve of these random and vicious raids on nearby villages and farms. She heard of what happened when Burel led some of the French out of the valley through the pass onto Seljuk terrain. They even reached the gates of Nicea some thirty-five miles away, trampling through pasture and village, mowing down fences and huts like a whirlwind, rustling herds and flocks, and, according to Peter's information, viciously abusing the Christian inhabitants of the region.

Christians! This Addie could not understand. Roasting babies on spits. The rumors circulated darkly. She didn't believe it. Her own countrymen could not be guilty of such crimes, she insisted to her brother, and, if they were, their faith was a kind with which she was unfamiliar. She was not particularly fond of the Greeks, but living in Provence, far removed from ecclesiastical centers and isolated from any influence the Eastern church may have exerted, she did not harbor the prejudice of the clergy who had made the pilgrimage. It was difficult for her to understand that such actions could be justified against a people who revered the same Lord, who venerated the same holy places, who worshiped the same God. But she had noticed that things which often made sense to the priests — never made sense to her. That Jewish mothers had died to protect their children had been pain enough for Addie to absorb; these events sank like stones to the bottom of her heart.

Geoffrey Burel was rich in enthusiasm, but poor in experience, she thought. But whatever her opinion of Burel, he stood higher in her estimation than Reginald, the pompous, petty Italian, who was the leader of the Alemanni and Italians. Reginald reacted with envy when Burel returned from Nicea with cartloads of shoes, tools, grain and scores of livestock. He vowed that the Italians would not be outdone by the French in flaunting their genius for looting and robbing.

About the third week in September, Reginald assembled a regiment of Alemanni and set out for Nicea to, at the very least, duplicate the feat of the French. A great cry arose as they rode out of the camp. They fancied themselves the inheritors of Charlemagne; their gold and white standards floated in the morning breeze.

Addie heard nothing of them again for over a week. Not even Peter had any news.

September passed into October. The woods, withering in the dry autumn, took on a dry, dusty appearance. About ten days after Reginald rode out of the camp, a local villager, a Christian, brought news that a castle called the Xerigordon, about fifteen miles from Nicea, had been captured by the Alemanni. The inhabitants of the castle had been caught by surprise, and the Alemanni were able to hold it. To their delight, they discovered the castle to be well-stocked. Reginald thereupon decided to hold the castle and use it as a center from which they could scour the countryside for even more loot.

Reginald's excursion into Turkish-held territory and the capture of a Turkish command post, however poorly defended, constituted the first legitimate victory for the peasants. In any case, Peter and his sister were eager to regard it as such, and indeed, this was the general feeling of the camp.

This news was followed by an even more marvelous report a few days later. Two men, villagers from some distance away, had wandered into the camp by chance (they had been fishing in the river), and in their conversation with some of the pilgrims they reported that Reginald and the Alemanni had mustered forces for an assault on Nicea and that they had sacked the city and were now in possession of it!

"Do you know what this means?" Peter asked his sister excitedly. Addie's enthusiasm was generally late in catching up with the vigor of her brother's. "Hildy, come over here," he shouted, beckoning the girl to leave her chores. "It means," he continued when he had their attention, "that we'll be moving to Nicea soon! Markets, food, shelter!"

It was, indeed, stunning news, almost beyond belief. Even Burel found it difficult to understand because he had been to the gates of the city himself. He had seen its defenses bounded on the west by Lake Ascansius, and the massive outer and inner walls which ambled several miles in circumference around the city. But now was not a time for petty jealousies. Burel spread the word throughout the camp that a regiment of soldiers would prepare to reinforce Reginald and that they would relocate to the ancient Roman provincial capital of Nicea, site of the First and Seventh Ecumenical Councils of the Holy Mother Church. *Deus vult!*

The expedition staggered to its feet again like an old cow and prepared to lumber out of the Dracon River valley. Amid swirling rumors of greatness and glory, the women and children began the task of gathering their possessions, thus creating the illusion that there was some order to their worldly affairs. Addie and the girls worked happily and frantically; they consoled each other that it was a happy chore that they would be doing many times before they reached Jerusalem.

It was, therefore, a rude surprise, even a shock, when Peter, not a day later after the news of the capture of Nicea, came running to their camp, stumbling over firewood and yelling like a madman,

"Lies, lies, lies!" he shouted angrily.

Addie looked at her brother. His eyes were weak at the corners and the skin of his face was tight and pale like it had been bleached and cured. His hands trembled nervously and tugged at his shirt as he spoke. "What lies, Peter?" Addie asked evenly.

"They were spies, Addie, they were spies," he cried. He grabbed a box and began to throw clothes and tools into it indiscriminately. "We've got to get our stuff together at once and get out of here!"

"Who were spies, Peter?" she asked, taking her brother by the arm, not understanding what Peter was saying. "Who were the spies?" Lettie repeated, dashing over to the two of them to hear the conversation.

"The two fisherman, we can't find them anywhere. They must have been spies. Their testimony was a total lie. Absolutely false!"

"A complete fabrication?" Hildy asked. Peter looked at her crossly, but said nothing. Instead, he threw himself on the ground and sat under a birch like Jonah under the gourd, face between his knees.

Addie touched him on the shoulder. "Start from the beginning. What happened?"

✠✠✠

Peter's news was not good. He told them that a messenger had arrived that morning by horseback from Nicea. This fellow was a Christian, his word could not be doubted. The messenger confided that Reginald had captured the Xerigordon precisely as they had heard. What they had not heard was that when the Alemanni seized the Xerigordon, the Turkish commander Aban Arslan, ordered a strong squadron to the castle to lay siege to it. The castle had a well, but it ran dry in the summer. The only well was outside of the castle and the Turks controlled it. So they surrounded the Xeriqordon and waited, telling Reginald and the Alemanni that they must surrender and that they must also renounce their faith or they would be killed. After eight days, Reginald surrendered."

"Surrendered?" askd Bernard, "and—"

"—and Arslan killed them all except those who recanted. Reginald himself renounced the faith; they sent him to the east. He was never seen again."

"And Nicea?" Bernard asked.

"Reginald never even thought of going to Nicea, much less launching an assault on the city. The story was made up because Arslan thought they would

move the camp and march on Nicea, which they almost did. The monk left by ship for Constantinople to get some help from the emperor. Burel wanted to attack immediately, but the monk said that he had the Devil in him and that God would not honor such a foolhardy plan with His presence. Burel, he said, should wait for reinforcements to arrive from Constantinople.

"It was Geoffrey Burel's fatal weakness that he lacked discretion; he did not know when to stay back and when to move forward. He often mistook foolhardy presumption for bold faith. At dawn, on the morning of October 21, Burel led the entire armed force out of camp and up the Dracon River valley: two hundred mounted knights, the rest, peasants and ploughmen armed with staffs, daggers, and in some cases rusty swords salvaged from the nobility when peasants had trudged through the Rhineland. These were, to be sure, the weapons of the flesh, and they could not (they believed) be compared to the weapons of the Spirit with which they considered themselves to be invincible. As they marched toward the pass in the hills above the Dracon River delta, there wasn't a knight or pilgrim among them that didn't believe that this very day was a date with destiny and that ere the sun had set upon their ragged multitude, they would clasp to their bosoms the sweet knowledge of victory."

✠ ✠ ✠

Addie rose early to build a cooking fire to feed some of the men before they departed. The meadow was filled with plumes of blue smoke rising in the early autumn morning. Peter stopped by to say farewell. Addie clutched his arm and wished him Godspeed.

"And don't forget the old castle, sister," he reminded her, brushing a tear from her cheek. "You must go there as soon as you can."

"Tell me again, Peter," she said, struggling to control the impulse to cry.

"Follow the river toward the sea until it widens. You'll see an island in the river. There will be a path to the left that will lead you to the sea only another mile away. There you will see the castle on a low cliff above the sea. Flee to it, and I will meet you there tonight before the sun sets."

"And what if you don't come as you say?" she asked.

"Then I'll come as soon as I can!" Having said this, he skipped away, joining Pons and Guy who with a score of others were acting as trailers to gather up any fleeing Turks who might retreat to the sea when routed by the peasants.

Burel marched his troops under the banner of the cross in six regiments of several thousand each, many of whom were themselves wearing the sign of the cross on their clothing. They were marching directly for the plains of Nicea, the fertile ground between the lake and the hill country that surrounded this city. It was on the north shore of Lake Ascansius, Burel decided, that he would confront the sultan, Aban Arslan.

There would be no confrontation. Less than three miles from the Civetot, Arslan, lying in ambush, attacked the peasants from both sides of the river before they had reached the pass. When Burel heard the alarm, he ordered his men to form flanks on either side to face the Turks as they charged out of the woods toward the river.

"Walter, to the north, and I to the south," he cried, spurring his horse.

Tragically, Burel's men were farmers, not soldiers. In the confusion that followed, the lack of military training and discipline became not only obvious, but a liability. The only military strategy with which these ploughmen were even vaguely familiar was retreat, a futile option because the Turks had closed ranks behind them. Escape was impossible.

Burel, for his part, had acted precisely as Aban Arslan had hoped he would. While the report given by the spies was a false report, it was perfect for Arslan's purposes. Had the peasants believed the report, they would assemble their entire force and set out for Nicea unaware that they were putting themselves at risk.

If, on the other hand, the report was somehow compromised (and it was), the pilgrims would either be immobilized by fear, or mobilized by foolishness. The latter proved to be the case: Burel chose a course of action which could not have played into Aban's hands any better than if he, himself, had devised the plan. The peasants, panicked at the mere sight and sound of screaming infidels on horses, turned and ran. The slaughter began.

It would be a misstatement to say that the pilgrims fought bravely. That they were in this battle at all was bravado, not bravery. They were peasants on foot, fighting soldiers on horses. Their sticks and stones were no match for spears, lances and swords.

An arrow knocked Burel from his horse; he hit the ground clutching the wound from which his life poured out onto the earth. Blood stained his yellow hair; his face tightened with pain. "This was a mistake," he said in a raspy, failing voice to Walter who had seen him fall.

The Penniless held his head up. "You are going to die a martyr, my brother," he said.

"Tell the monk—" He was cut off in mid-sentence. A Saracen pounded by the two of them and drilled a lance into Burel's chest. As Walter bent over the slain man, another Turk rode past, and with a tremendous thrust, pushed a lance through Walter's back pinning him to Burel.

The peasants' fall was rapid. Man after man went down by the sword. Headless bodies lay strewn like fallen timber throughout the valley. Some drowned in the river, attempting to flee the slaughter. Their bodies floated downstream until they snagged on tree roots at the river's bank, or log-jammed on a shallow gravel bed. Thus, thousands perished, and thus the pilgrimage of Peter the Monk came to an inglorious conclusion. There would be no further pilgrimage of the peasants: There were no more peasants.

✠✠✠

When Arslan saw that the battle was theirs, he sent several legions toward the encampment in the delta. While the bodies of the fallen peasants yielded no booty, the camp of the women and children was another matter.

Addie, with Clare, Lettie and Hildy, had already left the encampment when the Turks swooped in like hawks in search of flesh. Addie and the girls fled through the woods and undergrowth, wrapping their skirts tightly about them, and then out into the high grass of the delta. She wondered if Peter was safe, or whether he had been spared one death, only to be lost in another. Suddenly, Turkish soldiers broke into the meadow making for the sea. The four of them dived into the grass unnoticed and hid behind a mossy boulder as they passed by.

When the Turks had ridden out of sight, they slipped noiselessly back on the path and moved onward until they came upon a widening of the river and the island Peter had mentioned. "Here is the way," Lettie whispered urgently. Addie grabbed Clare and they began the diversion toward the sea.

But moments later, the tall rushes parted and four Turks, all mounted on huge horses and heavily armed, wearing high helmets topped with falcon wings, surrounded the women. They had not been unnoticed after all. They laughed heartily, while Addie, fearing not for her virtue, but for her life, grabbed the girls, and fell to the ground, praying.

The soldiers dismounted and removed their sword belts, helmets and outer shirts in a sort of perverse ritual ceremony. They stood above the women, talking excitedly in their own tongue. Then, one approached and seized Lettie by the arms and raised her to her feet. The girl began to scream in earnest, kicking and beating her captor as he carried her to his black stallion. Addie leaped to her feet and began to pound on the soldier whose comrades stood by laughing.

The Turk dragged the struggling Lettie to his horse, but when Addie continued to resist, he drew back the flat of his hand and struck her across the jaw sending her reeling to the ground with a bloody face. Lettie was thrown over the horse, gagged, and hands and feet bound. The Turk did not wait for his companions. He mounted his charger, and rode away, disappearing quickly into the grass.

The others flew at Addie, tearing at her clothes like vultures, picking her flesh each in their turn until her body lay bleeding and raw; they circled her prostrate form, waddling about patiently, flapping their arms and screeching raucously until her own screaming stopped. Addie's strength ebbed slowly, although, even after she was subdued, she quivered against their bodies, and raised her arms to strike them, but her arms were now too heavy to be used as weapons and they fell helplessly to her side. Then, she was quiet again, seeing nothing, feeling nothing, indeed, willing nothing, not even to live. She saw their faces, dark and bearded, and she saw their eyes, red and darting wildly. Then there was only a whiteness, cold and unending, settling over her.

They left Addie for dead, tossing her aside like useless, picked-over carrion, and grabbed Hildy and treated her the same way: the beating, the tearing of the clothes, the restraints, the rape. But Hildy did not cry nor did she resist. She had no illusions as to what was going to happen and what the outcome might be. She chose, therefore, to give herself up to the inevitable, believing there was no particular virtue in resisting what was evidently the will of God.

The men were scarcely talking now. They attacked Hildy as though this was their vocation. The assault elicited neither groans of lust, nor shouts of excitement: Rape, mutilation, abuse and kidnapping was the stuff of war, and the madness had degenerated into a mere wartime obligation. They had the power; they exercised it as they were supposed to, and the Turkish soldiers had no doubt that, were the Christians the victors, their women and children would be treated the same way. Both Allah and Yahweh were stern executors of judgment, bearing grudges, taking defeat without grace, and victory without mercy. So, it is not surprising that, having discarded the limp bodies of Adelaide Bartholomew and Hildegard, they now descended upon the child Clare who had crawled away through the sand and mud to the edge of the tall grass clearing. They grabbed her roughly and threw her to the ground and began to rip off the already tattered clothes of the girl, who immediately transformed into a whirling, churning animal of flying feet and hands, screaming for her mother.

But before this final atrocity against the child could begin, Pons, Guy and Peter crashed through the grass like wild boars taking the

Saracens by surprise, and unable to move freely because their trousers were gathered at their ankles and their *membra concupisicentiae* still visible and erect. Before they could begin to defend themselves, Guy struck a furious series of blows to Clare's assailant, and with a quick slice, severed his manhood to the dust before thrusting his dagger into his heart. The man collapsed with an "aaaarrrgh" to the ground, dead. Pons and Peter engaged the two others who were skillful fighters, but no match for two men with rage in the hearts and revenge on their minds. Within minutes, the three Turks lay lifeless in the ground and Pons and Guy stood breathless, surveying the scene. "I'm not through with them yet," said Guy. Taking his dagger, he carved the genitals from the two who were still in possession of genitals, and stuffed them into their mouths. "When they're found, the Turks will know that they will answer to us!" Guy said.

Peter rushed to his sister, demanding to know of Lettie's whereabouts, but Addie had not awakened, nor could she be aroused. Pons came to his help, lifting Addie into his arms. "We can't stay here," he said. "We'll use their horses and carry them out."

Guy quieted a screaming Clare who had not experienced any physical harm, but whose spirit had been savaged. Peter dropped to his knees beside Hildy. As he began to restore her modesty, he saw something that made him gasp. On her left breast, he saw a very distinct insignia, the Star of David.

"Oh Mary, Mother of God," he whispered. He was stunned. He glanced quickly at Pons and Guy, but they had not seen his reaction. He put out his hand and allowed his fingers to touch the brand. It was black and felt rough and textured where the skin had been seared. He quickly covered her up, lifted her up into his arms, and carried her to a horse.

They rode away quickly, Addie riding in the saddle held in place by the strong arm of Pons riding behind her, Hildy riding in the same fashion with Peter behind her, and Clare with Guy.

When they reached the misty seashore, they saw the ruins of the castle situated on low basalt cliffs by the sea. They sped onward, hoping to avoid Turkish patrols that might be in the area still. Peter wished now that they had moved the bodies of the Turks into the undergrowth and out of sight.

At the base of the cliff they found a path almost hidden by the undergrowth that led in a winding fashion to the top where the castle sat rooted in the rock, like a lone, gnarled pine that had weathered centuries of wind and storm. But Pons saw something that made him halt.

"Someone's in there," he said, staring at the crumbling edifice.

"I saw it, too," said Peter.

"Come on," Pons said to Peter, dismounting. "You stay here, Guy. We'll be back."

They scrambled up the path as light of foot as possible. Peter looked back. "The horse, the horse!" he hissed. Pons' palfrey had started back down the trail with Addie slumped over its rear. Guy, with Clare hanging on, raced after it and caught it within a minute. Peter sighed, and the two of them turned again toward the ancient fortress.

The glory of this mossy castle was well spent, but it still had a heavy door with massive iron hinges in its vaulted entrance. When the two men arrived, they found that access to the interior was best served through the door. They pushed it open.

"Let's stay together," Peter suggested when they had stepped inside. Pons had withdrawn a dagger and had it at the ready. The castle had obviously been abandoned for many years. Pons assumed it had served as a garrison guarding the entrance to the Dracon River. The stones of the walls were covered with dust, and the timbers upon which they walked when they stepped into the keep, were weak and rotten. They avoided the holes and peered below into a cellar. They heard a whimper. Peter had a hunch.

"Don't be afraid," he said. "We are friends." He listened, but heard nothing. He repeated his message again and again.

Out of the darkness, a woman and child appeared, and then an aged man, two other women, and another child.

"You are safe here," Peter said. "I am bringing my family and three friends inside, and then we'll talk. You will be safe, you'll see."

There were twelve of them now, an old man, five women, three children, and three men. Addie was breathing well, but still not awake. "She must rest," said one of the women.

✠✠✠

That night, while the twelve huddled before a small fire, Peter took stock of their situation. They had some food for a few days. The people who had also fled to this site had come prepared. They could survive under all conditions except one: If they were discovered by the Turks with sufficient manpower, they would not be able successfully to resist. Their position was favorable in that a hostile party could not approach unnoticed unless under the cover of darkness. But Peter doubted that the Turks would patrol the seacoast at night, especially if they had no reason to believe there were any survivors. Again, Peter wished they had removed the bodies.

"What are you going to do now?" Pons asked.

"We must get back to Constantinople," he said. "There's nothing else we can do. We can't stay here or the bastards will feed us to the vultures.'

"The bastards," Guy muttered.

"I hope the monk persuaded Alexius to help us," Pons said. "If he didn't, it will be a hard journey back."

"He'll be back soon with troops. We have to stay somehow until then."

"The monk will be able to persuade the emperor to let us remain in the city until the nobles arrive?" asked Pons.

"Certainly," Peter answered. "Alexius was prepared to let the entire expedition stay and would've if the Alemanni hadn't started creating so much trouble. If it weren't for them, we would all be alive and well in Constantinople."

"Reginald was a fool," said Guy.

"Reginald and Burel were both fools, and we were fools for following them," Peter said.

"The mistake was in crossing the Bosporus. The only person with the voice of reason has been Alexius. We should've listened to him all along. And we should have firmly disciplined the rabble-rousers who created all the trouble for us."

The conversation drifted off and soon sleep settled upon the weary pilgrims, who alone were left after the day's slaughter. They slept, like the small band of King David's huddled in flight half expecting Saul and his men to camp in the mouth of their own cave.

Then Peter heard voices, familiar voices. They were not angelic voices. He opened his eyes quickly. He was lying on a rough-hewn oak floor. Across the room he saw a figure kneeling over a woman, his sister, Addie. He sat up and crawled quickly across the floor to where she lay.

"Addie, Addie," he whispered. He stroked her bruised face with his hand.

She grasped his hand, and looked at him, smiling wanly. "I wished I had died," she said, turning away to face the wall.

"No, Addie," Peter said, tears filling his eyes. He pulled her toward him.

"Lettie is gone," she said, tears at the corners of her eyes again. "She's gone and she'll never be back. Oh, the poor child." She began to sob uncontrollably.

Peter turned away now too, and walked to the window which overlooked the coast line. Hildy appeared beside him. "Losing someone you love takes away both the desire to love and the desire to live," she said. "Your life is so bound up with the other's that when it is gone a part of you is gone, too, and you wish you could be complete and whole again." Peter tried not to think of Lettie, of what had become of her. She was probably alive, but what kind of life was it to live as a servant to these bastard infidels?

Peter climbed the interior staircase to the top of the east tower and searched the coast line for signs of the Turkish enemy. He saw smoke from the fires in their old encampment. They must have quartered there for the night, he thought.

When he checked two hours later, what he saw disturbed him. On the coast, a regiment of Turkish soldiers were massing on the beach and another regiment was joining them.

Soundlessly, Peter ran down the cold, granite stairs and summoned Pons and Guy who raced back to the tower with him. The Turks could be seen filing along the coastline like a trail of ants on the march. They no doubt had reason to believe there were still a few Christians hiding out in the tall grasses and marshlands or in small caves in the basalt cliffs.

"It won't take them long to get here," Pons said.

"We have to move into the forest, quickly," said Guy. "It's our only chance."

The Turks, however, showed no signs of moving a regiment toward the castle. Instead, they appeared to hesitate; some of the troops were reversing themselves and moving inland toward the encampment. Peter was the first to observe this puzzling occurrence, and he put his hand to his brow to shade his eyes from the brilliance of the mid-morning sun. Peter scanned the horizon, for, although he said nothing to his companions, he knew there could be only one reason why the Saracens were not racing their steeds toward their castle.

"Look!" he shouted, pointing wildly out to sea. "Ships!"

Pons and Guy immediately strained to see what Peter saw. "Where?" they both asked.

"Ships!" Peter repeated. "The monk is back!"

Indeed, white sails, like the wings of angels, were carrying a small fleet of three ships directly into the mouth of the Dracon River.

ANNO
DOMINI
1097

CHAPTER EIGHTEEN

Down to the Sea

HE SAD STORY OF THE PEA-
SANTS *cast a pall over Bernard and the
coterie of monks that had gathered around us in
the gardens at Cluny. One cannot help but feel
sympathy for those who, with the best of
intentions, begin a great thing, only to have it
ultimately fail. Rather than stopping the narrative
and thereby allowing the mood to settle perhaps
permanently, I chose to continue on a new tack. I
suggested we stand, and walk through the gardens.*
Nearby, my younger friends were hacking at the epinards, choufleur and
tomatoes; digging up stubby, fat carrots with granules of black soil clinging to
them; and harvesting white onions which they dropped into their baskets.

As we strolled among blossom and flower, I resumed the story of my notes
and the Gesta Francorum. *Although the peasants had died, I said, the
nobles had come to life. Short Breeches, with the Count of Saint-Valery,
Girard of Gournay, Hugh of Saint-Pol, and the sons of Hugh of Grant-
Mesnil, and Odo, the bishop of Bayeux, had begun the journey south. He even
had knights and a considerable host of foot soldiers from England, Scotland
and Brittany, in spite of the king's (his brother) personal animosity.*

Robert of Flanders put his affairs in the hands of his countess, Clementia of
Burgundy, and left for Italy at about the same time. Stefan of Chartres and
Blois departed from Pontarlier, traversed the Alps into Italy and met the pope
in Lucca. In Rome briefly, they met the anti-pope—after a fashion. Stefan and
some of his party entered the Church of Saint Peter and placed gifts on the
altar, whereupon the men of Guibert suddenly appeared with drawn swords and

stole the offerings, while at the same time, henchmen situated above the nave began to rain stones upon Stefan and his men. One of the towers was occupied by men loyal to Urban, and they began to withstand these adversaries. But Stefan, not wanting to further hostilities in the church, left quickly, and continued on his journey along the Via Appia, through Campania, stopping at Monte Cassino, arriving finally at Bari where they prayed in the chapel of Saint Nicholas. Some, however, now weak with cowardice, left and returned to their homes.

As it was early December, it was too late in Stefan's judgment to make a safe crossing of the Adriatic. But Robert of Flanders insisted on risking it nevertheless, and they landed safely in Dyrrachium, arriving weeks later in Constantinople where they awaited the nobles who stayed behind ...

✠✠✠

The Nones of April,
Which, in this year, falls on the Holy Day of Easter
Brindisi, Italy

The ships at Brindisi, down from Venice, were ready for embarkation. Boarding had begun.

That anything at all had begun was, in itself, something of a miracle, because, if the long winter sojourn in southern Italy had been necessary to ensure their physical safety, it had been disastrous for morale. Short Breeches had taken the cross less out of devotion to the Holy See as out of distaste for the administration of his duchy. Stefan's enthusiasm, always lukewarm, had languished even more in the tropical, Italian climate, for precisely the opposite reason: possessing the skill and temperament for governing and administration, he had no desire to give it up.

One does not say "No" to the daughter of the Conqueror, Stefan thought ruefully, as he watched the ships anchored offshore being loaded with horses, mules, cheese, wine, grain, treats and tools. His was a marriage in which temperament won over reason, outbursts over thoughtfulness. Stefan discovered, early in their marital life, that his role as husband was to be a Ruth to her Boaz, following his wife into the harvest gleaning what she had neglected, and hoping at the end that she hadn't forfeited the kingdom with her profligacy. To avoid aggravating her ill humor, he had begun to live the most banal of existences, speaking neither his mind nor his heart to her, but instead uttering whatever bland platitude would please her most, giving in to whatever whim it was her curious fancy to indulge. He was gone from her now, however, and spending an entire winter with little to do but to ponder the dreadful calamities. It was almost too much to bear.

He had not even written to her, unwilling to evoke a response that might darken his spirit further. He scribbled in his own hand at least three letters to Anna Comnena, however, on the ostensible grounds of advising her of their progress. The troubled count smiled as he thought of those letters. He knew he was one of those men who required a woman for conversation, the probing of two souls in search of the same truth. Words bounced off Adela like arrows off a stone wall. They talked *at* each other, not *with* one another. Their words had first lost the power to caress, arouse or enlarge their souls, and then had dropped off altogether. And Stefan felt strangely disabled, as though he were hobbling about on one foot, requiring the support of someone else to get about. Anna, in his own mind, had come to symbolize that support, even if, in fact, he had no reason to suspect whatever that the daughter of Alexius could provide it.

"I don't like this wind," Stefan said to Alexander, his chaplain, and Fulcher who had walked by. He glanced at the cloudless sky, and back at the priests with Anna choking in his throat. Stefan saw that Fulcher carried his writing board. "Are you noting this well, Fulcher?" he asked.

"I am noting it well," replied the young priest. "I have not had much to note," he added wryly. "But we shall land in Epirus, you'll see." Stefan nodded and said nothing as Fulcher sauntered down the dazzling beach, a black robe against the white sand. Stefan dug his feet into the grainy sand, digging to the moist layer several inches below the surface. A grey-white gull swooped with a screech to a bleached piece of driftwood close by, then bobbed, and floated back into the sky again. Stefan pitched his arms out imitating the gull, as though he, too, might jump off the earth and live like the birds in the heavens. He put his arms down heavily and sighed.

Alexander was preparing to say Mass. He had a box and wine. Other chaplains would say Mass this Holy Day of Easter elsewhere on the beach and the religious as well as the irreligious would attend, the latter as a wager against the possibility that perhaps there was a God after all. Alexander began to pray: *Te igitur, clementissime Pater, per Iesum Christum, Filium, tuum, Dominum nostrum, supplices rogamus ac petimus uti accepta habeas et benedicas, haec dona, haec munera, haec sancta sacrificia illibata, in primus, quae tibi offerimus pro Ecclesia tua sancta digneris toto orbe terrarum: una cum famulo tuo Papa nostro Urban et omnibus orthodoxis atque catholicae et apostolicae fidei cultoribus.*

Alexander spread his hands now over the bread and wine. Stefan watched the flotilla in the bay as the sailors raised the topsails. Alexander took the host in his hands and consecrated it: *Qui pridie qnam pateretur, accepit panem in sanctas ac venerabiles manus suas ... accipite, et manducate ex hoc omnes: hoc est enim corpus meum.*

The priest genuflected, showed the Sacred Host to the worshipers and genuflected again. Then, consecrating the wine, he said: *Hoc est enim Calix Sanquinis mei, novi et aeterni testament: mysterium fidei: qui pro vobis et pro multis effundetur in remissionem peccatorum.*

The harbor was dotted with galleys as the embarkation continued. Alexander showed the chalice to the celebrants. Away from the mystery of transubstantiation, cross-marked pilgrims gathered their possessions, clambered into lorries, and were ferried to the ships, which lay in the bay like beached whales. One ship was fit for sailing with jib and topsails in position. Earnest men still were rolling barrels on board other vessels, and horses pranced against their pens on the beach awaiting transport.

Stefan's chaplain made the sign of the cross three times over the chalice with the Sacred Host and twice between the chalice and himself, and then raised the Host and chalice slightly, and began to chant: *Oremus—Pater noster, qui es in caelis, sanctificetur nomen tuum. Adveniat regnum tuum. Fiat voluntas tua, sicut in caelo, et in terra. Panem—*

A tremendous crack, like a boom of thunder that breaks through the clouds and then dissipates to a distant rumble, burst upon the thousands on the beach. It was followed instantly by loud screams of distress. The worshipers at Alexander's service turned immediately toward the sea. "The ship!" someone cried. The celebrants abandoned the sacred drama and raced toward the water. Inexplicably, the largest ship, which had been boarded first and was ready for sailing, had snapped in two like a piece of dry kindling and was taking on water. Caro, Stefan's man, ran along side. "It's gone," he whispered. Stefan agreeing, said nothing. He could see people climbing upon the bow and stern, main mast attempting to stay above water or to cling to something that might stay afloat when the ship had gurgled to the bottom. The main mast quickly buckled now and the sails were in the sea, collapsing on top of those who had plunged into the water to escape. The heavy material fell upon them like a burial shroud, wrapping each one prematurely and bearing them downward to their cold, green tomb.

"The boats, Caro!" Stefan cried hoarsely. "Save as many as you can." Stefan called for his horse, mounted it quickly, and galloped down the beach. Thousands had crowded the shore, lining the ocean's edge like ants at water. A few had dashed in to reach a struggling survivor, but most could be nothing more than spectators. It was too awful to watch which was precisely why it must be watched. No one could turn away, for there was someone who would be saved, and their salvation would be the redemption of them all. In one, the many are saved. So they pushed, and jostled one another where the waves crashed upon the shore, and soon a body washed up on the beach.

"What happened?" Stefan demanded of the Genovese, who had built the ship. They were little men, with big palms. They shrugged. "We don't know," they answered, feigning grief.

"The ship was old and in need of repair," Stefan roared from his perch in the saddle. "The damned ship hadn't been repaired!"

"The ship was old, but it was a good ship."

"It snapped in two like a reed in the wind," Stefan cried. "How can it be a good ship? It just fell apart before our eyes. I've probably lost six hundred lives in this disaster, and you tell me it was a good ship? It wasn't even seaworthy, just sitting in the bay, scarcely had the main jib up and fell apart when a mere breeze shook it."

The merchants were not convinced. "Perhaps my lord over-boarded the ship and burdened it beyond its capability," one of them suggested. To be more deferential would've been obsequious; to be more pointed, rude.

"Overloaded? Are the rest of your ships going to fall asunder as this one did?"

Stefan pulled on the reins, flung his cape about him, and yelled at the men as he raced away: "I expect full restitution!"

The two sections of the poor vessel had now disappeared; the only evidence of their existence was the large and ever-widening circle of debris that could be seen where they sank: timbers and clothes washed to shore, and casks and barrels of oil and wine bobbed in the rough water. Friends and relatives gathered frantically around each body as they tumbled toward shore in three-foot breakers.

"The Holy Day of Easter and six hundred people die, Father," Stefan said to Alexander. "How does one interpret such an event?"

"God's way are not our ways, my lord," he replied.

"I'll grant you that," Stefan countered, "but if this is His way, what are we to make of it?"

Alexander was silent. "I'll tell you what those pilgrims are going to make of it. They're going to think it's a very bad omen. A very bad omen."

"It is very odd," Alexander allowed, "a day of death on the day of resurrection."

"You're not going to tell me it's a bad omen, are you, Father?"

"It's not a good omen."

'It's not an omen at all."

"It's more likely a test of our faith and devotion," the chaplain suggested. "And these who have died, have died victoriously in their faith."

"I like that, Father," Stefan said, pleased. "I want you to say Mass for those who perished, and to repeat what you have told me."

✠✠✠

"Some reported that when the bodies floated to shore, they found the sign of the cross on their backs," I said, sitting down wearily.

"But you don't believe it?" Bernard asked.

"I didn't see it, and I was there."

✠✠✠

"How unsearchable are his judgments and his ways past finding out," began Alexander, raising his voice above the wind to the assembled mass of Robert and Stefan's army. "What those who were living bore on their garments, it was fitting with the Lord willing that the same glorious sign should remain with them in death. They were occupied in his service under a pledge of faith, and it is by this miracle, those dead should by God's mercy obtain the peace of everlasting life in the clearly evident fulfillment of the prophecy which had been written: the just, though taken prematurely, shall find peace."

Then, beating his breast three times and bending low over the altar, Alexander said: *Agnus Dei, qui tollis peccata mundi: miserere nobis.*

The funeral mass began.

CHAPTER NINETEEN

Becalmed

NYTHING YET, CAP-
TAIN?" COUNT STE-
FAN shouted, address-
ing the Genovese pilot
of the ship.

The old man touched
his cap and wiped the
damp hair from his face. Large eyes,
like a sea bass, blinked at the count. His lips
pushed away from his beard as he spoke. "Not a
breath, m' lord," he replied in a gravelly voice.
"We're stuck here like flies in honey."

Stefan looked into the face of the water, flat
and glossy like a mirror, reflecting the hull of the
ship and its three masts. The water was a tepid
shade of pale green and far away the horizon was
colorless where it touched the bleached sky, a
heaven so empty that the blazing sun seemed to
hang without moorings, as though it might
crash into the sea at any moment. The only—
only—redeeming feature of the experience was that no one could
desert now. They were captives in a crowded castle on a crystal sea
and neither the strength of Man or the breath of God had moved
these vessels a single meter for two days.

"Do you think we should rig a square sail?" the count inquired. A whistling sound came from the old man's mouth of cracked, yellowed teeth. "A square sail would be of no use, m' lord, unless we had a strong wind dead aft, and we's not likely to have tha' kind o' wind when things get t' blowin' agin. These lateen sails are all w' need to fill'em with wind, sir."

The captain spoke the truth. The cargo ships were powered solely by wind in the sails. Stefan half wished he had ordered a fleet of galleys with square and lateen sails, but more importantly—with galley slaves. One was never becalmed in a galley and they were fast.

"Aye, that's the problem with these cargo ships in the open sea," said the captain, reading his mind. "You're at the mercy of the elements, for sure. You git becalmed at sea and there's nothin' you can do 'bout it except pray your supplies last. Now, one of these little galleys would get you across in no time ... only twenty meters long, couple meters high, plenty of manpower to adjust the yardarms and sails." The old seaman strutted a few steps surveying the nautical fief that was his kingdom. "But, you had no choice, m' lord," he declared, turning to the count again. "W'all these knights and horses ... a cargo ship can hold near six hundred tons, crew of a hundrid, a thousand people, even a hundrid horses. Gotta have a cargo ship."

Stefan turned away from the rail. "Makes me feel like Noah in the Ark," he said to the old man. He looked wistfully to the top of the main mast. The sails hung limply now as they had for hours. His eyes followed the length of the yard for the main mast. It was made of two spars fished together and was longer than the length of the boat itself.

"Noah weren't much of a shipbuilder, m' lord," said the captain. "Now how's that, old man?"

The captain twisted his lips strangely, puckered and expectorated savagely upon the deck. "The way I understand it, that ship of Noah's wasn't built for sailing. It was built for shelter. What Noah had, m' lord, was a big barn, you know—seaworthy for sure—but a big barn with no sails. And that's the difference between us and Noah, m' lord"

A smile broke at the corners of Stefan's mouth when he saw an extra spar on the first deck, and another set of sails, a reserve in case there was a change in the weather. There was little chance they would be needed, he thought ruefully.

"What's the difference between Noah and us?" he asked, turning back to the captain whose toothy grin startled him.

"We thought we was building a ship, m' lord, jist like Noah. But we was building a barn, only—unlike Noah—we's got sails! But that's all we got, sitting on this sea going nowhere, all's we's got is a big barn with limp sails."

Stefan said nothing.

"Great ships," the old man added, "but that's why I don't like takin' 'em out in the open sea. You stick close to land, you's more likely to have a wind, and besides, it's safer staying close to the shoreline. The Venetians run their galleys in these waters and cargo ships are not easy to defend."

"You keep your needle ready, because we're going to have a wind soon, I just know it!" Stefan said, turning back to the rail.

"Aye, but m' lord, we don't use a needle anymore. We got a fancy compass. It's a needle but it's cal'brated and fixed on a dry pivot and used with a chart. So if we can't see the stars or the sun, we can still get to port with the compass." The old man was proud of his knowledge of the new science.

"Well, then, captain, keep your compass close by, because there's a wind a-coming," said the count.

"I hope so, m' lord," said the seaman. "We've got the lower hold full of horses, grain, salt and four to five hundred in the castle aft, and two or three hundrid in the castle fore, and that's close quarters, m'lord, and tonight they'll be sleepin' out on the main deck and the soldiers and children git tired and weary, m' lord, and the women and old men are uncomfortable. So if you say there be a wind a'comin', well, that's good news for me."

✠✠✠

The old man left to inspect the rigging on the main mast and the mizzenmast. The lateen-rigged sails had been readied for a southeasterly wind.

That evening when pilgrim and crew alike had fallen asleep—it was better to be asleep, than to be awake bored—Stefan sat at a fragile desk in the captain's bunk, secured parchment and ink and began to pen a letter to his wife, the first since he had departed from the Loire River valley, his only letter in eight months. *Stefanus comes Adelae comitissae, dulcissimae amicae, uxori suae. Quicquid mens sua melius aut benignius excogitare potest.*

The count put the stylus down and lowered his head to his hands. The strain of doing nothing now prevented him from doing *anything*, even writing a letter to his wife. He had heard nothing from her or of her. He was fortunate, he decided, to have a wife who could read his letters privately and respond to them. Her training had been a gift from her indulgent father who was not afraid of educating a daughter. Stefan's education was typical of a noble family of means. He was sent to the new cathedral school at age eleven and had he been a man of the spirit he most assuredly would have remained in a Cluniac monastery. But he was not a man of the spirit … or not primarily so.

The count stood up and stretched. Then, stooping through the doorway, he walked down a narrow passage to steps leading up, as out of a deep crypt, to the main deck. The steps of rough planks were dimly lit, but he found the door latch nonetheless and climbed out quickly into the salty air. For a moment he stood still. The sky was thinly overcast and the sea was still. People were huddled fore and aft below the castles and a few had found corners and niches along the sides where, with the aid of a blanket, they had found rest. The night was silky smooth and he felt lonely.

Stefan strolled away from the main hatch toward the main mast, the hard heel of his boot hitting the oaken planks firmly. People stirred nearby. He paused at the main rigging and looked up to the maintop and main-top mast. A sudden urge gripped him, and securing a handhold on the rigging, he began to climb. The rigging's hemp felt dry and slightly frayed. His hands fit around the rope snugly. Hand over hand, step by step, he spidered up the web-like rigging, swinging and swaying until he reached the maintop. Cradling the mast with one hand, he secured a grip on the rigging for the maintopmast with the other.

From here he had a view of the entire ship, the castles fore and aft and the second and main decks now brilliantly lit by the flooding moonlight, but then quickly shrouded by rolling fog. For moments Stefan was himself above and in the fog, perched above the ship as though suspended. As he looked toward the forward mast, it suddenly stood out in its cruciform shape. Stefan whirled and the mizzenmast on the other side appeared as a cross also— mast and yardarm. With a start, Stefan realized he stood or clung precariously to the center cross, standing on the yardarm and in that moment he saw himself on the cross, he saw the Christ, the Christ of Chartres, the Bleeding Savior, the Christ of the Sword, his sword, Fortissimus! Stefan closed his eyes as the scene faded. Opening them again, the fog had parted and the ship was again visible and the moon shone in the blackness like the sun on judgment day.

Peace sailed down upon Stefan like a gentle zephyr. The crusader embracing the cruciform mast and filling the orb of the moon with his silhouette, had accepted this chapter in his destiny, a destiny that involved redemption, he as the redeemer. "I did not come to bring peace, but the sword," the Christ had said. Yet, the Christ had never produced a sword, Stefan thought. He refused the sword; he died rather than use the sword. Then Stefan understood. What the Christ had not done or could not do, Stefan must do! Stefan saw a continuity in all of this, that he was a part of a larger plan now, that in the ways of God there is a time for peace and a time for war, a time for embracing and a time not to embrace, a time for living and a time for dying. Stefan now had the sword and would use it as a cross, as an instrument of redemption, the redemption of both the infidel and the holy places.

The crusader understood now. *Deus vult.* Surely God is with me, he thought. He has given me his sword and his strength shall be my strength. *Fortissimus!*

The count swung happily around the mast in a dance of inspired enlightenment, suddenly not feeling tired and eager to return to his cabin to continue his epistle to his adventure-loving wife. She would understand this moment, he thought. I'm fortunate to have a wife like Adela, he considered. They rode together, they conversed together, they slept together—they were always together, he mused. Who is she with now? Thinking about this made him uneasy, and loneliness washed over him again reminding him that he had often been lonely when they were together. There was always an apartness in their togetherness. He stopped dancing on the mast. He stared into the infinite emptiness of the pale moon and longed momentarily to sail away, like the ships now cutting across the golden swatch of light on the sea, to some distant port, far away from both Adela and his newly understood destiny.

Ships? Ships? Stefan stared wide-eyed in nervous excitement across the sea. Coming toward him, traveling in the light of the moon, were two, perhaps more, galleys. "Venetian galleys?" Stefan murmured in amazement. Pirates! They were rigged with square sales, but there was no wind in them. The vessels were close enough that he could see the uniform movement of the oars as they slapped the water, but not close enough to hear them. Stefan now saw a third and fourth galley slip out of the darkness into the brightness of the night gliding noiselessly toward his ships like ravens in the keep of his castle.

The count hesitated. Yet, there could be no mistaking their intention. Deftly, he jumped off the main-topmast onto the rigging and, nimbly sliding down the webbing, descended within seconds and before reaching the bottom, swung himself over the netting and jumped lightly to the main deck. He ran to a nameless knight sleeping in a corner of the forecastle and shook him roughly. The young man awoke with a groan; Stefan slapped his hand over his mouth.

"Sshh! Quiet!" he whispered to the startled knight. "Pirates! Do you understand?"

"Pirates?"

"Venetians."

"Venetians?"

"Venetians! Don't repeat everything I say—just listen!"

"How many?" The knight was fully awake now.

"Don't know. At least four galleys headed our direction and they're going to be here in less than twenty minutes." Stefan looked about the deck quickly as though some of the scoundrels might be clambering aboard at that very moment. "This is what I want you to do."

"What?"

"Quiet! I want you to get all the women and children below deck immediately. Keep everyone quiet as possible. Tell the knights to go inside the fore and aft castles and we'll need some archers and pitch. We'll let 'em board, then, on command, attack from both castles and put archers on the mast and set fire to their galleys. Quickly now!"

Stefan ran across the deck to the aft castle, glancing across the sea. He couldn't see the ships now. He raced down the ladder to the lower berth and entered his cabin.

"Ah, there you are," he muttered as he spied Fortissimus sheathed in its scabbard and hanging from his chair. He dashed to it and strapped it hurriedly about his waist, firmly, snugly. He drew the sword and held it before him admiringly. Then he put the pommel to his lips and kissed the pelican figure upon it and re-sheathed it immediately.

"Everard! Caro!" he said, shaking his captains out of their slumber. He rapidly explained their harrowing situation. "Caro, you take the forecastle and you the aft. The bastards will board and when I sound the alarm, we'll attack from both sides."

"How many men do they have?" Caro asked, pulling on his boots.

"Four ships, maybe more, but I think we have more manpower if we can get into position quickly. I want twenty archers ready. At the alarm, they should go up the mizzen, main and foremasts and light their arrows and shoot. Questions?"

"Do we board the galleys?" Everard asked.

"No. We don't want to capture them, we just want to defend ourselves. They believe they have the element of surprise. That works in our favor. Now be off and Godspeed!"

Within moments, the ship had become a buzzing hive of muted confusion. Stefan pushed through the crowded lower deck, slapping knights on the shoulder and giving them encouragement. The beamed ceiling was low and the lights were dim below deck; it was difficult to distinguish faces.

"Pirates, Stefan?" said a voice from behind.

The count whirled and saw the face of a young priest. "Ah, yes, Fulcher," he replied, looking at the cleric keenly. In the shadows, the priest's high cheekbones were accentuated making his face appear hollow and skull-like. "This ship is going to be a battle zone within a few minutes. Keep your wits about you." Fulcher tugged at his sleeve.

"Then you are confident?" he queried.

"Absolutely!" Stefan said, smiling broadly. "Keep your eyes open. Tomorrow you will be filling your notebook with the glorious story of our victory!"

Stefan left him and passed through others until he came upon a lad of about twelve. The boy was lacing his shoes and looked up when Stefan tapped him on the shoulder.

"Come on, son," he said. "And bring your horn."

The boy reached within a large canvas bag and quickly produced a cornet. "Stay with me now. Quickly!"

They went out on the main deck which was damp; the fog continued to roil about in ephemeral patches. Stefan glanced heavenward. It was darker now and the moon was visible above the mast, wafer-like through the mist. The Host and the Cross, Stefan thought. He peered into the fog on the starboard side of the vessel.

"There they are!" he whispered to the lad. "Do you see them, Achard?"

The youth nodded. "Yes, there are two of them." Indeed, there were two of them about three hundred yards off, oars still.

Stefan raced to the port side. "Two more, m' lord,' the boy said.

"Right you are, lad, and they're moving in." The count glanced quickly around. The deck was empty and silent. Stefan hoped the soldiers were in place in the castles because the Venetians would be boarding within minutes. "Come on," he muttered. "We've got to get in place."

Stefan and Achard took a position behind the foremast rigging atop the forecastle and waited. Minutes passed. The boy shivered. They stared at the sea through the latticed rigging. Shadows in the vapor caught his eye; the square sails of the galleys appeared like death in Hades. The boats, being low and flat, were dwarfed by the cargo ship, but the four masts on both port and starboard side indicated that four warship galleys were about to launch a pirating foray against this, the largest of the crusader's small fleet.

Stefan listened for voices on the galleys, but it was quiet. They would be preparing gangplanks or rope ladders for boarding. More minutes passed—as interminable as the days they had been becalmed on this sea. Achard nudged Stefan to point out a lone figure slipping over the rail on the port side aft. Bending low to stay in the darkness and away from patches of moonlight, the man, whom Stefan presumed to be a Venetian, snaked along the side walls to deploy a rigging extending from both ships to the walls of the larger vessel. Completing this chore, he ran to starboard and repeated the maneuver. Then quickly, Venetian seaman were clambering over the netting and springing lightly to the main deck. They will wait until all their men are on board, Stefan thought. He knew that their objective was not the cargo, but the considerable sums of money—gold and silver—that were aboard this vessel. Indeed the armies of Stefan and Robert were the wealthiest of the four armies that had left France. *But how could the Venetians possibly know this,* Stefan wondered.

Stefan reckoned that the pirates could only have about 250 men, if that. No more than sixty per boat, whereas Stefan had in excess of four hundred soldiers if they were ready. The ambush had been laid, but if the alarm were sounded prematurely, the advantage of surprising their surprise would be nullified.

"Get ready lad," Stefan whispered to Achard. The lad raised the horn to his lips. The metal felt cold and moist. Achard rolled his tongue inside the mouthpiece, wetting it to ensure no false notes. The Venetians were gathering on the main deck in four groups according to the galley to which they were attached. Each were equipped with swords and some were helmeted and shielded. Almost a hundred now, but Stefan dallied, knowing he could not dally much longer. Timing was critical, but for Stefan timing was nothing more than sheer providence; the count was waiting for providence to intervene.

And then it happened. The fog capriciously banked and coiled away like the waters of the Red Sea, so that the entire main deck was swathed in the cool lunar luminescence of the brightest moon Stefan had ever seen. The Venetians themselves stirred at this development. Stefan glanced toward it and saw again the form of the mast casting its cruciform shadow upon the main deck, like the *labarum* of Constantine! He knew that this was the precise moment!

"Now!" he hissed at the boy. Immediately the lad filled his youthful lungs with brisk Adriatic air and expelled it explosively through the horn at his lips. A high tenor blast sliced through the air like a knife; it was followed by another and another and ere the third blast had tailed away, the fore and aft castles had yielded their snarling inhabitants; the knights were upon their startled attackers like jackals on a rabbit.

✠✠✠

"To the rigging," shouted Stefan at the archers who had already started up. The count leapt to the second deck with Fortissimus in one hand and the *misericorde* in the other. Archers with torches ascended the latticed rigging to the lower top yardarm and securing the torches began to light their pitch-soaked arrows and jettison them across the water to nearby galleys. Within five minutes the sails on all four galleys were in flames.

Stefan dispatched one raider, then another, whirled about to catch another with his dagger, and tossed one off the second deck with a firm kick of his boot. With a cry, he jumped off the deck and followed another man to the flooring, and finished him with a thrust to the chest. A body crashed against him; Stefan threw him off. He collapsed dead with a dagger in his back. Stefan looked up: Caro was waving above him. Stefan saluted him with Fortissimus and returned to the fight. At the starboard rail, he propelled an attacker over the edge, and saved one of his comrades from an attacker's blow.

Unlike many of the crusaders who had had the time to don their cone-shaped helmets and grab a shield, the count was unprotected except by his wits and Fortissimus. Movement was key. It was better that his feet be nimble than his hands be quick. He had planned to sever the rigging connecting the galleys to his ship, but it was an idea quickly abandoned when two Venetians accosted him. They worked him away from the rail, blow and parry, thrust and counterthrust until he had been forced again to the second deck. Fortissimus continued to slash, while its user ducked and whirled as the conflict required. He warded a blow with his dagger, thrust with the sword, following it quickly with the dagger again. Stefan felt a rhythm to his motions that was usually unerring: this man would not be breathing much longer. As his opponent deflected another parry, Stefan swung quickly and truly with Fortissimus bringing him to his knees, and then to the damp deck dead.

The sky had taken on an amber hue as the galleys continued to burn. Beyond this illuminated acre of purgatory, it faded to blackness. The Venetians were routed. Many pirates thought to escape by leaping into the sea where sharks had already begun to feed on bodies which were floating like driftwood. Stefan hurried up to the second deck for a broader view of the melee, when he was distracted by movement to his left. Achard! The lad had been hiding under a pile of rigging, but now the netting had been cast aside and the frightened child dragged from the webbed grotto by a villainous Venetian who had a blade at the boy's throat.

Stefan reacted instantly. "Leave the boy alone," he shouted.

"And you must be the count," the man sneered, tightening the dagger against the pale, thin throat of Achard. His coarse dark hair was pulled back and tied at his shoulders. His eyes skittered about anxiously in shaded, skull-like sockets. He faced Stefan with his left foot forward, leg bent at the knee, right foot back, a fighting stance.

Achard was whimpering incoherently in the grasp of the Venetian. "You're going to be safe, lad," Stefan said grimly. "Have no fear of that!"

"Tell your men to lay down their arms, or the boy dies," the man snarled. Achard clutched his horn to his chest.

"If the boy dies, your soul flies," Stefan said, advancing a step toward the villain.

"No further!" he shouted, menacing the boy again.

"Coward! Hiding behind a boy!"

"Tell them to lay down their arms. The boy lives and we will leave."

Stefan looked down to the main deck where some fighting continued, even though the outcome was clear. The Venetian was acting to save his men.

"Your horn, Achard."

Achard brought his horn out from under his wrap slowly, his eyes full of questions. The pirate still had him in an arm lock. The boy put the horn to his lips but he could not summon enough air to make even the slightest sound.

"The boy can't breathe," said Stefan fingering his sword carefully.

The pirate relaxed his hold on the child and in the instant when the villain glanced away and lowered the dagger's blade, Stefan lunged with a shout, bringing his sword quickly to the pirate's arm and severing it with a dreadful crunch. The boy backed away in horror, shaking the bloody appendage to the deck. The dagger clutched tightly in the pirate's lifeless hand fell loose and clattered inches away. Stefan kicked it away. The Venetian, who had drawn his sword, dropped it to clutch the ragged stump of his arm. His cold, white hand could not stem the flow of blood; it ran hotly through his hand onto the deck. Then he fell to his knees, and then, collapsed prone on the planking. Stefan walked to the fallen man and stood over him. The Venetian looked at him soundlessly, mouth agape. Stefan drew the *misericorde* and dropped to one knee over his foe. He placed the point of the dagger on a spot beneath his heart and then thrust quickly upward driving the blade to the hilt. Stefan withdrew the rapier and wiped the blade on the Venetian's clothing and returned it to its sheath within his jacket. With nimble fingers and quick hands, the count began to rifle the pockets of the dead man's clothes. The Venetian carried nothing in his trousers. Stefan examined an upper pocket in his shirt. His fingers felt something there; he withdrew a small piece of parchment.

"He knew who I was," Stefan muttered. "He knew who I was.' Stefan turned the parchment over. *Stefani comitis Carnotensis. Brindsi. P.*

✠✠✠

The moonlight bathed a lonely figure on the topmast. The battle was over. The galleys were at the bottom of the sea, the Venetians were in the bellies of the sharks, and crusaders were still chattering, too excited for sleep or cleaning the main deck. Stefan was again puzzled, as he was so often. Life was a mystery which needed continual explanation, and it was not enough to be told that mystery was the character of life; that mysteries defy explanation; that it is meant to be so. Stefan chafed at the puzzling elements of his life, which, like the stars above him, usually sparkled with promise, but not revelation; Stefan was not an astronomer, and the secrets in the stars were no more apparent to him than the mysteries surrounding his own life. The truth was there to be discovered, he was sure; he simply lacked the tools by which to find it.

He felt a coolness on his brow, standing here in the same place where earlier he had seen the Host and the Cross. There was a lightness in the air, a whisper of movement. Perched high above the deck, he would be the first to sense the slightest tilt of the ship's hull. He sensed the ship sway. For a few moments he stood transfixed again on the upper topmast. Then, he felt it again. Providence was giving a sign. The pillar of fire was moving, the Israelites were summoned to break camp and march! A wind was arising from the northeast!

"Captain!" He hollered at the men below. "Captain! We have a wind! The sails! The sails!" The captain quickly ordered a crew to the rigging to set up a single lateen sail on each of the masts and prepare sets of smaller yards and sails. Soon the sails were rigged and the rudder men at the rudders. The ship lurched and tilted to port slightly as the wind began to fill the canvas.

"We have a wind!" Stefan cried, thrusting Fortissimus into the star-bright sky. "Blow ye mighty winds, blow!"

And they blew, becoming stronger with each passing minute. "Sound the alarm, Achard!" Stefan shouted to the lad. Achard, who had taken a position on the foremast, jumped quickly to the rigging and climbed to the fore-topmast. He clutched at the mast carefully and then raised the cornet to his lips. Two quick notes, and a third long blast was carried high on the winds and into the billowing sails, and to the aft castles where even below deck the sounding could be heard. *Deus vult* sounded the quick, brass notes. *Deus vult!*

The ship cut through the Adriatic, plowing a course to its inevitable destiny. Stefan, his face against the wind, smiled broadly, and sheathed his sword.

CHAPTER TWENTY

Pons Sits on the Emperor's Throne

May 1, 1097 A.D.

ONS AND GUY MADE THEIR WAY into the city by an artful subterfuge. Guy posed as a blind man and Pons as a mute. They secured a barrow and, taking it to the Romanus Gate, Guy hopped in, and Pons wheeled him through the gate and past the guards who assumed they were proceeding to the Forum Constantini where beggars of their kind gathered daily.

Instead, they disappeared into a narrow, cobblestone street, and when they were unseen, abandoned their disguise and assumed new ones.

"This robe doesn't fit," Guy said petulantly of the garment that folded into the dust of the street.

"That's because it's my robe, not yours," Pons said, eyeing his stouter friend with amusement. They exchanged garments and secured the fasteners. "How do we look?" Pons asked.

"We need rings," Guy answered. "We're supposed to look like wealthy merchants. How can we look like we're rich without jewels?"

"We have jewels—you've forgotten—from the Jews in Mainz, here, see them!" Pons produced four rings of diamonds and jasper. "These will finance our journey to Jerusalem!"

They placed the rings on their fingers until they were satisfied that they were as aristocratic as possible. They passed out into the open street and the commerce of Constantinople's daily life.

"This is one of the crazier stunts we've attempted," Guy noted. "The emperor ought to hire you as the court fool. You should just stroll into the imperial court with a sign front and back: '*Le Duper de Provence.*'"

"It is not foolish," Pons said. "Perhaps a bit risky, but not foolish. We're just going to get inside the palace and look around, that's all."

"I hope the gods are with us."

"I don't expect the gods to be with us," Pons said. "The best we can hope for is that they won't be against us."

"You go in the palace and look around. I'll stay out here."

"Get going!" Pons said, pushing his friend down the street. "Feeble-hearted and feeble-minded!"

Blachernae Palace, the imperial residence, had been built by Emperor Anastasius in the fifth century. It was a palace of three stories and was wedged between the Theodosian walls and the Middle Byzantine outer wall, and its entrance was attractively designed with a decorative pattern of white stone and red brick. On the first level, access was gained through two double arches supported on columns, and above, each of the other floors had round-headed windows in the walls.

South of the palace, immediately adjacent, additional rooms and courts were being added. The Comneni were determined to expand the size and splendor of the palace and had devised a plan of construction which would involve builders for many decades.

"We shall say we are inspecting the construction," said Pons, "and in due course we shall espy a means of entry to the main palace itself. Come along."

They turned into the uncompleted wing of the palace, looking about widely and innocently, hands folded before them reflectively and wandered slowly toward the completed north wall, nodding superciliously to the peasant laborers, stone cutters and masons.

"Here," Pons whispered. He had found an unattended doorway and moved toward it. They ducked into the doorway and glanced about quickly. They were in the imperial palace of the High Potentate of the Eastern Roman Empire.

✠✠✠

A pair of massive doors, twelve feet high, of imported oak, swung open slowly, but soundlessly. Into the marbled corridor the emperor's entourage emerged followed by Stefan, Count of Blois and Chartres; and Raymond of Toulouse. "I'm pleased that this matter of the oath poses no difficulty for you," said Alexius as they walked through the Fourth Court toward the Hall of the Emperor for the ceremony. Alexius' regal head bore a small crown studded at its base in diamonds and on its tips with rubies. He was attired in precious fabrics of brocade, taffeta, satin and silk. His flowing cape of velvet with a border of white ermine was joined at his neck by a gold necklace. In his hands he held the imperial mace.

Stefan slowed his stride to match that of the emperor. He, too, wore a cape, but it extended only midway to his calves which were laced over dark stockings. He was wearing soft leather sandals, and his walk and movements were lithesome and agile. Fortissimus was strapped to his side.

"Our allegiance is first to God, and then to the Holy Father," said Stefan. "Since that presents no problem to you, the oath presents no problem to us."

"I have made this a requirement of all the armies, although Raymond here—" Alexius turned to smile at the Count of Toulouse—

—"needed considerable convincing."

"We understand," Stefan broke in, "that this pilgrimage represents the temporal interest of Constantinople. As such, the oath is reasonable."

"Yes, yes, of course," Alexius beamed.

"We also realize that as sworn agents of the empire, we may depend upon the utmost support and assistance of the emperor," Stefan said smiling.

"There is no question of it."

"Food."

"Of course."

"Supplies."

"Yes, yes."

"Horses."

"Absolutely."

"Gold."

"Whatever you need, I shall supply," said the emperor. "And you yourself, Stefan, shall be my guest in my palace until all the armies are across the Bosporus. You already have the maps and charts of Nicea. My daughter, Anna, is personally responsible for the comfort of your stay. You have met her already, as I recall. She will see that you lack nothing while you are our guests in Constantinople." The count smiled.

✠✠✠

"They've painted all the walls, Pons!" Guy exclaimed. "Who are all these people?"

They stopped below a fresco of Christ Pantocrator and the Mother of God.

"Don't know," said Pons unconcerned, "but this is probably the Emperor Alexius and his queen. You can tell by the gold circle about his head, you know."

"The mouth is too small, the nose is too long, and look at the oval eyes."

"That's the way people look over here," said Pons.

"Quiet! Someone's coming!" They bolted to a nearby doorway for cover and then slowly peeked around the corner. Two palace guards walked into view, and the Provencal peasants snapped their heads out of sight. A thick carpet-like veil hung in the doorway. Pulling it aside, they eluded the sentries by passing into a cavernous hall. Its ceiling was vaulted and overlaid, as were the walls, with thousands of individually crafted ivory tiles. The floors were huge marble slabs inlaid with gold. At one end of the hall was a small apse adorned in delicately painted frescoes in the center of which was a four-sided platform of five steps on which was a four-legged throne of simple design, but overlaid with the most precious and beautiful stones and jewels. On the seat of the throne was a cushion of velvet exquisitely embroidered with gold and silver thread.

"Ecce homo!" said Pons, staring at the vaulted ceiling.

"Ecce homo?" Guy repeated. "What's ecce homo?"

"It's Latin," Pons explained. "I think it means 'Behold the home.' I heard it somewhere. I mean, look at this place! How'd you like to live here, Guy?"

✠✠✠

The emperor and the counts of Chartres and Toulouse and their courtiers left the Fourth Court and entered another room.

"I call this the Audience Chamber," said the emperor to his guests. "I have brought you here before proceeding directly to the Great Hall because I believe you might be interested in this." They strolled across the richly appointed room where the emperor pointed out a case in which lay a complete set of military wardrobe many centuries old.

"The sword, shield and helmet of Constantinus Magnus," Alexius announced. Stefan and Raymond murmured appreciatively as they stood in silence. Seeing the effects of the great emperor and champion of the Christian faith put the counts in a mood of historical introspection. It momentarily reduced whatever notions of self-importance Stefan had been entertaining. He was but a mere count, an insignificant link, if that, in a long line of illustrious warriors whose contribution to the empire and the advance of Christendom would always and forever outshine his own, however courageous his own effort might be.

The room was a veritable museum of expensive and ancient artifacts. Alexius proudly presented his collection of fine Eastern porcelain, golden candelabra, jade vases, weapons encrusted with precious stones, the throne of Justinian (walnut, with mother-of-pearl and tortoise-shell inlays), a pendant of emeralds and pearls belonging to the Empress Irene, and many other treasures of inestimable worth. Never had the lords of France seen wealth on an order and scale as Alexius was showing them in this room alone, let alone the entire palace itself.

✠✠✠

Pons, look at this tooth, and this sword!" Guy was looking at a case along the west wall of the Great Hall. Pons was still inspired by the vaulted ceiling, but was now examining a gilded chandelier which hung from the dome.

"Those are relics," he said when he joined Guy.

"Whose?" Guy asked. "There's a tooth, some hair—perhaps from a beard—and this sword. Look at the stone in the hilt!"

"And the crown," Pens added. "From this we can surmise a king or emperor."

"If these relics are so valuable, why are they left unguarded?"

"They aren't left unguarded," Pons answered. "The entire palace is overrun of guards. We're not exactly invited guests here, remember?" He paused in front of the imperial throne.

"What are you doing?" Guy asked.

"I've always wanted to sit on a throne," Pons said, glancing toward the doors. "Haven't you ever wanted to be a king, ever? Think how different it would be if you were a king."

Guy pondered the impossible. "I shouldn't have to eat roots and berries again," he said finally.

"You wouldn't like royal food, Guy. But think of the maids and mistresses. You could lie with every bride in the kingdom before her husband. Guy, fetch the sword and crown!"

Guy stood transfixed at the meaning of Pons' words. "Oh, no, Pons, this is a very bad idea. A very bad idea."

"Fetch 'em, Guy!" Pons ordered. "I shall be king and you shall become my knight."

✠✠✠

Alexius and the counts, having lingered over the treasures of the Audience Chamber, now departed for the Great Hall of the Emperor for the ceremony.

"These paintings are very recent," said Alexius, commenting on the frescoes on the upper walls and ceilings of the long corridor in which they were now walking. "We have brought to Constantinople some of the finest artists and craftsmen of the empire. You see here a mosaic in progress, and when the project is completed, and I do not expect it to be finished in my lifetime, we will have the entire story of the gospels portrayed on these walls." He stopped the procession.

"Here, for example, is the birth of the Virgin, and here the First Steps of the Virgin." Alexius turned and pushed through the entourage to the other wall. "And here is the Return of the Holy Family from Egypt, and here, Jesus in the temple."

✠✠✠

This cushion is lumpy," complained Pons. He picked up the royal pillow and fluffed it. Then he replaced it and slowly eased himself into the imperial throne of the Eastern Potentate.

"You may approach the throne, you miserable wretch," Pons intoned. "I hope you shall be grateful that I deign to elevate you from your wretchedness to knighthood."

"Pons, I don't think—"

"Up the steps," Pons the Emperor commanded. "What's this?! Methinks this crown is ill fitting." Pons adjusted the crown, but it still sat low on his brow.

"Methinks you should take off the crown and abdicate your throne."

"Kneel, you ungrateful fool!"

"Pons, I—"

"Bow and kneel, you knave!" Pons said. "How can I make you a knight if you don't bow?" Guy bowed with as much ceremony as he could muster and then knelt humbly before his sovereign. Pons leaned forward and holding the sword in one hand while balancing the ill-fitting crown with his other, rested the tip of the sword on the right shoulder of his good friend who knelt before him.

Raising his voice, Pons announced: "By virtue of my authority as Supreme Impotentate of the Empire, I dub thee ..."

✠✠✠

"So then, gentlemen, are we ready?" Alexius inquired.

"We are ready," replied Stefan.

"Then, let us enter," he said. At that, the pages swung open the doors and the entourage of the courts of Constantinople, Chartres, and Toulouse, swept into the Great Hall.

"... Knight of Every Maid's Night and may your weapon be always at the ready!" Then he saw Alexius. "Hullo!" he whispered.

The emperor's wrath blazed like sudden lightning.

"What is this outrage?" he thundered. "Who are these villains! After them!" Pons and Guy made a half-hearted attempt to escape, like rabbits skittering in the shadow of a hawk. It was futile. The guards caught them within moments, subdued them and brought them to the emperor who was standing by the throne.

"The sword and crown of Charlemagne!" he cried. He whirled on the peasants. "Do you realize what you've done? Can you tell me why I shouldn't have you executed for this crime?" The guards tossed the men on the cold, marble floor and put a foot on their chests and a sword to their throats. The nobles crowded about the two men in a circle that was sometimes two, three people deep. Alexius, Stefan, and Raymond stood within the group in addition to the guards. "This is an insult of the worst kind! An affront to our people," the emperor huffed. "Release them," he ordered.

The guards stepped away from the peasants. Guy rubbed his neck where he could still feel the sting of the sword. Pons, however, remained motionless.

"Stand up!" shouted Alexius. "Up! Up!" The adventurers sat up nervously, and got to their feet while onlookers strained for a glimpse of the audacious intruders.

"Who are you?" Alexius demanded.

"We are here in your service to fight the infidel and liberate the holy places," Pons said, keeping his eyes down. "I am Pons de Rodez and this is Guy de Monteil."

Stefan looked sharply at Raymond. It was obvious from their speech that the men were from Provence.

"Where are you from?" Count Raymond asked, taking a step toward them.

"We are from Rodez of Provence," Pons answered.

"How did you come to Constantinople?"

"We traveled with Peter the Monk and arrived here last summer. We were taken to the Civetot, and we fought the Turks when our armies were defeated in October. Pons turned to Alexius. "You brought those of us who survived back to your city to await the arrival of the armies from France."

"But the armies have arrived, and I have transported them back to the Civetot and to the plains of Nicea where they are now preparing for its siege. Why are you here and not there with your fellow crusaders?" Alexius asked, continuing the interrogation.

"We missed the boat?" Pons suggested. Regarding this reply as impertinent, a guard smote Pons across the head and the peasant went crashing to the floor.

Raymond turned to Alexius. "Your excellency, this man is from my country. He and his friend are my responsibility. I shall order their execution ere the sun sets upon the city."

"My friend," Alexius replied in softer tones, "such a punishment is too severe. They shall face death soon enough against the Turks. Surely there is some other penalty you can apply in this case."

"Then they shall be flogged in the camp, and taken to the mews where they shall supply flesh for my falcons, six ounces from the two of them! Take them away!"

The people who had encircled the pair now broke rank as the guards grabbed them and began to drag them away. "I told you this was a bad idea," Guy whispered to Pons. But Pons paid no attention.

"Wait!" A different voice broke through the confusion, like sun through morning fog. A woman's voice. "Wait! Wait!"

Stefan of Blois knew the voice well. He turned and saw a woman who stood alone. He took a step toward her but stopped. She saw him and looked at him. Not a glance, not a sighting, but a look. Not a look that beckoned; not a look that rejected. Rather, a gaze that acknowledged him, that took his measure and comprehended his soul in an instant. He looked away.

"These men have done us a great service," she said. The emperor drew his daughter to the others as though to display his finest treasure of all. "My daughter, Anna," he said. "Raymond of Toulouse." The old count smiled and bowed slightly. "Stefan of Blois, with whom you're already acquainted." Stefan, following custom, bowed and expanded upon Raymond's gesture by securing the woman's hand and kissing it lightly, allowing his lips to linger long enough for the extra moment to be noticed by the recipient. And long enough, too, for his lips to receive in that fleeting tactile impression a sense and fullness of her that would remain with him for days.

"What do you mean, a great service?" Alexius grumbled.

"Father, Constantinople is a great city, none like it in the world. No city is as well fortified as ours. And this palace is also great and beautiful, and for its protection you have at your command the finest soldiers and guards the army can provide. But these ignorant peasants breached our defenses and advanced to the very throne room of the empire unmolested and undetected. And who knows what damage they might have inflicted upon our property and upon our persons had they truly been men of evil intention, if they had been, for example, Turks?"

The room was quickly stilled by this opinion. Anna continued: "They have done us a great service because they have shown us our weakness."

Alexius had always been of the persuasion that ignorance of one's strength was always beneficial, but that ignorance of one's weakness could be fatal. Now two mortals had ascended Mount Olympus, and the gods were angry and would condemn them like Prometheus to have their flesh plucked by the fowl of the air. He waved at a page who stepped forward bearing a cushion on which was a walnut, diamond-encrusted money case. The emperor withdrew a dozen gold bezant coins and dropped six one by one clinking into the eager palms of the two peasants. "My daughter has spoken the truth," Alexius said, "You have done us a great service."

Turning to Raymond: "Have these men flogged if you will. This is your affair. But may I suggest that you allow me to supply whatever flesh your falcons may need. You will require these men to be healthy in your upcoming campaign."

Raymond bowed stiffly: "As you wish, my lord."

They left with Pons and Guy speaking: "I'm a miner and an engineer," said one. "And I can ride a horse," said the other.

Stefan stood still until the others left, watching the woman disappear. His heart was a sea of emotion seeking an outlet. He wanted to follow her, to talk to her, for his greatest pain in life was that there was no one, and had been no one, who would listen to him, or, if listening, would understand. His importance as a person had always been measured by his sword and his wealth, but never by his words and his heart. Adela always cared about what he did, but never what he thought.

Before she turned away, she looked back and their gaze intersected, an amorous highway over which traveled a thousand questions and no answers. For once, Stefan felt frustration that what was the most important matter in the whole world could not be. "There will be time," he thought. "There will be time."

CHAPTER TWENTY-ONE

East Meets West

NNA LOVED HEIGHTS. IT CREATED a certain distance from her everyday life. Not that her privileged status was so unbearable. It wasn't. In fact, she wrote about it, recounting in her chronicles not only her own life, but that of the empire and the Comneni as well. The vista from this rocky promontory above the city and lowlands restored her perspective as a writer, as though living too long at the same level as the history she was writing skewed her ability to write it. The view was always the same: woods of oak and evergreen, the rough hewn cliffs, the Bosporus, and the city in the hazy distance. Invariably, however, she caught a new idea, saw something she hadn't seen before, mostly because from the cliffs she saw her life and world as a whole, whereas in the city her eyesight literally and figuratively was limited by the closeness of everything. When she was in Constantinople, she saw not the city but only her experience of it. Running away to the cliffs raised her perspective, freed her spirit and somehow lifted her above her limitations. She loved heights.

Today, she was not alone. Nor had she been alone yesterday, or the day before that. Once again she was the Norman's personal escort rambling about the largest city in the world, a bursting aggregation of several hundred of thousands. Together, they had explored the city known as the jewel of the empire because of its architecture, the security of its tripartite walls, for the beauty of its situation on the Bosporus, and for the treasures it had gathered from around the world, especially Alexandria.

She eagerly told him how such a city is administered. She showed him the water supply that came from the Belgrade forest and was transported by the aqueduct of Valens to mammoth, underground cisterns. She led him through narrow streets and spacious gardens; she took him to the maize and spice markets, to the Egyptian obelisk, the Serpentine Column and Constantine's Column.

Most impressive was Saint Sophia, the Church of the Divine Wisdom and spiritual center of the empire. They entered the church through its colonnaded forecourt and the west entrance where just inside the narthex they saw stunning mosaics of the Mother of God enthroned with the Christ Child, and of the emperors Constantine and Justinian, the former holding a model of a walled city representing Constantinople, and the latter holding a model of a church depicting St. Sophia. From the narthex, they walked through the Imperial Doorway into the massive nave. It is here that the uniqueness of St. Sophia could be truly seen. "The design has never been successfully imitated to this day," she told him proudly. It was a marvel of architectural engineering, and, as with all such marvels, there were problems, chief of which was its immense scale. Byzantine architects had some experience in building domes before, but not a dome more than one hundred feet in diameter and a dome, moreover, that did not rest on solid walls but four pendentives which distributed weight to the walls below, causing the dome to appear to be "hanging in air" as one architect described it. To the Norman who stood beneath it, the dome seemed to hover above the nave, floating on the light of the forty windows which encircled it.

They walked through meadows of variegated marble admiring columns of exquisite porphyry and Proconnesian marble. She showed him more mosaics and frescoes: Michael the Archangel, St. Ignatius the Younger, St. John Chrysostom and St. Ignatius Theophorus, all wearing the omophorion with the three crosses. They touched the legendary Sweating Pillar, the dampness of which was said to have curative properties. They visited the Hippodrome where thirty-thousand spectators could watch the imperial games.

The day was cool and bright, the sky infinitely deep, and the view across the Bosporus infinitely wide and detailed like a hand-stitched tableau. Beyond the far hills lay the ancient Roman road to Nicomedia and the road to Nicea where, even now, tens of thousands of crusaders had pitched their tents awaiting instructions for an assault upon the Seljuk city. Tomorrow, the Norman would join them. No more tours of the city, no more sampling the food of the street vendors, no more selecting silks and cloth in the bazaars, no more laughing in the markets, no more wild rides through the inland woods, and no more—she stopped and turned toward Stefan.

He was standing at his horse in a large grassy and flowered meadow that sloped toward the cliffs above the Bosporus. Anna's dog, a short-haired glossy foxhound with floppy ears, lay nearby. A falcon was perched on his saddle. Stefan tugged at the gauntlet pulling it on his right hand, and then placed the "bird of the fist" on his arm. Anna put the *campanelle* and jess into a small pack on the horse.

"Time for dinner, little pet?' Stefan said, speaking in sweet tones to the trained bird. The falcon flushed its wings, spread its talons, and took a step on the count's tough, leather glove. He removed the *chapel* from the bird's head so that its hooked beak was free. Stefan stroked the neck of the falcon, talking to it softly. Then he held his right arm away from his body, level and steady.

"Go!" At Stefan's command, the peregrine shrieked, extended his wings and swooped into the sky, catching a draught of lusty wind, soaring higher in widening circles until he was almost out of their sight.

"Soon now, my little pet," Stefan whispered. But the bird continued to soar above them and away from them. Anna felt a twinge of wistfulness. What freedom! she thought. To fly like that, to mount up with the wings of eagles, to soar, to see what others cannot see! *Sometimes I fly like that falcon! I see what others cannot see. I feel free and light. Soaring and happy.*

Suddenly, the falcon dipped his wings and with a single flutter wrapped them tightly to his body and darted to the earth with the speed of an arrow. Faster it plummeted, swooping in an unerring line toward the far end of the meadow. Stefan and Anna watched in fascination as the falcon dropped its feet at the last moment and extended its talons, hitting the earth. They saw it tumble and a spot of dust blew into the air.

Stefan knelt beside the hound. "Go!" he said, and the eager dog dashed toward the falcon, securing its catch in his mouth. The bird cawed again and flew swiftly to the gauntlet on Stefan's right hand. Soon the hound had returned with a small quail.

"This is your dinner, little bird," Stefan said releasing the animal. "You are a fine hunter!"

While the falcon consumed its prey, Anna, Stefan and the hound returned to the palfrey by the woods. Stefan produced some bread, wine and cheese. They spread a blanket in the sun away from the horses.

"Tell me what you think of the crusade," Stefan said, munching on a sesame roll.

"What?" Anna was startled. She was watching the falcon.

"What do you think of the leaders? Bohemund, Raymond, the others? You're a student of such things."

"I don't know—"

"Yes, you do. Tell me."

"Hugh is silly. But what he lacks in skill he makes up in eagerness."

"Go on."

"Godfrey de Bouillon, young and strong, an excellent knight, but given to passions ..."

"Tancred?"

"Bohemund's nephew?"

"Yes."

"Undisciplined, over-indulged youth—"

"*Enfant terrible*," Stefan suggested.

"Yes, yes ... rash because he hasn't tasted the misery of war. Raymond of Toulouse seems prudent, sincere—unwilling to choose war unnecessarily. Perhaps it is his age—honest and very compassionate. He values the truth above all else; he shines, as my father says, like the sun in the stars of heaven. The bishop is very much the same way."

"They both share a dislike for Bohemund." The falcon had risen in the air above the bones of his prey and was shrieking to the wind. Stefan put his fingers to his lips and gave a sharp, prolonged whistle. At this, the bird soared and circled above them while Stefan dashed to the horse to retrieve the gauntlet. The bird descended from the sky and landed gracefully on Stefan's arm. Anna brought the *campanelle*, jess and swivel and lashed the falcon to its perch on the saddle.

"Bohemund would like to be Grand Domestic in Asia, commander of all the imperial forces," Anna continued.

"What is your opinion?"

Anna was silent, and then shrugged. "I don't like him. You know, he and my father were enemies a long time ago at Durazzo and Larissa. When Alexius asked him about this he said that it was true, he had been an enemy, but now he had fled the ranks of the enemy and was a friend. And he swore an oath of fealty."

"But Alexius still doesn't trust him?"

"I'll tell you what happened." She rolled to her back and placed her hands on the flat of her stomach and began to speak to the thin clouds stretched across the sky like lace. "After Bohemund swore the oath of fealty, my father arranged for his passage and quarters at Cosmidion. He prepared a lavish dinner; tables were laden with food and condiments of all kinds. The cooks came out to Bohemund and showed him the uncooked flesh of various animals and birds and told him that they had prepared the food he saw on the table according to the skills and customs of this region, but, if he preferred, he was welcome to prepare this food, still uncooked, in any way he desired."

She paused. "Do you know what he did?" Stefan shook his head.

"My father knew Bohemund had a suspicious nature. At least he used to, and he doubted very little that the Italian prince had changed. So Alexius specifically ordered the cooks to give Bohemund this choice, so that not the least suspicion could be cast upon the empire. When the cooks gave Bohemund this choice, he immediately—-he is very shrewd—took the prepared food, and without even touching it with the tips of his fingers, or tasting it, distributed the prepared food to all those around—under the pretext of courtesy; in other words, dividing the cup of death among them. Then, he summoned his own cooks and had them prepare the raw meat after the manner of his own country. The next day, he asked his men whether they were ill or well. They replied that they were very well indeed, that not even one of them felt in the least indisposed. And when they asked Bohemund the reason for his inquiry, he had the temerity to give them an honest reply about his own deceit. He told them: 'The emperor and I were once at war against each other, and I feared lest perchance he had intended to kill me by putting deadly poison in my food.'"

"He understands military strategy," Stefan countered.

"Perhaps, but Alexius thinks that some of the nobles like him are more interested in carving out little kingdoms for themselves than they are in either liberating the holy places or liberating imperial territory."

"Bohemund, unable to have his own kingdom in Italy, wants to find one somewhere else. Is that what Alexius thinks?"

Anna was silent. *Wants to find one somewhere else.* Her eyes glistened. "Yes, that is what he thinks. The man is cunning, ruthless, cold-hearted, merciless, callous, and—"

"—a damned good general," Stefan said.

"No, he is a bad general, because, when things are quiet, he stirs up trouble to go to war. He rejoices in blood rather than peace. If he had to choose between winning a war with nobility and justice and winning by battle and bloodshed, he would choose blood. My father is not like that. He would rather let peace have her victories than go to war, and my mother Irene … even her name means peace."

Anna laughed and sat up suddenly. "Enough of this talk. Give me some wine to drink—from your cup." She moved close to him and playfully raised her chin to receive the cup of wine he offered. When she had drank, she wiped droplets of wine from her ruby-red lips with her tongue and said: "I've been talking too much. Now it's your turn. Tell me, of everything you have seen this week, which did you like the best?"

Nearby, the foxhound stretched out languidly in the grass, his head upon his paws, eyes pushed shut. The afternoon ambled pleasantly if unnoticed toward evening. Stefan responded to Anna's query by saying he loved an alabaster box with jade stones upon its lid. It was his favorite. It was a choice that pleased the princess, who expressed continued amazement that a barbarian like Stefan should have such fine taste.

"It has simple lines," Stefan said surprised. "I like it."

"I like that you like it," Anna said. She threw the wine goblet into the grass and propped her arms upon his chest and looked into his eyes. "You are a poet I think, and not a true soldier."

"Do you like that?" Stefan asked. He put his tanned hands upon her fingers lightly.

"I don't know," she said. She frowned at him, thinking. "It makes you different from the rest, I know that."

Stefan stood up quickly and dashed to his horse and returned waving Fortissimus wildly. "You are wrong," he cried with mock indignation. "I am a soldier, not a poet. You mistake my soft manner for weak character. You think I am an easy victim." He sat down beside her again and squeezed her hands, smiling. "But it is a trap. I lure them into carelessness and then my sword or my words cut them down."

"No, you are a poet," she said, sitting up, and leaning across his body on one arm. "A poet likes the simple instead of the complex, the inside instead of the outside, the small rather than the large. Soldiers ask what but you ask why. You are a poet."

"Am not," said Stefan.

"Are too!" Anna leaned closer. Stefan's hands embraced her hesitantly.

"Am not," he said weakly.

"Are too!" Her hazel eyes were soft and her lips parted slightly, but only to breathe, as her face sank imperceptibly closer to his— like the sun setting below the horizon behind them.

Just then, the dog yawned expansively, making the sound of a squeaky oxcart wheel. He stared impassively and uncomprehending at his master and the woman as their lips touched lightly, like a dewdrop sinking upon a leaf. The dog flopped over in the tall grass with a heavy sigh, rolling away from them, and closed his eyes again, unworried.

CHAPTER TWENTY-TWO

Pons and Guy Report a Deception

May 23, 1097 A.D.
Nicea, Anatolia

BAN ARSLAN IS RETURN-ING," SAID Bishop Adhemar to the noblemen of the Council of Knights.

"I thought he was a thousand miles east," said Short Breeches.

"He *was* a thousand miles east," Bohemund said roughly, "'cause his experience with those misbegotten bastards of Peter the Hermit's 'army' convinced him he had nothing to fear from any force originating west of Greece. He had better battles to fight. Those miserable pilgrims at least did us the favor of making us look like unskilled, uncivilized barbarians—"

"We'll not speak ill of the dead," the bishop interjected.

"—But now, my lords and ladies—" he paused to nod in the direction of Elvira, "—his spies have indicated that perhaps his judgment was in error." The Italian Norman searched the faces of the knights for a reaction. Their countenances were dark and hollow in the half-light of the flickering lamps and candles and expressionless. "Too bad for them and good for us—"

"Good for us?" asked Short Breeches.

"Good for us, because Aban Arslan is the head without which the Seljuk body cannot live. Cut off the head, and the body will twitch and die! And the sooner the better. We should tarry, not hasten, at Nicea—delay our attack until he comes."

"Perhaps he will cede Nicea and face us in the salt desert," Godfrey de Boullion suggested, speaking to the others.

"He'll come," said the blond Bohemund grimly, crushing a hazelnut between his fingers. "He'll come. His wife and children are inside the city at this very moment."

Robert of Flanders spoke: "The question is where he will attack our lines."

"The south," said Stefan. "He won't attack at the eastern gate because he would then be vulnerable to a counter-attack from the north and the south. The valley narrows and he won't bring his army past our armies on the east to attack the north. Nor will he swing behind the mountains to come in from the north because that will bring him too close to Pelecanum where the emperor is sitting with his troops. So he will attack the south from the south."

"Ha! That's what we *think* he'll do," Bohemund sneered. "You never know what a Seljuk infidel is up to."

"Alexius is at Pelecanum?" Robert asked.

"To ensure that supplies flow freely and to be available if the surrender of the city can be arranged by treaty," Stefan said.

"By treaty?" Hugh of Vermandois now entered the conversation. "By treaty? I don't trust Alexius," he said looking around at the others. "I don't trust Alexius."

"I thought Anna Comnena was at Pelecanurn for that purpose," Bohemund said sharply, looking at Stefan. The count shrugged, feeling a pang of pain. If he loved Anna, as he did, he knew that— by the very nature of things—it must be a secret love and, therefore, a *desperate* love. But he also realized that lovers want their love acknowledged and anything short of total recognition leads to nothing but despair. Stefan was prepared to be miserable.

After leaving Anna, Stefan had rejoined his army across the
Bosphorus. Stefan himself led the subsequent march in which the
army was protected on left and right, front and rear flanks by
mounted knights. They marched under the standards of Blois and
Chartres, and his captains, Caro, Everard, Geurin and Geoffrey
rode with him.

They sat astride war horses of the Ardennes that seemed as large
as elephants, so massive that they struck terror into the heart of any
foot soldier unfortunate enough to be in the way. The horses as
well as their riders were in full armor because Stefan was not willing
to take the chance that their passage to Nicea would be without
incident. Indeed, when they reached the Civetot, they saw the
bleached bones and skulls of the pilgrims who had met their deaths
a year before. The flesh had been picked clean by the birds of the
air and beasts of the field. Some skeletons lay on the shores of the
sea where they had vainly fled. In the bony hands of some were still
the stones they would've thrown at their attackers. Stefan had
dismounted in disbelief and had wandered through the death field
staring at the bodies, while the image of their enemy loomed larger
than ever, like the rising smoke of a burning field.

✠✠✠

I shook my head sadly. "I remember so well that passage through the Dracon,
the absolute horror of it when we realized the awful scale on which this
slaughter had occurred. But we were convinced that God would be with us. We
did not stop to consider the troubling question of why God had apparently
abandoned the pilgrims whose bones now lay at our feet. Nor did it occur to us
that God might similarly abandon us. I suppose we thought that while victory
was ultimately assured, it was never at any given point guaranteed."

"Were the knights afraid seeing this ... this destruction?" Bernard asked.

"We had never seen the enemy, but now we saw his work. No, we were not
afraid." Then I quoted Scripture. "We regarded these fallen pilgrims as ones
who all died in faith, not having received the promises, but having seen them

afar off, and persuaded of them, they embraced them, confessing that they were strangers and pilgrims upon the earth."

Bernard leaned over the *manuscript of the* Gesta Francorum. *"Let's continue," he said.*

"So we shall," I said.

✠✠✠

Stefan had led his army through the pass where wooden crosses had been erected at irregular intervals by scouts and engineers along the way to commemorate the dead. It was a huge army, marching through a forested corridor like an amorphous living organism snaking its way through the pass, its ranks so large that when Stefan broke through to the lake valley, the rear guards had yet to enter the pass behind.

The troops filed out of the divide into the flat, fertile fields that bordered Lake Ascanius on the north. They spent a night there where the air was fresh, and the mountains across the lake bedazzled them with their changing shape and color. The fire in the sky of that sunset, causing the evening light to dance upon the pale lake water, somehow bode well for the soldiers, rebalancing the horrors of the day. They took their evening meal in quiet optimism, even though they knew now, as they had not before, that they were well beyond the comfort of their native home, beyond the borders of the empire, and that they were not only *strangers* in a foreign land, they were *enemies* on a hostile frontier.

The lake was long and narrow extending east and west about twenty miles. At its extreme eastern end lay the Seljuk provincial capital, the ancient city of Nicea, home of the first and seventh ecumenical councils of the Church, and the city of Athanasius, Eusebius, Hosius and Arius. Strongly fortified by inner and outer walls, it was situated in a valley bounded on three sides by mountains and the fourth by the lake. It sat on an old Byzantine road and its recapture was critical to future success in Anatolia.

Godfrey and Raymond's troops had been at Nicea for several weeks and, until Bohemund's arrival, food had been scarce. One loaf of bread was selling for thirty denarii. Bohemund, however, was able to secure through Alexius a steady stream of supplies that came by both land and sea so that, from that time forward, the army at Nicea did not lack for food.

"This is Nicea," the bishop was saying as he stood over a map of the city which revealed an uneven pentagon with its west walls rising directly out of the shallow waters of the east end of Lake Ascanius. "You see the walls here some four miles long. Originally built in the fourth century, the Byzantines have kept them in constant repair which, of course, works to our disadvantage now. There are over 240 towers, and each one is equipped with *ballistae* making approach to the walls very difficult. We are preparing siege machines and building towers of our own at this very moment. We are hampered by moats here and here," he said, pointing to the eastern and southern gates.

"I'm sending miners and engineers in here," said Raymond, demonstrating where the southern wall joined the western wall near the lake.

"Good," said Adhemar. "The city is now under siege, effectively sealed off. No one goes in or out. Bohemund and the Allemanni are north, Geoffrey and the Franks are east, and Raymond and myself are south. For the city to survive, Arslan must break through our ranks. Our penetration of the walls is not critical to our success, but failure to do so will be time-consuming, delaying our advance into Anatolia."

✠✠✠

Guy thrust his long-handled spade into the earth and muttered: "I'm tired of dirt, aren't you?"

"Enough dirt to build a damned road to Jerusalem, I swear," said Pons, wiping his forehead with a grimy arm and leaning on his shovel. They were working the night watch, and along the walls of

Nicea small fires flickered, and from where they stood, a warm glow emanated from below the wall where the chink of axes and awls, blades and shovels could be heard. Above the two men, the sky was cloudless and deep, the stars bright and low. And when the wind stirred, it felt cool to the brow of these sweating laborers.

Count Raymond had indeed sent miners to the tower at the conjunction of the south and west walls. Their tactic was to burrow beneath the tower, supporting their work with great timbers until the wall and tower had been completely undermined. They would then set fire to the timber with the result that when the wood was consumed, the tower would collapse from a lack of support, thereby allowing the crusaders access to the city.

They made no secret of their intentions; the defenders of the city were quite aware of the objective. This made the beginning of the mining operation the most difficult, for the defenders attacked the miners ferociously, raining missiles and projectiles upon their heads. Raymond called for archers to periodically assail the defenders with a hailstorm of arrows while the miners built a wooden roof above the area where they would be working. Still, it wasn't uncommon for huge boulders to crash through these wooden ceilings injuring or killing the workers underneath, or for flaming bundles of straw to be cast upon the roof consuming it in fire.

The work went better at night when the defenders were hampered by darkness, when the miners could continue the sabotage with the aid of lamps and fires. Workers had been quickly assigned tasks, and the unskilled were given duties no more difficult than moving timber from beyond the walls to the subterranean cavity, or hauling dirt away in carts. The dirt was reserved nearby to be used to build a ramp over what they imagined would soon be the remains of the tower and that section of the wall.

"Let's make a break for the lake," Pons suggested, panting from exertion.

Guy agreed. "They won't miss us," he said.

"Where you off to?" called out someone as they walked off.

Guy turned back and shouted. "You want me to piss on your shovel, eh?" And then he disappeared behind some trees and ran swiftly for the lake nearby.

They washed their arms and faces in the cool water, splashing it upon their heads, letting it drip from the brow and soak in their beards. Pons could feel the slick growth of lake moss on the large stones inches below the water. He picked up a pebble and would've thrown it out upon the lake, but Guy restrained him. "Fool!" he said.

They sat on the shore in darkness a few feet from the tiny wavelets that splashed steadily on the rocks like a ticking clock telling the time of night. "Big lake," said Guy dreamily. "Never seen a lake this big ... Have you seen a lake this big, Pons?"

"Not this big, just ponds, small lakes, never a lake you couldn't see the other side of."

"Some people in the village had been to the ocean and they said it was huge and that you couldn't see the other side, but it couldn't be much bigger than this."

"Ten times bigger, dolt!" They were silent for a time before Guy spoke again.

"I fell in a lake once and nearly drowned when I was just a boy. We built a raft, wasn't even as good as the rafts we built at the Sava, and we only got it out about a fathom and the damm thing fell apart. I got real scared and just about died except someone pulled me out. My friends saved me only to turn me over to my father who nearly killed me. From that day I don't know whether I was more afraid of the water or my father. But I know I been powerfully a-feared of water ever since."

"Never saw my father," Pons said. "Killed in a fight before I was born."

"Well, I've been in trouble all my life." A loon called out across the lake. "You need a wife in your life, Pons!"

Pons turned and laughed. "Ha! I can't afford a wife and who'd have me?"

"You can arrange your own marriage—"

"I'm not meant for marriage," said Pons. "Some people are supposed to marry and some aren't. I aren't."

"Little Ponlets on your hearth. A woman with wide, childbearing hips, strong and stout, eh?" Guy grinned.

Then they heard sounds. "Ssshhh!" Pons whispered. Muffled sounds, voices far away and heavy sounds. They looked at each other in surprise and stepped quickly away from the shore to the western wall. The wall veered from the south tower to the lake and ran due north and south along the east end of the lake. Pons and Guy crept along its base hugging it tightly to avoid detection from sentries above.

Soon they were at the point where the wall met the water's edge. Here they bounded away behind some boulders near the large escarpment in the shallow water. They waited.

Across the pale distance they could make out a shape. "A boat, Pons!"

"Come on, let's get closer."

They drew close enough to hear voices distinctly, but not in a language Pons and Guy could understand. It was obvious that whatever was happening, it was a clandestine operation. Shadowy figures of men formed on the deck, moving about like phantoms on a ghost ship. Above, they heard the squeak of pulleys and winches; they saw in the moonlight, great bundles dragged up the walls, lurching and banging against the ancient stones to the top. "They're unloading … there's another boat … see there on the wall, they're hoisting stuff over the wall."

"What does it mean, Pons?"

"Quiet! Wait!"

They watched for about thirty minutes until the galley they were observing pulled away from shore and slid silently out to the open lake. It had no sooner departed than two more such ships oared to the western wall and the unloading began again.

"They're resupplying the city!" Pons exclaimed.

"Who they? Who?"

"Fool! The Turks!" He started to leave. "Come on! Count Raymond must be told!"

Guy protested as he clambered over the rocks to keep up with Pons. "Are you crazy? He just about had us killed in Constantinople and you want to wake him up in the dead of night?"

"We've got to tell him," said Pons. "He'll thank us."

Pons and Guy returned to the wall, thirty feet high, and darted along its base, touching it to steady themselves, feeling its water-smooth surface polished by centuries of weathering. They followed it to the south tower where they could hear the mining still in progress.

"We need horses," Pons said.

"I don't think this is a good idea," Guy complained. "And the last time you had a good idea, we were publicly humiliated and very nearly publicly mutilated as well!"

"Beaten to death, you mean," Pons corrected. "That was a *bad* idea; this is a *good* idea. Come along."

They found the horses hobbled in a stand of poplars. At the approach of Pons and Guy, they began to shuffle about nervously. Above them, the breeze rattled the poplar leaves, covering the sound of the conversation. Pons grabbed the reins of one and leapt upon its bare back nimbly. He spurred his steed and was prepared to dash away, but Guy was still struggling to get on his horse.

"Quickly now, friend. Quickly!" Pons urged.

"I'm trying, as God is my witness," said Guy exasperated.

"Haven't you ridden a horse?"

Guy was indignant. "Of course I have."

"Then get on the blessed animal and let's ride."

Guy struggled with a horse that would not cooperate, whatever his intentions for it. But, momentarily, he was astride the animal quite pleased with himself.

"Are you ready now?" Pons asked.

"I'm ready." At that, Pons hunkered over his horse and galloped into the night. At the same instant, Guy's horse bolted after Pons in a sudden start that jolted Guy to his back. Thus, with his feet in the air and laying flat on his back, Guy sallied forth toward the camp of the count.

They drew close to the camp, a city of tents spread out on the south plain, an army asleep while sentries posted guard at points on the perimeter warming themselves at fires. They approached one such guard station.

"We must see the Count of Toulouse immediately," cried Pons. "Can you tell us where his camp is?"

Said the first guards "I can tell you, but that doesn't mean I will."

Said the second: "It's only the third hour, and you wake the count?"

"On my mother's grave, you may have my life if I do not have the most urgent news," Pons said quickly. "Where is his camp?"

When they had elicited the information from the sentries, they rode off again, and within minutes, after convincing more guards of the importance of their mission, they stood inside the count's large and, by all accounts, luxurious tent. The interior was soft with low lamp light; pillows were strewn about on the carpeted ground; a table and chairs were positioned in the center of the room. To the side, a veiled passageway led to the count's bedchamber. They heard movements within and protests when he was awakened by a servant. Then he stood before the Provencals, tall, angular, and filled with the stupor of sleep. Pons and Guy dropped deferentially to one knee but the count would have none of it.

"Stand up, stand up," he said. He peered at the men intently as the lamps were turned up. "Yes, yes, I remember you two," for the servant had forewarned him. "What sort of trouble are you in now?" He sat down heavily at the table, and rubbed his face vigorously as though by massaging it to resurrect some life in it.

Pons was surprised now at how old the count appeared. His hair was thin and gray and beneath the high cliff of a forehead, the rest of his face seemed fallen, like an avalanche, sagging about the chin and cheeks, only a nose protruding and unmoved amid the facial rubble. Feeling overwhelmed, Pons began: "Begging you pardon, m' lord, your humble and loyal servants have witnessed something that may be vital to the suc—"

Guy broke in: "The Turks are resupplying the city, m' lord." The count's hands stopped their massage, and he moved them away from his face, staring at the men. "The Turks are doing what?" he said.

"The Turks are resupplying the city," Guy repeated.

"Impossible! The city's sealed and it's been sealed for almost a fortnight now. No one and nothing is getting into the city."

"By the lake, m' lord," Pons said. The count was awake now. "The Turks are resupplying the city over the lake by night. We saw so tonight with our very eyes. They're unloading at this very moment. We can take you there."

The count and his men dressed and within ten minutes they were ready to depart. Pons made a suggestion. "Our spying must be in secret. It requires silence and cunning. Perhaps there are too many of us. We can show you the way."

The count looked at Pons quizzically as though the notion of Pons and Guy being involved in anything cunning and quiet was strange beyond belief. Nevertheless, he waved the men away. They were about to ride when Pons said, "My lord," and nodded toward Guy who was attempting to mount his horse. Raymond looked at Pons who shrugged. A guard, understanding the situation, gave Guy a boost and the three rode away.

The three men concealed themselves below the towering west wall in the large stones and boulders that were scattered beneath it. The barges were still being unloaded. They could see the thick hemp ropes swaying from the western battlements to the boats in the shallow water, Slowly, supplies were inched heavenward to unseen hands high on the ramparts.

✠✠✠

Thus, Pons and Guy became heroes in the eyes of Count Raymond of Toulouse. Gifts were thrust upon them which they attempted to refuse, but in the end, gladly accepted. Pons took the opportunity to remind the count of one thing.

"I was one of your chief engineers at one time, begging your pardon," he said.

"Where?" asked the count.

"Compostella," said Pons, encouraged.

The count glanced to the ceiling of his tent, trying to recall. "Compostella ... hmmm."

"The siege tower ..."

"Ah, the siege tower!" he exclaimed. "I remember now. You designed a tower with an additional floor to give us the height to scale the walls. And what has happened since then?"

"After the war, I returned to Provence, but there were famines, I had to sell my tools, and live by my wits, and I don't have many of them you know." He laughed nervously.

By this twist in the providence of God, Pons and Guy hoped their fortunes would now begin to change. Their exploits, in any case, were proclaimed far and near throughout the camps. A stunned Council of the Knights sent Bohermund of Tarranto to Pelecanum to confer with the emperor. Alexius quickly dispatched imperial ships to the lake and within days the city was again sealed and under siege.

Bohemund returned to Nicea from Pelecanum with Anna Comnena under his escort. She had won the trip over the objections of the emperor by arguing that her presence would indicate to the impatient troops that the armies had the full support of the empire, in spite of the emperor's apparent lack of support for the earlier pilgrims whose bones now were scattered throughout the Dracon valley and had been seen by all. It was a flimsy excuse, and Anna was certain her father regarded it as such, believing she had made such a proposal only as a way to spend time with her escort, Bohemund.

Their entourage was small but heavily armed and scouts preceded their way to Nicea. Bohemund assumed his role as protector jealously even though Anna would scarcely converse with him. They rode swiftly in slow silence until it was necessary to stop to refresh the horses.

Anna was taking nourishment when Bohemund strolled into the grassy clearing where she was resting. "There is a sun in the sky but a cloud on your face," he said in Norman French, hoping to goad her into speech.

She did not answer him at first, but then she said: "I do not know what is on my face but I know what is in my heart."

"And what is that, may I ask?"

"You have asked two questions," she replied, looking at him. "Which do you want answered?"

"I am permitted but one question?"

"The latter."

"Yes."

"Yes, I may ask?"

"Yes."

"And what is that?"

"And what is what?"

"And what is it that you know is in your heart."

"I cannot tell you."

"You said I could ask."

"I did not say I would answer."

"You could tell me, but you will not tell me."

"Either way, what is in my heart is not for you to know," she said.

"You should not keep secrets from the man who will be your husband," he said.

Anna looked at him again, nervously aware of his handsome appearance, the strength of jaw and subtlety of his eyes. "You shall not be my husband," she said with conviction.

Bohemund shrugged. "I don't know much about matters of the heart," he said, "but I do know about the affairs of state. I shall be your husband. It has been decided."

"Be my husband if you wish, Bohemund, but I shall not be your wife. It's as simple as that."

"You talk in riddles," he said, grinning. Then in Greek he said that he loved her.

"But I do not love you," she answered, "but then, as you pointed out, this has nothing to do with love. It is a political arrangement, nothing more, and certainly much less. You marry me, but will love someone else. I marry you, but will love someone else."

"Exactly!" Bohemund exclaimed. "A marriage is always made not out of love but out of convenience. Friendships are made out of love."

Anna stood. "As for me,' she announced, "I shall neither marry you for convenience, nor be your friend out of love." She strode to her horse.

Bohemund stood and followed her, matching stride for stride and speaking as he walked. "You have no choice," he shouted at her.

"Why not?" she asked, taking the reins of her horse.

"You cannot disobey your father. Can't you see? We were enemies, but now we are friends. Our marriage will unite the empire with the west. You must choose marriage or death. There are no other choices."

"There is one other choice."

"What is that?"

Anna mounted her horse and looked down at the prince of Tarranto. "I shall not marry you."

"Then you will die," he said.

"Or you will die," she said. "That is the other choice." She spurred her horse and galloped away.

CHAPTER TWENTY-THREE

The Emperor Makes a Surprise Announcement

May 21, 1097 A.D.

NEWS REACHED CAMP THAT THE sultan's army was only miles away in the southern hills. It mattered not whether the army was ten miles or two miles: The announcement was greeted with both enthusiasm and rising apprehension. They had seen devastation and death, but like the wind, they had not seen the force which had caused it. Now they were about to. Most were anxious to dip their swords in Saracen blood. They had waited long and endured much for the opportunity to kill a Turk, recounting, as they waited about the campfires at night, the tortuous march across the Alps, the long journey through the Rhineland, Thrace and Macedonia, strange customs and irritating inconveniences.

The battle would be fought on the open southern plain. Raymond spread out his army there. Women, children and noncombatants were moved to the eastern valley. Tents were collapsed and trenches dug. War horses were reshod and swords and lances sharpened. Archers filled their quivers with new arrows and restrung their bows. Red crosses were painted on shields of white. Half albs of linen were prepared with the crosses stitched on front and back to be worn over coats of mail. Banners and standards bearing the cross were also readied.

Early on the morning of May 20, Adhemar served communion to the soldiers with the assistance of many hundreds of priests. The army then mounted and awaited their enemy. But the sultan did not appear. By noon, the crusaders disbanded; their victory or martyrdom postponed, they prepared for battle on the morrow.

The next day, communion was again given to the warriors and the great Ardennes war horses were readied. Adhemar took command of the right flank, while mounted knights numbering ten thousand assembled according to their legions on the plain. Foot soldiers were in rank behind the knights, and archers readied their arrows for flight over the front ranks.

The sultan's army appeared this time as quietly and suddenly as a cloud casts a shadow on the earth, out of the southern woods and hills growing larger, deeper and darker with each passing minute. A murmur swelled through the ranks of the crusaders. The spirit had become flesh, the incorporeal corporeal.

But in the very moment the shadow became substance, all fear deserted them and courage came to their aid. The white banner of the cross flashed in the wind. A trumpet sounded the alarm. A voice called out, "Deus vult!" This cry was repeated and it soon took on the sound of a song.

Horse and rider raced toward each other, and the plains of Nicea shook under the thunderous pounding of hoofs. A western army, thousands of miles from its homeland, butting heads with an eastern army fighting on its own soil, the world enduring yet another spectacle of armies on an open battlefield such as they had witnessed before at Thermopylae, Carthage and Poitiers. Cain striking Abel; it would certainly not be the last such battle. Steel upon steel, sword slashing flesh, and lance piercing armor. Horses panicked, knights were knocked off their mounts and fell heavily to the ground. Unable to arise in their suits of armor, they struggled in the churning earth until they were trampled to death, or smitten by a mortal blow.

The cross the crusaders bore was soiled as it was in every battle, by either blood or dirt. Christians perished beside Moslems who perished beside Christians. The frequency of death and the apparently infinite availability of soldiers on either side made the outcome of this contest initially unclear. The Saracens assaulted the southern army with wave after wave of mounted warriors, but Raymond was able to match foe with foe. Had Godfrey and Bohemund from the north been able to join forces with Raymond, the conflict would end quickly in favor of the empire. But they could not leave the defense of the northern or eastern gates.

Raymond's forces, however, were tired. This is the news that Count Stefan of Blois received late in the morning. Stefan decided to take action.

"We'll swing southeast beyond Raymond's flank in an encircling maneuver," he argued, studying his maps. "If Arslan has left troops in reserve in the eastern hills and brings them into the void, Godfrey and Bohemund will drop down here attacking from the north … What do you think, Caro?"

Stefan's lieutenant stood beside him bending over the charts for a better look at the plan. He was dressed out in chain mail, leather vest, the white and red, sword buckled and at the ready. His face was young and his eyes were eager. "I think he has put all of his men into the assault here, my lord, pointing to the south. "I also think he has underestimated our strength, and I do not doubt that when he sees he is overmatched that he will retreat and concede the city."

"Everard?

"I agree," he said, looking up from the map. "Our second battle with Arslan will be the true test of strength because then he will be certain to match us in strength and cunning. He'll not make the same mistake twice."

"Then, we'll do it," said Stefan with finality.

✠✠✠

Caro's assessment proved to be prescient. When Stefan, mounted on his high-stepping steed, led his enormous army into the conflict, his hand on the hilt of Fortissimus, the Turks were thrown into confusion and could not join the battle on two fronts. The sultan quickly ordered the withdrawal, and retreated into the southern hills, leaving Nicea to its fate.

The elated soldiers of Count Raymond's army, now imbued with renewed strength, chased the marauders back to their camp and beyond, a response against which Alexius had sternly admonished them. In this case, the impulse was harmless for the Turks had not prepared an ambush, confidently believing that one would not be necessary. Indeed, when the soldiers overran their camps they discovered wagons and carts piled high with the very ropes the Turks had intended to use on their captives to bind them and carry them into captivity. The discovery of these ropes gave particular joy to the weary soldiers who attached the carts to Turkish horses and drove them back to their own camp where the arrogance of the Saracen could be displayed to all.

The attempt to undermine and collapse the south tower had still not succeeded. Now, however, a consensus developed that such an effort was unnecessary: the city would surrender since its leaders knew they were utterly without help. To hasten that conclusion, that very same day Bohemund ordered the heads of the Turkish dead to be posted on pikes outside the walls where defenders could plainly see them from the battlements. Catapults were rolled up to the south wall, while vegetable wagons heaped high with Saracen heads like a load of cabbages were brought out. Soldiers grabbed each bloody head by the hair and flung it upon the catapult and launched it over the city walls in an attempt to discourage the general population. The carcasses of dead horses were likewise placed in giant catapults and jettisoned over the walls in the hope that the decaying bodies might spread disease among the inhabitants. All of these actions were accomplished with great joy and alacrity. The sultan had been humbled and convincingly so; the mood in the camp that night was euphoric.

Euphoric, and more so, as flagons of wine were filled and emptied by adventure-starved Christians who believed that in the bloody carnage of the day, they had defended the honor of Christ.

The soldiers drank, the women danced, and the children sang. Addie clasped her daughter in her arms, stroking her golden hair away from her face and watched. She sat away from the fire and the dancing and rocked her child.

"Mother, now will we be in Jerusalem soon?" Clare asked.

"Perhaps." The child nodded. Just then a man strode briskly toward them and exclaimed: 'What now, Addie? You're not celebrating with the rest?" Addie shook her head and smiled.

"Come on, then," said Pons, "You must dance with me tonight, or we may never dance again!"

Addie refused. "Clare is tired and—"

"Give the child to me," roared Guy happily. "I'll make sure she sleeps in this confusion!" He reached for the girl and hefted her lightly in his arms and began to rock her as he sang:

Close your eyes and sing this song,
The sky is dark and the night is long;
You are sweet and an angel's light,
A gift from God, a star so bright;
Close your eyes and sing this song,
Your mother's here, your fear is gone.

Addie followed Pons into the boisterous center of the wine-sotted revelers, and uncertain at first, began to dance swaying slowly, then lifting her arms and clapping her hands. Soon she was grabbing her skirt and kicking up her feet, pounding the earth with wild abandon as were the others. She lifted her mouth to the spray of wine and felt it burn her tongue and flow down the corners of her mouth. She wiped it away, and took more.

Then she yelled at the top of her voice, but scarcely heard by others in the din of the celebration: "Look at me, Pons!"

Pons looked at her and it was not for the first time.

"I'm dancing!" She twirled and swayed, jumped and skipped, laughed and hollered, sang and drank. And when Pons took her in his arms later that night and kissed her full upon her mouth, an incredible fever possessed her by which she truly believed that there was no sorrow that was not worth this one moment of inexplicable joy.

✠✠✠

The next morning, the camp of the Israelites awoke, groggy and ill, to discover that while the walls of Jericho were still standing, imperial banners were floating over the battlements. They blinked in disbelief; it could mean only one thing: the city had surrendered to the Byzantines during the night.

The Council of the Knights met that afternoon in the emperor's residence at Pelecanum. They sat at a horseshoe-shaped table and listened while the emperor explained.

"You acquitted yourselves with courage and bravery at Nicea," Alexius began. "I commend all of you. Last night, the Seljuk authorities, on instructions from the sultan Aban Arslan, turned the city over to our intermediaries. Briefly, the terms of the surrender were these: The transfer of power will take place in an orderly and peaceful manner. No Turks will be held for ransom, there will be no sack of the city, and Turkish dignitaries including the wife and children of Aban Arslan will be transported to Constantinople with the promise of safe conduct." Alexius sat down.

This news was greeted with silence as cold as a mountain wind. Council members began to confer with one another until their malcontented murmuring had swirled into a boisterous storm of protest. "You have betrayed us," Short Breeches brayed.

Alexius raised his hands for silence. "I have not betrayed you in any manner," he said.

Tancred, the nephew of Bohemund, arose, and pointed at the emperor. "We were promised the city," he shouted.

"We should have been informed of the negotiations," Godfrey de Boullion complained. "Our losses were heavy against Arslan; we invested many lives in this assault."

"No negotiations could have forestalled the battle against Arslan," Alexius returned. "It was only after the battle fought so brilliantly and a victory achieved so decisively, that the city agreed to come to terms. Until then, they still believed that the sultan would come to their aid and collapse the siege."

Tancred stood up and spoke: "But you have given the Turks safe conduct, escorted them and their possessions out of the city. You are treating them as friends when it is certain that they would not have treated us as friends had the battle gone the other way. We have the ropes with which they would have bound us and sent us into captivity. You give them their possessions and their lives; they give us fetters and death."

Cheers and applause followed these comments, but Alexius countered: "The battle was against the Turks, but *Nicea is essentially a Christian city*. It would not be proper to pillage and sack a city that, except for the past few years, has been our city with our citizens living in it. Our citizens have lived in peace with the Turkish garrison posted there. It was no more than right to treat them with respect and courtesy."

"Still, you betrayed us just like you betrayed Peter a year ago," Tancred reminded.

The room was instantly still again. Alexius would not let this pass. The emperor walked swiftly into the open end of the table to where Tancred stood. "I did not betray Peter," he roared, slamming his hand upon the table. "Peter and Walter arrived *uninvited* in Constantinople, and *I did everything in my power to keep them there*. But the barbarian behavior of their people made this impossible. I moved them across the Bosporus to the Civetot only as a last resort, and *if they had stayed at the Civetot*, they would have been safe. Instead, they wanted to fight the Turks. They went against all the advice I gave them, and you have seen the results! Do you, too, want to go against my advice, Tancred? Are you at your age so wise?"

Alexius whirled away from Tancred and returned to his place at the head. Then he continued, finger wagging in Tancred's direction, determined to embarrass him. "You are nothing but a young pup who has done little but soil the dignity, respect and reputation of your countrymen. You complain about having nothing, and you are entitled to nothing, and you shall get nothing until you understand that: you are fighting for the emperor at the request of the Holy Father, in my country, and for the return of my lands."

Tancred squared his jaw, stood straight and spoke without a quaver: "Then we are entitled to nothing from each other, for you shall have nothing more from me unless you fill a tent brimming with gold and present it to me and do the same for the others here."

It was the purest impudence and recognized as such by all including a guard standing nearby who protested Tancred's remarks. Tancred, turning to leave the hall, shoved him out of the way. But the guard grabbed the youth and threw him to the floor. Instantly Godfrey, Short Breeches and others rushed to his aid, while everyone stood prepared to join the melee. When the shouting had stopped, Bohemund was standing before his nephew who was shaken and disheveled. Alexius had not moved. Others crowded around the two.

Bohemund and Tancred exchanged glances, one of reproof, the other of defiance. Then, without warning, Bohemund raised his hand, brought it across his body and smote Tancred on the side of the face. The youth's head snapped violently, but he did not move or cry out.

"You have a lot to learn about manners," said Bohemund. "You have misspoke and offended. You owe the emperor an apology." Tancred continued to stare insolently at his uncle for a few moments. The veins in his temple pulsated, his mouth opened slightly to breathe, the nostrils flared. He looked at the others in the room and finally at the emperor himself; bowing slightly in his direction, he whirled and left the room.

The Council of Knights resumed their places. Bohemund's behavior had been apology enough. Alexius Comnena resumed. "I understand your frustration. In this case, there was no other way. In future campaigns, you yourselves will be required to negotiate the terms of surrender; you will decide how to treat your vanquished foe. I will not be with you, but I caution you to treat your enemy with respect. Having conquered them in war, do not abuse them in peace. If you deal harshly and unjustly with them, they will deal harshly and unjustly with you or your children someday. You'll sow seeds of destruction that your children will harvest.

"I will keep supply lines open, but I can go no farther with you. I have made arrangements for every crusading soldier to be presented with a gift of food. In addition, I am making the sultan's treasury available to you. I do not need it. You will each, with the exception of Tancred, be given more gold and jewels than you will have need of. Distribute this wealth to your soldiers, or keep it for yourselves. It is none of my affair. As for Nicea, your soldiers and non-combatants will be allowed to visit the city in supervised groups of ten. That is all."

The Council of Knights now felt embarrassed and ashamed of their earlier petulance. The venerable Count Raymond of Toulouse reminded the Council: "Perhaps we have forgotten that we are in the service of God and the Holy Mother Church. We are pilgrims to the sacred sites of the Holy Land. We have sworn to fight the infidel and the antichrist, not accrue riches for ourselves." The Council was rebuked and chastened. The meeting was over.

Bohemund stayed behind after the others left. "Your daughter appears to be uninterested in marriage," he said to Alexius. "Her love is difficult to win."

Alexius smiled. "My daughter is obedient, but not *blindly* obedient. An unfortunate byproduct of a good education is that, in learning how to think, one forgets how to obey. It is not necessary for you to win her love but to win her obedience."

"But she will not obey me until she is my wife," the prince of Tarranto replied.

"And she will not be your wife until she obeys me. Is that what you mean?"

"Precisely, my lord!"

Alexius laughed. "Then do not fear. She shall be your wife. But in matters of love as in matters of war, patience is a virtue. We will announce the betrothal at the dinner tomorrow night."

Alexius and the Comneni feted the western princes and their consorts in the home of the sultan in Nicea. Its walls were inlaid of beautiful blue tiles from the pottery mills near Nicea. The floors were of Polycronnesian marble, and the domed ceiling was supported by graceful, fluted marble columns. The emperor ordered entertainment in the form of dancing girls and troubadours who played Anatolian music on flute and lyre. The tables were overlaid with linens and silks, and burdened with racks of lamb, venison and many delicacies native to Nicea and Anatolia. Anna Comnena sat beside her father and on his left, Bohemund. Beside Anna sat her uncle George Palaeologus, while to Bohemund's left was the youthful and dark-haired Elvira, wife of Count Raymond of Toulouse seated next to her.

Stefan ate little. For love of France, he had been unwilling to leave Chartres, and now for love of Anna, he was unwilling to leave Nicea. Love, it could not be love! Was he dreaming? How could these thoughts be in his head? Still, why could he think of nothing but her? Why were his eyes constantly following her like a bird follows the sun. He looked at his food. He did not want food; he wanted love. And food, like life itself, without love, was tasteless. He felt sick.

Alexius stood and begged for a moment to speak. The great hall grew still like a dying wind, and when the last wisp of conversation had ceased, he said: "I have news of great joy and happiness to me and our empire. For it is the announcement of matrimony bringing together the kingdoms of the east and of the Italian and Norman states."

Anna gasped and put her hand to her throat. Her eyes widened at these words. Stefan watched her curiously. Bohemund leaned forward slightly and smiled at her.

"There are many fine princes and nobles among this notable gathering tonight, but most of you are already worthy husbands who have forsaken the love of wife and warmth of the hearth to defend our lands and rescue the holy city. But there is one who has distinguished himself as a soldier for many years, and promises to be a leader of his people for many years to come, and it is to Bohemund of Tarranto that I have given the hand of my daughter in marriage!"

Stefan gripped the edge of the table. The room grew dark amid the sounds of the applause, and shouting faded in his ears. A film covered his eyes, and his breathing felt constricted, lie choked; his food lodged in his throat. He pushed at the tightness around his neck and moved away from the table. He tasted treachery, and the worst of it was he couldn't be sure of its source, although he was blindly loath to admit that Anna might have been party to it.

The princess arose trance-like when her father spoke these words and walked carefully to the center of the room where her father now stood and where he now expected her to be. She joined him amid the wild cheering and waited while Bohemund likewise stepped to his side where Alexius brought together their hands in the sign of betrothal. Anna felt his touch as the brand of a hot iron and removed it immediately. Bohemund, unknown to many until his participation in the pilgrimage, had quickly established himself as a battlefield strategist and was generally well-liked, although some of the princes had been initially repulsed by his blatant attempt to be named the commander-in-chief of the Anatolian forces. Alexius' announcement, judging from the enthusiastic response, seemed to be well-accepted.

The news effectively capped a week of tremendously encouraging events for the crusading force. That the endeavor was a success was now beyond dispute. The idea and ideology of the crusade was sound, the wisdom of the Holy Father and the eastern emperor could not be challenged. And with the news of this engagement, the commitment of Alexius to the enterprise of the soldiers could no longer be doubted.

When the shouting and applause had dissipated, Anna begged to be excused on the grounds that she was ill due to the excitement. This Alexius seemed to understand. Anna arose, and without saying a further word, departed from the hall.

Minutes later, a page appeared at Stefan's side and would have given him a message, but Bohemund, who was moving about the room conversing with guests, intercepted the message, and opened the folded note. It read: South tower. West wall, ninth hour. Hurry. But it was in Greek and Bohemund didn't understand a word of it. He gave it back to the page and walked away.

Stefan read the note carefully, understanding immediately. Not long after, he, too, left the hall.

✠✠✠

They met at the south tower. Anna was astride her horse. She said nothing, but instead began to ride, her cape fluttering in the wind. They galloped away, Stefan and Anna, riding hard against the wind, outracing the moon until they were far away on the south shore of Lake Ascansius. Then they dismounted and wrapped each other in their arms.

"Why didn't you tell me?" Stefan wailed.

"I wanted to, but I couldn't!" They kissed long and fearfully. "I didn't know this was going to happen tonight, I didn't know!"

"We are but three months from Jerusalem," said Stefan. "When we arrive, I shall send for you."

"And I shall come, *carrissimus*. I shall come!" Anna threw her arms about his neck and clung to him desperately.

CHAPTER TWENTY-FOUR

The Long March

The kalends of August, 1097 A.D.

he previous month began with a battle that was critical to the fortunes of the Christians. A failure to defend at Dorylaeum would invalidate every triumph large or small hitherto achieved. This Stefan and every captain and foot soldier of the army knew well, doubling their efforts with courage and determination. Women and children hauled water to the front lines fearlessly, every ploughman turned soldier raised his shields defiantly. The battle on this day was a contest for souls and for the soul of the pilgrimage. If man, woman and child had strength to give, it was given; if they had breath, they breathed it; if they had voice, they raised it.

Their courage, however magnificent, was matched sinew and soul by the Turks themselves. They kept coming and coming, even after high numbers of their own had been knocked off their mounts by Christian arrows. The bodies of the Saracen dead as well as the Christian dead lay face down in the white, powdery Anatolian dust. The wounded had no one to attend their needs except for Fulcher the priest who, with other clerics, gave extreme unction where it was warranted. The sun waxed warm; the sky seemed dry, not wet or cool, and the soldiers knocking away Saracen arrows could taste blood on their parched, thick tongues. Some fainted in the sun, collapsing in their armor. Others, who had no armor but only shields, were more frequently shot. Even those with armor sustained mortal wounds, for Arslan's archers shot high and low. Selecting a target, a pair of Turks would raise their bows. The one shooting high forced the defender's shield up, whereupon the second Turk zinged a arrow low in the belly or thigh.

When the armies of Adhemar and Raymond of Toulouse appeared on the flank, the outcome of the battle of Dorylaeum was no longer in doubt. The Saracens not only retreated, but retreated in panic, as Adhemar marched his army resolutely down the crest attacking them from the rear and closing them in. Stefan, meanwhile, began a sweep with right and left flanks in an attempt to attach with Adhemar's right and left thereby enclosing the Saracen army. But the Saracens realized immediately the consequences of any hesitation in retreat. They broke rank quickly, leaving behind their fallen. The attempt to contain them on the field of battle failed.

✠✠✠

Arslan was determined not to have his intelligence fail him one more time. The Danaishmends and Cappadocians had not arrived in time. Their representatives were now in his tent. They wanted to attack at once.

"I have lost Nicea, I have depleted my stock of arrows and weapons, the greater part of my treasury is now in the hands of the barbarians, and you want me to attack them again. Fools! You are too late. The Franks are strong, stronger than we thought ... more courageous than we thought. They could be good Turks." The sultan stood up, called for his horse and stepped outside into the hot, afternoon sun. The tribal captains and emirs followed him.

Arslan shielded his eyes and looked across the shimmering expanse of the Great Salt Desert. A foot soldier brought his black stallion. He mounted.

"The Franks cannot be beaten right now," he announced. He turned his horse about. "Only one thing can defeat them, one thing and only one thing and it's not us."

"Who then?" called out one.

"Not us, but the land," he said, motioning toward the desert with a sweep of his arm. "The land."

"The land?"

"Look at this land. What do you see?"

Puzzled, they looked into the empty, flatness of pale dirt and dry brush. The wind swelled and blew rootless weeds across the Roman road, and swept away a layer of dust from the highway.

"Nothing," they said.

"Precisely," Arslan said. "Nothing can conquer the Franks at this moment, and nothing is precisely what shall conquer them after all!" He laughed out loud. "Nothing!" he shouted, "Nothing shall be their conqueror! Nothing shall defeat them! They shall attempt a crossing of this great Anatolian *nothing* and they shall die. I shall order every city and village evacuated and burned to the ground, all the granaries and supplies of food destroyed. The fruit of the orchards shall be plucked. The wells shall be poisoned. Our flocks and herds shall be moved together with our people. And there will be nothing!" He laughed uproariously again. "Nothing," he cried, stretching out his arms to the desert. "Nothing!"

✠✠✠

Addie peered at the scrap of leather tied to a birch thirty paces away. The leaves stirred with a puff of wind, branches swept across her vision. She raised the bow imperceptibly higher and closed her left eye. Then she sighted down the length of the arrow focusing momentarily on the fine red thread securing the sharpened flint to the shaft. The bowstring sank into her fingers as she forced it back. She steadied herself, checked her sight, and released the arrow.

It flew with a whirr toward the tree and nailed the leather patch with a twang and a thud! "Good shot!" cried an exuberant Pons.

"I have a good teacher," Addie shouted at him triumphantly as he removed the arrow from the tree.

"You're right there! But a good teacher with a poor student is wasting his talents," Pons said, returning. "You—" he poked her in the shoulder, "—have the gift!"

Addie blushed. "I *am* pretty good, aren't I?"

Pons laughed. "Good, but not the best. Come along. I have something else for you." He took her by the hand and pulled her away from the clearing and into the woods. She flung the bow and quiver over her shoulder and followed. They ducked beneath branches and padded lightly over the soft earth along a path that was lined with rotting tree limbs. Minutes later they emerged in another small meadow in an upper slope of the hills north of Dorylaeum.

"Now you stay here," Pons said. Addie waited as Pons ran ahead to the base of a tree where he had fastened a piece of twine and stretched it across the meadow. To this twine he had secured a piece of rabbit fur about twice the size of a man's hand, which he could then pull by means of another string across the meadow about a foot above the grass.

"When you see the rabbit," he told Addie, "remember the speed of the arrow, plus the distance away from the target, then sight just in front of the target and shoot. Get off two shots if you can."

Addie nodded, got in her stance and checked to make sure her quiver was positioned properly over her shoulder. Pons returned to the rabbit. "Are you ready?' he called out. "I'm not going to tell you when."

"I'm ready," Addie shouted.

"Keep your bow down," he yelled. Pons wanted to duplicate as much as possible actual hunting conditions. Addie dropped her bow, and stood out of her stance relaxed but waiting. Then suddenly the gray patch of fur jerked and dashed along the twine.

Pons had it running too fast, she thought. She leaped into her stance and brought her bow up with her left hand, while at the same time she reached over her shoulder with her right hand and grabbed an arrow, clamping it immediately to the bowstring. She sighted along the shaft, aimed and released the arrow. It flew through the air like a bolt of lightning, but past its mark, and before Addie could get off another shot, the rabbit had disappeared into the brush.

"You missed," said Pons smiling. "Don't take so much time to aim. Go with your instincts."

"You pulled the rabbit too fast."

They tried it again. This time Addie got off two shots but they both missed their target. They tried again, and again she shot twice and missed twice. "You only need to hit a rabbit once, but with larger game you need two shots and you have to hit the target both times," Pons said. He wasn't making it easy for her. "You're deadly with a stationary target; this will come, you'll see. Keep practicing." He patted her on the back and returned to the rabbit. "Don't hit me," he joked.

She glared at him darkly and reviewed the steps in her mind. She saw the rabbit and missed—twice. She saw it again and missed. She saw it a third time and missed even when Pons pulled it slowly. She gave up.

"That's enough," she said, tired. "I'll try again tomorrow. I'll learn, you'll see." She pulled up her leather boots until they were snug again, and tugged at her wool shirt, impatient with herself and ready to leave.

"Think of a moving target as actually stationary for a brief instant in time," Pons explained. "You just have to hit it in that split second of time and know where the target is going to be ... you'll do—"

"Wait!" Addie whispered. "Look!" She jumped into her stance, brought the bow up, snapped an arrow to the bowstring, and drew it back with her right elbow high and level. Pons saw a full grown rabbit bound out of a thicket and into the meadow, running a twisting, irrational course through the grass, stopping briefly and then hopping away again. Addie's bow was ready, the bowstring taunt. She released the arrow; the string snapped with a twang. Immediately she notched another arrow, shut her left eye and squeezed her right eye until it had only the quarry in sight. Aiming along the shaft, she suddenly saw the rabbit as a stationary target in a moving frame of time. She released the arrow which journeyed swiftly to an unlikely spot, but which, when it had reached its destination, found the rabbit there, too. The dart—this time—was deadly. They saw the rabbit tumble into the air and hit the ground with a flop and a squeal.

Addie's eyes widened in disbelief. "I got it!" she shouted, jumping proudly. "I got it!"

"Come on," said Pons as they ran toward the rabbit. He found the animal with an arrow thrust completely through its body at the shoulder. He whistled in admiration.

"The poor creature didn't have a chance," he said.

Addie struck him on the shoulder. "Now don't you try to make me feel bad," she teased. "Tonight we're having stew."

And they did. "Your mother shot this rabbit," Pons said to Clare a thousand times.

Two weeks later, they were on the third road of Tacitus, the road that skirted the southern edge of the Salt Desert from Philomelium to Iconium. They had been walking for twelve days under a hot August sun. Addie could not abide the heat. Her feet were swollen; putting on and taking off her boots was a painful ordeal. In any case, her boots would not last long. They already were in need of repair. Hildy's feet were lacerated and infected.

✠✠✠

"Many of the knights had been reduced to traveling on foot because their horses had died," I said. "They themselves suffered heat prostration, passing out, becoming ill, or even dying, because they had to travel in their suits of armor,

there being insufficient room on the baggage wagons to carry it. Some knights rode atop oxen. It was humorous for the pilgrim to behold, but humiliating for the knight to experience. A knight in full armor mounted on an ox! A proud knight on a humble ox. Such sights kept morale high. Pope Urban had envisioned an army of mounted knights riding off to Jerusalem, but not an army of knights mounted on oxen! And those who could not ride on some animal walked on foot, while dogs, goats and sheep were used to pull carts when necessary.

"And who was blamed for these difficulties? God? No, no, not at all. Why blame an ineffable God when you can blame the insufferable Greeks! The Byzantine guides were certainly doing their best, but after twenty years of warfare, numerous raids, and with roads and bridges falling into disrepair, the guides, who were often unfamiliar with the local roads anyway, frequently suggested poor roads and wrong turns. Of course, the pilgrims believed it was done intentionally. Not having a cloud by day and a pillar of fire by night, they were forced to accept Greek guides, and they were not always happy about it. But—they would see a comet in the sky, and everything would be wonderful again.

✠✠✠

"Are you coming then?" Stefan looked up. He was checking the shoes on his horse. The rocky roads through Anatolia were hard on horseshoes. He dropped the left foreleg and straightened up to his full height. The muscles in his lower back were stiff, and he groaned when he stood.

"He is no better?" he asked, referring to Count Raymond.

"Worse," said Adhemar. "I am giving his last rites now. Are you coming along?"

Guy de Monteil was bedridden with a fever after being severely injured in a fracas with a bear. No bones had been broken in his tussle with the beast, but his wounds were severe. His arms and legs were wrapped in bandages.

But Count Raymond's case was more severe. He had been ill for over a week. No remedies seemed to avail. The best possible cure was no doubt relief from the heat, but the end of the scorching temperatures was not in sight. Elvira, whom, in his delirium, he did not recognize, endeavored to nurse him back to health, but with no success. The bishop of Le Puy, legate of the Holy Father, believed that Extreme Unction should be administered without delay.

Stefan rode with Adhemar to the tent where Raymond lay dying. Other leaders of the pilgrimage were already present as they arrived: Godfrey, Baldwin his brother, Tancred, Bohemund, Robert of Flanders, Short Breeches and Hugh. Elvira, red-eyed and tired, greeted Stefan as he entered the tent, laying her head upon his chest as he embraced her and then he let her go.

The dying man seemed decades older than the fifty-five years he was. His cheeks were hollowed by the illness, and his gaping mouth gasped for air. His head was tilted back, and, with his jaw ajar, he had the appearance of one waiting to be fed. His arms, bony and fleshless, lay still beside his body and above a sheet now soaked with perspiration. Around his neck a silver amulet encased a relic of an unknown saint. A crucifix had been placed above his head on a pole.

There was no resemblance here to the man who had led his army in a furious chase over hill and valley to rescue the beleaguered forces at Dorylaeum.

The bishop donned a stole and withdrew a vial of oil from a fold in his vestment. He began the ritual: *In nomine patris, et filii, et spiritu sancti. Amen.* He touched the closed eyes of his longtime friend with the oil and intoned dispassionately: *By this holy anointing, may you be forgiven of all sins you may have committed through the sense of sight.* He then anointed Raymond's ears: *By this holy anointing, may you be forgiven of all sins you may have committed through the sense of hearing.*

Stefan was thinking of Anna and realized with embarrassment that his thoughts had not been holy. What law is it, he wondered, that decrees unholy thoughts at holy times, behavior most unsolemn at the most solemn times, laughter when levity is the most unseemly? The bishop is giving Extreme Unction, Raymond is dying, and I'm thinking of Anna. He tried to shove her out of his thoughts. He would not remember that it had been six weeks since he had seen her, one week longer than he thought it would take to get to Jerusalem. He would not think of the mountain range that still stood between himself and Antioch. He would not think of the cities to which he must lay siege. He would not think of Jerusalem … of the months—he knew it was months—before he would see Jerusalem and see her again. He would not think of it. He had little heart for the pilgrimage in the beginning and what he had now was slipping away. He, Stefan, a nobleman of France, one of the wealthiest men of Europe, languishing in the heat of Anatolia, chewing on thorn berry bushes, watching old men grow older and women and children suffer—all for … what?

"By this holy anointing," Adhemar intoned, "may you be forgiven of all sins you may have committed through the sense of touch. May the Lord Jesus Christ absolve you, and by his authority, I absolve you of all your sins."

CHAPTER TWENTY-FIVE

Through the Pass to the Iron Bridge

October 1, 1097 A.D.

The Anti-Taurus Mountains

AYMOND, COUNT OF TOULOUSE, DID not die. After the bishop's anointing, he lingered more than a fortnight at the portal of death refusing to enter therein until, at last, unable to wait for him either to die or recover, Adhemar ordered the pilgrimage to resume. Women tenderly bound and bandaged the old count's gaunt frame, and pilgrims conveyed him over terrain flat or rugged, until in late August they arrived with the count, bone-tired and exhausted at Iconium. The town was deserted as was every other village they had encountered, the result of Arslan's scorched earth decree. But nearby, in the fertile valley of Meram, clear streams of gushing water cooled the parched throats of the pilgrims, and orchards that Arslan had not destroyed, nourished back to health sun-bronzed bodies emaciated by deprivation. They could not believe their good fortune.

Raymond's countrymen laid him under a desert pine, like Elijah under the juniper tree, where his feverish brow caught the cool morning breezes that floated down from the foothills. They bathed his face in the waters of Meram and gave him small pieces of fruit to eat. Within a week of his arrival at Iconium he had revived. Within two weeks, he could mount his horse.

Guy, likewise, did not die from his wounds sustained with his tussle with the bear. His scalp had healed but some of his hair would never grow back, and he took pains to let his good hair fall over the scar where the bear had torn his flesh. He walked with a limp now, but at least he walked. The rest at Iconium enabled him to recover not only his strength but acuity of mind, and thereafter, he was never loath to regale the children with the brave, if not exaggerated, account of his battle with the bear.

Thus the time in Iconium, the city of Saint Paul, was spent in eating and drinking, storytelling and dancing. Peter the Monk and other clergy took the opportunity to preach, exhorting the pilgrims *qua* soldiers to repentance and courage, always reminding them of the proximity of the city of Christ and of the enemies who presently dwelt therein.

✠✠✠

"The Christians would remember those days in Iconium fondly," I said to Bernard. "With the exception of Heraclea, they would not experience such comfort and plenty again. Generally, Arslan's policy had been successful: towns and markets were deserted and destroyed; wells were blocked or poisoned. Occasionally, however, the pilgrims found small settlements of Armenians who were friendly and who endeavored to help them.

"When they left Iconium, they took enough water to last until they reached Heraclea. Beyond this valley, the road to Antioch branched in two directions. The one, laying to the south, requiring a journey through the narrow Cilician Gates, was, in the judgment of Tacitus, unsuitable for a large army. Cilicia was firmly in Saracen hands, and in September, the climate was highly unfavorable.

"Tacitus argued that the alternate route should be taken, namely, the road leading to Caesarea-Mazaca, and from there over the Anti-Taurus mountains to Marash, and from Marash along the easy road to Antioch by way of a wide pass known as the Amanus Gates."

Bernard, who had been studying the Gesta, *now looked up. "But?— "*

"But the leaders of the crusade sided with Tacitus on this matter, except the ill-tempered Tancred, nephew of Bohemund, and Baldwin, the brother of Godfrey de Boullion, who both refused to heed his advice and broke with the pilgrimage to seek their own fortunes. Tancred left with about a hundred knights and two hundred foot soldiers, and Baldwin took a larger force of five hundred knights and two thousand foot soldiers. Most of the nobles and captains of the army were happy to see them leave.

"Along this chosen route, the crusaders occasionally encountered resistance from bands of Turks, but the infidels were defeated consistently and villages and territories were then remanded into the custody of local Armenian princes who were at least nominally under the suzerainty of the emperor. Once, when the Armenians welcomed the crusaders into their village, they asked Tacitus, as the emperor's legate, to name a governor to rule the town for the emperor. Tactius chose a certain Peter of Aulps, a Provencal knight of distinction. This gesture did much to demonstrate to the Franks that Constantinople desired to cooperate and assist the pilgrims as much as possible.

"The footsore pilgrims travelled to Caesarea which was deserted, and on to Placentia which was under siege by the Turks, who fled as the Christians approached. From Placentia they moved to Coxon where they remained for three days gathering supplies for the last passage over the Anti-Taurus mountains to Marash."

✠✠✠

Bohemund rode with his captains at the head of a small band of five hundred mounted knights on the road to Marash. They travelled under the banner of the crusader cross, and each of the knights carried a ribbon-tipped lance set vertically in a holster. They wore chain-mail armor and their cone-shaped helmets with nasal were in place. Three hundred shields bearing the sign of the cross protected them.

The prince held up his hand and immediately his lieutenants signaled the regiment to halt. He pointed to his left to a great basalt wall that stretched along the valley leading to the Great Sea. Halfway up these cliffs, one could observe caves and dwellings that from this distance looked merely like the clay nests of swallows and other fowl of the air.

"The monastery," Bohemund said with a sigh.

The others nodded. "How do we get up there?" one asked.

"Only two goddamn ways," Bohemund replied. "From the top by ropes, or from the bottom by hand and foot."

The regiment made a bivouac in the marshy field by the roadside, while Bohemund and two of his men, Albert and Arnolf, began the journey to the monastery. At the lower elevation, an indistinct trail appeared to lead them to the top, but as the cliff became steeper, and the talus and scree from the towering wall above them more treacherous, the trail vanished and the climb became a desperate scramble until they reached The Ladders.

The Ladders were a series of contrivances by which the earnest seeker of truth could, by dint of determination, arrive at the monastery. Ladders, ten to fifteen feet high, constructed of birch or sometimes hemp, and leaning against or fastened to numerous sections of wall, comprised the final section of the vertical "trail" the three had to ascend. When at last the final ladder had been scaled, they staggered breathless into the monastery compound, which, of course, was larger than could be seen or imagined from far below —and, with its herb garden and narrow cloister, more beautiful.

The men walked rapidly toward an arched entrance in the cliff. "Cistern," said Bohemund as they passed a stone doorway that led underground. "Granaries here," pointing to other buildings. "Look at the rigging there," he said. "Food and supplies are lowered in baskets from above by ropes and pulleys."

They rang the brass bell at the entrance, and moments later the small barred window in the center of the door opened and two large eyes appeared, rolling back and forth like marbles on slate. The window slammed shut, the heavy door swung open, and a monk in the cowl stood before them. "I am Bohemund of Tarranto, and these are my friends. We are on pilgrimage to Jerusalem. We would like to speak with your abbot, please," Bohemund said.

"Who are these monks?' asked one of his men.

"Paulicians," he replied, striding briskly to keep up with the monk leading the way. The corridors inside the cave were narrow, dark and labyrinthine. Lamps were used sparingly, so that, while a lamp was always in sight, most of the tunnels themselves were in darkness. "They're a small sect, Syrians probably, broke away seven or eight hundred years ago. I don't know ... heretics, I guess."

They heard the sound of tenors singing Gregorian chants, perhaps a dozen voices, but there may have been more, or perhaps less, but because the music reverberated so, it was difficult to tell.

They arrived in a small chapel without chairs, adorned by a crucifix above the altar, and illuminated by many candles and lamps. Beneath each station of the cross was a small rack that contained whips used for self-flagellation. They genuflected and waited.

A low door to the side opened and the abbot stepped through. Bohemund expected an old man of full beard, with revolting personal features, and crippled and withered. Instead, the abbot was bald, clean-shaven, and quite young, about forty. His eyes were keen and open, not half-covered by drooping eyelids as the other monks.

"How may I help you?" he asked cordially. He did not appear to be the kind of monk who would choose voluntarily to live a lifetime in a cliff dwelling away from human society. Indeed, his manner suggested that he had frequent contact with the outside world, for his speech and his comportment were courteous and correct.

"Information," Bohemund said, getting to the point.

"What kind of information?"

"About the Holy Lance."

"Ah, the Holy Lance!" The abbot turned away from them and knelt at the altar and said a prayer. Standing again, he faced them and said, "What makes you think that I can tell you anything about the Holy Lance?"

"Because the Paulicians have been the custodians of the holy relics of Antioch—"

"And?"

"And if we could find the Holy Lance, we could return it to you for its safekeeping."

"And why would you want to do this?"

"We are making a pilgrimage to Jerusalem to liberate the city and its holy places, by this action we could ensure God's blessing."

"Excuse me," the abbot said as he left the room.

"He doesn't know anything," whispered one of the men.

"We'll see," said Bohemund. "I think he is a crafty little man. I don't trust him."

The abbot returned bearing a small reliquary in the shape of a simple hand-carved, wooden box. He gave it to Bohemund, and while the Italian held it, he opened it and removed a piece of parchment. "You're welcome to look at this," he said. "It is all I have for you."

Bohemund unfolded the parchment. On it were written the words: *Si quis vult post me venire, abneget semetipsum, et tollet crucem suam quotidie et sequatur me.*

"That's it?"

The abbot spread out his hands in a gesture of helplessness. "That's it."

"What does it say?"

The abbot took back the parchment. "These are the words of Jesus according to the third gospel. It says: 'If any man would follow me, let him deny himself, take up his cross and follow me.'"

"There's nothing more?"

"Nothing more."

"May I keep this?"

"I have another copy."

"We'll go then," Bohemund said, turning to his men. "May I offer a donation?"

"You may, but I'd refuse," replied the abbot.

"Very well, good day." Bohemund started toward the chapel door and had just pushed on the latch when the abbot called out. "Oh, begging your pardon, did anyone mention that, although our monks were kind enough to escort you gratis into this cave, there is a small charge to escort you out! Godspeed, then." The abbot stooped to depart through the low door and was gone.

"I told you he was a clever one," Bohemund muttered. "Let's go."

An hour later, a Paulician monk found the three of them in a deep cavern sitting dejectedly under an oil lamp. At the sight of the monk, they jumped happily to their feet. Bohemund began to count gold bezants into the hands of the frowning monk, first one, then another, until after ten coins had fallen into his purse, the monk broke into a wide smile. "Follow me," he said.

✠✠✠

On this day, October 1, Caro came to Count Stefan with news, "Bohemund has left camp for Antioch," he said matter-of-factly. The young captain, always eager, stood before the count with sword strapped to his side, jaw set, and eyes alert.

Stefan, writing a letter, looked up. "He did what?"

"He heard a rumor that the Turks have abandoned Antioch, so he set out full speed to occupy the city until we can arrive."

Stefan jumped up and began to pace. "It's a trap for sure. Doesn't he know this is a favorite ploy of the Turks, to spread rumors hoping to coax us out beyond our defenses? How many men did he take?"

"Five hundred knights."

"And Raymond is still chasing Turks at Placentia?"

"True," said Caro, nodding.

"Therefore," said Stefan, "we have a grand total of about three hundred horses actually with us in the camp at this very moment." He looked at Caro. "How many did we lose on the march?"

"They died like flies in the heat, no water ... left us with about a thousand all told, my lord."

The count began to shout: "Not only are we unable to rescue Bohemund, but we ourselves are vulnerable with only three hundred damned horses left! Whom did he notify?"

"No one, my lord," Caro answered. The captain took a step backward anticipating another outburst. But he was surprised. The count said nothing.

Later that day, Raymond returned to camp having failed to capture any of the fleeing Turks at Placentia. When he heard of Bohemund's action, he, too, was furious.

They didn't wait long to hear from the Italian Norman. He rode into camp with his knights the following day. When Stefan heard the news, he mounted his charger and rode off in search of him. "A meeting of the Council of Knights, my tent at sundown," he said tersely, and galloped away.

Inexplicably, Stefan's anger dissipated by the appointed hour of the meeting. Perhaps it was the brief encounter with Bohemund that again reminded him of Anna and of the letter he had been writing. It softened his attitude. Instead of delivering a personal rebuke, he allowed Raymond to express the general disapproval of the leaders. The success of the military venture, he suggested strongly, was dependent upon the cooperation of each army. This required that they, as leaders, must act in concert one with another and not independently of each other. The crusade, Adhemar reminded him, was like a body of which Christ through the Holy Father was the Head. A body whose individual members act in disobedience to the head is a grotesque thing, full of evil. Such is the army when its leaders fail to live in harmony with each other.

Bohemund took this rebuke silently and darkly and then gave the leaders news of his own.

"We came to a small monastery not far from the Orontes," he announced. "Held by some Paulician heretics. There we learned that the rumor we had heard was false. Had the rumor been true we would be in possession of Antioch at this moment."

"*You* would be in possession of Antioch," Godfrey corrected.

"If I possess Antioch, we all possess Antioch," Bohemund retorted heatedly. "This is a war, my lords, a campaign. We haven't the luxury of abiding here or there until the weather or the conditions suit us. We seize, as always in a battle, the opportunity when it presents itself. In Provence, perhaps you can afford to wait for the ideal; you have the numbers for it. In southern Italy, we make up in cleverness what we lack in size—"

"You'll not lecture me on waging war!" roared the count of Toulouse, bringing his fist down on the oaken table like a hammer to an anvil.

Bohemund arose and stood stiffly at these words, and leaned on his fists over the table toward Raymond: "Then you'll not lecture me when I propose to keep this damn beast of an army—"

Adhemar broke in: "—We have no quarrel with what you propose," he said with cold intensity, "only with what you dispose. We applaud your genius but demand that you share it. We are not four or five armies but one. You propose, and we'll dispose. There is no other way in which divine providence—"

"Providence," Bohemund shouted, "is less a matter of divinity than it is a matter of timing. We traversed Anatolia during the *worst possible* time of year, and lost horses and soldiers as a result. Providence or stupidity? We are now in the mountains during the rainy season. Providence? *Providence?* We should've crossed the desert in the spring and the mountains in the summer, and then our horses would be fresh, and our soldiers alive!"

A man stepped out of the shadows. "You are in no position to cast judgment on the providence of God." The voice was low and quiet, the eyes had recovered their fire. The words were laced with prophetic authority. Peter the Monk was back: "Providence hinges not on fortuity but upon obedience and obedience upon a teachable spirit. You have at least twice been disobedient to instructions that were quite clear to you. In spite of this, God has brought us to this place. We bicker like the Israelites and, if we continue, God will set us loose in this wilderness of iniquity to perish in our sins like the Israelites, and leave to our children the responsibility of liberating Jerusalem. This was the great sin of those who died at the Civetot. Each leader believed in the wisdom of his own plan and not in the strength of unity. In the multitude of counselors there is strength, saith the Lord. But they were like sheep led astray and like sheep they went to the slaughter at the hands of the infidel. We have a thousand horses and you foolishly take half of them for your own unannounced purpose. In time, the sin of one man will be visited upon hundreds, and the sins of two upon the thousands, and our bones, too, will lay bleaching in the summer sun like those of our brothers and sisters in the Civetot." The monk ended his tirade standing squarely in front of the Italian.

Bohemund sat down. "The Turks are not abandoning Antioch—" he paused. "They're reinforcing it."

"How many troops?" Stefan asked.

Bohemund shrugged. "I think they're preparing an ambush between here and Marash. This is what I heard from the Paulicians, and they have no reason to lie to us. There's a small road to the south which will take us to Marash and avoid the ambush." He stood and pointed out the way on the map to the others.

"That is difficult terrain," observed Raymond. "Not as difficult as ambushed terrain," rejoined Bohemund. Stefan arose and addressed the Council of Knights. "My lords," he said, "I agree with Raymond. An ambush is not an ambush if we know of it. Indeed, the element of surprise is on our side because they have lost the single device upon which they are depending to defeat us. Moreover, we have never been defeated by the Turks, and knowing aforehand of their intentions, we would be victorious again. The road is wider and smoother. And—" he looked in Bohemund's direction, "—I don't trust the intelligence. I don't believe the Turks want another pitched battle with us in the mountains." Stefan walked deliberately around the noblemen at the table and leaned into their circle to point to a charcoal spot on the map which indicated to him the next point of conflict. "It is more likely that they're reinforcing Antioch to make the final defense there because they know that, beyond Antioch, there is no obstacle to our march on Jerusalem." He punched the chart with his finger, and backed away. "It is at Antioch, not a pass in the mountains, that the Turks will attempt to stop us."

Godfrey stood up. "Stefan has spoken well. On the other hand, the Turks may very well be aware that we have suffered major losses and are not as strong as we were three months ago. Even if they plan to make a strong defense of Antioch, they may be reasoning that an ambush on the road to Marash will at best prove successful and at worse weaken our resolve and thereby enhance their prospects beyond the Orontes River." Godfrey spoke in the even and literate cadences of the count of Blois, matching his intelligence and civility with that of his own.

Godfrey's response was thoughtful and in the end prevailed. When the tally was taken, Raymond and Stefan's advice was rejected. The thirty thousand pilgrims, soldiers and noncombatants would change course and march through the narrow, southern hills to the plains of Marash.

They started out two days later. Like an awakening giant, the pilgrimage lumbered awkwardly to its feet—stiff, sore and complaining. The baggage trains, comprised of fewer carts, were loaded higher than ever. Carts of weathered timber, and wagons, held together by ropes, pegs and prayers, creaked forward defying logic that dictated their immediate collapse. Addie walked with a large pack on her back beside a cart bearing some of the few possessions she could still claim as her own: a pair of shoes she had been given by the emperor when she was reunited with Peter, clothes for herself and Clare, some grain and wine. Not much, but she stayed by her stuff, one hand grasping a walking stick, the other steadying the load when it seemed to shift dangerously to the side.

Peter and Hildy travelled with her, pounding their staffs steadily into the damp mountain soil, pushing themselves forward and upward, and when a cart became mired in mud, or when its way was impeded by a boulder, they lowered their shoulders and pushed the cart along until the next breakdown or impediment. Clare helped other children, most of them older than she, to herd the horses which were rider-less to keep them fresh. She carried a switch in her hand and tweaked a steed now and again as though without her childish ministrations the herd might be lost.

The road they had chosen from Coxon to Marash was actually
little more than a well-used trail for horses and carts. It provided a
link from Marash to small Armenian conclaves in the mountains
and now a few monasteries. It had never been a Roman road as
had the other route. There were no foundations of cobblestone and
brick; no curbs to mark the way or provide drainage. As the route
became narrow, the great company of pilgrims, once encamped in
Coxon in large rings of concentric circles, now stretched itself
through the hills like a serpent snaking through grass. In the gently
sloping hills, travel was not difficult, but it could be perilous when a
wagon with a broken harness careened down the path until
upended by a boulder or a curve in the road. Ascending the hills
was equally frustrating and more than one animal had to be
unyoked at the peak and returned down the slope to pull another
wagon to the top. The roads in this country, not being crafted for
travel such as this, came to be regarded by some as one of the
labors of Hercules, but the pilgrims had neither the strength nor
the inspiration of a Greek god, nor (they began to feel) the one
True God. The monk exhorted them with the words of David: "I
will lift up my eyes unto the hills from whence cometh my help."
But Pons, looking at the mountainous terrain, would always
whisper, "He means 'from whence cometh my hell.'"

✠✠✠

Bohemund, lean and fit, travelled alone out of the Anti-Taurus
mountains to Marash by night and knocked on the door of an
innkeeper called Fat Peasant. Inside, he met a confederate.

"You met with the Paulicians?" the man asked.

"Yes," replied Bohemund. He was tired and thirsty. "Bring me
some ale," he said, calling to Fat Peasant. The innkeeper had the
face and beady eyes of a mongoose, and the body of a cow. He
brought mugs for both of them.

"And what did the abbot say?"

Bohemund quaffed half a mug heartily if not sloppily, and slammed it down on the table. "Not much," he said, panting. "He gave me this." Bohemund pushed the parchment across the table.

The man seemed disappointed. "Third gospel," he noted.

"That's what the abbot said."

"We can't know what it means," said the voice, "without the complete Paulician Parchment."

Bohemund was surprised. "The complete Paulician Parchment?"

"What's that?"

The Italian's guest leaned back in his chair to tell the story. "It's not possible to determine the location of the Holy Lance with what you have," said the man. "It is merely Scripture. It might as well be Plato. Centuries ago, during the invasions of the Vandals and Visigoths, after the period when Rome itself was sacked, the intruders entered Palestine, raiding and plundering what they could. Many of the sacred relics were kept and protected in a treasury in Antioch by the Paulicians who had a monastery there. As the city was falling around them, the Paulicians fled, eventually establishing a new house on the cliffs which you visited. While they were able to take many relics with them, they thought it was wiser to leave the Holy Lance behind and hide its location. It was such a valuable relic, they feared that if they took it with them, they would be pursued and hounded until they surrendered it.

"So they left it to an old and clever monk to take care of it. He hid it and disclosed its whereabouts on two cryptic scraps of parchment, one of which he gave to his superior, and another, as the barbarians were closing in, to a group of monks on pilgrimage, returning to Gaul, and who later went to the Isle of Iona off the coast of Britain. There it remained unnoticed for hundreds of years.

"When Pope Urban announced the armed pilgrimage to Jerusalem to liberate the holy places, a venerable monk, who virtually lived in the Scriptorium, recalled the parchment about the Holy Lance. He gave it to his abbot who in turn journeyed to Canterbury and presented it to Anselm of Bec, the archbishop, as a gift for the pilgrimage, thinking that what better time to recover the Holy Lance than on the very pilgrimage that would once again restore Jerusalem into Christian hands.

"Anselm traveled to Clermont for the pope's sermon, and was going to give it to Adhemar, the papal legate, or Count Raymond of Toulouse. But he became involved in a spirited conversation with Adela, the wife of Count Stefan of Blois, and when she assured him that the count was taking the cross and could be entrusted to recover the Holy Lance better than any of the others, he gave it instead to her.

"Adela shared her information with the king, and they immediately devised a plan, the details of which are known to you. But, ironically, they trusted no one to carry the Paulician Parchment, except Stefan himself. So she gave it to Stefan without his knowledge, and he has brought it unwittingly with him to Palestine. Without the Paulician Parchment, we can do nothing."

Bohemund listened with rapt attention. "So where is it?" he asked. "Let's get it!"

"The Paulician Parchment is safe," the collaborator said. "I know where it is, and when we're ready to act, we'll recover it from Stefan. But the time is not yet right." He paused, his voice dry. Reaching for more ale, he said, "One more thing."

"What's that?"

"There's a Jew in your camp masquerading as a pilgrim."

Bohemund sat up and leaned forward. "A Jew?"

"A Jew."

"How do you know?" he asked, intrigued.

"I overheard a conversation in which she—"

"—A Jewess?"

"—confessed it, told her story. Adhemar is thinking of proclaiming a fast and other measures of purification. But as long as that Jewess is in the camp, the pilgrimage is defiled." The man drank again and laughed. "But I'll take care of her, you'll see," he murmured. "I'll take of her."

✠✠✠

When the monsoons began on the third day out, the road turned to mud making descent by foot or wagon treacherous and ascent well-nigh impossible. Indeed, during the rain, all travel stopped. The long train of tens upon thousands of pilgrims sank immobile into the mud of the Anti-Taurus. They sought refuge under trees and large boulders, and hastily erected their tents on level spots carved out in the side of the mountains. Some huddled under their wagons.

Not that they nurtured hope of staying dry. The afternoons became as night and leaden clouds hurled rain like arrows, pelting the pilgrims relentlessly. Some, already weak, took cold and died.

When the rains abated, the pilgrims emerged quickly from cover and began preparations to begin the journey anew.

"Over here," shouted Pons, "some help, my friend." Guy heard the call and came mucking over to the wagon Pons was attempting unsuccessfully to free. "The beast does not want to help us," he said. It was true. The ass refused to move forward.

Guy limped over to the animal and peered into its doe-eyed face. "You are choosing a bad time not to cooperate," he said with disgust. He grabbed the halter and yanked on it quickly several times, but the animal would not budge.

Pons called out again: "Addie, over here!" Addie was in a far tent changing into dry clothes. When she appeared, Guy gave her a switch which, at Pons' command, she laid across the back of the beast. Although Pons and Guy both pushed, the wagon wheels were mired firmly in the clay. They would need a better effort from the beast.

The switch was laid across the animal's back several times, but to no avail. They arrived at the moral stopping point at which they agreed to make an attempt one more time and failing, withdraw to consider another approach. Pons yelled at Addie to beat the beast again but before she could lay the switch across the animal, it brayed loudly and sprang into action, causing the wagon to lurch forward and throwing Pons and Guy face down in the grainy sludge.

"Oh, what a fine sight you are!" cried Addie, laughing. The ass brayed again, pulling back its lips and baring its teeth. Pons and Guy struggled to their feet covered head to foot in mud, scarcely able to see.

Addie stepped closer. "I've seen you before," she said, unable to contain her mirth. "Constantinople, the Garden of the Gods. A god! Yes, a statue of a god!" She circled around the immobile Provencals, mocking. "A god, a Greek god. Stand there, O ye gods!" She backed away from them as though to view them better. "In a few moments, this fair breeze will harden the clay upon your bodies and transform you into gods and only the kiss of a pure maiden will return you to your human form."

"And where shall we find a pure maiden?" Guy asked.

Addie whirled away from them. "Not I!" she crowed.

The two men began to peel the clay and sludge from their bodies until Pons had gathered a chunk of it in his hands. "To be a true statue, a Greek one at least, we should have to be naked," he said wickedly, leering playfully at Addie who had taken a few steps closer. Pons began to work the clay in his hand and in moments he fashioned a god-sized phallus which he positioned carefully. For a few moments, the clay member remained rigid and firm. Then it began a slow descent and suddenly dropped off and fell with a plop into the puddle at his feet.

The men laughed uproariously while Addie turned away to hide the color in her cheeks. Unwillingly, she smiled and tried not to think about symbols and realities, but that night she thought of little but Pon's clay phallus.

The next day, the road became even narrower. It led them for several miles along a muddy ledge above a deep ravine and the mood among the pilgrims became as dark as the clouds hovering above them. Every step they took displaced a murky mixture of water and earth which then splattered upon their legs and clothing. The mud dried upon their clothing and skin, giving them a ghost-like appearance as they plodded toward Marash.

"I don't understand why the Syrians are forever complaining about too much sunshine," Stefan said as he trudged along the slippery incline with Caro. Their elevation was higher here, the cliffs and ravine deeper and more severe. Stefan walked ahead of Caro who was leading his horse which was carrying their armor. Ahead of them a baggage train of animals was tied together and slipping erratically along the trail. The rains had been so heavy that even bushes along the path were losing the soil into which they had cast their roots. Occasionally, they would see the ground give way and a bush slide slowly downward and then tumble into the gorge.

"We may never see the sun again," Caro said, "like a lot of things we'll never see again."

"Is that so?" said Stefan. "Like what?"

"We may never see the sun again, we may never see home again, we may never see our wives again, our children, or Rouen, Chartres, Paris." He paused. "Do you miss her?"

"Paris?"

"No, your wife."

Stefan lied. "I never knew it was possible to miss another living person as much as I miss her," he said. Actually, he had not thought much of Adela. His wife was taking care of business, he thought grimly. He wasn't sure whose business she was taking care of, but somebody's.

"So what keeps you going?" Caro asked.

He was about to say "love," but checked himself. Actually, love was weakening his resolve. When he left France, he had believed that without love the journey was impossible. It was love of God that had taken him to Constantinople ... no, it was shame ... he had been shamed into taking the Cross. For love of God, he would've stayed in France. He had thought that love of Anna would strengthen him for the rest of the way. Instead, he found his enthusiasm waning, his spirit listless, his body enervated. Love was sapping his moral strength, leaving him shivering in despair, like a man naked in the rain on a dark night.

"Love." He said it anyway. "It's our passions that drive us, you know. Some stay at it for love of God, like Raymond, for example. That man truly believes. It is love of money that compels others, like Tancred and Baldwin and most of the knights. Or the love of glory, like Bohemund. But it's passion, not just love, but passion. Hatred of the Saracens, devotion to the Virgin Mary, love of God, obedience to the Holy Mother Church, love of a woman—all passions, and the successful person is the one who discovers which passion is needed for which objective."

His passion for Anna was not the proper passion. Fear. Fear of failure would keep him marching through his mud. Respect. He coveted the respect of his peers. This would spur him forward. Adventure. The thrill of the battle would entice him to Jerusalem. Fear. Respect. Adventure. But not love. Not love for God or Anna. Not love of God, because he was too irreligious to be moved forward by it; not love of Anna, because he was likely to be tugged backward by it.

"Hold on, what's this?" His thoughts were interrupted at the sight of two forlorn knights sitting trailside with their armor stacked in an unsightly heap beside them.

"What are you doing, lads?" Caro asked.

"Alas, we are doing nothing," one replied.

"We would like to be selling this worthless pile of metal here," said the other, "but no one wants it and we shall soon be obliged to discard it in this ravine."

"Perhaps your price is too high," suggested Stefan.

"I think not," the knight answered. "We can't give it away. Who would want to carry this burden through these mountains in such a confused state of things?" He looked sadly at his armor caked with mud.

"Where are your horses?" Stefan asked.

"Lost them long ago."

"Before Iconium," said one.

"Can't be much of a knight without a horse or armor," Caro said pointedly. They said nothing and Stefan and Caro resumed their march.

They were not yet out of the sight of the two horseless knights when Caro's horse suddenly lost its footing. Passing too close to the edge, the earth gave way and the horse slipped.

Caro, who still had the rope in his wet hands, whirled instantly to aid the panicked animal. Its ears were laid back, eyes dilated, nostrils flared, and mouth open, lips peeled back disclosing enormous yellow teeth. It was neighing in short staccato bursts. The back legs were slipping far below the path, chopping at the sodden earth, splaying the grainy mud in all directions. But it could not fight its way back to solid ground. Caro whipped the line taunt, jerking its regal head around, but it continued its downward movement, its legs spread in four directions. The earth moved under its belly.

Stefan glanced nervously to the void far below as Caro pulled and released rope as the animal descended. Stefan could not come to his aid, but saw clearly that the animal was lost. "Let go," he shouted. "Let him go!" The horse was threatening to pull Caro into the chasm. But Caro would not relinquish the line, struggling vainly to secure leverage as the falling horse inexorably dragged him closer to the muddy rim of the trail.

As quickly as this crisis developed, another one unfolded. The pack animals which had been travelling ahead of Stefan and Caro began a fierce braying. Stefan pivoted in time to see a portion of the trail give way beneath them plunging them all into the chasm. In seconds, animals bearing grain, armor, wine and tools vanished before his eyes as though they had never been there at all. Where a path was once, only a scar of fresh, wet, textured soil was now.

Stefan had neither the time nor presence of mind even to call out. What had been in his vision only moments earlier was now but a memory. They were gone. He stood like a statue mortared in rock, unbelieving, staring to the valley below. And when he turned back, Caro, too, had vanished. Only a large tear in the earth marked where he had been dragged down the incline and over the precipice by his horse. Stefan saw Caro far below, quite dead, with his horse. The rains fell now, softly wetting Caro's hair, running over his closed eyes, and across his ruddy face, cleaning and cleansing it until—much later—mother Earth covered him with soil as though with a thick blanket when one falls asleep.

Stefan threw off the broad leather hat he had been wearing and lifted his dirt-streaked face toward the gray, torpid sky. He closed his eyes and felt the raindrops play off the weathered skin of his face and flow over his chin and upon his cross-marked tunic. Slowly he sank to the earth, on one knee and then the other, feeling the wetness of the soil soak through his breeches. He knelt alone in the middle of the trail, shoulders stooped and his arms dropped helplessly at his side as two horseless knights watched from afar.

He was decidedly alone, yet without fear. Without hope.

Without love. Without passion.

As do all men when passion is gone, he wept.

ANNO
DOMINI
1098

CHAPTER TWENTY-SIX

Bohemund Prepares a Feast

Antioch
January 1098 A.D.

BAN ARSLAN STOOD ON THE BATTLEMENTS of the Citadel which overlooked the sloping north ridges of Mt. Silpius and the city below. On this cold, wet day, the distant north walls of Antioch were barely distinguishable, but he could see through the mist the cathedral tower of St. Peters and the palace to the west. These were situated on the main road that divided the city east and west from St. George's Gate at the west to St. Paul's Gate at the east. The markets would be busy now, he thought, in all three quarters of the city: Christian, Armenian and Syrian. He took another sip of bozo from his mug. He was amused with the irony of the situation. Moslems living in peace with Christians, Armenian sects, and fanatical Syrian Nestorians, Paulicians and the like. But the Franks, unaccustomed to a multiplicity of cultures and religious beliefs, hierarchically and religiously bound to an autocratic papacy, loved uniformity over diversity, and preferred to persecute heretics rather than teach them, live with them or learn from them. The barbarians! He spit over the ramparts and watched his sputum twist and sail in the swirling winds that swept the upper, rocky ridges of the mountain.

Here we are then, he decided grimly, defending a town that has no quarrel with the Franks, that is comprised mostly of Christians like themselves, so I, a Shi'ite Moslem, defending a city of Christians against Christians!

He dropped inside the Citadel Tower.

"The Franks are running out of food," he said. "I want the Christian inhabitants of this city to be allowed to come and go through the gates to visit the camps and resupply them with food to the extent that our own supplies allow and to the limits, of course, of their own Christian generosity."

Hatem, a captain, protested. Arslan raised his hand to stop the objection and sat down, calling for more bozo. "This is not a purely humanitarian gesture," he said, smiling. "The Christians will bring back information about their morale, their armies, their plans, anything useful. And to ensure their information is correct, I'll send some of my own people disguised in the clothing of the Armenians to mingle among the people and walk in the camps. We'll find out what they're doing and how they're doing it. But in the dead of winter they're hungry, our own supplies are low, and I doubt that they're in a position to do anything."

Then, inexplicably, he remembered he had not seen his wife and children for over eight months.

✠✠✠

"You have returned from Sens?" I inquired, as my visitors entered the library.

"Yes," replied Bernard wearily, sitting opposite me. In the sallow candlelight, his face seemed haggard and his spirit in tatters. As it was late, I suggested we wait until the morrow before resuming our examination of the Gesta Francorum.

"Oh no," he said. "Believe me, your commentary on the Gesta *and the manuscript itself are both enlightening and stimulating, a welcome relief from the tedium of heresy."*

"I've always thought of orthodoxy as tedious and heresy as—if not stimulating—intellectually challenging." I had become bolder in my conversations with Bernard, respecting him no less, but trusting him more.

"Challenging in the same way a fever is a challenge, the difficulty being to get rid of it."

"A fever?"

"Aye, the febris carnalis," *he replied. "Tertullian's term in* de Praescriptionem Haereticorum." *I knew little of Tertullian, except that as a Montanist he was regarded as a heretic himself by some. "But now, my friend, continue the story. The pilgrims are at Antioch, are they not?"*

"Well, yes," I said, confused as to where precisely to begin. *"Arslan, by forced marches, managed to reinforce the city before our armies arrived—which was October year of our lord 1097. Crossing the Orontes, we met resistance at the Iron Bridge which is heavily fortified by two towers flanking its entrance. But with Adhemar leading the attack across the bridge, the Franks were able to prevail, capturing a huge convoy of cattle, sheep and corn on its way to resupply Arslan within the city.*

"They laid siege to it then, and clashed with the Saracens on numerous occasions ... small little excursions ... chasing a regiment here, avoiding an ambush there, sacking a local village, that sort of thing. Horses lost, soldiers killed ... a very costly month in which they gave little effort and paid a high price."

We were interrupted by the appearance of Eustace, our cellarer, who brought us a red wine from the nearby Bordeaux region.

"In vino veritas," *he said, smiling as he poured.*

"Ah, in vino sola veritas," *said Bernard.*

I resumed. *"The weather became unbearable. Winter set in with torrents of rain and increasing cold. Food ran out, so raiding parties were forced to travel farther to find provisions; horses were in short supply so parties often went on foot. This, however, made them vulnerable to ambush and attack, but if they took horses and lost them, their situation was more desperate than before.*

"Antioch, an ancient city, so-called after Antiochus Soter who lived two centuries before Christ, formerly the third city of the world, and where the disciples were first called Christians, was inhabited, like Nicea, by a primarily Christian population—Greeks, Syrians and Armenians. The city itself is situated on the Orontes River some twelve miles from the sea and surrounded by

huge walls built by Justinian. These walls follow the Orontes on the north some three miles, ascend Mt. Silpius on the east and west and run along the southern summit ridge. Over four hundred towers lined these fortifications, all within a bowshot of each other. On the summit ridge guarding the valley in general and the city in particular, there was a large fortress called the Citadel. As you can see, the city was impossible to surround. Its conquest posed a severe tactical problem for the Franks.

"Arslan believed that the Franks would begin an immediate, massive assault on the city which is why he ordered the forced marches. And, in fact, this is the strategy for which Raymond and Stefan argued strenuously. Arslan's forces were thin and depleted, they said. And while the walls were thick and heavy, they were also too extensive for him to defend uniformly well. Being freshly supplied with food (as they were at that time), they were strong and healthy and, moreover, the onset of winter would make a long siege difficult to maintain.

"Bohemund said little. But the others contended that the troops were weary after the journey from Dorylaeum to Antioch. Moreover, they were expecting Tancred to arrive soon from Alexandretta and more reinforcements were expected from the emperor by sea.

"To Arslan's surprise, therefore, they did not mount an assault upon the city, but instead deployed their troops about the valley walls. The Council assigned Bohemund to the sector by Saint Paul's Gate, Raymond to the Gate of the Dog and Stefan and Godfrey to the field below Duke's Gate. The rest of the Franks occupied an area behind Bohemund while the forces built a bridge of boats spanning the river behind Stefan's camps, providing a link to the village of Talenki and the roads leading to Alexandretta and Saint Symeon. Later, they established a camp north of the river, beyond the Bridge of the Boats. The Bridge Gate and Saint George's Gate were, for the moment, left uncovered. Stopping the flow of goods into the city through these gates would have to await the time when reinforcements arrived."

✠✠✠

Bohemund was distressed, and being a hasty man by nature, he actually preferred the emotion of impatience to that of anxiety. The source of his uneasiness was, as usual, a strategic one: the camps were afflicted with spies who wandered at will in and out of bivouacs like pests. Bohemund thought them to be everywhere: on the decrepit carts travelling north from Jerusalem; or old women on nags from the coast twenty miles away; the witch; the child; the vintner; or harlot—all indistinguishable from the local inhabitants of the Syrian villages in the region of the Orontes River Valley. Indeed, they were merely villagers, Bohemund understood, who had taken up spying for the Saracens besieged inside the great walled city of Antioch. They passed on information about troop strength, morale, horses, food and such matters, and like most pests, were more annoying than dangerous.

Bohemund vowed to deal with the spies. "Prepare a fire," he told his warriors, "and announce to all the settlements that Bohemund is preparing a great dinner tonight in our camp near Saint Paul's Gate and the Gate of the Dog."

✠✠✠

"Mother, I'm cold," Clare cried. The child was lying in a corner of their small tent and was covered with many blankets already. Addie had to borrow these, and she couldn't make Clare warmer by adding more covers. Her stomach, she said, felt like rocks—heavy, tight and painful. Clare had been ill for two days, her forehead feverish, her face ashen, her body thin and emaciated.

Addie ran out of the tent, a tent for which she was grateful—grateful but not satisfied. It leaked dreadfully when it rained and it did not prevent drafts from blowing through. Sometimes, the days were bitterly cold. Other days, it merely rained and soaked everyone to the skin bringing on coughs, congestion and for some, death. Every day, people were buried in the cemetery beyond the Bridge of Boats.

She grabbed her bow and quiver, a bow and quiver she had made herself and the arrows too. She cut the sapling, devised it for her own height and strength, whittled and planed, crafted arrows of birch precisely straight and with her own mark on them. Taking the Roman road to the Iron Bridge, she soon came to the woods two miles beyond Antioch, stepped off the road to a small path and prayed for a rabbit to hop into view. Today was like most winter days at Antioch: gray skies, biting chill in the air, and a hint of dampness. The ground was layered with leaves, and the trees, skeleton-like, stretched their bony limbs into the misty sky. She paused by a huge tree whose trunk was larger than she could put her arms around, resting against its crusty, rough and damp surface as though it were a friend upon whom she could lean. She watched and waited.

The count cannot take care of us all the time, she thought. Raymond gave the poor as much as he could. There was no nobleman more compassionate than he. But it wasn't enough. She thought of their arrival in Antioch in the fall ... when the trees still had fruit, when crops were still in the field and could be harvested, when sheep and cattle were slaughtered and no one went hungry. And then it was over. Suddenly, there was nothing. Had they expected that the food would last forever? Did they think they could arise every cold autumn morning and find manna on the ground and quail in the air? Did they suppose that the oil would never run out, or the flour never be consumed? They needed a Joseph to ration their food in the seven weeks of plenty so that they would have food in the seven weeks of famine. Instead, they ate greedily, as though they were unaware of the approaching winter.

One does not adjust readily to the daily experience of hunger. Addie didn't know which was worse: the hunger or the fear of hunger. Where would she get food for Clare and for herself? If there is such a thing as providence, God will send a rabbit along right now!

A hand touched her shoulder. Addie jumped away and screamed. She turned around to face a human being who looked half-man, half-animal. Addie cried out again and stepped back, brought her bow instantly and notched an arrow aimed directly for his heart. The bearded man was dressed in tattered leather and animal skins, and, although he was now about eight feet away from her, she could smell the foul stench of his body. His shoulders stooped and his head craned forward as he looked at her.

She heard a noise to her left. She didn't want to look. Holding the bow steady, she glanced aside. Another one! And on the right, another! Three men, looking equally frightful, grunting a strange and unintelligible language, closed in on her, their intentions plain. Addie darted away from them about ten paces and then whirled, arrow drawn. They drew up quickly, and stopped, talking among themselves.

Tafurs! Addie had heard of them. A sect of pilgrims who were extremely poor, had broken off the pilgrimage, elected their own Tafur king, raided villages, ate berries, and some said even ate human flesh. The pilgrims in the camps were terrified of them, for they were absolutely fearless in battle and without any known scruples. She would have to teach them scruples now, she thought resolutely, leveling her arrow.

The first one grinned and stared directly at Addie, who returned his gaze. He stepped forward menacingly and without hesitation, she lowered her bow and shot an arrow into his thigh with such force that the missile went completely through the flesh instantly disabling the man and throwing him to the ground. He screamed, clutching the arrow in his leg while the other two looked at the woman with shock. The universe was stranger than they had imagined. A woman had shot at them and was preparing to shoot again. They were diviners of mysteries, interpreters of signs, observers of comets and stars, but they were not prepared to understand a woman who had fought back. The men glanced down at their companion and then looked back at Addie and lunged toward her with rasping cries. Addie released the arrow and faster than the men could blink, notched another and shot it as well. The first arrow went directly into the chest of the one Tafur, causing him to fall back, and the other arrow pierced the right eyeball of the second man. It was not luck; she had aimed.

Addie fled with their screams ringing in her ears and kept running until she was within a bowshot of the road. She threw herself down on the ground and began to quake, fear finally catching up with her. She was not the same woman the Turks attacked at the Civetot, she thought. She had taken a grasp of her life; she could not trust it to any other person, neither a man nor a god. She would be responsible! But, she lamented, perhaps neither man nor God, or even herself could ultimately deliver her from this wretched experience.

Her thoughts were interrupted by an animal crossing the road and making for the woods, nose to the ground exploring scents and tree stumps. A dog! Addie sat up straight and slowly reached for her bow. She notched an arrow and sighted down the shaft. It was not a Christian dog: they had all disappeared within a month of winter. It must be a Syrian dog from Talenki. The mongrel raised its head and looked toward Addie. Disinterested, it resumed the course its nose had previously dictated. Addie's arrow whizzed through the air and caught the dog in the shoulder. It yelped and fell to the ground and was still whining when Addie reached it. She put an arrow through its heart, whipped out a knife and skinned it right then and there, quickly, deftly, slicing meat from shoulder, haunch and rump. They would have meat tonight. Even though she had heard Bohemund was hosting a feast, she knew it was not for the poor and penniless such as herself. Still, if she attended, she might be able to glean scraps for her family.

She left the carcass for the wild animals.

✠✠✠

Anna strode determinedly through the palace, long strides and swinging arms, toward her father's stateroom. After putting her off for several months, he had promised to review her objections to the marriage between herself and the prince of Tarranto. Melissenus met her at the door.

"He's receiving a delegation," he warned, shaking his head.

"Fine," she answered, pushing the door open and striding into the room. Four people (not counting an interpreter), three men and a woman, were seated in decorative chairs in front of the imperial desk behind which Alexius himself was seated. At her sudden entrance, all sprang to their feet.

"Excuse me," Anna said to the visitors. Then to her father: "I had thought we were going to talk about that other matter."

"And we shall, my dear daughter, we shall," Alexius cooed in a tone that was cloying and irritating to Anna. "These guests are from Normandy and the Ile de France: Gratian and Rainald in the employ of the King of France, and Gerard of Blois, who is chief vassal in the service of this beautiful woman, Lady Adela, wife of Count Stefan of Blois and Chartres." He folded his hands obsequiously, pleased with himself.

This is Adela! The princess could barely suppress a gasp at this sudden revelation. She stepped back, like a wild animal stunned by an attack, but primed to begin clawing. Her mind had been so preoccupied with the problem of Bohemund, that she had not considered seriously the female impediment that blocked the realization of her fondest fantasy. Now the other half of the problem had materialized before her very eyes, doubling in difficulty the effort to live and love as she chose.

She instantly sensed that in Adela, of golden hair and alabaster skin, she faced a shrewd and resourceful adversary. The woman possessed a fine figure, and was wearing a well-tailored gown, string of pearls and ruby earrings. But it was the feline face and especially the eyes that warned Anna of the rivalry between them. She held her head high, and hadn't bothered to turn her body to face the princess, but instead had merely turned her head; her gaze was unwavering and innately suspicious.

The emperor continued, addressing his daughter: "You know Adela's husband, of course—"

"—She has been with my husband," snapped Adela to Gerard in Norman French that she supposed no one else understood. "I know it!"

"—and she brings us the sad news that—"

"—that we miss him very much," Adela said, interrupting the interpreter. "We are hoping to convince the emperor to accept an offer of more mercenaries and substantial cash incentives in exchange for the opening of our borders to increased trade. Our markets in Rouen, Paris, Chartres, Lyons, and Orleans, to name a few, are eager for goods from the East."

"Yes, yes," added a startled Alexius.

Anna turned to leave. "Je suis enchantee d'avoir fait votre connaisannce," she said to the gentlemen. Then to Adela she said in rapid French: "Yes, you are right. I *do* know your husband. You can rest assured he is utterly devoted to you." She did not want to cause problems for Stefan, but perhaps she overplayed her hand. She wasn't sure. Why wouldn't Adela assume her husband was devoted to her? By mentioning his devotion, did she plant in Adela's mind the very doubt she wished to remove?

The men murmured upon hearing their own tongue, but the expression on Adela's face did not change.

That night, Anna found Gerard in the inn of Vasil the Robber, a tavern near the quay on the Golden Horn. A fire blazed at one end of the room, while opium smoke filled the other. Everywhere, men sat about with stems of ale on their tables and wenches in the laps. The Normans were drinking together, leering and laughing obnoxiously, taking as many liberties with their wench as could be allowed. She accosted Gerard by pushing the startled man back in his chair and leaning into his face thereby allowing him to have a calculated and full view of her ample cleavage, a gesture which she surmised might be interpreted by the barbarian as an amorous overture.

"I am Anna Comnena," she said, staring directly into his eyes a scant few inches from her own. "I want to speak with you."

Gerard laughed nervously. "I know who you are!" he exclaimed in a high-pitched wavering voice. "With me?" Anna nodded and backed away, motioning for him to follow.

"Certainly, certainly," he said, his tongue thick with ale.

Anna nodded to the innkeeper, and passed through a bulky curtain to a back room of low oaken beams and stone walls. She sat him down, and poured him another mug of ale.

She took a gold coin out of her pocket, passed it before his eyes, and laid it on the table. "What did my father mean this morning when he said that Adela had brought the sad news? What sad news?"

"I don't know, I don't know," he stammered. "I don't even remember this morning."

"Yes, you do, my friend," Anna said. "What did he mean?"

"Sad news?"

"Sad news."

Gerard shook his muddled head as though to dislodge forgotten memories. "It was Stefan," he mumbled.

"What about Stefan?" Anna said sharply. She grabbed his head and forced him to look at her. "What about Stefan?"

Gerard moistened his lips and passed his hand over a five day growth of beard. "Why, that Stefan was dead, of course!"

Anna pushed him back in his chair, grabbed the hair of his head and pulled his head back. "What do you mean Stefan is dead?"

She let him go, and stepped back, stunned.

"I mean Stefan is dead," Gerard answered, in a whinny, singsong voice.

Anna thought for a moment, organizing a line of questioning. She put another coin on the table and sat down. "How did he die? How did Stefan die?" she demanded.

"Well," Gerard began to explain, "he isn't really dead—"

"You just said twice that Stefan is dead," Anna screamed, "now you say he isn't. Is he or isn't he?"

"Well, yes and no," Gerard muttered. Anna raised her hand and slapped him across the face with all her strength sending the hapless knight sprawling to the floor. She pounced on him like a panther and wrenched his face around to hers and hissed slowly and distinctly into his ears:

"Is ... Stefan ... dead ... or ... is ... he ... alive?"

Gerard, frightened by this display of feminine ferocity, whimpered a reply. "He is alive, but he is going to be dead."

"Why did you tell my father that he is dead?"

"Because he had to believe he could deal with us and not Stefan."

"Why don't they want him to deal with Stefan?"

'Because if Stefan is alive, they don't get the money." Gerard was beginning to sober up. Anna allowed him to retake his seat. She threw another coin on the table. He scooped the three of them into his pocket.

"And if Stefan is dead?"

"Adela gets half, and the Church gets half, and King Philip gets its all."

"How does Philip get it all?"

Gerard sputtered, exasperated. "Lady Adela gives it to him, of course!"

"And what does Adela get out of all of this?" Anna was still searching for the full picture.

"Philip invades Normandy and then England itself, and deposes William Rufus and sets up Adela, daughter of William the Conqueror, as the first Queen of England!"

It will never happen, Anna thought. Never happen … not if I can do something about it. "So Stefan is alive for now, but not for long, is that what you're saying?"

Gerard nodded. "Why do you care?" he asked. "Is it proper for me to tell you these things?"

"Never mind," she said, answering his first question. "Yes it is proper," she added, answering his second. "Now where is the Church in these plans?"

Gerard grinned. "The Church is quiet."

"Because the Church gives Adela their inheritance from Stefan's death."

"Why would the Church give up their share of Stefan's inheritance?"

"To build the world's most beautiful cathedral," he whispered.

"Where?"

"At Chartres."

'But they'll need money," Anna said, confused. "Why give Adela their half of Stefan's wealth if they intend to build a cathedral?"

Gerard explained. "It's an exchange," he said. "They give us their share, and in return we give them something even more valuable."

"What?" asked Anna impatiently.

"The Holy Lance!"

✠✠✠

The feast attracted the attention of the Turks and general population within the city. They began to gather in the late afternoon upon the battlements between St. Paul's Gate and the Gate of the Dog. The citizens of Antioch had not themselves experienced the pain of starvation for the walls of their city encompassed considerable arable land and there was a river which ran through the city from the Iron Gate on the slopes of Mt. Silpius and out beneath the walls between the Duke's Gate and the Gate of the Dog. Moreover, the crusaders had been unable to seal off the city, so supplies still flowed freely through St. George's Gate.

The preparations they viewed this day from the wall were extraordinary only because they seemed extravagant for a beleaguered force with no visible lines of support. They saw animals slaughtered by the dozens, skinned, eviscerated, and placed over roasting spits. By evenfall, the carcasses were ready for consumption. The leaders of the pilgrimage gathered at Bohemund's quarters and several hundreds of their vassals and lower lords. Beyond this crowd were the desperate and poor, who believed that even if they couldn't eat, they might be nourished by at least the scent of roasting flesh. Like Addie, they, too, thought they might glean scraps when it was all over.

Addie was tired, her body weak and limp like a withered plant. She sat alone on a patch of grass near the fire pits. Bohemund's servants were filling several fresh pits with timber in preparation for additional roasts. She watched in a detached, uninterested manner, knowing that all of this activity had nothing to do with her. She became passionate about very little these days; hunger was a great neutralizer of emotion. Guy was watching Clare; Pons was somewhere looking for food himself.

Peter and Hildy ... she didn't know where they were. They had married. The four of them could not share a tent together, and sleeping together in the same tent was not possible. They had been inseparable; it seemed only reasonable. Addie approved. Fulcher the priest performed a brief ceremony in the Church of St. Peter inside of the city. He had requested special permission from Bishop Adhemar to do so, and the bishop sent emissaries to the acting governor of the city (for Arslan had temporarily departed). Peter found the experience genuinely moving, examining the church carefully, whereas Hildy seemed terrified. Fulcher attributed her reaction to a fear of marriage rather than a fear of being in a Christian church. In any event, he extracted no promise from Hildy other than to love and obey and to be a faithful wife. She took the sacrament but did not swallow it, and later spat it into her hand.

Addie smiled wanly. Peter a husband! That dreamer! How would Hildy abide his visions and prophecies? Hildy! Her sister-in-law! Well, she liked Hildy and she understood Peter's love for her. You could see the intelligence in her eyes and she had a face that was more beautiful when it was sad than happy. Her hands were brown and expressive; her long, slender fingers spoke a language for Peter beyond what her eyes could suggest or her lips could voice. She was an enigma and some men like mystery; Peter was definitely one of those men.

She could see from her vantage some of the leaders of the crusade. She did not know all their names except for her own lord, Count Raymond. She recognized Bohemund who had been pointed out to her. The tall one. And she knew Count Stefan by sight. They had met briefly once in Iconium. She was sitting by the roadside when he had passed with his entourage. She called out offering him an orange. But he had declined and passed by.

Armenians, Syrians, Moslems and Christians crowded the battlements watching the spectacle in the fields below. The campfires, providing warmth and light for knights, foot soldiers and servants, cast shadows upon the great, moss-covered walls of Antioch, creating a giant tableau of twenty-foot shadows walking and dancing about on the surface of the wall like the scene on Plato's Cave. Then Addie heard Bohemund call out: "Bring in the prisoners."

✠✠✠

"Bring in the prisoners?" Godfrey questioned. "What's this?"

"You'll see," Bohemund replied, filling his cup with wine and avoiding a direct glance at Godfrey. The captain shouted another order and a few moments later, soldiers escorted a dozen Turks into the arena by the campfires.

"Where did these come from," Godfrey asked.

"Up the Orontes, on a raid. They are spies."

"We can't feed ourselves, why should we feed prisoners?" asked Hugh of Vermandois.

"True, my friend," Bohemund shouted, raising his voice for the others, "It is time the Turks started feeding us, wouldn't you say?"

The leaders did not know what he meant by this, for none of them had begun to eat. But now they were watching intently. Bohemund raised his tall, sportive frame erect and walked across the clearing to the unused fire pits. The fire builders had rubbed pitch on several of the faggots and now, as they lowered their torches to the kindling, the pits came alive with fresh incendiary light, six of them. These were roasting fires, and the spits were prepared for the lamb or hog.

The Turks, their hands lashed behind their backs, were young with dark beards and flowing hair, fine bodies, and bound to each other by ropes around their necks. The guards lined them up in the center of the arena and then went from one to the other stripping them of their clothes which were gathered and thrown on a nearby fire and quickly consumed.

When the men had been stripped, Bohemund, dressed in hauberk, cloak, heavy woolen breeches, and his sword strapped to his side, passed by the lot of them looking each square in the eyes until he had reviewed them all. At the end of the sixteen, he turned, the breeze catching his cloak and twirled it about him. He looked down the row of them, saying nothing.

"We are going to have entertainment," said Hugh.

"Games," said Godfrey.

"Murder," said Stefan.

Bohemund walked down the row of the sixteen men again. Then he spoke to the guard. "Kill them," he said.

Addie saw the guards order the Turks to their knees. With their hands tied behind them, some lost their balance and fell prostrate upon the earth, struggling like a capsized turtle to right themselves. Addie knew then they were going to die and she knew that they knew they were going to die. What might it be like to know you are going to die? she thought. Was it envy she felt? Envy of these men who were staring death in the face, who knew that in moments their spirits would take flight to Allah? Mortal lives at an end ... whatever they had experienced of life and love was now all subsumed in the horror of this very moment. Their mothers had held them as infants and nursed them. They had played common childhood games with their friends as children. They had grown strong bodies and fought hard. They had loved women and been comrades with their boyhood companions. Now their lives were at an end. They would fly away as martyrs and Addie would continue to be hungry. She would continue to breathe mortal life and struggle to find a way to feed her daughter. Addie knew that keeping her daughter alive was keeping her alive, for without Clare, she would have no desire to live, not like this.

Heads rolled. The executioner's axe cut roughly. The body, separated from the head, fell off balance to the earth where it lay convulsing and bleeding. A guard picked up each severed head and with two hands, one over each ear, lammed it roughly over a spiked pole which had been set up near the Antiochan walls and plainly within sight of the observers on the ramparts above. These spectators, many of them women, began to wail, throwing their cries upon the winds, as they watched the slaughter of their countrymen take place.

When the eleventh victim had been slain, Bohemund arose and strode to the bloodied site and watched the execution of the twelfth. Then he stayed the death of the remaining four and ordered them to be tied together as they had been when they were first brought out.

Addie sensed a horror was beginning to unfold. The slain Turks were now lifted, each in turn by their ankles and hoisted upside down by ropes over a beam so that their headless bodies swayed like carcasses of meat. The guard then approached each corpse, disemboweled them, slicing through the belly so that the viscera spilled on to the ground. Addie averted her eyes. The leaders in the canopy watching this horror, shifted uneasily in their seats. They were accustomed to thinking of their enemy as less than human, but their form was human and now twelve human forms were strung up and swinging freely by their ankles and each one sliced open and cleaned out.

The bodies were lowered to the ground and placed side by side not far from the butchering area. The guards then brought large grates on which each human flitch was laid over the six spits, six to a roasting pit. Bohemund cooked the bodies, his intentions clear. "The Turks shall feed us," he had said. Twelve infidels roasting over Christian fires to feed hungry pilgrims. Nearby, the four reprieved Turks were compelled to watch as their brothers, slain before their eyes, were now baked over open fires. It was not long before the sweet, pungent smell of human flesh wafted over the surrounding company.

After about an hour, Bohemund shouted, 'Bring me to eat!" A guard drew his blade and approaching the well-roasted, singed corpse, sliced through the thigh and placed the slab of cooked flesh upon a plate and brought it to Bohemund. The other leaders watched in disgust. There wasn't one among them who would eat human flesh and there wasn't one among them who wasn't certain that Bohemund would.

The prince accepted the plate on which lay a slice of human thigh still simmering in pink juices. Taking it, he arose and walked to where the remaining prisoners were bound.

"Loose them," he ordered. The captives rubbed their wrists to ease the pain where the ropes had been.

Bohemund crouched before the first prisoner and put the platter of human flesh in his face.

"Hoc est corpus suum," he intoned, "Take, eat, for this is his body broken for you." The Turk grimaced and refused to open his mouth or take the meat with his hands.

"Eat it," Bohemund screamed. "Eat it now!' The Turk shook his head wildly and begged to be excused.

Bohemund withdrew a dagger and pulled the man's head by his long, black hair and placed the tip of the dagger upon the flesh of his throat.

"Eat it," he whispered, his eyes glazed with evil, "Or I will be eating you!"

The Turk, crazed by fear, grabbed the meat and tore at it with his fingers. He broke off a small chunk and put it in his mouth.

"Chew!' said Bohemund. But the Turk did nothing. "Chew!' He screamed again. The young man began to chew. But not for long. A pained expression came over his face and suddenly his mouth opened and he spewed out the entire contents of his stomach. His friend likewise vomited. Within the space of a few moments, all four of the prisoners lay retching in their own vomit.

Bohemund stepped back and watched this impassively. He made a motion with his hand and the guards severed the ropes binding them to each other and loosed the remaining men.

The Italian spoke to them through an interpreter: "Go home tonight, and tell your people that we shall dine this evening on the flesh of our enemies. Tell them that this is the fate that awaits each and every spy who enters our camp to learn of our affairs and to do us damage and harm. Tell them that our God is great and mighty and that no one can stand in the face of his wrath. And tell them that we shall eat upon the flesh of the next spy who dares to come into our camp and attempt to deceive us. Go from us now, and tell what you have seen."

Bohemund finished his screaming and the frightened men scrambled to their feet and staggered away uncertainly as the entire camp watched. Then they began to sprint into the darkness toward the walls of their home, soon lost in the shadows beyond the flickering light of the campfires.

By all accounts, however, the savagery of his action was unheard of. No one, poor or nobleman alike, could remember anything comparable in their recent, storied past. The strategy achieved its intended result, for the news of this incident was soon spread far and wide and Christians gained the reputation for being a fierce and intractable people. It was reasoned that Christians, who in their secret worship allegedly ate the body and drank the blood of their prophet, could also be expected to cannibalize their victims. Such barbarianisms were to be expected, they whispered, from the less civilized west, perhaps not of the Italians where an ancient Roman and Tuscan tradition of laws and civilization was in place, but certainly from the extreme edges of the civilized world such as Gaul, Normandy, and Britain. What would one expect of the Franks, the most cruel and brutish of the races?

They feasted that night on the calf, wild boar, sheep and lamb, not on human flesh. But Bohemund continued the deception by having the soldiers occasionally butcher the Turkish bodies so that those on the walls would believe that on this cold winter night, the Christians were feeding on the flesh of spies. When the festivities were concluded, the nobles went to their tents. But out of the darkness crept the Tafurs who fed upon the bodies of the Turkish infidels like jackals. The next morning, observers could see the smoldering fires on which lay, in the flaky white ashes of the fire, the fresh, skeletal remains of the Turks, the flesh of their bones picked clean by the Tafurs.

Addie's hunger was unassuaged. She felt tired and weak and when she went to pull her cloak about her more tightly, she noticed her hands were shaking. Then she could feel her heart drumming as though it were beating out the time remaining of her mortal life. She slumped to the earth in repose, quietly and unnoticed, and remained there as the night temperature dropped and the revelers returned to their camps. The wind played wildly under a full moon and blew Addie's cloak over her head so that to a passerby she appeared to be nothing more than a pile of rags, or to be what she was, a poor wretch who either had no place to sleep or was too ill to get there.

She might have lain there throughout the night had it not been that one knight only narrowly managed to avoid trampling her with his horse. He dismounted and knelt beside her and gently rolled her over, removing the cloak from her face. The light of the Syrian moon illuminated the Gaullic features of a face that to Godfrey de Boullion still had considerable, if emaciated, beauty.

The knight mounted his horse and said to his aide: "Take her to my tent," and then he rode toward Duke's Gate.

CHAPTER TWENTY-SEVEN

Addie Receives a Proposal

ODFREY INSERTED HIS SLENDER HAND into the folds of the oriental tapestry that served as a partition between his bed chamber and an outer room. He pushed the divider apart slightly and peered carefully into the inner room. There was a single cot in the room, and a small table with a wash basin. On the bed lay a woman sleeping—deeply and heavily. Godfrey's chamber ladies had dressed her in a white linen sleeping robe. She lay as though on a funeral bier, her head propped high on an embroidered pillow and her auburn hair spread across the cushion in haphazard fashion.

Godfrey guessed her age to be about twenty-eight although the rigors of pilgrimage can age one prematurely, he thought. She was very thin, yet her beauty was not diminished by the obvious impoverishment through which she had been compelled to pass. Hers, he thought, was the kind of beauty that withers evenly no matter what the age or the phase through which she is passing.

The knight from Lorraine stepped into the bedchamber where she lay. He stood quietly by the cot looking at her: her mouth, smallish and thin-lipped, was parted slightly; her white hands lay peacefully beside her. He knelt beside her and with the fingers of both hands touched her hair. It felt dirty, clotted with mud and clay. He would have his servants wash her hair tomorrow. He put his open full palms against the sides of her face and tilted her head toward him. She groaned and moved slightly, but remained unaware of his presence. His hands slid down across her cheeks to her neck. He felt the narrowness of it and with his thumbs grazed the outline of her chin and jaw. Trembling now, he removed his hands from her neck and pushed them slowly over her upper chest and then her breasts. He caressed them lightly, smiling fainting. His tongue moistened his lips.

His desire ungratified, he tugged at the drawstring at her neck. He opened the bed shirt and pulled it away from her neck revealing the pale bounty of her chest. Placing his wavering hand in the valley between her breasts, he could feel the warmth and the downy texture of her skin. He slid his palm to her breast and touched it, grazing it as though by accident, and then—in full commission of his sin—took the tender mass in his full hand feeling the fluidity and suppleness of it. He brushed the nipple, expecting to find it taut but instead found it flaccid.

Addie slept through this assault quite innocently, unmindful of either what was occurring or what intentions prompted it. Godfrey stayed at her side kneeling in this manner for several minutes, his hands moving constantly albeit imperceptibly. Suddenly, the knight removed his hands, but supporting himself with them, he brought his head to her chest and kissed her breasts. His tongue flicked at her nipples, lingering and making them wet. Then he retied the drawstring and stood. He studied her again carefully and abruptly quit the room.

Such encounters as Godfrey's with Addie were only one reason Pope Urban II had strongly discouraged women from joining the pilgrimage. He had argued that the dangers and demands of such a journey were rigorous even for the most able-bodied of men, but were absolutely perilous for women. In truth, Urban had less the mortal life of women at heart as he did the moral life of men. Women, he said, would distract from the purpose of the pilgrimage. They would inevitably invite temptation and render a pure pilgrimage impossible and a pilgrimage infected by impurity would ultimately fail to achieve its goals. Adhemar had already begun to suggest that the recent misfortunes of the crusaders were due to immorality.

Pope Urban must have known that there had been no pilgrimage in recent times that had not been accompanied by a certain number of camp followers, women who were present in the camp to be women for men who had no women. A woman who would be a woman, Godfrey thought. Not a woman who would be a soldier, not a woman who would be a pilgrim, not a woman who would be a saint, but a woman who would be a hungry, salacious, leg-spreading love-pumper. This was the role of women after all: useful in loving, farming or cooking. Beautiful women should be lovers, strong women farmers, and those who were neither beautiful nor strong should cook. Sometimes these roles were assigned by providence: a woman ugly from birth, if strong, learned to till the fields; a woman without beauty or strength from her youth learned culinary crafts. Other times, these roles developed chronologically: the woman in her youthful beauty gave herself away in love, but when beauty faded, yet her strength being strong, she could still do the haymaking, weeding, mowing, or transport the grain, drive the oxen, or break stones for road mending. And when her beauty and strength was gone, she could retire to cooking and sewing.

God created woman for man, Godfrey mused. It could not be so much of a transgression if he, Godfrey, a knight of Lorraine, joyfully accepted what God himself had ordained. In any case, his merits as a pilgrim on this wretched journey more than offset the venial offense that would be charged to his account because he was simply a man wanting to be with a woman, or in other words, because he was precisely the kind of man God had wanted him to be all along.

The next morning after Godfrey had slept on those thoughts, he visited Addie once again in her bedchamber. He found her very much awake this time and eager to depart.

"I must leave and return to my family," she said anxiously when Godfrey appeared. "They will be very worried about me." Then her eyes widened with curiosity. "Who are you and why am I here and how did I get here and why can't I leave?" She posed the questions quickly and peevishly.

"Hold on, now," said Godfrey. "You must return at once to your family and friends. I found you as though dead last night, lying alone in the grass near the clearing—" Addie seemed puzzled by this account. "—Where the feast was, where the Turks were killed." Addie nodded.

"I remember," she said.

Godfrey continued. "I brought you to my tent and my servants gave you some new clothing and washed your hair. I asked them to keep you here until I had a chance to greet you personally. Are you hungry?"

Addie dropped her eyes and stared at her hands. She did not want to betray how hungry she actually was. "I am not hungry," she said, looking at him again, "but I have a child who is not well. She is very weak, and there no food for her."

"What is her name," Godfrey inquired.

"Clare—and she is all that I have."

"You have but one child then?"

"I had a sister, Lettie, but she was taken by the Turks at the Civetot." Addie choked back the tears. "I pray for her every day. I know she is still alive somewhere."

"I'm sure she is," Godfrey said. "Excuse me for one moment." When Godfrey left, Addie sat quietly, uncertain yet as to why she was there and to what circumstance she owed the good fortune of meeting a nobleman like Godfrey de Boullion. The prince returned and put three rolls into her hands, and gave her a basket of barley cakes and cheese.

"Here," he said, "eat and take the rest to your child."

Addie sighed in happy relief at the sight of such wholesome food. "You are so kind," she stammered. "I am so undeserving of your kindness."

Godfrey smiled. "Not at all," he said. "Now tell me about yourself." Addie recounted the tale of her wanderings, their life in

Provence, the preaching of Peter the Monk, and why they had answered the call to establish a new millennial order in Jerusalem. Godfrey listened in fascination. This woman was ignorant but by no means without intelligence.

"You are a beautiful and brave woman," he said. Addie blushed and looked away. It was the first time a man had called her beautiful since Ollo had died. Pons treated her as though she were beautiful, but he never said it. She did not think of herself as possessing either beauty or bravery. There was little she could do about the former designation and little she had done to merit the latter. If the alternative to being a coward is to be brave, then she reckoned herself brave, but it was more apt simply to say she had thus far survived.

"I want to help you," Godfrey announced.

"You do?" Addie said. She did not know this man, nor he her.

"Yes, I do." Godfrey paused, unsure of how to proceed. Lust overcoming doubt, he said: "You are in a desperate situation, with a child to care for, not to speak of your own health to safeguard. If your health fails, your child is left alone in this world." He paused to see if his words were striking a chord. They were.

"You are forced now to beg for your food, and, even when you are successful, there is very little for you. Your brothers and sisters are dying for lack of food. Others have joined the Tafurs—" Addie shuddered and put her hands to her ears and bowed her head. "—and eat rodents and maggots in horse dung." Godfrey leaned forward and grasped her wrists and pulled them away from her face. He saw that her eyes were reddened and that tears had made a wet course down the dry skin of her checks.

He continued, holding her hands so that her palms were open, as though ready to receive his largess. "You are in desperate need, and I am in a position to help." He stopped, staring still at her tear-streaked face.

"Would you?" she asked, sniffling. "Would you help us?"

"Mais oui," Godfrey answered. They were speaking French.

"But would you prefer to receive my help as a gift or would you rather help me in return?" Addie looked up sharply at those words. Of course, she would be overjoyed to be employed in the service of a lord; she could call him her lord. She would feel useful again!

"Oh, yes," she said smiling broadly through her tears. "I could sew and bake for you, clean your armor, sharpen your weapons, feed your horses. It doesn't matter. Anything!"

"Anything?" Godfrey asked. He took her hands again. "You have a great need and I have the resources to relieve that need, soften your pain. But I have a need and you have the resources to meet that need. I can help you and you can help me." Addie brushed away the hair from her face and sat up straight upon the bed. "I will help in any way that I can. Just give me the work and I will do it. I am very strong and useful, there is nothing that I can't do that even a man can do," she said proudly.

Addie thus assumed a very resolute and direct posture. Throwing her shoulders back, she awaited his verdict with determination, confident that there was no task or requirement he could name that would be too difficult for her to perform. Godfrey, for his part, stared as unobtrusively as possible at her heaving bosom, remembering the sight of her breasts lifting and falling in slumber only a few hours before.

He stood and walked away from her. "I am a man," he said almost inaudibly, "and you are a woman." He turned around and faced her again. "You must give me your woman-ness. You must give to me what only you can give, and I will give you what only I can give. We are twice blessed in both the giving and the receiving."

There. He had said it. He waited.

Addie leaned away from him in shock and clutched the drawstring of her blouse instinctively. She wasn't completely sure what it was that he had just proposed, but if it was what she *thought* it was, she could not for life or breath consider it a moment further.

"You want me to—"

"—give yourself to me," Godfrey said. "It is my need and your plenty. I will feed you and Clare, for it is your need and my plenty.

Nothing could be more fair."

Addie stood quickly. "But the laws of pilgrimage demand abstinence," she objected.

"Yes, I know," Godfrey admitted. "Pilgrimage demands many things that cannot be fulfilled."

She attempted to leave, but Godfrey stepped in her way.

"I must go now," she said, sobbing. "You mustn't stop me."

Godfrey grabbed both of her arms by the elbows and pulled her close to him. He could feel her breasts pressing against his chest. She turned her head away from him, but he spoke into her ear. "Think carefully," he whispered. "You have your daughter to think about as well as yourself. Don't be so selfish that your daughter has to suffer for your moral scruples. God wants you to use the gifts he has given you and he has given you the gift of beauty. Use it!" He relaxed his grip, but did not let go. "Think about it now and come back to this tent when you're ready. And you will never suffer lack, I promise you!"

Addie broke away from his grasp and pushed aside the tapestry and made her way out of the tent and into the early light of morning. Her bare feet carried her swiftly down the trodden path and across the misty grassy clearing to the encampment of the Provencals. Behind her loomed the walls of Antioch. Tears blurred her vision as she ran, her world glistening with tear-sparkles that laid on her eyelids like the dew on the grass beneath her feet.

She cried for two days. And when for brief periods her eyes were dry and the raging tempest in her heart was still, she asked herself whence and wherefore came her tears. She wasn't sure. But she knew and was afraid to admit to herself aloud that it was less the suggestion that had been made to her as it was the *reasonableness* of it that so maddened her. She wept because harlotry seemed such a plausible way out of her distress when there appeared to be no other way out, and wept that she could even think such thoughts. She never would have weighed such a proposition in other, more prosperous, circumstances. But, in another situation, she would not have been required to solicit help at this price. For which would

God now condemn her: for allowing her child to suffer when she had the means to alleviate the suffering, or for giving her love to a man in exchange for her child's life?

This was a choice she did not want to make; she was not schooled in the laws of casuistry and moral theology. She only knew that she was a good person. She dared to be angry with God that her condition could be reduced to such a state of moral rubble, and she was angry with Godfrey who, by his proposal, had created an ethical dilemma in which she appeared to sin whatever choice she made. How could she stay by her fire with a few berries and roots to eat and watch Clare grow weaker by the day when she was capable of providing for her needs in a more bountiful way?

These questions wearied Addie until she could think no more of them. No one had ever made such a proposal to her before. And she had not loved a man for — how long had it been? Three years? She didn't want to count. Too long! There had been no man with whom she had wanted to share her love except Pons, and they had not come even close to consummating their friendship in this manner. She was willing, she confessed. She had thought about Pons as a lover, and she suspected that Pons would leap into her bed if she suggested it. But it had not been suggested. She had not been with Pons, or anyone.

Godfrey's proposal effectively reduced Addie's life to a repetitive cycle of events which no longer had meaning for her. Her walk was wooden, her expression drawn in despair, her gaze aimless and glazed. Neither Peter nor Hildy could elicit the cause of such behavior from her. She spoke only when spoken to and seldom smiled. She arose each day, labored as she could, rested, and slept. She ate little, for there was little to eat. She preferred to leave it for Clare.

Thus, she wavered between heaven and hell, believing essentially that Godfrey, whatever he had done, had removed the possibility of heaven and had consigned her, whatever her choice, to hell. She hated him for that. Hated him, not because he thought her body could be purchased for a few handfuls of grain, but because he had sent her soul to hell. He had robbed her of innocent suffering, of an unmolested martyrdom. She could have died virtuous and pure; now she would die either a harlot with a warm heart, or a mother with a cold one.

It was this realization that helped Addie determine her mind. If she was going to hell unable to save *herself*, she must then by all means save Clare.

She appeared at his tent exactly one week from the time he had talked to her last. She did not know what she should wear; she had nothing exquisite and certainly did not feel that she needed to please him in the choice of her clothing. In any case, she didn't have the luxury of choosing her raiment. She wore what she had: a full skirt tied at the waist by a cord of rabbit fur, a loose-fitting cloak and a cape with a cowl.

Thus attired, she stood shivering in the early morning at the nobleman's tent with her cape wrapped tightly around her. A maidservant much less beautiful than herself, Addie thought (thinking more this week about her own appearance) emerged in the entranceway. It was early morning, and Addie, shivering in the cold, wrapped her cape tightly about her and told the maidservant to tell her master that a woman of Provence had a gift for him. This news was conveyed and shortly Godfrey greeted her warmly but did not want her. Instead, he gave her some rolls and grain and sent her away with instructions to return the next day at eventide to a tent at a different location, a tent marked by his personal standard near the Orontes River by the Bridge of the Boats. She would recognize his banner as the white one with a lion of gold in the center surrounded in four corners by a cross, a crown, a chalice and a pitcher.

But the events of the next morning changed her plans. A herald, sent by Bishop Adhemar, rode into camp puffed with self-importance, and read a decree from the bishop to all the camp-dwellers. All women, by this decree, married or unmarried were to be removed from the camps and relocated in a separate camp beyond the river near the cemetery between the river and the road to Alexandretta. The statement went on to reaffirm prohibitions against using false weights and measurements, fraud, theft, fornication and adultery. The offenses were punishable by beatings, brandings and imprisonment.

As though to emphasize the point, a small procession came into view of six naked persons including three women, all caught in adultery and stripped of their clothes. Bound together and their hands lashed behind them, they were marched through the camp while men appointed by the bishop laid a reed to their backs. One woman was very young with small breasts that had never suckled a child. Another, much older, marched with her eyes closed and her face to the sky, willing to allow the person in front of her to lurch her forward step by step. The men marched with their heads bowed as though to hide their faces in their beards and hair. One man's belly was so large that only the tip of his penis could be seen hanging beneath it, while the flaccid penis of a taller and thinner man swayed with each step, slapping his thighs.

Addie stood unblinking and curious as they disappeared from view, wondering if any of those women had been in Godfrey's tent. She hadn't time to consider such questions as the relocation of the women began immediately. Addie began the work of collapsing the tent undaunted by the inconvenience of it all, and gathered her possessions which consisted merely of the tent itself, poles, clothes and a box of personal treasures.

"We're moving," she said to Clare when she picked up the child.

"I don't want to move," the child complained, watching her uncle Peter stroll into view.

"The bishop," he said, "has also ordered a three day fast of purification."

"A three day fast?" she said, astounded, dropping what she was doing to stare open-mouthed at her brother. "I've been on a three *month* fast already. How can he tell us to fast when we are already dying of starvation?"

Later in the day, she saw Fulcher visiting the women and children, the sick and the needy. "Will God forgive them, father?" she asked of the priest in the long, black cassock.

"Forgive who?"

"Those men and women who passed through our camp this morning."

Fulcher clasped his hands behind his back and invited Addie to walk with him. They strolled down to the river. "God will forgive those whom the Church forgives," he said.

"And does the Church forgive them?" she asked.

"There is only one sin that cannot be forgiven and that is blasphemy against the Holy Ghost."

"So will the Church forgive them?" she said, repeating her question, pressing him for an answer.

"If there is evidence of contrition signified by the completion of penance, the Church readily forgives," he said, smiling. "And they must forgive themselves."

"What do you mean?"

"I mean that sometimes a person can feel too much remorse, like they are walking with a sack over their heads in total darkness with someone's hands at their throat choking them. They can't see, they can't breathe, they can't enjoy life anymore, even after penance. That person hasn't forgiven himself, hasn't remembered that, after all, we all are human."

"And what if those women were forced to do what they did? What if they had no choice but to sin?"

Fulcher sat down on the bank of the river and plucked at the grass. The Orontes flattened out here, pocked by sandy shoals, so that its depth was no more than two or three feet. Its banks were grassy and protected by reeds and cattails, home to muskrats and waterfowl. The current was slow and lazy, bearing small limbs toward the sea where someday they might be carried to the shores of Africa. The sun, shining indistinctly through a veneer of gray clouds, cast a sheen upon the gray water.

"What if they had no choice?" Addie asked again.

"There is always a way in which sin can be avoided," he said.

"So it is possible not to sin?"

"Yes."

"But no one has ever done it?"

"No one but the Lord."

"Not even you?"

Fulcher laughed. "Not even I!"

"So it would seem *not* to be possible."

"Yes, it would seem so," Fulcher said, turning to look at her. He raised his finger to emphasize his point: "But each sin is decisive and calls for an act of the will. You must decide to sin, and, in the moment of decision, you can decide not to sin. If you did that consistently, you would not sin."

"But Father, sometimes, I sin against my will, I don't want to, and sometimes I do without thinking."

Fulcher cited Scripture: "There is a prayer in Scripture that says, 'Search me, O God, and see if there be any wicked way in me and lead me in the way everlasting.'"

"Who said that?" Addie demanded.

"David, King of Israel."

"Was he a sinner, too?"

"He committed adultery with Bathsheba."

"He DID?" Addie let this piece of intelligence filter into her heart. "And did God forgive him?"

"Yes, but he paid the price."

"What was that?"

"The child died."

Addie was silent. Then she said, "That doesn't seem fair."

"No."

"So the child dies, but then God forgave him?"

"He is called a man after God's own heart.'

"Thank you, Father!" She leaned toward him and embraced the startled priest fully and passionately. When she released him, she said: "Can we talk again?" Fulcher nodded, lost for words.

"Please do come by again," Addie said, as she rose and ran away from him.

Curiously, her conversation with Fulcher only strengthened her resolve to accept Godfrey's proposal. Her decision did not signify that she hated Godfrey less; only that she loved herself more. She now believed that while what she was about to do was in the eyes of the Church wrong, in the world in which she lived, it was very right. She would risk the opprobrium of the Church to gain the well-being of her family.

It was with a strong sense of mission that Addie stood that same night in the darkened chambers of her new lord, Godfrey de Bouillon. She fancied herself a *sanctimoniale*, about to offer her chastity for a higher good. And if, in the pursuit of righteousness as she understood it, she erred, God would show her the pathway to redemption. Salvation had become for her no longer an abstract notion relating to a future state, but a condition she herself must work to achieve in this world, this lifetime.

Therefore, she stood before Godfrey in the cracked moonlight as a *mediatrix* between life and death. She put her hands to her throat and tugged at the laces there. In a smooth, flowing motion, her robe slipped to the floor. She stood mute and naked in the pale, lunar light. Her right hand dropped slowly down her chest, covering for a moment her full breast. She went to him and he grabbed at her in his need. She winced, and cried out, but did not stop him.

When she left an hour later, she was—as he had said—twice blessed, both in the giving and in the receiving.

CHAPTER TWENTY-EIGHT

The Harlot

Antioch, May 27, 1098 A.D.

"WHAT I AM PROPOSING, MY LORDS," said Bohemund, exasperated, as he stalked around the table of the Council of Knights, "is that the city of Antioch be given to whoever takes the initiative to seize it. One among us must remain in power when the pilgrimage continues to Jerusalem, and I suggest that person be the one who takes it, and since none of you appears willing, I think that person will be me!"

Raymond, who opposed Bohemund on most matters, arose before the Council to oppose him again. "Tacitus tells us that the emperor is gathering an imperial force to join us in the siege. It would be foolhardy to attempt an assault now when our numbers are low and most of our knights are without mounts." He took a deep breath and pompously continued, frame erect and chin high. "In any case, what we capture is for the emperor and not for ourselves, and the lord from Tarranto should know that better than anyone else."

"My impending connection with the imperial family is all the more reason to approve this idea," Bohemund said quickly, hearing from Raymond an argument which he himself had overlooked.

So went the conversation in the late winter months. But the Council of Knights did not approve of Bohemund's plan and the siege continued into its eighth month. For most of this period, the presence of the western pilgrims before the Byzantine walls of Antioch could be called a siege in name only. The view generally held was that the city could have been captured in late October or early November had the crusaders the verve to strike quickly. Bohemund had been uncharacteristically reluctant to launch an offensive at that time, and camp gossip had it that the Italian had his heart set upon snatching the city for himself.

The bleak winter months, then, had been quiet militarily. The crusaders had fought, it is true, but not to gain the city but rather to preserve their lives. The skirmishes in which the army found itself from time to time were over food and supplies and not over territory. Raiding parties roamed as far as a hundred miles searching for food. Famine was widespread and hundreds had died and many hundreds more had deserted and returned to Italy or France. Those who remained were either foot-soldiers or knights who hoped to better their lot in Palestine and continued to believe in the ultimate victory of their endeavor, or they were the poor who had no place to go, or in any case, no means by which to get there. In both groups, the apocalyptic vision stayed constant; most firmly believed that, as Fulcher was wont to tell it, "the suffering of this present world was not worthy to be compared to the glory that would someday be revealed in them." They would at the latter day, he told them, stand white-robed on the Mount of Olives, on the neck of the Antichrist, and gain their eternal reward.

In the spring, however, the presence of the army began to take on the appearance of a siege once again. The leaders of the crusade elected Stefan of Blois as their *Ductor*, a move which pleased him very much, but a move nonetheless that only recognized the sagacity of his administrative, not military, skills. As a landowner of immense holdings in France, he knew how to manage large affairs.

Nevertheless, the crusaders began to tighten the blockade of Antioch and the effects were clearly being felt within the city. This was made possible by two developments. First, Adhemar had been in contact with the orthodox patriarch of Jerusalem who was living in exile on Cyprus. Symeon, no particular friend of the West (indeed he had published a treatise against the Latin rite), was still less a friend of the Turks. Reasoning that an enemy of his enemy had to be a friend, Symeon was eager to help the crusaders. That Adhemar had given him the titles and authority of an independent pontiff no doubt helped. In return for these overtures made by the papal legate, Symeon secured all the fruit, bacon and wine that he could and sent them to Antioch to help feed the famished army.

Second, a fleet arrived at St. Simeon from Constantinople. The ships were manned by Englishmen and carried a contingent of Italian pilgrims anxious to join the crusade. It had sailed into port at Constantinople and there picked up siege materials for use in the Palestinian campaign. The Turks tried to capture these goods as they were unloaded at St. Simeon, but Bohemund and Raymond successfully defended the supplies, leaving the Turks to bury their dead in the Moslem cemetery across the river. Not willing to let the dead rest in peace, Bohemund ordered the bodies dug up and dragged from their graves. They were looted for jewelry, ornaments, bezants, cloaks, and bows and arrows. They were then decapitated, the corpses tossed into an open pit, and the heads taken to the Norman's quarters for an accurate count.

With the new siege materials, the crusaders began to construct towers to guard the major entrances of the city in order to complete the blockade. The first such fortress was built near the Fortified Bridge, also near the Moslem cemetery and in full view of the road leading to St. Simeon or Alexandretta. They called this tower "The Mosque" or La Mahomerie. It was placed under the control of Count Raymond. Another tower was built close to the Gate of St. Paul, and called the Tower of Malregard. It was given to Bohemund to garrison. A third tower was built close to the Gate of St. George, and it was given to Tancred. The city was now effectively shut up. The only access to the city was now over the steep slopes of Mount Silpius or the Iron Gate. In any case, food convoys would no longer be able to enter the city.

With the advent of spring, food became more plentiful but, while the plight of the pilgrims eased somewhat, inside the walls the situation worsened for the Antiochan inhabitants. Starvation grew in their bellies like yeast in bread. The army was acutely aware that a battle for the city could not be far in the offing. In fact, food was not plentiful for the pilgrims, but it was available in greater quantities than before.

This posed a new dilemma for Adelaide. She could no longer justify the services she was providing to Godfrey. She knew that the arrangement Godfrey had made with her would have to be terminated not because Godfrey was no longer in need of her, but because she no longer was in need of him. Still, food continued to be a problem, and it would not become plentiful until later in the summer when harvests would begin. Moreover, she saw the need, as she hadn't before, to lay in a store of money to keep her through those lean periods that this pilgrimage seemed inevitably to encounter.

Addie had become the woman of preference for the leaders of the crusade. They came to her because, after having slept with her, they did not feel ashamed. While with Addie, they were with a woman who wasn't ashamed of her behavior and, therefore, they themselves did not feel shame. Addie had given to her harlotry a kind of redemptive cast that enabled her to participate with—if not enthusiasm—at least active acceptance. Her liaisons with the northern French leaders therefore took on a salvific dimension. She no longer saw herself as going to hell; no one can be a good lover while sliding into the jaws of perdition. Instead, she had come to believe that she had been elevated in the eyes of God to a place of special favor. She could do nothing else but receive these men as though she were receiving Christ himself, and, in so doing, she became the bride of Christ, performing only what was her duty to perform and what, in any case, she could by no means avoid. Therefore, in every encounter she gave herself anew to Christ, receiving every body as His body. Once, when her blood stained the bed sheets, she put her finger upon it and with two strokes painted a sign of the cross.

She had not received Christ to her bosum in the person of Count Raymond, however. Nor Count Stefan of Blois and Chartres, nor Robert of Flanders. She was thankful not to have seen the count of Toulouse in her bedchamber. Raymond was, she imagined, too old and too devout to even consider satisfying his needs with a visit to her tent. And he had Elvira. As for Stefan and Robert, she did not speculate. But she gave them a measure of respect for maintaining their absence, being vain enough to believe that if they had not slept with *her*, they had not slept with anyone else. Nevertheless, she had little respect for those who had received her ministrations in spite of the manner in which she had been able to sacramentalize each encounter. It was important to understand that, while in each erotic communion she received the body of Christ, her partners themselves were not sacred: thus the need for sacramentalization. Her lovers were reprobate and ungodly whoremongers who would have to answer for their own sins.

This notwithstanding, there were times when she felt compassion. The men who loved her also loved to talk to her. They told her fondly of their wives at home. They spoke in longing tones of their children, the homeland, their farms and animals. They regaled her with tales of personal exploits on the pilgrimage, of the passions which drove them and kept them alive. They continued to believe in the ultimate victory of the crusader army, hoping that God, having led them this far, would not abandon them to their persecutors. Addie listened attentively and, as she did, her own heart echoed the sentiments she heard, for on her face were written the lines of suffering and sorrow, a face which, when read by her lovers, captivated them and opened up the pages of their own hearts even more.

These matters would all come to an end, she knew, because her changing circumstances would demand it, or because she would be discovered (or betrayed), stripped and flogged, and marched shamelessly through the camp as had many others in her place.

In fact, her circumstances changed sooner than she expected

and in a tripartite and most unexpected manner, a manner in which she would cause the death of one man, save the life of another, and assure the fall of Antioch.

Primo. One night late in May, when she had finished rubbing a sweet-smelling ointment over her body and combing out her luxuriant auburn hair, she heard steps approaching outside the sheepskin door of her bedchamber. Immediately Bohemund was at her side pressing his lips against hers and then pushing her away, smiling arrogantly. Adelaide took no offense, for this was Bohemund's way, as a child forcing his will, teasing, expressing petulance and shifting moods. She stood wordlessly before him and then slowly sank to the padded mat on the floor and stretched out upon it expecting the Italian to lay beside her.

But he did not. Instead he stood over her uncertainly, hesitating between activity and passivity, between what he might do and what he might want done. Addie observed him now as though it were the first time she had seen him, decidedly not the case. He was tall. It was the most striking feature of his physical appearance. His hair was blond, and fell curling to his shoulders which were broad and creased with strength. His face was washed with Italian kindness, and fashioned with rounded features. He had amorphous eyes that were fixed with neither mischief or evil but, Addie thought, a mixture of both.

"Have you said your prayers?" he inquired, still looming over her. He stooped slightly, his head grazing the top of her tent.

"No," she replied, uncomfortable bringing God into her tent. She sat up. "Have you said yours?"

Bohemund smiled. "No, but I'm ready to begin." He leaned toward her with his arms extended and raised her to her feet. He pressed her closely to him, raising her slightly off her feet until her upraised face was near his. "Don't you kneel when you pray?" he asked impishly.

She nodded. He pushed her to her knees in front of him and put his hands on his hips and waited. She knew what he wanted. She fumbled with the buttons on his breeches and then, closing her eyes, she opened her mouth to pray. And indeed, she prayed, furiously and desperately, thinking not of the crescending passion her supplications were invoking, scarcely mindful of the power of her stroking fingers, nor did she wonder why this warrior weakened with the wetness of her kiss. She prayed to the Virgin and St. Anthony and would have proceeded to St. Anne were it not for a cataclysmic shudder that injected fluid into her throat and spewed it across her aching face when she gagged.

When he had composed himself, Bohemund sat down facing her, waiting while Addie cleaned her face with a cloth, got dressed, and combed out her hair. "I want you to work for me," he said casually.

She looked at him with tired eyes. "I am stopping this," she said. "I do not need this anymore."

"Why not?"

"There is food now, the crops are planted. There will be harvest—" Her voice cracked. "I do this for my Clare. I do not care about myself. I do it for her."

Bohemund nodded. "Very admirable," he said. "But if you work for me, you can stop these shameful matters in two weeks—or less."

"But Godfrey de Boullion—"

"Two more weeks for Godfrey at the most. What I want you to do is something entirely different."

Speak, for I am the handmaid of the Lord. Addie turned to him, frowning. "What are you talking about?" she asked.

Bohemund shifted his weight toward her and spoke to her earnestly. "I have been gathering information about the defenses of the city for many months now—hopeful that someday I may discover something valuable, something decisive." He looked at her solemnly. "Now I think I have it! There is a section of the wall between the Gate of the Dog and the Gate of St. Paul that is commanded by a Turk called Firuz from the Tower of the Two Sisters. When he was a child, he was orphaned, and some pilgrims returning from Jerusalem, took him with them back to Provence where they settled and he was raised. When he was a youth, however, he returned and has been here ever since adopting

Moslem habits and customs. He is a treacherous little fellow and would sell his own children to the devil for a profit. Now he has discovered that his Armenian wife has been seduced by a Turk, and I have been told he is angry enough to bring down the entire city in revenge."

Addie was not clear where this was leading. Bohemund continued. "I want you to establish contact with Firuz and carry a message from me to him and return with his response. If we dress you as an Armenian, we can get you into the city. I will show you where to go. You must speak to him with my message. I will tell you what to say. We'll give him a reward, and assure him of his own personal safety if he will open the Gate of St. Paul during the dead of night. Our troops will enter and open the other gates and the city will be ours before the inhabitants can mount a defense."

Bohemund's account sounded farfetched to Addie's ear. "You will show me where to go and tell me what to say?" Addie said.

"Yes."

"And you will tell Godfrey that he no longer requires me?"

"You must continue as always for a couple of weeks so as not to arouse suspicion. No one knows of this plan, not even the other leaders. I have taken you into my confidence as I must."

"And this is my only reward? That I don't have to work for Godfrey after this is all over?" she inquired.

"That should be reward enough," Bohemund answered. "You haven't any choice."

Addie was of a different mind. "But I do have a choice, and I choose not to do it, and I choose to tell Stefan and Raymond about your little plan."

Bohemund's mood changed swiftly. In a flash, he grabbed her hair with his left hand and put a dagger at her throat with the other.

"And I choose to slit your throat, you impudent little tart!"

Addie spoke quietly and carefully, awkward as it was with her head thrust backward and her throat white and extended. "And if you do, you shall have Godfrey to contend with, and the blood of another innocent person on your hands." Bohemund relaxed his grip slightly. "All I want is fair compensation for what you say is a very important mission."

Bohemund dropped his dagger and released her. He realized that it was precisely this brazen quality that made Adelaide the ideal person for his mission. He promised to reward her suitably when the city fell.

"And you are an honest man?" she asked.

"As honest as you," he replied.

"Give me your amulet," she said abruptly, holding our her palm. Bohemund put his hand to his throat quickly. "My amulet?"

"Your amulet," she repeated, her anger rising. "I'll accept it as payment for this favor you ask and for all the other services I have performed for you."

"But it has the Holy Nail—"

"Holy Nail, Holy Snail! We could build a pissburnt bridge across the golden ocean with all the Holy Nails around! Now give me the goddam amulet, you Norman arsehole!"

She spoke a language the Italian could understand. They made a pact, and he assured her that within two days, she would be inside the walls of Antioch with the fate of the city in her hands.

Secundum. Shortly after Bohemund departed, a knight of means came to see her. He was a Norman and that's all she knew about him, except that he was either the commander of an army, or one of the chief captains of one. She had seen him only a few times, but frequently enough to remember his likes and dislikes and his fondness for jewelry. He would not tell her his name and she did not need to know.

On this occasion, however, he had brought some friends with him who had waited outside during his rendezvous with her. When he returned to them, they renewed a vigorous albeit muffled conversation, the gist of which was not entirely lost upon Adelaide who, while not attempting to see who the participants were, attempted to ascertain what they were saying. She pressed her ear to a seam in the hanging skins of her tent. Someone was going to be killed, deserved to be killed, it must appear to be accidental, and it must be soon. They would meet at midnight on the morrow, in the olive grove by the Fortified Bridge.

They left and Addie shuddered, wrapped her cape about her and returned in the darkness to her camp alone. Only later did she realize how this event changed her life.

✠✠✠

A low, mottled sky hung over the city of Antiochus Epiphanes portending a late spring rain. Even the brooding Mt. Silpius was hidden by airy stone-colored clouds that blew across its eastern slopes, momentarily disclosing a view of its southern haunch, and then closing it off only capriciously to reveal another aspect of its bulk. Addie gathered the wool shawl about her shoulders and face, tying its corners neatly beneath her firm chin and glanced anxiously toward the heavens. She preferred a God who was visible, and under the open skies and deep, star-strewn heavens, she always took comfort from the fact that God was there straddling the east and the west, sitting upon the girth of the earth, hands upon the sun and the moon and his eyes upon her. She did not like these gray, godless days as though she were shut up in a dark closet being punished, being isolated from her parents by her parents, or now, from God by God. But she should have known; this is a trial, and God demands that trials be experienced alone. God is funny that way; when you need him most, he disappears and when you are quite comfortable without him he obtrudes into your life, moving you toward yet more misery and isolation.

She stepped lightly into the cart, waving high one hand for balance and pulling adroitly at her skirt with her other hand to avoid falling. Three women in the ox-powered conveyance stopped their chattering long enough to watch curiously as she situated herself among them. They were ample-bodied Armenian Christians with sun-creased rounded faces framed by their shawls like aging Madonnas. Their fleshy hands lay at rest upon the girth of their bodies, fingers interlocking as though to contain the rolling flesh that strained against skirt and blouse. She settled by one of them as the little Syrian driver cracked the whip and the wagon lumbered forward. On the floor between her and the two women facing her were earthen jugs of water, a cask of wine, three bottles of oil, and other sacks containing unknown wares. At her feet lay a mongrel dog, whose tail thumped vigorously upon the oak flooring of the wagon, like the pounding of a drum, whenever Addie was glancing its way.

The cart bumped along the path toward St. Paul's Gate, each revolution of the cartwheels bringing Addie closer to her rendezvous with the tower-keeper. Gradually the walls, built of ancient, storied stone and flecked with pigeon droppings and pocked and chipped by countless assaults of stone and rock projectiles, loomed larger until they arrived at the gate itself and were compelled by Norman guards with lances to halt. The soldiers, in helmet and halberk, inspected the cart with drawn swords, poking and probing for foodstuffs, but seeing no grain allowed the cart to pass. Wine was permitted but bread, fruit and grain of any kind was not. Better that Antioch starve in a drunken stupor and surrender, than starve sober and fight.

They passed cautiously through the city gates thirty-five feet deep that were flanked on either side by massive towers. Addie sat impassively allowing the uneven movement of the cart to sway her body with its jagged rhythms. Inside the city, Turkish guards glanced at them casually but let them pass without stopping. Addie jumped out of the cart when they were out of sight of the gates and glanced backward at her companions. She wondered if they had been given any instructions by Bohemund. They had not said anything to her and could not have believed her to be an Armenian woman as she was dressed to be.

The city streets were narrow here and defined by houses and shops built ramshackle upon each other. She ran up the street woman-like, feet lifting to the side, seeking a sense of direction. People glanced her way but she feigned indifference and walked on. Finding an alley that led her close to the gate at which she had

entered, she paused at a corner, looking carefully across the street
at the interior side of the city walls and the flight of stone stairs
about a cubit-width that led to the wide top of the ramparts. At the
base of the stairs, dusty-faced children were playing a spirited game.
The streets were crowded with people as midday approached,
milling in conversational groups and flowing toward market places
full of empty stalls. Their faces were war-tired and Addie could see
in the eyes of many the sunken effects of hunger.

She stepped into the street and walked against the flow of the
clangorous throng, dodging herds of children and women, and old
men sitting on benches as though they were permanently stationed
there. There were young men, Turks, recent arrivals from other
parts of the caliphate empire; the old men on the benches were
Syrians whose ancestors had lived in these environs for generations
and whose black-robed priests of the dwindling Nestorian sect still
believed in the heretical notion of subjugating the divine nature to
the human nature in the Christ. Addie peered through the surging
mass and spotted a low, recessed entry in the aged walls. And at the
same instant, the weathered door moved, and a small, bearded
man, stepped into the cobblestone street. The Turk glanced quickly
up the street in both directions, unsure of where he wanted to go.
Then he set out, walking briskly along the town walls, his sullied
white tunic flowing behind him. Addie kept a rapid pace herself,
following at a discreet distance, bobbing in and out and around
townspeople to keep her quarry in view.

Bohemund's assignment was, of course, a fresh experience for
her. She had never trailed anyone, although she could say that she
had herself been pursued more than once. Chasing this little man
was like chasing the pigs and chickens back home. She could
usually catch them, but when she did, she knew what to do with
them. This was different: she wasn't sure what she would do when
she caught up with him.

The man was quick and nervous, bobbing and pecking his way
through the crowds. His journey took him through a labyrinthine
maze of alleys and passageways until the crowds had thinned and

the din of their voices had begun to fade. Suddenly they were alone, this man and she on the street. Family sounds could be heard within the Antiochan homes of mud and timber; children laughing or crying and their voices passing from hearing as she moved on. She stayed back and away now, walking not too fast, but she did not lose her prey. Eyes and head low, she wandered in apparent aimlessness and once when the man glanced back her way she did not even slow her gait or turn aside her head; she walked confidently forward as though this man was nothing to her and she cared nothing about his affairs.

Then he disappeared. Addie stopped in open-mouthed astonishment. One moment he was in the street a short distance in front of her, and the next he had vanished. She quickened her step and soon was near the spot where she had last seen him.

She sat; she rested; she waited. It began to rain, softly at first. She felt a few drops upon her head and then noticed a few others fall to the dust in the street and bead into tiny dark globules. The mist released a scent of freshness which Adelaide savored, breathing in the aroma deeply. She welcomed the coolness and the freshness. Rain had never been her enemy, she had rather feared the wind and the heat. The wind played havoc with sheds and lines and gardens and huts back home, and the heat could cause the crops to wilt and could make working in the fields unbearable. But the rain had never caused her an anxious day in her life, except last October in the Anti-Taurus mountains. That was frightful. But this rain was pleasant—inconvenient—but pleasant.

The rain began to pelt her with greater intensity, and she realized that she could not remain where she was without arousing suspicion. She stood, prepared to walk away, when suddenly he appeared again, slipping quietly into the street. He walked as quickly now as he had before. Addie matched her pace with his and soon they were again on the wide streets which had been so crowded earlier. Addie walked faster. She became short of breath because, although he was a diminutive man, he walked rapidly, and it was all that Addie could do to keep pace.

When she believed she could get no closer, she decided the time to act had come. She spoke in Provencal French: "Deus vult!" she called out. The little man whom she had been pursuing swerved to the side of the street and turned around. He stared wide-eyed at the woman standing twenty yards away. Then he started back up the street without saying a word.

"Please, sir, I must speak with you," she said pleading. The man slowed down without turning around. She walked faster and soon caught up with him.

"What do you want?" he said irritably, also speaking in Provencal French.

"I have a message from a friend," she said as they continued to walk.

"Who is my friend?" he asked.

"I have a gold bezant for you if we can find a place to talk," she replied, ignoring his question. "It is a most urgent matter. Then I will explain everything."

Her reference to the gold bezant sparked interest. He said that he would meet her at the Tower of the Two Sisters in fifteen minutes. They should not be seen traveling together. To this Addie agreed.

Addie took to the foot-worn stone stairs at the appointed time mounting them each deliberately and wondering wearily how she had becoming involved in this and so many other exciting affairs of her young life. As she ascended, the city of Antioch unfolded gradually. She could see the small gardens and larger fields on the slopes of Mt. Silpius, and she saw stretching out before her the length of the Byzantium fortifications until they turned toward the mountain at the Gate of St. George. At the top, she ambled to the ramparts and battlements from which she could gaze down upon the fields and encampments along the Orontes. Everywhere she looked, as far as she could see, the pilgrims dominated the view from the walls—their tents, huts, wagons and carts and she understood now how oppressive it must be to be shut up within the walls a captive in one's own city.

She strolled along the ramparts until she came to the third tower. There was a walkway around the circumference. She strolled about and finding a door, stooped slightly and entered without knocking. Addie looked about. The room was murky but illuminated by a single, narrow shaft of sunlight which cast its luminous stream on the wooden floor. Not everything could be seen in the shadows. There were barrels aplenty and piles of arrows and long bows hung on several racks. Lances were leaning against the wall; to the side she noted buckets of sand, several piles of large rocks, and tubs of oil. The room was an armory. She wondered if each of the three hundred towers was so equipped.

The man coughed and spit on the floor. "What do you want with me?" he asked roughly, approaching her. Addie backed away. Had she not been able to smell his foul breath from several feet away she might have thought the fellow was merely an apparition, a creation of her fearful imagination. His swarthy features made him blend into the dimness and when he spoke the sound seemed to come from nowhere until, that is, he stepped menacingly into the light. Addie retreated again, but this time backed into a rack of spears. They clattered to the floor in cacophonous pandemonium. She put her hands to her ears. The man didn't move but stared at her and spit again.

"My lord Bohemund sends his greetings to you," she began, moving away from the wall. "He respects your skills as a warrior and expresses his sorrow over the recent embarrassment you have suffered—"

The man was not amused. "What embarrassment?" he growled.

"Your name is Firuz. Your wife, an Armenian, played you for a fool. The news is all over the town. Bohemund feels your pain and he offers you his sympathy."

Firuz laughed. "Bohemund is a blood-thirsty barbarian. Sympathy! Ha!" He spit again and took a few steps closer to her. "So Bohemund has sympathy! Next you'll be telling me he says his prayers every morning!"

Adelaide thought grimly of the prayers Bohemund enjoyed. "God is with us," she said.. "Your city will fall. There is no question of it. Every battle and every city we have attempted to

take, we have taken with the help of God. It has been a long
winter. Our soldiers are now very eager to carry the battle to the
walls. Emperor Alexius at this moment is marching across Anatolia
with an invincible force to assist us. When he comes and when our
knights and soldiers attack, the city will fall and you will die. There
is no question of it. In the meantime, your people are suffering a
shortage of food. But in their suffering, they have found something
that warms their heart and makes them glad. Something that brings
joy into the despair and hollowness of their drab, dreary existence.
The wife of Firuz, the tower-keeper, has slept with a man not her
husband. Her husband was not enough of a man to keep her at
home; now everyone knows, she found someone else!"

Firuz sprung at her like a cat and clamped an iron-like vise
about her throat with the sinewy fingers of his left hand. He threw
her against the wall sending barrels and arrows flying in the
confusion. His hand forced her chin high and to see him she had to
glance down along the dark hairy arm to his green eyes. She
struggled to breathe, her chest constricting with sudden terror.
With his right hand, Firuz tore the scarf from her head and grabbed
her breast pushing her harder against the wall.

"You filthy whore! I'll tear out your tongue, you cheap barbarian
harlot!" With his left hand, he slammed her to the wall again. Addie
grappled weakly, albeit desperately, attempting to free herself from
the suffocating grip he had upon her throat. His arm was like an
iron pole and his fingers could not be peeled away from her neck.
She began to beat upon his arm and body with her hands,
pummeling him with ineffectual blows, until her hands suddenly
came to rest upon his head and then Addie found surprising new
strength in her fingers even as her own energy was ebbing. She
thrust her fingers into his hair so they were interlocked deep within
his scalp. Then almost immediately she jerked his head in an
upward and backward motion while at the same time brought the
full force of her knee between his legs. His small body lifted slightly
from the ground and then folded in front of her. Even as Addie
felt his fingers release and fresh air rush into her lungs she brought

her clasped hands crashing down upon his neck and sent him sprawling to the floor. Screaming in pain, Firuz lay in a fetal position until Addie kicked him over on his back and fell to the floor beside him, her fingers again in his hair and a dagger at his throat.

Her voice was husky, but Firuz understood every word. "You pathetic little worm," she snarled. "Who's the whore you're visiting down the street, you self-righteous arsehole? Bohemund offers you a chance to live and get revenge upon your faithless wife and every Turk who has been laughing behind your back. He even offers you a gold bezant just for listening! I should slit your throat right now, you dirty infidel! What do I care? You touch me again, Bohemund will find you tomorrow, or the next day, or next week, or next month and when he finds you—you know what he'll do to you, my little weasel?" The dagger's edge was still on the skin and Addie's dark, flashing eyes were inches away from his frightened face. "He'll skin you alive and give your every limb to the Tafurs for dinner." She released him, stood up, and backed away from him. Firuz stayed curled upon the floor with both hands between his legs. Addie walked away from him and massaged her throat and took several deep, cleansing breaths. She felt better now.

Firuz rolled over on his side, groaning and holding his groin. Somehow he managed to get to his knees. Addie saw him but had no pity. "Get to your feet," she said. She flung the gold bezant to the floor at his feet. He watched it roll to a stop, but did not attempt to pick it up.

"Do you want to listen, or not?" she asked. Firuz nodded.

"You are in command of the Tower of the Two Sisters, correct?" He nodded.

"This is the plan. At a pre-arranged time under the cover of darkness, Bohemund and a party of men will scale the walls under the Tower of the Two Sisters with your consent. The men will open the Gate of St. Paul to allow the army to enter the city. The city is surprised and captured before they realize what has happened. We pay you handsomely. Your life is spared and that of your family. If you refuse, we simply wait. We wait for your suffering to increase, we wait for Alexius to arrive, we put our miners and engineers to work, we employ our battering rams and siege towers, we send disease into the city with our catapults, we capture the city, and you die along with the others. I suggest you accept Bohemund's offer. It is the best offer you'll get." She turned to leave.

"How much money?" he asked in a thin voice.

"More than you have seen in your lifetime," she said, grasping the latch on the door. "I'll be back tomorrow for your answer, and one more thing."

"What?"

"We'll need to have your son as a hostage until the city is in our hands."

"You butchers! I'll never see him again!"

"If you do not practice deceit, you shall have both the money and your son. Think about it." Then she was gone.

They negotiated a deal within the next three days, and when it was done, Addie, too, had more money than she had seen in her lifetime.

Tertium. On the night of June 3, she returned to Godfrey's tent to get some of her clothes and personal belongings. Although she was not expecting anyone, she heard movement outside the tent and turned in time to catch sight of an agile-looking, tall, sportive figure standing soundlessly in the opening. He began to leave, perhaps thinking better of it.

She arose quickly from her mat and sprang to him and taking him by his hand brought him within the candlelit comfort of her tent.

She dropped his hand and faced him. His face was honest and slightly embarrassed. She smiled, and lowered her head deferentially, saying: "Good evening, my lord. It is an honor to meet Stefan, the Count of Blois and Chartres."

CHAPTER TWENTY-NINE

The Betrayal

DDIE LIT A LAMP AND INVITED Stefan to sit at the table with her.

"I am Adelaide Bartholomew of Provence," she said gently, smiling. Stefan was glumly unresponsive, like a man for whom life was a hollow and unbearable existence.

"You are either homesick or lovesick," she continued.

"Do you think so?" he asked, turning to look directly into her cavernous eyes.

She didn't speak immediately. "You know," she began, "Loneliness, of all the human afflictions, can disguise itself in other forms ... like boredom ... or apathy ... or even rowdiness and debauchery ... Tonight, perhaps ... —"

"—concupiscence?" Stefan volunteered.

She nodded, and arising, led him to her private chamber, and pushed him carefully down upon her bed. Leaning low, she slid her right hand beneath his neck and raised him slightly to position a pillow under his head. Quietly, she lay beside him, and propped herself on an elbow facing him.

"You are obviously sick," she went on. "There's a redness to your eyes, your complexion is pale—" she touched his eyes and drew her palm across his face—"and you have no life and no desire in you. Believe me, I have seen this many times before." She dropped her head on a cushion near his. "These past seven months have been the most difficult," she whispered in his ear. "Two years we have been away from home, and for two years I keep my hope and my faith. In Hungary and Thrace, my feet were swollen and my mouth parched. I nearly lost my brother in the Sava River, and my daughter and I were nearly roasted alive by the Pechenegs. We barely escaped from the Turks at the Civetot, and my sister was abducted. But I kept going ... all the time I kept going and I try not to think about Provence, about my little village, or my friends who thought I was mad when I packed up a few belongings and left the village to follow Peter the Monk to the other side of the world. I kept going, but I think about home anyway. But the hardest time has been these past seven months. Because here we sit in the rain and the cold without food. Many of my friends have either died or deserted. And I keep thinking about Jerusalem. I know that I will get there with my child. I have done nothing else in my life, but this is one thing at which I will succeed: I will complete my pilgrimage to Jerusalem. I will pray at the tomb of our Lord. But this waiting is very hard. It is so long."

She sat up. "And it is long for you, too. That is why I say you are either homesick or lovesick, because you are not sick in your body but in your heart. It is very plain to see." She patted his chest playfully.

"And you do not like being here with me, do you?" Stefan smiled faintly.

"I am a good person," she said. "I do not want to do this, but I had no—" Stefan pushed himself up halfway, and clamped a hand over her mouth.

"You do not need to explain," he said. "I understand. You are ... a good person."

Silence passed between them as a bond of mutual understanding.

"You have a wife?" she asked. Stefan nodded and lay down again. "And you have not seen her for almost two years?"

"That's right, almost two years."

They were silent. Adelaide broke in. "So you are both lovesick and homesick?"

The count sat up, sensing a desire to talk. "Yes, that is probably true."

"It is a long time to be faithful."

Stefan frowned. "But I haven't been faithful."

"You haven't?"

"I am homesick for home," replied the count, "but I am lovesick—as you put it—for ..." his voice trailed off like a mist fading in the cool night air.

"For someone else," Adelaide suggested. "Someone not your wife." Stefan nodded.

"And you haven't been faithful to your wife, but you have been faithful to your lover, until tonight when you thought—"

"—When I thought being with someone else would distract me, might be some sort of tonic for my soul."

"Instead you found—"

"—Instead..." Stefan swung his feet over the side of the cot and sat with his back to Adelaide who had laid down. "I never knew it would be this way. I never bargained for this in the beginning. I had not anticipated the pain, the incomprehensible sorrow of loving her. Because when I was with her, I felt things ... I experienced passions I never knew existed. There was no risk I wasn't willing to take, no price I was not willing to pay to be at her side, to hold her in my arms and know the inexplicable joy of the bonds of love, because I was bound to her by whatever it is that binds human beings together, bound to her by the everyday, commonplace strands of experiences we shared, that, though common, were mysteriously made memorable by our having lived them together. And when I left her, I promised to return quickly. I never bargained for the delays, the ineptitude that keeps me from her." He climbed aboard the bed again, and laid beside his new companion. "I don't know why I'm talking to you," he confided.

"I would rather have you talk to me than ... well you know," Addie said, embarrassed. "You treat me as a friend ... Listening to you, I feel like a woman ... not something else, and I thank you for that." She took his hand and gripped it tightly, laying it across his chest.

"What are you going to do?" she asked.

"About what?"

"About your wife."

"Actually I think it is less a question of what I'm going to do about her as it is a question of what she's going to do about me."

Addie lay on her back next to Stefan and studied the flickering shadows upon the coarse ceiling of her tent. She could feel the entire length of his flawless body and it felt pleasant, particularly so because there would be no demands of that body upon hers, no pain, no degradation and no shame. Then she thought of Pons and that she had never laid with him like this, never felt the reach of his body. She made a resolve to change that as soon as possible.

"What do you mean—it's a question of what she's going to do about you?" she asked, snuggling closer to him.

"My wife is very attractive," Stefan said, also conscious of the body next to his. "She will suffer no want of lovers if she chooses to have any and I have no doubt that she has made me a cuckold, a cuckoo who has left his nest for others to rob. But I am in no position to know. She is a very forceful person, strong, stubborn, and opinionated. We met at Rouen in the Church of Saint Maclou where we were attending a funeral for Roussel, a captain in her father's army. She had been in England with her father, and when he returned she came with him. My father, his name was Theobald, he encouraged us to marry. We did. I think she saw a lot of her father in me, but I turned out to be far less driven than he. She now has the vast responsibility of managing our estates, and I haven't the faintest idea what has become of everything. I tend to fear the worst."

"Which is?"

'Which is that she has been manipulated by unscrupulous rogues and lost everything." Stefan rolled to his side and faced her, smiling lamely.

"You don't trust your wife?" Addie asked.

"I had to trust her. Actually, you are right, I don't trust her. Unfortunately, I had no choice but to leave her in a position of trust. But Adela is a very capable person. It will be difficult to get the better of her."

Adelaide stiffened at the mention of Adela. She had heard that name before! In the silence that passed between them, she begged her mind to divulge to her memory why the name of Adela was so important. The intuition that she was about to remember the significance of this name was so real that it was frustrating for her to pass the minutes struggling to do so.

She sat bolted upright beside him and clutched his hand. "You are a very wealthy man with many castles?" she queried apprehensively.

"Yes, I have many castles," he acknowledged.

"About three hundred and sixty?"

"You are right," said Stefan, surprised, sitting up now. Addie turned away, wringing her hands.

"What's this all about?"

"Do the names Ivo or Gerard mean anything to you?" she asked.

"Ivo is the bishop, and Gerard is my chief vassal—"

Addie jumped to her feet. "Oh my God, Oh my God!" she cried. "You're in grave danger!" She clasped her hands over her mouth and turned to him, her eyes wide with dread.

"What do you mean?" Stefan demanded, standing and approaching her. "Speak to me!"

"They are going to kill you!" she said. "I heard them talking last night outside of these walls."

"Who is going to kill me? When? Why?" Stefan said, agitated.

"I don't know who. A man came to my tent last night. I had never seen him before. He wouldn't tell me his name. He had friends waiting outside. They talked. They didn't know I could hear them. They thought you would be dead by now. They have been told that you must die in order for them to legally seize your affairs back home. It must look like an accident or else the Church will not be able to approve. I don't know, I don't know. That's all I know," Adelaide wailed, feeling miserable. "Is there something you can do?"

"Of course there is," Stefan replied. "God has sent you to save me, like a Rahab on the walls. When is my death supposed to occur?"

"Tonight!" she exclaimed. "Listen!" She just remembered. "Tonight the city is going to fall!"

"Antioch is falling tonight?"

"Tonight, into the hands of Bohemund. The city is being betrayed by Firuz the Turk in command of the Tower of the Two Sisters near the Gate of St. Paul."

"Bohemund! How do you know this and not I?"

"It's a long story but I'm telling you the truth of it. I swear!" Adelaide cried. "Tonight, perhaps even now, Bohemund is sending out a sizable force of troops as though they are going on a raid. He will assemble the soldiers in plain view of the towers so that the city will know what he is doing. And then he will lead them to the north along the river and away from the city to trick the inhabitants into believing he has left. But under the cover of nightfall, they are going to double back and be in position. During the early watch, ladders will be set up near the Gate of St. Paul. Some of Bohemund's troops will ascend the ladders under the protection of Firuz in the tower. They will then open the Gate of St. Paul to allow the entire army to enter in, and the city will be taken by surprise."

Stefan stood and brushed his hair from his face and placed his hands on his hips thinking. The pope had argued for this pilgrimage partly on the grounds that the fighting which was rending the seamless garment of Christ should properly be directed against the infidel and not brothers both in blood and faith. He had now traversed thousands of miles risking body and limb at a tremendous personal cost, only to discover that the bellicosity which had so plagued them at home had fevered the hearts of men abroad as well.

The news came as a personal affront. He had been involved in frequent altercations over minor boundary disputes in the Loire River valley back home. But never had he been the target of a deliberate attempt on his life. Not that he knew of at least. If he should die, let him die a valiant death in battle, let him be slain by his superior, let him fall as a warrior in honor. These were the traditions of combat, these were the realities of his life. He could die honorably against a foe who declared himself, but what sort of a snake would wrest from him, not only his life, but the opportunity to die with honor? And what sort of a coward is it that so fears him that he is unwilling to face him and openly? His foe, Stefan decided, was a coward who could not kill him with honor and was so lacking in scruples that he would not hesitate to do it with dishonor.

"And how am I to be killed?" he asked bleakly.

Addie spoke rapidly. "The ladders. They've marred a ladder so that it will collapse under the weight of a regiment of soldiers ascending it. They will send for a small band of your troops with a message from you saying to come at once. These men will fall to their death on the rocks beneath the walls. But you will not fall; you'll already be dead. They will come to your tent tonight and tell you of the plans to capture the city. This man, I overheard, will drink wine with you to celebrate the impending fall of the city, but your goblet will be poisoned. They will take your body and abuse it with blows to your head, break your legs and throw your body surreptitiously upon the pile below the walls. You will be found dead among your men and everyone will claim it was an accident." She took a deep breath.

"I didn't know who they were talking about. They didn't mention your name, or I would have come to you at once. I only heard others mentioned, and now, when I heard your wife's name, I recalled what had been said. Please believe me!"

Stefan and grabbed her by the shoulders. "I believe you! There's never been any doubt of that. God has sent you to save me. I will not die. God would not go to the trouble of bringing you to me or me to you if He did not intend for me to live and the evildoers be punished." Stefan was a firm believer in economical providence. God does not waste time. He always moves in a straight line from point A to point B. His providence can be recognized as such if one is cognizant of this simple truth: life is simple geometry. Everything in life involves an equation, and one can generally solve the particular, if not the general equation, provided one has at least one or two of the factors. In this case, had it been God's will for him to perish at the hands of these men, he—Stefan—would not have become privy to the plan.

"You were a part of the providence of God tonight, Addie," he said. Providence fails without foreknowledge, he believed, and foreknowledge breeds invincibility. Stefan could not fail now: God had forewarned and, therefore, forearmed him.

"When are they coming for me?" he asked.

"They are meeting by the oak tree at the Fortified Bridge at midnight," she answered. "They will ride from there."

"How many are there?"

Adelaide put her hand to her forehead thinking. She looked at Stefan, her brow furrowed. "I really don't know. Last night it sounded like there were only four or five men. There could be more." She dropped her arms in despair. "I just don't know."

"It will be the hour soon," Stefan said. "You will come with me to my tent. You will see that God has not sent you to me in vain." Stefan picked up his cloak and threw it about her shoulders. "Come now, quickly, we must ride and make plans. Not a moment to lose!"

Together, they fled the tent belonging to Godfrey de Boullion. Adelaide never returned.

✠✠✠

The count sat at a fine oak desk, the gift of Symeon, the patriarch of Jerusalem. The prelate, administering his office from Cyprus, had received letters from Constantinople advising him of Stefan's presence at Antioch and sent gifts to all of the nobles of the crusade in addition to the corn, grain, oil and wine for the pilgrims themselves.

Stefan's quarters were commodious owing to the liberal use of wood from the forests beyond Marash and the luxury of time in which to build. Stefan had himself stripped and cleaned many of the beech poles used to frame his quarters, and had supervised the tanning of the skins, and the construction from its start to finish. He had furnished his own bedchamber with a bed built a foot off the floor and sumptuously fluffed with cushions, soft blankets, and satiny sheets. His masons had built a fireplace in the bedchamber and also in the outer room where he received visitors and guests. A delicate Egyptian stand stood by his bed, and the room was lit when necessary by two large beeswax candles, on thick oak-hewn stands about three feet high, and many other candles and lamps as well.

Stefan had laid down Turkish carpets over the rough flooring, and placed two chairs in front of his desk. A chest sat far opposite, over which, attached to a beech beam, hung a crucifix. Over his head a single beam extended across the length of the room. From it to both walls were strung smaller poles and an overlay of rough boards, thickets, skins, and dried mud. Across another wall the count had fashioned some shelves on which sat several mugs, a crystal chalice, wine goblets (blown in Antioch and given to him by the Paulicians), Persian bowls and two coned-shaped helmets. His leather boots were near the door, and on a nearby table sat a box of candles. Three swords and his lance stood in a corner. Nearby, he had placed his shield and, over a chair, a coat of mail.

The flickering light of tallow candles cast shadows across the desk where Stefan sat motionless, his shoulders rounded and drooping, hands folded and fingers drumming nervously.

He looked across the room to the bedchamber and sighed, wondering how long it would be until he could rest. It was now well past the hour and the night was dark and leaden. There were no sounds afoot, only the hooting of a distant owl, and the night music of crickets.

Stefan bestirred and walked over to the corner where his armor was stacked and took the scabbard down from a hook on the knife slashed pole. He withdrew Fortissimus from the sheath slowly and thoughtfully and ran his finger across its brightly burnished surface. Its edge was still razor sharp. *How often wilt thou keep me from death's door?* Stefan thought. He lifted it close to his face and peered into the depths of its reflective surface. He could see his visage there and studied hard the eyes he saw, his eyes, his life and being; eyes that had not seen Anna for almost a year now, that had not seen his beloved Blois for over two years; eyes that had not seen Jerusalem ever. Would they ever see Jerusalem? Should they ever? And would it matter? What if he left and returned to Constantinople for Anna? Would she return to France with him? Of course it was out of the question. He would have to divorce Adela. That would almost certainly mean excommunication. Moreover, the church would claim his lands and castles because he failed to fulfill his vow. Nor could Anna leave the court of Constantinople, nor should she.

Stefan brooded over these unpromising matters. The covered floor, soft beneath his slippered feet creaked loudly as he paced. The night was still and close, the air thick and damp. A fly spun noisily out of control around the room. Stefan wiped the moisture from the back of his neck, looked at his palm briefly and then dried it with a quick motion across his shirt.

Then he heard a distant rumble. He listened intently. Horses were approaching, several riders judging from the heavy mix of the beat. He waited unsure. Many times he had faced his personal mortality without warning or the luxury of preparation.

But he had never had to wait for Death to approach. It had always sprung out at him in surprise, and he had to this point successfully fought it off. Now Death had sent him an invitation to the Feast, and was galloping toward him to keep the rendezvous.

Was he better prepared with the notice of its coming, or would he have reacted more keenly without counsel?

His visitors were close. Stefan bounded adroitly to the desk, and laid Fortissimus across its surface and sat down, slightly slumped, in a disinterested sort of way. He must not convey to his nocturnal guests that he was in any way expected or that he was prepared for them. He was tired and restless, he couldn't sleep. That is what he would say; that would be enough. It would, in fact, be true.

The riders pulled up thunderously outside of Stefan's quarters. Their horses wheezed deeply; Stefan could hear them prancing and snorting. There were words among the men and then quietness.

Stefan dropped his head upon his chest and closed his eyes. Someone approached. The door latch rattled ominously and a man stepped into the room. His heavy boots hit the floor. The intruder was armed and wearing a shirt of mail; Stefan recognized the familiar sound of the scabbard tapping the chain-links.

"Stefan!" cried strong, jovial voice. "Stefan! Wake up you sleeping fool!"

Stefan snapped his head to attention and opened his eyes slowly, feigning drowsiness. Then he examined his visitor carefully. He was medium height, and his weight which he carried at his waist gave him a stocky appearance. The face was globular, jowls hanging on mid-sized cheekbones on either side of a spherical nose planted quite in the middle of his face. A mole in the crevice between nostril and cheek marked this otherwise unremarkable countenance. Bushy eyebrows hung like willows over deep set eyes and his head was crowned with thick, dark hair.

Stefan smiled. He was in no danger from this man. He was no enemy, and he certainly was no swordsman. The man before him was his brother-in-law, Short Breeches, Count Robert of Normandy, son of William the Conqueror and brother of the King of England.

"I couldn't sleep," Stefan said, "so I got up and polished Fortissimus, and the next thing I know, you are here putting the bloody fear of God into me!" Stefan arose and walked around the desk to greet his kin by marriage. They embraced each other and then Stefan offered Robert a chair at his desk.

"No, no, I came by to celebrate, offer a toast to victory," he said. "Tonight the city of Antioch is ours!"

Stefan looked at him keenly, seeking signs of insincerity or notes of falseness. "I had heard a rumor to that effect, but I gave it no credence," he replied irritably, "because I didn't think military plans would be drawn up without my knowledge or consent."

Robert laughed. "You forget the agreement we all made. If any one of us could arrange for the collapse of the city, it was ours for the taking. Especially after Tacitus left."

'So this is Bohemund's idea?"

"Yes, and if the plan works—and I think it will—the city will have the banner of St. Peter and the Christian cross flying atop the walls by sunrise." Robert leaned back in his chair revealing a portly belly that hung limply over his sword belt. "So I'm here on behalf of Bohemund, a fellow Norman, to urge you to join your men in position at the walls immediately." His eyes narrowed and his voice lowered: "Bohemund is not telling Raymond or the others; only myself and you—Normans, you know. My men are already at St. Paul's Gate and—"

The villains, Stefan thought. Bohemund was behind this treachery, he was sure of it. And his own kin! And what enticement could Bohemund have offered this wretch to persuade him to betray kin? A snake and a scorpion! And how was Robert going to accomplish his death? He was to end up in a pile of dead bodies beneath the walls of Antioch. Robert certainly is not going to overpower him. He cannot use a sword, he is mortally slow and would never instigate swordplay. Will Robert offer to accompany me to the walls to join my troops who are already there? Perhaps I will be ambushed outside by the men he has there.

These questions nagged at Stefan even as he listened to Robert carry on, nervously loquacious. It could not be a question of receiving his just desserts. He did not customarily treat people unfairly. There are only two answers, he thought, as he watched

Robert gesture grandly: money or power, perhaps both. His wife! Robert could not possibly be party to this action without the informed consent of Adela! Or could she be ignorant of this matter? How will Robert explain his death? An accident in the siege of Antioch? He would be declared a martyr. A candle would burn in perpetuity in Chartres Cathedral; a new cathedral would no doubt be built with grants from his estate. A special mass would be said on the anniversary of his birth.

"Stefan!" The count looked up. "You were thinking of something else?" Robert asked, annoyed.

"I'm sorry," Stefan mumbled as he stood. "Let's proceed." He picked up Fortissimus. "First, I must put on my armor, and it's so bloody warm tonight—"

"There is time, brother!" said Robert. "First we must celebrate!" He reached into his sack and pulled a bottle of wine, already opened, the cork visibly protruding. Robert leaned toward Stefan and winked: "I've already had a little myself," he said, slurring his speech, "and it won't hurt to have a little more." He staggered to the shelves, reached for the Antiochan goblets putting them on the table in front of him.

Stefan stepped up to Short Breeches and before he could protest, swiped the bottle from his hands. "No guest in my house drinks his own wine," Stefan said. He put Robert's bottle on the shelf and produced a flask of his own.

"No, no," Robert insisted, "Take my wine, it is my pleasure!"

"Nonsense!" Stefan replied. He poured his own wine into their chalices, and proposed a toast. "Deus vult!" he cried.

"Deus vult," Robert mumbled. Stefan smiled and wondered what contingencies had been prepared in the event that the wine failed.

Robert's face brightened. "Since you are so generous with your wine, may I invite the rest of the men inside?"

"Of course," said Stefan, sitting down at the table. Robert disappeared through the door and conversed with his allies outside. When a few minutes had passed during which Stefan surmised that fresh plans were being laid for his demise, Robert entered his quarters again and following him, single file, were three huge knights attired for battle. Robert stood aside while the men moved to separate corners of the room. Then, on cue, they all drew their swords and held them tips down.

Stefan remained seated at the table. It was not yet time to take action. But we're getting close now, Stefan thought. "What's going on here, Robert?" he asked, finding it hard to believe that the skunk would be honest with him, even now.

Before Robert could answer, another man, shorter than the others and dressed in the habit of a monk, stepped through the door and into the light. The man pulled back his cowl. The face was long and narrow, the beard patchy, the nose beaked, and the eyes dark.

"Peter!" exclaimed Stefan, genuinely surprised. "Are you involved in this grisly affair too?"

Peter the Monk said nothing but walked to the shelf, retrieved Robert's bottle, and slowly poured a portion of its contents into Stefan's chalice. "Not many people get to choose their deaths," he said as he placed the chalice before the count. "I think you know what the choices are."

Stefan pushed it away. "Really, Peter, and you, too, Robert, you insult me by coming here with three men, well, four, counting you, Short Breeches, and expect me to quiver and quake, to do your bidding, to actually drink this cup of hemlock. I can take all of you with a sword in one hand, and this chalice in the other and not spill a drop. Two of you will be dead, and the other two will run like rabbits. Come now, what is the meaning of this?" Stefan's tone was soft and condescending. Robert glared.

"If I may examine your sword, Stefan," said Peter. Fortissimus was lying on the table before Stefan where he had been polishing its blade.

"You may examine it, but by no means have it," the count replied.

"As you wish," said Peter. "Hold it for me then." Stefan grasped his sword by the pommel and held it toward the monk, tip down. Peter fumbled with the pommel and hilt, removed the leather binding, snapped a hinge and opened the pommel. He bent over slightly to peer into the cavity and then thrust his fingers inside and withdrew a piece of parchment.

Stefan was again surprised. *This is a night of revelations*, he thought.

"The Paulician Parchment," the monk announced, as he meticulously opened the fragile document fold by fold. When he had done so, he smoothed it out on the table and examined it, with Robert peering over this shoulder. On the parchment had been drawn a symbol that looked like a cross. There was nothing else.

"St. Peter's Cross," the monk muttered. He folded the parchment and slipped it inside his habit.

"It's time to leave," he said, pushing the goblet toward Stefan.

"Why didn't you just ask for the sword, for the parchment?" Stefan asked. "I'd have given it to you. In fact, how did it get there in the first place?"

"Your wife," Short Breeches sneered.

"Adela?"

"Adela."

Stefan tried to understand the implication of what he was hearing. "Why would she hide this ... Paulician Parchment and not give it to me outright?"

"Never mind!" roared Short Breeches. "Drink the wine!"

"Wait, wait," cried Stefan. "Why do I have to die for this piece of parchment?"

Peter the Monk held up his hands to silence Robert of Normandy. "This fragment," he said, "is the second of two pieces that will lead us to the most holy and sacred relic of all Christendom, the Holy Lance."

Stefan nodded. "And what does this have to do with me?"

"With the Holy Lance, do you think there is any doubt that the people of this pilgrimage would again turn to me as their leader? Do you think for a moment they would follow you or any of you worldly knights who have blasphemed the Cross of Christ by joining this pilgrimage for your own personal gain, who think you shall increase your material and worldly goods, and do so at the expense of the holy shrines and the very ground upon which our Savior walked? And what does God think of a people who harbor a Jew in their midst, the very killers of Christ, and of those who do business with Jews, and employ Jews to increase their personal wealth? Well I shall take care of that Jew, I will take care of her!" The monk's voice rose both in pitch and volume. He began to pace the floor becoming more distraught with each utterance, but returning to the table where Stefan sat to thunder a final round of imprecations: "The Lord sits in judgment upon all of you, you all deserve to die for your avarice, wickedness and lascivious ways. You are the first to die, and the Lord will take the others. May God have mercy upon your soul."

Stefan scratched his head. "Begging you pardon, Peter," he said bewildered. "You mean that you think with the Holy Lance you are going to become the leader of this pilgrimage? That behind your leadership you are going to have all the princes and nobles of this enterprise killed?" He chuckled, noting the mounting fury on the monk's livid face.

Stefan leaned forward on the table so that his hands were only inches away from the hilt of Fortissimus. "Now I understood that this Holy Lance of which you speak was going back to the Ile de France where my wife and the King of France were going to sell it to the Bishop of Chartres. I don't think, Peter, the Holy Lance is going to stay here at all. In fact, I think you are a dead man!"

"Shut up!" roared Short Breeches. He pushed the monk aside, raised his sword, and rushed upon Stefan. In that instant, Stefan grabbed Fortissimus and swung it to ward off Robert's blow, but the blow never landed. Thwang! An arrow whizzed through the air and caught Robert in the shoulder. Short Breeches dropped his sword and cried out. Immediately a second arrow plunged with incredible force into the thigh of the knight standing at the door. He, too, dropped his sword and fell to the floor clutching his wound.

"Jesus Christ," Stefan muttered in amazement. He turned in the direction of the arrow's source. Crouching in the doorway of the bedchamber was Addie with her bow. She winked, and notched another arrow.

"Jew-lover!" shouted Peter the Monk when he saw Addie. He leveled his finger at the woman, and shouted again. At the same time, the other two knights sprang toward Stefan, and the door opened admitting three more knights who had been waiting for matters in Stefan's quarters to conclude. Hearing the uproar, they decided to enter the fray. Stefan was now fully in action, wielding Fortissimus deftly, making each stroke count, warding off one blow and disarming a knight with a single blow of his own.

Suddenly there were shrill shouts at the door, and three more men rushed into the room. Stefan had no idea who they were, but they were on his side, for they immediately began to defend him. Steel flashed upon steel, bodies jarred bodies as the men paired off, dancing with mortality. Shelving and desks tumbled in the tumult. The arena became a dim chamber of combat as one candle after another was sliced in half by an errant swing.

Addie wanted to help. She let loose with another arrow. She crouched in the doorway following the action in the faint light while the struggle continued. She saw little but heard voices—some guttural and desperate. But she also recognized the tones of a voice she loved. A voice that she loved. The thought startled her. It was revealed to her so simply as though it had been in her heart for so long. *A voice she loved.* Pons—her Pons, she now realized—her Pons was here, and with him Guy.

She readied her bow to get off another shot. She drew back the bowstring and sighted down the shaft, being careful to hit the right target. Seeing her man, she followed him as he danced across the room. She released the arrow! But instead of hitting her target, it sank into the buttocks of the Count of Blois just as he pirouetted to avoid a slashing blow.

Stefan cried out and clutched the arrow with his left hand and looked back painfully at Addie. "Oh Mother Mary, what have I done?" she wailed. She dropped her bow and would have run to his side, but he was continuing to fight while he still had strength and could stand the pain.

She heard Pons shout "We have'em," but at that moment, a candle fell to the floor and ignited the oil that had seeped from a fallen lamp. The fire grew slowly, but it was only minutes before curtains, and the dry flooring and beech poles were aflame.

"Get out, quickly," Stefan shouted to Addie. He could feel the arrow in his posterior with every movement he made. Pons rushed to her aid, tongues of fire licking at his heels. Stefan turned from Addie in time to see an adversary bound at him with dagger drawn. But before he could sink it home, Pons' and Guy's unknown companion thrust his sword into assailant's back and flung the body to the blistering floor. "Come on," he said to Stefan in a light voice, "Let's get out of here!" Together they fled the blazing structure, Stefan feeling quite amazed at the extent to which divine grace had preserved his life on this night.

"Someone get Short Breeches, and pull him out," Stefan shouted as he stumbled out into the fresh, midnight air.

"I've got 'im," cried Guy. He stooped to grab the toppled noble, saw a corked bottle of wine with the contents intact and slipped it into his vest pocket, and dragged the portly villain to safety.

"Are you all right, Addie?" Pons asked when they were safely outside. They sat under a willow tree exhausted, and he took her in his arms and held her.

"I love you," he whispered in her ear. The night air was bracing and the branches of the willow swayed in the breeze in a peaceful and sweeping motion, like the waves of the sea.

Addie swung around to face him. Her eyes glistened with hope. "Oh, Pons," she cried, "I love you too!" She flung her arms tightly around his neck and looked up through the willow at the half moon above them. "I shall never forget this night, never," she said, meaning it with every fiber of her being.

They had all gathered under the tree: Short Breeches with his shoulder wound, Guy enjoying the wine, and Stefan, grimacing in pain so intense it was close to rendering him unconscious, laying on his side with his head in the lap of the knight who had come to his aid and befriended him. Addie's arrow still protruded from his buttocks.

"Begging your pardon," Pons said to the stranger who had charged into the tent with him and Guy, "but who are you?"

"Who are *you?*" Stefan interjected, speaking to Pons. He knew no one except Addie.

"These are my dear friends, Pons and Guy, from Provence,' interjected Addie. "They are like family to me. But this friend here, I have no knowledge of."

"In that case, I, too, would like to know who you are," he said to the stranger. "You saved my life in there, and I must admit, I needed a little help."

The soldier lifted his helmet from his head and laid it aside. He put his hands behind his head and bending it slightly, fluffed his hair and let its locks fall carelessly around his head and upon his shoulders.

The soldier smiled. "My name is Anna Comnena, Imperial Princess and daughter of Emperor Alexius Comnena, Supreme Potentate of the Eastern Roman Empire." She looked down upon Stefan, and touched his face tenderly. At these words, the Count of Chartres, who had endured more surprises and shocks in one night than should be expected of any mortal man, passed peacefully from consciousness to restful sleep.

Through her tears, Addie beamed.

CHAPTER THIRTY

The Flight of Stefan of Blois

HAT NIGHT, GUY DE MON-
TEIL died in the arms of his life-
long friend, Pons, poisoned by the
wine of Robert of Normandy who was
alive to watch the entire agony. Pons
attempted to take his revenge then and
there, but was restrained by Stefan,
Addie and Anna who assured him that
Robert would be turned over to the
proper authorities. Stefan, for whom the
poison was intended, was grief-stricken,
and Addie, whose actions had contributed indirectly to Guy's
death, refused to be consoled by the knowledge that those self-
same actions had led directly to another's man's salvation.

The cry of the loon flying across the marshy fields in the half-
light of the half-moon, calling for its mate, echoed the mournful
wail that passed through the strictured throats of Addie and Pons.
It was a night of acute, indescribable sorrow, full of the kind of
anguish that cannot be assuaged, particularly not by references to
the loving providence of a transcendent deity. She would never
understand God who saved one life, only to take another. Addie
fervently wished that she could lose her faith altogether, for it
would be better, she thought, not to believe in God at all, than to
believe in God and know that this is what God is like. There is a
God, and God is a monster.

✠✠✠

"I've got to see Bohemund," Stefan said, after Anna had extracted the arrowhead from the count's buttocks.

"You won't be able to ride for another week," Anna reminded him.

"I know, I know," he said, grimacing. "Let's find a cart, and you can haul me to St. Paul's Gate like a sack of flour."

Servants quickly located a light cart to which Stefan gratefully hobbled and crawled inside. The hoofs of the little colt clattered rhythmically as they pushed through the camp on a cobblestone roadway toward St. Paul's Gate. Stefan could see in the distance a warm, orange glow. Bohemund had lit fires along the ancient walls. His men were no doubt already scaling the ramparts if not in possession of the towers.

"Wait here," said Stefan when they arrived. Bohemund was directing the assault from a field tent, and Stefan could see him standing behind a high table, inspecting maps of the city, and barking out orders. He stood at the portal of the tent unnoticed until, after a few moments, Bohemund glanced up. Stefan thought he detected a look of surprise when Bohemund saw him. But the Norman resumed his examination of the charts, and called for an aide.

"Malam Coronam," he bellowed. A soldier, so-called because a horse had kicked him senseless in the head, quickly pushed past Stefan and to greet Bohemund. "Ride now to the armies of Duke Godfrey," he said, speaking slowly and plainly, "and the count of Flanders, the count of—"

"—Duke Godfrey, the count of..."

"—the count of Flanders, the count of St. Gilles, the bishop of Le Puy, the count of—"

"—the count of Flanders, the..."

"—the count of St. Gilles, oh, never mind," Bohemund said exasperated. He spoke to a secretary. "Write this down for him. You've heard what I've said, and add the count of Normandy."

"The count of Normandy has taken ill," Stefan interjected. Bohemund stared at Stefan sharply. "He may not recover," Stefan added, smiling.

Bohemund turned to the secretary and said in a low voice, "Disregard the count of Normandy." Turning to Malam Coronam he said: "Tell them to prepare to enter the city, for on this night the city is delivered into our hands."

Two soldiers burst into the tent with a small boy in tow. "Firuz is panicked because he thinks we don't have enough men on the walls."

"How many towers do we have?" Bohemund asked.

"Three."

Bohemund grabbed his cloak and swept past Stefan and went outside, not noticing the cart-driver nearby. The soldiers dragged the boy out with them. "Where are the bloody ladders?" he yelled. "Get more ladders on those walls, and more men. Let's get those gates open! I have three thousand men at St. Paul's Gate pissing in their breeches waiting for the goddam gates to open." He headed back for the tent. "Holy Mother!" he muttered.

"What do you want us to do with this child?" the soldiers yelled after the commander. Bohemund halted and turned about to see the little boy. Walking back to him, he squatted to see him at eye level. He touched the boy's face gently and patted him on the head. "Hold him until we are sure his father hasn't betrayed us," he said, glancing up at the walls. "When we get inside the city, take our banner to the mountain facing the Citadel and make it fly there. That is all."

"If you take the city for yourself, Alexius will not only cut us off from any further aid, but will cut you off from Anna as well," Stefan said quietly when the Italian had returned. They were alone.

"Alexius has no further plans of coming to our aid," Bohemund said crisply, his eyes glazing like ice on a winter pond. "We have already given him more territory than he can possibly defend anyway." The warrior sat down with jaunty confidence, as a man who not only possessed authority, but as one who had taken authority. Bohemund was making the strategic move of his life. He would live or die by the decisions he had made this night and by the success or failure of his cunning.

Outside, Stefan could hear the muted sounds of battle-axe and sword, and the pounding of battering rams. The battle was on. He sat down wearily—and carefully—opposite the man.

"What's the matter?" Bohemund asked, noticing Stefan's halting manner.

Stefan smiled weakly. "I took an arrow in the arse," he said. "A bit painful."

"Get shot running away?" Bohemund tittered, laughing.

"Not funny."

"Anyway, Tacitus has left us. Do you think Alexius will invest any more soldiers or imperial bezants in this campaign? Alexius has no further interest in this affair. It's the figging pope's affair now. He betrayed us at Nicea (my nephew was right you know); he has what he wants, and now we are on our own!"

"And Anna?"

"Ah, Anna!" Bohemund's mouth twisted into a smirk. "Anna doesn't fit into my plans. I don't want her, I don't need her." He paused, watching Stefan absorb this news. "But you will never have her either," he said.

"That is not your affair," replied Stefan, warming up.

"True, certainly true. You will never have her and it is none of my affair."

"False," Stefan retorted. "I already have her and she has me."

Bohemund raised his hands to the air. "God be praised!" he hooted, smiling broadly. "Then you are happy, she is happy, and I am happy." His countenance clouded, and he leaned forward. "But, she shall never be your wife," he warned, "and maybe that is best."

"What do you mean?"

"What do you mean 'What do I mean'?"

"That perhaps it is best."

Bohemund laughed. "Stefan, Stefan. Do you know what your problem is? Do you know what your problem is? You are too good a man for either love or war. This war, for example. Your heart is not in it, I can tell. You would rather be at home in Chartres taking care of your affairs. You attack the integrity of the pilgrimage constantly, you see the pope as a manipulative, power-hungry old fart, which he is, by the way. And as for love, you think your wife should be someone whom you love and when you do not love your wife or when she does not love you, you worry and fret. *C'est la vie*, Stefan! And what is worse, you think that when you find someone you love, that you are required by some strange law of the universe to make that someone your wife—which, in your case, is difficult because you already have a wife. A wife is not for love, Stefan. You must have a wife for children. You must have a wife for the affairs of state and to manage your household and servants. You must have a wife to occupy the conjugal bed. But it doesn't matter if you love her or if she loves you. She is a wife, not a lover. You need a woman who is not your wife to be your lover. Ha! Am I not right? Stefan, you old fool!'

Stefan was silent.

"Eh?" Bohemund prodded him, teasing.

"I have no wife," he said.

"No wife?"

"If a wife is only what you say she is, then I have no wife. I have no children, I am not in the conjugal bed, and she is not managing the affairs of my household, at least not with my interest at heart. And further, if she does not love me, and I do not love her, then I have a wife neither in the sense which you convey nor in the meaning that is dear to me. I have no wife."

Stefan arose to leave. The decision that had been forming in his mind had achieved clarity as he had been speaking. There was fire in his stomach. He tightened his jaw with resolve.

"I'm leaving," he said, stepping toward the tent portal. "I'm leaving the pilgrimage and returning to Chartres to take care of some matters."

"You're leaving?" Bohemund asked, truly caught off guard. "You can't leave. You're our *Ductor*. You're breaking your vow."

"Not breaking my vow, but postponing the fulfillment of it. I'll be back."

"Antioch? Jerusalem?"

"Antioch has fallen or will. There is no doubt about it ... I'll be back before the pilgrimage gets to Jerusalem."

Suddenly, two aides rushed into the tent. "A ladder has collapsed," they shouted breathlessly.

Bohemund stood quickly. "How many men?"

"About fifty, maybe sixty," they said, wide-eyed. "Damn," Bohemund muttered aside. "Forgot to replace that ladder."

"Go, go," he said to the men, sweeping them out the door.

Stefan continued out the door. He was leaving anyway. Foot soldiers rushed by him bumping and jostling him, sending darts of pain down his leg. He crawled into the cart, knowing that the events of this night had altered his destiny, and that where he was needed most was where he was wanted least.

But he would return and keep his vow. He would say his prayers at the Church of the Holy Sepulcher. Maybe not this year, but certainly next.

As Bohemund rushed past the cart, Anna removed her cap. "Goodbye, Bohemund," she said, amused. Stefan watched with a mixture of curiosity and pride. Bohemund stopped dead in his tracks and turned around. Anna snapped the reins, and the cart lurched forward.

They returned to his camp and slept for a few hours and then in the faint light of morning, left quickly for Alexandretta with a small force of men. They boarded a Genovese vessel for Tarsus which sailed later in the afternoon, arriving in port the next day. In Tarsus, they secured fresh horses and began the journey to Iconium where the pilgrimage had been almost a year before. They travelled along an ancient Roman road still serviceable and marked by the granite blocks that formed a curb beside the road. Parts of it had suffered from disuse and were overgrown of weeds and brush; the flagstones had been hauled away to serve some other building purpose, or had been buried by slides and debris from storms of the millennium past. They galloped over the road of Saul of Tarsus, the highway which the apostle had no doubt traveled with Timothy, Silas, John Mark, Luke and others. John Mark! Stefan winced at the memory of his name, recalling the stories of the parish priest about this writer of the gospel who as a youth had fled the company of the apostle fearing for his life and unwilling to suffer the hardship of The Way. Desertion was no doubt the interpolation that would be given to his absence when it was discovered. The apostle, Stefan, remembered, had had nothing to do with Mark after that episode, even though others had come to his defense, blaming his indiscretions upon his youth. If St. Paul could not forgive the errors of a young man, how could he expect others, less sanctified, to understand him now?

Their criticism be damned, Stefan thought, riding high in the saddle, his wound still smarting. Fortunately, Antioch was in crusader hands. He had not left them without a leader, nor had he deserted them in an hour of distress. While God may have ordained that Antioch fall to a horde of invaders, he did not believe that it was the will of God that Blois and Chartres should fall into the hands of interlopers. And while he may someday give his life as a martyr, it was not the will of God that he die as the victim of an assassination. Whoever was involved in this sordid mess underestimated his devotion to the Church. He would have no difficulty settling accounts with both the secular and sacred arms of authority. This time, they would settle matters on his terms, or he would die trying.

✠✠✠

When the sun rose above the eastern horizon, the awaking pilgrims saw the crusader flag fluttering in the uncertain breeze atop the battlements of Antioch. As the morning unfolded, pilgrims and soldiers lined the lofty ramparts dancing gleefully upon its broad pavement and shouting joyously to the distant meadows and fields of the pilgrim camp along the Orontes.

✠✠✠

I placed my decrepit hands on the top of the desk, and pushed myself up. "So, Antioch had fallen!" I said. "Incomprehensible! Bohemund and the Count of Flanders entered the city via St. Paul's Gate, Raymond by the Gate of the Dog, Godfrey with Stefan's troops via Duke's Gate, and Tancred via the Bridge Gate and St. George's Gate."

"And Arslan?" asked Bernard, observing me as I shuffled toward the Scriptorium window. Copyists worked nearby at their elevated desks, scratching meticulously the works of Augustine upon the parchment before them.

"We're coming to that," I replied. "Arslan had left the city, but had not abandoned it. Instead, he left it in charge of Yijid Sagin, who realized very early in the morning that the city had been betrayed. Sagin understood the folly of attempting to resist the flood of frustrated crusaders who would be pouring into the town. Gathering as many of his soldiers as he could, no more than one hundred, he fled to the Citadel atop Mt. Silpius. From here, he could watch every move Bohemund made, and easily defend himself until reinforcements from Arslan arrived.

"Bohemund attempted to prevent the flight to the Citadel and made the Citadel his primary military objective once he entered the city. But Sagin sprang like a cat to the fortress where Bohemund could do nothing but yelp like a dog beneath its ramparts. He had treed the quarry, but not captured it; Bohemund slunk away to sulk and wait for another opportunity.

"Bohemund's star, however, was never brighter. He became the people's commander, a warrior who was both cunning and courageous, willing to take a risk while the other princes dawdled. Stefan, contrarily, was deemed a coward who had fled when the pilgrimage needed him most. But even the news of Stefan's defection from the pilgrimage could not dull the luster of this moment. The pilgrims, ensconced on these plains for eight months, were ecstatic.

"Sadly, Christian exuberance translated into a terrible atrocity. The soldiers ran into the city like starving wolves, fangs bared and devouring whomever crossed their path. Turks were slain wherever they were encountered, being vastly outnumbered. The citizens of the city fared no better." I paused, remembering the scene. "Let me put it another way. The able-bodied, whether knight or foot soldier, rampaged through the city like a swollen, flooding river

carrying away everything in its path and leaving destruction in its wake. They entered homes without invitation and dragged the occupants into the streets to slay them or slaughter them within the shelter of their abodes, or while they were yet lying in their beds. Armenian women were slain with their little children ... It seems like wherever the hand of God falls the blood of the innocent is shed."

Bernard rose and stood by me at the window. "The fault lies not in the hand of God, but the heart of man, my brother," he said quietly.

"They will never forget," I said, still shocked by the memory.

"Who will never forget?"

"The Turks, the Armenians, the Moslems. They will never forget."

✠✠✠

In a small tree-lined bed of the Orontes River, not far from the Bridge of Boats and across the river from the cemetery, a small company of people gathered not to celebrate but to mourn. Addie and Pons, with Clare, Peter and Hildy, and a few other friends stood by a freshly-hollowed grave bareheaded. Fulcher, standing at the head of the mound of moist earth, gave Guy a Christian burial. The forenoon air was still. Fulcher's black garb hung stiffly; his words fell like stones.

Guy had been a True Friend, the one constant of Pons' life throughout the many changes he had experienced. They had searched for each other's happiness and rejoiced upon finding it. They had engaged in schemes good and bad, had defied authorities benign and evil and had known women both passionate and indifferent.

There was a regularity to their friendship, a sort of astronomical constancy to it. As the stars appeared in the heavens, as the sun rose and set, as the rains fell, and the mountains stood unmovable, so Guy had been to Pons. Guy's devotion had been strong and un-changing. Pons had suffered many things, but his world had never been altered, his life had never changed. Now, however, Pons understood that a fundamental shift was underway. His life without Guy would seem anomalous, strangely tilted and off balance.

Addie stood by him, her arm about his waist. She rested her head upon his shoulder. The cost of the pilgrimage had again become personal and expensive. Pons needed her now, and despite her own sorrow for Guy, she knew she had a greater duty to Pons whose own soul was dying. She understood Pons and that revelation melded her spirit with his. They had been brought together by a remarkable series of events which, she now understood, had served to bind their lives together in a bond unfailing and true, experiences which woven together had created an adhesion hardy and indissoluble. She did not fancy that she could act as a substitute for Guy, nor did she want to. Guy was irreplaceable, as all friends are.

So Pons and Addie forsook the river bank and the grove of willows, leaving the mortal remains of their friend by the flowing water and trudged away into a different, somewhat diminished world, less friendly, less hospitable. They found a room in Antioch

"When the sun rose above the eastern horizon, the awaking pilgrims saw the crusader flag fluttering in the uncertain breeze atop the battlements of Antioch. As the morning unfolded, pilgrims and soldiers lined the lofty ramparts dancing gleefully upon its broad pavement and shouting joyously to the distant meadows and fields of the pilgrim camp along the Orontes" (p. 384)

where they flung their few possessions, and there they would live until it was time to move again, this time to their final destination in Jerusalem.

This blending of their possessions was an important step in their own friendship. It happened without ceremony or comment; it seemed apparent to both of them that their lives had become so entwined that they were hopelessly a part of each other in a way in which neither one of them wished to undo and that to untangle themselves from each other would be painful and foolishly unnecessary. Moreover, they acknowledged that to stay apart from each other when there was nothing in the world they desired to do less, would not achieve disengagement even if they wanted it.

Peter spent the afternoon with the Peter the Monk constructing a cross.

"A cross?" Addie asked.

"He wants a cross to overlook the city of Antioch as a sign of its liberation," Peter explained. "So I helped him hew the timber and strip the bark, and dig the hole to drop it into—"

"—You stay away from the monk," Addie warned. "He's an evil man. He is responsible for the attempt of Count Stefan's life, and if it wasn't for him, Guy would be alive today. Just stay away from him!"

Peter was vexed by his sister's remarks. "I'll help him drop it," he said stubbornly. "He paid me, you know."

Addie and Pons returned to the river the night of the day they buried Guy, walking along its banks and occasionally down at the water's edge where the stream flattened out like a Roman road. The night air had not yet cooled. The excitement between them was unspoken but not unfelt. He caught her looking at him, her eyes steady upon his, not questioning, not evaluating, but simply gazing. Pons saw her look, a look that was fatal to the reserve he had hitherto exercised in his careful relations with her. They stripped themselves of their clothes and stood on the stony shore of the river quite alone and quite naked, their bodies moist to the touch and cooling in the night air, their souls parched for love and warm with anticipation.

They swam in the river, in a crook where the river dammed and backed up. Quietly. Floating in and out of each other's presence, wordlessly approaching and touching briefly and then drifting apart, until that eternal pull that pushes and pulls at the ocean tides, pulled them together, powerless to pull them apart. They embraced in the flowing water feeling upon each other points of certain interest, and then, kissing, they sank beneath the rippling surface.

Later, upon a grassy swell near the river, he called and she responded; his call and her arching response; his call and her response—again and again, until spirit, soul and body quivered at the brink of crisis, like a vessel that can be filled no more—but, being filled, its liquid overflows its rim and pours out upon the sides randomly and chaotically, flowing where it will and at will, stretching out upon the surface for the farthest distance.

Addie felt a fire in her thighs as she lifted her torso high against his unrelenting body until, suddenly, the fire spread throughout her body, quickening it in spasms of the most inexplicable radiance and brilliance of her lifetime. In its warmth she cried out, clutching at him, and then dropped her arms heavily upon the grass.

They lay together until their strength returned. Then they dressed and before the moon had ascended the atramentous heavens above them, they wandered away.

✠✠✠

Stefan and Anna sat in the emperor's quarters outside of the city of Iconium, thousands of imperial troops encamped about them.

"The city is Bohemund's?" the emperor asked.

Stefan nodded. "But Arslan is approaching from the west, the largest army he has ever brought against us. We spied the army while en route from Tarsus.

"Danishimends, even some Syrians," Anna added.

"So Bohemund's advantage is only temporary?"

Anna continued. "Arslan has never defeated the crusaders on the open field, except for the Civetot, a completely different situation. He has decided to reverse the field position. He now has the pilgrims shut up behind walls with little food and no possibility of escape. Bohemund fought hard to stumble inside the trap but he finally succeeded. The bird is in its snare and the hawk is swooping down upon them."

"He won the battle—," Stefan said.

"—But he's going to lose the war," Anna finished.

"He should've waited until our forces arrived," Alexius mused. "Another week, but Bohemund is not a patient man."

"I'm also afraid that he's not going to honor the alliance which was proposed at Nicea," Stefan mentioned.

Alexius laughed. "I do not think my daughter will object, will you, dear?"

Anna smiled but said nothing.

The emperor ordered the imperial army to return to Constantinople.

That night, Stefan slept with Anna.

✠✠✠

Two days after the row in Stefan's barracks, Addie learned in the street outside of their temporary quarters, that Hildy was missing.

"She's with the monk," Peter said.

"For how long?" she demanded.

"About an hour."

Addie ducked quickly into the doorway. "You get that horse," she said to Peter, pointing down the street. "I'll be back in a minute."

Peter was baffled. "What's going on, Addie?"

"Get the goddam horse," she screamed.

Inside, she frantically packed a satchel, grabbed her bow and quiver. Outside, Peter had the horse.

"He's going to kill her, Peter," she muttered as she mounted the horse. "Get on."

"He's going to kill her?" Peter repeated.

Addie snapped the reins and spurred the horse. "He knows that Hildy's a Jew," turning back to yell at her brother as they galloped up the street. Peter put his hands on Addie's hips and hugged her close as they rode.

"Where're we going?"

"You tell me," Addie shouted. "Where have you been for the last two days?"

"Oh my God!" Peter whispered to himself. "This way," he cried, thrusting his arm and pointed finger past Addie's face. "Toward the Citadel" The pair was soon outside of the city itself but yet within the walls of Antioch, bolting up the gravel road that led to the fortress.

Peter wished now that he had observed more carefully the route he and the monk had taken on their trips up Mt. Silpius. He searched for landmarks as they traveled up the road but could not be certain they were taking the most direct route. Ahead and above them, though, he could spot the ridge where the monk had hoped to plant the cross looking down on the city below and facing the Great Sea.

They pounded up the road as fast as the surprised horse could take them. The air in the late morning was still cool and thin and the horse, exerting itself with two riders, labored under the demands of this emergency. Their path twisted and turned, following the contours of the flank of the mountain, a road which gained elevation gradually and required long circumventing loops around downward ridges that flattened out just above the city itself. Peter and Addie thought about none of this; they only hoped they were not too late.

But Peter, whose singular trait was his propensity to daydream, had obviously been unaware of their route up the mountain. In time, it became clear that the road they were now on was unfamiliar to him.

"Where should we go?" Addie pleaded. "You've got to remember." They rested the horse while Peter scouted the mountain side for clues.

"Over there!" he shouted. They galloped up the road apace until Peter said, "Turn off here."

They turned into the forest, ducking to avoid branches and followed a small path. The evergreens were close; the interior darker. "Is this the way?' Addie asked.

"No, no," said Peter, "but it will get us there."

They continued to travel until they could clearly see the pale sky through the forest. When they broke out of the forest's edge, they stood upon a rocky crag above a small but unpassable ravine. Across the divide, on a point that overlooked the city, perhaps two hundred yards away they saw the monk and Hildy. Addie groaned in despair. There was no way they could get to them without retracing their steps and circling around the head of the ravine.

"Hildy!" Addie and Peter shouted. "She's alive," Addie exclaimed when she saw Hildy struggling. The large cross was still laid out on the ground where Peter and the monk had worked on it. Hildy's clothes had been removed and she was on the ground with her hands and feet bound to four stakes, spread-eagled in the cross-like shape. The monk had already removed his habit.

"Goddam bastard, he's going to violate her," Addie said. "We're going to try to get him right here, Peter," she explained, but if we can't, we'll have to go around. One way or another, the monk is a dead man. I'm going to kill him if it's the last thing I do in this mortal life. Let's pray that we can keep Hildy alive."

Peter nodded. Tears rimmed his eyes, partly because he was embarrassed that he was so utterly dependent upon his sister in this attempt to rescue his wife, and partly because of the unfairness of it all. Sniveling, he stood by helplessly as Addie reached for her satchel, bow and quiver, and dashed to the farthest-most prom-ontory and peered across the divide. Crouching on one knee, she whipped out her bow and notched an arrow and sighted down the shaft. The monk had mounted Hildy who was screaming Peter's name. Addie saw the monk rear back and strike her across the face, glancing over his shoulder across the ravine to where he knew Hildy's rescuers were.

Addie had brought along her largest and strongest bow. Actually, it was not hers but Pons'. It would require all her strength to draw back the line, but now she locked her left arm, held it true in front of her with the bow grasped tightly in her fist, and drew back on the string, bending the sapling wood the full length of the arrow and when she had the monk in her sights, she released the arrow toward its target.

The arrow whizzed like lightening across the void, flying level and on its mark, but alas, short of its mark, falling harmlessly on the rocks of the far cliff. It was futile to try another, as Addie knew she had utilized all the power that the bow and her arm possessed.

She reached into her satchel, fumbling nervously, and pulled out a strange looking apparatus. "What's that?" Peter asked.

"An arbalest. A crossbow." Addie explained as she started to assemble it. "A new invention that Pons lifted from a baron in the Rhineland for some of St. Antony's bones." She snapped the bow on a shaft of wood. "The bow lies cross-ways like this, and you sight it horizontally." She hefted the stock of the bow and sighted down the shaft. Placing the string of the bow in the notch, she turned a handle and cranked the string back until the bow was stretched as far as possible. "This is called a trigger," she said, "and when I pull on it, it releases the string and pushes the arrow which is guided by these grooves to the target. It has greater distance than an ordinary bow and better accuracy."

She crouched again with the crossbow set and laid a shorter, but thicker arrow into the groove and pushed its notch in the string. Lifting the stock of the cross bow to her shoulder, she propped her left elbow on her left knee and held the bow with an even, steady hand, the butt of the stock against her right shoulder. Beyond the end of the bow she saw the monk straddling Hildy and beating her again. This has to work, Addie thought, terrified. She could not be sure if the monk had penetrated yet, but she could see his white arse flashing like the rump of a white-tailed deer. She thought grimly of what she might do to him if he was alive when she found him.

She knew that if her bow was powerful enough, she could hit him. She was vain enough to believe that it was not a question of her skill but of her weapon. Hildy's deliverance had been reduced to and was dependent upon Addie's vanity. Without it, Hildy was lost.

Addie took careful aim and pulled the trigger. The arrow flew out of the bow with such force that Addie fell backward. It fell wide of its mark and Addie had to set up again. She braced herself and shot again. This time, as an open-mouthed and wide-eyed Peter watched, the arrow flew with incredible power across the ravine, farther than any arrow had ever flown before, still moving with speed and force, losing none of its power even when it entered with a slam into the bare back of the monk two hundred yards away.

Peter and Addie whooped when they saw the arrow hit its mark. The monk jerked straight up immediately and brought his arm around his back, attempting to pull it out. Addie crouched again and inserted another arrow into the groove of the crossbow. She fired just as the monk had stood in paralyzing pain to face the direction whence the arrow had come. As he turned to face Addie and Peter across the way, he took Addie's second arrow squarely in the chest where it penetrated his heart. The Monk's eyes widened in surprise. He clutched the arrow in his chest, staggered for a couple of steps toward Addie and Peter unaware of the chasm at his feet and, taking a step too many, plunged to the rocks fifty feet below.

"He might have been dead before he hit the ground," Addie said later. "That second shot was lethal."

They found Hildy shaken and sobbing incoherently, but otherwise unharmed except for some bad bruises. Together, they peered into the ravine at the body of the Monk. "God's just going to have to get along without the Monk," Addie said. She put her arm around Hildy. "The god this man believed in is not the god I believe in," she said soothingly. "As I see it, we all come from the same parents, so that makes us all brothers and sisters."

"So sister," she added, smiling, "let's go home."

From then on, Addie called Hildy "Sister."

CHAPTER THIRTY-ONE

The Redemption of Adelaide Bartholomew

Early June, 1098 A.D.
Antioch

HE WESTERN PRINCES AT-
TEMPTED TO restore to the city a
sense of calm and order. The dead were
buried in an orchard along the north wall.
Each of the nobles had accepted by
consensus an area of the city assigned to
him and his army, and within these areas, the
pilgrim, whether knight, foot soldier, woman
or child, settled for at least the time being.
There was no talk as yet about leaving the
city; they had only now possessed it, and
some believed they should maintain proprietorship of the city for
as long as they had suffered attempting to get in.

This question clearly was not on the minds of the Council of
Knights. There were issues of control and authority to settle and a
large body of princes believed that the pope now needed to
become involved, particularly since the emperor appeared to be
walking away from commitments he had earlier made. Bohemund
had already announced his claim to the city. He argued that the
defection of Tacitus, the imperial legate, and, in addition, the failure
of the emperor to provide reinforcements at crucial points in the
siege, effectively cancelled all rights or claims the emperor may
have had on the city and that further, his behavior had in effect
nullified any oaths of allegiance they had made to him in
Constantinople. The fecundity of their oath rested, he argued, upon

the emperor's ability to provide support and material assistance. This he had failed to do and in this failure, lay the seeds of Bohemund's claim.

Bohemund also reminded the nobles that the city had fallen through the negotiations which he and he alone had arranged, and that without his intervention, the pilgrimage would still be outside of the walls of the city, unprotected by the emperor and vulnerable to attack. The city belonged to him, and he intended to assert his claim, defend his claim, and keep the city for the crusaders and the Holy See as the pilgrim entourage proceeded to Jerusalem.

Count Raymond of Toulouse, his bitterest foe, received this news with surprising good cheer. He was of the opinion that Bohemund's argument, while the fruit of despicable motivation, was essentially unassailable, and that the Italian count's position offered the further benefit of restricting him to this locale while he, in turn, could proceed, sans Bohemund, sans Stefan, to Jerusalem, the holiest city of all. This then, was the settlement of the matter: Bohemund was declared Protector and Governor of Antioch, and the venerable Raymond, while not elected commander, with these two defections became by default the *Ductor* of the pilgrim armies. In this way, then, the future of the city was decided. The Council of Knights, however, did not anticipate seeing what they saw on the morning of June 14.

That morning, when the rising sun was still a large flaming orb teetering on the edge of the eastern horizon, sentries posted at St. Paul's Gate peered into the blinding light and detected the faint outline of several legions of Turkish soldiers marching abreast toward the city on the road to the Iron Bridge. They immediately sounded the alarm with a trumpet signal, sending it quickly along the hundreds of posts atop the walls. They then discovered to their terror that the Turks were also approaching from the north along the road to Alexandretta. Before the sun was above them, the Saracens had stationed legions of soldiers at the east, and at several points along the northern wall, but on the far side of the Orontes.

It was clear that they neither expected nor desired an engagement on this day, but the distress within the city was palpable.

In the early stages of the siege, the crusaders believed that they would be able to endure indefinitely provided sufficient crops could be grown within the city and the water supply was adequate. But the crops had already been planted by the Turks; it was too late to plant anything else, and water was very scarce and had to be rationed. That food and water was scarce was alone sufficient to drive the nobles either to war or the negotiation table. But the additional knowledge that no reinforcements were on the way, and that whatever deliverance they might experience would have to come from themselves and themselves alone, created further despair within their ranks.

Thus the news of Arslan's siege was greeted with universal consternation, and most of the noncombatants believed that they would die in the city just as the pilgrims had been slaughtered at the Civetot. Bohemund's reputation suffered as these events unfolded. It would have been better, thought most, to have remained outside the walls where the enemy could be engaged freely, than to be shut up surrounded by the infidel with no place to go. Further, the Citadel was still in the hands of the Turks, and Arslan would be sure to use the Citadel to his advantage in subsequent military endeavors. The aspect of the present situation looked bleak.

✠✠✠

One day, Fulcher, the young priest, came to Adhemar the bishop and the Council of Knights and said: "My lords, listen to a certain matter which I saw in a vision. One night, I was lying in the church of St. Mary, Mother of God. I was in the garb of confession and, after obtaining pardon, began to sing psalms with some companions. While the rest were sleeping, and while I watched alone, and having just sung 'Lord, who shall dwell in thy holy tabernacle, or who shall rest in thy holy hill?' our Lord Jesus Christ, the Savior of the world, appeared to me with His Mother and St.

Peter, prince of the apostles. However, I did not recognize them. He appeared to me as a certain man, beautiful beyond all description. This man said to me, 'Man, who are these people who have entered the city?'

"I answered, 'Christians.'

"'Christians of what kind?'

"'Christians who believe that Christ was born of a Virgin and suffered on the Cross, died, and was buried, and that He arose on the third day and ascended into heaven.'

"At this the man said, 'And if they are Christians, why do they fear the multitude of pagans?' Then he added, 'Do you know me?'

"I answered 'No,' and at these words, a whole cross appeared on His head.

"A second time, the Lord asked me, 'Do you know me?'

"To Him I replied, 'I do not know thee except that I see a cross on your head like that of Our Savior.'

"When I scrutinized him intently, I saw a kind of cross much brighter than the sun proceeding from his head. Then I knew it was the Lord and I immediately fell at His feet, humbly beseeching that He help us in the oppression which was upon us.

"The Lord said, 'Who is the lord of the army?'

"And I replied, 'Lord, there never was in the army but one Lord, for rather they do put their trust in the bishop.'

"And the Lord said to me, 'Say this to the bishop that I have helped you in a goodly manner by conducting you hither to this point, and I am grieved at the misery which you have suffered in the siege of Antioch. But these people have wandered far from me by evil-doing. They are committing evil pleasures with Christian and depraved pagan women whereof a stench beyond all measure arises unto heaven. I say to you, return to me and I will return to you. You shall be my people and I shall be your God. And when you enter into battle, you will say "Our enemy is assembled and they glory in their own bravery. Destroy their might, O Lord, and scatter them, so that they may know that there is no other who will fight for us except Thee, O Lord."'"

"And when he had finished these words, he added: 'And say this also to them: "If ye do whatever I command you, within five days I will send you great help. Only you must daily chant the response *Congregati sunt*, all of it, including the verse."'"

Adhemar, bishop of Le Puy, became uncomfortable with this narrative, passing a hand impatiently across his bearded face. His astute eyes narrowed with suspicion upon the young priest in their midst. His impression of Fulcher dating to their first encounter in Clermont was favorable. But Adhemar didn't care about this. He viewed visions and ecstasy with a certain kind of native skepticism. He was a scholar by training and a churchman by profession. A prophet is tested by whether his words come to pass, but visions are generally unarguable. This was the uncomfortable part. The bishop could not tell the priest that he had not seen what he claimed to have seen. Dreams and revelations are private affairs and relatively harmless ones until they arrogate to themselves the teaching office of the Church. Adhemar was untroubled within the pages of Scriptures, ill at ease outside of Scripture, and occasionally hostile to flights of fancy that dared to bypass divinely ordained channels for hearing the word of God. Adhemar was a bishop of apostolic succession. God spoke through the pope in concert with the bishops. Anything else must be regarded carefully.

"These are mere ravings," he said. "How long has it been since you have eaten, Father?"

"Bishop," Fulcher replied, "if you do not believe that this is true, let me climb up into this tower, and I will throw myself down, and if I am unharmed, believe that this is true. If, however, I have suffered any hurt, behead me, or cast me into the fire." The priest's eyes blazed with conviction; his smooth-skinned jaw was struck defiantly and set like the Citadel of Mt. Silpius.

Adhemar nodded. He turned to the chaplain guard: "Take him to the South Tower, and let him fling himself off the walls."

Fulcher paled at these words, but spoke quickly. "My lord, what I say is true, just as what I said when I spoke with the Holy Father in Clermont concerning Peter the Monk was true. I was a faithful witness then, as indeed I am now, as I am sure you recall. You were there."

"He speaks the truth," Count Raymond said. "There is nothing in his message but what we need to hear. Sin and immorality fills the camp. How long will God tolerate this iniquity? When Israel so sinned, God sent pestilence and death among them, saved only by a bronze serpent in the wilderness. Moses slaughtered thousands who rioted before an idol. We must listen to these words."

Fulcher's face sagged slightly in visible relief at this affirmation. Raymond's cutting words had slashed through the pretense of every excuse, and lay the groundwork for what the leaders knew would be a sweeping program of prayer and fasting.

Hearing these words from his trusted friend, the bishop of Le Puy ordered that the Gospel and the Cross be brought so that Fulcher might take an oath that what he had said was true. At the same time, the leaders were all counselled to take an oath that not one of them would flee, either for life or death, as long as they were alive. Stefan's defection and that of others was still hot in their memories. Bohemund was the first to take this oath, followed by Raymond, Duke Godfrey, and the Count of Flanders.

They announced a three-day fast and ordered all the women once again to be separated from the men, including wives from their husbands. While fasting and throughout the remainder of this ordeal, there would be no fornicating nor would they take the risk of adding dependents to the general population by allowing husbands and wives to lie with each other. No man would know a woman until the Lord had given them the victory. In addition, all known harlots were to be gathered for judgment and sentencing.

By some circumstance, Addie was caught in this latter edict and with others was herded like chattel to a square in front of the palace where the roads to St. Simeon and the Iron Bridge converge. Many, if not most, were younger than herself, she only 24. Their faces were streaked with fear and marked by hollowness and hunger. They huddled together like sheep in a storm. Addie did not feel she was like any of them, but she had learned now not to sit in judgment upon the unfortunate. She stood apart quietly waiting to see what would happen, believing fatalistically that she would experience the same punishment that she had seen imposed upon others from time to time.

She sighed. Whenever the soldiers lost a battle, a harlot was beaten and persecuted; this had become an accepted fact of life. But whenever there was a great victory, the harlots were busier than ever. In this sense, no wars could be fought without women: their presence explained defeats, and, on the other hand, made victory sweeter. Without the camp followers, no army could be controlled and pacified. And by declaring a fast and a period of abstinence, Adhemar ensured, as he well knew, an army of soldiers who would fight harder in order to have the ban lifted.

As they waited in the square, a crowd began to arrive, who had recognized who they were. Addie moved away from their gaze and tried to hide in the shadows along the walls of the palace. The crowd became noisy and taunting accusations were cast upon them like stones upon the biblical adulterers. The fallen women, ill dressed and undernourished, huddled closer, casting quick, dark glances out upon the throng. Curses rang out as the mob realized that the women were being blamed for the misfortune they were now experiencing. A few picked up stones and hurled them at the women who flinched as they bounced off their backs. The soldiers moved in to protect the women who were deemed unworthy of such protection. This was the atmosphere in which Addie, with the others, was ushered inside the judgment hall.

The taunts and jeers faded as they walked through the marble corridors of the ancient palace, home to Roman procurators, and Constantinopolitan governors. They were escorted to a hall in which the leaders of the crusade were seated upon small thrones. The plight of the pilgrimage was so severe that the particular measures proscribed by the bishop and the Council of Knights had to be announced abroad and made known to all. This was the place where the process began, and Addie realized as she looked about the room, that there would be no mercy from these men.

The soldiers bade them stand in a line and one by one they stepped forward to hear the charge of fornication read and to receive a guilty plea. Addie took the last place in the line and stayed close to the girl in front of her (who had not yet reached her sixteenth year), and kept her head bowed and her shawl drawn about her face. The voice of the bishop's adjutant was harsh and accusatory. The responses were low and muffled. After each woman answered she stepped aside and the next harlot stepped before the bishop and into the ring of leaders and nobles. One by one the women responded and stood with the condemned nearby until there was only two, and then only one, and Addie herself stepped forward to face her accusers.

When she had advanced far enough into the circle of knights, she threw back her shoulders and stood proudly erect, pushing away the scarf that had hidden her countenance. She dropped it to the floor and stood dauntless before Adhemar and the Council. Addie examined each of the nobles one by one. The Count of Flanders. He did not know her. His face was impassive. Godfrey de Boullion. He glanced away nervously. Hugh of Vermandois. Tancred. Raymond of Toulouse. Adelaide could see no hope in his maturely drawn face. Bohemund. The Italian was jittery. He stared hard at her in consternation, obviously shocked to discover that she was among this coterie of harlots.

The accusation was read. "What say you to this?"

"Not guilty," she replied. The adjutant looked up sharply as Adhemar leaned toward her, peering over his papers. "We have made a mistake, is that it?" he asked.

"Yes," she murmured.

"Execute them all!" Bohemund shouted. This outburst generated considerable excitement from the observers in the room so that in the ensuing clamor the voice of the bishop calling for order could not be heard. Raymond, indignantly shouted that execution of these people was not warranted in this situation. But others agreed, shouting "Fornicators, adulterers," and "Deus vult."

Addie stood impassively and motionless throughout this melee like a lamb before the slaughter. Adhemar arose quickly, veins pulsating, countenance darkened with anger.

"This is an ecclesiastical proceeding, and you, gentlemen, will speak when I give you leave! Is that understood?"

The room quieted, and the bishop sat down and continued. "Now then," he began, "we have made a mistake in your case, is that correct?"

"Not just in my case, my lord."

"And what do you mean by that?" asked the bishop, curious.

"Begging your pardon, my lord, may I speak freely?" At these words, Bohemund and Godfrey again began to protest. But they were silenced by both Adhemar and Raymond who was never loath to take a position against the Italian count if there were no compelling reasons not to. The papal legate gave her leave to speak.

"None of us here are guilty," she began, glancing to the herd of harlots huddled nearby. "Not guilty because the crimes of which we are accused were not committed by us but by others. For every woman you see here, there is one or more criminals who are free to enjoy what they have stolen, because every woman here has had her honor and her dignity take from her. We are vessels, my lord. We can only be filled. We cannot ourselves fill anyone. We are the passive victims of the crimes of which you accuse us, not the perpetrators of them. Execute us if you choose, but you shall not in so doing, eradicate the crime, because you are not executing the criminals. Separate the women from the camp if you want, but the real culprits will find other women to rob and victimize."

"You did not have to commit this indecency," Adhemar interjected, impressed by her testimony.

"And if I refused? I could have been beaten, raped or killed. And given the choice I was offered, how could I refuse?"

Adhemar sensed that the observers in the room were listening with rapt attention. "And what was that choice?" he asked.

"I could do as I was told, or I could refuse and watch my child starve to death. Had I chosen to reject his offer, my soul would go to hell for refusing the only remedy that could save the life of my child. But in yielding to his proposal, I sent my own soul to hell. He is a criminal who forces us to make such choices, who robs from us the possibility of eternal life and what greater criminal is there than a man who robs us of our salvation?"

Her words were powerfully expressed, carried on a clear soprano voice which crashed through tense air with petrifying force. Addie continued: "If you must punish us, then justice demands that you punish our partners. And if you are unable to discover our partners, then release these girls and deal with me, for I assure you that justice can be done in my case."

The condemned women standing nearby looked upon Addie with amazement and newfound hope. The glint of redemption shone in their eyes like the sun after the rain. No one had ever spoken on their behalf before and they looked upon Addie with respect and admiration.

"And can you tell us who your lovers are?" the bishop inquired.

Addie looked at the circle of men. "Lover, not lovers," she said resolutely. "Who my lover was."

"One man?" Adhemar asked, "No more?"

"One man, no more." The princes were absolutely silent, fearing that any word of protest might appear unseemly and cast unnecessary suspicion upon themselves. In truth, such a thought was furthest from the minds of those present, for none suspected that the princes were in any way involved with this woman. Adhemar, himself, was laudably interested only in apprehending the partner of the immoral liaison so that the two of them could be prosecuted and punished as Addie herself had suggested.

"And can you tell us who that man is?" he asked, leaning forward in anticipation of her reply.

The hall hushed, straining to hear Adelaide's response. The face of Godfrey de Boullion was drained of color, and his pallid hands fidgeted nervously in his lap. Bohemund appeared relaxed but his gaze was riveted upon the woman.

Addie reached into a pocket of her dress and withdrew a small cloth which had been folded carefully several times. As she unfolded the fabric, she began to speak.

"The man whom I knew, who robbed me of my honor—" she succeeded in unfolding the material, "—is the owner of this amulet!" She gave it to Raymond of Toulouse who examined it carefully and then looked up quickly.

"Why, it belongs to Bohemund! I've seen it many times!" he exclaimed. Cleverly, Addie had given the amulet to Raymond not only because she knew he could identify it, and not only because he was her lord as a Provencal, but because she knew of the antipathy between the two leaders. She knew he would pursue the prosecution of this matter with a holy vengeance.

"This is an outrage!" roared Bohemund who stood quickly.

"This woman is a devil and a liar. You cannot possibly believe her!" Adelaide looked at Bohemund knowing that their eyes would meet. She wanted him to see her watching him. She knew that if he would look at her, he would know that she was redeemed and free, that fortuitously, she had been led into a circumstance that had promised certain condemnation, only to discover, that in this regrettable affair, God had planned her redemption. Fulcher told her later when discussing these events, "Like Joseph told his brothers who had sold him into slavery, 'You intended it for evil, but God intended it for good.'" Bohemund did look at her, believing that if she saw him looking at her she would know that someday he would exact his revenge. But when the exchange took place, he saw in her eyes not fear, but triumph; not shrinking, but courage. He knew that he had been bested.

Adhemar ordered the women released, believing that the ordeal had been enough of a torment to them, and he ordered Bohemund to be subjected to the same punishment to which any man would have been subjected had he been caught in the act of fornication. He would be bound and stripped, and compelled to walk backward through the streets of the city, with a herald announcing the nature of his crime. Adhemar enjoined Bohemund from mobilizing his troops to prevent such a fate, and demanded that Raymond of Toulouse summon the resources of his army to ensure that no altercations took place, and that the Italian army did not prevent the sentence from being carried out.

Sitting quietly throughout all of this was Godfrey de Bouillon who when he saw Adelaide, looked at her gratefully. She smiled; Godfrey was not evil, just a man. Bohemund, she believed, was an evil man.

But she was not evil, she exulted, just a woman. A good woman, free and whole.

CHAPTER THIRTY-TWO

The Holy Lance

June 12, 1098 A.D.

HE VERY NIGHT OF THE DAY of Addie's vindication and Bohemund's shame, there appeared in the sky an enormous, brilliant star hanging over Mt. Silpius like a diamond pendant. No one had seen anything like it. Christians young and old, women and children, knights and foot soldiers came out of their houses and huts to gaze in awe upon it. They sat upon tree limbs and hillsides, crowded the city battlements for a better view. For they truly believed this celestial portent was a sign from the Lord that God would favor the crusade and that his anger for the sins of the people had been, momentarily at least, assuaged.

After a short time, the star divided into three parts and appeared to fall into the camp of the Saracens. This was cause for great rejoicing as the leaders of the crusade privately began to believe that in five days the Lord would indeed send another sign.

The next morning, a raucous procession left from the porch of the Antiochan provincial palace, the promenade of penance in which Bohemund fulfilled the penalty proscribed by the papal legate. They had granted him the dignity of a loincloth. No young girls would be glancing at his swaying member, no older women in shriveled maidenhood satisfying their curiosity about the valiant and handsome Norman prince from Italy. He was made to march backwards unbound through the streets of the city along a predetermined course, with a herald announcing his sins; allowed to walk freely, if not awkwardly.

Dogs yapped and women wagged. The requirement that the sinner be stripped of his clothes worked to Bohemund's advantage in this case because the person who was compelled to march through the streets bore little resemblance to the prince who ruled the armies. It might have been to his greater shame had they commanded Bohemund to march about Antioch under the watchful gaze of its conquering inhabitants fully clothed in his knightly attire. This man, whose tall shoulders were rounded and whose frame was stooped seemed not at all like a prince. His blond hair fell on his shoulders in stringy strands like wilted flax. He walked deliberately, carefully lifting his feet high to avoid stumbling, the mighty muscles of his calves twitching with every flex of his leg. His eyes never left the pavement at his feet. Not once did the man glance up to look into the eyes of the people who now jeered him, who were eminently pleased with this verdict, who believed for the first time that the laws of God were meant to be obeyed by all people not just those who were at the lowest stratum of human society. This man, it was clear, had not escaped the condemnation of the law, and his punishment, taken for the sins of every noble who had sinned, was right and fit in the eyes of the peasant pilgrim who had suffered the want of all things, including the occasional gratification of the flesh so freely afforded those in higher places.

✠✠✠

About this time, Peter Bartholomew, after consulting with Hildy, sent an urgent message to Count Raymond of Toulouse and Adhemar, bishop of Le Puy. It read: "Andrew, apostle of God and of our Lord Jesus Christ, has recently admonished me a fourth time and has commanded me to come to you and to give to you, after the city was captured, the Holy Lance which opened the side of the Savior. Today, moreover, when I had set out from the city with the rest to battle, and when caught between two horsemen, I was almost suffocated on the retreat. I sat down sadly upon a certain rock, almost lifeless. When I was reeling like a reed from grief and fear, St. Andrew came to me with a companion and he threatened me much unless I returned the Lance to you quickly. Therefore, I must speak with you at once."

Later in the day, Adhemar and Raymond received Peter in the palace near the church of St. Peter.

"Tell us how this all began," Adhemar started. "From the beginning."

Peter related this story: "At the first earthquake many months ago when the Franks were first besieging the city, such fear assailed me that I could say nothing except 'God help me.' For it was night and I was lying down; nor was there anyone else in my hut to sustain me. When, moreover, the shaking of the earth had lasted a long time, and my fear had ever increased, two men stood before me in the brightest raiment. The one was older, with red and white hair, black eyes, and his stature medium; the other was younger and taller, handsome in form beyond the children of men. And the older said to me 'What are you doing?' and I was greatly frightened because I knew that there was no one present. And I answered 'Who are you?'

"He replied 'Arise and fear not, and heed what I say. I am Andrew the Apostle. Bring together the bishop of Le Puy and the count of St. Gilles and say these words to them: "Why has the bishop neglected to preach and admonish and daily to sign his people with the cross which he bears before them?"' And he added, 'Come and I will show you the Holy Lance of our father, Jesus Christ, which you shall give to the count. For God has granted it to him ever since he was born.'

"I arose, therefore, and followed him into the city, dressed in nothing but a shirt. And he led me into the church of the apostle of St. Peter through the north gate, before which the Saracens had built a mosque. In the church, indeed, were two lamps, which gave as much light as if the sun had illuminated it. And he said to me, 'Wait here.' He commanded me to sit upon a column which was closest to the stairs by which one ascends to the altar from the south; but his companion stood at a distance before the altar steps. Then St. Andrew, going under ground, brought forth the Lance and gave it into my hands.

"And he said to me 'Behold the Lance which opened his side whence the salvation of the whole world has come.'

"While I held it in my hands, weeping for joy, I said to him, 'Lord, if it is thy will, I will take it and give it to the count!'

"And he said to me, 'Not now, for it will happen that the city will be taken. Then come with twelve men and seek it here whence I drew it forth and where I hide it.' And then he hid it.

"After these things had been said, he led me back over the wall to my home; and so they left me. Then I thought to myself of the condition of my poverty and your greatness, and I feared to approach you. However, when the city was taken, I came to you. And now, if it please you, test what I say."

Adhemar tapped the arm of the royal chair impatiently. He looked the part of a bishop on this morning, resplendent in an ivory cassock and purple chasuble. A jeweled cross, a gift from the Holy Father himself, hung around his neck. He looked at it now, lifting its emerald-studded *patibulum* to his eyes for closer inspection. It was a habit of his when he was impatient and fearful of saying things he would later regret and of which he might be in need of confession. He remained silent.

His silence, however, clearly suggested that he thought little of the words of Peter and could not give them credence. "We might call for the Gospel and the Cross, my lord," said Raymond. The count and the bishop of Le Puy had known for each other for many years.

"The Gospel and the Cross!" Adhemar growled. "Have I done anything this week except trot out the Gospel and the Cross to elicit affirmations of honesty from food-starved visionaries who see in every shadow St. Andrew or St. Peter, and hear in the slightest moan of the wind the voice of the Blessed Virgin!" Standing, the bishop strode in agitation toward Raymond. palms outstretched in a gesture of supplication. "Why, Raymond, the pastoral office is scarcely needed now. We hear from the saints and apostles directly. God speaks through peasants and serfs and not through the Holy Father or the bishops of the Holy Mother Church!" He turned away from his friend. "I'll have no part of this foolishness!"

Raymond's eyebrows arched: "Does memory serve me well in reminding me that God once spoke to a prophet (not a bishop like yourself of course), through the mouth of a donkey?" There was a smile in his voice.

"Before the age of the Holy Church, my friend, before the age of the Church, and the Jews would sooner listen to an ass than they would the prophets anyway!"

Peter dropped to his knees before the bishop. "Your reverence, what I have said is the truth. I would not risk your enmity or the disfavor of my lord to make statements such as these."

"He is a Provencal, Adhemar—"

"I was assigned to Peter the Monk to guard the treasure chest. I served him well."

"Peter the Monk! Ha! I won't hold that against your account." But Adhemar dropped the hand-wrought cross upon his chest and, unswayed in this dissimulation, quit the marbled room in mutterings and disgust. The two Provencals watched him depart; then Peter turned to the count to see what might happen next.

"You can lead us to the spot where the Holy Lance is buried?" the old knight asked, stroking his beard thoughtfully.

"Yes, my lord. There is no doubt."

✠✠✠

That night, the conspirators gathered at Bohemund's quarters in the Armenian section of Antioch. Tancred was present, as was Robert of Normandy now fully recovered, Eustace of Rouen, Baldwin of Boullion (brother of Godfrey), and Bohemund himself.

Quaffing wine, they huddled in the light of a hanging lamp over the enigmatic contents of the Paulician Fragment which was smoothed out before them in two pieces like scraps of untidy linen.

Si quis vult post me venire
abneget semetipsum et TOLLAT CRUCEM
suam quotidie et sequatur me.

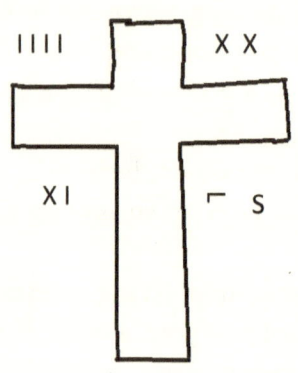

"This parchment is a relic in its own right," Eustace said, unable to explain the meaning of the fragment.

"Come, come," Bohemund said testily. "This fragment, now torn in two pieces, was deemed by the monk of antiquity to provide all the information necessary for the recovery of the Holy Lance."

"So where do we start?" Short Breeches asked.

"We start where all discoveries begin," Tancred said. "With questions."

"And the first question?"

"Is location," Tancred continued. "The fragment has to reveal location."

"Obviously," said Short Breeches scornfully. "That's why we're here."

"He means 'starting point'" Baldwin interjected. "The fragment has to give us a place to start. We know that the old monk was housed in a Paulician monastery which no longer exists. What if he hid the lance in the monastery?"

Bohemund answered quickly. "He wouldn't have done that, because he knew that his order was fleeing to the mountains. Why hide the most precious relic in Christendom in a monastery that is being abandoned? No, no, he would hide it somewhere he believed it would be safe for centuries to come." Bohemund reached for a closer look and then picked it up, holding it to the light. He put it down unsatisfied.

"Look at these letters here, how large they are," Tancred observed. "TOLLAT CRUCEM ... *bears the cross.*"

"It means something," Short Breeches said as Bohemund continued to examine the other segment.

"Six, seven hundred years have passed," Baldwin said. "The lance could be anywhere. The monk could've thrown it in a well or hurled it over the wall, who knows?"

"Nonsense," said Short Breeches. "He both hid it and revealed it—hid it so the barbarians couldn't find it, but revealed it in this fragment so that we could."

"And what if we can't?" asked Eustace.

"Then someone smarter than us will find it."

"Wait a minute!" Bohemund exclaimed. "What do you see here, Tancred?" He pushed the fragment in front of his nephew.

Tancred looked at it carefully trying to see what his uncle saw. "I see ... a cross, and the numbers four, twenty, eleven, and the sign 7S."

Bohemund twirled the parchment upside down. "Now, what do you see?"

The men clustered over it again with hawking eyes, mixing their wine-bated breath. "I see SL and the numbers nine, twenty, and four," Tancred said.

"And?" Bohemund nudged.

"And an upside-down cross." Then Tancred had an inspiration. "St. Peter's Cross!"

"So if the question is 'location' or 'starting point' what does this suggest?"

"St. Peter's Church!"

"But the SL?" Baldwin asked.

Bohemund answered. "Secundum Lucam nine twenty-four. It's the reference for the TOLLAT CRUCEM on this fragment."

"But what does it mean?" Baldwin persisted.

"I don't know for sure," Bohemund said. "TOLLAT CRUCEM ... bearing the cross ... in large letters. Hmmmmm. It's supposed to tell us something." They were silent again.

"The second station of the cross," said Eustace.

They stared at him in disbelief. "Of course!" exclaimed Bohemund. "What does one find in a church besides an altar and saints?"

"The stations of the cross!" said Tancred.

✠✠✠

Twenty minutes later, less than two hours before midnight, five men bearing oil lamps stood beneath the second station of the cross in the Church of St. Peter. In a niche three by five feet, they saw a carving in olive wood of Christ being compelled to bear the cross while passersby look on. On the stone ledge beneath the carving were etched the words TOLLAT CRUCEM.

"Tollat Crucem," said Eustace, a man who, doing his thinking out loud, was nonetheless known as a quiet man.

"The lance can't be buried here," said Baldwin. "We still don't know where it is."

"But we're closer than we were before," snapped Tancred.

"It's in this church, I know it," Bohemund said, looking around. They were standing in the aisle near the altar close to the north transept. Bohemund stepped into the nave, the aura of golden light following him as he walked. "Somewhere, O King, is thy lance!" he muttered. "And somewhere, Bohemund is thy reward!" he added.

"Let's examine the parchment again," he suggested. They met again beneath the TOLLAT CRUCEM. Bohemund reviewed the obvious. "A cross ... an upside-down cross ... St. Peter's cross ... the second station of the cross ... Careful now ... This church has a cruciform shape, does it not?" The men agreed. "If the cross on this fragment is in the form of the church, then we are standing here," he concluded, pointing to the parchment.

"That's no help," Baldwin objected.

"Shut your mouth," Bohemund snarled. "I'm thinking."

Tancred spoke. "The numbers must give the precise location since the text gave us the general location."

"Nine ... twenty ... four ... nine twenty four ..."

"Thirty-three," Eustace said unthinking.

Bohemund's head snapped up. "What?"

"Nine plus twenty plus four equals thirty-three," he said. "The age at which Christ died."

Although they did not know what it meant, Eustace's revelation seemed significant to them for they all began to speak immediately and continued to do so until Bohemund intervened.

"Quiet!" he hissed. "Eustace has something here."

"Thirty-three steps from the TOLLAT CRUCEM," Baldwin suggested.

Tancred scoffed. "Whose steps? A tall man, a short man? The old monk isn't going to mark off steps. Every man's stride is different."

"Besides we don't know in what direction," Short Breeches said.

"Wait," cried Bohemund, "I have a hunch. This church is in the form of a cross, therefore, where the beams of the cross intersect is where the transepts and the nave intersect, correct?"

They nodded. "Go stand directly in the center of this intersection, Robert, and await our instructions." Robert did as he was told. The four men beneath the TOLLAT CRUCEM watched as Robert of Normandy walked, carrying his lamp, into the nave and toward the altar until by looking in both vertical and horizontal directions he ascertained the precise point of intersection.

"Are you there?" Bohemund asked in a muffled shout.

"Yes," came the reply.

"Now walk away from the altar in a straight line until you are even with us." Robert took four or five steps until he was in the nave directly even with them at the TOLLAT CRUCEM.

"Now take one or two steps away from us, but even with us, until you are standing in the middle of the next floor slab."

Robert lowered his lamp to reveal the marble floor of the church, and stepped to the left several feet. "Are you in the middle of the slab?" Bohemund yelled. His voice echoed in the empty stone church.

"Yes," Robert answered.

"Stay there, don't move." Bohemund turned to Eustace, Baldwin and Tancred. "Gentlemen, I believe Short Breeches is standing over the spot where the Holy Lance is buried!"

✠✠✠

A small band of thirteen hardy men gathered in the darkness in front of the palace where Bohemund's procession had begun earlier in the day. They assembled a cartload of shovels, picks and spades and began the trek through the city toward the Church of St. Peter on the road that led to St. Paul's Gate. Few of them dared to believe they would actually succeed in their mission; such a dream was too incredible. Discover the spear that had pierced the side of the Savior while he was yet upon the Cross? Could it be possible? Was it probable that they, pilgrims from a faraway land, the land of the Franks, could have been brought from such a distance to uncover this, the most sacred of treasures? Except for one youth, Peter, they did not believe so, and as they pushed and pulled the creaking cart toward the church, they laughed and joked among themselves about their lives, their labors, and their loves. They did not give much thought to what they were seeking; it was in the course of their pilgrim lives but another duty to fulfill as they had many times before. Dig a trench here, burnish the armor here, dig a hole there, mine this wall, build that hut, transport these supplies.

There was a dreary and commonplace reality to this undertaking which they accepted well enough, but to which they attached little importance.

In the group was Fulcher, the priest, who wanted to be present to record the endeavor whether it succeeded or failed, and who, in any case, understood the mystical possibilities; the youth Peter himself; Count Raymond; also the bishop of Orange; a Pontius; a Feraldus of Thouars; and other men of able body and willing spirit making thirteen.

Peter watched these proceedings with mounting apprehension. It now seemed to him one thing to have had a vision in which reality seems somehow so "real," and quite another to be awake and ordering one's life on the basis of it. Still, the vision had been vivid—the colors, the strength of the voices he heard, the countenance of St. Andrew, all foreboding and ominously real ... vivid enough to send him to the count and the bishop ... real enough to cause him to quake in fear during the day when he thought of it and to dread nightfall lest he be visited again. But now, looking at the spades with their chipped and slivered handles; and the picks and hammers laid out, the instruments with which to carry out his orders; seeing in his mind the hard-packed earth settled by centuries of tradition, chipped and violated and flung on an unconsecrated cloth; the dread of it all settled upon Peter like a heavy burden.

✠✠✠

How can you possibly know that?" Tancred exploded.

"I can't," Bohemund answered. "It's a hunch. Robert is standing approximately where the SL is located on this fragment. My guess is that there are thirty-three marble slabs between the Second Station of the Cross and where he is now standing." He stood with his back against the wall beneath the TOLLAT CRUCEM and peered through the ring of light to the floor. "This is one," he said, walking toward Robert, with Tancred, Eustace and Baldwin following, making sure of this count. "Fifteen ... twenty ... twenty-five ... thirty ... thirty-one, thirty-two, thirty-three!" They were standing with Robert in the nave.

"Move away," he ordered. He knelt on the floor of the church while the others gathered around him in a circle enclosing the light within the ring of their bodies turning the church into a virtual cavern of darkness. With his hand, Bohemund dusted off the three-foot square section of marble, pushing aside dirt and soil carried there by pilgrims and penitents. "More light," he said. They leaned closer as he swept the ancient and polished surface clean.

"There it is," he said quietly. The men dropped to their knees. Bohemund's finger pointed to a spot in the center of the stone where someone had hastily scratched in small letters SL. The men gasped excitedly.

"Secundum Lucam," said Eustace in awe, touching the stone.

"No," said Bohemund firmly, "not Secundum Lucam."

Tancred looked up into the half-lit face of his uncle. "What then?"

"Sancta Lancea!" The men gasped as though they'd been touched with a hot iron.

"We're rich!" Tancred whispered.

Suddenly they heard a commotion at the west of the nave. "What's that?" Bohemund asked, startled. They whirled about staring into the darkness toward the far end of the church.

"Someone's trying to get in," Tancred said.

"Blow out the lamps," Bohemund said. They had no sooner done so than one of the west portal doors opened, and Bohemund and his men saw lanterns and the dim shape of men carrying them enter the church.

"Quick! Robert, you and Baldwin to the south transept. We'll to the north! We'll wait and watch there."

Peter's band of men illuminated the nave, lighting the lamps by all twelve stations of the cross, and bearing lamps into the nave itself near the altar while Bohemund watched, impatient and furious. When they were ready, the men stood apart while Peter, standing before the altar, closed his eyes to pray and to recall the vision of Saint Andrew. Minutes passed and then the lad, his eyes still closed, moved away from the altar, wandering slowly and aimlessly. When he stopped, he was standing in the nave and facing the altar. He closed his eyes again, but did not move.

"This is the place," he said, awaking. He marked the spot where they should begin to dig. With iron bars and fulcrums, they lifted several marble slabs like coffin lids exposing the earth beneath. Soon, a substantial pile of dirt had been thrown on the canvas nearby as the hole became deeper.

"How did he know it was there!" Tancred complained, scarcely believing what he was seeing.

"I don't know," Bohemund muttered. "His sister, Addie, testified against me, and now he is about to steal the lance right from under our noses."

"Let's just take it!"

"There's thirteen of them!"

"We'll take it when they remove it from the church!"

"Maybe."

By midnight, the hole was large enough for two men to work in. They took turns at the labor to keep their effort fresh. Doubts, the size of a small cloud, began to appear on the horizon of this enterprise. First, a good-natured question that expressed in jocular form the suspicion that they were digging in the wrong place. Then came the suggestion that Peter in his state of ecstasy may have mistaken the altar steps for the choir steps, or that St. Andrew had been misinformed by the archangel, or unaware that the Holy Lance had already been removed. These comments Peter endured with passable good humor. But he was young; it bothered him. The old visionary learns never to expect others to believe in his dreams. The old men shall dream dreams, declared the prophet Joel, because old men never presume that anyone will take them seriously. They are humored as are children engaged in games of make-believe. People smile at old men and children, thinking them clever either in their infancy or their dotage for having the imagination to fashion out of nothing elaborate divinations and visions of prescience. The old man need not be taken seriously. But the young man dreaming dreams must be reckoned with, and if his fancies come to pass, he is accounted a seer. If they fail, he is rebuked and made a laughingstock. Peter understood, therefore, that ridicule and scorn were tests of his prophetic and mystical calling.

The bantering increased as the midnight hour lengthened and soon a discussion ensued debating the merits of their labor. Peter removed himself to a statue of the Virgin Mother. There he prayed alone, not doubting the vision of St. Andrew, not doubting that God had sent the saint to speak to him, not doubting God, but not knowing why God should at such a crucial time abandon him and leave him to his own devices, leave him with a crew of doubt-mongers who would have him curse God and flee.

Peter looked at his hands and trousers. They were clean and unsoiled. His role was not to dig but to pray and encourage. But now Peter thought, as he looked up into the cerise eyes of the Virgin's tilted head (was she taking pity on him?) perhaps it was time for him to dig, to allow the saint to direct his spade whither it should go.

The work had proceeded for several hours yielding nothing. Both Bohemund, hiding in the transept and the men working in the nave, began to believe that a mistake had been made. The thirteen refused to work longer. When Pontius at last flung away his spade on the mountain of dirt now rising from the floor of the nave, the search was at an end. But Peter would not be deterred. He jumped into the pit, now over six feet deep.

"What are you doing?" asked Pontius, sitting down to rest.

"I will continue to dig, for the lance is not far from discovery," said Peter. "Hand me the trowel." Feraldus threw the small instrument into the cavity which Peter caught in flight and began quickly to apply it to the soil. Observing this, Feraldus jumped in as well, joining him with a shovel. The spear would be found now, or it would not be found at all.

Then everyone in the church heard Peter strike metal against metal. The two men in the pit stopped working and looked at each other fearfully, afraid that what they would find upon closer examination would be nothing more than a nail, or a horseshoe fallen from an ancient Roman steed in a bygone epoch when Italian legions had opened highways from Tarsus to Caesarea. Or did they fear that what they had struck was indeed the spear with which Longinus had pierced the Savior in the side, or did they fear that power by which Peter had been led to the precise spot where this lance had lain buried for almost a millennium? No matter, they looked at each other with a mixture of hope and anticipation, and then in an instant flung themselves upon their knees while their blistered fingers worked at the soil about the tip of the trowel. Their fingers now were sensitive to every hardened module of earth, feeling for any abnormality, casting to the sides of the pit the dirt that was rejected by their expert hands. Deeper and deeper they probed, fingers touching the edge of the trowel and working down and across its blade, until, by a miracle, Peter exposed the metal point of an object which he loudly proclaimed to be the lance of the Lord.

"I have found it!" he cried. "I have found it!" At this, his hands badgered feverishly at his discovery. Feraldus jumped in opposite Peter, working just as hard. Within minutes, they uncovered the ancient spear lying horizontally at a depth of about seven feet, and removed the relic from the pit. The lance itself was wrapped in a shroud that now was in tatters, a rotting and decaying fabric that had once been as carefully wrapped around this relic as it would now be unwrapped. Peter held it aloft for the admiring pilgrims who had fallen to their knees to venerate it.

Peter handed the Holy Lance to Fulcher the priest who placed it on a white linen cloth secured for this very purpose. Carefully, they laid the spear across the crimson Crusader Cross where, as it touched the fabric, soil falling from the holy shaft peppered the embroidered cloth.

There are moments of such extraordinary excitement that emotions and enthusiasm cannot be contained but must be expressed vocally and loudly. Such was the shouting and excitement when the gates of Antioch had opened to the crusaders. Such also was the thrill when a white-robed Adhemar appeared on the crest behind the Turkish army at Dorylaeum. But there are also moments of such exquisite sacred intensity, that any sound is sacrilegious and any vocalization superfluous. This was such a moment.

The spear was about eight feet long, including tip and barbs. The tip was covered in a malleable metal, which was frequently replaced. Fulcher wondered if it was simply his imagination that he could see the wear on the shaft of the spear where Roman soldiers had checked the spear for balance, and where Gallic hands had grasped this javelin before hurling it in thousands of practice tosses or before heaving it into the breathing chest of a Jewish rebel, or into the belly of a Bedouin woman. And how many persons had suffered death by this very instrument after Longinus had thrust it into the side of the Savior? Fulcher stooped lower, maneuvering among those who pressed close, to examine the relic. He could see the longitudinal strokes made by an adze where some unknown craftsmen had whittled and shaped this slender beam of lightweight acacia wood into an implement that would wound the Savior. It had no doubt been balanced carefully.

Bohemund and his men were never able to apprehend the lance for it never left the church itself. All of their intricate plans, delicate negotiations, all of the miles ridden and conversations undertaken, came to naught.

The men who had helped to uncover the Holy Lance became known as the Twelve Discoverers, not counting Peter himself. The Twelve Discoverers. There was significance in the number: twelve apostles, twelves Sons of Israel, twelve spies in the land of Canaan, and twelve signs of the zodiac. God had given the pilgrims still another clue of His presence.

The next evening at vespers, a large assembly converged near the steps of St. Peter's. The crowd was told when they would be able to view the relic themselves. Since Raymond had believed the Provencal youth who had discovered it, the lance was given to the count for its protection and safe-keeping. As for Peter, he was introduced to the throng amid a great swell of cheers and accolades. Peter nervously beckoned for them to be quiet. Then he said, holding aloft the newly discovered relic:

"'I have found it!' he cried. 'I have found it!' At this, his hands badgered feverishly at his discovery. Feraldus jumped in opposite Peter, working just as hard. Within minutes, they uncovered the ancient spear lying horizontally at a depth of about seven feet, and removed the relic from the pit" (p. 421)

"Behold the lance which pierced the side of the Savior, he who was wounded on the Cross for us. The Lord commands that you celebrate the day on which He gave us the lance. And since it was found at vespers, He commands that we celebrate the solemn festival next week at the same time, and thereafter each year on the day of finding the Lance. We are to conduct ourselves henceforth as we are taught in the epistle by the saint of this church, Peter, which is our reading for today: 'Humble yourselves under the mighty hand of God.' And let the clerics sing when the lance has been presented: *Lustra sex qui jam peracta tempus inplens corporis.* And when the clerics have sung, *Agnus in cruce levatus immolandus stipite,* they should finish the hymn on bended knee."

"You are a man of letters?" asked Fulcher, later when they were walking away. He had found most persons subject to visions to be ignorant, often peasants. Perhaps Peter was an exception in this case. Peter, believing that Fulcher would not believe him were he to tell the truth, replied that he was unlettered. In fact, Peter was so ignorant at that hour of what he knew and didn't know that any answer would have in good conscience been the truth. He had not learned letters, but did know the *Pater Noster, Credo in Deum, Magnificat, Glory in Excelsis Deo*, and *Benedictus Dominus Deus Israel.* He remembered nothing else even though he had at one time known much. And though he would later be able to recover some of his learning, it was only through great effort.

✠✠✠

"It was a vindication of sorts for you, as well, wasn't it?" Bernard asked. "You had said that in five days the Lord would give them a sign. And that is exactly what happened!"

I nodded, smiling ruefully. "I confess, that I was relieved when the lance was discovered because I, too, had made my integrity an issue. The truth is, the discovery of the Holy Lance was the pivotal point in the pilgrimage. Its impact was absolutely immeasurable. The army and the morale of the people was so strengthened that they believed passionately for the first time in over a year that their destiny was totally and completely unalterable and that they as a people of God were invincibly and inexorably directed toward Jerusalem. No longer would the armies of the Turks strike fear in their breast. The presence of the Holy Lance removed fear and doubts. Henceforth, they would sally forth into battle convinced that God was their captain and that the victory had already been secured. It remained only for them to claim it."

CHAPTER THIRTY-THREE

Duel on the Plains of Antioch

June 27, 1098 A.D.

ETER BARTHOLOMEW WALK-
ED RELUCTANTLY ALONG the
cypress-lined colonnade, a thorough-
fare which stretched about two miles
north and south from the St. Paul's
Gate to the Gate of St. George. It
was dawn in Antioch. The western wall and towers
were bathed in the flush of cool morning light,
while he himself traversed the roadway in shadows
and silence. The sun had not yet peered over Mt.
Silpius and the Citadel was still dark. Few had
ventured out on this morning, preferring to stay shut
up inside their newly acquired houses resting and
conserving energy for what would be another day of
scorching heat. Supplies were exhausted, and the heat
was enervating.

The leaves on the cypress trees were still. Peter
passed a passel of women gathering them. They would
be cooked and eaten. Provencal women were especially
adept at transforming mundane fare into spicy delicacies
that in other hands would slip past the palate in utter blandness.

Life was at a standstill. The street dogs lay in corners of
doorways, their pink tongues hanging languidly. Horses too weak
to stand were lying in the fields. Today several more would die. The
proud army of the Franks now consisted almost entirely of foot
soldiers, warriors who would sooner eat their horse than attempt to

ride it into battle. Peter brushed a fly away from his face. There were millions of flies that seemed healthy enough, feeding on decaying flesh, resting on open wounds, and lighting on the swollen and malnourished eyes of children who inexplicably seemed neither to notice or care. They stood quietly along the street, those little ones and watched Peter saunter by, some with no clothes at all, and they looked into his deep eyes, apparently unaware of the flies perched on their own eyes, sucking and feeding, mating, and biting their tender flesh. Peter the Visionary looked away. Above the sloping hills of Silpius, iron-clawed buzzards hovered motionless in the pale air, waiting for a horse to die, or searching for carrion on which to spend the morning feeding.

"We cannot wait any longer," said Raymond in the Council of Knights. "The longer we wait, the more horses we lose and the weaker we become."

"We are not ready to meet Arslan," said Hugh of Vermandois.

"We will never be stronger than we are today," Raymond countered, glaring at the Norman. Hugh's influence among the princes was no greater than it had been two and a half years earlier in Clermont.

Since the discovery of the Holy Lance, Peter Bartholomew had been invited to attend the Council of the Knights as an observer. So far he had said nothing. The council began vigorously to debate the merits of various military options. In fact, it appeared that the alternatives were very few. They could attempt to endure the siege and establish a life within the city walls, hoping to tire and discourage the enemy until the fall and winter weather approached. Or they could assemble their army and march out to face Arslan in a battle which would decide who controlled Antioch.

The first option was quickly discarded. The city had no food. Attempting to survive until autumn and then throughout the winter was impossible. They must face the enemy whose force was superior to theirs in numbers, horses and supplies.

"Arslan is not going to flee when we march out of the city," observed Godfrey.

Adhemar glowered thoughtfully, forefinger tapping his brow. "We are assuming that Arslan expects a fight. Perhaps he is hoping that we will simply surrender the city without a struggle."

"Begging your pardon, my lords," Peter interjected, twisting his cap in his hands, "That is correct. Arslan expects us to surrender the city."

Stony silence greeted Peter's words. "How do you know this?" Bohemund inquired.

"He told me so yesterday when I went to see him."

"You saw Arslan?" chimed several voices at once. Bohemund and Raymond leaped to their feet and leaned toward the youth studying carefully one who had dared to do what they themselves would not have dreamed of doing. Peter nodded.

"You have our attention," Adhemar said. "Go on."

Peter hesitated and then began: "Begging your pardon again, my lords, but we sit here on this mountain like the children of Israel before the camp of the Philistines. Their Goliath mocks us every day asking where is our God. Yesterday it became clear to me that, in this dire circumstance, God wanted me to speak to our enemy, the infidel. Accordingly, I slipped away on the road to their camp, and when I arrived near their encampment, several of their soldiers met me and escorted me to their leader."

"What was he doing?" asked Short Breeches.

"Playing chess—"

"—Chess, chess, what is chess?" they all asked.

"—a crude game played on a board made to resemble a battlefield, with two sides, black and white, and many pieces representing soldiers, horses, and castles. When Arslan inquired as to the nature of my visit, I replied by asking him a question. 'Why,' I asked, 'have you entered the land of Christians in such a haughty manner? Perhaps it is because you wish to become Christians yourselves,' I said, 'or if not, you have come hither for the purpose of harassing us as much as possible. If this is the case, you must leave at once, and if you do, you may take your horses, mules, camels, sheep and all other belongings that you wish. Unless you remove your armies from the Orontes River valley and evacuate this region which at one time belonged to Christians, we will surely begin a war against you within three days.'"

Hugh leapt to his feet. "By what right do you utter such statements on our behalf?" he cried.

"Silence!" roared Bohemund. "Let the boy finish," he said. "Whatever has happened, has happened. Let's discover more of this, and then we can make our judgment of this matter." Turning to Peter, he smiled darkly, and said, "Please continue."

Peter resumed his narrative. "I was not surprised when Arslan rejected this suggestion for the impious do not believe in the strength of the Lord. He sent me back with this message: 'Say to Bohemund who is now for a short time the king of Antioch, "On what do you base this great confidence of yours? Do you think you can win this war with mere words? Have you formed an alliance with another power so that you have more men and horses than we? I will make a wager with you. If you can supply the men, I'll give you the horses to put them on. Then come into battle against us so that the war might be fairly fought. You are all doomed. You do not have a cavalry. Your infantry is weak and tired of war. Your people are doomed to eat their own excrement and drink their own piss. Listen to me. You unjustly attempt to occupy land that is not yours, and seek to possess land which was never your inheritance. We marvel that you call this land *Christian* land. It was never so. Even your prophet Jesus was a Jew, not a Christian. Therefore, if you wish to convert to the true God, Allah, and if you wish to deny the god who leads you into such injustice and oppression, if you wish to forsake your cruel laws and customs, you will have food to eat, horses to ride, and you will enjoy the fruit of the vine and the crops of this valley and the water of our cisterns. None of you, I promise, will be foot soldiers; you will all be knights, just as we are, and we will consider you our friends. If you do not, you will all surely die or be led in chains to Chorsan to serve us and our children in perpetual captivity.' This is what he said to me, and I left his presence."

At these words, the council was thrown again into dissension. It is one thing to receive the conditions of surrender; it is quite another to be taunted in the process. Some were of the opinion that Arslan did not want them to surrender. By this taunting, he wanted instead to goad them into a fight which he believed they would surely lose.

Adhemar, Bohemund and Raymond listened to the others chatter wildly, realizing that those who were speaking the most were those whose opinion mattered the least. Raymond knew that Arslan's assessment was militarily correct. But he also knew that military strength alone does not always win battles.

Adhemar the bishop was not nearly as religious as Raymond the count. He was less confident in the power of the Holy Lance in the bosom of the Church and more confident in the efficacy of an unholy lance in the hands of a crusader. God, he believed, seemed to prefer strength in numbers and arms, and right now, they had neither.

Bohemund received Arslan's words as a personal challenge. They were after all addressed to him. Aban Arslan had insulted him in front of his peers. Whatever the outcome, Bohemund thought, Arslan will answer to me.

"He is pissing in the wind," said Raymond at last. "He's never beaten us yet ... he's hoping we won't fight, and if we do, he'll retreat."

"Turks never run from a fight," Bohemund replied.

"The Turks expect to fight and we expect a miracle," Robert added.

"It's happened before," Adhemar said. "Once when Elisha was a prophet in Israel, Ben Hadad the king of Syria besieged the city of Samaria with thousands of soldiers, horses and chariots. When Elisha's servant saw it, he feared that they and the city would be destroyed. But Elisha prayed and asked God to open the eyes of his servant. And the Lord did so, and the servant saw that the mountains were full of the armies of the Lord, of horses and chariots of fire. The next morning, four beggars went into the camp of the Syrians to beg, believing that they were going to die anyway and it wouldn't matter if they died outside the walls of Samaria or by the hands of the Syrians. And perchance, the Syrians would take pity and give them food. But when they arrived at the Syrian camp, the place was deserted. That night, the Lord had made the Syrians hear the sound of chariots and horses, the sound of a great army, and they said to themselves, 'Israel has made a treaty with the king of the Hittites and the Egyptians and now they are come upon us.' So they fled in terror leaving behind their tents, horses, donkeys, raiment, their silver and gold. The Lord was with them that day."

The knights were quiet. Then Adhemar said to Bohemund. "There may be a way for you to get your hands on Arslan, if you really mean it."

✠✠✠

Arslan sat with his advisors in his tent. It was richly appointed with carpets made in Anatolia and delicate curtains of Persian silk. He was playing chess with one of his commanders, Muluk-Dukak of Damascus. Watching the contest were others of his council: Amisoliman, Tughtikin, Janah ad-Daula, Arslan Tash of Sanjar, Sulaiman ibn Artug and a few other emirs. The chess board of marble with mosaic inlays supported pieces made of Egyptian alabaster. The game was going against Arslan.

"You are waiting for me to make a mistake," said Muluk, "But I am a patient man."

"But patience without cunning is cowardice," replied Arslan, grinning. "You are afraid of my knights."

"As you are afraid of the Franks?" Muluk asked, pushing the point.

"The Franks are effeminate weaklings," Arslan sneered. "They have been here on these plains since October and what do they have to show for it? Antioch. They captured a city that has no food or water. Ha! They fled like a deer into the snare. Now they think by their puffing to scare me into fighting them. I will wait. They will die, or give up. You will see. The Franks have no stomach for war if they know they will die. They are not willing to become martyrs." Castle to queen castle five.

Muluk considered his options. Pawn to queen four. "You underestimate them. You do not know Bohemund."

Arelan brushed aside the criticism. "Why should we attack Antioch now and lose thousands of men in the process, when we can wait, enjoy the valley, rest, gain strength and let time and nature do our fighting for us?" Knight to king five. "Every day that passes, they grow weaker and weaker. Every day we get stronger and stronger." He smiled at Muluk. The bastard, he thought. In control of Damascus and wants more. Muluk was threatening his queen.

They heard the drumming of horses approaching. Moments later a messenger, Amirdal by name, entered the chamber and whispered briefly into the ear of the commander. Arslan's eyes registered surprise. "Bring them in." Amirdal bowed and left their presence and returned straightaway with Peter Bartholomew and his riding companion, Roger of Barneville.

"It's customary to bow," said Muluk, looking up from the game board.

"I bow only in the presence of God and not seeing God here, there is no requirement that I bow," Peter announced. A guard moved behind Peter and brought the flat of his hands across Peter's back and sent him sprawling to the carpeted floor of the tent.

"Good to see you again lad," said Arslan laughing heartily. "Take his friend outside while we converse." Roger was escorted away, leaving Arslan, his advisors and Peter alone. "Now we can talk, although such extreme prostration was not necessary. I surmise you have delivered my message?"

Peter stood and cleared his throat as though to confirm that he had a voice with which to speak. "I have," he said returning Arslan's gaze directly.

"And what, may I ask, was the response?" Arslan motioned to have the chess game removed.

"Our leaders consider you to be an effeminate sister who is afraid to engage our forces in battle." Arslan did not flinch at this verbal sally, but his council of advisors hovering nearby cast quick sidelong glances at each other as Peter continued. "We view a battle as inevitable and believe there will be a great loss of life on both sides. Since you profess to be interested in preserving the lives of your soldiers, we propose that you personally represent your army in a battle against one of our soldiers who will represent us. The winner takes the city and promises to respect the lives and property of the losing side. This way the inevitable resolution of this problem can be handled without controversy and without bloodshed. Surely this is as pleasing to your god and customs as it is to ours."

Arslan looked at his advisors, smiling gamely and attempting a laugh. "You do not want to fight us. We are superior to you in every way. You are searching for a way of escape to avoid losing in a battle to us. It will not work. Tell your leaders to prepare for war. I am a patient man. But if war is what they want, war is what they will get. Bring in the weapons they brought with them."

A guard left the tent and returned with a sword covered with rust, a well-worn bow, and a crooked lance. Arslan examined them carefully. "These are the weapons with which you would fight us?" He laughed. "Amirdal, take down this letter to the Caliph. 'To the caliph, our Lord Sultan and valiant knight in Chorsan: Please receive with rejoicing these three weapons which we recently took from a squadron of Franks. Now you know with what arms the barbarian host comes against us; how very fine and perfect they are compared to our weapons which are twice, thrice welded, purified like the purest gold and silver. Know also, that I have the Franks shut up in Antioch and that I hold the Citadel at my free command, while they are below in the city. I shall make them undergo the sentence of death or lead them into Chorsan in the harshest captivity because they think to drive us out beyond upper India, as they have done with our brothers in Pomania and Syria. Now I swear to you by Mohammed and Allah that I will not return to Chorsan until I have restored to the glory of our empire the city of Antioch, all of Syria, Bulgaria, Romania and even Apulia.'"

Peter was not daunted by these words. "It is as my lords said it would be. You lack the courage to fight. You prefer to not fight at all, or to write letters, to threaten us with mere words, the sound of air moving between your lips. And when you do venture to fight, you send your soldiers to the front lines to do the fighting for you. You are a coward. You are afraid to do battle with one of our men. I will tell them what you said, and they will laugh and say that you are an effeminate sister." He turned to go.

"Wait," said Arslan. "To the death?"

"At the discretion of the victor."

"Weapons?"

"All's fair."

"The armies?"

"Full army support. The losers lay down their arms and the victors take possession of the city. Each army retains their own belongings."

"When and where?"

"The tenth hour tomorrow, west of the river, north of the road to Alexandretta. You will see us, of that you may be sure."

Arslan spoke to his guards. "Take this rusty sword and return it to its owner." They nodded and left, escorting Peter out of the tent while Arslan consulted with his advisors. When he was taken inside once again, he learned that Arslan had acceded to the plan offered by the crusaders. The Frankish council had been correct: Arslan was too proud to be considered a coward, especially by his enemies. Personal pride for once interfered with correct military strategy, while Arslan's advisors, it can now be said, approved of the Frank's plan, not because they thought it bode well for them, but because they believed it bode ill for Arslan. The commander was not beloved of his army.

"And who will be my opponent?" he asked as Peter prepared to depart.

"Bohemund, prince of Antioch," he said.

This news seemed disconcerting to Arslan, but he corrected himself as a guard approached bearing a burlap sack dripping with

blood. He turned to Peter and said: "Then take this gift to Bohemund and tell him that he shall be as your friend now is." The
guard put the sack at the feet of Peter who looked at Arslan per-
plexed. The sultan smiled. Peter leaned over the sack and untied.
Inside was the severed and mutilated head of Roger of Barneville.

"It would not have been nearly so difficult were not the sword
so rusty and dull," said the guard.

✠✠✠

That evening in Antioch, Adhemar the bishop, sent out orders by
heralds to all the soldiers of the army of God that each one should
lay out as much grain as possible to supply and feed his horse, so
that those carrying riders on the morrow would not become too
weak in the event of a battle.

In the church of St. Peter that night, he proclaimed mourning
for Roger of Barneville who was beloved by many. Moreover,
everyone was to say five *Pater Nosters* for the five wounds of Christ.
If any soldier should refuse to fight he was branded a Judas, a
betrayer of the Lord, who deserted the apostles and sold his Lord
to the Jews. He announced that Bohemund would be fighting
Goliath on the morrow, and that God would surely give them the
victory. However, they suspected treachery, and if a battle ensued,
they were to go into battle crying "Deus vult." This would be their
battle cry. All the brothers who have died in this pilgrimage will be
with us tomorrow, Adhemar preached.

The next morning, all partook of communion and gave themselves to God and to death if God willed it, gave themselves to the
Holy Mother Roman Church for the glory of the race of the Franks.

Four days before the kalends of July, the army marched out of
the city in double lines of infantry and cavalry. Thus, the banners of
squadrons, troops and phalanges went first. Among these first lines
were priests and monks dressed in white vestments who, weeping
for all the people, sang hymns and psalms to God and poured out
many devout prayers.

With these priests in the first lines were the troops of Adhemar, who himself was dressed in white and carrying the Holy Lance aloft as they left the city. With him was an army of Gascons and Provencals. Raymond, being deathly ill, remained in the city to watch the Citadel with a small band lest the Turks descend from it into the city. Then followed Robert of Normandy, Hugh of Vermandois, and the rest of the Normans; then Robert of Flanders, Duke Godfrey and the Burgundians, Germans and Lotharingians; then the people of Bohemund and Tancred. All soldiers had been instructed to remain with the princes of their own people. In this way, the crusading army left the city of Antioch early in the morning to meet the enemy, led by Bohemund personally, followed by clerics, priests, monks and the bishop with the Holy Lance, all carrying crosses and praying, while on the ramparts of the city behind them stood priests and people arrayed in white with crosses and singing. And thus protected by the sign of the cross, the army departed the city over the Fortified Bridge.

✠✠✠

So it was, in the providence of God, that the fate of the pilgrimage should come to this specific point in time and rest upon the shoulders and upon the arm of one man: a murderer, adulterer and a fornicator. Fulcher wanted to evoke images of David and Goliath as he watched Bohemund prepare his armor. Certainly it was not difficult to make a comparison between the Turks and the Philistines. Arslan's defiance of the pilgrims rang true with the ridicule the ancient giant had heaped upon the Israelites in the valley of Elah. And likewise, it did not stretch the bounds of credulity to suggest the comparison between the pilgrims and the Israelites. But associating Bohemund with David was not so facile. Young David, although accomplished with stones and slingshot doing battle against wild beast as a shepherd protecting his father's flock, had never been a soldier. And, while he, too, was a murderer and adulterer, these were sins committed after his encounter with

Goliath. Bohemund had been both a skillful sinner and soldier for many years now.

The sun was above Mt. Silpius as Bohemund adjusted the leather cuirass. He would wear no armor on this day, deeming it too awkward and cumbersome. His arms, sinewy and rolling with strength were bare and bronzed. His head was uncovered because he wanted maximum visibility. A helmet with nasal would be obstructive, and moreover, a blow to the head, even with a helmet, would no doubt send him to the ground where his opponent could finish him.

He was clad in soft shoes and leggings in the ancient fashion. His legs were covered with trousers that extended below the knee and were bound by the leather straps. He wore no belt and now as he stood prepared to meet Arslan, he had a sword in one hand and a dagger in the other. He would not mount a horse, because any horse he might have would be inferior to the horse Arslan could ride, and he could fight better alone than he could on a weak horse. He positioned a lance nearby and a pole, but doubted that he would need them. He stood in front of the lines of Adhemar the bishop, Fulcher, and the priests. Behind them were the rank and file of the rest of Raymond's army, and the Franks, the Germans, and finally, his own men, the Italians.

In front of him, Arslan had arrived and was preparing to meet his foe. The army of the Turks had assembled behind him in lines as well, and with Arslan was a squadron of elite soldiers to ensure that the contest proceeded as it had been announced. Arslan appeared to place his confidence in armor and horses to a greater extent than did Bohemund who viewed this with contempt. Arslan does not trust his own skill, he thought. He wore a conical helmet without a nasal, a sword belt at his waist, and would use a weapon Bohemund had rejected: his horse. The saddle was adjusted, stirrups set at the right length. The horse itself was protected by a blanket and armor on its haunches and head. It was not a war horse; it looked to be a palfrey, extremely sleek, no doubt fast; a horse, Bohemund thought, that had been battle tested. It appeared spirited and restless for action. A soldier held it by the reins as Arslan prepared to mount.

On the ramparts behind the crusaders, thousands of the remaining noncombatants crowded for a view of the battleground. The Turks were not arrayed in divisions lined up behind the other, but in squadrons placed asymmetrically in a half-moon fashion opposite the crusaders. They stayed their positions in what would be the first staged battle of the two-year pilgrimage to Jerusalem. Nicea was a siege and the battle had descended upon them quickly and frighteningly. Dorylaeum was an ambush and strategy was improvised and makeshift. Today, however, the plans had been carefully drawn, decisions made and executed. There was a small chance that little blood would be shed, that the crusaders would win, retain their control of Antioch, and the Turks would retire gracefully and go home to Damascus, Aleppo or Chorsan.

"If we win this battle, we will see Jerusalem soon," Addie said to Clare as they peered into the distance toward the hills beyond the river. Far away, the tents of the Turkish encampment pocked the plains like a city in search of walls. Peter was in the field with the foot soldiers as was Pons. They would return this night in flight or in fortune.

Arslan mounted his horse with a ribbon-tipped lance in its holster and trotted briskly fifty yards away, his back to Bohemund. Then he pivoted on his steed to face his opponent from Italy. In this brief pause hung the balance of many fortunes, papal dreams and schemes, the fancy of nobility, the defense of Saracen strongholds held for many years, the sway of religions, and the hopes of the devout. Soldiers hushed and a silence settled over the valley as the two men surveyed each other, assessing for a final time the possibilities against the probabilities; weighing risk against certainty, strengths against weaknesses. Each man was as convinced of the rectitude of their position as the other. No man believed he was fighting in an unjust cause or for inglorious reasons. For the one, the fight was against an enemy who had appeared uninvited and unprovoked, and whose only justification for doing so was the thinly veiled excuse of the liberation of sacred sites. For the other, the enemy was a cruel unbeliever, a tool of Antichrist, who had persecuted believers of the true God and denied adherents free and unmolested access to holy sites and shrines, and whose unbelief, in any case, justified their slaughter lest unbelief grow and spread.

Arslan gripped the reins in his leathery left hand and fingered them familiarly but anxiously. Bohemund stood as a small man not far away, facing him, sword drawn and ready for the battle.

Arslan waited. His steed pranced impatiently. Arslan looked at Dukak beside him, and the guards flanking him. Dukak watched him impassively. Arslan looked away and back again to the figure before him. He could see the battlements of Antioch in the distance and the rank upon ranks of crusaders who were now arrayed against him. Once again, he had underestimated their size and strength.

Whatever faced these two men as they stared at each other across the turf of the river valley, it was not Death. Neither believed he was going to die on this day, and neither believed the other had the skill or strength to defeat him. Both wore their invincibility like another layer of armor. Arslan tightened the reins. His charger tossed back his head eagerly and reared slightly off the ground and then dropped his head between his legs, whipping it high again and rearing up in the air, his black forelegs flailing the air. Arslan snapped his legs tightly around the flanks of the horse and when the forelegs touched the ground, gave the flanks a jab with his heels and urged the steed forward. The horse sprang into action with the fluidity of a leopard, and bolted toward Bohemund a scant few seconds away.

The valley erupted in shouts and cheers. Bohemund watched Arslan direct his horse toward him. Arslan's spear was ready, but Bohemund could see that it would not be thrown. Arslan would use it to knock him off his feet. Indeed Bohemund stood his ground as the charger raced toward him unsure of whether the horse would bolt to his left or right. At the last second, Bohemund leaped to his left, rolled several times and jumped lightly to his feet while the horse thundered by. Everyone cheered wildly.

Arslan rode away for a second run and came at him again. His spear was positioned for another sweep and again, Bohemund jumped out of the way to rousing applause from the ranks. Arslan retreated again for yet another pass. Bohemund threw his sword to the ground. At this point it was useless. Arslan advanced. His spear leveled Bohemund like a maid sweeping out the cat. Bohemund fell to the ground and Arslan reined his horse and whirled upon the fallen prince. Shifting the spear expertly in his hand to grip it for throwing, he tossed it with heavy force toward Bohemund who had turned on the ground in time to see Arslan's arm cocked for a throw. He rolled out of the path of the spear just as it pierced the earth beside him. Arslan grimaced as he saw his miss, and galloped away for another spear, while Bohemund pulled the Saracen spear out of the ground and tossed it aside.

Arslan readied himself again, and raced in the warming sun toward the crusader. Bohemund, not faint of heart as he stood in the pathway of the horse coming upon him, did not leap out of the way of the horse this time but instead stepped deftly aside, twirled about and with his gloved hands grasped the lance that Arslan had again dipped low and wide and feeling it secure, fell heavily to the earth jerking the lance with him and toppling the rider to the ground as the horse rode away.

The chant of "Deus vult" now picked up renewed strength as the knights saw their fortunes increased by the horse being removed as a weapon in the contest. Bohemund jumped to his feet casting the lance aside and quickly retrieved his sword and dagger. Thus armed, sword in right hand and dagger in left, he crouched in an attack position, knees bent and hands high as Arslan prepared to fight.

The Turk removed his helmet and flung it upon a grassy knoll nearby. He had tied a scarf around his head to tie back his long flowing black hair. His face was clean-shaven, revealing strong jaws and finely-shaped cheekbones. His countenance was fierce with the pride he felt for his ancestors and his heritage.

Sword met sword, steel upon steel, parry and thrust—each man perfectly matched for the other, each leaping to a new defense, each avoiding the thrust of the other until, at intervals, they both wearied and there was a pause in the fighting as though by mutual consent they waited until some rest had been achieved and some respite gained. After a half an hour of fighting, their hair and bodies dripped with perspiration. Bohemund removed his leather cuirass and stripped off his shirt. Both men now were bare-chested, wearing only shoes and short pants. They had thrown away their sword belts; they had reduced their defense to what they could carry in their hands and what was dictated by modesty.

Behind the fight, the men of Arslan's army had dropped off their horses and stood or sat to watch the fight. The foot soldiers on either side prevented their respective soldiers from advancing closer. The two men had a large arena in which to stage this battle on which hung the fate of the city. The crusaders remained mounted, although the foot soldiers in the front ranks had pressed somewhat closer and Adhemar and the priests, clothed in white with red crosses affixed to their vestments had also nudged their steeds forward.

As the two men prepared to resume their fight, Bohemund suddenly tossed his sword to the ground and stared at Arslan. Arslan lifted his sword slowly and then dropped it to the earth as well. They circled cautiously, each taking the measure of the man. Bohemund's hands were open, Arslan's clenched. Arslan swung and Bohemund deftly dodged. Then the Italian lunged at the Saracen and he too missed. They continued to stalk each other, stepping side to side, like starving hunters chasing the last deer of the forest. Then Arslan hit Bohemund on the chin with his right fist, and followed it up with a blow to his body. Bohemund grunted at these blows and responded powerfully with counter-punches of his own. Arslan's head snapped back when Bohemund caught him squarely in the nose with his right. Then more blows to Bohemund's head and soon he could sense that the eye was swelling. Both men's blows to the head were beginning to inflict damage. Blood was streaming from Arslan's nose and one eye was puffing, while Bohemund had been cut under the eye and it was closing.

The men were staggering now, but even so, Arslan had the strength to send Bohemund reeling with an unseen blow. Arslan lunged after him, but Bohemund caught him with his feet and tossed him aside, not unlike he, himself, had been thrown from his horse.

The crowd of warriors, cheering or groaning with each blow, began to sense that the fight was nearing an end and that their fate was soon to be determined. The Turkish soldiers, however, were noticeably less enthusiastic. The crusaders clearly had the moral advantage, or so it seemed to Adhemar. The two fighters could no longer stand erect. They could stand, but not erect. They could see each other, but not well. Their eyes, if not closed from swelling, were covered with blood and perspiration. Their faces, once clean, handsome and unblemished, were now ashen and bloodied, the flesh had been pounded like one might flay a cut of beef. Their hands, arms, and legs were marred with lacerations. They came at each other uncertainly, like old men unable to see their way. They staggered and lunged, swung wildly, occasionally connecting with a feeble blow, but even a feeble blow when landed against one even more feeble, can be highly effective.

Such was the case when Bohemund touched Arslan with a glancing blow that sent the warrior again to the ground. Bohemund stood over him, unwilling to pounce upon him this time out of fear of being unable to rise again. He waited for Arslan to stand up, but Arslan was slower to arise this time. That he would again be on his feet, there was no doubt. How long it would take was highly questionable, but Bohemund preferred to allow his opponent to stand; better to strike him to the ground again.

Suddenly there was a swift whirring sound, a thud and a sharp cry. An arrow had been shot hitting Bishop Adhemar. He immediately cried out and fell from his horse with the arrow stuck firmly in his shoulder, blood flowing and staining his white vestments like wine poured in snow. As he lay writhing on the ground clutching the arrow, a great cry rose in the ranks of the knights and foot soldiers. They moved forward en masse toward the Turkish garrisons that had now leapt to their feet and mounted their horses.

The Provencals led the charge. The foot soldiers moved forward, fitting arrows into their bows as they advanced with such haste that the Turks were unable to get off a single shot of their own. Quickly, however, the Turks broke off to the sides as was their familiar practice to shoot their arrows from many different positions, attempting to attack upon the crusader's flanks. This tactic was quickly recognized and the crusaders responded to it by sending reinforcements upon their flanks to minimize the damage.

The Turks seemed to lose heart for the battle and began to break rank. Dukak, no friend of Arslan, was the first to retire from the fight and flee for more familiar territory but not without first setting fire to the grass of the plains in an attempt to keep the crusaders at bay. Then the others, whose loyalty to Arslan was slight at best, quit the fight, and soon the entire Turkish army, the largest that had been amassed against the pilgrims, was fleeing the valley.

The crusaders would have chased them but for the few horses they had with which to do so, and out of a fear that the Turkish retreat was a tactic to lure them into the mountains where ambushes had been laid. This in fact was the case, for Suliman ibn Artug and Janah ad-Daula had been sent for this very purpose. But they, too, fled. Although an attempt was made to pursue them into the mountains, it was quickly given up. Instead, the crusaders were happy to race through the abandoned camp of the Turks who had left their valuables, gold, silver and jewels, and to re-equip themselves with horses, weapons and food. The soldiers collected what wealth they could for themselves, gleefully reminding themselves that Alexius had deprived them of this opportunity in Nicea, and when they came across the women that the Turks had left behind, the soldiers perpetrated no evil upon them, but were content only to thrust spears through their bellies.

CHAPTER THIRTY-FOUR

The Pope Receives a Letter

September, 1098 A.D.
ROME

UGH OF VERMANDOIS, ANNOUNCED THE page in a loud, modulated voice.

The pope arose, motioning for the man to be ushered in. He met him halfway between his desk and the door. Hugh knelt and kissed the pope's hand, and stood again, waiting. Then they sat down.

"You bring news of the pilgrimage?" asked the pope. It was more a statement than a question.

Hugh nodded. "The Council of Knights entrusted me with a letter to your Holiness." He touched his large, mottled nose slightly with his hand, and brushed his hair behind his ear. Then with a flick of his head he said: "But the news is not all good."

The pope's expression did not change. "I didn't think you traveled this distance to give me good news," he said. "What is it?"

"Bishop Adhemar is dead."

Urban's mouth opened slightly, and his hands, folded in his lap, tightened. His small eyes, fixed on Hugh, looked away toward the pallid morning light streaming through the windows. He felt a stricture in his throat and a tightening in his abdomen. He pressed his hands there to relieve the pain.

"When did it happen?"

"The kalends of August."

"And how?"

"He was hit by an arrow. In the heat of the summer, his wounds would not heal. He then contracted a fever which rendered him even weaker. He couldn't recover."

The pope was silent. "He was a valiant warrior," Hugh said. The pope nodded.

"Where is he buried?" he asked.

"In Antioch, in the crypt beneath the altar in the Church of St. Peter."

✠✠✠

"The loss of Adhemar was a stunning blow to the pilgrims," I said to Bernard. "In his absence, the Council of Knights realized the extent to which he had been the true leader of the crusade. He had been the single unifying force and personality of the enterprise. It was he who was able to check both the temper and the ambitions of Bohemund. It was he who had provided inspiration on more than one occasion when the crusaders had given up hope. It was he who had stressed the necessity of purity. Without Adhemar, the leaders worried privately how to proceed. He had been the one person who claimed the allegiance of all."

✠✠✠

"You have the letter?" the pope inquired. Hugh produced the parchment and handed it to the pontiff. Urban rose and strolled to the window. Then, unrolling the document, he read it.

It seems that some sorrow is ever upon us and now the burden of sorrow has increased since the bishop of Le Puy whom you committed to us as your vicar died on the kalends of August, after the battle in which he had taken an honorable part was over and the city pacified.

Now, therefore, we, your sons, bereft of the father committed to us, bid you, our spiritual father, who started this expedition, who by your sermons, caused us all to leave our lands and all that was on those lands, commanded us to take up the cross and to follow Christ—we bid you complete the task which you urged. Come to us and persuade all whom you can to come with you. For here the blessed Peter was enthroned in the church which we see daily, and it was here that the followers of Christ were first called Christians. What could be more proper than that you who stand forth as the father and head of the Christian religion should come to the first and chief city of the Christian name and complete on your part the war which is your own?

We bid you therefore, again and again, our most beloved father, come as father and head to the place of your fatherhood, and, as the vicar of St. Peter, take your seat in his church and have us as your obedient sons in well doing. Root out and destroy heresy and complete the expedition of Jesus Christ, begun by us, and preached by yourself. And likewise, open to us the gates of both Jerusalems, and make free the Sepulchre of the Lord and exalt the Christian name above every name. For, if you will come to us, and with us finish the expedition begun by you, all the world will be obedient to you. May He Himself cause you to do this, who lives and reigns, one God for ever and ever. Amen.

But the pope did not go to Antioch, and the leaders of the expedition to Jerusalem pondered what to do next.

✠✠✠

October, PARIS

"He's been in France for two months and I still haven't seen him," Adela announced petulantly. She stood at a draperied window of the Grand Palace looking out upon a small courtyard below where maidservants clucked and fussed, and a gardener cut back a cherry tree. Beyond the wing of the palace she could see the Seine twisting away from the city under a pale, gray sky. She was talking to no one and yet everyone.

"And are you disappointed?" asked the bishop.

Adela turned about and glared at the bishop seated heavily in a large, ornate chair. She disliked him and made no attempt to hide the fact. It was as natural an animosity as a cat feels for a mouse, she the cat, he the mouse, the skinny little mouse, the skinny little useless mouse. She said nothing.

"Are you surprised?" Philip asked. The king was standing near a center table on which were trenchers of fruit, nuts and wild fowl.

"I am neither surprised nor disappointed," she replied tartly. "I was merely making an observation the significance of which seems to be lost on the two of you." She approached the table and picked up an apple and hefted it in her hand as she walked away.

"And what is that?" asked the king.

"He obviously knows more about this situation than we had originally thought. The plan is discovered, I'm afraid, and now we must decide upon a course of action."

"The course of action depends entirely upon him, my dear," the king crooned. "We don't know yet what he intends to do. Is he coming to Paris? When is he returning to Blois? Does he have revenge on his mind, or is he merely interested in restitution?"

"We know what he intends to do," Adela murmured. "Already he has reassembled an army. He has seven hundred knights riding with him now. And everywhere he goes, he enlists the help of tradesmen and ploughmen who support him because they see him as a gentle overlord who has been cheated out of his land by ruthless, selfish, greedy and overbearing blackguards. He has recovered already over a hundred of his castles, and you say that we don't know what his intentions are."

"Small little castles, largely unprotected and that offered little resistance," Philip scoffed.

"Philip, darling. I love you, but this is not the way it was planned," Adela said. The bishop, hearing this, sighed.

"We laid a snare and the quarry has eluded it, and if we're not careful, we shall be caught in our own device," cautioned the prelate.

"Stefan has gone too far," said the king. "He thinks by challenging me he shall recover what he has lost but it is too late. He had little chance of surviving in Palestine, but he has no chance of survival in France. It would have been better for him to have stayed where he was."

"My dear friends," said the bishop of Chartres, "while the count was in Palestine on the holy crusade, it mattered little to the church if he was killed in a battle. Indeed, it would have been to the eternal benefit of his soul if he HAD died, for he would have died the death of the martyr. And in that case, as you have so frequently observed, the Church and the widow would inherit his considerable wealth, and as for you, there would remain no ecclesiastical obstacle to your marriage—except for the small little matter of Bertrada."

The bishop climbed out of his chair, stood erect, and strolled about the room continuing his lecture. "Now, however, we have a different situation. It appears that Stefan has abandoned his solemn vow when he took the cross several years ago. In that case, his possessions revert to the Church as provided for under the provisions of the charter. This is an even more acceptable scenario to the Church, for the Church is under no obligation to share his holdings with anyone. Therefore, you can understand that the Church prefers only to discourage Stefan, not kill him; whereas you two prefer precisely the opposite!" The bishop sat down again.

"You do have a grasp of the situation, Ivo," Philip observed.

"Unless, of course, you can deliver the Holy Lance," the bishop added.

"We shall know soon of its whereabouts," said the king. "And when we find it, you shall have it and your new cathedral."

The bishop rose and prepared to leave. "I will remain at Chartres and expect to hear from you about the disposition of these matters. You will inform me of your plans?"

"We shall inform you," the king said, nodding gravely.

The bishop paused. "As for your marriage, the annulment of Adela's marriage to Stefan will hardly secure smooth sailing into the matrimonial harbor for the two of you, since you, Philip, are still excommunicated because of the Bertrada affair."

"The pope is ill. There is a chance a new pope will look more favorably upon my circumstances."

"And why is that?" the bishop inquired.

"Urban is less interested in my morals than he is in my resources for his crusade," the king said, standing and approaching the bishop at the door. "A new pope with less ambitious designs on Christendom, will be inclined to look at my situation somewhat more—shall we say—dispassionately."

"We shall see," replied the bishop as he left. "We shall see."

"He should look after his own soul, not mine," said Philip closing the door behind him.

Adela was upon him in an instant, flinging her arms about him, kissing him frantically. Philip responded wordlessly, clasping her face in his hands holding her mouth on his until Adela, gasping for air, sank with him in delirium upon the brocaded carpet of the locked anteroom where in haste layer after layer of clothes were peeled away like the petals of a flower.

"I can't see you again, Philip, until this is all over," Adela said.

"And it will be over soon," he whispered.

"Not soon enough," she said. "What do we do now?"

"We wait," said Philip. Adela winced. Waiting was not something she did well.

✠✠✠

Count Stefan rode hard toward Blois where his wife had sequestered herself in the castle. He had with him more than a hundred knights assembled at Chartres and points along the way. He and his band approached Blois from the south, driving their steeds across the bridge over the Loire River and loudly clattering up the cobbled streets of the small town, winding uphill to the castle that overlooked the valley and whose walls rose high above the precipitous slopes of the bluff above the river.

Stefan left the bulk of his forces at the river. Sentries spotted the arrival of the smaller force, and when the band arrived at the gates of the castle, the drawbridge lowered in time to receive them at full gallop. They rode loudly into the courtyard and quickly dismounted.

Stefan patted Fortissimus sheathed at his side and glanced up at the keep of the castle where he knew that in all probability his wife was watching him at this very moment. He strode briskly toward the broad arches of the keep beneath which were heavy doors leading to the rooms of their castle home.

His feet pounded hard upon the oak flooring as he stepped into the Grand Hall. He looked quickly about and then retreated to the hallway and turned up the narrow stairwell that wound darkly around the keep and up several flights. Their bedchamber was just below the top of the tower. Bending low, he entered the room.

Adela was at the window as though she had been watching and waiting as he supposed. She turned slowly and faced him. Stefan had wondered if, when he saw her again after an absence of two years, he would love her or hate her. In fact, she was more beautiful than ever and if Stefan hated her for anything it was that. Her face had matured into the ripe beauty that graces a woman's face as it evolves a heartbreak or two beyond youth. Her golden hair was thicker and longer, her skin less pliant and more experienced. But seeing her, Stefan realized he neither loved nor hated her; one cannot love or hate a stranger.

"Why have you come back?" she demanded.

"You're not too happy to see me," Stefan. "Even from an enemy, I might have expected some sort of greeting. But I walk into our bedchamber to greet the wife whom I haven't seen for two years, and the first thing she wants to know is why I'm back."

He made no move to approach her or touch her, separated by the space of the room between them and by the space of the worlds that divided them.

Adela said nothing. Stefan continued, "Or is it that you've forgotten how to behave as a wife, or forgotten how to behave as MY wife?"

"I am glad to see you because I have not seen you for so long," Adela said carefully. "Two years is a long, long time. But I would prefer to see you under different circumstances."

"I'm sure you would," Stefan countered.

"You took a vow," Adela said, her voice rising, moving now toward him. Her palms were facing up, outstretched toward him. "What happened? Why do you disgrace the family, our name and reputation, by abandoning your solemn oath, leaving the battle in Palestine so that everyone thinks you are a coward?"

"My reputation seems to be something you have not been too concerned to protect," Stefan replied hotly. "And no one I've met in France in the past sixty days seems to think I'm a coward for returning, or foolish for being here."

"You took a vow," Adela screamed. "You're a coward, you fled the battle!"

"And what do you know about battles?" Stefan shouted. "What do you know about fighting the Turks? You know nothing, Adela, nothing about battles. All you know about warfare comes from your father who beat up on the Brits. Oh yes, verily, a great conqueror, a conqueror of the English! Let me tell you something, my sweet pet, the English are like children when compared to the Turks. The English don't know their right hand from their left. What do you know about cowardice and courage, about war and peace, about death and life? I was there at Nicea, I was there at Dorylaeum. I watched our soldiers suffer. I saw women and children die from hunger, women and children who kept their vows." Stefan marched toward her menacingly. "And what do you know about vows, whore!" He raised his hand and slapped her across the face with a force that sent her sprawling to the floor. Adela cried out in shock, but jumped defiantly to her feet.

"What do you know about vows, solemn vows, wife?" Stefan repeated.

Adela backed away from him without taking her eyes from him. The Stefan challenging her now bore little resemblance to the Stefan that left Blois with the crusading knights three years ago. Adela felt suddenly weary. She turned from Stefan and walked to the bed and slowly sat down upon it, and looked up at her husband.

"I know nothing about vows," she said. "What is it that you want?"

"What do *you* want?" Stefan asked.

"I don't know what I want," she said. Then she changed her mind. "No, I want you to go back, fulfil your vow in Jerusalem, and then return."

"You want me to go to Jerusalem, but you don't want me to return, Adela." Stefan moved swiftly to his wife and knelt before her, forcing her to look him directly in his eyes.

"You sent your brother to kill me, Adela," he said. "Instead, I killed him. I know everything. The Paulician Fragment, the Holy Lance, Philip, everything. Your breaking of our vow released me from mine. I had no choice but to return. You know that."

Tears swelled in her eyes. She dropped her head into her smallish hands and wept. The plans she had laid had clearly gone too far, although she did not consider the irony of weeping for a brother who was dead and weeping at the same time for a husband who was alive.

Stefan grasped her by the shoulders, but she brushed him angrily away. "You killed my brother," she screamed, beating upon Stefan with her fists. "You killed him."

Stefan stood up angrily and slapped her hard across the face again. She fell violently against the bed, and then crawled away from Stefan in fear now of her life. "You lying, hypocritical wench. You plot my own death, you plot to rob me of my possessions, you give your love to another man, and now you can only accuse me of forsaking a vow and killing your brother!" He climbed on the bed and grabbed her and dragged her to the floor and picked her up so that her face was nose to nose with his. "I ought to kill you right now, throw you out on the streets as an adulterer, a Jezebel and let the dogs lick your wounds and eat your flesh." He threw her back on the bed.

"You are not a good woman, Adela," he said, panting. His face was flushed, and his spirit emotionally charged. He had never treated Adela or any woman this way. But she had brought it upon herself, he would reason later. In any case, he was in no mood to temper either his thoughts or his actions. "What happened?" he asked. "Was it the loneliness? Power? Greed?"

Adela continued now to cry in racking, heaving sobs. Stefan sat on the bed beside her. "What happened to all those things you told me long ago? How you would never leave me, that you could never hurt me, that our souls were bound in kindred unity, that you loved me because I was more *you* than you yourself, that you would always love someone who knew you so well?"

"You were not here, Stefan," she sobbed. "You left me—"

"I didn't want to go."

"You had to go, I knew that, but you weren't here, and I didn't think you'd ever be back. When I said goodbye to you I was convinced I would never see you again. You were gone and Philip was here."

"You never sent word to me, and I wrote you letters. You knew I was well and alive."

"But Stefan, you weren't here. It was wrong, but I started to live my life as though you were dead. I didn't plan for it to turn out this way. It just happened."

Stefan shook his head, tired of hitting her now, he turned to her and tilted her head toward his. "You're still lying. You planned this before I was gone. It's why you were so insistent that I leave. You knew the pope was going to announce a crusade before I did, because of his prior conversations with Philip. You conspired with the church to deprive me of my estates. The bishop gets a new cathedral provided he gets the Holy Lance as a relic for his church, and you inherit my land. You hid the Fragment in the hilt of my sword. I don't know when Robert became a part of this, but he became involved. Your lying, deception, thievery and greed has cost you your husband, and your soul is going to burn in hell."

"What are you going to do?"

"I'm going to drive Philip out of the rest of my castles and land, and after I have dealt with Philip, you can have him if you want him."

Adela shook her head. "I don't. I want you. I've always wanted you."

"Don't lie, Adela. You're stronger than that. And I am stronger than that. You can tell me to my face that you love Philip and not me. In any case, you can't have me. I'm going back."

The countess stopped sniffling and looked at her husband wide-eyed. "You're going back?"

"Yes, back."

"Back to Jerusalem?" she asked. "You're going back to Jerusalem?"

"Back to Jerusalem," he answered with a slight smile. "I never intended to forsake my vow. I made a vow and I am going to keep it. I'll reach Jerusalem in time for the final assault."

"And the Holy Lance?"

"I have it."

"You have it?"

"Yes, I have it and I am going to present it to the bishop soon."

"When?"

"Soon," he said, getting up from the bed.

"Where are you going now?" she asked, sniffling.

"I have business to take care of with the king of France. You will see me once before I go. It may be several weeks. But you will see me again."

"How can you be so sure? The king is a powerful man."

"The king is outnumbered. God is with me," he said smiling, as he turned to bow out of the room. "And incidentally, your brother is alive. I could've killed him, but I didn't. Deus vult!"

Then he left.

CHAPTER THIRTY-FIVE

Count Stefan's Surprise

HE ROMANESQUE CATHE-
DRAL AT CHARTRES was teem-
ing with baker, cobbler, scullery maid,
ploughman, serf, baron, vassal and
knight at the mid-morning Sunday
mass. Rumors had floated deliciously
through the small farming village like the
scent of freshly baked bread, that the
bishop would reveal on this day the Holy
Lance which had been carried back from
Palestine. The village population had
swollen in the previous three days like a
river during the rainy season. Peasants and princes alike had made
the journey from great distances to the village of sheep and wool, a
few muddy streets and an inn. The people, standing, pressed
against each other, filling the length and width of the nave from the
north and south aisles and from the western doors to the altar itself
and into the north and south transepts and around both sides of
the high altar. Families who had not attended mass in months were
present today. Men whose duties kept them from proper religious
observance had found time to drop what they had been doing and
join their wives at mass. The aged, who by reason of their weakness
could not faithfully attend, had found friends to carry them to the
church. The halt and the blind, young and the old, mothers nursing
their babies, knights, lords and vassals, and their mistresses were
there, expectant—expectant in an age when expectancy had
vanished from religious observance. One fulfilled one's religious
obligations with an air of resignation. Life was predictable,

mechanical, full of rhythmic cycles without surprises. Life was the fulfillment of law—natural law, secular law and ecclesiastical law. There were no exceptions, no deviation from the natural, secular and ecclesiastical norms. The sun rose, the sun set; crops were planted, watered and harvested; children were born, they married, gave birth and died.

But this day, the cycle had been broken. Anticipation settled upon their sensate awareness as strongly as did the rose-scented incense of the priests. New wine was being poured this day. God was doing a new thing, and they, the poor and humble, the rich and advantaged, were together, expectant.

The mitered bishop of Chartres paused before ascending the steps of the High Altar. His face was flushed and the veins in his red neck were engorged with blood. He could feel his heart thumping against his white linen alb. He put his hand to the cross on his chest as though to keep it steady. Today, the journey toward the erection of a new cathedral would actually begin. It would be a cathedral surpassing all others in perfection of design and exquisiteness of beauty. It would be constructed in the new style of the finest materials and by the best master builders available. Its stained glass would be produced by the finest craftsmen, and its statuary rendered by the most talented of artisans. Its size and its height would go beyond anything the human mind had dreamed possible. And it would be financed by the most stupendous, awe-inspiring relic in all of Christendom: the Holy Lance! Not a piece of it, not a sliver, not merely its tip or the shaft, but the Holy Lance itself. The bishop had not seen it, but he had been told that Count Stefan would produce it today. Thereafter, it would be protected under perpetual guard in the Treasury, and the public would pay many coins to see it, to receive miracles for body and soul, to offer prayers to the Virgin Mary while they adored it. And with their coins, coin by coin, the cathedral would be built—block by block, arch by arch, window by window. Well after he had been laid to rest in the crypt beneath the cathedral, the crowning achievement of his life would be this cathedral begun in his lifetime.

It would even be built on this very site. The foundations would surround this present edifice, the walls would gradually rise around and above it. The new geometry would permit dazzling new experiments with height and vaulting.

The bishop turned his back to the worshipers and began the service. His voice, sonorous and mellifluous, filled the heavy church with solemn tones of divine weight, pleading the throne of God for forgiveness and mercy, excusing the foibles of human nature. The choir chanted the responses with Gregorian clarity while altar boys waited expectantly to serve at appointed times. But the bishop could not keep his mind on the solemn mass. He would say *Hoc est corpus meum*, but *hoc est ecclesia mea* was clearly what he was thinking.

The massive crowd stirred. At the rear of the nave, the great western doors of the cathedral began to swing open. The disturbance caused the bishop to halt the service. In the blinding light, there appeared an enormous white steed, a war horse magnificent in the perfection of its proportions, a long and full mane as white as the driven snow, and covered with a richly appointed maroon blanket attached beneath its neck and draped over the rump where the beast's floor-length tail swished and flashed regally from side to side. Upon this horse sat a knight in chain-mail armor sans helmet with a bejeweled sword strapped to his side and a beautiful lance held vertically and set in the lance rest. On his left hand was a leather gauntlet on which was perched a falcon, and with which he held the reins. With his right hand, he gripped the lance. His hair was golden like the flaming sun; his skin bronzed like that of a god. Out of his eyes flashed the zeal of righteousness. Ivo's heart fluttered erratically: it was Count Stefan, Count of Blois and Chartres.

The count nudged his horse forward. Its mammoth size dwarfed the worshipers as he pushed into the crowd. Like a living organism, the throng parted to receive him and just as quickly engulfed him as the horse and rider drifted up the center of the nave as though floating toward the altar on waves of human joy.

Stefan could not see, nor could he know, that one pair of eyes, shrouded by a scarf, watched in fascination from behind a north aisle pillar: It was Adela.

At last he reached the altar. Turning, he faced the crowd and with a swift, smooth motion, produced his gleaming sword Fortissimus and held it aloft crying: "Deus vult! Deus vult!" The multitude, hearing this, responded with a long, loud and lusty cheer that evolved into a chanting shout of "Deus vult" just as some had cried in Suger's field three years earlier when the pope had preached his sermon.

Stefan lowered his sword and replaced it in its sheath and then raised the lance and held it aloft with two hands and again cried "Deus vult" and this time with similar results. The heart of the bishop was warmed and cheered by this response for he knew he was a witness not only to the most holy relic in all of Christendom, but to the holy enthusiasm that would build for Christendom and Chartres the most impressive cathedral the world had known, to the eternal glory of God.

Then Stefan sprang to the back of his horse, standing agilely thereupon, one foot upon the rump and the other on the saddle. He motioned for silence.

"People of God," he shouted, "tomorrow I return to the Holy Land to raise the siege of Jerusalem where even now the Franks are gathering to reclaim the city of our Lord for the glory of Christendom and the glory of France!" Again a great cheer swelled among the people. Adela's heart swelled with pride, and tears began to well in her eyes.

"This lance has shed the blood of the infidel and has driven the unbeliever out of the holy places in the Holy Land!"

"God bless you," someone shouted.

"Death to the infidel," shouted another.

"We have found the lance, the Holy Lance by which our Savior suffered and died. It was found in the church of St. Peter in Antioch, the city where the disciples were first called Christians." Stefan paused, looking over the crowd who now awaited his next words eagerly. He turned to the bishop, who nodded and smiled. Adela too, clutched her throat.

Stefan continued: "People of God, you have been betrayed. I have been betrayed. This is not the Holy Lance. The Holy Lance is in the possession of those who will revere it and adore it. Your bishop, my bishop, has betrayed us all. He placed wealth and possessions above his duty to serve us. He conspired with the king to take my lands, he plotted against my life. The bishop wanted the Holy Lance more than he wanted my life. The bishop wanted my lands more than he wanted me alive. The bishop wanted a cathedral of stone more than he wanted a church of living flesh. And he wanted you to pay for his selfish dreams, to pay for the privilege of seeing the Holy Lance, to spend your money and put it in his coffers.

"People of God, he does *not* have my lands, he does *not* have the lance, and he does *not* have my life, because my life belongs to God! Deus vult!" Stefan, standing tall upon the white horse, thrust Fortissimus into the air again, the glint of its Toledo steel flashing in the light streaming through stained glass. "Deus vult!" he cried again, and again. Then, reaching for the reins, he turned the horse toward the western doors still standing astride its back. Then the count on his horse moved forward into the crowd toward the back of the nave, waving triumphantly to the cheering throng.

Indeed, the cathedral was in an uproar. While the people cheered the count, they jeered the bishop, who, hearing ugly comments and cries, began to fear for his safety, himself shocked by this unexpected turn of events. He turned and disappeared into the narrow stairwell near the rear of the altar and descended quickly into the subterranean crypt from whence he fervently prayed he could escape to safety.

✠✠✠

Late that same afternoon, before the sun had set, but after the chill of the autumn day had returned, Stefan and Adela took a walk along the river below their castle. On the bluff across the way and downriver stood the cathedral, the scene of the tumultuous events earlier in the day. It seemed dark now. Adela shivered. Everything was cold. It was a cold day, a day of unspeakable, inexplicable sadness. A suffocating horror had settled upon her soul as though the Devil himself were sitting upon her chest, producing a impermeable melancholy with which, she thought, she might forever be afflicted. She needed someone to lie to her, to tell her that she had not behaved so unreasonably, that her life was merely a response to the times. She was not a good person, Stefan had told her. She had thought much about that since. He was right, and the ugly realization had thrown her into a malaise from which she neither cared to be released nor could be released. Men had always been her special province; there wasn't a man on earth whom she couldn't bend to her will, and the events of the past three years had proven her correct. That men found her attractive and fascinating, that they found themselves drawn to her like moths to light, imposed on her a deathless sense of personal significance which never left her. Her every gesture and comportment of her person was unconsciously, if not consciously, tailored to this unalterable perception of herself. She was a "man's woman," her father's daughter, and the great glory of womanhood was the ability to push a man beyond reason, to afflict a man with foolishness, to revenge the Adamic accusation, "The woman hath caused me to eat." And so she had exercised the powers of Eve by defiantly acknowledging her unreasonableness but demanding she have her way nonetheless. No man had refused her nor had she refused a man who could better her station in life. God had given her gifts to fare well in the world and she was never loath to use them: a keen mind, a hard heart, and a soft cleft between her legs.

"There's not much to say, is there?" she said. They sat down under an oak on a bed of dry leaves on the river bank. They did not sit close to each other.

"No," he said, tossing a twig into the slow moving stream, "there's not much to say."

She waited for a few moments before continuing. "You said I was not a good person. No one has put it quite that simply to me before. I mean, I am used to not being liked by people, of having bad things said, but when you said that, it was the first time I really heard it, really understood myself differently. I am not a good person, and I apologize for that."

She didn't know what he'd say. What was there to say? "My father taught me that anything worth achieving in life is worth it at any price. He never committed himself to a battle unless he was convinced the objective was of military or economic value. But once that decision was made, he spared no expense. He made a total commitment to the goal regardless of the size or relative importance of the goal." She looked up to see if he was listening. "It's a good philosophy of life," she said, "but he didn't teach me how to decide what's important, how to determine what one should go after. For him it was always the next town, or the next city, the next hill or bridge, or crossing the channel, or London. He didn't teach me about fighting for love, fighting for life, about making sacrifices for anyone other than oneself."

She moved closer to him, crawling toward him on her hands and knees until she sat near him staring at his profile as he gazed into the gray depths of the stream water. "Philip was like him. At first, I thought you were, too. You're right, I always wanted you to be someone you weren't. And when you left, I thought I'd never see you again, and Philip was so much like the man I thought I would love, and it was only later that I realized that both Philip and the bishop had more in mind than I realized and by then, I, the strong one, was too weak to protest, and … and … I'm sorry, I don't know why I'm telling you all of this. It doesn't matter anymore. I'm saying it for myself. I need to say it; it needs to be said."

She fell silent waiting for him to say something. She could see slight movements of his lips, an expression in his eyes that indicated he had something to say. Then he spoke. He looked at her briefly, wistfully: "You know, Adela, I've never backed away from a fight, but I didn't have anything against the Turks. I didn't care whether they were infidels or not. I thought and think today that the crusade was begun for many reasons other than the noble ones mentioned by the pope. But I thought it was my duty to acquiesce to the plan. But when I discovered what was happening back here, none of that mattered anymore. I just wanted to get home. Vow or no vow, home was where my true obligations lay. I suppose that will always be the way I look at it." He stopped to allow Adela a chance to say something. But she remained silent.

"But now I have no home ... not here, anyway. A home is where love is. And there's no love here. The affairs of my estate are here, and I shall always have to be in France to take care of worldly matters. But such things do not give one a home. Love gives a man his home." He shrugged his shoulders.

"There's no love left," he said.

"I wish we had had children," she said.

"Maybe you will," he said.

"Not with Philip," she replied. "I haven't been with Philip since you came back two months ago, and I won't ever again."

"Come," he said, standing, "you are my wife. Tonight I will sleep with you and tomorrow I depart again."

That night they slept together for the first time in years rediscovering if not their love for each other, at least the lust that the two of them could create as naturally as fire creates heat.

The next morning, Stefan's band of knights met him early and Adela could see from her castle window the crimson Crusader Cross fluttering on their flags as they marched astride their palfreys through the gates of the fortress and away from her. Faraway, on the road just before he passed out of her sight, she saw him turn and wave. Quickly thereafter, he was gone.

Then, as do all women who lose something it had been in their power to keep, she wept.

ANNO DOMINI
1099

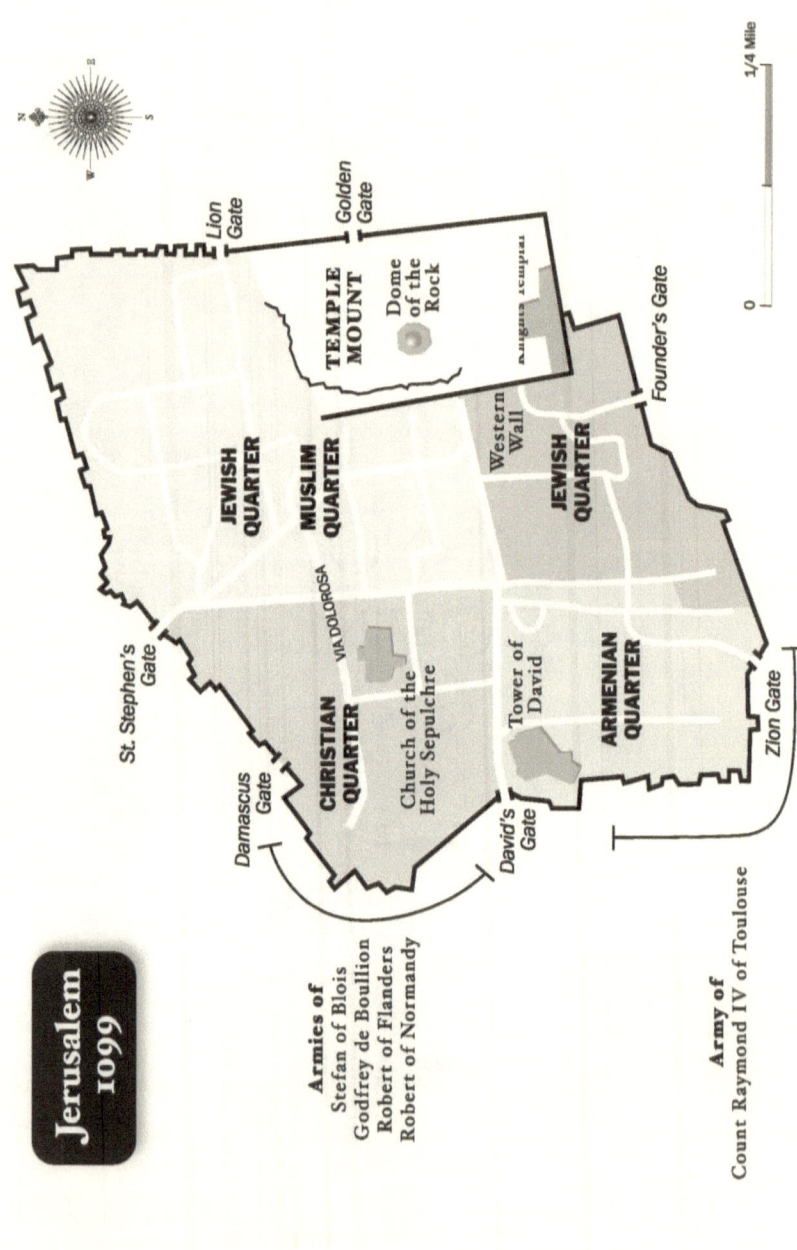

Jerusalem 1099

St. Stephen's Gate

Lion Gate

Golden Gate

TEMPLE MOUNT

Dome of the Rock

Ancient Temple

JEWISH QUARTER

MUSLIM QUARTER

Western Wall

JEWISH QUARTER

Founder's Gate

VIA DOLOROSA

CHRISTIAN QUARTER

Church of the Holy Sepulchre

Damascus Gate

Tower of David

David's Gate

ARMENIAN QUARTER

Zion Gate

Armies of
Stefan of Blois
Godfrey de Boullion
Robert of Flanders
Robert of Normandy

Army of
Count Raymond IV of Toulouse

N
E
S
W

0   1/4 Mile

CHAPTER THIRTY-SIX

Jerusalem

Constantinople

HE EMPEROR WAS ANGRY. HE had repeatedly under-estimated the resourcefulness of the pilgrims against the intransigence of the Moslem infidel—a misjudgment based either on misinformation or his own lack of faith. The report of Stefan several months earlier had been true, but the crusaders had proved their mettle beyond even the emperor's expectations. Now, he had been betrayed by Bohemund, the very man to whom he had promised the hand of his daughter in marriage, and this self-same man was occupying Antioch with no intention of surrendering it to the legitimate control of imperial forces. Alexius looked at Count Stefan standing attentively nearby. He liked Stefan's straightforward approach to affairs, his analytical mind, his honesty and basic integrity. His eyes never wavered when you talked to him; he looked directly at you with the courage of a man without guile.

"I will send Tacitus back to the crusaders and inform them of my decisions. We will send reinforcements to Jerusalem by ship. They must be within days of the city now. A siege will take months. My ships will arrive most auspiciously with siege engines, ropes, tools, weapons, animals and food. I will send Tacitus with this news. The ships are even now sailing out of our harbors." He gazed toward the azure waters of the distant glassy sea, the southern region of the Bosporus. While repairs on St. Sophia continued, his palace, situated atop one of the southern hills of Constantinople, stood guard over the straits of the sea watching ships ply the winds to and fro.

The imperial court did not like what they heard. Stefan knew that the choice of Tacitus was a poor one. At one time, it may have been the best choice, but now the situation was radically different. Tacitus was loyal, but he was also aloof and curt in his manner with the crusaders. Although strong and capable, his inability to bridge the natural suspicion that existed between the Greeks and the Franks had led to mistrust and misunderstanding, and had had the further disastrous effect of allowing Bohemund to exploit the weakness.

"There may be someone more appropriate than Tacitus," said Anna. Alexius looked at his daughter curiously. "Better than Tacitus?" he echoed. The emperor's daughter chose her words with her father carefully. When with him as a father, she was carefree and unafraid of both her words or her actions. When with him as the emperor, she was not afraid, but she was not carefree; she understood the limits and extent of her influence.

"Tacitus does not enjoy the trust of the crusaders. They blame him for the Nicea affair and the long difficulties at Antioch. Sending Tacitus would indicate to them that imperial policy is unchanged and that, from their point of view, they can expect more of the same, which to them is more treachery." Anna spoke clearly and quickly, with authority.

"Tacitus is an envoy," Alexius said. "He will do and say as he is directed." Stefan looked away. He knew that Alexius' greatest weakness was an inability to appreciate the nuances.

"But he will not be believed," Anna rejoined, with no hint of argument. She moved to his side and put a reassuring hand on her father's shoulder. She could see that her father was tired. He wore greatness heavily, she thought, as she looked in his eyes, eyes that now seemed deeper set beneath eyebrows that had thickened like a hedge—hidden eyes retreating as her father was retreating. Alexius had become less interested in the affairs of state and more interested in the affairs of life as he had grown older. But when matters of state intruded into the life he loved, her father still was capable of flashing the old zeal, the familiar contempt of incompetence, and could bark out imperial commands with the same strength with which he had led his armies in former times.

✠✠✠

The hour was late and I sensed that Bernard of Clairvaux was tiring. His companions had slipped away leaving only the two of us in the monastery's high-ceiling library. The goblet of wine was drained and its effect was beginning to induce sleep. Or so I surmised.

I set aside the Gesta Francorum *and said, "Perhaps we should finish tomorrow?"*

To my surprise, the abbot leaned forward alertly and insisted we continue. "The pilgrims appear to be advancing to Jerusalem in spite of the emperor rather than because of him," he observed.

A novice entered the library and presented us with a cloisonné tray of fruits and cheeses. "When this has disappeared, we will break off and resume tomorrow," Bernard said laughing. I looked at the mound of food heaped upon the platter. "That might not be until tomorrow," I said.

"Go on," he urged, tugging at the manuscript.

I hesitated. "Let me interject here a few words about Anna." The abbot nodded and I continued. "Anna loved Stefan. Nothing was clearer to her than this truth. It was a truth as unalterable as the rising of the sun over the Bosporus. Now she was on the verge of realizing the fulfilment of a plan that would place her with Stefan perhaps for the rest of her life. She had lived with these plans since Stefan had left her for France. Only a hope, only a thought, a mere seed planted in the fertile imagination of one deprived of the most important thing in her life. No plan grows so well as one plan nurtured by spiritual desperation. After years of loving Stefan, Anna felt reckless. She had nothing to lose and everything to gain. Her father needed a legate in the Levant to represent the interests of the empire, to not only communicate those interests but to ensure that those interests were protected and that imperial policy was carried out.

"Tacitus was out of the question. The crusaders would slay him on sight. Any other general that Alexius might send would either meet with a similar fate or be ignored altogther. There was only one person who could restore to the empire its ravaged interests, only one person the crusaders would not destroy, only one person to whom they might listen and who might be able to convince them of the emperor's sincerity. Anna had this calculated like a finely-reasoned Pythagorean theorem; there was no doubt. It was a truth that shone as brightly and clearly upon her soul as the light flowing through the leaded glass of St. Sophia. Someone who would journey to the Levant, who would talk to the princes of the crusade, who would convince them of the nobility of her father's intentions, who would save the east for the empire!"

✠✠✠

"Then, who? Ekkehard, Baldric?" Alexius asked.

"No, none of them," said Anna with finality. She faced her father and looked directly into his eyes, her hands upon his shoulders. "Father, they will believe ... me. Send me, father."

She could not only do it, there was no one else who could! She stood now before her father as an Esther before Ahasuerus; she would save her people, she would save the empire, she would save—herself, Oh! Could this be the hour?

Stefan was amused. Alexius did not appear to be surprised. But he did not give her the answer she had hope to hear.

'No," he said, and turned away from her.

"Of course, this is the answer," Anna cried.

"It is not the answer," Alexius replied. "I can't send you to Jerusalem only to have you captured by the Turks and held ransom for half the empire. It just won't do, daughter!"

Anna ran to her father and faced him again. "Yes, father, it will do," she said. "Listen to me. I'll travel only through territory already held by our forces. With the exceptions of a few stretches, this will enable me to reach Antioch safely. From there, it is but a short distance to Jerusalem."

She continued. "Moreover, you shall send me to Jerusalem under the protection of—" she turned to the count—"the Count of Blois, Stefan!" She turned back to her father. "You see? It is the perfect plan. It cannot fail!"

In the end, the emperor relented. He was powerless in the face of such irrepressible logic. He needed someone whose credibility was beyond question, someone whose authority was equally undisputed. Given the abysmal state of the relations between the crusaders and Constantinople, there was no doubt that, if Alexius was to send anyone at all, only one person fit the criteria and that one person, he reluctantly conceded, was Anna Comnena, his daughter.

Stefan could scarcely believe the words he was hearing. Was this the shy young woman he had first seen three years ago? Was this the beauty with whom he had fallen in love? Would they now be together again and forever? Did she love him more than her life and he love her more than his kingdom?

Of these and other matters of grave consequence they discussed that night into the dim hours of the morning, until he, who had no right to ask the question, asked it nonetheless: "Will you be my wife?" And she, who had no right to answer, replied joyously and without hesitation: "Oh, Stefan, yes, I will, yes!" That night they slept together and for the first time she felt as though she were his bride while he pondered the penance for his sins.

✠✠✠

They were a ragged, motley bunch that struggled toward Jerusalem. Even though their numbers had been severely reduced in the three years they had been traveling from France, over twenty thousand of them still remained. To Addie, the numbers were incomprehensible. As she gazed down the winding road from Ramla, the stream of pilgrims stretched as far as she could see, over this hill and past the next to the distant ridge: Normans, Brits, Englishmen, Germans, Lothingarians, the Flemish, Italians and Provencals like herself. Behind her and before her trudged a sanctified procession of *crucesignati* who, amid perils of land and sea, through battles large and small, in spite of fears, hunger and death, who had come so tantalizingly close to the most holy of cities. Here she was with Pons, Clare and Hildy and others of Raymond's army. She smiled wanly, her face hollowed by grief. Army! A few hundred knights perhaps. She touched her hair.

It felt stringy and dirty. She looked at Pons. He still walked tall and without a limp like most. The sun had bronzed his skin; it looked like leather. He looked strong and in his face she saw hope. In her face, she was sure, was only despair.

Despair—for Peter was gone. A dispute had arisen about his visions. He'd been challenged by a certain Arnold of Chocques. Peter was brash and indignant. "If it is a test you want, a test you shall have. I demand the Ordeal by Fire!"

The request was shocking and surprising. The Ordeal had not been invoked since the pilgrimage left Europe. It was generally reserved for situations in which the guilt of the defendant was stronger than this present case, cases in which the guilt was so far assumed that *only by the miracle of surviving the ordeal* could a person's innocence be established. Peter, while hotheaded and a visionary, was not so clearly guilty as to be put to such a test. But it was his request, and not Arnold's suggestion.

Addie had been distraught. "How could you have said such a thing? You are so stubborn! Let them believe you are a fool, that your dreams are only dreams and not visions from the Lord. What difference would it have made? Have I lost a sister, only now to lose my brother also?" She had wept and had turned away from Peter and would not be comforted by him.

The next day, Arnold of Chocques ordered a band of yeoman to stack two piles of cypress and cedar faggots in a narrow and hollowed-out passage. The wood was dry and tinder had been scattered at the base. A bishop of Provence, in the dark purple vestments, solemnly consecrated the logs. They were set in the ground in such a way that the person undergoing the Ordeal would be compelled to run through the entire passage and could by no means escape should he have a change of heart.

Peter made it to the end of the blazing gauntlet but, at the last, he lacked the strength to step out of the flames themselves. His tunic was ablaze as was his hair. He stood in the fire, unable to get out and indeed would have fallen back upon the pyre had not Pons alertly reached for him, preventing him from collapsing in the flames. Pulling him out of the fire, they laid him to the ground and threw cool blankets over him, smothering the fire. The visionary was unconscious, and it was obvious to all who could see him that he was mortally wounded.

Still, the word quickly spread that the lad had survived the Ordeal, which indeed he had. Hildy took him to her tent where she and Addie bathed his scarred and blackened body and nursed his wounds. His skin soon began to peel and boil off in layers, rendering his body a mere slab of raw flesh. This went on for eleven days during which Hildy and Addie never left his side. He regained consciousness only for brief moments at a time but never spoke. On the twelfth day after the Ordeal, he died.

The band of pilgrims pushed onward, a collection of rags hung on frail frames of flesh lurching down the rocky road to Jerusalem. It was a silent company, silent because they were suffering. One might complain when one is the solitary sufferer among many, but when one is among thousands who are companions in suffering, one keeps quiet and bears the pain and presses onward. Except now. They stopped to rest. The mother examined the feet of the daughter. The soles of her feet had been leathered by the much walking, but cuts old and new and brackish bruises covered the tops of her feet and lower legs. Addie examined her face. She winced at the sight of Clare's swollen lips and parched mouth. In the absence of water, Addie could taste it and smell its scent, recalling its coolness when it coursed down their throats. She was thirsty; her tongue lay thickly silent in her mouth. She would take a drink, the next time they were rationed a little, and let it swirl about in her month for a few moments and then swallow it drop by drop until there was no more. She would enjoy it better next time. She glanced up at the sun. It lay languidly in a pale blue sky to her left. It was not yet noon, but the heat was becoming uncomfortable, already beginning to drain her energy. Her feet could not dance, and her mouth could not sing. She had no song.

Presently, Fulcher the priest happened by. He, too, was barefoot, but wearing priestly black even in the June heat. Over his shoulder he had slung a sack which he said contained his parchment and quills, a book and a psalter. He fell into step with the four of them.

"I have something for you," he said, smiling. He pulled three little hard rolls out of his bag. "Chew on these for a while," he said, "It will give you strength." Clare reached for one eagerly and took a bite. It seemed like days since she had had anything to eat and even then the porridge had not assuaged the hunger.

"Thank you," Addie said gratefully. Pons and Hildy likewise received a roll with relief. A long time ago, Pons had ceased to be concerned overmuch about the source of his sustenance. He knew that on a venture such as this it was impossible not to accept the friendship and beneficence of those inclined to help you and you could only receive it humbly, throwing away your pride and self-reliance, regaining your dignity, in some measure, by helping others when you had a chance. But there was one thing he could not do, he thought as he tore off a chunk of the bread. No matter how starved he was, he would not eat human flesh as others had done. He shuddered in disgust at the thought. At Archas, the army had been so hungry that when the Saracens were defeated, some of the soldiers had carved up chunks of flesh from the buttocks of the vanquished Turks and after roasting them over a fire, had eaten them. I should rather die, thought Pons.

"We found a lot of grain at Ramla which the Saracens left when they fled before we arrived," said the priest. "So don't thank me, thank God."

They munched on the rolls greedily. "When will we get to Jerusalem?" Addie asked, breaking the silence, and realizing at the same time that her question echoed Clare's continual complaint.

Fulcher laughed. "The hardest part of a three year journey is the last three days," he said agreeably, handing her his water skin. "Those days seem to stretch on forever, don't they?"

"For more than forever," Addie said ruefully, gulping thankfully, forgetting her earlier vow to sip and savor.

Fulcher continued: "We'll probably arrive at the walls by evening tomorrow. So you see, it is not far off at all!"

"It probably won't be any different from the towns we've already passed," said Clare.

Fulcher passed his thin hand gently over her golden hair and down the back of her head to the nape of her neck. "Oh, but Jerusalem is not just another city," he said.

"What's different about it?" Clare asked.

"Some people call Jerusalem the navel of the world, because it's the center of the world," Fulcher replied, smiling. "Do you have a navel?" he asked.

"Yes," said Clare.

"And others say Jerusalem is our Mother because the apostles, martyrs and holy preachers who lived and died before us gave birth to us in the faith of Christ. And it is different from other cities because it is a holy city: it was at Jerusalem that Jesus died and was buried and rose again."

Hildy stood up and walked away as Fulcher watched. Then the priest squatted down before Clare and took her hands in his and looked into her breathless blue eyes. "Clare, do you understand that you are going to walk on the very streets on which Jesus walked?" He touched her feet. "Your eyes will see exactly what he saw." He touched her eyes. As he spoke, Addie could sense a mounting emotion in her heart. For an instant, she remembered her enthusiasm when Peter the Monk had preached on the bridge back home in Provence. She remembered now his power and the strength of his word. She remembered the passion she had felt then when he urged her to make the pilgrimage to the Holy City before it was destroyed by the Antichrist, to be a part of the people's army to liberate it from the infidel and thereby save her soul. Jerusalem was not just like another city. It was a city in which she would walk even though she having paid an awful price to do so. All for this city. Not for Nicea, not for Antioch, but for this city. This city alone among the cities of the world. This city!

"And it is not just a city on earth," he said. "Jerusalem is a city in heaven which we can see only through the eyes of faith." He reached into his sack and withdrew a small book. "Haymo of Halberstadt," he said. "Listen to what he says:

"Hierosolymitana est visio pacis." The priest glanced quickly at the three and then translated: "Jerusalem is a vision of peace. It refers to the Holy Church of God which we see only with our understanding, which consists of angels and human beings who already reign with Christ, and those saints who are still on their journey to God on earth. It is said to be above us, because while our bodies are on earth, our understanding is in heaven. *Nostra autem conversatio in caelis est.* 'For our life is in heaven,' writes the apostle." He closed the book. "I am boring you," he said as he replaced Haymo in his satchel.

"No, Father, please, we want to hear more," said Pons, standing up, signaling others to prepare to resume the walk.

"Perhaps we will have time tonight," Fulcher replied. "We could eat, perhaps I could find some wine, and we could talk more of this heavenly as well as earthly city." He paused. "I could bring some grain with me, and you might bake up some more rolls and little cakes?"

"That would be glorious," Addie cried. "Please find us tonight!"

"That I will, I will," said Fulcher, waving before he disappeared ahead of them among the travelers on the road to the Holy City.

✠✠✠

Count Raymond of Toulouse believed the worst was behind them. They had been fortunate to discover so much grain at Ramla. Moreover, they were traveling at a time when this road linking Jerusalem to Galilee wasn't congested with merchants. They would also be able to feed on the harvests along the way, although, in this hilly region, crops were not as plentiful as they had been in the coastal meadows and valleys.

Raymond was anxious to fulfil his vows at the Church of the Holy Sepulcher. He was not a young knight like the others and the Egyptians were a worry. Perhaps Godfrey had been right. He had argued in the Council of Knights at Ramla that the Egyptians were the real threat; they should be confronted first before laying siege to Jerusalem. They were marching a substantial army from the south to Palestine. Since they lacked siege engines anyway, they ought to engage the Egyptians and then turn their attention to Jerusalem, hoping that siege material would arrive by sea in the meantime.

Raymond conceded now that there was wisdom in Godfrey's words. He thought fleetingly of what Stefan of Blois might have said. Stefan was a genius in strategy, an idiot in courage. Confronting the Egyptians, he would have argued, is not expedient. Sometimes the wisest course of action is the least feasible. The army was impatient to reach the emotional and military objective of the crusade: Jerusalem. They believed that, if the Egyptians wanted to fight, they were welcome to advance on Jerusalem to join the battle. By the time the southern army had arrived in Palestine, Jerusalem would be safely in the possession of the crusaders and not even the Egyptians would be able to wrest control of the city from their hands.

Raymond sat tall upon his courser, still strong for an older knight. He glanced up the ranks of the forward contingent he was with. They had been able to acquire more horses and animals in the past few days, and now the procession was full of camels and other beasts of burden, sheep and goats. Even dogs were used as pack animals since the wagons were heavy with grain, olive oil and wine. Other trains were bearing timber from the northern forests, mining equipment, rope, nails, canvas, blankets and tools. Still other carts were crammed with weapons: lance tips, spears, bows, arrows and arrow tips.

As he inspected the long rows of wagons and carts ahead of him, he spotted a cloud of dust in the distance. Riders. Perhaps five or six. No doubt lieutenants from the front with fresh information. The horses and their mounts soon appeared, and fell into step with Raymond. Three knights and two men.

"Envoys from Bethlehem, my lord," said one of the knights. Raymond glanced at them sharply. They were not soldiers; they appeared instead to be simple town folk, men of about thirty years, attired in trousers and outer shirt. Raymond guided his steed out of the procession and halted, facing the new arrivals.

"What do you want?" he asked. His horse snorted and stepped about.

"We are indeed from Bethlehem," replied one. "The city of our Savior's birth, location of the Church of the Nativity built by Helena, mother of Constantine. Our population is entirely Christian but administered by Moslems."

The other broke in. "They do not keep a garrison at Bethlehem. Most of the forces have been moved to Jerusalem. We beg you to come to Bethlehem and remove the few remaining Moslems and liberate the city."

The news both encouraged and disturbed Raymond. The possibility of an easy capture of a city so sacred to Christians could boost the sagging morale of the troops and be a genuine accomplishment no matter how easy the conquest. But the news also indicated that the Saracens understood their military objective to be Jerusalem and had already begun to refortify the city and make preparations for their arrival. Perhaps they were raising the walls at this very moment! The siege of the holy city promised to be everything they had thought: a battle for the future of Christendom.

Raymond acted quickly. "Take these men to Tancred, and tell him that he is authorized to take Baldwin of Le Bourg and a hundred knights, and move immediately to Bethlehem and claim it for the Church."

"Yes, my lord!" They pulled on the reins and reversed their direction and rode hard away. Raymond smiled. Tancred, he knew, would jump at the chance for great glory with little risk.

✠✠✠

Fulcher had a sack of grain delivered to Addie, and ere the night had fallen, she had pounded the grain, separated the chaff, and with the help of a little olive oil made some cakes which she shared with her neighbors. She took a deep breath now as she leaned over the fire of dead olive branches, the only fruit tree that grew and survived in this part of Palestine. She filled her lungs with the pungent scent of the oil heating upon the pan on her fire.

Darkness like velvet slipped over the encampment and Fulcher appeared at their fire. As they were eating and the fire blazing, Addie said: "Tell us about Jerusalem."

Fulcher's first words were muffled by the grain cakes in his mouth. "The city of Jerusalem is situated in a mountainous region in the midst of a barren and rocky plateau, being one of the most stony and least fruitful districts of the region, lacking in streams and springs except for the pool of Siloam which is a bowshot from the city.

"There are many cisterns in the city which store the winter rains so that even in summer there is an abundance of water for both the inhabitants of the city and strangers who pass through its walls.

"It is not a big city; Antioch is much larger. The height of the walls is about thirty-five feet, but this varies because the city is set on hills and the walls in some places are very steep. To the east of the city less than a half mile away is the Mount of Olives."

Fulcher paused. "Pons, le vin, s'il vous plait." He refreshed his palate and continued. "To the west, at a place where two corners of the walls come together is the Tower of David, constructed of the finest limestone masonry and sealed with molten lead. If it were filled with adequate supplies, fifteen or twenty soldiers could defend it from every side.

"There is no temple in this city for the Moslems have built a mosque on the site where Solomon built his temple and where Herod replaced it. The Church of the Holy Sepulcher, the most holy church in all of Christendom, is in this city, round in form and is never covered and can always be seen from above. The streets are of fine pavement from the time of Hadrian, and there are gutters by which rain water and dirt are washed away."

They plied Fulcher with questions even though Fulcher's knowledge was second hand. He had never been to the city himself. But he knew more about it than the peasants of Provence.

"What's a cistern?" Clare asked.

"It's a large cave where water collects during the rainy season so people can drink it later," he replied.

"Where did cisterns come from?" Clare asked her mother. Addie glanced at the others and shrugged, revealing plainly that she didn't know the answer to the question. Hildy broke in: "Most of the cisterns were carved out of soft limestone. Sometimes tunnels were cut out of the rock so that the water could flow from an upper cistern to a lower one and from there to pools throughout the city. There was once a king, a long, long time ago—" Hildy lowered her voice as though to share a dark, mysterious secret— "who built a tunnel from a spring outside the city to a pool within the city. Do you know why?"

The flames danced in the eyes of Clare as she stared wide-eyed at the woman. Hildy pulled her cloak about her tighter. She shook her head. "So that when the city was attacked by an enemy, they would always have a supply of water no matter how long the siege. It was a secret tunnel then, but we know about it today. King Hezekiah's tunnel, it is called. But there are many other tunnels under the city spreading out like a honeycomb. Secret tunnels and false passageways where kings and emperors saved their families, hid their treasures, or stabled their horses."

Fulcher stretched his bony fingers over the flames of the fire. They licked at the palms of his hands. "The Virgin's Fount," he said. "I have heard villagers and town folk talk about it. No one knows precisely where it is. People around here call it Ain Sitti Miriam or Spring of the Lady Mary. I learned about it as the Virgin's Fount. Women used to bring their water skins into the cavity under the steps of the Fount and fill them completely and many miracles happened there. A Paulician monk in Antioch told me last year that the entrance to the underground Virgin's Fount could be found at the steps of the Seven-Sevens of the Apocalypse which—leading downward beneath the city—directs you to a small platform covered by a Roman arch, and the twelve Steps of the Apostles which ends at a small opening above another cistern called the Great Sea. This mammoth cistern lies directly beneath the Temple Mount and contains over a million gallons of water!"

Addie relaxed. She hadn't realized how tense she had become as Fulcher was telling his story. "How do you expect a child to be able to sleep when you tell such exciting tales?" she asked Fulcher.

"I beg your pardon," Fulcher apologized. "I will calm her spirits with a song."

"Perhaps you should tell another story," Pons jested.

"I feel the point of your rapier wit, Pons, and accept your challenge," Fulcher replied, his eyes sparkling gaily. "Give me some music!" Pons retrieved a wind pipe from within his tunic and began to play. After a few notes, Fulcher began to sing in clear, bell-like tones:

Jerusalem, my happy home, name ever dear to me!
When shall my labors have an end, in joy, and peace, and thee?
When shall these eyes thy heaven-built walls and pearly gates behold,
Thy bulwarks with salvation strong, and streets of shining gold?
There happier bowers than Eden's bloom, nor sin nor sorrow know:
Blest seats, through rude and stormy scenes, I onward press to you.

"There! What do you think," said Fulcher as Pons put away his pipe.

"Oh, that was beautiful," Addie whispered. "And look!" She pointed to the sky where the moon full and round began to shrink.

"Lunar eclipse!" Fulcher said.

"Isn't that a bad sign?" Pons asked.

"No, no," Fulcher assured them. "A solar eclipse is an evil omen, but a lunar eclipse is a good sign."

"Your singing has produced wonders in the sky and on the earth," Addie said. "See?" She nodded toward her daughter snuggled in her arms. The child had fallen soundly asleep dreaming of hot rolls and strawberry preserves, roast chicken and apple sauce. Jerusalem was not a city with streets of gold or pearly gates, but a city of roast duckling, trenchers of fruits and salads and plenty to drink. Wouldn't it be grand to sit down like a queen with her mother and father, her sister and her uncle, and Hildy, and eat—all of them—until they could eat no more, forever and ever? Yes, it would be grand beyond words!

CHAPTER THIRTY-SEVEN

Stefan's Revenge

Antioch

ITTING ON HIS THRONE IN THE palace, Bohemund was full of good cheer. The year so far had been a prosperous one for the inhabitants of Antioch. The spring rains were torrential; the crops were planted, and grain would be plentiful. Pastures were green, sheep were lambing, and the flocks would increase. Cattle would have feed, and the orchards would be laden with summer fruit. Trade on the Roman roads between Antioch and Aleppo and Edessa had never been better. Venetian, Genoese and English ships were plying the coastal waters. Under his suzerainty, the city had recovered from the wars of previous years and was enjoying peace.

Still, Bohemund had the uncomfortable sense that, although the town folk were enjoying their newly found affluence, they were not particularly fond of the leader who had brought it to them. Petty ingrates! The Christian and Syrian population still regarded the Italian prince as an outsider. Bohemund scarcely had the respect, let alone the love of the people, and respect did not guarantee friendship; it only meant that in a war, your opponent will not underestimate your strength. Respect—Bohemund never had trouble fighting for respect. Indeed, the only battles he lost were in love, not war. In the latter he had invariably gained respect; in the former, only contempt. Bohemund himself agreed that he'd never really loved anyone. Anna was the one person who came closest to receiving what Bohemund called love, but she was such a brassy bitch, spoiled at her father's court, never learning how to be a woman. "She'd be giving me orders right now," he thought.

The Italian prince brooded in this manner whenever he saw the tangible success of his policies. Such fortune always pointed, like the hands of a sundial, to the true nature of his life: abject failure, not as a person, but at least as a man. And if, therefore, he could not command the love of a good woman, he would command the respect of every man, woman and child, Syrian, Christian or Turk. It mattered not. Human or beast, they would fear the ground he walked on and they would leap to obey his most capricious request. It mattered not that he loved not; there wasn't a woman in Antioch, matron or maiden, who wouldn't satisfy his needs whenever and however he demanded. This, Bohemund thought, is good fortune. Better to feck a whore without regret, than a wife with remorse.

There was a knock at the door. A page entered.

"Well, what is it?" Bohemund said.

"There are visitors," the lad replied.

"What kind of visitors?"

"They wouldn't say, my lord. Wished to keep it a secret, they said."

Bohemund's eyes registered surprise at this news, but then his brow furrowed and he said: "Send them away."

"They anticipated your response, my lord. I am to tell you that Princess Anna of the imperial court of Constantinople brings you greetings."

There was no mistaking the surprise, perhaps a trace of alarm, that crossed the Apulian face of the count now, like clouds over the Alps. Anna! He should have been prepared for something like this, having only thought of her name moments earlier after months with scarcely a recollection. Why is she here? Alexius is no doubt determined to advance his claim over the city! Tribute perhaps. Does she bring a garrison with her? Surely not, or his scouts would have informed him.

"Where is she?" he snapped.

"In the Great Hall, my lord," the page replied.

Anna! The name stirred the old desire he had felt before. The mountain never climbed, the river never forded, the desert never crossed, the ocean never sailed. Now she was in his palace. She had come to him! They always do, he thought, but not without unease. Why? Surely she was not alone?

"You said 'they.' Who's with her?" he asked. Then suddenly he realized. Stefan of Blois!

"Count Stefan of Blois, my lord," came the expected answer.

Bohemund stood up swiftly and reached for his cloak.

"That's all, page," he said as he prepared to leave. "I shall be down shortly."

He ran out of the throne room, down the corridor of alabaster and marble, to the circular stairwell leading to the lower level of the palace. His heart raced from the sheer excitement of it all: the Woman was within his walls, the one woman whom he had ever wanted and the one woman who had so plainly rejected him. Even as he flew down the flights of stairs, hands pushing off the stone walls right and left, keeping his balance, he knew that whatever the outcome of this visit, she would not leave this time without being his.

When he saw her, he realized that she was already someone else's. He paused at the door. A servant held it ajar and he peered into the Great Hall. She was here! And more beautiful than ever! Still in her riding clothes, outer tunic, boots. She's wearing trousers like a man! Yet on her they seemed in place, for she exuded royalty of bearing and the poise and confidence of one who knows her superior station in life. Clothes, even rags, could not demean this woman; she would look like Helen of Troy whatever she wore. He caught sight of her pearly white teeth when she laughed and the black, full tresses of her hair when she turned to Stefan. Stefan touched her. And instantly and to his surprise, Bohemund realized that he hated this woman. This was not an admission that he didn't want her, just that he didn't love her. Indeed, not loving her, made him want her all the more, for his desire, now liberated from the restraint of love, could bolt unrestrained. It was no longer a contest of the spirit but of the flesh, and he had never lost contests of the flesh. He strode into the room with authority and welcomed his visitors with civility without cordiality.

"What a surprise," he said. "I do not generally enjoy surprises but this is the exception! You are both faring well, I see?" It was a statement more than a question, but Stefan answered it nonetheless.

"We are well, thank you, after a long trip."

Bohemund was not interested in their trip, its length or their health. "A long trip? And what, might I inquire, is your destination?"

"We are en route to Jerusalem where even now the crusaders are laying siege to hasten its liberation," replied Anna. "I assured Stefan, who was not anxious to stop here but preferred to proceed toward the Holy City itself, that our old friendship, while disagreeable, was a thing of the past, and that a person of your station in life would not hold a grudge even as my father held none toward you when you lately joined the crusade at Constantinople."

He respected her intelligence, but did not love it; he loved her body, but did not respect it. Aha! The world breaks down into what one fears or loves, he thought. You cannot love what you fear and will not fear what you love.

"And for that I am grateful, and you are entirely correct," said Bohemund, bowing slightly. "Please, sit down." He pointed to a set of lounges nearby, and they sat down, servants and pages hovering close by with wine and fruit.

"You enjoyed your stay in France?" he asked, turning to Stefan.

"No, I did not enjoy my stay in France, but I accomplished there what I set out to do." He paused. "It was not pleasant, but I succeeded."

Bohemund wanted to inquire about his wife, but thought the better of it. Not even he was without discretion; at times it was his greatest skill.

"And you?" he inquired of Anna. "What is your present occupation?"

Anna noted the condescension in his voice but did not respond to it. "I am making the journey to the Holy City as the imperial legate traveling under the protection of Stefan of Blois. I have certain news to impart to the forces fighting there that will bring them encouragement in their time of need."

"Your father's offers of help, for all his many virtues, always seem to arrive too late to be of benefit," Bohemund rejoined tartly. "I suspect in this case that the crusaders, having advanced thus far without imperial aid, will not think they need it now."

"Perhaps you are right," Anna replied. "In that case, it is their decision. I have not come to *enforce* my father's will, only to *advise* the crusaders as to what it is. They may bear the consequences themselves whatever their decision." Her words were final. Bohemund could see that she would broach no further discussion of the subject. But Bohemund was curious.

"So you have not brought an imperial army with you then?" he asked, laughing nervously.

Anna answered quickly. "We are here with a hundred knights. The way has been quite safe you know, and these are some of the finest."

"But the emperor is well aware of our plans along the way, including our stop here, which he heartily endorsed," Stefan interjected.

Bohemund caught his breath. Anna had erred by giving away her strength. And Stefan had immediately lied to cover up the obvious indiscretion. Bohemund also knew that Stefan was aware that he understood the significance of Anna's revelation. Stefan was *en garde*.

After an awkward moment of silence during which Anna came belatedly to the same realization as the other two, Bohemund spoke up again: "You must meet me for dinner tonight. We will feast royally. It will be splendid," he said, smiling broadly.

"I must decline your offer," she said. "I will not speak for Stefan here, but if you wish to feed me, you may order something brought to my chamber this evening, and I would be grateful. Otherwise, I shall spend my time here resting, and tomorrow be off for an early start southward."

With this announcement, the meeting broke up. Bohemund gave instructions to his servants, and they were escorted to parts unknown in the palace, leaving Bohemund standing in the Great Hall pondering the extraordinary turn of events.

✠✠✠

It does not take long for a plan to formulate in the mind of an evil person. Goodness takes time, but evil spawns like mosquitos in a marsh. She should not have objected to our marriage, Bohemund reasoned. Had she been an obedient child, she would now be my wife. I am only claiming what by imperial authority should have been mine anyway, and what by the laws of the Church can in no wise belong to Stefan. And the beauty of this, he chuckled as he walked up the stairwell toward Anna's chamber, is that Anna will never breathe a word of this to anyone. She cannot tell Stefan, for he will act rashly and imperil her honor, and she cannot tell her father that her virtue has been compromised by the man he had intended her to marry. He reached her door. Anna had stationed four imperial guards on either side of the door. When Bohemund arrived with food from the kitchen, recognizing him, they allowed him to pass.

He knocked on the door.

"Who is it?" came a voice within.

Bohemund motioned to one of the guards playfully. "Tell her it is her dinner," he whispered.

"Your dinner from Lord Bohemund," shouted one of the guards past the heavy, oak door.

"One moment, please."

Bohemund turned to the guards while he waited, smiling broadly. "She will be surprised, eh?" They laughed in agreement.

"Come in," came the order. Bohemund winked at the guards and then pushed down on the iron latch and pressed against the door, and entered the bedchamber while holding aloft a charger of steaming food.

She was sitting on her bed with her back to the door while a chambermaid sat beside her brushing her hair. "Put it on the table there, please, and thank you," she said while the girl continued to stroke with her brush. Bohemund, never taking his eyes off of her, went stealthily to the table and set the charger upon it, and stood motionless until, at last, Anna, sensing something amiss, froze momentarily. She turned to see with a shock that her visitor was none other than Bohemund himself.

"What are you doing here?" she demanded, standing up as she spoke. Her eyes flashed with imperial ire, a look that Bohemund had forgotten until now.

"Voila!" he said, as he raised the lid of the silver charger from its base to reveal roast ducking, fruit, pomegranate sauce, and fresh bread, butters and jams.

"Thank you," she said. "Now if you will please leave!"

Bohemund made no effort to move. He was noticing instead that Anna had been preparing to retire. She was dressed in a short, linen under-tunic that revealed all the dreams and fantasies he had ever had about this woman. He could feel that feeling again.

"If you don't leave now, I will call the guards who will throw you out with no regard to the privileged station you may enjoy here in Antioch!" She spoke firmly as though the sound of authority might jolt the Italian prince into the action she desired. But he said nothing. Instead, he began to arrange the food on the table so that two could eat of it.

"I want to eat alone," Anna declared. "Please leave the food and leave this room." But Bohemund persisted, acting with the confidence of a man with the key to the storehouse treasury.

"I'm calling the guards," Anna said, striding toward the door with a backward glance at Bohemund. She paused at the door half expecting him to stop her, but he did not. With a lunge, she pulled at the door and stepped swiftly into the door frame and into the arms of a guard, but not one of her guards!

"Who are you?" she demanded. "Where are my men?"

"Your men have been, shall we say, relieved of their duty! Isn't that right?" The soldiers laughed while Anna, shocked to the core, turned back into the room, slamming the door behind her.

She was annoyed. "We shall eat, and then you shall go," she announced. "Anything else and I shall report you to the highest authority in the empire and they shall spare neither men nor money until the worms are eating your body and the city is leveled to the ground."

She did not see it coming. Bohemund drew back his hand and smote her across her face with a blow so powerful that her head snapped and she was sent reeling across the room, on the floor to the wall. The chambermaid screamed. "Stay there on the bed!" he snarled at her before rushing to Anna.

Anna touched her face and knew in a vague sense that he had struck her, but she was so dazed that she didn't think of the awful implications of the fact. She saw Bohemund grinning at her as she slid out of his arms. She heard in the distance the cry of her chambermaid, a long, shrill wail. The girl brought her hands slowly to her mouth; Anna saw Bohemund turn to the girl and say something, but then, suddenly and mercifully, it became cold and light fled from the room. Was she dying? Is this death? Where is Stefan? Where?

✠✠✠

Stefan was ill at ease. He did not like being away from Anna. Not ever, and certainly not now. They were vulnerable in Antioch as the guests of a person like Bohemund who had reneged on his oath to the emperor, who had reneged on his oath to God, and would have no hesitation in withdrawing any promises made to them. Anna should not have told him about their security arrangements, but she had and there was nothing to do about it now. Bohemund's character seemed no more noble than before; to the contrary, considerably less so. The hardships of pilgrimage and battle had failed to mold character in him; instead it had chipped away at it like hail on limestone. He would not be at ease until they had left these walls and had the city of Jerusalem in sight.

As he was thus thinking, there came a knock at the low door of his chamber. He looked quickly to Everard who merely shrugged. One of the other guards answered it, and a tall, Norman knight of Bohemund's army, bowing low, stepped into the room.

"Good evening, my lord," he said.

"And good evening to you, man," Stefan replied. The fellow had a sincere face, dressed in leather halberk, gloves, and riding trousers, and boots. Stefan was curious. He did not have to wait long.

"I'll not take up your time, my lord. Bohemund has asked me to give you a tour of our city, including an evening ride of the walls and an inspection of the Citadel. Since you were here during the siege last year, he thought you might appreciate such a view, especially since you are leaving tomorrow."

Stefan thought this a cordial invitation. "But where is your lord?" he inquired. "I would prefer the journey to be with him."

The soldier hesitated and in that precise instant of vacillation, Stefan caught a whiff of danger. "My lord has taken a fever, and cannot accompany us, but does not want to appear inhospitable. Please do come."

Stefan appraised the situation immediately. He was to go on a ride including the Citadel on Mt. Silpius. That would remove him from the palace for a number of hours. Remove him from the palace and from Anna. Bohemund would not be with him on Mt. Silpius. He would be with Anna in the palace, fever or no fever. To refuse this offer, if treachery is afoot, will enjoin a dangerous response, but to agree to it, would be even more dangerous.

"I think Bohemund's idea is splendid," he said, smiling. The knight smiled and seemed relieved. "But I must make some preparations. Who are we meeting and where?"

The knight answered: "My name is Reginald, and we are meeting Hugh and Michael at the Church of St. Peter. From there we will travel south to the Gate of St. George and from there along the southern walls to the Citadel itself."

Stefan beamed as he approached the tall one. "Fine, fine. I will need just a few minutes to make preparations. You go join Michael, and I'll be there in fifteen minutes."

The soldier hesitated, but he could not find a flaw in the plan. "Alright, then, fifteen minutes at St. Peter's." He turned to go, but in a flash, Stefan was upon him with a dagger at his throat, its razor edge on the tight, pale skin.

"Not a word, or I'll stick you like a pig," said Stefan. "Tie him up and gag him," he said to Everhard. "Get his clothes off first." The men began to work rapidly on Reginald. "I thought we could've met them at St. Peter's and overpowered them there, but I didn't want to take a chance of creating a disturbance." Reginald's boots and trousers were off. Stefan went on: "I don't think this Michael knows what I look like. You, Henri, wear my clothes and take my place. Agree to go with him, and make up an excuse about Reginald here. Take a squad with you so that in case they give you trouble at the church, you will be safe. Otherwise, proceed with the plan. I believe they will take you to the Citadel and show you around, and bring you back when they think enough time has elapsed." Reginald was trussed and immobile, clad only in cords and his under-tunic.

Stefan addressed the prisoner. "And now, Reginald, about how much time were you going to keep me away from the palace. And why?"

Reginald was not yet gagged, but said nothing.

Stefan whipped out his dagger and put it to his throat again, pulling back the prisoners head by the hair. "Reginald," the count said in his most soothing voice, "I don't have a lot of time. I also am a man of my word. If you do not answer my questions I will—

on my word—slice off your ear, and then your other ear, and then I will slit your throat. By my same word, I am not a violent man and have no desire to see you die. You mean nothing to me unless you refuse to cooperate with me. Then you mean something to me: you're my enemy. Now tell me: where is Anna, and where is your lord?"

Reginald paled considerably during this entreaty. He was now willing to talk.

"I don't know," he cried. "I don't know. I swear by the Virgin Mary, I don't know."

"Sit him up and gag him," Stefan ordered. Henri gagged him, and then Stefan jumped behind him, knelt, grabbed the Norman's hair and yanked his head backward. With a swift, blurred motion he brought the dagger past the side of Reginald's head. The soldier uttered a muffled scream as the top half of his right ear fell to the floor. Blood trickled down his neck and stained his white under-tunic.

"I am a man of my word, Reginald," Stefan said. "It is your choice. You know what I said I would do next. What is more important: to protect an evil master who does not treat you well, or to enjoy the love of a good woman again? Now, tell me: where is Bohemund and what is on his mind." Reginald nodded, terrified. Henri removed the gag.

"We're listening," said Stefan.

Reginald began. "He is with Anna. In her room, I believe. There are four guards at the door—"

"What happened to her guards?" Stefan asked.

"Either removed or killed," Reginald replied.

"Go on," said Stefan.

"I believe he intends to have his way with her, but he will not kill her," Reginald added.

"For Bohemund to have his way with her is worse than death," Stefan said, anger rising in his throat like bile. "And he is there now?"

"I believe he is there now." Stefan looked away from the men. How could he have been so stupid? Why did he not better understand human nature, particularly when it came to a man like Bohemund? This is the man who carved up Turks and roasted them over open fires. A man to whom power was more important than principle! God! He needed to do something! He had to stop regretting and take action.

"The bedchamber, Reginald, what story?"

Reginald clearly did not want to cooperate, but his loyalty to his own person proved greater than that to his lord. "Fourth story, my lord, the top story. We are on the second and the Great Hall, as you know is above us."

"And there is no other way to gain access to the fourth story except by the staircase?"

"And it is easily blocked, my lord," the prisoner added.

This, Stefan knew, was true. The defender always had a distinct advantage when protecting upper stories because the only route from floor to floor was via a narrow, spiral staircase. Not only was the stairway easily blocked but it was often designed so that a right-handed man standing above, could easily use his sword while his body was shielded by the central newel of the stair. The attacker, below, while not immobilized, could only flail with awkward strokes without the protection of the wall.

"We must find out for ourselves," Stefan said. "Stand him up and strip him naked." When Reginald was standing, Stefan said to him: "I believe you've told me the truth. But if you haven't, you know what will happen. So before I leave, is there anything else you want to tell me?"

"No, my lord," he said, crying.

"I need four men, plus another to stay with Reginald here." He turned to Henri who had not yet left for the Church of St. Peter's. "Go to the storeroom and fetch me two or three more men. Everard and I will stay here until you return. Quickly now!"

Stefan pondered his situation. Anna was in peril only two flights above him. Directly above him. Bohemund was with her. *What did he want? Surely his intentions were both licentious and evil; but he wouldn't kill her, would he? He was brash, but not stupid. Would he abuse her and then simply let her go, and send us on our way? Bastard! I will not be sent away by Bohemund!*

Henri reappeared with the soldiers. Stefan and Everard and two others left the room quietly, while Henri stayed with the prisoner. Stefan started up the constricted passageway first, stepping stealthily upon each weathered, stone step. Then, when they were all in the stair well, he danced lightly two steps at a time, nimble of foot, until they were a step below the Great Hall. The sound of voices could be heard within; probably cooks and servants in the kitchen. Stefan leapt past the closed doorway and bounded up another few steps. Guards would be posted ahead of them. They were getting closer now.

As the small band neared the fourth story and the low doorway to the upper chamber, Stefan paused to listen for sounds. But he heard none. Silence was of prime importance. He would not want his sword to bang against the stone walls alerting the guards to his presence. Stefan looked behind him. Everard was beneath him by a step, and Roger behind him, but Richard was not visible, hidden by the curvature of the staircase.

Stefan moved into position, that precise point at which the doorway would come into view. Hugging the cold inner wall, he edged his head around the boss of the limestone block. No guards were visible yet. He shifted his weight and placed his soft-soled boot on the next step and inched his body higher and further around the curvature of the wall. Still nothing.

Becoming bolder, he moved more quickly until the doorway was in plain sight and realized that the doorway was unguarded. There were no soldiers at the door! With a quick motion of his head, he signaled Everard to follow him. They positioned themselves on either side of the oak, metal plated door. Stefan withdrew Fortissimus from his scabbard. He nodded to Everard who had also drawn his sword. Everard placed his gloved hand upon the door latch. It gave! The door was not barred. He pushed it open just a crack but enough for its creaky hinges to announce their presence to the wide world, Stefan thought. With a great thrust, Everard batted the door opened and the men rushed into the chamber.

An empty chamber! Anna was nowhere to be found. Stefan strode quickly throughout the room, quickly inspected the garderobe, but she was not there. "Where is she?" he asked in exasperation.

"If she was here, she's not here now," said Roger, stating the obvious.

"She was here," Stefan said, picking up a hair brush from the floor and noting the tunic and clothes upon the bed. "These are her things."

"Then she has been moved," said Everard as he inspected the room. "The question is where."

"And why," added Richard.

"If he only wanted to force himself upon her, why would he move her?" Everard asked. His observation of the room had taken him to the far wall, where he was examining some marks on the floor and wall.

"I don't know," Stefan muttered.

"Blood," said Everard.

"What?" Stefan rushed to Everard who was pointing to a spot on the wall.

"Notice here, my lord," he said. "Blood." Stefan touched the dark stain and withdrew his finger. There was indeed fresh blood on it. "Look," said Everard. He took Stefan's hand and held it while he withdrew a few hairs which clung to the count's finger.

"Anna's?" he asked. Stefan knew it was possible. "My lord, there was a struggle here. Look at the bed, the clothes on the floor and the brush which was on the floor." Stefan had noticed this, too.

"It's possible," Everard continued, "that Bohemund has not yet forced himself upon her, that in fact, she resisted and in the struggle she struck her head here. Such a blow may have rendered her unconscious and Bohemund, taking advantage of the swoon has removed her to another location."

Everard's explanation made sense. "But why not keep her here?"

Everard looked at his lord in silence as though pondering whether to speak his mind or not. Stefan repeated the question, returning Everard's gaze directly. "Why not keep her here?"

"I think there are two possibilities," Everard answered as he resumed his examination of the room. "First, Bohemund likely does not want to force himself upon her unless she is conscious of it. He wants her to know she is vulnerable, that he is having his way with her when she had so long refused him. Second, we must not dismiss the further possibility that he sees an opportunity to revenge his treatment by Alexius by holding Anna hostage for ransom."

Ransom! Of course! While Stefan was unwilling to accept the truth, he recognized when he heard it. "Where have they taken her?" he lamented.

"If I was Bohemund, king of Antioch, and had a very important person I was holding for ransom, there is only one place I would even consider keeping my prisoner, the most impregnable fortress in the Levant," Everard said, letting Stefan come to his own truth.

"The Citadel!"

"The Citadel," Everard said, concurring. "There can be no question that Bohemund has taken Anna Comnena to the Citadel."

In the moments that followed, the group devised a plan of action, a plan that would at least carry them through the next few hours before a specific design could emerge for liberating Anna from the Citadel. Stefan's knights actually outnumbered Bohemund's by a few score since most of the army had proceeded to Jerusalem. The army that remained consisted of local inhabitants enlisted to defend the city, their own city. The important fact was that Syrian Christians were loyal to the city and not necessarily to Bohemund. He was an Italian of a different church, a different rite and certainly a different culture. In short, Bohemund represented an occupying force, and the townspeople had no particular loyalty or affection for him.

"This," Stefan explained, "is critical. We will seize the palace and summon the leaders of the town, including the military leaders. We will offer them incentives to help us oust Bohemund. He has Anna in the Citadel, but we will make him a captive in his own tower. The city is ours, while the Citadel is his."

☩☩☩

"Ahmad, what can you tell us about the Citadel?" Stefan asked when they had retired to Bohemund's palace hall. Ahmad, of strong face and dark complexion, was only too eager to offer his knowledge of the Citadel, having been the commander of the fortress himself.

"The battlements have a large fighting platform and the battlements facing away from the city had well-constructed hoardings. The roof is protected by a high encircling wall. And the base of the tower sits on a deep-battered plinth."

Stefan and his men listened carefully. "The entrance doorway is protected by a stout, oak portcullis and a door secured by two timber beams. The portcullis is operated from a small chamber over the doorway. From the entrance there is a passage which leads to the central chamber of that floor, primarily a store room or guard house. Opening to the right of the passage there is a spiral stairway which ascends to the battlements seven stories up. To the left is a circular mural chamber with a domed roof. And around the central chamber there are three wide recesses and two doors, each of which lead to smaller domed chambers similar to the one to the left of the passage."

"Is this the pattern on each of the floors?" Stefan asked.

"The second story has neither recesses nor mural chambers, but on the third, fourth, and fifth stories there are two large recesses, a mural chamber near the stairway and one or two latrines. On the sixth floor, there is a passageway that follows the curve of the tower that leads abruptly to the crown of a deep circular dungeon—"

"The oubliette," Everard interjected.

"Yes, the oubliette, which is built into the massive walls and is about twenty-five feet deep. There is no exterior entrance to the Citadel, but the interior entrance is protected by a large machicolation which rises some twenty feet above the doorway through which boiling pitch, stones, darts and other projectiles can be thrown upon anyone attempting to burn the doorway, or gain access."

"The storehouse is full of grain, oil and food?" Everard asked.

"Fully stocked," Ahmad replied, "and there is a well, of course."

"On what story is she likely to be?" Everard continued.

"Probably the seventh. The top floor. Bohemund has the best view of the terrain, and can move her quickly to the battlements if he needs to. The room itself is large, with a domed roof. Yes, she's probably on the seventh floor," Ahmad concluded.

"So, gentleman, the Citadel is invulnerable, and we haven't weeks and months to lay siege," Stefan announced. "If we cannot open the gate of the Citadel ourselves, we must get Bohemund to open it for us himself!"

"And how can we do such a thing?" Ahmad asked.

"Surely, Bohemund does not expect the townspeople to be aware of what is happening," Stefan explained. "He would not find it unusual for routine deliveries to continue on their normal schedule, would he? The carter, or baker or cellarer, or blacksmith or carpenter? Certainly one of these tradesmen are expected yet today—and it is better today, because tomorrow, he will be more suspicious."

✠✠✠

Anna eyed her tormenter warily. In spite of the faults she had always seen in him, she had at least thought him handsome at one time. Now she was embarrassed that she had ever believed so. He wore his external appearance like the mask of a Greek actor, and underneath the golden body, and finely chiseled face, existed the monstrous form of a vile-looking brute. She shuddered in revulsion as she turned away from him. She touched her face and felt the damp texture of her skin where her tears had flown as he had taken her. He has not taken me, and I have given him nothing, she thought. Maybe someday I'll live in a world where the weak are strong and the strong are weak, a world in which women need not be afraid because they are women. Or at least a world where the strong and weak are equal in their strength and weakness.

"Can I go now?" she asked. She had no idea where she was. She only knew it wasn't the room she had been in when she first saw Bohemund. She remembered him hitting her, and the next thing she recalled was awaking in this beautiful domed room, the top floor, she reckoned. Stefan! Where is Stefan?

"You are going nowhere," her captor announced. "You will fetch a handsome price from the emperor—"

"Ransom? Surely you jest?" Anna said. "If the emperor ever gets word of this, you may say your prayers at once, for your days will be surely numbered!"

"The emperor will not have time to send an army, but he will have time to send money. If he doesn't, it is you who will be saying prayers."

"You are not as bright as I thought!" Anna laughed. "You have a strong body, but a weak mind. Even if my father sends the money, an army is sure to follow. There's no place on the face of the earth that will be safe from his wrath. You must pray he never hears of this, and if you release me now he shall not hear of it from either myself or Stefan, that I promise you."

Bohemund ignored her insults. "I am not through with you yet. You are begging for favors; but I take what I want and what you think of me hardly matters anymore, now does it?"

"It is a cruel twist of nature that God should give such a feeble-minded simpleton the brute strength to take what he wants. So we have a world that exists at the mercy of those least capable of governing it while those with the wisdom to govern languish without the power to do so. You will go to hell for many sins, not the least of which is that you traveled in this life where you did not belong; in the next life, you shall not enjoy that privilege again." Drawing the sheet up about her, she turned away from him. "You may go to hell, and the sooner the better."

✠✠✠

Stefan was gambling that they had acted more quickly than Bohemund would think possible. If their plan worked, once inside the Citadel they would have more men and better men than Bohemund. They had to get inside; this was crucial. A thousand men outside could not do the good of ten men inside.

Stefan wrapped the cowl of a cellarer's garb tighter about him. No one but Bohemund would recognize him. Ahmad was along to help. Him they knew. The count glanced behind him. His wagon was bearing oak barrels of wine, and the wagon behind him was laden with vegetables, a weekly supply to refortify the small contingent of servants and guards who maintained the Citadel. He looked back to the Citadel itself. They were so close to the massive tower that only the first thirty feet of it could be seen without looking up, and Stefan did not want to do that now. No doubt, they were being watched at this moment by the guard in the chamber above the portcullis and by guards in the machicolation above the entrance. For now, he stared intently at the doors of the tower and the lattice-like portcullis which protected it.

As he was watching, the doors swung open heavily and the portcullis was raised a few feet from the ground. An armed guard slipped beneath the portcullis and approached Stefan and the wagons. He had drawn his sword. The guard, medium height, rough, unshaven face, and a bulbous nose that bespoke too many tankards of ale, poked about the wagon with his sword, parrying holes into defenseless piles of vegetables.

The guard swaggered back to the portcullis and, with a wave of his hand, ordered it raised. Slowly the iron portcullis inched upward until it was high enough to permit movement freely beneath it. Stefan maneuvered the wagon close to the entrance while the vegetable wagon behind him moved forward as well.

"Help these men with the wine," said Ahmad. "Where is Bohemund?"

"What do you need with Bohemund?" asked the guard in a surly manner, unhappy to be ordered about by someone of Arabic descent.

"I want to know what he wants me to do with a hundred imperial knights. Where are they to be housed? How are they to be fed? What am I supposed to do with these guests? He runs off without saying anything. Now help these men!" And he disappeared inside.

Stefan had lowered the sides of the cart and had erected runners on which to roll the casks of wine to the ground from whence they could be rolled through the entrance into the tower. The other wagon was being emptied of its vegetables. Stefan struggled to be patient. A good plan is worth the time of its execution; impatience had destroyed many a well-conceived device, he knew.

Suddenly, Ahmad reappeared demanding to know if there was a key to the mural chambers where the wine would be placed. The guard produced a key and Ahmad and Stefan put their shoulders to the final cask of wine and rolled it beneath the portcullis and through the doorway, down the passage into the central room where about a half dozen guards were seated playing dice.

"Into the storeroom, guards," Ahmad ordered, "and make a clear place for these casks." The men grumbled about the interruption, but ambled off to the storeroom and began to move the casks to make room for the additions. When they were inside, Ahmad closed the storeroom door and twisted the key in the lock.

"Whoa!" cried the guards, "Open the door!" They pounded on the door. At this, Stefan, ran to the entrance and shouted "Deus vult." Immediately from beneath the wagon without and the casks within a dozen of Stefan's men appeared as though by magic. The astounded guard immediately cried to the guard in the portcullis chamber to let it down, but the guard lay in his little room with his throat slit, the handiwork of Ahmad. Stefan's men came in freely, dragging the resisting guard with them. They would have killed him, but Stefan restrained them.

"Tie him up, gag him, and put him in the mural chamber room." This they did.

Stefan then noticed a commotion coming from the stairway. Guards from the third and fourth floors had evidently heard the clamoring below and were coming to investigate.

"To the stairs," cried Stefan. His men rushed to the stairs to keep the soldiers from entering the central room of the first story. Stefan quickly ordered the portcullis to be lowered to prevent reinforcements from arriving, and ordered his banner to be flown from the machicolation above the entrance. His own forces would arrive within the hour.

Ahmad and Stefan led the first group up the stairway fighting Bohemund's guard. They were not interested in advancing up; they wanted only to hold their ground. But, in the course of the fighting, the guards clearly had no stomach for advancing their position and quickly retreated.

Stefan ordered his men to split into two groups. "They'll try to flank us after we've passed one story," he said. "You'll come after them at their rear."

In a stairwell fight, one's forces are only as good as the lead man. If he falls, the fight goes to the man behind him. In this case, Ahmad led the first group up the stairs followed by Roger and Richard, while Everard and Stefan led the second group. Stefan did not want to fight until he could fight Bohemund himself.

As Stefan had predicted, the first group was attacked from the rear by soldiers lying in wait on the floor below them. But Everard and Stefan, hanging back for just such an eventuality, put them to the sword, and soon the stairwell was strewn with the bodies of slain guards.

The men secured the third and fourth floors, and then inspected the fifth and sixth, placing servants and maids in mural chamber rooms on lower floors. They then began a stealthy ascent to the seventh floor and the battlements.

✠✠✠

Anna rued her temperament. She had relied entirely too much upon her own wisdom. This realization came to her when it became clear that her captor intended to compromise her virtue. *I am such a fool! Aha! If I am so smart, why am I in this room with this beast? Why did I compromise the success of this mission? Because I did not have the grace to consider the wisdom of somebody else, especially someone else I loved and cherished. Am I so vain that I couldn't listen to advice? If, if if, if I had listened to Stefan we would be on a road somewhere between here and Jerusalem. What are the chances of us getting there now? I am the stupid one!* She pulled the sheet up about her nervously as Bohemund began to disrobe.

There was a knock at the door. Bohemund was instantly alert.

"Who is it now?" he shouted. "Go away!"

"Lord Bohemund, it is I, Ahmad-ibn-Marwan."

"What do you want?" Bohemund began to button up.

"The Greeks," Ahmad shouted. His voice sounded distant, muffled by the oak door. "There are a hundred knights, horses, servants. Where do you want them? You tell me nothing. First, you are in the palace and then you are gone and I have to guess what has happened to you. This is no way to govern a city, we have no knowledge of what—"

He was interrupted by the door opening quickly. Bohemund stood in the opening, glaring at his visitor.

"Why are you bothering me with this, Ahmad?' he said impatiently. He turned away from the door and Ahmad stepped in.

"Ah, I see you have been busy," Ahmad observed, spying Anna in the bed.

"Never mind," said Bohemund, facing Ahmad again. "I have to get back to the palace, take care of the Greeks, especially take care of—STEFAN?" His sentence was interrupted as Stefan himself stepped through the doorway and into the room. Fortissimus was in his right hand, its six-foot blade gleaming in the lamplight. He stood quietly, legs apart as though straddling already the corpse of his adversary. His eyes were like furnaces of fire, his face like the stone of Gibraltar. He advanced slowly toward Bohemund who backed away equally as slowly. As Stefan moved, Everard, Roger, and Richard moved in behind him.

"Stefan!" Anna screamed. The count came to her side while his men kept an eye on Bohemund. "Stefan, you are here, you're here," she sobbed as he placed his arms around her.

"I'm here, and I shall never leave you again, as God is my witness." He kissed her and then pulled her arms away.

"Draw your sword, you villain, for I will not send a defenseless man to his Maker," he said to Bohemund. The prince reached slowly for his weapon, and hefted it menacingly in his hand, testing again its weight, its balance.

Stefan turned to his men. "This is to be a fair fight. You are in no case to interfere. If Bohemund should be the victor, you shall guarantee him safe passage to the city where the townspeople can determine his fate, and you shall in any case provide for the safety of Anna and conduct her to the Holy City." He turned to Bohemund, and laying his sword in the flat of his palms, he read aloud what was inscribed on one side of the blade: "Do not draw me without a cause." He turned it over. The other side read: "Do not ensheath me without honor." Then, taking the sword by both hands, he raised its hilt high above him and thrust the tip into the timber floor so that the sword took on the form of a cross, casting its shadow across the room toward Bohemund. Placing his hand upon the hilt embellished with velvet and silver, he swore an oath: *This day, O man, shalt thou die, Or my soul shall fly to the sky.*

Stefan yanked Fortissimus out of the flooring, and raising it in the air with a two-handed grip, he brought its tip to meet that of Bohemund's sword. There, briefly, the lives of the two men stayed in the balance, their swords creating a protective firmament over all beneath it. But suddenly the weapons came clanging down as metal clashed upon metal and the fight began.

The strokes of each man were quick and sweeping, each alertly parrying the thrust of the other and leaping out of harm's way. For moments, they exchanged violent, ringing blows. Stefan did not underestimate his opponent. Indeed, he knew of his reputation as a swordsman. Moreover, he was familiar first hand with the ferocious nature of Bohemund in battle. The Italian was a transformed man when in combat. His face became a commentary on each movement of the arm and body: a grimace, and a frown, the facial muscles twisted and elaborated the progress of the fight.

Bohemund, like Stefan, did not suffer a lack of enthusiasm for this contest. Stefan had long been a rival ever since arriving from Norman Italy three years ago. The obvious favoritism shown to him by Alexius. The certain knowledge that the emperor favored him over Bohemund. The knowledge that Stefan would've been Anna's designated husband were it not that he was already married. Stefan's reputation as a keen strategist of war, and as a superior swordsman himself. All of these factors, while not considered individually now, nonetheless comprised the emotional framework which allowed, indeed, compelled Bohemund to harness all the savage power he could.

Thus, evenly matched in both skill and motivation, the bout would be won by the person who was able to discover a weakness and exploit it. No such weaknesses appeared at the present moment, however. The two men fought as though they could fight all night; they wasted not a moment, nor did they seem to be saving their strength for later. They fought as though they might vanquish their foe with the next thrust.

At first, Anna refused to watch. She sat on the bed with her head in her hands crying out of fear and despair. But as it became clear that the match was not going to be decided quickly, and that the match, whatever was at stake, was a thing of artistry and skill, she began to watch while praying fervently that Stefan would be given the strength of Hercules to complete at least this one task. The combatants, she observed, were tight, coiled like cobras, springing to an offensive position, leaping away from a dangerous thrust. Knees bent, body forward, left arm parallel and extended fully for balance, feet nimble and light, taking the body where the mind willed it to be. The match will be won or lost in the feet, she thought. Better to be quick of foot than of hand or eye. Many a swordsman has been saved by having feet more skillful than hands.

But Stefan's hands were fast and strong. He wielded Fortissimus with his two-handed grip effortlessly, his wrists snapping fluidly to whip the blade of the sword to its intended target. He whirled his sword above his head and brought it crashing upon Bohemund's sword driving it into the timber. But he was unable to follow through with another quick jab before Bohemund had retrieved his sword and renewed the fray.

Then, suddenly, he was cut. The blow was aimed at his shoulder. Stefan dodged it and gamely endeavored to bring his sword to the left so that the blow would be deflected, but in this he had only partially succeeded. His blouse was torn, and the blade sliced the flesh in his right arm, the arm of his strength. Bohemund now seized the moment and with quick advancing steps moved into Stefan's defense and began to back him toward the doorway. The advantage was a real one, and Stefan was unable to do anything but defend.

Anna was more alarmed at this turn of events than Stefan. The latter, while conscious of the wound, felt no pain nor weakening of his condition. He did realize, however, that the blow had given the advantage to Bohemund, but he did not make the mistake of attempting to counter too quickly. He realized that in this stage of the match it was his obligation to defend himself until the defense was clearly established and the opponent would gain no further advantage by pressing.

Bohemund drove Stefan out of the room to the landing at the head of the stairs. Stefan shouted for his men to stay in the chamber; they would be in his way should they attempt to view the match in the stairwell. The match was even again, although Bohemund was able to force Stefan down the stairs to the next story.

The landing on the sixth floor was larger and Stefan was able to maneuver into a passageway to his left, rather than down another flight of stairs. The narrow, damp corridor was unlit, except for what light came into it from the stairway behind them. Soon the stairway itself was out of sight and they fought alone, shadowy figures in a dance of death upon slabs of granite six storys up in the

Citadel. Stefan began to feel the pain now, throbbing and distracting. His strength would ebb if he didn't gain the offensive soon. Bohemund, he could see, was confident of victory, evidently convinced that the battle was his.

Stefan became more conscious of technique. He planted his right foot perpendicular to the wall and his left foot toward his opponent and attempted to hold his ground. But Bohemund was a stroke ahead of him. Stefan's right foot inched backwards, Bohemund lunged forward, Stefan countered, the right foot back again almost imperceptibly until, he realized to his horror, his next step would be into a void. His right foot was over the edge of a step. This was a stairway down. No! His chest tightened as though an iron fist had gripped it. His heart skipped a beat in panic. The oubliette! The dungeon for The Disappeared, The Forgotten. A black abyss of twenty-five feet where even now lay the rotting flesh and broken bones of sorry victims.

For the first time, Stefan realized his peril. His death was imminent and no longer an abstract notion or mere possibility. It was now a very real probability, and as much as he hated Bohemund, he had relied too heavily on what he believed were his superior skills, not underestimating his opponent, but overestimating his advantage, and he was now about to crash to his death.

He heard a quiet laugh; it was Bohemund. He looked at his face, and suddenly his lungs filled with air and he cried long and loud: "No!" And at the same time, he dropped his two-handed grip and holding Fortissimus in his right hand, he reached for his dagger with his left hand and began anew with two weapons.

There are not many knights who can wield a ponderous sword in one hand leaving his other hand free for combat with another weapon. Those who are so skilled are greatly admired, and Stefan was one of those who could. The dagger, the *misericorde*, usually reserved for the *coup de grace*, now was put into action. Stefan wielded Fortissimus with his right hand, his wrists still strong and every sinew and tendon in his lower and upper arms stretched and utilized to its maximum potential in spite of the earlier wound.

Bohemund was startled by this maneuver, and the brief hesitation his consternation produced allowed Stefan to regain the edge and push Bohemund back, and himself away from the oubliette. Indeed quickly now, he jabbed and parried in a frantic flurry of blows until a very frustrated Bohemund found himself in the stairway and backing down the stairs.

Stefan, not wanting to go down the stairs lured him back by giving him a slight advantage. But when he had Bohemund on an equal plane again, he lunged forward in a fury of six swift strokes during which the tip of his dagger found its mark underneath the right arm of Bohemund, for the dagger being in Stefan's left hand went directly forward to the right hand of his opponent facing him. Bohemund cried out, but Stefan pressed the assault with a vengeance until it was Bohemund who was on the defensive, backing up in the passageway of death.

Bohemund was aware of the strategy and cursed himself for being lured back up the stairs, even though fighting below an opponent on a stairway is awkward too. Stefan's feet moved forward rapidly now, as the dark, rock-lined passageway rang with the sound of sword on sword. Stefan would have watched Bohemund's eyes, but in the dim light, he could not see them clearly. He could only see the brightness of steel and do his best to anticipate the blows.

He was tiring, however. The sword was heavy, and his movements slow. Bohemund's retreat was imperceptible. Then, it was his misfortune to be wounded again, this time at the hip. His carelessness had allowed it; for a moment, he had taken his eyes off Bohemund and was looking behind him. The wound angered and empowered him. On he pressed, not giving an inch, and then suddenly, he was able to deliver two quick blows with Fortissimus and follow through with the dagger. Bohemund lay on the stone floor stricken.

Stefan relaxed and waited for him to arise and when he did, they exchanged blows again, but Bohemund's heart was not in it and had Stefan been able to see into his eyes he would have seen there a pale malevolence perhaps illuminated by the self-knowledge in those final moments that he was about to die. Stefan struck again, blow, jab, thrust and counterthrust. Bohemund blocked, struck, and retreated and then—tripped into the *oubliette*. Stefan heard his fading cry as he vanished from view.

Stefan collapsed right there in the murky darkness of the passageway to the *oubliette* and leaned heavily against the clammy wall. In an instant, Everard was at his side and with the help of Roger and Richard, he was carried back to the bed where he had last seen Anna. Now he saw her again. She sent the others out of the room. He saw her tear off his tunic and bind up his wounds. He saw her take off his clothes and her own, and he saw her naked, slipping into the bed with him, pulling up the blankets over them, where in safety she stretched out her warm body upon his, kissing him full upon the lips. She took great pleasure in giving freely to Stefan upon the same bed, what Bohemund had aspired to take.

But Stefan, weary and wounded, was unable to wield his sword in this encounter, so Anna lay beside him stroking his body and comforting him.

"Beloved, is this the Holy City?" he once asked, coming out of his sleep.

"Yes, darling," she replied. "This is the Holy City."

CHAPTER THIRTY-EIGHT

PONS LE CHEVALIER

TEFAN AND ANNA FIRST SAW the city of David from the crusty ridge of the Nabi Samwil in the late morning under a hot sun. Not the largest nor most beautiful city of the world but a city steeped in antiquity; a city old beyond its years, one which by all accounts should be nothing but a pile of rubble and overrun of sheep and goats, and nattering crones casting dire imprecations upon the solitary traveler. To enter its ancient precincts was to journey into the history of many civilizations past, reliving its tortured existence.

"Shalom," said Anna. "The city of Peace."

"The ancient Salem," Stefan murmured, as their company came to a halt. "I wonder how many sieges and battles these walls have withstood."

Anna nodded. "Plenty," she said, resting her hands on the pommel of her saddle. "Some of those stones date from Nehemiah. The Hasmoneans extended the walls out and Herod built them higher. The Romans tore some of them down; Constantine and others built them up again. The Saracens have strengthened them, the Egyptians repaired them. I guess the entire world has laid stones on the walls of Jerusalem at some time. And I daresay, if we're like the rest, we'll add a few of our own."

They rode hard toward the sprawling camp of the crusaders. The pilgrims had cast themselves along the western and northern fortifications since the eastern and southern walls were naturally protected by the two steep valleys, Kidron and Hinnom. The relatively flat areas before the western and northern ramparts were crowded with tents and hastily erected domiciles. Construction had already begun in large level fields of siege machines and catapults; corrals and pens for horses, sheep and goats had been swiftly erected. The pilgrims had arrived at their destination; the activity in the camps clearly showed they had no intention of leaving any time soon.

Stefan and Anna rode slowly through the camps attracting attention from bystanders as they proceeded. It was hot; old men sat in the shade of shrubbery, and women and children pounded grain, carried water, or stripped wood. The Council of Knights posted a large tent at the Quadtrangular Tower (at the north-western corner of the city where the two walls join) at a judicious distance from the battlements so that catapults firing missiles from the tower would be unable to damage it. As they approached the tent, they could easily hear a boisterous discussion in progress, the exact details of which were obscured by the confusion.

"Nothing's changed," Stefan laughed. "Still arguing."

Stefan and Anna dismounted. He was uneasy; a lion padding into a coliseum of bloodthirsty Christians. Would they want his hide, or would they be in a forgiving mood? Thumbs up or thumbs down? Anna appeared to be completely poised.

"Can you see it?" he asked cryptically.

"See what?" she asked. She held his gaze for a moment.

Stefan lowered his voice. "Can you see—on my face—that I love you?"

She smiled. "No, it is okay," she said. "You look very much like you do NOT love me."

Stefan waved his hand at Everard asking him to accompany him within. The three of them stepped beneath the canopy, Everard leading the way, and pushed their way through the milling aggregation of knights and soldiers straining to overhear the discussion of the princes.

Stefan could see Raymond who stood taller than the others. He was speaking, but he could not yet make out what he was saying. But whatever it was, it was being received disagreeably. Stefan squeezed Anna's hand as he tugged and pulled her through the crowd. He was beginning to feel excitement. He was again in the arena of activity that seemed natural for him. He could sense the scent of battle hovering in the atmosphere, an erotic musk that engorges a soldier and allows him to raise his weapon and penetrate an enemy's defenses. He could feel the raw emotion of it now coursing through the body of this company: the tightening tone of the muscles, the timbre of voice, the passion and artful declarations of love and loyalty. Another city to rape.

They pushed into the inner circle, and as they did so, the conversation stopped. The knights were assembled about a large, low table on which was an enormous parchment map. It was a map of the latest style, made by a cartographer of Cambrai who had developed the technique of using black crenellated lines drawn with a number of squares along it, representing small, specific sections of the city. In a quick glance, Stefan could see that the walls were clearly marked, and the discussion was without doubt centered on the vexing problem of how to breach those selfsame walls.

Stefan glanced from face to face upon the visage of his familiar friends and former companions in arms: Raymond, Tancred, Robert of Normandy, Robert of Flanders, Godfrey, Conant of Brittany, Hugh of St. Pol, and lesser knights: Arnulf Malecorne, the chaplain of Robert of Normandy; Fulcher, priest and chronicler; and other religious. They wore expressions of surprise and shock— and traces of resentment.

"You have returned," Raymond said without emotion. Stefan detected an edge of irritation in his voice.

In a quick, swift motion, Stefan withdrew Fortissimus from its sheath. The princes jumped back awkwardly in consternation.

Stefan, as he had in Antioch, seized the hilt with both hands and thrust the sword into the floor. "I have returned to pay my vow at the Church of the Holy Sepulcher," Stefan said, answering the question he knew would be asked. The men averted their gaze. "I have escorted Anna, princess of the empire and daughter of the emperor, to Jerusalem," he continued undaunted. "She is here as the imperial legate and speaks for the emperor."

The silence was shattered. The nobles spoke all at once. Anna edged nervously toward Stefan. The sound of the rabble was unfriendly; Stefan was not surprised. Nevertheless, they would have to listen to her and suffer the consequences of their actions whatever they might be.

"We're surprised to see you, Stefan, and you Anna," shouted Godfrey. "To be honest, we thought you were a coward with a heart of snow which melts in the heat of the battle."

The youthful Tancred bullied through the crowd and stood face to face with the count of Blois. Stefan knew he could not expect civility from this rogue. "You fled like a coward at Antioch, you forsook your solemn oath for secular concerns, you fornicate with a woman not your wife—"

Stefan pulled back his right hand, shaped it into a fist of iron and sent it crashing with bone-crunching force into the left side of Tancred's olive-skinned face. The soldier, hefted off his feet by the force of the blow, reeled back and crashed to the ground. Before the startled onlookers could intervene, Stefan was upon him lifting him back to his feet. He threw him like a rag doll into the crowd of soldiers who caught him and prevented him from falling again. Tancred touched his face where Stefan's fist had landed. It was possible Stefan had broken his jaw. In any case, Tancred could not speak.

"Don't lecture me on morality, Tancred, and do not show disrespect for the imperial legate!" Stefan said quietly, as a man utterly self-assured. Turning to the others, he said: "I left Antioch because I had been told by Bohemund himself that the city would be betrayed into his hands that night and as you know Bohemund wanted Antioch for himself. If I was fleeing from anyone or anything, it was not from my vows. I returned to France because the Church which had promised to protect my lands had failed to do so. So don't give me platitudes about the secular or the sacred. I have returned because, in fact, I never forsook my vow; I only delayed its fulfilment."

Stefan paused and looked at the circle of knights. "I can see that in the time I've been gone I haven't missed much. I left when Antioch was about to be delivered into your hands, a city a mere three week's journey from here. Three weeks! That was a year ago. Since then I've been to Constantinople, to France *and back*, while you have scarcely managed to get your arses down to Jerusalem. So don't speak to me of cowardice, unless you're prepared to explain why it took so long to journey such a short distance. And as for secular interests, why not ask Bohemund who has deserted the pilgrimage to stay in Antioch and why not ask Tancred why his banner is flying over the Church of the Holy Nativity in Bethlehem at this very moment!"

At this news there was a great outcry. Raymond restored order. "We welcome you back as a Christian brother, and while we confess that we did not understand your motives, we shall leave that matter in the hands of God. Still, our forces have been divided up, and I shall not reassign men for you to lead. Instead you will attach yourself to the count of Flanders, and meanwhile, your advice on our situation will be invaluable." Raymond was gracious.

Stefan bowed slightly, and Raymond's speech seemed to win the approval of the rest. "I shall want a tour of the walls as soon as possible," said Stefan.

"You shall have it," said Raymond. "I, myself, shall lead you on an inspection of the walls. We can complete it in a couple of hours. I suggest that we break off for today and convene another meeting tomorrow morning."

✠✠✠

Stefan and Anna, with Richard, Roger and Everard, followed
Raymond on horses to the Quadrangular Tower. "This tower,"
Raymond began, "is the highest point of the city, right here at its
northwestern point." Stefan scrutinized the elderly commander. He
was a man of remarkable vigor who had no doubt come to stay; he
was too old to return to France. The count, Stefan remembered,
had sold much of his land and donated it to the Church. He would
carve out a patrimony for himself in the Levant and stay until he
died. Yet, there was nothing retiring about this battle-weary soldier.
He was a knight in the finest tradition of the word, a gentleman,
and a man whose own people loved and respected him, someone
known as a friend of the poor and honest in all his dealings.
Stubborn, but a good man nonetheless.

From the Quadrangular Tower, they rode along the north wall.
"After the Seljuk Turks conquered the city in 1073," Raymond said,
"they ordered the destruction of all the monasteries and other
buildings which were beyond the walls of the city, and used the
materials to erect these outer walls, the *antemurale* or *barbican*. You
will see that this *antemurale* extends for the entire length of the
northern wall and must therefore be breached first before we can
assault the main walls with scaling ladders or siege machines."

The defenses were impressive. The party rode to the north of
the *barbican*. "What's the size of the garrison inside?" Stefan asked.

"The name is Iftikhar-ad-Daulah," Raymond replied. "Fatimid
Egyptian. He's expecting reinforcements from a large Egyptian
army moving north toward us. Hopes to last until then." Stefan
understood then that it was imperative that the crusaders occupy
the city as soon as possible. "Iftikhar is smart. He has control of
Roman cisterns that are full of water. He has gathered up flocks
and herds from the region and herded them inside the walls. He's
expelled all Christians—orthodox or heretics—doesn't matter. Just
means fewer mouths to feed and no possibility of betrayal as at
Antioch. The Jews are still inside, primarily in the northeast quarter
over there—" he stopped to indicate the direction. "Juiverie, it's

called. Over here outside the walls, all the wells are poisoned. Don't try to drink from them or you'll die or end up a sick man—"

Anna broke in: "Barbarous! Where do we get our water then?"

Raymond smiled. "Not barbarous. Smart. We get our water from neighboring villages. It's more work, but there's water for everyone. Iftikhar knows that the making of war is harder for an army that is already working hard simply to survive. And he's right. He's clever. He's got better arms, and he has been strengthening his towers, and I imagine he has lots of sacks of straw and hay, and plenty of Greek fire. It's going to be a bloody fight. No doubt about the outcome, though."

"You sound optimistic," said Stefan.

"Of course I'm optimistic," Raymond responded strongly. "What other choice do we have but to be optimistic? We are about to fulfil our destiny! I didn't come this far to fail at Jerusalem having succeeded at every point along the way."

Raymond was right, of course. The crusaders would find a way to take the city. Any other outcome was unthinkable. "What about the moat?" he asked.

Raymond pulled on the reins. They stopped. Pointing east in the direction they had been traveling he said: "The moat starts at the Citadel on the eastern wall—we'll see it later—and continues north to the Quad tower and then east to this northeastern corner and for a short distance south along the east wall. It's about fifty feet wide and twenty feet deep. When the attack comes, we'll have to cross the moat, breach the outer wall, then the main wall—in that order."

"If we attack from the north," Anna added, understanding that one does not launch an attack at the enemy's point of strength.

"If we attack from the north," Raymond repeated, "and we may have no choice, although there will no doubt be an assault from the south as well." They rode around the northeastern corner of the wall and began a descent into the Kidron Valley.

"This valley," Raymond said, as he continued his description, "is also known as the Valley of Jehoshaphat. You can see there is no way the walls can be breached from the east." It was true. The walls were as formidable here as on the western side, but the steep shoulders of the Kidron valley made it impossible to set up catapults, use scaling ladders, or siege machines. The eastern wall was impregnable. As they rode deeper into the Kidron, Jerusalem arose higher and higher, its walls looming massively and invincibly above them. The defenders of the city would waste no men attempting to defend these walls; the natural defenses of the land and walls would be enough.

They began to travel west, climbing out of the Hinnom valley along the south wall by taking a trail which switched back several times to gain the higher ground near the southwest corner. "As you can see, the east and south walls are virtually impervious to attack, except for this area of the south wall here," said Raymond as they cantered easily now on the level ground near the Zion Gate. "We can bring siege machines up against this section of the wall, and deploy a siege tower against a section of the north wall as well, and I'm afraid these are the only two sections of the defenses where towers are feasible."

They galloped ahead for several hundred yards until they had made the turn at the southwest corner of the wall. They were now among the armies of Raymond himself, Godfrey and Tancred. "As you can see, an attack here will be very difficult. The initial deployment of our forces here was made in order to lay siege to the Citadel. We were discussing this when we were interrupted by your arrival." Stefan looked at Raymond directly to judge his manner, but the crusader was gazing at the fortifications of the city. "The Citadel, also known as the Tower of David, is surrounded by a moat which you see here dividing it from the city although it is connected by a bridge. Robert of Flanders and Hugh of St. Pol are supposed to supervise the walls here where they slope to the fields, but there's little supervising to be done. This damned wadi which follows the walls north and splits off to the west will make it very difficult to attack here."

"Why attack here?" Anna asked.

"Because it appears to be key to the defense of the city. Capture the Citadel and you capture the city. And there's no *antemurale* to break through and the moat can be filled."

"But you cannot fill the ditch without exposing your men to the defenders on the battlements," said Stefan. "You can't throw enough men against this moat or these walls because of the terrain. The Egyptians will pick you off one by one."

Raymond nodded. He saw that in Stefan he may have an ally in the council.

✠✠✠

Addie sat beside a small fire near a sheltering cypress. The night air had cooled, and she felt refreshed for the first time this day. Hungry, but refreshed. Wood was scarce. She made this little fire from scraps of kindling lying about; the olive and cypress wood was hard and gave off strong, lasting heat. But she knew the soldiers were having trouble finding wood for their towers, catapults and machines. I don't care, she thought, I'm here now with Clare, Pons and Hildy, and I've no place to go. This is all I want. With this I shall be happy until my fortunes improve—if they do. She looked about for Clare. The little girl was with friends nearby. Addie could hear her laughter even now. They were camping with the Provencals under Count Raymond's command opposite the west wall not far from the Jaffa Gate. Not far? Far enough. She could see the gate, its rounded arch, and the towers above it. But there was a large sloping wadi between her and the walls, and she was perched atop the ridge while thousands were camping in terrace-like rows and randomly scattered clusters on the slopes of the dusty wadi itself. She and Clare and Hildy would live or die with the crusaders. "I'm ready," she said out loud. "I'm ready for life or death. Either way, my prospects are going to improve. If death, my sorrows are ended; if life, I enter Jerusalem to say my vows."

"Ready for what?" asked a familiar voice from the darkness. Addie peered beyond the glow of her campfire. "Ready for what?

For whom? For me?" asked Pons as he stepped into the warm circle of firelight.

"Pons!" Addie exclaimed. He was wearing military garb, a coat of mail that approached the knee, gathered by a heavy leather belt, and a sword was sheathed at his side in its scabbard. In his hand he carried a helmet. "What are you doing with all this, this stuff!" she asked, leaping to her feet and touching his chest. Her nimble fingers ran over the tiny links of steel before stroking his beard. It was really him. Pons grabbed and swung her around laughing.

"Je suis Pons le Chevalier," he said. "Pons, the knight!" Addie was astonished.

"A knight!" she cried, clutching at him. "You are a knight? How did this happen? Tell me, tell me," she begged.

The knight unbuckled his sword belt and placed it carefully on the earth beside the campfire and sat down. "Count Raymond," he said, looking at her happily. "The leaders had a council last night. Raymond said he was moving his army to the south wall, to Zion Gate. He said that an assault against the Citadel would be too difficult, that the south and north were the best areas for machines."

"So what does this have to do with you?" Addie pressed. Pons raised his hands motioning for patience.

"He's had deserters, soldiers going over to Godfrey and Hugh, he needs knights, and he picked me!"

"He picked you! How wonderful, Pons!" Addie laid her head against his shoulder as he swung a knightly arm around her. "He picked you!"

"No more mining," Pons added. "No more mining, because you know what, my dearest? Raymond made me commander in charge of all mining operations at the south wall!"

"No more mining?" Addie could scarce believe her ears. She realized she had been repeating everything Pons had said. "No more mining?"

"No more mining! I'll have men who will be doing the work for me. I'll have to direct the progress, make sure we have the timber for the supporting beams, the axes, shovels and equipment. And

Raymond gave me this armor, and he gave me my own horse! Can you believe it, we have a horse!"

It was almost more than Addie could bear. What good fortune had smiled upon them! She squealed with delight and threw her arms about her friend the knight and squeezed him long and hard as was fitting for a woman who had never so lovingly squeezed a knight before in her life. "Where is the horse?"

"Tis yonder," he replied. "Want to see him?"

"Oh, yes, oh yes, I want to see him." They bounded to their feet and Pons, taking Addie by the hand, led her away from the camp, down a short pathway and around a turn, to see their new horse.

"He's beautiful," Addie said in awe. "He's so beautiful." The animal was a handsome chestnut that appeared to be well fed in spite of the recent shortages of grain. "A fine animal," said Pons admiringly as he ran his hands across the withers and down the forelegs. "He'll be a good horse in battle, and if—" Pons corrected himself "—when we get into the city, he'll be very valuable to me."

"What's his name? He must have a name!"

"I'm going to call him Pilgrim, because he's come a far distance just like us, Addie, haven't you, Pilgrim?" he said patting his nose. Pilgrim nuzzled his hand, looking for grain.

"Pilgrim! What a splendid name," Addie said thoughtfully. "A splendid name!"

"An entirely new strategy is being proposed," said Pons when they had returned to their campfire and he had shed his knightly attire.

"How's that?" asked Addie, curious but not captivated by the news.

"The Citadel is no longer considered important. The armies are going to focus entirely upon the north wall and the walls at the southwest corner." Pons seized a stick and began to draw a map in the dust of the ground by the fire. First, he outlined the pentagonal shape of the city. "The north wall is by far the longest and it angles slightly—here—to give the city a five-sided appearance. Raymond is moving here—" he said, pointing to the area at Zion's Gate in the south, "and all the others, all of them—Tancred, Robert of Flanders, Robert of Normandy, Hugh of St. Pol, Conant of

Brittany, Godfrey de Bouillon—all are being placed at points along the north wall. The terrain there is flat as it is here in the southwest corner. This is where the assault will take place, and if God is with us, we shall break through at the south while they are breaking through in the north, and once in, we'll fan out against the interior walls and proceed through the city, trapping their forces."

"And when does this all begin?" Addie asked, worried lest Pons be exposed to danger too soon after his new commission.

"Don't know. The Council of Knights heard that there is an old hermit who lives on the Mount of Olives. He is said to be a prophet and a wise man. The council is making a pilgrimage to see him tomorrow. We'll know more then." They fell into silence each thinking about the future, their particular future, and their future together.

"Have you seen the Antichrist?" Addie asked.

"The Antichrist?"

"The Antichrist. The monk said when we were in Provence, that the Antichrist was in Jerusalem, and that we must go there to fight him. Have you seen him or heard of him?" Pons said nothing.

"There is no Antichrist, is there?" Addie asked.

"No," said Pons, "I don't think so."

"So, here we are, and nothing is coming to an end. Adhemar is gone, we don't have the first, middle or last emperor, and the only thing that has come to an end is hope, and faith—"

"But not love, my sweet," said Pons nuzzling her neck. "The greatest of these is love."

✠✠✠

Then, based on the advice of a seer, the "hermit of the Mount of Olives," the crusaders suddenly launched an assault—the day after Stefan's arrival. Three and one half years after Pope Urban II had preached at Clermont, the Militia Sancti Petri would attempt to seize their objective: Jerusalem.

CHAPTER THIRTY-NINE

The Attack

ERNARD OF CLAIR-
VAUX, WITH HIS *friend
William of St. Thierry, returned to
Cluny after an absence of a week. I
had not been well; my skin was the
color of flour; my hands trembled
and my legs were unsteady. My
brow felt warm and moist; the night
passed fitfully. Our abbot, Peter, has given me extreme
latitude and allows me to get the rest I need when I need it.
So it wasn't until the twelfth hour that I hobbled (O
wretched body!) into the dining hall where the brothers were
serving hot lentil soup and steaming, fresh rolls.*

"So, you are back from Sens," I said, greeting my visitors.

*They smiled wanly and nodded. Bernard's face was haggard, and his
eyes dull; the experience had no doubt been a trying one.*

I dipped my ladle into the bowl of soup. "And Abelard?" I inquired.

*"Condemned on all nineteen counts," William said with finality. After a
pause, he added: "In absentia."*

"In absentia?" I thought that Abelard would be present at the proceedings.

*"He refused to listen, and walked out, shouting and arguing with the
judges," Bernard said.*

*"Abelard is very impatient with those he deems his intellectual inferiors,"
William explained. "He does not suffer fools gladly." Bernard glared at him
and William, caught in his indiscretion, stammered, "No, I didn't mean ..."
His voice trailed away.*

"All nineteen?" I said, echoing *William's earlier statement.*

Bernard nodded. *"All nineteen. Had he stayed to contest the charges, the outcome would have been the same. He knew and wisely decided to leave and not waste his time."*

"What happens now?" I asked.

"He cannot teach Catholic faith and doctrine, his writings are condemned, and students who attend his lectures flirt with heresy themselves."

"His condemnation may cause a controversy," I said.

"Not for long," Bernard said wearily, fingering a roll but not eating it. *"Heresy is a weed that grows quickly into a large, noxious plant. But when it is plucked, it just as quickly withers away."*

"We are nearing the end of the Gesta Francorum,*"* I said, changing the subject.

"But he'll find a way to circumvent the order of the council," Bernard continued, speaking to no one in particular and everyone in general. *"This is not over, I'm afraid."*

We sat in silence as though to allow the pathos of the moment to linger and remain, or lift and blow away. Then Bernard looked up quickly, his eyes wide and alert, and jaw firm and resolute. *"Yes, the* Gesta! *We shall resume immediately."*

And we did. Finishing our lunch, we retired to the library and began our examination anew. *"The assault on the walls of Jerusalem,"* I began, *"commenced at sunrise only hours after the visitation to the Hermit of Olivet. The Council of Knights believed that the defenders of the city would be surprised and unprepared by the sudden attack, coming so soon after arriving in the region. After all, this was the most heavily fortified city of the Levant. Surely the Christians could not expect to do in eight days what they had been unable to do in Antioch for eight months.*

✠✠✠

June 20, 1099 A.D.

While it was still dark and under cool, heavy clouds, Stefan assembled a legion of soldiers and led them into position at the northwestern sector near the Quadrangular Tower. Tancred's troops were located here, and since it had been Tancred who had found the timber (in a cave near Jerusalem) with which the only ladder in their arsenal of weapons had been constructed, it was Tancred who requested the right to ascend the ladder first when the assault got underway. This unusual request was summarily denied, but the assault took place nonetheless at the Postern of St. Lazarus opposite his position. Stefan was not convinced that his troops would even see any action, but if they were called upon, he was determined that they should be ready. Count Raymond's forces were entirely unavailable for they were in the process of moving to the southwest corner near Zion Gate, and it was felt that Raymond's activity would lull the defenders into believing that a general offensive against the city would be several days if not weeks hence.

Tancred's forces were joined by Robert of Flanders and Robert of Normandy in the initial attack. The remainder of the crusader forces would be held in reserve until the walls had been penetrated.

The military objective was three-fold: First, render the moat ineffective; second, destroy the *barbicon*, or outer wall; and third, scale the inner wall. The incursion began with a march to the moat by fearless and strong-bodied foot soldiers of Tancred and Robert of Flanders, who donned their helmets and marched to the moat pulling carts laden with stones, rocks and all manner of debris with which to fill it and provide access to the outer walls. The troops following those who filled the moat marched forward carrying an overhead ceiling of shields, followed by an equally impressive force of more soldiers armed with iron hammers and mattocks with which they began to beat the outer walls. Their efforts brought down upon them a mighty barrage of stones, arrows and other projectiles which went flying over both the inner and outer walls inflicting heavy losses. Nevertheless, the crusaders were able to breach the lower walls and reach the higher inner walls the scaling of which would mean access to the city. Carrying the only ladder in the possession of the crusading army, the troops succeeded in attaching it to the wall in spite of heavy bombardment by the defenders from the battlements above.

✠✠✠

I had to pause because my sense of mirth overwhelmed me. "There we were," I said to the others, laughing, "facing the strongest city of the Levant armed with a single ladder! One ladder! We were like David and his slingshot only without the stones! We either had faith to move mountains or we were incredibly presumptuous!"

✠✠✠

The defenders of Jerusalem were taking heavy losses, too, for without the protection of hoardings on the ramparts, the defenders exposed themselves to the arrows from crusader archers who, assembled several ranks deep beyond the moat, plucked many Saracens out of the sky with their superior marksmanship. Their accuracy was legendary.

Leading the charge up the ladder was a certain Reybold, a strong-armed knight of Chartres. He, in fact, reached the top of the inner wall but his hand was cut off by a Moslem defender and he was forced to retire from the battle. He was later carried by a carter to Tancred's camp where great and justifiable praise was heaped upon him.

By noon, the crusaders' losses were so great, and the prospects so disheartening, the assault had to be abandoned. Stefan sent his troops back to their camps, and the armies of Tancred and Robert of Flanders began to assess the damage, bury their dead, and take care of their wounded.

The Council of Knights met two days later on June 22.

"Ladders," said Robert of Flanders. "We failed for want of ladders."

"One ladder is worth ten hermits telling us we don't need ladders," added Tancred pointedly. The Council was not in a cheerful mood. Clearly, something had been misunderstood theologically. As a group, they had trusted the word of a man of God rather than their own military instincts. In light of this setback, they turned to their own history. Past victories had been ascribed to the help of God and not military strength, and past defeats had been blamed on moral failure. Requisite to military success was holiness: without holiness in the camp, there could be no victory in the city. Even now there was talk of fasting and prayer; the military effort must be preceded by a spiritual effort, they reasoned.

This sentiment, however, evoked a spirited discussion. "We need ladders, and no attack by soldiers with one ladder, however holy the soldiers and consecrated the ladder, will succeed!" Godfrey argued.

"Agreed!" cried Conant of Brittany. "If it is holiness that wins battles, let us round up all the monks and hermits from the Dead Sea to Galilee and throw them against the infidel!" There was heavy laughter, but it was underscored by a sobering reality: unless the crusaders could build towers, mangonels, catapults, battering rams and ladders, the siege of the city was doomed to fail.

"The Egyptians are coming from the south," Raymond observed, "and they will surely be upon us in six to eight weeks. If we are not in the city by the end of July we'll be forced to fight the Egyptians on the open field, and at the same time defend our position outside of the city. We'll be trapped by the army from the south and the Saracens in the city to our rear."

The situation became even more critical because there was a severe shortage of timber with which to build the necessary war machinery. This shortage of wood was caused by the Egyptian siege of Seljuk Jerusalem only the year before. And, in any case, this southern region of Palestine was naturally barren and rocky; houses, churches and towers were built of stone. What timber had been available had regrettably disappeared. The only answer was to form parties to travel far and wide into the forests of central Palestine and haul the beams south to Jerusalem. This plan was not only dangerous, but more importantly, it was time-consuming. Still, there was no other possibility: the crusaders would have to begin wood-gathering expeditions immediately.

Then the unexpected happened. A fleet of six ships, two Genoese and four English, put into the harbor at Jaffa laden with foodstuffs, ropes, saws, hammers, casters and rollers, nails and bolts for making the siege machines and ladders. While this unanticipated turn of events did not resolve the question of wood, it gave the crusaders a much-needed boost in their morale.

Tancred and Robert of Flanders set out immediately for Samaria, and although it was a district heavily populated by Moslems, they made many captives and compelled the prisoners to transport the timber they secured back to Jerusalem. Within days, Italian and Provencal carpenters were beginning the construction of towers and ladders filling the wadis and fields north and south of Jerusalem with the sound of hammer meeting nail, and plank being slapped upon plank.

Working conditions were difficult. The weather was hot and sultry. Water was scarce and had to be hauled to Jerusalem from the north as the wells in the surrounding districts had been poisoned. Christians who happened to live in the area were helpful in pointing out springs, but even these were far from camp. Many pack animals died of thirst. Just when it seemed that conditions could get no worse, a sirocco blew in which helped plunge morale to its lowest point since reaching Jerusalem.

Work on the towers and machinery was slow. But Pons, now in command of the work on Raymond's towers, was exhilarated by the challenge. He had quickly divided the manpower into several working groups. Some were assigned to construct sheds and deploy them for use while filling up the ditches and low areas before the wall. They would need level ground in order to wheel the tower into place. The sheds would protect the workers who were filling in the ditches from stones and Greek fire hurled upon them, from the battlements above.

He then appointed a squad of men to strip and plane the lumber that had reached them from the forests of Samaria. They needed beams, planks and rollers. *Artillatores* built projecting machines. Many versions of these contrivances would be used in the siege.

Some machines projected large flaming arrows at the enemy from a fixed position on a tower or on land. Others cast stones or balls of iron at the walls and the defenders on the battlements. This not only inflicted heavy damage on the walls, but forced defenders to back away while the attackers moved forward. This artillery for ejecting stones mainly consisted of a perpendicularly suspended beam which was held down at one end by means of twisted ropes and balanced at the opposite side by a heavy weight of stones or metal which caused a tremendous recoil of the beam as soon as the rope was released. Pons figured that these petraries and mangonels would be an important element of the attack once it was begun.

Runners kept the carpenters and other workers constantly supplied with materials and a ration of water. The work was done primarily in the cool hours of the morning, and late afternoon and evening. Any attempt to work throughout the midday hours was counter-productive; men collapsed from exhaustion. The work was hindered rather than helped by attempting to do too much too soon.

The tower that Pons designed for Raymond's forces and with Raymond's approval was like a wooden castle on wheels or rollers. It was approximately thirty feet in width and had a height of about fifty-five feet, or in any case, higher than the walls they wished to surmount. The precise height would not be known until the attack was under way. Iftikhar might begin to raise the height of the wall when he sees us building the tower, Pons thought, and we must be able to extend the height if necessary.

The tower would consist of several floors each holding about a hundred soldiers. The first level normally would house a battering ram which, when swung on a pendulum would create a breach in the lower wall. But Pon's tower would have no battering ram, for they intended only to go over the walls and having secured a portion of the wall, they would throw down scaling ladders for the rest of the army. The tower's first level would be open on both ends permitting the movement of the rollers or logs from one side to another as the tower was rolled into place. The movement of the tower would be accomplished by two large windlasses which required twelve men each to operate. The tower would be slowly inched into place on rollers. As the tower moved away from one log, it would be picked up by strong men, placed into the tower, rolled to the other side and dropped in front of the tower as it proceeded forward.

The top of the tower would be fitted with a large bridge which would at first serve as an embrasure to protect the soldiers, *arbalisters* and archers. At the right moment, the bridge would be lowered into place, and the crusaders would rush across the bridge to the top of the walls in an attempt to secure the wall. Soldiers within the tower would move up through the tower on a staircase in an unending onslaught as the battle progressed.

Another meeting of the Council of Knights was held on the morning of July 6. "The Egyptian army is somewhere between Pelusium and al-Arish. They could be here by the end of the month," said Raymond gravely, standing before the map. "Let's have the reports."

"Work on the tower is almost complete," announced Duke Godfrey de Boullion. "The battering ram is finished and ready for transport. But we are reconsidering the point of attack. The Damascus Gate is heavily defended, and the terrain is not as level as we would like. We are thinking of moving the tower to the east, past Herod's Gate, and I believe we can do it without Iftikhar knowing. The ground is level, and the walls are among the least defended and most vulnerable." Godfrey looked into the features of pilgrim-weary princes. "We hope so, anyway."

"Pons de Rodez report for me," said Raymond, turning to the startled Provencal.

Pons cleared his throat and stood. The experience of speaking to more than one or two people at a time struck fear into an otherwise brave man. His throat seemed paralyzed and he could feel a heavy pounding in his tightening chest. He labored for a deep breath and began: "The tower on the south side is likewise nearing completion. But we've been unable to build it away from the walls as you have on the north side. We've been catching fire from volleys of flaming arrows. To counteract this, we've covered the tower with wet hides, and our men are working under sheds filling the moats. Even with these difficulties, we are virtually ready to mount an assault." The tightening in his chest started to ease, and in fact he felt proud of his effort.

"The biggest problem is morale," reported Robert of Flanders. "The soldiers are underfed, there is little water, and this sirocco has the men fighting with each other."

"When Jerusalem is ours, we will need a king to govern it," said Conant. "We should elect a king from among us now rather than waiting until we've captured the city."

"Outrageous," Robert of Flanders retorted. "Tancred has already offended us by putting his banner over the Church of the Nativity. These places are too holy to be ruled by a secular lord."

"I agree," proclaimed Fulcher of Chartres, speaking for the first time in the Council. "No man should be declared king in the city where Christ was crowned and crucified." In the uproar that followed, a single voice could be heard above the others: "I've had a vision of Adhemar, bishop of Le Puy." At first the bedlam did not subside. The voice was heard again, and then again: "I've had a vision of Adhemar, bishop of Le Puy." Then the council became quiet and the speaker was thrust into the center. He was a man named Peter Desiderius, a Provencal who had had visions before in support of Peter Bartholomew. They gave him leave to speak.

✠✠✠

Addie dipped a patch of linen into a small jar of water which she reserved under a rock to keep it cool. "Here," she said to Clare after passing it across her fevered forehead, "Suck on this. It will help make you better." Clare was languishing in their small tent, wilting like a flower in the heat of the summer. As far as Addie knew, no one had yet died of a known disease since they had arrived at Jerusalem. But some of the older men and women had died for lack of food and water. Frail in health to begin with, the harsh demands of the present siege were difficult on many who had survived the trip. But Clare was not sick, just exhausted.

"I'm fine, mother," said Clare. She did not want to distress her mother. But her mother was not easily worried. *Pilgrimage drives all the worry right out of you*, Addie thought, as she mopped Clare's forehead. Addie had not known that taking the red cross on white linen and tying it across her shoulders would signify the loss of so much. *But, if you carry a cross, I reckon you don't carry much else. A victim of crucifixion doesn't need much by way of earthly possessions. This is what it means to be a pilgrim: you are walking to your own crucifixion. You start out with much and end with little and each loss is another nail in the cross. You finally die of suffocation—that's what Father Fulcher said—you can't breathe anymore; it's too much, the burden of mere breathing, of sheer living, is too great and you just die, you just stop pushing up for more air. You're too tired and you don't care.*

She sensed movement nearby and, looking up, saw Pons coming toward her. He strode into camp appearing tired as he had for the past two weeks.

"You work too hard, Pons," she warned him, helping him sit down. "Take a sip of this. " She offered him a drink of her water. He took the two-handled clay jar from her and lifted it to his lips and drank a small amount, letting it cool his tongue and swirl about in his mouth before it slipped down his dry, parched throat.

"Thank you," he said, leaning back against a large rock. "That's good." He wiped his face and beard with his hand, drawing it down from his forehead to his beard and then stared into her deep, brown eyes. "How's Clare?" he asked.

Addie smiled wanly. "She's the same. Hot and tired, and a little feverish. It's this weather and this wind. Can't get away from this hot wind." Addie looked away, south toward Bethlehem. The wind was from the east, coming up in the valley south of the Mount of Olives from the Dead Sea and the Jordan Valley—strength-sapping and arid wind, picking up dirt and flinging it everywhere. Addie touched her hair and dug her fingers deep into its roots. She could feel the grime not only in her hair but on her face, arms and hands as though it had been painted and baked on her skin in a clay oven.

Pons touched her face. "The council and clergy are calling for a fast," he said wearily. "Starts immediately."

"A fast?" Addie snapped. "Have they lost their senses? How can they call for a fast when we don't have any food as it is? What good's a fast?"

"Don't be angry with me, Addie," Pons said. "If I could change it I would."

Addie stood angrily and walked away from their camp. She stopped suddenly with hands on hips and looked toward the Hinnom Valley. The hills in the distance across the valley were turning a sweet lavender in the fading light of day. Pons caught up with her. Addie turned to him. "I do get angry and when I do, you're often around. It's circumstance, that's all." She turned back

"The processional march began as scheduled on the evening of the third day of the fast, Friday, July 8. The host of people stretched from the northeast corner at the top of the Kidron Valley across the northern walls to the Quadrangular Tower and beyond. ... The bishops clad in full episcopal regalia went first carrying crosses and relics, followed by the rest of the clergy ... Then came the princes ... then came knights, followed by foot soldiers, and finally the noncombatants—every one. No one was excluded from this procession" (p. 533-34).

to the valley and spoke again. "It's just that I don't understand religion the way the priest does. I wish he could explain to me why God will be pleased with people who are already starving and hungry from a lack of food refusing food entirely for another three days. Why does that please God?" She turned to Pons. "Tell me that? Why does that please God?"

Pons said nothing but took the precaution of crossing himself. Addie shouldn't talk that way and sometimes it made him nervous the way she carried on. Addie turned to Pons again and shook her finger in his face. "The only two classes of people in the entire camp who have enough food to eat are the clergy and the nobles. They are the ones who should fast if God needs a fast. Let them give their food to the poor when they fast. Then God will be pleased, and the army will be well fed and ready to fight!" She turned away from him as he tried to put his arms around her. "It doesn't make sense," she fumed.

"Friday evening, on the third day at the end of the fast, there's going to be a procession around the city by everyone, I mean everyone," Pons said. "Clergy, princes, knights, young and old. We're supposed to wear white if possible and our cross patches."

Addie sat down now. "Whose idea was this?" she asked. "Tell me more. I want to hear."

"There was a priest from Provence," he began, "—and incidentally, Count Raymond has made a very, very strong effort to get food to us. We're really fortunate—" Addie nodded in agreement. "A priest from Provence who had had some visions and last night he had another one. He said he had seen the bishop Adhemar—"

"—Old Adhemar has proclaimed more fasts since he was dead than he did when he was alive," Addie muttered. Pons crossed himself again.

"—and the bishop said he deplored the fighting and the selfish feuds among the nobles, and he ordered the entire army to hold a fast and then to walk barefooted around the city walls. He said that if we did, that within nine days the city would fall to them."

"And of course they believed him?"

Pons did not speak at once because he didn't want this to become an argument. This was a discussion and he was simply reporting what happened. Addie could respond in any way she desired. "This is a critical period for the pilgrimage. The Egyptians are definitely on the move and they'll be here, right here, Addie, by the end of the month. If we're not inside Jerusalem by the time they arrive, we're going to die. Chances are that if we get inside the city, they won't even attempt a siege. They went through that last year, I doubt they'll want to do it again. But the thing is, we're just about ready to attack. We need another week. But we're hot and tired and everyone is complaining and fighting. This fast has united the princes again, and the way I see it is that when the princes are agreed on something and cooperating on something, we usually succeed—"

"—And the way for them to succeed is to make the poor suffer," Addie said ruefully.

"As you said, Addie, we've already been going without food. Three more days isn't going to make much of a difference to us." He sat down beside her and taking her by the shoulders swung her back upon the ground and leaned over her and kissed her playfully. Then he kissed her again, longingly.

✠✠✠

The processional march began as scheduled on the evening of the third day of the fast, Friday, July 8. The host of people stretched from the northeast corner at the top of the Kidron Valley across the northern walls to the Quadrangular Tower and beyond. Stefan felt a surge of excitement course through his body as the promenade began. The bishops clad in full episcopal regalia went first carrying crosses and relics, followed by the rest of the clergy who were singing songs of divine aid. Then came the princes, the group with which Stefan and Anna were walking, both following the banners and standards of the empire; then came knights, followed by foot soldiers, and finally the noncombatants—every one. No one was excluded from this procession.

The Moslems watching from above on the ramparts of the walls laughed and hooted at the sight, but Stefan figured their laughter was a sign of fear; they did not know how to defend against faith, and the usual reaction of people to anyone of faith is to laugh and scoff. Indeed, the solemn procession around the city was unlike anything the Saracens had ever seen. Certainly the Egyptians had not engaged in such unusual behavior, and the Saracens themselves had never employed such a tactic in their own assaults upon walled cities and fortresses. If they had the faith and obedience to do this, something so foolish and by all accounts, senseless, then perhaps they would have enough faith to make the push over the walls and into the city when the moment came.

Stefan looked at Anna walking beside him. Her alabaster face contrasted with the purple shadows of the eastern Byzantine walls. She, herself, carried a banner of the empire while Stefan carried his ancestral banner of green and gold. Further back in the procession, Pons de Rodez walked resolutely and beside him, Addie, who, in spite of her irreligious tendencies, was pleased beyond expression to be with Pons in the march. Behind them, Hildy and Clare. For Pons and Addie, this was the most thrilling moment of their lives. The pomp and ceremony gave to them a sense of destiny, gave to them a feeling they were a part not only of their own destiny, but the shaping and the changing of the course of human history. He and Addie, humble peasants from Provence were walking with the *milita sancti Petri* in the Holy Land, in the very valley that Jesus himself had crossed on his way to Gethsemane the night he was betrayed, or on his way into the city on Passion Sunday, or when he journeyed from the city to Bethany to see his friends Mary and Martha and Lazarus. He, Pons, was now in this same valley, on these same roads, and he was a part, an important part, of the struggle to return these sites to a people and a faith who would guard them and take care of them. He felt proud then, even as his stomach ached, even though his throat was parched, he felt proud of this effort, of the suffering, and the glorious achievement to have made it this far if no further.

"Deus vult," he said to Addie.

"Deus vult," she responded. The pilgrims marching in front of them heard her, and repeated what she had said. Then the knight behind them, and before them, soon the cry began to filter from the rank and file to the bishops and to the non-combatants in the rear: "Deus vult! Deus vult!" They shouted. The cry rose into the air, like an arrow in flight. To the Saracens on the battlements above them, it was a cry that sent fear into their scoffing hearts, for it was the cry of faith and even they were beginning to understand that the cry of faith is the cry of victory.

CHAPTER FORTY

Blood in the Streets

July 13, 1099A.D.

"ATAPULTS!" GODFREY SHOUTED ANGRILY. HE was standing beyond the range of Moslem missiles directing the movement of the tower. He had ordered the siege tower to be moved from the Damascus Gate to a point farther east on the northwestern section of the wall. It had taken three days to move it. The assault was now underway. Today, he would be happy to get the tower in position and the walls softened. "Catapults! I want three catapults pounding the walls continuously ... keep those bastards back on the ramparts. Get to it now!"

Immediately, a large group of Lorrainers began preparing catapults for service. Crews wheeled huge carts into place laden with stones which would be hurled at the defenders atop the walls.

"Arbalisters! Where are the archers?" The Moslems were protecting their walls by lowering straw-filled sacks and huge ship hawsers on ropes to nullify the effect of the projectiles. "Get the archers over here, and set those sacks on fire. You know what to do, so let's get it done. Three days to move this tower, I don't want to waste the effort!" Godfrey was now oblivious to anything except the military objective. The walls had to be taken. It was now or absolutely never.

✠✠✠

Rome

In a grand room of an extremely high and painted ceiling, a single bed was positioned near a tall draperied window. The pale morning light revealed an aged man whose coughing could be heard by members of the Curia waiting in the sanctified silence of the corridors without. At the far end of the room, a tall door opened, and a priest in a black skullcap, attired in black and red robes, swept into the room, silver chains jangling. He swished swiftly to the bedside of the ailing man. He reached beneath the man's head and lifted him slightly, propping him up with several pillows.

"You'll eat better now," said the adjutant gently. Pope Urban II saw him and smiled wanly but waved him away. He was not hungry, nor had he been hungry for several days. His weight had dropped dramatically, his spherical face had assumed edges and lines, and the skin was sucked into deep pockets beneath his cheekbones. Atop his head, patchy wisps of hair hung over his eyes like errant clods of grass. His chin was elevated and he breathed through his mouth, each breath a victory.

"The *crucesignati* are at Jerusalem, your Holiness," the priest continued. "They will liberate the Church of the Holy Sepulcher very soon now, *gratia dei*." Urban closed his eyes at this news and smiled again. The priest nodded to the nuns hovering nearby and left the room.

✠✠✠

July 14

As the sun burst over the Mount of Olives, Pons rolled wearily on his back and propped himself up on his elbows. The southern walls, mottled by dirt and moss, pocked by the pounding of rocks and stone, were a flaming orange. He glanced at his tower. It had been a sleepless night. Sleepless because he feared the Moslems would attempt an attack on the tower in the dark. Their mangonels had already inflicted heavy damage against their catapults and as a result they were having great difficulty moving the tower to the walls. Today they would attempt the move again, but Pons was not optimistic. This clearly was a difficult section of the wall to surmount. Work still remained on the moat. It was only partially filled; the task was treacherous because the Moslem defenders relentlessly rained all manner of objects upon them as they worked, including flaming arrows which set the wood of the sheds on fire. Their catapults attempted to set the siege tower aflame and had already disabled one of Pons' machines. It would be a long day and the work would be hard, Pons thought, but there can be no victory without long days and hard work.

✠✠✠

It had also been a sleepless night for Godfrey, Stefan and the others mounting the assault along the northern sector of the walls. They could hear sounds of movement within the city, and they feared the garrison was active and preparing to strengthen their defenses, perhaps even to sally forth against them and the tower. Large regiments of armed sentries on both foot and horses patrolled the line that had been formed by the crusader forces, forces which had not yet been engaged in the battle. Only hundreds of men were involved to this point in the siege while the rank and file of the 12,000 foot soldiers awaited the moment when the walls were breached and they could enter the city.

At the first light of morning, Stefan and Godfrey reviewed their strategy. Stefan was somehow grateful to Godfrey. There was an unaccountable attitude in Godfrey that suggested understanding and sympathy. Godfrey understood quite clearly the responsibilities of a knight and the dangers of deserting possessions at home to fight for the unknown abroad. Stefan sensed in him a compassion he hadn't noticed before, a humbleness, something akin to what he had seen in Raymond's demeanor. It was becoming, Stefan believed, and he returned this unspoken acceptance with respect.

"They've lowered more sacks," Godfrey observed as he scanned the walls for signs of what the Moslems had been doing during the night.

"Is the tower ready?" Stefan inquired.

"The tower's ready, everything's ready," said Godfrey with an edge of eagerness in his voice. "By nightfall, we could be in the city."

"Archers, battering ram and tower," said Stefan, in a few words outlining the strategy for the day.

"Agreed," said Godfrey.

Stefan ordered the archers to form lines somewhat closer than a bowshot from the walls. He coordinated his movements with Godfrey who was assembling a squad of men to deploy the battering ram. Behind it, the tower was readied to begin its movement toward the walls.

Stefan gave the order, and the archers raised their long bows and fired flaming arrows wrapped in cotton soaked in oil toward the straw filled sacks hanging against the walls. Soon the sacks and hawsers were aflame and smoke was again swirling on the ramparts and along the walls. Under the cover of this smoke, and amid a hail of arrows and stone, the battering ram was brought forward by men of prodigious strength and courage. This huge device was made from a freshly-felled tree and the iron head of the instrument was shaped like a ram's head. It was operated in a pendulum motion and when the crusaders brought it against the outer walls, it made a breach quickly. With a great cry, the crusaders broke through the barbicans preparing the way for the ram to assault the main walls themselves and to level an approach to the wall for the tower. The tower was, in fact, moving directly behind the battering ram. Inch by inch, moving as the ram itself moved.

Stefan's heart raced as he saw the great blocks of stone crumble under the destructive power of the battering ram. He saw the soldiers working feverishly with iron mallets to pound stone into smaller pieces, he saw an innumerable host of others with little protection bravely risking their lives to move rock and stone to prepare a smooth way for the ram and tower. Stefan knew their hands were bloodied and raw, that the powder and dirt from rocks and soil would work its way into their hands, but he knew also that these men were now oblivious to pain and suffering.

Stefan and Godfrey entered the tower with their men. They would occupy the upmost floor, the *arx* or *coenaculum* superior, and conduct the battle from this floor. Scores more mounted the interior stairs of the tower to occupy the middle floor. The lower floor was filled with those responsible for moving the tower and defending its base.

The men were eager now, and in the cramped space of the upper story they were anxious for the fighting to begin. "Prepare to wait," Godfrey had told them as they mounted the stairs. "Patience will bring to us what presumption only promises." It would be hard for them to remember those words, Stefan thought as he mounted the ladders to the roof of the tower.

The battering ram was making havoc of whatever stood in its way. It was indeed a prodigious instrument and the Moslems properly regarded it with fear. Stefan leaned over the tower's guard rail and peered across to the walls. Amid the smoke he could see the defenders attempting to set the ram on fire using pitch, beeswax and sulfur as it approached the walls. If the ram could be ignited (although it would take some time), the timber would burn and destroy the ram and if it caught sufficiently on fire, those who were operating the ram would be unable to handle it and use it. But the crusaders were adept at protecting the ram with wet hides and other devices and it continued to operate safely until the unexpected occurred.

Stefan saw it with his own eyes. The men pushed the ram back for another thrust. With every ounce of strength they possessed, the soldiers slammed the ram upon the crumbling mortar already softened by previous blows. This time, it hit the walls with a thunderous crash dropping another pile of rock and rubble to the earth. But to Stefan's horror, the crusaders were unable to withdraw the ram from the wall. It was stuck! The ram's head had penetrated the wall so deeply that the soldiers were unable to remove it from the rock and mortar that had closed around it.

Stefan watched helplessly as the men attempted to extricate the ram from the wall, but their efforts were to no avail. The defenders atop the ramparts immediately ordered a halt to the Greek fire. Instead the fire was directed toward the tower itself and what was worse, Stefan saw that the Moslems were preparing a large coil of rope with a mangonel. He raced from the roof of the tower down the ladder to the upper floor.

"We've got to move the tower," he cried. "They're going to try to overturn the tower with ropes." Godfrey understood precisely what Stefan meant and sent orders below that the tower should be moved away from the walls, out of range of the mangonels until the question of the ram could be settled.

Unfortunately, the durability of the tower was suspect. It was built with fresh timber, true enough, but it had been built quickly. It had been moved a far distance in order to position it, and the movement had placed a great strain on the tower as it would on any edifice as large as this. And it was large. It exceeded the height of the city walls by at least a spear's length. Nor was it easy to budge, and when it did move, every movement weakened the supports and joints. Godfrey and Stefan both knew that it was not uncommon for siege towers to collapse or be overturned by ropes from defenders. The attempt in this case would require the Saracens to attach ropes to the tower by means of a mangonel. The rope would then be winched taut and from a severe angle, slowly forcing or tipping the tower to the ground.

"Why isn't this tower moving?" Godfrey roared. The question was relayed to the lower ranks and soon Eustace the Lothingarian appeared in the upper story.

"We've got a problem, sire," he said. "We cannot move the tower backward because the incline is too steep. It was possible to move the tower forward up the incline with winches and pulleys, but if we attempt to move it back down the incline, I'm afraid the winches won't hold and the whole thing will careen out of control."

Godfrey cursed.

"Move the tower to the side then," Stefan said.

"Cannot do that either, my lord, because we've built an elevated road to the wall expressly for the tower. It would tip over if we moved it more than ten feet in either direction."

"And we can't move it forward because the damn ram is in the way," explained Godfrey. "So the ram is stuck and we're stuck."

"Set fire to the ram," Stefan said.

"What?" said Godfrey surprised.

"I said set fire to the ram," Stefan repeated. "The ram is no longer useful to us and has become a Moslem weapon. They themselves have stopped trying to set it afire. Now we should try to succeed where they have failed. And when we succeed, since we cannot move the tower backwards or sideways, we must move it forward, so close to the walls that the Moslem catapults will no longer be useful. Their stones will fly harmlessly over our heads."

Godfrey turned to his lieutenants and issued the orders. "Set fire to the ram, and I want men on the roof prepared to cut the ropes if the Moslems succeed in attaching ropes to this tower."

The military situation was now reversed. Whereas the crusaders had been attempting to protect the ram from fire, they now endeavored to set it on fire. And whereas the Moslems had attempted to set the ram on fire, they now tried to protect the ram from the fire of the crusaders by raining water upon it and badgering the crusaders with arrows, rocks and spears.

✠✠✠

Addie sat at her camp rinsing clothes. It was impossible to keep anything clean. The sirocco had passed, but even the slightest breeze stirred up dust, dirt and grime. She tried to keep clothes and her body as clean as was feasible, and while the local wells had been poisoned, the water was still suitable for washing.

The camp was deserted except for women, children and old men too feeble to take part in the assault. Addie was simply thankful for being alive. *I spend most of my time thankful for being alive.* She liked that. It was better than wishing she was dead. At home in Provence, she had never wished she was dead, nor was she ever particularly thankful to be alive. She lived at home unaware of life. It was taken for granted. Life was what enabled you to go into the fields, harvest the crops, bake bread, cook meals, go to church, feed the chickens, milk the cows, mend and sew clothes. One didn't think about life; one thought about these other things. Life was neither good or bad, fair or unfair; it was simply a realm in which one functioned.

Now Addie was glad to be alive. She breathed the air deeply, she rejoiced in the smile of her daughter, she quivered at the touch of her man, she noticed beautiful things like the wing of a bird in flight, or the petal of a wild flower, or the sun setting over the western mountains or arising over the Mount of Olives. Tomorrow or the next day it may all be gone. This may be where life ends for me and for my child, she thought wearily. Or it may be where it begins.

She looked up from her washing when she heard horses. Pons was away; she hadn't seen him for a week and she might not see him ever again. It wouldn't be him. She stood. There were several horses and riders and banners flying above them. She recognized the imperial banner of gold and blue. The entourage approached and Addie bowed saying: "Good afternoon and God be with you."

It appeared to Addie that the procession would've passed her by, but at these words, the group halted, and one of the riders dismounted and approached her.

"Thank you for your greeting," said the voice, a woman's. "Your voice sounded familiar to me," she continued. "Do I know you?"

Addie smiled. "I'm quite sure I don't know you," she said, "except you are a woman in the clothing of a man."

"I am a soldier in the clothing of a soldier, but my name is Anna, the daughter of Alexius, emperor." She tried to say the words without appearing condescending, but it is difficult to identify yourself as a royal without appearing to be ostentatious.

To Addie also, the voice was familiar. The two women faced each other thinking. Then Addie remembered. "You are the one who appeared the night of the fire when our friend Guy died."

Anna's face lightened: "Why, of course! That's it. I remember you were so distressed at the loss of your friend, but it was dark and I didn't see much of you, but I remember now your voice and I remember the night quite clearly."

"As do I," said Addie. Anna stood awkwardly waiting, not knowing what to say. "Would you like to rest a while here with me?" she asked her royal visitor.

"That's a splendid idea!" Anna exclaimed. She summoned the others and they dismounted apace.

"You speak French very well," Addie observed when they were settled under a cypress tree.

"Thank you," said Anna. "I had good masters at the court in Constantinople."

"It would be very hard for me to learn Greek," said Addie apologetically.

"Not at all," said Anna. "You seem a bright person. It is only a lack of time and teachers that keep one from learning."

"Well, I reckon in Provence, I don't much need to speak Greek!"

"Agreed!" They ate barley cakes, the staple of the pilgrimage. "Tell me, you miss your friend very much?"

Addie appeared startled. "My friend?" she inquired, puzzled.

"Your friend," Anna repeated. "The one who died that night in the fire."

"Oh, Guy," said Addie. She was quiet for a moment. "Yes, of course I do. He and his friend saved my life and the life of my daughter once. We became close friends. Yes, I do miss him."

"And the other friend, he is still alive?" Anna persisted.

Addie smiled, "Yes, yes, he is very important in Count Raymond's army. He is a carpenter and engineer. He built Raymond's siege engine."

"Ahhh," Anna murmured. "I like that Raymond. He is a kind man, a bit old for this sort of thing don't you think, but a very good man, a gentleman."

"Yes, I like him too. He has been good to us."

"And this other friend, does he have a name?"

"Pons de Rodez."

"Pons," she repeated again. "I have a friend—"

"—Count Stefan of Blois," said Addie interrupting.

Anna looked up surprised, "Yes, Stefan. How do you know his name?"

"It's a long story." Addie was sure that Anna knew nothing of the particulars of that night. And she wouldn't share them.

"Yes, Stefan," she said. She stopped speaking. She wasn't sure she should say more. She felt a kinship with this woman because circumstances had at one time placed them in a sad situation together. And this woman did not seem to be unduly impressed with her station in life and Anna liked people who saw past the tiara, the clothes, the title, to herself as a human being. Somehow, Addie was making her feel like a woman and not a princess and she liked that feeling. She enjoyed conversing with a woman who was not an attendant or who was not otherwise dependent upon her or her father for support and approval.

"You are very close to Stefan, yes?" Addie asked sensing that Anna was in a mood to talk. Anna was surprised again. Addie's questions always seemed to hit the mark. She was perceptive, a trifle uncomfortably perceptive.

"Yes, close, very close," Anna replied. "It is very sad because we can never, never—-"

"—get married?" Addie offered.

"Yes, because—"

"—-he's already married, no?"

"Why, yes!" Anna said in amazement, "because he's already married!" She looked at Addie. "You know so much about Stefan!"

"We have been traveling for over three years," Addie said, laughing. "There's not too much that one doesn't know." She paused and then looked at Anna directly. "I could tell you stories! Stories you wouldn't believe. But I like your Stefan. Seems courteous, thoughtful. Not like the others, mostly brutes, you know. He doesn't love his wife, though, does he?"

"He says he has no wife. She made a cuckold of him while he was on crusade, but his Church won't give him a divorce and even if it did my Church wouldn't recognize it, and I can't marry without the blessing of the Church ... If I was an ordinary person, it wouldn't matter, but the crown is a prison ... I was supposed to marry Bohemund—"

"—Bohemund?"

"You know of him?"

"He is an evil man," said Addie. Anna decided against inquiring further. She would not be surprised if she and Addie did not share similar experiences.

"He's a dead man," Anna said. "Stefan killed him in the Citadel last month. Fighting for my honor, that sort of thing. Saved my life actually."

"Dead?" Addie could scarcely believe it. She raised her hands into the air above her head and clapped them joyously. She quickly sobered. "What are you and Stefan to do?"

"What are you and Pons to do?" Anna asked, wishing to shift the conversation away from herself for a while.

"Oh, yes, well we are lovers, you know," Addie confessed, blushing, feeling that she could confidently confide in Anna. The princess nodded her head knowingly. "We are lovers, and we hope that tomorrow or the next day we will say prayers in the Church of the Holy Sepulcher and then I don't know. We would like to go back to Provence. We'll stay here and earn enough money to go back."

"You'll get married?" Anna asked.

"Yes, I think so, but we are not sure when. Sooner than later I hope, though, because the priests already suspect, and the Church disapproves you know. And if they catch us they'll march us through the camp naked. Anything that goes wrong, you know, they blame it on the women in the camp. Adhemar especially.

Every time a horse was taken, or a soldier fell, the women were moved outside the camp and segregated from the others ... Adhemar could be fair, though," she said, thinking about her trial against Bohemund. "Pons is a good man, and I do love him. When Guy died, we became closer. I liked him terribly much before Guy died, but with the two of them, I guess I didn't let myself become too attached to Pons."

"I wish I could stay unattached like that," said Anna, "but the heart makes a bond of love and won't release you even when you want to be released. Of all jailers, love is the worst or the best because it holds you in obedience to your will or against your will. Love is so arrogant; it thinks it knows what is best for you. So here I am, in love with a knight who is already married and who cannot get a divorce and whom I cannot possibly marry! What am I to do?"

Addie felt sympathy for this new friend of hers. "Love him," she said. "You don't need an excuse to love someone, you know."

✠✠✠

"What's the situation now, Eustace?" Godfrey, Stefan and his men had forsaken both the *coenaculum* superior and the *coenaculum* medium and were awaiting in the evening shadows the outcome regarding the battering ram. "We can't dislodge it, sire, nor can we set it on fire. There's nothing that can be done about the battering ram. It is going to stay where we put it!"

Godfrey cursed and whirled about in thought, arms flailing the air in frustration.

"Lieutenant," said Stefan, "how much clearance is there on either side of the tower?"

"Clearance?"

"Room to move the tower," Stefan said impatiently. "How far can the tower be moved to the side, either side?"

"Six to eight feet on either side, my lord," replied Eustace. "You've seen it yourself."

Stefan ignored that impertinence. "And the tower is about twenty feet wide, correct? The youthful paladin nodded. "Then it must be widened tonight," he exclaimed. "We must be able to move the tower into position against the walls of the city tomorrow morning. We can do it if we build up a runway beside the ram so we can skirt it with the tower."

"But my lord—"

"—No arguments now," Godfrey interrupted. "There is no other way, unless you have one to suggest." Eustace shook his head. "Then gather a corp of the finest, able-bodied men who are rested and those who aren't, have archers and catapults standing by lest the Moslems harass them from the walls."

✠✠✠

Rome

The Holy Pontiff's condition worsened. The pallor of his face scarcely contrasted with the pure, white linen of the pillow cases and sheets upon his bed. His portly frame had shriveled and now lay lightly on a pallet of warm blankets and sweaty covers. Black-robed monks and imperious-minded archbishops and cardinals hovered ceremoniously about him in small covens of whistling conversations. Gregorian monks had arrived and would intone a dirge or two from the psalter, while the smoke of scented candles floated listlessly to the ceiling and the crucified Christ, looking down from his place at the twelfth station of the cross said, "Father, forgive them, for they know not what they do."

✠✠✠

July 15

Ere dawn appeared in the eastern sky, heralds blasted the sleeping out of their sleep. Stefan could see that the enemy had built a wooden curtain wall upon the wall itself opposite the tower but to each side, so that with its protection, they could continue to send flaming arrows and hurl Greek fire and other projectiles. Moreover, the curtain wall would make it difficult for the crusaders to ascend the walls and access would have to take place where the tower would meet the wall. Godfrey summoned Robert of Normandy and Tancred to take up positions on either side of the wall and to bombard the curtain wall with flaming arrows.

As this new construction faced a barrage of crusader arrows, Godfrey and Stefan ordered the tower to be moved to the wall itself on the new ramp that the midnight workers had prepared. The battering ram was still stuck in the stone wall like the quill of a porcupine. Soldiers repaired to the interior of the siege tower once again to prepare for the final assault. Stefan climbed atop the roof with a squadron of archers and foot soldiers and not a moment too soon, because he heard the characteristic whoooosh of a mangonel and the whipping sound of rope being released. Almost instantaneously, a coil of rope landed on the roof and was immediately retrieved by enemy soldiers in the hope that it would snag a pier, beam or scaffolding, allowing them to winch the tower over on its side. This time the rope slid harmlessly away.

"Be ready with those scythes, men," Stefan reminded them. The soldiers had attached scythes to strong beams by which they would, if necessary, sever the thick ropes that the Moslems were using.

The walls themselves had suffered serious damage. Gaping cavities in the walls were visible. Of course, the walls were so thick that penetration of their thickness was impossible. But it was possible to place beams from the tower into these cavities. But Iftikhar had another idea.

Stefan heard the sound of the mangonel again, but this time it was a rope being shot through the air. Iftikhar had bound faggots of wood and straw together with iron chains and cast them into the air toward the tower. Amid the smoke from smoldering curtain walls, and flaming sacks and hawsets, Stefan could see that the projectile was going to hit its mark.

"Run for cover," he cried, as the archers looked up and saw a flaming beam soaked in oil and pitch twisting horribly in the air toward them. It landed among them pinning several to the roof and splintering its oil-soaked and flaming contents across the entire area of the roof. Stefan shielded his eyes, and shook his hand vigorously to throw off sparks.

Aha, Stefan thought, if you think you have outdone us now, you are mistaken. He had heard the cheers of his counterparts on the walls. "Roll out the vinegar," he cried. He had learned from local Christians to use vinegar instead of water to put out such fires. Quickly he distributed vessels in which to carry vinegar and when they had spread it about the roof the fires slowly disappeared.

This crisis passed, the fighting continued between archers on the walls sighting Christians and dropping them with a single shot, and Christians pulling relentlessly closer to the wall. The tower creaked and groaned as every foot gained brought the crusaders closer to the moment when the walls would be scaled and a drawbridge dropped to the summit of the ramparts.

✠✠✠

Rome

They had prepared a small table in this large room. It was covered with a white cloth and placed near the sickbed so as to be within the sight of the pope, but the pope was not seeing. Nevertheless, a cross and two lighted candles were placed on the table, as well as a small vessel containing holy water and a sprinkler. Beside the holy water rested a dish with bread, and another dish with soft cotton cloths. Near the table lay a basin, water and towel so that the priest could wash his hands.

A simple parish priest had been selected to administer last rites. Attired grimly, and wearing the solemn expression of gloom, he approached the bedside of the pope. Crossing himself, he said:

Oremus. Introeat, Domine Jesu Christe, domum hanc sub nostrae humilitatis ingressu, aeterna felicitas divina prosperitas, serena laetitia, caritas fructuosa, sanitas sempiterna: effugiat ex hoc loco accessus daemonum: adsint Angeli pacis, domumque hanc deserat omnis maligna discordia. Magnifica, Domine, super nos nomen sanctum tuum; et bene (crosses himself) dic nostrae conversationi: sanctifica nostrae humilitatis ingressum, qui sanctus et qui pius es, et permanes cum Patre et Spiritu Sancto in saecula saeculorum. Amen.

The monks thereupon began to chant: *Oremus. Et deprecemur Dominum nostrum Jesum Christum, ut benedicendo bene dicat hoc tabernaculum, et omnes habitantes in eo …*

But the pope slept.

✠✠✠

At about the ninth hour when the men had been fighting for about five hours, two important changes occurred. First, the curtain wall was now completely engulfed in flames and the smoke was as thick as blood along the parapets. This had the effect of forcing the defenders either to drop back on the wide walls because of the flames and heat or to retreat laterally on either side until out of danger. Second, two men on the *coenaculum* medium nearest the wall, Ludolph and Engelbert of Tournai, seeing an opportunity to reach the ramparts, with the help of their countrymen, thrust rough-hewn beams into two cavities of the damaged wall. While archers rained a hailstorm of arrows from the roof of the siege tower upon the enemy above, the two Franks sallied across the beams toward the wall with scaling ladders in their calloused hands. Ludolph slipped and fell upon the beam as one would fall into a saddle, but he quickly regained his position and with Engelbert established a foothold in the crumbling stone of the ancient wall. Moments later, they were able to attach the ladders to the battlements by which they then scaled the remaining distance to the top.

At this precise instant, the drawbridge was lowered from the *coenaculum* superior and Godfrey and hundreds of his men stormed across the planking into the smoke-filled breach upon the ramparts, swords drawn and screaming "Deus vult!" with heart-stopping ferocity. Seeing this brave effort, Stefan ordered the archers to increase their assault on the defenders who were only six spear lengths away from them. The soldiers climbed up the stairs from the ground floor to the *coenaculum* medium and upward to the *coenaculum* superior, across the drawbridge, on to the battlements and down the inner stairs of the Jerusalem walls to the streets of the city, while within the hour, thousands of others used scaling ladders that had been hastily let down as the defenders fled for their lives.

Stefan remained on the siege tower until the enemy had fled and the tower had been emptied of its soldierly inhabitants. He, too, then raced across the drawbridge to the city walls, with Fortissimus drawn and at the ready. Foot soldiers and knights streamed by him as he stood atop the burning walls of Jerusalem, his fair beard matted with perspiration and soot. Moslem bodies lay everywhere: propped in life-like positions against the interior walls, slumped in death in a far corner, fallen in somersaults down the stone, weather-beaten stairs, hanging pitifully over the battlements, or strewn like shredded sacks of grain across the pavement. Stefan looked wildly about him and then with a whoop dashed down the blood-stained stairs to Jerusalem. But ere he reached the bottom, a Moslem, assumed to be lifeless, felt a quickening in the arm and feebly raised his sword upon which the unsuspecting Stefan rushed, receiving a wound in his belly. The prince of knights, the count of Chartres and Blois, clutched his wound and fell to one knee in anguished surprise. His hand relaxed and Fortissimus clattered to the pavement. Stefan collapsed upon the body of his enemy. *Terra Sancta, Urbs Sancti.*

✠✠✠

Rome

The monks sang: *Exaudi nos, Domine sancte, Pater omnipotens, aeterne Deus: et mittere digneris sanctum Angelum tuum de caelis, qui custodiat, foveat, protegat, visitet atque defendat omnes habitantes in hoc habitaculo. Per Christum Dominum nostrum. Amen.*

✠✠✠

Pons had never been in a battle like this before, ever, in his life. Thousands of Provencals were in ranks behind the siege engine, hundreds within the tower itself, and hundreds more were laboring beneath the walls, many being killed by stones and fire from the ramparts above. The southern wall was unyielding. The tower itself was near the wall, but the catapults and the fire from the enemy had virtually destroyed the upper section of the tower Pons had labored so hard to build. The timber was hot and smoldering. Burning ash and embers lay upon fresh timber and only by constant vigilance was the siege tower saved from further damage.

Still, they were unable to bring the tower closer to the wall even though they had moved the siege engine to another section of the wall. *What would Addie say to me now?* Pons wondered. *There must be something that we can do short of quitting the battle altogether.* Pons realized that as grim as their posture was at the present time, it wasn't hopeless: even if a retreat was sounded, the capture of the city was inevitable. *Wasn't it?*

The tower needed to be repaired. He told Raymond so. "The tower will not survive the rest of the morning or the day, my lord, without repairs," he said to the grunting, older knight who had journeyed down the interior stairs to the ground floor where Pons was directing the men who were moving the tower.

"How long and how much?" he asked the youthful engineer.

"The important thing, sire, is to remove the tower out of range."

They were interrupted by a disturbance to the east. They heard a blast on the horn and the sound of riders. Stepping quickly from the tower into the open air, they saw three horsemen approaching at full gallop shouting what at first sounded like incomprehensible ravings. As the riders drew nearer, Pons and Raymond exchanged glances of puzzlement when they recognized the battle cry "Deus vult!"

The horsemen soon were upon them while thousands of foot soldiers waited impatiently in the Hinnom Valley. "Count Raymond," they cried, panting, and not bothering to dismount or approach the count with proper respect. "We are knights with Duke Godfrey de Boullion sent to give you the glad tidings that the men of Godfrey, Robert of Normandy, Robert of Flanders, Stefan of Chartres, and Tancred are within the city! The city is ours!"

Pons and Raymond dropped their hands in utter astonishment as though life had suddenly seeped out of their bodies. The worry etched in the furrows of their chiseled faces vanished like clouds on a windy day and smiles appeared like the sun rising over Olivet. Defeat had been snatched away by this unlikely but welcome news. They clasped each other in a vigorous embrace "When did this happen, my friend?" the count asked.

"Only a scant hour ago," replied one of the knights. "Look to the walls," he cried. "The Saracen is gone!" It was true. They had disappeared. Pons was awestruck; the incredible had happened.

"Pons, your horse," said Raymond. "Bring our horses!" he shouted. Two lads appeared quickly with chesnut palfreys and Pons and Raymond mounted with other knights. Raymond reared high on his charger and shouted to his men:

"To the walls!" Then he dashed toward the towering fortress with Pons and the army in pursuit, soon crowding Zion Gate, a swelling tide of human emotion. Already, the men were chanting, "Toulouse, Toulouse," as they pressed against the ancient city. Pons glanced east along the wall to the smoking tower that now stood empty and alone, like an old soldier frozen in immortality, an abandoned wooden obelisk that would burn and crumble and be forgotten. Foot soldiers bearing the banners of the crusader cross were clinging to and climbing the walls like squirrels as though they had been doing it all their lives. Zion Gate would open momentarily; inevitably, it seemed. When it did, thousands of eager, blood-thirsty Christians streamed like a flood through the streets of Jerusalem with revenge on their minds and lust in their hearts.

✠✠✠

Rome

Then the priest said: "I confess to almighty God, to the blessed Virgin Mary, to blessed Michael the Archangel, to blessed John the Baptist, to the holy apostles Peter and Paul, to all the saints and to you, Father, that I have sinned exceedingly in thought, word, and deed; *mea culpa, mea culpa, mea maxima culpa.* Therefore I beseech blessed Mary ever Virgin, blessed Michael the Archangel, blessed John the Baptist, the holy apostles Peter and Paul, all the saints, and you, Father, to pray to the Lord our God for me."

Then the priest said: "May almighty God have mercy on you, forgive you your sins, and bring you to life everlasting." *Indulgentiam, absolutionem (crosses himself) et remissionem peccatorum tuorum tribuat tibi omnipotens et misericors Dominus. Amen.*

✠✠✠

I closed the pages of the Gesta, *and my own* History, *and looked wearily into the somber eyes of the monk from Clairvaux. "The slaughter was incredible," I said. "The crusaders, starved and humbled for so long, fell unrestrained upon the inhabitants of the city. Except for Iftikhar and his family, who made a special arrangement for their safety, not a single living soul, man, woman or child, survived. The innocent perished that day for no reason but that they had the misfortune to live in Jerusalem, their blood splattered like ritual sacrifices upon the white walls of their homes and mosques. Thousands fled but Tancred led a procession of knights and foot soldiers, beheaded them all and sliced their bodies open for the sheer terror of it. I tell you, if you had been in the mosque, the blood would have been at your ankles—such was the misery. Horses cantered through the streets stumbling upon human flesh and bones. Cries of mothers for their children went unheeded as swords opened their tender bellies. I have never heard of such fanaticism before, nor have I since, nor do I ever hope to again."*

✠✠✠

A choir of novices and boy sopranos sang the Kyrie Eleison:
    Kyrie eleison, Kyrie eleison,
    Kyrie eleison, Christe eleison.

The priest said the *Pater Noster. Pater noster, qui est caelim, sanctificatur nomen tuum … Et ne nos inducas in temptationem sed libera nos a malo.*
And then, while the blood flowed, the pope died.

"Not a single living soul, man, woman or child, survived. The innocent perished that day for no reason but that they had the misfortune to live in Jerusalem, their blood splattered like ritual sacrifices upon the white walls of their homes and mosques. Thousands fled, but Tancred led a procession of knights and foot soldiers, beheaded them all, and sliced their bodies open for the sheer terror of it. I tell you, if you had been in the mosque, the blood would have been at your ankles—such was the misery" (p. 555).

CHAPTER FORTY-ONE

Stefan Says His Vows

July 16, 1099 A.D.

"OME ON, NOW," SAID PONS. "I'm taking you into the city."

Addie, ignoring Pons, turned to Clare. "You stay with sister Hildy until we get back." Her daughter was already running away from the camp joyfully. "When will that be?" she called back.

Addie cupped her hand to her mouth and called out: "I don't know, but stay with sister Hildy until we're back. We'll find you, Clare, don't worry," she yelled again, but the golden-haired child was beyond hearing.

Hildy turned to follow her, but said before she left: "So the Christians have the city?" Addie and Pons, who were about to leave, hesitated, tripped in their path by the steely edge in Hildy's voice. They nodded, staring at her.

"And they claim the right to do this because it was their city before the Moslems'?" They nodded again. Addie noted that Hildy was not accusing them of being Christians.

"But it was our city, a city of the Jews before it was a city of Christians, and before that, a city of Ephraim; and before that, of

Canaan. This city can't belong to anyone, it belongs to the world! It is Jeru-*shalom*, a city of peace, not of death." She ran away from them crying.

Addie and Pons stood together in stunned silence as though someone had pounded them into a stupor with a mallet. Then Addie burst after her in a frenzied dash and swung her around. "What's the matter?" she cried. Hildy's face was flushed and damp. "You're my sister," Addie complained, pleading with her.

Hildy nodded and wiped her eyes. "You've been good to me," she said. They embraced. "And Peter ... he loved me ... but I've never witnessed a religion as harsh and cruel as ... as ... yours. Brooks no disagreement, no differences. Uniformity ... conformity at all costs, even in lands far away from your home. All or nothing, bend the knee or lose your head ... Today I know that mothers shall weep just as you have wept for Lettie, wives will weep for their husbands as I have wept for Peter. Jerusalem will weep for its children, but the children will die ... it's the children who always suffer and die. And for what? In God's name, for what?" Addie was crying now too. Pons approached them both and wrapped them in his arms. They sank to the earth and sobbed for those who had fallen as victims of another's god.

✠✠✠

The non-combatant pilgrims were streaming toward the city, shouting, cheering and jeering. "Jerusalem!" shouted a doddering old man to Pons and Addie as they passed him on the road. He was dressed in a simple cloak and trousers, but had a sword in a belt around his waist. He intended to use it.

"I'm going to kill one of those bastards," he crowed. Addie shuddered.

"There's no need to kill now, Christian," said Pons.

"Oh yes there is!" he cried, pulling his short sword out of its sheath and waving it in the air. "I didn't travel from Brittany to Macedonia to Anatolia to Jerusalem just to say my prayers." He laughed heartily. "I hear there's still a lot of infidels alive in the city, and I intend to find me one before the sun sets."

"You should say your prayers first," Addie reproved.

"What's the matter with you?" the old man asked. "They're going to hell anyway; might as well be now than later, I say."

"A dead man can't repent of his sins, friend," Pons said spurring his horse, Pilgrim. "God will take him when the time is right." They rode away leaving a billow of dust in their wake. Addie hugged Pons. "That man surely is no better a man than the one he's going to kill," she said to Pons. But Pons was silent.

As they passed through the Zion Gate, the crowd thickened. Horses jostled pedestrians as the mob moved through the massive gate and into the ancient city. Addie's nose quivered. There was a sweet, sickening scent that she recognized as decaying flesh. And then she started to see them. Corpses of soldiers lying headlong on the stairs of the interior walls or narrow streets. Their eyes protruded ghastly, mouths agape as though gasping still for a final breath; arms, legs and heads were sometimes severed. More than once, Addie saw horrific sights she wished not to see, and had to avert her gaze lest the horror be permanently impressed on her mind.

The two riders moved further into the city. The Christians had spread throughout the town and were hunting infidels like rabid dogs and slaying them upon sight. The fighting of the day before destroyed the army of Iftikhar, but the innocent population had been less affected. Now they were being slaughtered indiscriminately.

Pons lifted his arm and pointed. "Over there," he said. Addie saw three soldiers accosting an old, white-bearded man, and running him through with a sword. He fell wordlessly against the wall of his home clutching his abdomen. The soldiers entered the low door of the white-washed brick house and soon they heard screams from within. The family, the rest of the family. Addie bowed her head.

"Pons," she said, "I don't want to see any more of this. Can't we go home?" Pons nodded. They would go up this street, they

decided, and try to cut back through an adjacent street and go back
to Zion Gate. Their decision to leave did not spare them the sight
of further horrors, however. The Franks were a people out of
control. Their actions were precisely those they had ascribed to the
Saracens in countless conversations around campfires and over a
mug of ale and beer. They gave no quarter, and as they had
described the infidel as merciless, they, too, showed no mercy; they
had spoken of the infidels' thirst for blood, theirs, too, could not be
satiated; they had spoken of the awful atrocities perpetrated upon
children, they, too, on this day slaughtered children and babies;
they had told of the Saracen's ill treatment of women, and they,
too, spared no woman. Addie was ashamed and realized in a way
she hadn't before that religion didn't make anyone anywhere any
better than anyone else. And that being the case, she understood
with a shudder, it was possible for a Moslem, or a Jew to be as
good as anyone else. It was not religion that made her heart bleed
for these who were dying. It was a simple sense of decency, and
there was no greater obstacle to decency than religion.

"That's why the pope concocted this whole idea," Pons said, as
though he could read her mind. "Christians were killing Christians
in France, and he couldn't stop them from doing that short of
expelling them from the country and telling them to take their
killing elsewhere."

"Oh, Pons," Addie cried leaning her head against his back and
closing her eyes, "I think I have lost my faith. My faith, my faith,
my faith. My faith in humanity, my faith in God, Oh, Pons, this is
so terrible."

And it was terrible. From the moment they had passed through
Zion Gate, her ears had been filled with either the sounds of joy at
revenge fulfilled, or cries of terror as death visited household upon
household. Neither Addie nor Pons wished to see another body,
another severed head, or hear another cry, but as long as they were
within the city, such a prayer could not be answered.

They moved Pilgrim quickly now. The narrow, stone streets
were not so crowded here, but would no doubt thicken with

gawkers as they approached the walls. The moment they turned the corner, however, they spied two soldiers, swords drawn, pounding on the wooden door of a house. The door had evidently been bolted from the inside by the fearful inhabitants, and even now, Pons and Addie could see it giving as the hardy warriors put their shoulders against it.

Pons reined Pilgrim to a stop. The door began to give. "Stop them, Pons," Addie implored. But Pons was thinking the same thing. Addie dismounted quickly, and as Pons jumped from the horse, the doors went crashing down. With a whoop, the soldiers rushed in.

Pons withdrew his sword and ran to the doorway while Addie followed. At the door, he peered in. The room had a low-beamed ceiling, wooden floor, a fireplace and cooking hearth against one wall and a small table with chairs. It was already too late for an old woman who had been slashed with a sword, but was still breathing. She wouldn't breathe long, Pons thought.

Three other inhabitants remained alive, a young Saracen against whom the two were now fighting, and a young woman, probably his wife, and a baby. The Moslem was fighting bravely but was already wounded, and Pons knew he was doomed. They had no sooner thrown the infidel like trash into the corner, than the short one hefted the baby in the air holding it by its feet. The other brandished a dagger. His intention was obvious.

"Pons!" Addie screamed when she fathomed their purpose. At the sound of her shriek, the soldiers whirled about to see Pons towering in the doorway, Addie behind him.

"Don't harm the baby," Pons said. The soldiers, nonplussed, stood immobile for seconds, taking the measure of the man before them. One was stocky, with wide arms and hands seemingly without wrists and a bearded face below wide, wild eyes. The other, taller, was a man of moderate looking strength, low cheekbones that gave his head an elongated appearance and slightly stultifying look. The baby was still screaming, and its face was reddening as the short one continued to hold it upside-down.

"Give the baby back to its mother, and then leave," Pons said.

"And who's askin'?" the tall one sneered.

"Doesn't matter," said Pons, "do it." He took a step toward the men with his sword drawn. The soldiers were quiet again, clearly pondering their chances against this interloper. Addie sighed in relief as the Tall One turned away slightly as he tucked his dagger away. But when he faced Pons again, he withdrew his sword and squared off against Pons.

"I don't know who you are," he snarled, "but if you don't leave, the baby's dead."

"Wrong," said Pons, determined to see this through, "if you don't leave, one of you if not both of you is dead. I don't think you're the type to risk your lives for a baby because if any harm comes to either the baby or the young woman I will kill you both, and with pleasure."

He had spat the words out quickly, but he meant every word. They would stay or leave on his terms. Addie put her fist to her mouth and bit down nervously. There was death in this room and there would be more death in the next few minutes. An old woman dead, and a young man still breathing, but dying. Now Pons was risking his life for people he didn't know and for Saracens at that! He was in danger of dying at the hands of a Christian while defending infidels. *O God, O God, how tangled these affairs become! My mind is heavy with too much thinking!*

The Christian lunged toward Pons and their swords clashed quickly. The short one continued to hold the baby who was hollering as frightfully as before. Pons felt the muscles tighten and flex in his arm as his sword sliced through the air. He clenched his jaw and summoned long dormant strength, dormant only because it had not been in combat, but strong by reason of the daily labor he had contributed over the past weeks for Raymond.

Pons pushed him back firmly and with such ease, that it was clear even to Addie that her man would have the better of this fight. She could see that this truth was also beginning to dawn in the eyes of his foe. She sensed that he would make some sort of offer to quit the fight and retreat, and she began to believe that further blood would not be shed after all. Pons would not kill this man unless he left him with no choice but to do so. Indeed, Pons, knees bent and advancing relentless inches at a time, held the advantage. Suddenly, the tall one's sword went crashing to the floor after Pons delivered a crushing blow to the arm. In an instant, Pons had positioned the point of his saber at the throat of his enemy.

Pons was about to ease the rapier away from his throat, when he heard a thwack! The tall one's eyes widened silently and to Pons' utter astonishment, he moved forward slightly and then fell firmly upon Pons' sword, its tip sinking softly into the throat and disgorging a torrent of blood. Pons, bewildered by this, stepped aside and let the body fall off his sword. As it did, the tall one fell to the blood-stained wooden floor. A jewel-studded dagger protruded from his back, sunk cleanly to the engraved hilt.

"Holy Mary, Mother of Jesus!" murmured the short one. Pons looked about and saw the young Saracen's hand fall to the floor limply. It was the hand that had grasped the dagger firmly in the uncommon strength of a dying man, and had hurled it upon the enemy. He had died seeing the salvation of his child and the woman.

"It's time for you to go, isn't it?" said Pons to the Short One. He nodded. "The baby," Pons said, pointing with his sword to the young woman. The soldier placed the baby in the lap of the woman, and then straightened up and walked carefully around Pons and quit the room and the house.

The woman had taken her child in the folds of her skirt and pressed it close to her breast. She was hunkered down in a corner, her head covered by the Moslem *quitikar*, a shawl, and she rocked back and forth clutching her baby. Addie, who had stepped inside when the Short One left, stood with Pons watching mutely. Addie understood the human tragedy here. Indeed, she understood it so well, she wanted to leave. She tugged at Pons' sleeve. Craving the embrace of her little Clare, she wanted now to get back to her own child.

"Pons, let's go," she begged. She tugged at his blouse as he stood woodenly still observing the pathetic scene. "Come on, let's go," she whispered.

They turned to leave, but when they reached the door, they heard the woman begin to sing softly but in clear, flowing tones, like spring water seeping forth across the parched earth.

Chaterai por mon corage que je vueill reconforter,
Car avec mon grant damage ne vueill morir n'afoler.

Addie froze as though all the blood in her veins had turned to ice. Her chest tightened and she couldn't breathe. She put her hand to her throat. The somber timbre of that dulcet voice brought to her breathless heart the recognition of a voice long stilled. She whirled about to look at the woman huddled in the corner singing.

Quant de le terre sauvage—

"Lettie?" She whispered in a barely audible voice, taking a step closer to the girl. She put her hand to her mouth as though to utter those words after three years of grief was a futile gesture that would lead only to more suffering.

—ne voi nului retorner.

The sounds were French, Provencal, here in this room in Jerusalem thousands of miles removed from the hills and valleys of homeland. Addie squinted, peering intensely at the woman. The girl had stopped rocking, still clutching her child. Then she turned her face toward the visitors in the room. The shadows in the dim light obscured a clear recognition of the girl from Addie. But then the young woman began rock her baby and to sing again.

Ou cil est qui m'assoage le cuer, quant j'en oi parler.

Addie hesitated. *I will sing to comfort my heart, for in spite of my great misery I do not wish to die, and yet I see no one return from that savage land, where he has gone who quiets my heart when I hear news of him.*

"Lettie?" Addie rushed forward and flung herself on her knees before the girl. Grabbing the girl by the shoulders, she twisted her face into the light. There she saw a girl whose mature face belied the tender years she had lived. The eyes were Provencal blue. The nose still retained its familiar cast and her countenance evoked the murky Basque ancestry Addie herself shared. *The Lord giveth, the Lord taketh away, the Lord giveth again.*

"LETTIE! Oh, my Lettie!" she cried, throwing her arms about her, and pulling herself closely. The girl gasped for breath in the embrace and pushed away. "Do you remember me, Lettie?" Addie asked, weeping.

Deep calleth unto deep. The flood waters recede, and the dove floats on the cool breeze with the olive branch in its beak. The sky breaks and the blue pierces like a knife through the gray crust, and sunlight sweeps the earth. Flashes of the Civetot return. The image of horsemen, women screaming, a child crying, of her sister reaching out toward her. She can feel sand grinding into her scalp, feel the flesh of the man she mauls, and the jarring crunch of the horse as it carries her away. More impressions. A new tongue, unfamiliar faces, mysterious rituals—holding her child in one arm, she extended her hand to touch Addie.

"Addie," she said in a parched voice. "Is it truly, truly you?"

Addie threw up her arms and shrieked for joy and turned for an instant to Pons who was observing with astonishment. Lettie arose slowly and handed the child to Addie. "This is your nephew," she said quietly. She went to the dead youth across the room and knelt carefully beside him and put her head on his chest near the fatal wound. She began to sob.

"We're going to need another horse," Addie said to Pons, wiping her watery eyes.

"I'll get one," Pons said. "I'll be right back."

Addie dropped to the floor beside her sister, laid the child on the floor beside her, and put her arms around her sister. "Your husband?"

Lettie moved. She touched his hair, laid his hand across the abdomen, closed his eyes, and kissed his forehead. The sisters sat beside the body. "My husband," she said, brushing her wet hair away from her face. The sisters sat facing each other beside the body. "He's the one who took me away from you," she said, looking down upon him. "But he did not mistreat me. Ever. Even then."

They were silent for a few moments. Addie searched Lettie's face for understanding. "You married him?"

Lettie began to cry uncontrollably while Addie realized that these tears represented the pent-up emotions of three years of courage, faith, and the strength to seek her own way. "I never thought I would see any of you again," Lettie sobbed. The sound of her words were almost unrecognizable in her grief. "I never thought I would see Provence again. Nothing ever again. He was very gentle with me, everyone was and later he said he was sorry for taking me from my people but he couldn't take me back. It was too dangerous."

"You loved him?"

"Yes."

"Could you have left him?"

Tears began to fall again, like a soft autumn rain. "I don't know Addie. I began to understand some things I hadn't understood before. I had a new life, a man who loved me, and a child to take care of." She put her head down and rubbed her temples. "I just don't know."

They sat in silence for a few moments. Then Addie said:

"Peter's gone."

"Gone?"

Addie nodded. Her eyes reddened again. "How?" Lettie asked. "The Turks?"

"The Church."

"The Church?" Addie nodded, putting her hand to her mouth to stifle her emotions. Then she picked up the child and cradled him carefully. "And the baby?" she asked.

"Yaddie, we've called him," Lettie said, "but maybe I'll call him Peter, what do you think?"

"I think Peter's wonderful," said Addie, smiling, pulling back the cloth from his face so she could see him. "Oh, Lettie, it's so good to see you again. You must see Clare, how she's grown."

Suddenly, Lettie's countenance darkened, her eyes narrowed. "The money," she hissed. "We've got to get the money!"

At that moment, Pons walked in. "Horses waiting outside," he announced.

"You don't remember Pons, probably, but he saved our lives in the burning church, remember?"

Lettie nodded. "There was another one—"

"That's another story," Addie interrupted. She motioned for Pons to join them on the floor in their conference. "Now what about the money?"

"The money. We were rich, my husband's family was wealthy. He was a nephew to the Caliph, and when we came to Jerusalem because we knew the crusaders were coming here, we brought money, and when the city was collapsing we donned these disguises and moved to the common quarters because we thought the Crusaders would not destroy the common population but just the army, the soldiers!" Her face brightened at the thought that perhaps in this tragedy she would be able to bring some good news. "We have money!" she said hopefully, through her tears.

✠✠✠

Chartres

Adela threw open the shutters of the bedroom and looked out upon the vast expanse of lawn and woods beyond. The day in the early light was gray and unseasonably brisk for a July morning. The undulating hills clasped pillows of fog to its wooded bosom. The scent of rain was in the air. Adela placed her hands on her stomach and stared through the window of her castle chamber at the pastoral scene. Her thoughts drifted lazily to a knight in a far off country, a knight whom she felt intuitively she would never see again, but a knight who was brave, honest and true, and who was fighting with courage and inspiration.

She turned away from the light. The interior of the bedroom seemed dreary, but then her life seemed bleak. No, not bleak, she thought, just difficult. She didn't feel well, and hadn't for several days. She had stayed in bed and would continue to stay in bed until she felt better. She sat on the edge of her canopied bed, and took a deep breath, and sighed. Then, lifting her legs on the bed, she pushed herself to its center, laid her arms now beside her, and rested. Soon she slept.

✠✠✠

They left with little Peter and Lettie riding behind Pons. Addie mounted the fresh horse with renewed alacrity. They rode through the city again. It was shortly after noon, and the sun seemed to hang interminably above them, baking their skin until it was warm to the touch and making breathing unpleasant. Perspiration soon soaked their clothes. The hooves of the horses clattered upon the stone pavement, and Addie noticed above the staccato that she no longer heard cries of distress as she had earlier. The slaughter was complete. The dead are dead and the living are living; those who wished to die have probably had their wish granted. Soldiers were still on the prowl looting houses and bodies of their valuables.

Lettie directed the way. Soon they were in the southeast quarter of the city, not far from the Dome of the Rock. They pulled up quickly before an ancient, stone arch. Dismounting, they passed through the arch and proceeded along a colonnade until Lettie steered them left. Soon they were at the head of a long, weather-beaten stairwell leading scores of feet below the earth. It descended in a series of thirty steps and then turned, and turned again, twisting deeper into darkness. Pons grabbed a torch from a rack at the entrance, and they started down, slowly at first, but then picking up the pace, they fairly raced down the steps until they reached a tunnel.

"Hezekiah's Tunnel," Lettie murmured, as they huddled close, peering into the vast emptiness of the horizontal shaft before them.

"I don't like this one bit," Addie complained, shivering. They were far from the heat of the sun now. Addie touched the tunnel wall. It was damp with an edge of sliminess. She recoiled with a grimace.

"It doesn't get better," Lettie said laughing. She looked back and upward. They had made so many turns in their descent that there was no light from the entrance above them. She hopped down the final step and turned. "Come on," she said eagerly and she started out into the darkness.

The intrepid trio, not counting the child strapped to Lettie's back, began their trek through the stone-hewn tunnel. Pons could feel nicks and cuts in the rock as he touched them, balancing for support. They walked through a small stream of water that barely flowed now; standing water collected in uneven puddles here and there. The sound of their feet sloshing through the water echoed in eerie tones, and, when they talked, the tunnel amplified their voices but without an echo.

"Hello?" Lettie called.

"Ssshhh!" Addie admonished, "You might wake up—the RATS!" She shrieked as one of the demons scurried past her. "Rats, I don't like rats. And there's another one!"

"Leave them alone," Pons said, hoping to instill bravery into her. "They won't bother you."

"I forgot to tell you about the rats," Lettie confessed.

"What else did you forget to tell us about?" Addie asked fearfully, pushing ahead nonetheless, but following Pons now.

"That I have no idea how we're going to get these jewels and coins out of here!"

"Pons?"

"We take what we can in these aprons," Pons replied, "and what we can't retrieve, which sounds like it could he considerable, Count Raymond will guarantee."

"He will?" Lettie asked unbelieving.

"Sure," said Pons confidently. "Why not?"

"Why should he?"

"Count Raymond hired Pons to build the siege tower," Addie explained, still trying to spot rats and avoid them. Her feet were cold. "He trusts and respects Pons. I agree, the count will help if he can."

They now were moving in a beam of torchlight about twenty feet long that traveled with them as they traversed the tunnel, darkness before and behind them and they at the center. Soon Lettie motioned for stillness and they stopped. The shaft seemed to veer and Lettie touched the walls looking for something.

"Hold the light higher," she urged.

Pons raised the light not sure what Lettie was searching for.

"Ah," Lettie murmured, "There it is." She pointed above her to faint writing in the rock. There were a series of the figure seven etched in the stone. "The seven sevens of the Apocalypse," she said. "Help me," and she began to run her fingers along the cut in the rock. Within moments, there was a snap, and the sound of a latch releasing and the wall of the tunnel seemed to give way.

"Push with me," Lettie said. Pons pushed where Lettie indicated, and the wall moved away like a door and they stepped through to a small landing at the top of another staircase leading further into the bowels of the earth.

"More stairs," Addie groaned. "I'm not looking forward to the return trip."

"Nor I," said Lettie. "It's a long one. Forty-nine stairs here though."

Pons noticed the stairwell was lit with torches. "Who lights the torches?" he asked curiously.

"I don't know," Lettie said. "Makes it easier for us though, huh?"

They rushed down the stairs after adjusting the sling in which Peter was being carried. He was making the journey on Lettie's back with admirable ease.

"Do you want me to carry Peter for you?" Addie asked.

"No, no," said Iettie, "he's fine for now and he's not heavy."

"Why the Seven Sevens?" Pons asked.

"The seven seals, the seven bowls, the seven trumpets, the seven angels, the seven churches," Lettie responded, "I don't remember them all. They're there though."

They traveled down the stairs of the Seven Sevens in silence and were soon at the base of the stairs that dropped them in the middle of another shaft. Lettie directed them left. The bottom was rocky and their feet began to feel the pain after being softened by the continual grinding of the stones. They were tiring, but Lettie urged them forward until they saw a brighter light ahead of them. As they walked closer, the tunnel widened and soon they were close to a large arch that opened to a small cavern bathed in brilliant light. They were standing at the top of a short flight of stairs.

"Twelve Steps of the Apostles," Lettie announced. As they descended the steps their eyes focused on the central feature of the cavern, a beautiful fountain of onyx and alabaster about eight feet in height and three feet in diameter. It was perfectly proportioned and carved and molded in the Roman style. It glistened and gave off the appearance of sparkling radiance.

"The Virgin's Fount," Addie whispered in awe.

"That's right," Lettie exclaimed. "How did you know?"

"A priest told us about the legend," she said.

"There's no water in the fountain," Pons observed.

"Only once a day," Lettie said. "At least that's what the emirs have told me. No one has ever seen it work and lived to tell about it."

"Why not?" Pons asked.

"Because it works only when there is enough water pressure, and when there is enough water pressure, the channel fills the shaft with water and you drown. There! Understand?"

"Sort of," Pons muttered looking about.

"Where does the water come from?" Addie persisted.

"I don't know," Lettie said, slightly exasperated. "I think the Romans found an underground spring and channeled the water into an upper reservoir somewhere and contrived a spring-loaded mechanism that daily diverted a portion of the water to hidden, underground cisterns so that in the event of a siege they would always have hidden reserves of fresh water. I don't believe these stories about dragons and devils, do you?"

"Where's the chest of coins?" Pons asked, not answering her question.

"See there," Lettie said, pointing. "The tunnel leading away, there's a very small cave there. We hid it there less than a month ago."

"Let's go," said Pons. They walked slowly toward the new shaft and stooping slighting, they entered the tunnel and walked a few paces before they noticed the cave Lettie mentioned. Stepping inside there was scarcely room for more than five or six people and the cave was bare except for a high ledge and on the ledge was an exquisitely carved wooden chest.

"Open it," said Lettie, handing Pons an iron key. Pons climbed up a few feet on the protruding rock of the cave, inserted the key into the lock, and lifted the lid of the chest. He gasped. It was full of coins, jewels, and precious stones.

"It's here," he cried.

"It's ours!" Lettie exclaimed. Pons swept his hand into the grainy depths of the coins. "Unbelievable!" he murmured.

"And it's all mine!" said a low, strange voice in Arabic behind them. Lettie, Addie and Pons whirled about to behold in the entrance of the cave a swarthy looking man in eastern attire standing menacingly before them, scimitar drawn.

"Who are you?" Pons asked, sizing up the man. To the utter astonishment of all, including the erstwhile robber, Lettie repeated the question in Arabic. Pons and Addie looked at Lettie with disbelieving eyes, not comprehending where the strange sounds had come from. The thief cocked his head quizzically, but then replied:

"I am Vehip-ba-Hatin, an officer of the Halqa commanded by the Emirs of Ten, commanded by the Umara al-Mushara, Men of the Sword, governed by the Sultan, governed by the Caliph of the Mamluks of Damascus."

"So what do you want?" Pons asked, pushing between Lettie and Addie to shield them from any possible disturbance. Lettie continued the translation.

Vehip laughed nervously. "What do I want? What do I want?" His sword lowered slightly as he struggled to put into words his response. "I am here because it is the only place in Jerusalem to be safe from the barbarians and now here you are. I want my life and your money, that's what I want and that's what I shall have. Now move out of there all of you."

Pons stepped slowly out of the cave and into the shaft and allowed the women to pass before him. They started toward the Virgin's Fount. Pons walked backwards still holding the torch aloft and keeping his eye on Vehip who urged him forward with his scimitar.

"You can have your life, but you cannot have the money. It is ours."

"It is not yours, you lying scum!" Vehip snarled, pushing them into the larger cave containing the fountain.

"It certainly is not yours!" Lettie argued, whirling about. "It belongs to us. My husband was an officer of the Bayt-al-Mal, the treasury in Damascus, governed by the Wazir, the same Mamluk Sultan and the same Mamluk Caliph. We do not want your life, but we do want our coins!"

"What did you say?" Pons asked, hands spread out before him inquiringly. He saw that Vehip was taken aback at this forceful speech.

"You would not kill me?"

"No," said Lettie gently.

"We won't?" said Pons looking sharply at Lettie.

"No, we won't" Lettie replied. Turning to Vehip, "Put that thing away. You are safe with us, but you mustn't threaten us. Besides, we will give you some money to help."

"We will?" Pons interjected.

"Yes, we will," said Lettie determined. "In fact—" she took Vehip by the arm and walked away from the group chatting with Vehip in Arabic—"we will help you get out of Jerusalem. Stay with us and we will guarantee your safety."

From about ten feet away, Pons and Addie watched this drama unfold. The conversation ended when Vehip's eyes widened and brightened. He chattered rapidly and made a series of short quick bows to Lettie.

"What did you tell him?" Pons asked rushing over to them.

"I said that we would guarantee his safety out of Jerusalem."

"YOU WHAT?" Pons and Addie shouted. Vehip jumped.

Lettie braced herself before them, hands on hips: "Look," she said, "my husband didn't deserve to die. I think you know that. He was a nice man, the father of my son. His people have been in this land and in this city for hundreds and hundreds of years. They don't understand the passion and devotion we have for this city that is thousands of years old. This is just their homeland, that's all, and we've invaded and destroyed it. Vehip isn't an evil man, just a man that fears for his life. He will do us no harm. He is a Moslem, yes; we are Christians, yes; but the Moslems in the three years I lived with them never asked me to convert and I never did."

"They raped me and took you away—" Addie snapped.

"And none of your soldiers and men didn't do the same to Moslem women?" Lettie demanded. "No Moslem woman has been raped in Jerusalem in the past two days by Christian soldiers?"

Addie bowed her head. Lettie continued. "There are rotters among us all. And what my husband did was wrong. But it happened, and I had to make the best of it. I've learned a lot in these three years, and I know that we don't know Vehip here at all, but I trust him. He certainly is not like those two Christian men in our house today. We'll help him, and that's the end of it!"

Pons and Addie looked at each other, trying to read the level of trust in each other's eyes. They turned to Lettie and nodded. She said something in Arabic to Vehip, and he immediately smiled and nodded.

"Let's go then," said Pons gruffly and he headed back to the cave where the wooden chest lay undisturbed. Soon he reappeared with an apron of jewels. "Are you going to give me some help here, or have we lost interest in the money?"

Just then they paused, for they heard a deep faint rumbling while, at the same time, they felt drops. The Virgin's Fount had started to spray a stream of water which reaching its apex came down in a beautiful circling pattern raining upon the water already in the pool and upon the dry heads of the pilgrims gathered around it.

They stared in wonder at its beauty before coming to the startling recollection only moments later: "The water," Lettie cried. "We're going to get caught in the flood!"

Pons looked about at the cavern and realized for the first time that the cave was not a cave at all, it was in reality a cistern, and not a particularly large one at that. Perhaps, he thought, the cistern had been carved out of the rock, or out of an existing cave, to create a safe place for the relic. The cistern was actually a giant and ingenious reliquary that had a built-in mechanism for protecting its relic. Now they had removed the relic, the birth clothes of Christ, but were in danger of dying for the privilege of seeing it.

They had entered at the Steps of the Twelve Apostles and that is where the rushing torrent would enter the cavern. It would exit the cavern from the shaft above them where they had climbed to find their treasure, and the flood would then continue until it emptied into an unknown cistern somewhere.

"Let's go," Pons shouted. "We've got a little bit of time left." They turned and ran toward the steps leading to the cave shaft. As they began to ascend them, they heard the water entering the cave behind. A small stream of water cascaded down the Steps of the Twelve Apostles, but even as they watched the flow steadily increased in size and strength.

"Come on," Pons yelled. They rushed up the stairs and, upon reaching the top platform, they turned about for a final look. The shaft at the Steps of the Twelve Apostles exploded with a rushing flood of continuous water spilling into the cave and beginning to fill it. They turned into the shaft and darted into the cave.

"What are we going to do?" Addie cried, sobbing.

"We can't out run it," Lettie said. "We're going to get caught in it."

"Not necessarily,' said Pons who was glancing about this tiny cave. "The chest of money is on the ledge, right?" They nodded. "It's there," he went on, "because the height of the ledge is higher than the top of the shaft and the ceiling of the cave. When the water passes through the shaft, the water level in this cave will only go as high as the height of the shaft itself. There's room for two people up there if we take the chest down."

"We're going to lose the money?" Addie asked.

"I don't know, we can come back, but better to lose the coins than our lives," Pons replied briskly. He had donned again the mantle of messiah; he would find a way to save them all. It was difficult because of Vehip. Without the Moslem, the two women and child could stay in the cave and he could strike out on his own and hope for the best. But he could take Vehip with him.

"You and Lettie and Peter climb up on the ledge, and Vehip and I will continue as far as we can," he said.

"No, no," said Addie, "if something happens to you, Lettie and I will have no one to help us."

"Can't we get three people up here?" Lettie asked.

"No we can't," Pons replied, "and we must decide now."

"Then I will go with Pons," said Addie. "We've come this far, we can survive this."

"No, no, you mustn't—"

"Yes, that is the best," interjected Lettie. "Pons and Vehip can't communicate with each other. So Vehip will stay here with Peter and me, and when the water passes we will catch up with you. Now hurry."

There was no more time for arguing, for they could hear the rush of the water filling the cistern behind them. Pons grabbed Addie and ducked out of the cave. "Get Vehip to knock that chest off the ledge and get up there, we've got to go now."

"I love you, Lettie!" Addie cried as she departed.

"Come on," said Pons, tugging her down the shaft. They set off running as fast as they were able along the rocky-bottomed shaft which they knew would certainly fill with water at any moment. Addie stumbled and tripped, falling to her face, putting her hands out in front of her to protect herself. Fortunately her fall was broken when her hands landed on something soft. A rat! Addie screamed in terror as it scurried away. Rolling over to get away from it, she suffered the further terror of several more crossing her body as she lay on the floor of the tunnel.

"Get up, Addie," Pons pleaded, grabbing her arm. "We've got to keep going."

"I can't do this, Pons," she sobbed. She wrested her hand out of his grasp. "I'm going to die and I don't care."

Pons straightened the flat of his hand and laid it firmly across her face stinging her smartly. Addie's eyes widened in astonishment, and she stiffened and then realized what he had done. She raised her chin, and lifted her skirt, and taking Pons proffered hand, began to run again, sobbing faintly.

The sound of the water grew louder and Addie wondered if her sister would be alright, and if, surviving the water, she would really be alright with that … that Moslem fellow. Lettie's instincts were probably correct, she surmised. The roar intensified until it was pointless to attempt communication with Pons. It was a roar of judgment, of a final attempt on their lives.

The water was now up to their ankles as they sloshed through the tunnel toward what they earnestly believed would be safety. Pons was secretly entertaining the hope that there would be another cave such as the one in which their coin chest had been located. If they could find such a place with sufficient interior height, they would be saved.

The water continued to rise. Both Pons and Addie knew that it was pointless to attempt to outrun the flood now. Pons glanced at the ceiling of the tunnel looking for air pockets, some place where they could place their heads to breath. He also knew that, unfortunately, the power of the current would probably make it impossible to hold a position long enough to outlast the flood.

Pons stopped. Turning about, he grabbed unseeing in the darkness for Addie and put his mouth to her ear. "This tunnel has to let out somewhere. The best thing to do now is to go with the current, swim if we have to, get as far as we can as fast as we can. Come on."

Pons stretched his frame forward in the tunnel and began to swim even as the current carried him swiftly forward. Addie followed his example trying to make her strokes as powerful as possible. But the flow was now upon them in earnest. She could not travel any faster by swimming than the current was now taking her. The powerful pulse of the water pushed her both forward and then beneath its surface, slamming her against the wall of the shaft. She felt the rough rock beat her side and tear at her arms. She was like a not-so-buoyant log, powerless to affect her own destiny, completely at the mercy of this the most basic element of the earth: water. She had nearly died from a lack of it, and now she would die from a superabundance of it. Clare, Pons, Lettie, little Peter. What a life it might have been!

She scolded herself for thinking such thoughts. She should be thinking about how to save herself. But in truth, remedies of salvation were gone. She tucked her arms about her body with her hands over her head and let the stream carry her. It had not yet filled the shaft completely. She bobbed along roughly, attempting most of all to keep her head above water and when it was possible to take huge gulps of air. Normal breathing was not possible or advisable. She willed to breathe when it was safe to do so and hoped that the breath she took would not be her last.

Sometimes, she gulped at the wrong time and got instead a mouthful of water. Instinctively she swallowed it rather than attempting to cough or spit it out. There wasn't time. She swallowed and then gulped again when she believed her mouth would safely engulf air, not water.

Suddenly her eyes were blinded by intense light. She closed them immediately and just as suddenly the buffeting and pounding ceased. She felt only air and the sense of falling. She thought instantly that this is what death feels like. She heard her name called out. She was not dead! It was Pons! She opened her eyes in time to see that she was indeed falling and headed toward a huge pool of water. Could she straighten her body in time to enter the water feet first? She tucked her head and rolled her body in the air and brought her feet about. Her skirt flew up about her neck and obstructed her vision. But it didn't matter; the moment her feet were pointed downward, she hit the water. It was cold, and colder as the momentum of her fall carried her deep. She hadn't taken the time to inhale before hitting the surface so now she could feel the need to breathe pounding in her chest until the fatal impulse to breathe would inexorably overpower the will not to breathe. She kicked with her feet and strained her face toward the surface of the water. She opened her eyes in the hope of seeing light and thereby gauging how far to the air above the water. She could see light! Kicking harder, arms tucked snugly at her side, she propelled herself silently upward as though flying like an angel toward heaven. And then, miraculously she was in a new world where she could breathe clean, cool air, where there was light and sound again, where the darkness had fled. She treaded water furiously, gasping rapidly, as her lungs drank in the freshness of this new atmosphere, taking in swiftly vast quantities of air of which it had been deprived. As her breathing relaxed, she felt strong arms grasp her about the waist.

"Pons," she cried. Tears welled in her eyes and melded quickly with the water flowing from her soaking hair. She turned about in his grasp and threw her arms about him. For a moment, they sank and thrashed beneath the surface of the water. They emerged soon laughing. "Here again to save me, eh, Pons?" she asked.

"Someone has to do it!" he said, laughing. "If not I, then who?"

"No one," Addie said smiling through her tears. "No one at all."

"Look," Pons said. He pointed above them. Water was still spewing forth out of the tunnel high above them. It looked like a waterfall.

"We came out of that?" Addie asked.

"That's right," Pons said. "Fell about thirty feet. That was a hell of a somersault you made when you came over, landing in the water feet first. It was beautiful!"

"When I saw the light, I thought I had died," she said, laughing, so glad to be with Pons. "But when I opened my eyes, I could see I was going to hit hard unless I did something quickly."

"We used to have a swimming hole near Avignon, you know, and I could jump from a good height, not this high, but high."

The waterfall was dying out now to a trickle. Within moments it stopped altogether and it was quiet. They had fallen into a massive underground cistern, a rock-cut cavern with columns left in place for support. Pons saw steps climbing in a circular fashion along the side of the wall at the far end of the cavern where the light was streaming in.

"Let's swim over to the steps. Can you make it?" They swam to the wall of the cistern and slowly clambered up on the steps utterly exhausted.

"Why are there steps like this in a cistern?" Addie asked, panting for breath again.

"How do you think the workmen who hollowed out this cistern went home at night to their wives and families? They made steps to get down into the cistern in the morning and to get out at night. If we could dive to the bottom of this cistern, we could follow the steps all the way down.

"It's huge," Addie murmured. "Our voices echo in here."

"Hello, down there!" Someone was shouting from above. Pons and Addie looked up to see Lettie and Vehip peering over the edge of the shaft high above them. Lettie held little Peter up for them to see.

"Lettie!" Addie yelled in joy. "Are you safe?"

"Yes," the voice echoed back. 'Everyone is fine!" Vehip waved at them happily. "How are we going to get out of here?" she called.

It was a good question. There were no steps leading downward from the opening of that shaft. Of course they could jump; that's how Pons and Addie had done it, unwillingly of course, but it was effective. But this was not possible with little Peter being a part of the group. But Pons, cupping his hands to his mouth, had an answer: "I'll go for some rope and come back. I'll shoot a thread to you with the long bow and you can pull up the rope. We'll get you down here and then you can climb the stairs."

And that is how they were saved from the cistern known as the Great Sea. When they stepped out of the cistern at its entrance on the Temple Mount, they rejoiced, and agreed that it was the best day of their lives!

✠✠✠

Anna showed them where to lay him. The soldiers (Normans from Rouen) brought Stefan into a dark room, dimly lit so as to be kind to his eyes, and laid him gently on a soft bed covered with ornately embroidered blankets and coverlets. It was evening and Stefan, wounded at the northern wall near Juiverie was discovered and protected by Everard and brought to what had been the home of an officer of the Halqa. He lay as one dead but not yet dead, rescued by those who did not wish him to be dead.

"Gently, please," Anna said. "Thank you," as the soldiers left. She stood above him, her head bowed and eyes closed. The armor had been removed, the wound bound. She could see the crimson stain where the bleeding had not yet stopped. She knelt beside him and put her head on his shoulder and cried for a while.

When she looked up, she saw the scarlet flow and put her finger on it and looked at it, rubbed it between her fingers thoughtfully. Swords. Arrows. He had been wounded by the sword, but smitten by an arrow. As had she. *Sagittas amore. Sagittas mors*; arrows of love and arrows of death. They had been wounded by both and no matter how hard they had tried to remove the arrow, it had remained lodged quite firmly, in their hearts, their deepest consciousness. And it would always be there. She had heard of soldiers who had lived with broken arrows in their bodies. The tissue heals over and covers the wound but never the pain. A sudden movement, an unexpected jolt, and the pain suddenly returns.

Anna put her bloodied fingers to her chest. This was a wound she would always feel. I must either stop loving in order to avoid such pain, she thought, or I must be willing to suffer the pain. *Is it possible to love without pain, to love without bonds?* She crawled up on the bed beside Stefan and lifted his arm so that she could lie down within his embrace.

The movement momentarily awoke him. "Is this Jerusalem?" he asked in a voice hazy and indistinct. Anna snuggled firmly against him and lifted her face to his and smiled: "Yes, my love this is Jerusalem."

He smiled crookedly. "This is the New Jerusalem, now, isn't it?"

"Yes, the New Jerusalem," said Anna in a hushed voice, "coming down out of heaven like a bride adorned for her husband and there shall be no more pain, nor sickness, nor crying, nor death, for all things are new."

Stefan lay restlessly upon his bed at these words, clutching his chest, grimacing in pain. Then it subsided and he was peaceful again.

"I will be your husband," he crooned, "and you shall be my bride."

"I will be your bride and you shall be my husband," she echoed, her eyelids becoming heavy with sleep. And so they slept and roused in turn, each afflicted by their respective wounds and tormented throughout the night by them until the faintest light began to sneak over the eastern ridge.

At dawn's early light, Stefan awoke suddenly and sat up.

"My vows! I must say my vows!"

Anna, awakened by this, was too sleepy to comprehend what he was talking about.

Stefan turned, not surprised to see her, and said: "I must get to the Church to say my vows! I haven't said my vows yet, have I?"

"No, but you must wait until you are stronger," she said, fully awake now.

Stefan was insistent. "I must get to the Church! Get a cart and driver, and a priest. Get the priest and take me by the Via Dolorosa to the Church of the Holy Sepulcher."

Anna arose and tucked Stefan beneath the blankets again. "You are feverish and cold," she said solemnly, tears in her eyes. "We must be careful. But I will get a cart and make the preparations. Promise me you will try to rest now until the driver comes."

Stefan nodded. "Quickly, Anna, quickly."

✠✠✠

Chartres

Adela could feel nothing but pain now, the most riveting pain she had experienced, but she knew it would be over in moments. These pains had been coming spasmodically for six hours, only now they were more frequent than before. She had been in bed for two days, too weak to walk and feeling that the time to deliver would shortly be upon her. Today would be the day, she believed, and it appeared she was right.

She had called for the lady-in-waiting to assist her, and the physician had already arrived. There was not much to do now except to wait and endure and hope. She would be delighted with a baby daughter, but she fervently hoped the child would be a boy, a son. This child was hers and Stefan's. For once, she had kept her word; she had known no man since she had been with Stefan the night before he had departed. This was Stefan's child and she hoped it would be a son with Stefan's blue eyes and golden hair, a son she could raise in the image of his father. Four years ago she would not have said that. The only man by which men were measured was her father. Years and tangled experiences had changed this. Her father's image was not discolored by the passage of time, but time had rather enhanced her image of her husband. It had blended into strength the faults she had previously seen with such clarity; what had been seen as such glaring defects not long ago had now become lost in the fog of time. What she saw now was the bold and strong outline of his character and stature even if the particular features were blurry and indistinct. The prophet, not being in his own country, had recovered his honor.

"Good morning," she said, when the pain had subsided. The physician entered the room briskly, nodding to the attendants. "I am going to have a child soon now, am I not?"

"It is very possible," he said as he prepared to make an examination. He placed his hands upon her abdomen applying pressure here and pressure there. After making a visual inspection he announced: "Yes, it will be quite soon," thereby affirming what the patient already knew.

✠✠✠

"Per istam sanctam unctionem et suam puissimam misericordiam indulgeat tibi Dominus quidquid per visum deliquisti," Fulcher intoned as he touched the eyes of Stefan. They were in a small cart drawn by two fine sorrel horses clattering through the quiet streets of Jerusalem early in the morning. The vendors were not in their shops, the animals were in their stalls, the olive presses were silent. Anna sat beside Stefan who lay stretched out on a makeshift cot. Fulcher sat on the other side administering rites. He had been hastily summoned and he grabbed a vial of oil, donned black vestments, had thrown the driver onto his perch and they were off.

May the Lord forgive you by this holy anointing and his most loving mercy whatever sins you have committed by the use of your hearing. Amen.

They traveled to the northwest of the Dome of the Rock. Anna could see the porticos of the temple mount and the light brightening behind its dome as they fled away from it toward the Church of the Holy Sepulcher. The homes that they drove by would be empty unless already occupied by pilgrims, emptied at least of their Moslem occupants. The city was still a city of death, a cemetery with walls, the most well-fortified cemetery in Christendom, Anna thought, seeing still the dead now and then.

Fulcher continued to administer the sacrament: *Per istam sanctam unctionem indulgeat tibi Dominus qiuidquid deliguisti. Amen.*

The heads of the horses bobbed rhythmically as they strained against the harness propelling the cart and its occupants across the width of the city, from east to west, the rising sun at their back. They must reach the Church quickly, Anna thought. Quickly now!

Benedictio Dei omnipotentis, Patris, et Filii, et Spiritus Sancti descendat super te et maneat semper. Amen.

Anna was surprised to see other pilgrims at the church when they arrived. It was still early, but Christians had begun to fill the Church for it was the cool part of the day and because they no doubt believed it would be crowded later in the morning. Fulcher and Anna helped Stefan out of the cart. With great difficulty he was able to walk and he seemed to be strengthened with the knowledge that he had arrived at the church. He paused to look about the impressive structure first begun in the time of emperor Constantine. The structure was large and rambling, a collection of towers and domes, added on by emperors with varying degrees of religious fervor. The tomb of Christ had been isolated and enclosed within a rotunda below a large timbered dome. To the west was a colonnaded court which enclosed the rock of Calvary. The group of three walked through the outer court of the church, up a series of stairs and into the nave. To their left was the high altar and to their right was the tomb of Christ under the dome.

Stefan pointed to the tomb and the three staggered haltingly toward it. When they arrived, they lowered Stefan to his knees beside the wall of the tomb itself which consisted of thick stone. The count touched the wall and looked at Anna. Tears streaked his face.

"My knife," he whispered to Anna, holding out his hand. Anna gave him his knife, noticing a group of people nearby who were watching with curious interest.

Stefan took the knife carefully and grasped it firmly, putting its blade to the rock of the wall. Then he began to scratch some lines on the walls, a vertical and horizontal line, many of them, until they were but two thick and deep scratches in the rock.

The Crusader Cross, Anna thought. When he finished, he fell off his knees and sat wearily against the cross-marked wall while two pilgrims, a man and a woman, approached them.

The woman looked at Anna. The princess recognized her as the woman she had talked to only a few days earlier. She smiled nervously at Anna, and then looked into Stefan's uplifted eyes.

"Count Stefan, remember me?' she asked simply.

Stefan, very weak, looked at her steadily, and his lips struggled to form the words. "Addie," he murmured.

"Yes, Addie," she replied. She knelt before him, took his hands, and looked deeply into his soul-blue eyes. "I want to give you something to have or leave with whomever you choose. She took a leather pouch from Pons and opened it while Stefan, Anna and Fulcher watched. "We found this at the Virgin's Fount, and removed it lest it fall into the wrong hands. Look!"

She held up the cloth unfolded for everyone to see. On the cloth, Fulcher saw the dark shadings of a face, gradations of charcoal and empty places, an unmistakable pattern of the face of the crucified Christ. It was quite plain to see. The others saw it too. "The Shroud of Christ," Addie confided, "his burial cloth. Take it, Stefan. Make sure it is safe." She glanced up at Anna and Fulcher and shrugged. "We cannot protect it, you know." Taking his hand, she kissed it, and then arose and bowing slightly to Anna, turned away and disappeared among the crowd.

Stefan took the cloth and ran his hands over it slowly in awe and then lifted it carefully to Fulcher who took it from him. "Take it, father, it belongs to the Church." He turned to Anna, and said, "I'm going to pray now, and then we can go back."

Falling to his knees, he began to pray with faltering voice the *Pater Noster.* He did not finish for as he prayed he saw the Lord coming toward him in a high mountain meadow where lilies and daisies sprung quickly and bloomed gloriously. He was dressed in the finest white, and his face shone like a thousand suns, his golden hair flowed to gentle, sloping shoulders and his eyes were warm and tender.

"My Lord!" called Stefan, falling off his knees.

"Oh, Stefan," Anna cried, sinking quickly beside him cradling him in her arms. Stefan's gaze was focused upward into the eyes of the Christ unseen by all but him. The Lord produced a brilliant sword and put it before Stefan. "My sword," he murmured.

Anna motioned to Fulcher who abruptly departed. Stefan did not notice. Rather, he heard the Christ say: "Well done, good and faithful servant. Enter into the joy of your reward." The Smiling Christ extended his hands toward the fallen warrior and Stefan lifted his arms and extended his fingers as though to touch him.

"My Lord, my Lord!" he cried, as tears once again creased his face. Fulcher returned and rushed to Anna and Stefan. Producing Fortissimus, he stood the shining sword on its point in front of the pilgrim soldier so that Stefan could see its cruciform shape.

He struggled to his knees again with Anna's assistance and grasped the hilt in his hands and pressed it to his lips. Then he fell back into Anna's arms and closed his eyes.

He did not open them again. Fulcher choked and turned away, his eyes moistening, while Anna pressed Stefan's head deep into her bosom and caressed his hair earnestly and hopelessly. She, too, closed her eyes and lifted her head to the heavens. She remembered the Gospel: "Why stand ye here gazing into heaven? He is not here ..." He is not here. He is not here. HE IS NOT HERE. Oh God, he is not here! She lowered her head on his and held him tight.

✠✠✠

Far away, the lusty cries of a newborn baby stirred in the tapestried chambers of Stefan's castle at Chartres. Adela held her infant son for all to see. "He shall be called Stephen," she announced joyfully, laughing until the tears welled in her eyes and coursed freely down her cheeks. "And you, my little one," she cooed, "shall be a great one—just you wait!"

Adela laughed, but at the Church of the Holy Sepulcher, Anna, kissing the freshly carved Crusader Cross, cried unabashedly.

Like all those who have lost something worth more than life itself, she wept.

INCIPIT EPILOGUS

I closed the pages of my *Historia Hieroso-lymitana* and the *Gesta*. Bernard was silent. I could hear his breathing. The library was quiet. The lamplight was low. I could not surmise whether my words had been encouraging. I closed my eyes. I leaned back in my chair and waited.

"That's it?" he said presently, without looking at me.

"That's it," I replied.

He said: "Anna, did she stay?"

He wanted to know more!

"No," I said, leaning forward into the fluttering light. "She left Palestine almost immediately, return-ing to Constantinople where she married Nicephorus Byrennius Caesar. But she did not love him, although, when her father died in 1118, she tried to place him on the throne instead of her brother, John Comenus. She failed. He threw her in a convent where she wrote the *Alexiad* and where she is now finishing out her days."

"And the others?"

"Raymond was hoping to be the secular leader of Jerusalem, but his vanity perversely moved him to refuse the crown when it was offered. He was then incensed when it was given instead to Godfrey de Boullion. The count of Toulouse took his forces and left. Never returned to Jerusalem and he died in Tripoli. Godfrey, meanwhile, piously believed the Holy City should be under ecclesiastical rule, but nonetheless took the title of *Advocatus Sancti*

Sepulchri, Advocate of the Holy Sepulcher. But he died less than a year later in 1100.

"And Bohemund—this is interesting. Bohemund did *not* die in the oubliette of the Citadel as Stefan and Anna believed. Loyalists rescued him and treated a broken arm and leg. He retained control of Antioch but was captured nonetheless by Malik-Ghazi in 1100 and held for three years in prison. Tancred, becoming Governor of Antioch, displayed a remarkable lack of interest in ransoming his uncle. Alexius, however, wanted him as a hostage, but so did Aban Arslan, who was now the sultan of Iconium. Bohemund offered to form an alliance with Malik-Ghazi against both Alexius and Arslan in return for his freedom. This was granted and Bohemund promptly returned to Antioch and deposed his nephew.

"In 1105 and 1106, Bohemund toured Italy and France where he was hailed as a hero of the crusade. Amassing a fortune in Europe, he laid siege to Dyrrachium with 34,000 men. Alexius threw up a blockade on land and sea and Bohemund was forced to sue for peace. He took an oath of vassalage and returned to Italy a broken and humiliated man. He died about 1111. The Norman count, more than anyone else, was singlehandedly responsible for destroying any hope of new understanding between East and West."

"What of the Bartholomews?"

"Addie and Pons returned to France wealthy and happy. They were married in Chartres Cathedral. I know. I was there as the presiding priest at the wedding mass. They made a home in Provence, had children, and now have grandchildren. Clare, however, entered a Benedictine convent at the Paraclete—"

"—where Heloise is abbess." Bernard was interested now.

"Yes," I continued, "the convent Abelard built. Hildy stayed in Jerusalem in the Jewish quarter, but was killed during the campaign of 1101. Lettie returned with Addie and Pons to Provence with Peter, her child. But she found her position there misunderstood. She left soon after and returned to Syria where the child was again known as Yaddie. She remarried and converted to Islam."

Bernard left in a disagreeable mood. But when I saw him the next morning he was bright and cheerful again.

"Oh yes," he said, as he climbed into his carriage. "I forgot to inquire of Adela's child."

I waved goodbye as they left. "Stephen II?" I called out. "Why he's the present King of England, of course!"

I never saw my friend again. But I hear through channels—I have my sources—that he is raising a second crusade. Someone else will chronicle the death and destruction this expedition will bring forth. Not I!

Deus vult!

EXPLICIT EPILOGUS

Afterword

The historical stage for this novel is the First Crusade, 1095-1099 A.D. The 1095 A.D. date marks the beginning of the novel, because it was in November, 1095, that Pope Urban II proclaimed the crusade in a sermon at a Church Council at Clermont, France. The inspiration for the novel comes from some letters written between Count Stephen of Chartres (and Blois) and his wife, Adela, the daughter of William the Conqueror, and sister of the current king of England. Stephen was not altogether enthusiastic about signing up as a *crucesignatus,* even if the pope had, for the first time ever, offered a plenary indulgence for participation in the crusade.

The First Crusade, however, was a polymorphous affair. Enthusiastic peasants, under the leadership of Peter the Hermit, Walter Sans Avoir, et al., started out for Jerusalem fairly soon after the pope's sermon, going through the Rhineland, slaughtering Jews along the way. It was an ill-fated venture, however. The peasants had scarcely stepped on Asian soil when they were destroyed by the powerful Turkish armies in the area. Meanwhile, the nobles prepared to leave under the standard of several leaders. They made their way to Constantinople where they met and they proceeded *en masse* to Jerusalem, a journey that took about three years. The "pilgrimage" suffered many setbacks and defections, but in July of 1099 A.D. Jerusalem fell to the Crusaders. Stefan and Adela, although in my story were lucky to have *one* child, in true life had *eleven!* Stefan did, in fact, leave the pilgrimage early, as my story reveals, and he did return, but in my story, he returns a bit earlier than the historical record confirms.

This is the canvas on which my tale is portrayed. The broad strokes are true or faithful to the primary sources. Although the noblemen are historical figures, the peasants are fictional characters, although they are composites of what we know of the commoners who enlisted in what was also known as the "People's Crusade." So, the finer strokes on this canvas including people, conversations, deaths and manner of deaths, may vary from the historical record if such a record about such particulars exists.

The First Crusade was not without its historians or chroniclers. Fulcher of Chartres was one. His version of the crusade is found in his *History of the Expedition to Jerusalem*. The *Gesta Francorum* was written by an anonymous chronicler. Many others wrote accounts as well, including Guibert of Nogent, William of Tyre, Peter Tudebode, Ralph of Caen, Anna Comnena's *Alexiad*, et al. I relied on Fulcher's account of Urban's sermon at Clermont, and used Fulcher's version of the crusade as a starting point—which is why I decided to bring him into my story itself as its narrator.

Lettie's song in "Anno Domini 1099, A.D." is taken from *Chanterai por mon corage, Chanson de femme, chanson de croisade*, found in *Songs of the Troubadours and Trouveres: An Anthology of Poems and Melodies*, edited by Samuel N. Rosenberg, Margaret Switten, Gerard Le Vot.

The historiography of the First Crusade is enormous, and I will not reproduce my sources here. Fortunately, for the interested reader, the efficiency, breadth and reach of the Internet today allows anyone to investigate whatever in particular should interest them.

Spelling issues. I changed the spelling of the Count of Chartres from Stephen to Stefan for no good reason other than whimsy. The name of the principle adversary of the crusaders while traversing Anatolia was the Turkish sultan Kilij Arslan. He became Aban Arlsan in my story for ease of reading.

I also had to make a decision about whether to use Moslem or Muslim. I went with Moslem. Although "Muslim" is clearly the preferred word to use today when referring to an adherent of Islam, this is only a recent development. As late as 1992, The American Heritage Dictionary asserts that "Moslem is the form predominantly preferred in journalism and popular usage." The American Moslem Foundation is not the American Muslim Foundation. Moslem, then, is a much better fit for a narrative that takes place in the late eleventh century.

Many thanks to my wife, Jeanie, for reading the manuscript, offering helpful suggestions and for her enthusiastic support, not only for this book, but for all of my writing projects; to copy editors Jane France, Joanna Loucky-Ramsey, Barbara Stimson and Ron Peters, for their amazing work; to Stace Wright of Eureka Cartography for the maps; to Ying Tuin of Shanghai for her work on the cover; and to Karen J. Hatzigeorgiou for her very helpful website containing countless images in the public domain, including the illuminated capitals used in this book. See her website at: http://karenswhimsy.com. And a special thanks to Chelsea Lee and Stanley Shao, two students at Shanghai American School, Shanghai, China, who worked hard on some art projects for the book that didn't pan out. I am grateful to them for their efforts and amazed at their skill.

The research for this novel took place at Speer Library, Princeton Theological Seminary; the New York Public Library, New York City; Chartres Cathedral, France; Cathedral of Clermont, Clermont, France; Bari, Italy; the Archaeological Museum, Istanbul; Nicea, Turkey (modern Iznik); and, of course, Jerusalem itself.

But all the research aside, my purpose in writing this novel was not to write a history of the First Crusade. That's already been done. I wanted to write a *story*, a couple of stories actually, and use the First Crusade as a backdrop or stage on which the story could be acted. The story's the thing. I hope you will not find the history daunting. On the other hand, those of you who enjoy medieval history will be doubly blessed with both the story and the *his*tory.

Thank you for reading my book.

—*Timothy Merrill*
Shanghai, China
December, 2014

www.ingramcontent.com/pod-product-compliance
Lightning Source LLC
Chambersburg PA
CBHW030921020726
47498CB00001B/50